The First Circle

'*The First Circle* asks to be compared to Dostoevsky. Solzhenitsyn is in the great story-telling tradition. When he introduces a character, he fills in the complete background. His portrait of a Soviet prosecutor and his family circle is unforgettable. So are chapters devoted to the brooding Stalin. A future generation of Russians will be able to come to terms with their history through books like *Dr. Zhivago* and *The First Circle*.' *David Pryce-Jones, Financial Times*

'Very impressive. Twenty years ago Koestler gave us his theatrically conceptualized account of Stalinism and the purges in *Darkness at Noon*; Solzhenitsyn makes the subject more spacious, and, as a real novelist must, places it in the lives of men and women. He shows the lives out of which opinion has grown. In his latest novel, *The First Circle*, he is quietly in command of powers that were scattered and now, like the great novelists, can control a beautifully orchestrated theme.' *V. S. Pritchett, New York Review of Books*

'A book of great sadness with deep veins of humour . . . It is at once classic and contemporary. Reading it, we know that it has been with us for years just as we know that future generations will read it with wonder and with awe.' *Thomas Lask, New York Times*

D1347426

Available in Fontana by the same author

The Gulag Archipelago

The First Circle

Alexander Solzhenitsyn

Translated from the Russian by
Michael Guybon

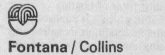

Fontana / Collins

First published by
William Collins and Harvill Press 1968
First issued in Fontana Books 1970
Nineteenth Impression June 1974

The publishers would like to express their gratitude to Penguin Books Ltd. for permission to quote from *Canto IV, The Comedy of Dante Alighieri* translated by Dorothy Sayers, and to The Estate of Sir Bernard Pares for permission to quote from *The Sabre Blade* from 'Krylov's Fables' translated by Bernard Pares and published by Jonathan Cape Ltd.

Made and Printed in Great Britain by
William Collins Sons & Co. Ltd., Glasgow

L. & M.

Although the central action of *The First Circle* takes place within a time-span of only three days, the book is rich in characters, most of whom are essential to the structure of the closely inter-locking narrative and many of whose Russian names may seem unfamiliar. A *dramatis personae* is therefore appended on the following pages in the belief that it will help the reader to enjoy the book. As is the Russian practice, most of the characters are given surnames, first names and patronymics, although to mini-mize confusion the name-and-patronymic form of address is used sparingly in the text.

The main locale of the novel is a 'special prison' (a techno-logical research establishment employing highly qualified political prisoners), situated in a converted country house in the outer suburbs of Moscow called MÁVRINO (the stress-accent is on the first syllable).

The characters are listed in alphabetical order and described by their status or function. Real personages are marked by an asterisk; those not directly involved in the action, but referred to, are shown within square brackets.

Characters in 'The First Circle'

*ABAKÚMOV, Víktor Semyónovich · *Minister of State Security* (d. 1954)

ADAMSÓN · *prisoner at Mavrino*

[BOBR · *prisoner at another special prison; engineer*]

BOBÝNIN · *prisoner at Mavrino; engineer*

BULÁTOV, Amantái · *prisoner at Mavrino; engineer*

BULBANYÚK · *General; senior official of Ministry of State Security*

CHELNÓV, Vladímir Yerástovich · *prisoner at Mavrino; professor*

*[CHIKOBÁVA · *Professor of Linguistics, Tiflis University*]

'Dásha' · *graduate student, Moscow University*

DOBROÚMOV · *Doctor*

DOF-DNEPRÓVSKY · *prisoner at Mavrino*

DORÓNIN, Rostisláv ('Ruska') · *prisoner at Mavrino*

DVOYETYÓSOV · *prisoner at Mavrino; engineer*

DÝRSIN, 'Ványa' · *prisoner at Mavrino; engineer*

Erica · *Hungarian graduate student at Moscow University*

GALÁKHOV, Nikolái Arkádyevich · *writer*

GERÁSIMOVICH, Illarión · *prisoner at Mavrino; physicist*

KAGÁN, Isaac · *prisoner at Mavrino*

*[KALÍNIN, Mikhaíl Ivánovich · 1875-1946. *Chairman of Presidium of Supreme Soviet, titular head of state*]

KAMYSHÁN · *Lieutenant; prison officer at Mavrino*

KHORÓBROV, Ilyá · *prisoner at Mavrino; engineer*

KLIMÉNTYEV · *Lieutenant-Colonel; governor of Mavrino special prison*

KLYKACHÓV · *Lieutenant; prison officer at Mavrino*

KNYAZHÍTSKY · *prisoner at Mavrino; professor*

KONDRASHÓV-IVÁNOV · *prisoner at Mavrino; artist*

*[KÓSTOV, Tráicho · *Bulgarian Communist leader*]

LÁNSKY, 'Alyósha' · *literary critic*

Ludmíla · *graduate student at Moscow University*

LYUBÍMICHEV, Víktor · *prisoner at Mavrino*

MAKARÝGIN, Pyótr · *Major-General; State Prosecutor*

MAKARÝGIN, Alévtina · *his wife*

MAKARÝGIN, Danéra · *his daughter; married to Galákhov*

MAKARÝGIN, Datóma ('Dottie') · *his daughter; married to Volódin*

MAKARÝGIN, Clára · *his daughter; 'free' worker at Mavrino*

MAMÚRIN ('The Man in the Iron Mask') · *prisoner at Mavrino; ex-colonel*

MARKÚSHEV · *prisoner at Mavrino; engineer*

*[MARR, Nikolái · *professor of Linguistics*]

MÍSHIN · *Major; Security Officer at Mavrino*

Músa · *graduate student at Moscow University*

NADELÁSHIN · *Junior Lieutenant; prison officer at Mavrino*

NÉRZHIN, Gleb Vikéntich · *prisoner at Mavrino; mathematician*

NÉRZHIN, 'Nádya' · *his wife*

Ólga · *graduate student of Moscow University*

OROBÍNTSEV · *prisoner at Mavrino*

OSKOLÚPOV · *Major-General; senior official of Ministry of State Security*

[PETRÓV · *official of Foreign Ministry*]

*POSKRYÓBYSHEV, Alexánder · *Stalin's private secretary*

POTÁPOV, Andréy Andréyevich · *prisoner at Mavrino; engineer*

PRYÁNCHIKOV, Valentín · *prisoner at Mavrino; engineer*

RADOVIČ, Dúshan · *Serbian Communist*

RICHTMAN, Max · *prisoner at Mavrino; Austrian*

RÓITMAN, Adám · *Major; officer in charge of acoustics research at Mavrino*

RÚBIN, Lev Grigóryevich · *prisoner at Mavrino; philologist*

RYÚMIN, Mikhaíl Dmítriyevich · *senior official of Ministry of State Security*

Serafíma Vitályevna ('Símochka') · *'free' worker at Mavrino*

SEVASTYÁNOV · *Deputy Minister of State Security*

SHCHÁGOV · *graduate student of Moscow University*

SHCHEVRÓNOK · *official of Foreign Ministry*

SHÍKIN · *Major; Security Officer at Mavrino*

SHÚSTERMAN · *Senior Lieutenant; prison officer at Mavrino*

SIMMEL, Reinhold · *prisoner at Mavrino; former SS Obersturmbann-führer*

SIROMÁKHA, Arthur · *prisoner at Mavrino*

SLOVÚTA · *Major-General; State Prosecutor*

SMOLOSÍDOV · *Lieutenant; prison officer at Mavrino*

SOLOGDÍN, Dmítry Alexándrovich · *prisoner at Mavrino; engineer*

*STALIN, Joseph Vissariónovich (real name Djugashvíli) · *Marshal; Chairman of the USSR Council of Ministers; Secretary-General, Soviet Communist Party*

[SYAGOVÍTY · *official of Foreign Ministry*]

STEPÁNOV, Borís Sergéyevich · *Communist Party secretary at Mavrino*

VERENYÓV, Pyótr Trofímovich · *Professor; civilian research adviser to Ministry of State Security*

VOLÓDIN, Innokénty Artémyevich · *Counsellor, Soviet Foreign Service*

YÁKONOV, Antón Nikolýevich · *Colonel; head of research, Mavrino special prison*

YEGÓROV, Spiridón Danilovich · *prisoner at Mavrino*

YÉMINA, Larísa · *'free' worker at Mavrino*

*[YESÉNIN, Sergéi Alexándrovich · *Russian poet (1895-1925)*]

[ZAVÁRZIN · *official of Foreign Ministry*]

ZEMÉLYA · *prisoner at Mavrino*

[ZHÁBOV · *literary critic*]

Zhénka · *young man, friend of Clara Makarygin*

ZHVAKÚN · *Lieutenant; prison officer at Mavrino*

CHAPTER ONE

The fretted hands of the bronze clock on the shelf stood at five to five. In the dying light of the December day the clock seemed almost black. Reaching to the ground, the tall window with its double panes looked down on the scurrying traffic in the street and the janitors who were shovelling the snow—freshly fallen but already soggy and dirty brown —from under the feet of the passers-by.

Staring at them blindly, Counsellor Innokenty Volodin leaned against the window-frame and whistled on a high thin note. His fingers turned the pages of a glossy, brightly coloured foreign magazine, but his eyes saw nothing.

The counsellor, whose rank in the Diplomatic Service equalled that of an army colonel, was tall and thin; he was not wearing his uniform but a suit of smooth material, and looked more like a rich young man about town than a responsible member of the Ministry of Foreign Affairs.

It was time either to put on the lights in the office or to go home, but he made no move to do either.

Five o'clock was not the end of the working day but only of its less important daytime part. Now everyone would go home and have dinner and a nap, but at ten the lights would burn again in the thousand upon thousand windows of the sixty-five Moscow ministries. Sitting up behind his dozen fortress walls, one man suffered from insomnia—and he had trained the whole of Moscow's officialdom to watch with him into the early hours. Knowing the habits of their sovereign, all three-score ministers sat like schoolboys, waiting for his summons. To keep themselves awake they summoned their deputies, the deputies harried their section heads, research assistants climbed step-ladders and looked up card indexes, clerks dashed up and down corridors and typists broke pencils.

Even now, on the eve of the Western Christmas, when all the embassies had been quiet for two days, their telephones silent, and the diplomats were probably sitting down in front of their Christmas trees, there would still be night work at the Ministry. Some people might play chess, or tell funny stories or fall asleep on their sofas, but there would certainly be work.

Quickly, aimlessly, Volodin's nervous fingers leafed through the periodical, while inside him the flicker of fear now rose to a small flame, now died down leaving him chilled.

How well Innokenty remembered Doctor Dobroumov from his childhood! This was before Dobroumov was famous, before he was sent on delegations abroad, before he was even talked about as a scientist—he was simply the family doctor whom Innokenty's mother always called in. She was often ill, and she trusted no one else. The moment Dobroumov arrived and took off his beaver hat in the hall, the whole flat seemed to fill with an atmosphere of kindness, reassurance, confidence. He would never spend less than half an hour by her bedside. He went painstakingly into every symptom, he examined the patient as though he had all the time in the world and explained every detail of the treatment. Nor, on his way out, would he ever pass the small boy without stopping, asking him something or other, and gravely waiting for the answer as though he genuinely expected it to be intelligent and important. His hair was already grey in those days . . .

Flinging down the magazine, Innokenty shivered and took a turn round the room.

Should he ring up Dobroumov or not?

Had it been anyone else—some specialist he had never met —it would never have occurred to Innokenty to warn him. But Dobroumov of all people . . .

If you telephoned from a box, could you possibly be identified? If you wasted no time, if you left as soon as you had finished? Could they recognize a muffled voice over the telephone? Surely they couldn't—there was no such technique.

He went up to the desk. In the twilight, he could just make out the top page of his new instructions. He was being posted abroad. He was to leave by air on Wednesday or Thursday, before the New Year.

The sensible thing was to wait. It would be reasonable to wait.

God! A shiver ran across his shoulders, so unused to carrying burdens. If only he had never heard! If only he knew nothing . . .

He swept all the papers off the desk and took them to the safe.

When you came to think of it, how could anyone object to what Dobroumov had promised to do? Like all gifted men, he was generous. A gifted man is conscious of his wealth and ready to share it.

Yet all the while, Innokenty's uneasiness was growing stronger and stronger. Leaning against the safe, he hung his head and rested, closing his eyes.

Suddenly, as though ignoring the last few moments of daily routine, without ringing up for his car, without closing the inkwell—he went out, locked the door, handed the key to the Duty Officer at the end of the corridor, put on his plain civilian coat and almost ran downstairs, past the permanent members of the staff in their embroidered gold braid, and rushed out into the raw dusk.

Passing the monument to Vorovsky in the half-enclosed courtyard of the Ministry, he looked up at the new building of the Greater Lubyanka and shivered. It held a new meaning for him. Its nine-storey grey-black hull was a battleship and the eighteen pilasters on its starboard side were eighteen gun turrets. Solitary and frail, Innokenty was drawn to it, across the small square, like a dinghy under the bows of a huge swift ship.

Escaping, he turned right towards Kuznetsky Most. A taxi close to the curb was about to pull away. Innokenty got in and sent it chasing down Kuznetsky Most, then left towards Petrovka where the lamps had just been lit.

He was still hesitating, wondering where he could telephone without somebody coming up and knocking with a coin on the glass of the kiosk. But to hunt for a quiet, isolated box would attract even more attention; better, perhaps, to choose one here, in the milling crowd, but make sure it's soundproof, built into the wall. . . . It also occurred to him how rash it was to go round in circles with a taxi-driver as a witness. He was digging in his pocket for a fifteen-kopeck coin when he realized that none of it mattered.

In the past few moments he had calmed down: he had

realized that he had no choice. Dangerous or not, he had to do it.

If you always look over your shoulder, how can you still remain a human being?

At the traffic lights in Okhotny Ryad he found not one but two fifteen-kopeck pieces in his pocket—it was a lucky omen.

Turning right after the university, the taxi raced up the Arbat. Innokenty gave the driver two notes and, without asking for the change, got out and walked across the square, trying not to hurry.

All the lights were on. In front of the cinema, a crowd was queueing up for *The Love of a Ballerina*. A grey mist veiled the illuminated red 'M' on the metro station. A woman who looked like a gipsy was selling small yellow bunches of mimosa.

Above all, he must be quick. Speak as briefly as possible and hang up. Then the danger would be minimal.

He walked very straight. A girl looked up at him as she hurried past.

Then another.

One of the wooden kiosks outside the station was empty, but he passed it and went inside.

Here there were four, built into the wall—all taken. But in the end one on the left, a dishevelled, tipsy lad was putting down the receiver. Quickly taking his place, Innokenty pulled the heavy glass door to, keeping it shut with one hand while the other, gloved, one he fumblingly dropped the coins into the slot.

After several long peals, the receiver was lifted at the other end.

'Yes?' said a woman's sulky voice as though doing a favour.

'Is that Professor Dobroumov's flat?' He tried to disguise his voice.

'Yes.'

'Could I speak to him, please?'

'Who are you?' The voice drawled, replete and lazy. The owner must be settled comfortably in her armchair.

'Actually . . . You don't know me. . . . But it doesn't matter. . . . Could you call him, please? It's very urgent.'

(All those extra words just for the sake of politeness!)

'But you can't expect the professor to speak to every Tom, Dick and Harry who rings him up.' The lady had taken offence. She sounded as though she might hang up then and there.

Beyond the plate-glass door, a yard from the row of cabins, people scurried past, overtaking each other. Someone was already waiting to come in.

'Who are you? Why can't you give your name?'

'I am a well-wisher. I have some important news for the professor.'

'What if you are? Why are you afraid to say your name?'

(It was time to hang up. People shouldn't have stupid wives!)

'And who are you? Are you his wife?'

'Why should I tell you first? You tell me!'

He would have left it at that. But not only the professor was concerned. . . . By now seething, no longer trying to disguise his voice or to keep it low, Innokenty pleaded excitedly:

'Listen to me! Listen! I've got to warn him, he's in danger!'

'In danger?' Her voice fell. She paused. But not to fetch her husband—oh no. 'All the more reason why I shouldn't call him. You may be lying. How can you prove you're not?'

The floor burnt Innokenty's feet and the black receiver with its heavy steel-wound cable scorched his hand.

'Listen to me! Listen!' he shouted in desperation. 'When the professor was last sent to Paris, he promised his French colleagues to give them something. Some kind of medicine. He's supposed to do it in a few days. Hand it over to foreigners! Do you realize? He mustn't do it! He must not give anything to the foreigners. It may be used as a provoca . . .'

There was a soft click, then dead silence, without the usual crackling on the line.

Someone had broken the connection.

CHAPTER TWO

'Look, we've got company!'

'They've brought in a new lot!'

'Where do you come from, friends?'

'Where are you from?'

'And what are those patches on your chest and caps?'

'That's where our numbers were,' said one of the new-comers. 'We have them on our backs and knees too. They ripped them off when we left the camps.'

'What d'you mean—numbers?'

'Gentlemen,' said Valentin Pryanchikov, 'would you kindly tell me what century we're living in?' He turned to his friend, Lev Rubin: 'Numbers on human beings? Is that what you call progress?'

'Don't start acting up, Valentin,' said Rubin. 'Go and have your dinner.'

'But how can I eat if there are human beings somewhere, going around with numbers on their heads? It's like something out of the Apocalypse, out of the Book of Revelations.'

'Hey!' said another Mavrino prisoner. 'They're giving us nine packets of Belomors[1] for the second half of December. You're in luck.'

'Belomor-Yavas or Belomor-Ducats?'

'Half and half.'

'The swine, those Ducats are poison. I'll complain to the Minister, that's what I'll do.'

'What are those overalls you're wearing?' asked the new-comer who had spoken first. 'Why are you all dressed up like parachutists?'

'They've put us in uniform now. The bastards are tightening up on us. We used to have proper woollen suits, and ordinary overcoats.'

More Mavrino men came out from the dining hall.

'Look at this new bunch!'

'They've brought in a whole lot of new ones!'

[1] Cheap brand of Soviet cigarettes.

'So what? Never seen real live prisoners before? You're blocking the gangway!'

'Good God, who's this? Dof-Dneprovsky! What happened to you, Dof? I looked all over Vienna for you in 'forty-five, I looked everywhere!'

'Look at them—all in rags and unshaven! What camp were you in?'

'River Camp. . . .'

'. . . Dubrov Camp . . .'

'I've been inside for more than eight years now, but I've never heard of those before.'

'They're new camps, Special Camps. They were only set up last year, in 'forty-eight. There was a directive from Stalin to tighten up on security in the rear . . .'

'Whose rear?'

'They picked me up right by the Prater and shoved me into a police wagon.'

'Wait a minute, let's hear what those new fellows have got to say.'

'No, let's go out for our walk. Out in the fresh air! That's the routine—even if there's an earthquake! Lev will get their story, don't you worry.'

'Dinner! Second shift!'

'Lake Camp, Meadow Camp, Steppe Camp, Sandy Camp . . .'

'You'd think there must be some great, unknown poet in the MVD, a new Pushkin. He's not quite up to a full-length poem, but he gives those wonderful poetic names to concentration camps.'

'Ha, ha, ha! Very funny, gentlemen, very funny,' said Pryanchikov. 'What century are we living in?'

'Quiet, Valentin!'

'Excuse me,' a newcomer asked Rubin, 'what's your name?'

'Lev Rubin.'

'Are you an engineer too?'

'No, I'm not an engineer, I'm a philologist.'

'A philologist? Do they even have philologists here?'

'Better ask who they don't have,' Rubin said. 'We've got mathematicians, physicists, chemists, radio engineers, telephone engineers, artists, translators, book-binders, architects, designers, and there's even a geologist who got in by mistake.'

'And what does he do?'

'He's all right—he got himself a job in the photo lab.'

'Lev! You say you're a materialist, but you always think people can live by things of the mind alone.' Valentin Pryanchikov said. 'Listen, friends! When they take you to the mess hall—we've put thirty-three plates for you on the last table by the window. Stuff your guts—but mind you don't burst!'

'Thanks very much, but what about yourselves?'

'We don't mind. Who wants salted herring and millet kasha, anyway!'

'Who wants what? Millet kasha? I haven't seen any in five years!'

'It's probably not millet anyway, more likely *magara*.'[2]

'You're crazy! Just let them try giving us *magara*! We'd throw it in their faces!'

'And how are they feeding people in the transit camps these days?'

'In Chelyabinsk. . . .'

'The new or the old place in Chelyabinsk?'

'I see you know your way around. At the new one. . . .'

'How is it there nowadays? Are there still no lavatories so that prisoners have to use buckets and carry them down from the third floor?'

'Yes.'

'What sort of a place is this?'

'How much bread do they give you here?'

'Who hasn't had dinner yet? Second shift!'

'We get four hundred grams of white bread, and the black bread is just put out on the table.'

'What do you mean—put out on the table?'

'What I say: it's put on the table, all sliced. You just take what you want.'

'Yes, but we have to break our backs for twelve and fourteen hours a day to earn our butter and Belomor cigarettes.'

[2] Coarse Siberian grain commonly fed to prisoners in the concentration camps of the Soviet Far East.

'That's not breaking your back! It's not breaking your back to sit at a desk. You break your back swinging a pick.'

'How the hell should we know? We're completely cut off in this dump. . . . Do you hear that, gentlemen? They say they've clamped down on the criminals[3] and that even in Krasnaya Presnya[4] they don't fool around any more.'

'They give forty grams of butter to the professor and twenty to the engineers. From each according to his abilities, to each according to his possibilities.'

'So you worked on the Dnieper Dam?'

'Yes, I was there with Winter. And that's why I'm here —because of the dam.'

'What do you mean?'

'Well, you see, I sold it to the Germans.'

'But it was blown up!'

'So what? I sold it to them after it was blown up.'

'Honest to God, it's like a breath of fresh air to hear all this! Transit camps! Prison trucks! Anything to be on the move! Take me back to dear old Sovietskaya Gavan!'[5]

'But not to stay, Valentin, not to stay!'

'No—only so long as they bring me back even faster, of course!'

'You know,' a newcomer said to Rubin, 'this sudden change makes my head spin. I've lived fifty-two years, I've survived fatal illnesses, I've been married to pretty women, I've fathered sons, I've won academic prizes—but I've never been so blissfully happy as I am today! Just think—they won't be driving me out to work in icy water tomorrow! Forty grams of butter! As much black bread as you like— *out on the table!* You can read books, you can shave and the guards don't beat you. This is a great day! It's like a mirage —or perhaps I've really died, and this is all a dream? I'm imagining I'm in heaven.'

'No, my dear sir,' said Rubin, 'you are in hell, just as

[3] Ordinary criminals, as opposed to the 'political' and other prisoners, were the aristocracy of the Soviet camps.

[4] Krasnaya Presnya—a Moscow prison, where conditions were comparatively lax.

[5] Sovietskaya Gavan—port in Far East round which there were camps.

before. But you have graduated to its best and highest circle
—the first circle. You asked me what sort of place this is.
Remember how Dante racked his brains to know where to
put the sages of antiquity? As a Christian he was in duty
bound to consign them to hell. But as a man of the Renaissance he was troubled in his conscience at the thought of
throwing them in with all sorts of ordinary sinners and con-
demning them to all the torments of the flesh. So he designed a special place for them in the Fourth Canto; it goes
something like this:

> "*A castle, girt with seven high walls around,*
> *And moated with a goodly rivulet*

> "*O'er which we went as though upon dry ground;*
> *With those wise men I passed the sevenfold gate*
> *Into a fresh green meadow, where we found . . .*

> "*Persons with grave and tranquil eyes, and great*
> *Authority in their carriage and attitude,*
> *Who spoke but seldom and in voice sedate.*"

'You came here in the Black Maria so you didn't see
that fresh green meadow.'

'You're too much of a poet, Lev,' said Valentin Pryanchikov. 'I could find a much simpler way to explain to the
comrade what a special prison is. You know what they're
always telling us in the newspapers: "It has been shown that
the better sheep are fed and looked after, the higher their yield
of wool." '

CHAPTER THREE

The Christmas tree was a sprig of pine wedged into a crack
in a stool. It was decorated with small, low-voltage coloured
lights on milky-white plastic-covered wires which had been
wound around it twice and connected to a battery on the
floor.

The stool stood in a corner of the room, between double bunks, and one of the upper mattresses shielded the whole corner and the tiny Christmas tree from the glare of the light bulbs in the ceiling.

Six men in thick, dark-blue denims, like those worn by parachutists, stood together near the Christmas tree and listened with bowed heads as one of them, a swarthy, thin-faced man called Max Richtman, recited a Protestant Christmas prayer.

There was no one else in the whole of the large room, which was crowded with double bunks welded together by the frames. After dinner and their hour of evening exercise, all the others had gone to night work.

Max finished the prayer and they all sat down. Five of them were filled with bitter-sweet memories of home—their beloved neat and well-ordered Germany where beneath the tiled roofs this most important festival of the year was such a joyful occasion. The sixth member of the group was a great hulk of a man with the thick black beard of a biblical prophet—he was a Jew and a Communist.

Lev Rubin's fate was bound up with Germany in both peace and war.

In peacetime he was a specialist in Germanic philology, speaking modern German perfectly and even able to cope with all the dialects. He could remember every German whose name had ever appeared in print as though he were a personal acquaintance. He could talk about little towns on the Rhine as if he had often walked their spotless, tree-shaded streets.

But all he knew of Germany was Prussia, where he had served—as a major in the Red Army—in a unit concerned with penetration, sabotage and psychological warfare. His job had been to select German POW's who were willing to collaborate, take them out of the camps and set them up comfortably in a special training school. Some he sent through the front lines with explosives and forged Reichsmarks, leave passes and identification papers. They blew up bridges, or just made their way back home and had a good time until they were caught. With others he discussed Goethe and Schiller, composed propaganda leaflets or got them to talk over loudspeakers mounted on lorries, urging their comrades, who were fighting on the other side of the lines, to turn their guns against Hitler. With others, again, he went through the lines himself and persuaded enemy strong-points to surrender, thus saving Soviet lives.

But he could not work with Germans like this without becoming one of them, without coming to like them and also, once they were defeated, to pity them. It was for this that Rubin had been arrested. People in the unit who disliked him had accused him of speaking out, after the offensive of January 1945, against the slogan 'Blood for blood and death for death'.

There was some truth in the accusation and he did not deny it; but the truth was so much more complicated than had been said in the newspapers or in the charges against him.

Two lockers had been pushed up against the stool with the lighted Christmas tree to serve as a table. The six men treated themselves to tinned foods from the *Gastronom* (inmates of special prisons were allowed to order goods from the best stores in Moscow and pay for them out of their earnings), home-made cake, and coffee that was already going cold. A sedate conversation started up, which Max firmly guided towards peaceful subjects: old folk customs, nostalgic stories of Christmas night. Alfred, a bespectacled physics student from Vienna, who had not been able to complete his studies, spoke with a funny Austrian accent. Gustav, a youngster from the Hitler Youth, who had been taken prisoner a week after the end of the war, sat, round-cheeked, his pink ears translucent like a piglet's, and stared wide-eyed at the Christmas lights, hardly daring to take part in the older men's conversation.

But they could not keep off the subject of the war. Some-one remembered the Christmas of 1944, five years before, when every German had taken pride in the Ardennes offen-sive—as in antiquity, the vanquished had turned the tables on the victors. They remembered how on that Christmas Eve Germany had listened to a speech by Goebbels.

Rubin, plucking at the bristles of his stiff black beard, said he also remembered that speech, which had been very telling. Goebbels had spoken with deep anguish, as if he had per-sonally shouldered the burdens under which Germany was tottering. He probably already had a premonition of his own end.

SS-Obersturmbannführer Reinhold Simmel, whose long body barely found room between the table and the double bunk, did not appreciate Rubin's tact. He found it unbearable that this Jew should dare to comment on Goebbels at all. He would never have sat down at the same table with him had he had the strength of will to deny himself the company of his compatriots on Christmas Eve. But the other Germans had all insisted on having Rubin. For this handful of Germans, thrown by fate into the golden cage of a special prison in the heart of this bleak and barbarous country, this major from the enemy army, who had spent the whole war spreading discord and destruction among them, was the only man with whom they had a common language. He alone could interpret the local manners and customs for them, advise them how to behave and keep them up to date on what was happening in the world by translating the news from Russian.

Trying his best to needle Rubin, Simmel said that in the Reich there had been plenty of rousing orators and he wondered why the Bolsheviks preferred to read speeches which were prepared and approved in advance.

The remark was all the more wounding for being true. How could one explain the historical reasons for it to this enemy and murderer? Rubin felt nothing but loathing for Simmel. He remembered him when he arrived at Mavrino after many years in Butyrki Prison, still in his creaking leather jacket with the marks on the sleeves where his SS insignia had been ripped off—he had been in the civilian branch, which was by far the worst. Prison had not softened the relentless cruelty of his face, stamped with the mark of Cain. Simmel's presence had made Rubin reluctant to come to this dinner, but the others had been so insistent, and he was so sorry for them in their loneliness that he could not bring himself to cast a shadow on their festivities by staying away.

Trying to keep his temper, Rubin quoted in German Pushkin's advice that certain people should not attempt to deliver judgments higher than their boots.

Max tried to stop tempers rising even more by saying that, with Lev's help, he was beginning to understand Pushkin in the original. He asked Reinhold why he hadn't taken some whipped cream with his cake, then turned to Lev and asked where he had been that Christmas Eve five years before.

Reinhold helped himself to whipped cream. Lev recalled that five years ago he had been in a bunker by the Narev bridgehead near Rozhan.

And as the five Germans remembered their torn and trampled Germany, decking it out in the richest colours of the mind's eye so too Rubin suddenly thought back to the Narev bridgehead and the dank forests around Lake Ilmen.

The little coloured lights shone in the six men's eyes. Once again, the Germans asked Rubin to tell them the latest news. But it was embarrassing for him to talk about what had happened in December. He could not play the part of a neutral, a non-Communist, nor could he give up all thought of re-educating these people, but there was no question, either, of explaining to them that in our complex age Socialist truth sometimes progresses in a devious, roundabout way. So he picked out for them, as he did subconsciously for himself, only those current events which showed the main trend, and passed over in silence those which obscured it.

But that particular December nothing positive had taken place, except for the Soviet-Chinese talks—though even they seemed to have got bogged down—and the seventieth birthday of the Leader of the Peoples. He could scarcely tell the Germans about the trial of Traicho Kostov, at which the whole blatant *mise-en-scène* had suddenly come unstuck in open court and the correspondents had been fobbed off, after some delay, with a false confession allegedly written by Kostov in the death cell. This was too shameful, and it would hardly have served the purposes of re-education.

So Rubin dwelt mostly on the historic triumph of the Chinese Communists.

Max listened and nodded agreement, his brown, olive-shaped eyes guileless. He was attached to Rubin, but since the Berlin blockade he had had doubts about the things he told them. Rubin did not know that, in the Microwave Laboratory where he worked, Max at the risk of his neck would occasionally put together a tiny receiver made to look like something else, and then dismantle it. So Max

24

already knew from Cologne and the BBC German service not only about Traicho Kostov—how in court he had repudiated the confession which had been forced out of him during his interrogation—but also about the plans for the North Atlantic Alliance and economic developments in Western Germany. All this, of course, he passed on to the other Germans.

So they just nodded as Rubin spoke.

Actually, it was long past the time for Rubin to go—he had not been let off the whole of the night shift. He said how much he had enjoyed the cake—the student from Vienna gave a little bow of gratification—and began to take his leave. The Germans kept him for as long as politeness required and let him go. Then they started to sing Christmas carols in subdued voices.

Rubin went out into the corridor, carrying a Mongolian dictionary and a volume of Hemingway in English under his arm.

The corridor was wide; it had a temporary floor of rough wood full of splinters. There were no windows, so it was lit day and night by electricity. It was here that, eager for news like the other inmates, Rubin had questioned the prisoners from the camps during the dinner break an hour ago. A door to the main prison staircase opened on this corridor, as did the doors of several cell-like rooms. They were rooms in that they had no locks, but they also qualified as cells because of the peep-holes—little windows in the doors. The peep-holes were never used by the warders, but they had been installed, as required by the regulations for ordinary prisons, simply because officially Mavrino counted as a 'Special Prison'.

Through one of these peep-holes one could catch a glimpse of another Christmas Eve party—the Latvians had also been let off work for the occasion.

The rest of the prisoners were at work, and Rubin was afraid of being found out, taken to Major Shikin and made to write out an explanation.

At each end of the corridor there were large double doors. One pair was wood-panelled and led through an arch into what had once been the sanctuary of the chapel in this former country house, but had now also been converted into a cell. The door was always shut and it was covered from top to bottom with sheet iron. It was known by the prisoners as the 'heavenly gates'.

Rubin went up to this iron door and knocked at the little window. From the other side the watchful face of the warder pressed up against the glass.

The key turned quietly in the lock. This warder happened to be one of the more easy-going ones.

Rubin came out at the top of the main staircase of the old building; the two flights curved outwards and converged again at the bottom; he walked across a marble-paved landing, past two old, unlit wrought-iron lanterns, into the laboratory corridor, and pushed open a door with a sign saying 'ACOUSTICS'.

CHAPTER FOUR

The Acoustics Laboratory was a wide, high-ceilinged room with several windows. It was untidy and crammed with electronic instruments on wooden shelves, shiny aluminium stands, assembly benches, new plywood cabinets made in a Moscow factory and comfortable desks requisitioned in Germany.

Large overhead frosted globes cast a pleasant, diffused white light.

In a far corner of the room stood a soundproof acoustic booth. Wrapped in a layer of straw covered with sacking, it looked very makeshift. The door, three feet thick but hollow as a circus clown's dumb-bells, was at the moment wide open, and the woollen curtain which usually hung over it had been thrown back to let in air. Next to the booth, rows of brass plugs gleamed on the black bakelite face of the control-board.

A girl sat at a desk near by, her back to the booth. She was diminutive and frail, her narrow shoulders barely covered with a shawl, a stern expression on her face.

The ten or so other people in the room were men, all dressed in identical dark-blue denims. Lit by the overhead lights and by additional spots of light from adjustable desk lamps, they busied themselves with their work, tapping and

26

soldering, walking around or sitting at the assembly benches or desks.

From different places in the room three makeshift radio sets, hastily mounted on aluminium panels without cabinets, blared competing programmes of jazz, piano music and Oriental folk-songs.

Still holding his Mongolian dictionary and his Hemingway, Rubin walked slowly through the laboratory towards his desk. Some white crumbs from the cake still adhered to his curly black beard.

Though the denims issued to the prisoners were all alike, each prisoner gave his an individual touch. One of Rubin's buttons had come off, and he had slackened the belt so that loose folds hung over his stomach. By contrast, a young fellow with flowing chestnut hair, who was at the moment standing in his way, had made himself look very smart. The buckled cloth belt was pulled tight round his thin waist, and he wore a blue silk shirt, a little faded from too much washing, and a bright-coloured tie. This young man completely blocked the way down one side of the room. Brandishing a hot soldering iron in his right hand, and resting his left foot on a chair and his elbow on his knee, he was studying a radio circuit in the American magazine, *Wireless Engineer*, and singing:

> '*Boogie-woogie, boogie-woogie.*
> *Samba! Samba!*
> *Boogie-woogie, boogie-woogie.*
> *Samba! Samba!*'

Rubin stood for a moment with a patient expression on his face. The young man did not appear to notice him.

'Valentin,' Rubin said, 'couldn't you move your hind leg a bit?'

Without looking up from the diagram, Valentin answered in a brisk staccato voice:

'Lay off, Lev! Why do you come here at night? What's the point?' He looked wonderingly at Rubin with his bright young eyes: 'What the hell do we need philologists for here? Ha, ha, ha.' He pronounced every syllable very distinctly. 'You're no engineer! It's ridiculous!'

Pouting his fleshy lips like a child and opening his eyes unbelievably wide, Rubin said with a lisp: 'There are engineers and engineers, my child. Some of them here used to do very well selling lemonade.'

'Not me! I'm a first-class engineer, and don't you forget it, my lad!' Valentin retorted sharply, placing the soldering iron in a wire stand and straightening up.

He had the clean, well-washed look of youth. Life had left his face unfurrowed and unmarked, and his movements were boyish. It was hard to believe that he had graduated from an institute before the war, that he had been in Western Europe, gone through the German prison camps and was now serving his fifth year in prison in his own country.

'How can I be a bad engineer? You know how mad I am about women!'

'Only theoretically, it would appear,' said Rubin in a bored voice, moving his lips as though he were chewing.

'And how I love spending money!'

'But you never have any.'

'So how can I be a bad engineer? Just think of all the money I need to spend on women! And how can I spend it unless I earn it? And how can I do that as an engineer unless I really know my stuff? So I have to be mad keen on it, don't I?'

Valentin's long face, thrust defiantly at Rubin's, shone with conviction.

'Lev!' cried the prisoner by the window, whose desk faced the young woman's. 'At last I've caught Valentin's voice! It's like a bell! That's how I'm going to label it: bell-like. You can tell a voice like that on any phone, through any amount of interference.'

He unfolded a large sheet of paper divided into columns and squares with headings under which different types of voices were classified.

'What a lot of nonsense.' Valentin picked up his soldering iron and it began to smoke.

He moved out of the way and Rubin went to his chair, but bent over the list showing the classification of voice types.

He and his friend Gleb Nerzhin looked at it for a while in silence.

'We've made some real progress, Gleb. If we use it in

conjunction with spectographs we'll have a good tool. Soon we'll understand exactly what it is that a telephone does to a human voice.' He gave a start: 'What's that on the radio?'

The loudest noise in the room was the jazz, but here, by the window-sill, it was drowned by the music from his own little improvised radio—a piece for the piano, a flowing melody in which the same notes kept fading away only to re-emerge more insistently.

'It's a miracle. That's Beethoven's Seventeenth Sonata in D Minor. For some reason it's hardly ever played. Do listen.'

They bent closer to the receiver, but it was hard to hear because of the jazz.

'Valentin,' said Gleb. 'Do us a favour, cut it out.'

'I've already done you a favour,' said Valentin. 'I made that receiver for you, but I'll unsolder the coil and that'll be the end of it.'

The young woman raised her eyebrows: 'Really, Valentin! It's impossible to listen to three sets at once. Do as you're told and turn it off.'

Valentin's radio was playing a slow fox-trot which the young woman liked very much.

'Serafima! I protest!' He seized the back of a chair and gesticulated as if he were speaking from a platform: 'How can any normal, healthy person not enjoy the rousing, up-lifting sound of jazz? You're all being corrupted by trash! You mean to say you've never danced the "Blue Tango"? You've never been to Arkady Raikin's[1] variety show? You just don't know the best things created by man. What's more, you've never been to Europe. Where could you learn to live? My advice to you is—fall in love!' He delivered this speech from behind the chair, not noticing the bitter lines round the young woman's lips. 'Anyone you like—*ça dépend de vous!* Think of the lights twinkling in the night, and the rustle of silk.'

'He's gone berserk again!' Rubin said with concern. 'We'll have to be firm.' Behind Valentin's back he switched off the jazz.

'Who said you could do that?' Valentin spun round,

[1] Popular Soviet comedian.

frowning, with an attempt at a threatening air. The flowing strains of the Seventeenth Sonata rose in all their purity, competing only with a homely folk-song from the third radio in another corner of the room.

Rubin relaxed and his brown eyes looked less unyielding. His beard was still dotted with cake crumbs.

'Are you still worrying about the Atlantic Charter, Valentin? Have you written your will? Who are you leaving your bedroom slippers to?'

His face suddenly serious, Valentin looked into Rubin's eyes and asked quietly:

'Listen, what the hell do you want? You're driving me crazy. At least in prison a fellow has the right to be himself.'

He was called away by one of the fitters and walked off gloomily.

Rubin sat down at his desk, with his back to Gleb, and listened to the music. But the soothing, plunging melody stopped abruptly, like a speech cut in the middle of a word. And that was the untimely end of the Seventeenth Sonata.

Rubin swore obscenely, but so low that only Gleb could hear him.

'Would you care to spell that? I couldn't hear properly,' said Gleb, his back still turned.

'Just my luck,' Rubin said hoarsely, also without turning round. 'Now I've missed that Sonata, and I'd never heard it before.'

'It's because you're disorganized, as I keep telling you.' So cheerful a moment earlier when he had recorded Valentin's voice, Gleb was listless and sad again. 'What a fine sonata it is. Why doesn't it have a name like the others? How about "The Sonata of the Passing Moment"? The mood keeps changing—everything in it is transient—the good and the bad, the sad and the gay—— just like in life. And there is no ending—that's like life too. It should be called —*Ut in Vita*. Where have you been?'

'With the Germans. We were celebrating Christmas,' Rubin said with a smirk.

They talked without looking at each other, the backs of their heads almost touching.

'Good for you' Gleb thought; he said: 'I like the way you

treat them. All those hours you spend teaching Max Russian. Though you have all the reason in the world to hate them.'

'Hate them? No, but of course I'm not so uncritically fond of them as I once was. Even that kind-hearted unpolitical Max—doesn't he, after all, have some share of responsibility for all the atrocities? He did nothing to stop them, did he?'

'You mean, just as you and I are doing nothing to stop Abakumov,[2] or Shikin and Mishin.'

'Listen, what am I in prison for? I'm a Jew and a Russian, but I'm also a citizen of the world, aren't I?'

'"Citizen of the world" sounds innocent enough!'

'Well then, cosmopolitan.[3] So I'm here for good reason, aren't I?'

'Of course you are. Although you're always trying to prove the opposite to the Supreme Court!'

From the radio on the window-sill came the voice of an announcer promising to give the results of the latest 'Socialist Rivalry' competition in half a minute. Before the thirty seconds were up, Gleb Nerzhin reached unhurriedly for the knob and switched it off.

His tired face was ashen.

Valentin Pryanchikov was by now busy working out what scale of amplification to use. He was humming cheerfully:

> 'Boogie-woogie, boogie-woogie,
> Samba! Samba!'

[2] Abakumov, Victor Semyonovich: a career official in the Soviet security police, Abakumov first achieved prominence in 1943 when he was placed at the head of SMERSH, the military counter-intelligence organization subordinate to Beria's Ministry of Internal Affairs. In 1946, when Beria moved up into an 'overlord' position in charge of all police, security and espionage activities, the Ministry of Internal Affairs (MVD) was headed by Sergei Kruglov, while Abakumov was made Minister of State Security (MGB). He was replaced in 1951 by Semyon Ignatiev. After Beria's fall and execution in December 1953, Abakumov was arrested the following year and condemned to death for complicity in Beria's abuse of power.

[3] A term applied to Jewish intellectuals during the anti-semitic campaigns of Stalin's last years.

CHAPTER FIVE

Nerzhin was the same age as Valentin Pryanchikov but looked older. Although his hair was still quite thick and had not turned grey, deep wrinkles had gathered round his eyes and mouth and ran across his forehead. His face was drawn and, for lack of fresh air, the skin had a faded look. But what really made him seem elderly was the slowness of his movements—that wise economy of effort by which nature husbands the strength of prisoners in camps. True, there was no great need for it in the relatively lax conditions of the Special Prison with its meat diet and freedom from back-breaking physical labour. But knowing the length of his sentence, Nerzhin was training himself in the knack of not wasting energy.

At the moment his large desk was piled high with Russian and foreign books, typescripts and files—magazines were lying open even on the working space in the middle. An uninitiated onlooker might have mistaken the scene for one of feverish scientific activity.

In fact it was all window-dressing. Nerzhin carefully arranged it every evening in case there was an inspection.

He had no idea what was on the desk in front of him. Pulling aside the light-coloured curtain, he looked out through the dark window. Moscow, far away in the night and hidden by a hill, threw up a pillar of pale, diffused light, filling the sky with a reddish glow.

Nerzhin's special chair with its well-padded back, his special roll-top desk of a sort not made in the Soviet Union and his comfortable place by a window facing south, would have told anyone familiar with the history of Mavrino Special Prison that he was one of its oldest inmates.

The prison took its name from the nearby village, which had long since been swallowed by Greater Moscow. It had been opened on a July evening three years earlier. A dozen prisoners were brought from the camps to this old country house on the outskirts of Moscow, which had been duly surrounded by barbed wire. The prisoners looked back to those early days as to an age of pastoral simplicity. They had been allowed to wander about the compound as they pleased; they could lie in the long wet grass—it was uncut although, according to prison regulations, it should have been cropped very short to prevent prisoners from crawling unobserved to the barbed wire. They could gaze at the stars—or, if Lieutenant Zhvakun of the MVD was on night duty, watch him sweat as under cover of darkness he stole timber intended for building repairs and pushed it under the barbed wire, so that he could later take it home for firewood.

At that time the prisoners did not yet know exactly what kind of research they had been brought to Mavrino to do. They were busy unpacking stacks of crates which two special goods trains had delivered, securing comfortable chairs and desks for themselves, and sorting equipment (telephone engineering, ultra-high-frequency radio communications and acoustics), all of it out of date and all broken in transit. In doing so they discovered that the best of the equipment and most recent technical documents had been pilfered or destroyed by the Germans. This had happened because the MVD major, sent to requisition the stuff from a German firm, knew a lot about furniture but had no knowledge of either radio or German, and had spent his time combing the suburbs of Berlin for furniture for his Moscow flat and those of his superiors.

For a long time now the grass had been kept short, and the gates closed except when a bell gave a signal to open them. The establishment had passed from Beria's jurisdiction to Abakumov's and had been allocated top-secret work connected with telephone communications. The job was to take a year but, growing ever wider in scope and more involved, and invading related areas, had already dragged on for two. The objective, as Rubin and Nerzhin understood it, was to find a way of identifying voices on the telephone and to discover what it is that makes every human voice unique.

No one, it appeared, had tried to do this before. At any rate, they could find no books on the subject. They had been allowed six months, then another six, but they had made little progress and now time was getting short.

Feeling unsettled, Rubin complained over his shoulder:

'Somehow, I just don't feel in the mood today.'

'You amaze me! You only had four years of the war and you've been less than five years in prison, and you say you're tired? You should get yourself a holiday in the Crimea.'

There was a silence.

'Are you doing something of your own?' Rubin asked quietly.

'Uh-huh.'

'Well, who's going to get on with the voices?'

'To tell you the truth I was hoping you would.'

'You're shameless! All that stuff you've got out of the Lenin Library, saying you need it for the job! Speeches of famous lawyers, Koni's Memoirs, Stanislavsky's Memoirs! And *Princess Turandot*—that really was the limit! Can you see a prisoner in camp with a collection like that?'

Rubin pushed out his thick lips in a way that always gave him a comic and foolish look.

'It's a funny thing but didn't I see you reading all those books, including *Princess Turandot*, and in working hours at that?'

'You did. I'd be working my head off now, if it wasn't for a couple of things I've got on my mind. To start with, I'm worrying about those parquet floors.'

'What parquet floors?'

'The ones in the MVD block of flats at Kaluga Gate—you know, the one with the round tower. It was built by people from our camp and I worked for the man who laid the floors. I heard today that Roitman lives there. I suppose it's a question of pride—I'd like to know if those floors squeak or not. If they do, it means I did a bad job. But here I am, and I certainly can't go back and fix them!'

'Yes, I can see you might lose sleep over that.'

'Exactly. And the other thing—isn't it bad form to work on Saturday night when you know that only the free workers will get Sunday off?'

'Yes,' sighed Rubin. 'They're enjoying themselves in town now, the bastards.'

'But do they know how to enjoy themselves? Do they really get more out of life than we do? I'm not so sure.'

Turning their backs to the room, they looked out of the window at the lights in the compound, the watch-tower faintly outlined in the darkness, more lights near the distant greenhouses, and the column of pale shimmering fire over Moscow.

Nerzhin was a mathematician who knew something about linguistics; when Russian phonetics became a subject of research at Mavrino he was put to work with the only philologist in the place, Rubin. For two years they had sat back to back twelve hours a day. Very soon they had discovered that they had both served on the Northwestern and the Byelorussian fronts during the war, and that both had been arrested at the front, in the same month, by the same SMERSH unit, under the same Paragraph 10, which was *universally applicable*,[1] that is, it was applied without regard to education, property qualification or material situation. And both had got ten years—like everybody else. There was a difference of only five years in age and one degree in rank between them—Nerzhin had been a captain. It was possible that before the war he had actually attended some of Assistant-Professor Rubin's lectures.

They looked out into the darkness. Rubin said sadly:

'It worries me that you have so few intellectual interests.'

'But I'm not trying to understand things. There's a lot of cleverness in the world but not enough goodness.'

'Here's a good book for you to read.'

'Hemingway? Is this another one about poor mixed-up bulls?'

'No.'

'Or lions at bay?'

'No.'

'I can't even make sense of people, why should I bother about bulls?'

'You really must read it.'

[1] SMERSH, organized during the war by the Director of State Security, Abakumov; a branch of the Secret Police particularly concerned with unreliable elements in the Red Army and counter-espionage.

Paragraph 10 of Article 58 of the Criminal Code relates to people engaged in propaganda against the régime, or other subversive activities.

'I don't have to do anything for anyone, and don't you forget it. "I don't owe nothing to nobody" as our friend Spiridon would say.'

'Hemingway is an intelligent, generous, totally honest writer—soldier, hunter, fisherman, drunkard and lover of women. He has an utter contempt for falsehood, is always simple, very human and has the innocence of genius. . . .'

'Oh, come off it!' Nerzhin laughed. 'I've lived thirty years without Hemingway and I can go on for a few more. First you tried to force Capek on me, then Fallada. My life is a shambles as it is. Don't try to make me go in all directions at once. Just let me find my own way. . . .'

He turned back to the window.

Rubin sighed. He was still in no mood to work.

He looked at the map of China, propped up against the shelf at the back of his desk. He had cut it out of a newspaper and pasted it on cardboard. All through the past year he had marked in red the advance of the Communist armies and, now that their victory was complete, had left the map there to raise his spirits when he felt depressed or tired.

But today sadness gnawed at him and even the big red expanse of victorious Chinese Communism failed to cheer him up.

Nerzhin, occasionally stopping and thoughtfully sucking the tip of his plastic pen, wrote in a hand so fine that he might have been using a needle, on a scrap of paper hidden behind his books and files:

'There is, I remember, a passage in Marx (I must find it) where he says that the victorious proletariat might perhaps achieve its aims without expropriating the richer peasants. This means that he saw an economic possibility of including *all* the peasants in the new social system. The Big Chief, of course, didn't even attempt this in 'twenty-nine. But then, has he ever tried to do anything subtle or intelligent? How can one expect a butcher to be a surgeon?'

The large Acoustic Laboratory was busy with its usual peaceful routine. The motor on the electrician's lathe hummed away. People ordered things to be switched on or off. One of the radio sets was playing a dreadfully sentimental tune. Someone was calling loudly for a 6K7 valve.

When she thought no one was looking at her, Serafima

glanced sharply at Nerzhin who was still writing in his microscopic hand.

The Security Officer, Major Shikin, had ordered her to keep an eye on him.

CHAPTER SIX

Serafima was so tiny that it was difficult to call her by anything but the diminutive of her name, Simochka. She wore a cotton blouse, always had a warm shawl round her shoulders, and she was a lieutenant in the MGB.

All the free workers at Mavrino were officers of the MGB.

In accordance with the Stalin Constitution of the USSR, they had a great many rights, among them the right to work. But they were entitled to do so for eight hours a day only, and their work was not productive but consisted in supervising the prisoners who, bereft of all other rights, were granted that of working a twelve-hour day. The free workers took it in turn to work late shifts in the laboratories so that the prisoners would be supervised during their additional four hours—from seven to eleven p.m.—as well as during the dinner break from six to seven.

Today, the birdlike Simochka was on night duty in the Acoustics Laboratory where, for the time being, she was the only representative of authority.

The regulations required her to see that the prisoners worked and didn't idle or use their working time to manufacture weapons, dig tunnels or take advantage of the radio equipment at their disposal to set up two-way communication with the White House. At ten to eleven she was expected to collect all top-secret documents, lock them in the safe and then lock up the laboratory.

It was only six months since Simochka had graduated from the Institute of Communications and, because her background was impeccable from the security point of view, had been sent to this top-secret research establishment, officially referred to only by a code number but which the prisoners irreverently called the 'monkey-house'. All free workers in it were automatically given the rank of officers in the security service and salaries higher than those of ordinary engineers. They also received clothing allowances and bonuses according to rank. In return, their only duty was to be dedicated and vigilant.

It suited Simochka very well that no one expected her to show any competence in her special field. Like many of her girl-friends there, she had not learned anything at the Institute—this for many reasons. The girls had done very little maths or physics at school. In their final years it had come to their ears that the headmaster was always reprimanding teachers for failing too many students, and they realized that they would scrape through even if they knew nothing. As a result, when the time came to go to university they were completely lost in the jungle of mathematics and radio-technology—and very often they had no time at all for study. Every autumn they were taken for a month or so to collective farms to dig potatoes. The rest of the year they attended classes lasting from eight to ten hours a day, so they had no time to digest their lecture notes. On Monday evenings they had political studies, and at least once a week they were obliged to attend some meeting. Then there were the obligatory 'civic' activities—helping to produce the wall-newspaper, organizing workers' concerts, sponsored by the Institute. Time had also to be found for housework, shopping and looking after their clothes—and for an occasional evening at a cinema, a theatre or a dance. If you don't have a little fun as a student, when are you likely to have it later in life?

When the examinations came, Simochka, like the other girls, wrote cribs, hid them in her clothes, smuggled them in and took them out and unfolded them at the right moment, so that they looked like legitimate sheets of rough work. The ignoramuses could easily have been shown up if the examiners had asked enough questions at the orals, but the teachers themselves were overworked—what with committees, meetings and writing various memoranda and reports for the Dean and the Rector. Failing their students meant extra work examining them a second time. Besides, if their students failed, the teachers suffered, just like factory workers turning out defective goods—on the well-known principle that there are no bad pupils, only bad teachers. No wonder that they didn't try to catch their students out but did their best to get them through as quickly as possible and with the highest possible marks.

In the last years of their studies, Simochka and her friends came to realize with a sinking feeling that they had no liking for their subject and indeed found it a terrible bore. But by then it was too late to change. Simochka trembled at the thought of actually having to do responsible work in radio technology.

Fortunately she was sent to Mavrino where this was not expected of her. But even someone less small and puny might well have had been overawed on entering this secluded citadel where specially chosen jailors and armed guards kept watch over important state prisoners. She was briefed, together with nine other girls who had all just graduated from her Institute. It was explained to them that the place they had come to was more dangerous than a battlefield—it was a serpents' nest where the slightest false step could be their undoing. They would be in contact with the dregs of the human race—people unworthy of speaking Russian, and the more dangerous because they did not openly bare their fangs but always wore a mask of courtesy and good breeding. If asked about their crimes—which the girls were categorically forbidden to do—they would weave a clever tissue of lies, trying to prove that they were innocent victims. Finally, the girls were told that they must never show their hatred of these vipers but, as good members of the Komsomol, and like the prisoners themselves, put on a show of politeness. On the other hand, they must not get into conversation with them (except on purely practical matters) or run errands for them outside the prison. At the slightest infringement of these regulations (or even the first hint of such a possibility) they must immediately report everything to the Security Officer, Major Shikin.

The major was a short, swarthy, self-important man with a big head, closely cropped grey hair, and feet so small that he wore boys' shoes. He told them that although the reptilian nature of these wicked men was obvious to him and to other experienced people, there might well be someone among the girls—completely new to this work as they were—who, out of the kindness of her heart, would waver in her duty and break the rules, say, by lending a prisoner a book from the library intended only for the free workers, or worse, by posting a letter for him outside. (Any such letter, though addressed to a Maria or a Tanya, was bound to be intended for a foreign spy centre.) He urged anyone who saw a friend going wrong to come like a good comrade to her help by reporting her action to him at once.

Finally, the major pointed out that to have an affair with a prisoner was an offence under the criminal code which, as they all knew, was very flexible and provided penalties up to a sentence of twenty-five years hard labour.

The girls were shaken by this bleak picture of the future ahead of them. Some even had tears in their eyes. But the seeds of mistrust had now been sewn among them and, as they left the briefing session, they did not talk to one another about what they had been told.

With her heart in her mouth, Simochka had followed Major Roitman into the Acoustics Laboratory, and instantly felt like shutting her eyes and as though she were falling from a great height.

In the six months that had gone by since that day, something strange had happened to her. It wasn't that she had stopped believing in the reality of the imperialists' dark designs, and she was still quite prepared to accept that the prisoners who worked in all the other laboratories were blood-thirsty villains. But as for the dozen or so she saw every day —these engineers and technicians, some with the highest university degrees—they seemed so grimly indifferent to the thought of freedom, to what was happening to them, to their prison terms of ten or twenty-five years, and they were so wrapped up in their work which brought them no return, that she simply couldn't bring herself to see them as desperadoes of international espionage—a type so easily identified by cinema-goers and so easily hunted down by spy-catchers.

Simochka wasn't in the least afraid of them, nor could she hate them. Their great learning, and the stoicism with which they endured their fate aroused nothing but her boundless respect. Though duty and patriotism compelled her to report all their transgressions to the Security Officer, she began to feel, for reasons that were not at all clear to her, that her role was a thoroughly despicable one and that it put her in an impossible position.

It was particularly painful in the case of her nearest neighbour and working partner, Gleb Nerzhin, who sat facing her across their two desks.

For some time now Simochka had been working closely with him, under his direction, on diction tests. At Mavrino new telephone circuits were always being tried out to see how well they conveyed the nuances of human speech. There was still no instrument which could accurately measure this factor and register it on a dial. From this point of view, the efficiency of a circuit could only be judged by someone listening while a second person read out test syllables, words and sentences at the other end of the line.

Nerzhin was responsible for the mathematical programming of these tests, which were working out so well that he had even written a monograph on the methods involved. Whenever he and Simochka felt that their work was getting on top of them, it was he who decided what was urgent and what could wait: at such moments he looked so young and self-assured that Simochka, whose mental image of war was derived from the cinema, saw him in a captain's uniform, shouting orders to his gun-crew in the blaze and smoke of shell-fire.

But, in fact, Nerzhin was decisive only because he wanted to get through his work as quickly as possible and relapse into idleness. Once he had said to Simochka: 'I am active because I hate action.' 'What do you like?' she had asked shyly. 'I like to think,' he said. And indeed, once an immediate crisis was over, he would sit still for hours, his face grey, showing his age and his wrinkles. There was no trace now of self-assurance, and his movements were slow and hesitant. He would think a long time before writing a few of those notes which Simochka, today again, saw on his desk among a pile of technical reference books and monographs. She noticed that when he finished he always put them in the same place on the left side of his desk, but not in the drawer. She burned with curiosity to know what he was writing and for whom. Without knowing it, he had become for her an object of sympathy and admiration.

So far, Simochka's life had been very unhappy. She was

not pretty. Her nose was too long; her hair was thin and grew awkwardly—she gathered it together at the back of her head in a straggly little knot. She was not just small, which can be quite attractive, but too small—more like a schoolgirl than a grown woman. Also, she was rather prim and proper, had no time for fun and games, and this also put the young men off. At twenty-five she had no boy-friends and had never been kissed.

A month ago something had gone wrong with the microphone in the acoustics booth and Nerzhin had called Simochka to help him fix it. She came with a screwdriver in her hand, then, in the soundless, airless room where there was barely enough space for the two of them, bent towards the microphone which Nerzhin was examining, and before she realized it, her cheek was touching his. She nearly died of fright at the thought of what might happen next. She should have drawn back, but she went on foolishly looking at the microphone. There followed the longest and most terrifying minute she had ever known—their cheeks were on fire as they touched, but he too did not draw away! Suddenly he seized her head and kissed her on the lips. Simochka's whole body felt exquisitely faint. She forgot her duty to the Komsomol and to her country; all she could say was:

'The door's not shut.'

They were hidden from the noisy room outside only by a thin flapping blue curtain in the window of the booth—anyone could have pulled it up at any moment. Nerzhin risked only ten days in the punishment cell, but for her, Simochka, her security clearance, her career, perhaps even her freedom, were at stake. Yet she had not the strength to draw away from the hands that clasped her head.

For the first time in her life a man had kissed her.

In this way, the cunningly wrought chain broke at the link formed by a woman's heart.

CHAPTER SEVEN

'What do you want?'

'I'm in a poetic mood. Let's talk.'

'I'm supposed to be busy.'

'Nonsense! I'm upset, Gleb. I was sitting with the Germans in front of their Christmas tree, and I happened to mention something about my dug-out at the bridgehead north of Pultusk. Suddenly, there it all was—the front, the war. It was so vivid—and nostalgic too. . . . Even war memories can be sweet.'

'They shouldn't be. According to Taoist ethics "Weapons are the instruments of misfortune, not of honour. The wise man conquers unwillingly."'

'Have you changed from a sceptic into a Taoist?'

'I've not decided yet.'

'Thinking about the war reminded me of my Krauts— the good ones, I mean—and how we used to make up captions for leaflets together. The mother hugging her children and the blonde Gretchen in tears—that was our masterpiece. It had a text in verse.'

'I know. I remember picking one up.'

'On quiet evenings we used to take loudspeaker vans up to the front line.'

'And in between the tangos they appealed to their fellow-Germans to turn their guns against Hitler. We used to climb out of our dug-out and listen too. But your appeals were a bit naïve.'

'Well, I don't know. We did take Graudenz and Elbing without a single shot.'

'But that was not till 1945.'

'Drops of water wear down stones, but it takes time. Did I ever tell you about Milka? She was a student at the Institute of Foreign Languages, graduated in 'forty-one and was sent straight off as a translator to our unit. A little snub-nosed girl, very keen and brisk.'

'Wasn't she the one who went with you when you accepted the surrender of a German strong-point?'

'That's the one. She was terribly vain, loved being praised for her work (God help you if you told her off!) and being put up for decorations. Do you remember, on the Northwestern front, just beyond Lovat, south of Podtsepochye, there's a forest?'

'Lots of them. This side of the Redya River or the other?'

'This side.'

'Yes. I know where you mean.'

'Well, she and I spent a whole day wandering about that forest. It was spring. Almost spring, anyway—March. We sloshed through puddles in our boots and sweated under our fur hats. There was that everlasting smell of awakening spring. We might have been in love for the first time, or a newly married couple. Why is it that every time you fall in love, you go through it all again right from the beginning, like a schoolboy. . . . That endless forest! Here and there, smoke from a gun-position in a clearing where there was a battery of seventy-sixes. We kept away from them. We wandered about till dusk—it was damp and the sunset turned everything pink. She had been driving me crazy all day. Then in the evening we found an empty bunker.'

'Above ground?'

'You remember? They built a lot of them that year, like shelters for wild animals.'

'The ground was too wet to dig in.'

'Yes. Inside there were branches of pine scattered on the floor, and logs smelling of resin, and soot from old fires. No stove. Just a hole in the roof. No light at all of course, just flickering shadows on the log walls if you lit a fire. Those were the days!'

'I've always noticed that whenever anyone tells a story in prison about an innocent girl, all the listeners—myself included—are just waiting for her to lose her virginity before the end. That's the whole point of the story for a prisoner. It's a kind of search for universal justice, don't you think? A blind man wants those who can see to reassure him that the sky is still blue and the grass still green. A prisoner needs to know that there are still real live attractive women in the world and lucky fellows who make love to them. . . . You call that a war memory? An evening with a girl in a shelter smelling of pine resin, with no one shooting at you! That same evening your wife was turning in her sugar coupons for a little sticky lump of sugar all mixed up with paper, and wondering how to share it out between your daughters so that it would last thirty days. And in Butyrki Prison, in cell seventy-three . . .'

'. . . On the first floor, down a narrow corridor . . .'

'Exactly. A young Moscow history professor, Razvodovsky, only just arrested and who of course hadn't been at the front, was arguing passionately and brilliantly—and convincingly, too—that war had its good side. He produced a whole battery of political, historical and philosophical arguments to back up his case. And some of the boys in the cell, who had fought on every front, were so furious they nearly lynched him. I listened and said nothing. Razvodovsky had some good arguments. Every now and then I thought he was right, and I did remember some good things about the war—but I didn't dare argue with those soldiers. The professor, you see, had been spared from having to fight. And as a reserve artillery officer, so had I—at least compared to those men, who had been in the infantry. You know how it was, Lev, you were at the front yourself—you had a pretty easy war in your little Psychological Warfare outfit. You were never in the sort of fighting where you and your men had to hold out at all costs. It was the same with me, or very nearly so—I never once led an attack. Our memory plays tricks with us, we forget the worst. . . .'

'I wasn't saying . . .'

'. . . . And we remember the things we liked. But that day when a Junkers dive-bombed us and nearly blew me up near Orel—there was nothing I liked about that. The only good war is one that's over and done with.'

'I wasn't saying it was good, only that I have some good memories.'

'One day we'll have some good memories of the prison camps as well. Even of transit camps.'

'Transit camps? Gorky? Kirov? Never!'

'You say that because they took your belongings away from you there—you're not being objective. But some trusty who had a soft job there—a storekeeper or a bath attendant, who maybe even had a woman as well—he'll swear there's no better place than a transit camp. Happiness, after all, is a relative term.'

'That's true. It's even proved by etymology. The word happiness is derived from "now", "this moment".[1]

'You're wrong there, maestro. Read Dahl. "Happiness" is derived from "part" or "share"—in other words, whatever you've managed to grab, or has come your way. You can't have any illusions about happiness if you know your etymology.'

'Just a minute! I got my derivation from Dahl.'

'That's odd! So did I.'

'I must look it up in other languages. I'll make a note.'

'You're a maniac!'

'Speak for yourself! Let me tell you something about comparative linguistics. . . .'

'I know—you want to tell me that Marr[2] claims that every other word is derived from "hand".'

'Oh, go to hell! Listen—have you read the second part of *Faust*?'

'Better ask me if I've read the *first* part. Everyone says it's a work of genius, but no one actually reads it. They only know it from the opera.'

'The first part is quite easy

> "*I care not for the sun and stars—*
> *I see but man in torment . . .*"

'That I can understand!'

'Or take this:

> "*What we need, we know not;*
> *What we know we do not need.*"

'Excellent!'

'The second part of *Faust* is heavy going, but the idea

---

[1] The Russian word for 'happiness' is *schastye*; the Russian for 'now' or 'this moment' is *seichas* literally meaning 'this hour' or 'the present time'. 'Part' is *chast*.

[2] Nikolai Marr: Soviet professor of linguistics who asserted, *inter alia*, that all languages in the world have a common origin. His theory was denounced by Stalin in 1950.

behind it is marvellous. You remember the pact between Faust and Mephistopheles—Mephistopheles will only get possession of his soul on the day Faust exclaims: "Oh moment, stay—thou art so fair!" So Mephistopheles gives him everything he can think of—his youth, and Margaret's love, an easy victory over his rival, boundless riches, knowledge of the deepest mysteries of being—but still Faust refuses to say the magic words. Years go by, Mephistopheles is sick of haunting his insatiable victim, he sees that nothing will make the man happy, he's ready to give the whole thing up. By now Faust is old for the second time, he's blind, but a great idea is born in his tired old brain—he wants to bring about universal human happiness. Mephistopheles the cynic thinks he's lapsed into second childhood. Faust commands him to summon thousands of labourers and make them dig ditches to drain the swamps. Mephistopheles orders his servants— the lemurs—to dig Faust's grave. Mephistopheles, who hasn't lost his sense of irony, fools him, telling him they're digging the drainage ditches. The *finale*, when Faust at last exclaims: "Oh moment, stay!", is always interpreted by Soviet literary critics in an optimistic sense: Faust has discovered supreme happiness in serving mankind. But I wonder if Goethe wasn't simply laughing at the whole idea of happiness? After all, Faust wasn't really serving anyone. He had been deceived, he spoke the long-awaited words when he had one foot in the grave, and the lemurs immediately shoved him into it. Is that a hymn to human happiness or is it a joke?'

'That's how I love to see you, Lev—when you talk from the heart, wisely, instead of sticking derogatory labels on to everything.'

'I thought you'd like it. But now listen—on the basis of this fragment from *Faust* I developed a theory in one of my lectures before the war—my lectures were very bold for those days. My theory was that there is no such thing as human happiness—either it's unattainable or it's illusory. Well, after I'd finished, I was handed a note from a student—a scrap of paper torn from an exercise book: "I'm in love and I *am* happy. What do you say to that?"'

'And what did you say?'

'What could I say?'

CHAPTER EIGHT

They became so absorbed in their conversation that they no longer heard the noises of the laboratory or the tiresome sound of the radio in the far corner. Once again Nerzhin swivelled his chair round so that his back was to the rest of the laboratory. Rubin twisted around, put his folded arms on the back of his chair and rested his bearded chin on them.

Nerzhin spoke very earnestly, as one whose thoughts have been a long time taking shape.

'When I was free and read books by wise men who wrote about the meaning of life, or of happiness, I made very little sense of it. I took them seriously, after all it's the business of wise men to think profound thoughts. But what can you say about the meaning of life? We're alive—and that's all there is to it. Happiness comes when things are going well, everyone knows that. Thank God for prison! It has given me the chance to think things out. To understand the nature of happiness we first have to know what it means to eat one's fill. Remember how it was in the Lubyanka and when the security people were grilling us? Remember that thin barley or oatmeal porridge without a single drop of milk? Can you say you *ate* it? No. It was like Holy Communion, you took it like the sacraments, like the *prana* of the yogis. You ate it slowly, from the tip of a wooden spoon, entirely absorbed in the process of eating, in thinking about eating—and it spread through your body like nectar. You quivered from the exquisite feeling you got from those sodden little grains and the muddy slops in which they floated. And you went on living like that, with virtually nothing to sustain you, for six months, or for twelve. Can you compare that with the way people wolf down steaks?'

Rubin could never bear listening to others for long. For him conversation was a process in which he bombarded his friends with his eagerly garnered scraps of wisdom and knowledge. Now he was trying to interrupt, but Nerzhin had

48

grabbed him by his denims and shook him every time he tried to get a word in.

'So miserable wretches like ourselves really do know from bitter experience what it means to eat one's fill. It's not a matter of *how much* you eat, but of the *way* you eat. It's the same with happiness—it doesn't depend on the actual number of blessings we manage to snatch from life, but only on our attitude towards them. The Taoists have a saying that "Whoever is capable of knowing when he has had enough will always be satisfied."'

'You're an eclectic,' Rubin said with a smirk, 'you're always picking up pretty feathers and sticking them in your tail.'

Nerzhin jerked his head and arm violently in protest. His hair hung down over his forehead. Carried away by his argument, he looked like a boy of eighteen.

'Don't try to confuse the issue, Lev. That's just not true. I draw my conclusions not from the philosophers I've read but from the stories you hear about people in prison. I'm expressing ideas I've arrived at for myself. Why should I discover America all over again? In philosophy, there's no unchartered territory. I read the ancient philosophers and in their books I find my own latest discoveries. Don't interrupt! I was going to give you an example. Whenever by a miracle they let you have a free Sunday in prison, particularly if it's a special prison like this—your mind thaws out, relaxes, and even though nothing has changed outwardly, prison life seems a little easier to bear, you have a good talk with someone or read something worthwhile, and then you're on the crest of a wave. You forget that you haven't lived a real life for years, you feel as though you're weightless, suspended in mid-air, disembodied. I lie on my top bunk and stare at the ceiling. It's very close and bare, the plaster work is bad—but I tremble from the sheer joy of existence! I go to sleep perfectly happy. No president, no prime minister can fall asleep so well pleased with his Sunday.'

Rubin grinned amicably, intending to convey partly agreement and partly indulgence for his friend's delusions.

'And what do the great books of the Veda have to say about that?' he asked, his lips protruding comically.

"I don't know about the books of the Veda,' Nerzhin said

49

firmly, 'but the books of the Sankhya say: "For those who understand, human happiness is suffering."'

'You've certainly worked it all out,' Rubin muttered into his beard. 'Has Sologdin been putting you up to all this?'

'Perhaps he has. For you I suppose it's just idealism and metaphysics. But listen! The happiness that comes from easy victories, from the total fulfilment of desire, from success, from feeling completely gorged—*that* is suffering! That is a spiritual death, a kind of unending moral indigestion. I'm not talking about the philosophers of the Veda or the Sankhya, but about myself, Gleb Nerzhin. After my five years on this treadmill I've reached that higher state where bad begins to appear as good. And it's my own view, arrived at by myself, that people don't know what they are striving for. They exhaust themselves in the senseless pursuit of material things and die without realizing their spiritual wealth. When Tolstoy wished to be in prison, his reasoning was that of a truly perceptive person in a healthy state of mind.'

Rubin laughed. He often laughed when he was in total disagreement with another person's argument.

'Listen to me, my child! All this is just your callow, youthful mind. You think your personal experience is worth more than the collective experience of mankind. Your mind has been poisoned by prison latrine talk—it's clouded your view of the world. Why should our views change just because we personally have come to grief?'

'You seem to be very proud of not changing yours.'

'Yes! *Hier stehe ich und kann nicht anders.*'

'Of all the pigheadedness! Talk about metaphysics! Instead of trying to learn something in prison, instead of looking at life as it really is——'

'What life? The life of people embittered by failure?'

'—You've wilfully closed your eyes, plugged your ears, you're putting on an act, and you think you're being clever! You think it's a sign of intelligence to refuse to develop!'

'To be intelligent means to be impartial.'

'You call yourself impartial?'

'Completely!' Rubin spoke with dignity.

'I've never known anybody less impartial.'

'Don't bury your head in the sand! Look at things in their

historical perspective. I shouldn't quote myself, I know, but:

> "*A moth's life lasts but a moment,*
> *An oak tree grows a hundred years*".'

'Doesn't the law of life mean anything to you? Don't you realize that everything is conditioned by immutable laws and goes exactly the way it should? So it's useless to root around and come up with this sort of corrupting scepticism.'

'Don't think for a minute, Lev, that scepticism comes easily to me. For me it's like a roadside shelter where I can sit out the bad weather. It's a long way of ridding the mind of dogma —that's its value.'

'Dogma? Don't be such a fool! How could I be a dogmatist?' Rubin's big warm eyes gazed at him reproachfully. 'I'm a prisoner like you—we were both picked up in 'forty-five. I had four years at the front—as the piece of shrapnel in my side reminds me. I've done five years in prison. So I can see just as clearly as you. What must be, must be. The state can't exist without an elaborate penal system.'

'I won't listen to that. I won't have it.'

'So much for your scepticism! Who do you think you are? Sextus Empiricus? Why are you so upset? You'll never make a real sceptic. A sceptic is supposed to withhold judgment. He's supposed to be imperturbable.'

'You're right,' Gleb said, despairingly clutching his head in his hands. 'I do always try to be restrained, to keep my mind on higher things, but I get carried away, I lose my self-control.'

'Higher things, my foot! You're always going for me because there's not enough drinking water in Jezkazgan, or something of the sort.'

'You bastard! That's where you should be sent. You're the only one here who thinks the Big Chief is right and that his methods are normal and necessary. You'd soon change your tune if they sent you off to Jezkazgan!'

'Listen, you!'—now Rubin grabbed Nerzhin by his denims. 'He's the Robespierre and the Napoleon of our revolution rolled into one. He is wise. He is really wise. He sees far beyond what we can possibly see.'

51

'Better to trust your own eyes. Listen, when I was still only a kid I started to read his books after I'd read Lenin's, and I just couldn't get through them. Lenin is to the point, so full of feeling and so precise, and then I came on to this mush. Everything Stalin says is crude and stupid—he always misses the most important point.'

'You made this discovery when you were still a kid?'

'When I was in the last year at school. You don't believe me? Neither did my interrogator. . . . But I'm driven crazy by his oracular style—and the condescending way he has of laying down the law. He really seems to believe that he's the cleverest man in the country——'

'But he is!'

'—and that he makes us happy just by allowing us to admire him.'

In the heat of their argument they had become careless, their conversation was overheard by Simochka; for some time she had been glancing disapprovingly at Nerzhin. She was hurt because he had not taken advantage of the fact that she was on night duty, had not even bothered to look in her direction.

'You don't know what you're talking about—you're just meddling in matters outside your competence! You're a mathematician, you don't really know anything about history or philosophy—so what right have you to make those sort of judgments?'

'Don't try to tell me that the people who could discover the neutrino and weigh Sirius-Beta, without being able to see them, can't take an intelligent view of simple human problems. What are we mathematicians and scientists to do if you historians don't study history any longer? I know who the people are who win prizes and get fat academic salaries. They don't write history, they just lick a certain part of a certain person's anatomy. So we scientists have to study history for ourselves.'

'How dreadful you make it sound! Don't exaggerate!'

'There's a lot to be said for the scientific method. History could do with a little of it.'

The internal telephone rang on the desk of Major Roitman, the chief of the Acoustics Laboratory, who was absent. Simochka got up to answer it.

'The interrogator just couldn't believe that my subversive activities as defined under Article 58 could be traced back to my early interest in dialectical materialism. I admit I've always been rather a bookworm and I don't know much about real life, but I have again and again compared those two styles, those two ways of presenting an argument, and in the texts——'

'Gleb Vikentich!'

'—in these texts I discovered errors, distortions and crude over-simplifications—and that's why I'm here.'

'Gleb Vikentich!'

'Yes?' said Nerzhin, turning away from Rubin and at last taking in that he was being called.

'Didn't you hear the telephone ring?' Simochka was asking him sternly. She stood at her desk, frowning, her arms crossed, her brown shawl pulled around her shoulders. 'Colonel Yakonov wants you to go to his office.'

'He does?' The wrinkles on Nerzhin's face fell into place again, the excitement of the argument had died away. 'Very well, thank you, Serafima Vitalyevna. You hear that, Lev? It's Yakonov. I wonder why?'

A summons to the office of the head of research at ten o'clock on a Saturday night was a very unusual event. Simochka tried to look official and impassive, but Nerzhin could see that she was alarmed.

The passionate quarrel which had been interrupted by the telephone might never have taken place. Rubin looked at his friend with concern. When the light of battle was not in them, his eyes were almost feminine in their softness.

'I don't like it when our lords and masters show an interest in us,' he said. 'It's best to keep well away from them.'

'But I think we do. This voice job we're on is not of major interest to them.'

'If Yakonov comes breathing down our necks, we'll get hell for that Stanislavsky book and the lawyers' speeches,' Rubin laughed. 'Or do you think it might be the speech tests in Number Seven?'

'But the results have already been turned in and there's no backing out. Just in case, if I don't come back——'

'Don't be silly.'

'What do you mean? You never know, with us. Burn that

53

stuff—you know where it is.' He closed his desk, gave Rubin the key and went off with the unhurried step of a prisoner in his fifth year on the treadmill who always takes his time because he expects things to be even worse in the future.

CHAPTER NINE

Passing under the bronze sconces and the ornate stucco ceiling, Nerzhin climbed the broad, red-carpeted stairway to the third floor, which at this late hour was deserted. He tried to look unconcerned as he went past the Duty Officer keeping watch over the outside telephones, and knocked at the door of the head of research at Mavrino, Colonel Anton Nikolayevich Yakonov. The office was spacious, well furnished with rugs, armchairs and sofas. A long conference table, covered with a bright blue cloth, stood in the middle of the room and Yakonov's desk and chair curved their brown bent wood limbs in the far corner. Nerzhin had sometimes attended conferences in this splendid setting, but it was a very rare thing for him to come here by himself.

Colonel Yakonov was over fifty but still in his prime. His height was imposing and his face looked as if it might have been lightly powdered after shaving. He wore a gold pince-nez, and he was suave and portly, like one of the princes Obolensky or Dolgorukov. With his lordly ease of manner he stood out among the other high officials of the Ministry.

'Be seated, Gleb Vikentich,' he said, preening himself in his large armchair and toying with a thick, coloured pencil which he held poised above the smooth brown surface of his desk.

This use of Nerzhin's first name and patronymic made it appear that the colonel was going out of his way to be courteous and amiable, but it cost him no effort since under the glass on his desk he had a list of all the prisoners with their names and patronymics; people who did not know this were astonished at his memory. Nerzhin bowed respectfully but not obsequiously, and sat down warily at an elegant lacquer

54

table. Yakonov's voice was deep and mellow. It seemed odd that this born aristocrat did not roll his 'r's' in the French manner, like the old nobility.

'You know, Gleb Vikentich, half an hour ago your name came up in a certain connection and I suddenly wondered what the devil you were doing in the Acoustics Laboratory, working under Roitman.'

Yakonov mentioned the name in a deliberately offhand manner, not bothering to give Roitman his title of Major. Relations between the head of research and his first deputy were so bad that there was no point in concealing it any longer.

Nerzhin was now very much on edge—these opening words had an ominous ring. He had heard the same irony in Yakonov's voice a few days before when he had said that Nerzhin, though fair-minded about the results of the work on the classification of voices, looked down on Number Seven as a very poor relation. Number Seven was Yakonov's pet project, but the work was going badly.

'. . . . of course I think very highly of what you've done for the technique of voice classification . . .'

(He was making fun of him.)

'. . . and I am very sorry that your original monograph on the subject has only been printed in a small classified edition so that you've been denied the fame of being the Russian George Fletcher . . .'

(He was blatantly making fun of him.)

'. . . However, I would like to put your work to better use—make it pay better, as the Anglo-Saxons say. Much as I respect theoretical work, I have to look at the practical side, you know.'

Colonel Yakonov was at the stage when, though he held high rank, he was not yet so close to the Leader of the Peoples that he need deny himself the luxury of showing intelligence or uttering opinions of his own.

'Well, anyway, let me ask you frankly: what are you doing at the moment in the Acoustics Laboratory?'

This was a sore point. If Yakonov had been able to keep a check on everything himself, he would have known the answer.

'All that parrot-talk—"cheese", "choice"—why should a first-rate mathematician like you to be doing that? Turn round.'

Nerzhin turned and half got up from his chair. There was a third person in the office. A modest-looking man in black civilian clothes rose from a sofa and came towards him. His round spectacles gleamed. In the generous light from overhead, Nerzhin recognized Pyotr Trofimovich Verenyov who, before the war, had been an Assistant Professor at his own university; but following the habit he had formed in prison, he said nothing and made no movement, assuming that Verenyov was a prisoner and not wishing to harm him by any hasty sign of recognition. Verenyov smiled, but seemed embarrassed. Yakonov reassured them in his purring voice:

'I must say I'm impressed by your reserve—it's like a Masonic ritual. I've always thought of mathematicians as Rosicrucians of some kind, and I regret I was never initiated into their secrets. Please feel at ease. Shake hands and make yourselves quite at home. I shall leave you for half an hour so that you can talk about the good old days and also hear from Professor Verenyov about our new assignment.'

Yakonov rose from his outsize armchair—his imposing, heavily built frame was accentuated by his silver-and-blue epaulettes—and moved swiftly and easily to the door. By the time Verenyov and Nerzhin had converged to shake hands they were alone.

Nerzhin had been so long in prison that this pale man with his gleaming spectacles seemed like a ghost illicitly returning from a forgotten world—a world long since overlaid by the forests round Lake Ilmen, the hills and ravines of Orel, the sands and marshes of Byelorussia, the rich estates of Poland and the tiled roofs of German cities. In the nine years which separated that forgotten world from today there had also been the bare, garishly lit 'boxes' and cells of the Lubyanka, dingy, foul-smelling transit prisons, stifling compartments in converted goods wagons, the cutting wind of the steppe. All this made it impossible for him to remember how it felt to write out the functions of an independent variable on the yielding surface of a linoleum blackboard.

Nerzhin couldn't think why he was so agitated.

Both men lit cigarettes and sat down, separated by the small lacquer table.

It was nothing new for Verenyov to meet one of his former students from Moscow or R—— University (where he had been sent before the war to impose the official line in a controversy between opposing schools of thought). But he too was affected by the unusual setting of today's meeting: the triple shroud of secrecy over this secluded institution in the suburbs of Moscow, the multiple barbed-wire fences set up around it and the strange, dark-blue denims worn by its inmates.

It seemed somehow right that all the questions should be asked by Nerzhin, the younger man, who had so little to show for his life, and that the older man should reply as if he were ashamed of his straightforward academic career —after being evacuated during the war he had returned to work for three years with K—— and had taken his doctor's degree in topology. Nerzhin, his lips tightly drawn, was inattentive to the point of rudeness; he did not even bother to ask what exactly Verenyov had written about this arid branch of mathematics in which he himself had done a little work for one of his courses. Suddenly he felt sorry for Verenyov. Topology belonged to the stratosphere of human thought. It might conceivably turn out to be of some use in the twenty-fourth century, but for the time being . . .

> '*I care not for the sun and the stars,*
> *I see but man in torment.*'

Nerzhin asked why he had left the university to come to this place. The answer was that he had been sent here. True, he could have refused the job, but they had offered him double his previous salary . . . and he had four children.

They spoke about the other students in Nerzhin's class, who had graduated on the day the war started. The most gifted had been killed or got shell-shocked—they were the ones who always rushed into action, without a thought for their own skins. Those of no promise were now either completing their post-graduate work or teaching in universities and institutes.

Then Nerzhin remembered the university's pride and joy—Dmitri Dmitrich Goryainov-Shakhovskoy. The old man had difficulty in keeping himself tidy in his old age—he was always covering his black corduroy jacket with chalk or putting the rag for wiping the blackboard into his pocket. He was a legend, a figure about whom innumerable stories were told. He had come to the industrial town of R—— in 1915, rather as one might come to a cemetery, from the Imperial University of Warsaw, where he had been one of the leading lights. When he celebrated the fiftieth year of his scientific career, telegrams of congratulations came from all over the world—from Milwaukee, Cape Town, Yokohama. And then, in the course of a campaign to 'put new life' into the university, he was 'purged'. He went to Moscow and brought back a note from Kalinin saying: 'Don't touch this old man!' (It was rumoured that Kalinin's father had been a serf of the professor's father.)

After that he was left alone—so much so that others looked on in terror. He was quite liable to produce a mathematical proof of the existence of God or, in the middle of a public lecture on his beloved Newton, suddenly to growl from behind his yellow moustaches:

'Someone has just sent me up a note saying: "Marx wrote that Newton was a materialist, and you say he was an idealist." I can only reply that Marx was wrong. Newton believed in God, like every other great scientist.'

It was terrible trying to take down his lectures—even with shorthand one was driven frantic. Because his legs were weak, he sat facing the blackboard; he wrote with his right hand, wiping out what he had written with his left, and all the time muttering to himself. It was impossible to grasp his ideas at the time, but whenever Nerzhin and one of his comrades shared the work of taking notes and managed afterwards to reconstruct what he had said, they were moved as one is moved by the shimmering light of distant stars.

Nerzhin asked what had become of him. Verenyov said that during the bombing of R—— the old man had suffered a concussion and had been evacuated to Kirghizia more dead than alive. He had come back but was transferred from the university to the teachers' training college. It was quite astonishing that he was still alive. Time either flew or stood still.

Then Verenyov asked why, actually, Nerzhin had been arrested.

Nerzhin laughed.

'No, but why actually?' Verenyov insisted.

'Because of my way of thinking, Pyotr Trofimovich. In Japan there's a law which says that a person can be tried for his inner thoughts.'

'But we don't have any such law, do we?'

'Yes we do: Section 58, Paragraph 10 of the Criminal Code.'

Nerzhin listened very inattentively to what Verenyov now told him about Yakonov's reasons for bringing them together. Verenyov had been sent to Mavrino to step up and systematize the research on cryptography and codes. For this they needed mathematicians, a lot of them; Verenyov was overjoyed to see among them a former student of his, and one who had shown such promise.

In answer to Nerzhin's casual questions on points of detail, Verenyov, gradually warming to his subject, explained what had to be done by way of setting up new approaches and revising old ones. But all the time Nerzhin was thinking about those little sheets of paper covered in tiny handwriting, the notes he had been able to write in such peace behind his false front of books and papers, with Simochka stealing loving glances at him and Rubin talking cheerfully in his ear. Those little sheets of paper were a kind of coming of age for him—the first fruits of his thirty years.

Of course, it would have been more gratifying to prove himself in the field of his first choice. Why on earth had he ventured into the lions' den from which professional historians had fled to take refuge in the distant past? What was it that drove him to try to solve the riddle of the grim monster who had only to move an eyelash for Nerzhin to lose his head? What had got into him? Why did he have to rush in where others feared to tread?

Should he now succumb, instead, to the octopus embrace of cryptography? It meant fourteen hours a day, with no time off at all, and his head would be filled, to the exclusion of all else, with theory of probability, theory of numbers and theory of error. It would numb the brain and wither the mind. What time would he have for thought and for reflecting on life?

On the other hand, it meant staying here, at Mavrino. It was better than life in the camps. There was meat for dinner and butter for breakfast. You didn't have to work till the skin came off your hands and your fingers froze. You didn't have to flop down at night half dead, in your filthy rope sandals, on the wooden boards of a bunk. At Mavrino you slept sweetly under a nice clean sheet.

What was the point of living out the whole of your life? Did one live just for the sake of living, just for the sake of one's bodily comfort? Comfort, indeed! What was the point of living if comfort was all that mattered?

His reason bade him say, 'Yes, I'll do as you wish,' but his heart said: 'Get thee behind me, Satan.'

'Pyotr Trofimovich, do you know how to make shoes?'

'What did you say?'

'I'm asking you if you can teach me how to make shoes?'

'I'm sorry, I don't understand.'

'Pyotr Trofimovich, you live in a fool's paradise. When I finish my sentence I'll be sent to the back of beyond, to spend the rest of my life in exile. But I don't know how to work with my hands, so how will I live? There's nothing but bears in the *taigo*, and nobody out there is going to need Euler's functions for the next three geological eras.'

'What are you talking about, Nerzhin! As a cryptographer, if the work goes well, you'll be released ahead of time, you'll be pardoned, they'll give you a flat in Moscow.'

'Pardoned?' Nerzhin cried angrily, his eyes narrowing. 'What makes you think I want such a favour from them? You think I want to be told I've worked so well that all is forgiven and I can go? No, Pyotr Trofimovich!' He rapped on the varnished surface of the small table with a finger that seemed weighted with lead. 'You're putting it the wrong way round. Let them admit first that it's not right to put people in prison for their way of thinking—and then *we* will see whether we can forgive *them*.'

The door opened and in came Yakonov, as princely as ever with the gold pince-nez on his large nose.

'Well, you Rosicrucians, have you come to an agreement?'

Without getting up, Nerzhin looked Yakonov steadily in the eyes as he answered:

'Do as you think best, colonel, but my own feeling is that I still have work to do in the Acoustics Laboratory.'

Yakonov was now standing behind his desk, and the knuckles of his fleshy hands were resting on the glass top. Only those who knew him well could have told he was angry when he said:

'Voice classification versus mathematics! You have traded the food of the gods for a mess of pottage. Good-bye.'

And with a thick, two-coloured lead pencil he wrote on his desk pad:

'Transfer for Nerzhin.'

CHAPTER TEN

For many years during and after the war Yakonov had held the post of Chief Engineer of the Special Equipment Section. His specialized knowledge had earned him the rank of Colonel and he wore with dignity his silver epaulettes with their sky-blue edging and three large stars. In his position he could direct the Section from afar and without going into details. Occasionally he read a learned paper to an audience of high officials; occasionally he commented intelligently and in elegant language on a finished model submitted by an engineer; thus he maintained his reputation as an expert and, while bearing no responsibility, drew a salary of many thousands of roubles a month. Whenever a new project was born, he made a speech at the christening, kept away during the childhood sicknesses and growing pains, and reappeared for the funeral or the triumphant coming-of-age.

Yakonov was not so young or so self-assured as to chase after the elusive glitter of a Gold Star or a Stalin Prize and insist on handling personally every new assignment from the Ministry or even the Boss. He was experienced enough and of an age to distrust ambition with its dizzy heights and yawning chasms.

As a result he had led a fairly untroubled existence until January 1948. In that month someone suggested to the Father of the Peoples of East and West the idea of a telephone for his exclusive use, fitted with a secret device that would prevent his conversations from being understood even if anyone managed to intercept them. Pointing the august finger with its tobacco-stained nail at the spot on the map where Mavrino was engaged in developing walkie-talkies for the use of the police, the Father of the Peoples uttered the historic words:

'What do I want those for? To catch burglars? Who cares about burglars?'

He ordered the scrambler to be ready by the 1st of January, 1949, but gave it a moment's thought and added:

'Very well, you can have till the 1st of May.'

The project had top priority and was unique in the tightness of its schedule. The heads of the Ministry thought it over and ordered Yakonov to see it through personally at Mavrino. He pleaded in vain that he already had too much work. The head of the Department, Oskolupov, looked at him with his green, feline eyes; Yakonov remembered his tainted record (he had served six years in prison) and stopped arguing.

Ever since—for almost two years—Yakonov's room at the Ministry had stood empty. The colonel spent day and night at the country mansion with its hexagonal tower rising above the onion dome of the disused chapel.

At first he had actually enjoyed getting down to the job —casually slamming the door of the car which the Ministry kept at his disposal, dozing as it sped him to Mavrino, past the saluting guards and the gate wreathed in barbed wire and, in spring when all is young and fresh, strolling with his suite of captains and majors under the century-old lime trees of the Mavrino grounds. So far his masters had required nothing from Yakonov except plans, plans, promises and more plans. In return the horn of plenty was tipped over Mavrino, showering it with Soviet-made and imported radio parts, equipment, furniture, a library of thirty thousand of the latest technical publications, specialists brought in from the labour camps, the very best security officers, filing-clerks experienced in handling secret material, and a guard detachment of picked men. The old buildings had to be repaired and new ones put up for the prison staff and for experimental machine-shops, and by the time all the lime trees were covered in fragrant, pale yellow blossom the listless voices of German prisoners of war in threadbare camouflage tunics could be heard beneath the shade of those giant trees. Still prisoners four years after the war, these idle fascists had little incentive to work. It was almost more than a Russian could bear to see them unload bricks from a lorry—passing them from hand to hand one by one, as though they were made of glass, and stacking them neatly in a pile. Installing radiators under the windows and mending rotten floorboards, Germans wandered in and out of the top-secret laboratories, peering at the German and English instructions on the equipment. Any German schoolboy could have guessed what the laboratories were for.

All this was stated in the report that Rubin submitted to Colonel Yakonov—a report which was accurate but highly inconvenient to the Security Officers, Major Shikin and Major Mishin (known collectively to the prisoners as Shishkin-Mishkin). What could they do about it? Report their own negligence to higher authority? It was in any case too late, because some of the prisoners had been repatriated and those who were back in West Germany could by now have explained to anyone interested the exact location and plan of the Mavrino research establishment and of each of its laboratories. So Major Shikin suppressed the report, but made sure that no laboratory knew more about the work of its neighbours than about market gossip in Madagascar. Colonel Yakonov was not allowed to divulge the address of the special prison, and if a colleague from another department wanted to talk to him, they had to meet in Moscow at the Lubyanka.[1]

The repatriated Germans were replaced on the building sites by men from the labour camps—prisoners too, but dressed in filthy rags and not given white bread. The new voices under the lime trees cursed everything indiscriminately

[1] Lubyanka: the central detention and interrogation centre of the Ministry of State Security branch (MGB), situated in Moscow on Dzerzhinsky Square. Before the revolution the building was the head office of the 'Rossiya' insurance company.

in good camp swear-words, reminding the relatively privileged inmates of the Mavrino special prison of the hell from which they too had come and to which they were some day doomed to return—the dreaded forced-labour camps. These men unloaded the bricks in such haste that most of them were broken in the process. In the evening, with a shout of 'One —two—three—heave!' they hoisted plywood hoods on to the lorries, crawled underneath and, cheerfully hugging the foul-mouthed women prisoners among them, were driven back to camp for the night.

So in that enchanted castle, unknown to the ordinary people of Moscow and insulated from them by an impassable perimeter, lemurs in black quilted jackets wrought a marvellous transformation, conjuring up running water, drainage, central heating and flowerbeds.

Mavrino expanded, even absorbing another establishment which had been engaged on similar lines of research. This second outfit arrived complete with its own desks, chairs, safes, files, its obsolescent equipment and its head—Major Roitman, who became Yakonov's deputy. Unfortunately its founder, guiding spirit and patron, Colonel Mamurin, head of the MVD's Special Communications Branch and a man of great consequence in the land, had disappeared in tragic circumstances.

Annoyed by the amount of static interference on the line when he was speaking to China, the Leader of All Progressive Mankind had rung up Beria and said to him in Georgian:

'Lavrenty! Who's this ass you've got in charge of Special Communications? Get rid of him.'

Mamurin was duly got rid of—he was thrown into Lubyanka Prison—but no one knew what to do with him next. None of the usual instructions had been received about whether to try him, and what to sentence him for and for how long. Anyone else would have been sent to Norilsk, sentenced to a prison term of twenty-five years and a further five of exile and deprivation of rights but, mindful of the saying, 'You today, me tomorrow,' Mamurin's former colleagues stood by him. They waited until they were sure that Stalin had forgotten him, then—untried and uncondemned—sent him quietly to a house in the country.

So, one summer evening in 1948 a new prisoner arrived

in Mavrino. Everything about him was unusual. He came in a Black Maria instead of a car; instead of an ordinary guard, he was accompanied by the head of the Prison Administration himself; and his supper was served on a tray, covered with a napkin, in the governor's office.

Prisoners (who are supposed to hear nothing but always hear everything) learned that the newcomer had refused salami and was politely urged by the governor to 'have something'. This was overheard from the passage by a prisoner on his way to the doctor. The indigenous population of Mavrino discussed the extraordinary event, decided that the new arrival was a prisoner all the same and, their curiosity satisfied, went to bed.

Where the new arrival spent that first night was never established, but early next morning a brash young lathe operator met him on the marble porch (which was later put out of bounds); he dug him in the ribs and said: 'Well, brother, where are you from? What did they get you for? Sit down, let's have a smoke.'

But the newcomer shied away in fastidious horror. The lathe operator stared at his blank eyes, thin, fair hair and bald patch, and said angrily:

'All right, you snake in the grass! Bet you'll talk when they've locked you up with us for the night.'

But the snake in the grass was not locked up with the others. A small room (previously a dark-room) was found for him off the main corridor between the laboratories on the second floor. Bed, table, cupboard, electric heater and flower-pot were crowded into it, and the sheet of cardboard stripped off the barred window—which didn't even face the light of day but a backstairs landing, which itself faced north, so that at all times the privileged prisoner's cell was in semi-darkness. The bars could, of course, have been removed, but after some hesitation the prison authorities decided to leave them. Not even they could make anything of the mysterious affair or adopt a consistent line of conduct towards their prisoner.

The other prisoners nicknamed him 'The Man in the Iron Mask'. No one knew his real name. No one could even talk to him. They saw him through the window, sitting with his head bowed in his solitary cell or, at hours when they were not allowed out, wandering like a lost soul under the lime trees. The Man in the Iron Mask was as thin and sallow as though he were half dead after two years of interrogation —but in view of his ridiculous aversion to salami, this could not be the true explanation of his state.

Only much later, when Mamurin had begun to work in Number Seven, did the prisoners learn from the free workers that this was the famous Colonel Mamurin, head of Special Communications who, in the old days, had forbidden anyone to pass his door except on tiptoe and would rush out furiously through his secretary's room, shouting:

'Whose office do you think you're tramping past? What's your name?'

Later still they understood the nature of Mamurin's suffering. Rejected by the world of the free he scorned the world of the prisoners. In his solitude he had at first taken to reading book after book—such immortal works as Panferov's *Struggle for Peace* and Babayevsky's *The Knight of the Golden Star*, novels by Sobolev and Nikulin, verses by Prokofyev and Gribachev[2]—until one day a wonderful transformation took place in him and he began writing verses himself. Poetry is known to be born of the torment of the soul, and Mamurin's torment was sharper than that of any other prisoner. In prison, untried and unsentenced for close on two years, he still lived by the latest Party directives; he still deified the Wisest of Teachers. As he confided to Rubin, it was not the prison food that worried him (as it happened, his meals were cooked specially), nor the separation from his family (once a month he was secretly taken home and spent the night at his flat), nor any other crude physical privation—what distressed him was the loss of Stalin's confidence and the fact that he was no longer a colonel, that he had been dismissed and disgraced. Such were the things that made prison infinitely harder to bear for men like Rubin and himself than for the unprincipled swine who surrounded them.

Rubin had been a Party member. But after hearing the confessions of his seemingly orthodox fellow-Communist and reading his verses, he began to avoid Mamurin, even to hide from him—he preferred to spend his time among men who

[2] Notorious Soviet hack writers of the Stalin period.

66

attacked him unfairly but who at least shared his lot as equals.

Mamurin was driven by the ambition, as nagging as a toothache, to rehabilitate himself by his work. Unfortunately, all he knew of communications, of which he had been the head, was how to hold a receiver. So he could not work himself; he could only direct others. What he needed was a successful project to direct; an ill-fated one would have done nothing to restore him to Stalin's favour. Luckily, just then, two promising schemes were taking shape at Mavrino: the 'scrambler' and Number Seven.

For some deep-seated reason which defies logic, people take to each other at once or not at all. Yakonov and his deputy, Roitman, had never got on and detested each other more with every passing month. Harnessed to the same cart by a hand mightier than theirs, neither could break loose; they could only pull in opposite directions. When two alternative lines of approach to the problem of the scrambler were developed, Roitman collared everyone he could to work in the Acoustics Laboratory on the scrambler, which was known in Russian as the Artificial Speech Device; Yakonov, in his turn, stripped every other team of its most gifted engineers and best imported equipment in favour of Number Seven. All other budding projects expired in the unequal struggle.

Mamurin picked Number Seven for himself. He could not bear to work under his former subordinate Roitman, and it suited the Ministry to have him glaring vigilantly over the shoulder of Yakonov, who was not a Party member and had a slightly tainted record.

From that moment, whether Yakonov was at Mavrino or not, the discharged MVD colonel, now a lonely prisoner with feverish eyes and hideously sunken cheeks, suppressed his passion for poetry, refused food and drink and slaved till two in the morning, forcing Number Seven to work fifteen hours a day. It was the only laboratory where such long hours could be kept, for Mamurin could be trusted to act as his own security officer, so no free workers had to be kept for an extra shift.

When Yakonov left Verenyov and Nerzhin in his office, he had gone straight to Number Seven.

CHAPTER ELEVEN

No one tells the soldiers what the generals are planning, yet they always know perfectly well whether they are deployed on the main line of advance or on the flank. In the same way the three hundred prisoners at Mavrino knew that Number Seven was the crucial sector.

No one was supposed to know its name but everyone did. It was called the Clipped Speech Laboratory. The expression 'Clipped Speech' was taken from the English, and not only engineers and translators but assembly and installation men, lathe operators and probably even the deaf carpenter knew that this piece of equipment was being built on the American model. But it was accepted practice to pretend that it was of Russian origin. So American magazines with diagrams and articles on the theory of 'clipping', which in New York were openly sold on news-stands, were here numbered, tied with string, classified and sealed in fireproof safes for fear of American spies.

Clipping, damping, amplitude compression, electronic differentiation and integration of human speech was an act of desecration similar to, say, cutting up a Black Sea resort such as Gurzuf or New Athos into a billion fragments, packing it into matchboxes, mixing them all up, flying them to Nerchinsk and there, inland, in the far north, reassembling the original, complete with its sub-tropical vegetation, the sound of the surf on the beach and the softness of the southern air and moonlight.

Speech was to be broken down into small groups of electrical impulses and reconstituted so perfectly that not only could each word be clearly heard but the Boss could also recognize the person he was speaking to by his voice.

In the special prisons—those pampered institutions where the snarl of the camp struggle for existence was unheard —it was a long-established rule that, when a difficult problem was solved, the prisoners most closely concerned with it were given everything they could desire—freedom, clean identity papers and a flat in Moscow—while the rest got nothing, not one single day of remission, or even a tot of vodka to drink to the lucky ones.

There was nothing in between.

Therefore, those prisoners who had most successfully acquired that camp tenacity by which, it seemed, they could cling by their finger-nails to a vertical mirror, did their utmost to reach Number Seven as a stepping-stone to freedom.

This was how Markushev had got there, an engineer with a brutal, pimply face, always panting with eagerness to die for the ideas of Colonel Yakonov; and others of his sort arrived in the same way. But Yakonov was shrewd enough to pick some men who had made no special effort to get there. Such was Amantai Bulatov, an engineer and a Tartar from Kazan, a straightforward fellow with enormous horn-rimmed spectacles and a deafening laugh, who had been sentenced to ten years for having been a prisoner of war and for having had connections with the Tartar leader Musa Djalil. Such also was Andrey Andreyevich Potapov, a specialist in ultra-high voltages and the construction of electric power stations. He had come to Mavrino through the mistake of a stupid clerk in charge of the GULAG[1] card index, but, being a good and whole-hearted worker, had quickly found his function and become irreplacable in the handling of the complex equipment for precision measuring of radio frequencies.

Another such engineer was Khorobrov, a great radio expert. He had come to Number Seven when it was still an ordinary section; lately he had wearied of it and now refused to keep up with its furious pace. And Mamurin had grown weary of Khorobrov.

The latest arrival was the gloomy genius Bobynin. He had been rushed post-haste from the famous construction site 501 near the settlement of Salekhard, from a punitive brigade in a labour camp, and immediately placed above everyone else. Snatched from the jaws of death, he would be the first candidate for freedom in the event of success. So he worked into the small hours, but with such scornful dignity that, alone of the whole group, he was never rebuked by Mamurin who was afraid of him.

Number Seven was a room similar to the Acoustics

[1] GULAG—abbreviation for the General Department of (Prison) Camp Administration.

Laboratory, one floor above it. Equipped and furnished in the same way, it differed from it only in not having an acoustics booth.

Yakonov visited it several times a day, so his appearance had none of the character of a commanding officer's inspection. Only such toadies as Markushev pushed themselves forward and bustled about more eagerly than ever. As for Potapov, he had set up a frequency meter in the one unoccupied space on the shelves cluttered up with instruments, which screened him from the rest of the room. He did his work on time and without frantic bursts of effort. Being up to date with his job, he was, at the moment, making a red plastic cigarette case which he intended to give as a birthday present to a friend next morning.

Mamurin rose to greet Yakonov as an equal. He was not wearing the dark-blue denims of an ordinary prisoner but an expensive wool suit, but it did nothing to enhance his emaciated figure.

The expression of his corpse-like, lemon-yellow face and bloodless lips was interpreted by Yakonov as joy.

'We have readjusted to every sixteenth impulse, and it's much better, Anton Nikolayevich. Here, listen, I'll read to you.'

'Reading' and 'listening' were the normal test of the quality of a telephone circuit. The circuit was altered several times a day by the addition, removal or replacement of some unit or other, and to set up a proper articulation test each time would have been a cumbersome procedure too slow to keep pace with the ideas of the engineers. Besides, there was no point in getting discouraging figures from a system which had once been objective but had now been taken over by Roitman's *protégé* Nerzhin.

Dominated as usual by a single thought, Mamurin, without asking or explaining anything, went to the far corner and, turning his back on the room and pressing the receiver to his cheek, read from a newspaper. At the other end of the circuit, Yakonov put on a pair of earphones and listened. They emitted dreadful sounds: Mamurin's voice was broken by bursts of crackling, roaring and screeching. But as a mother gazes lovingly at her ugly child, Yakonov, far from tearing the earphones from his tortured ears, listened closely

70

and decided that this dreadful noise was perhaps a little less dreadful than the one he had last heard when he had listened before dinner. Mamurin's voice had none of the tone of spontaneous conversational speech—it was measured and intentionally precise. Moreover, he was reading a piece about the insolent Yugoslav Border Guards and the self-indulgence of Yugoslavia's bloody executioner Rankovič who had transformed that peace-loving country into a mass torture-chamber, so that Yakonov could easily guess the words which he failed to hear; he realized that he had guessed them, forgot that he had guessed them and eventually persuaded himself that the audibility was better than it had been that afternoon.

He wanted to share his opinion with Bobynin. Massive and broad-shouldered, his hair cropped like a convict's—even though at Mavrino any kind of hair-style was permitted—Bobynin sat near by. He had not looked up when Yakonov came in and, bending over a long band of photo-oscillogram film, was measuring something with a pair of dividers.

This Bobynin was no more important than an insect—an insignificant prisoner, a member of the lowest class—while Yakonov was a high-ranking official. Yet Yakonov could not bring himself to distract Bobynin, much as he wanted to speak to him.

One can build the Empire State Building, discipline the Prussian army, make a state hierarchy mightier than God, yet fail to overcome the unaccountable spiritual superiority of certain human beings. There are soldiers of whom their company commanders are afraid, labourers who intimidate their foremen, prisoners who make their prosecutors tremble.

Bobynin knew this and, in dealing with authorities, made use of his power.

Every time Yakonov talked to him he caught himself out in a craven wish to play up to this prisoner, to avoid annoying him. It made him angry with himself, but he noticed that everyone else had the same reaction to Bobynin.

Taking off the earphones, Yakonov interrupted Mamurin. 'It's better, definitely better! I'd like Rubin to listen to it. He has a good ear.'

Pleased with an opinion that Rubin had given, someone had once said that he had 'a good ear'. The statement was seized upon and believed. Rubin had got into Mavrino by accident and had managed to hang on by doing translations. His left ear was as good as anyone's, but the right one had been deafened by concussion during the war, a fact which he now had to conceal. His reputation strengthened his position and he finally established it by his magnum opus, *The Audio-Synthetic and Electro-Acoustical Aspects of Russian Speech*.

So they rang up the Acoustics Laboratory for Rubin. While they waited, they listened again for the umpteenth time. Markushev, brows knitted and eyes strained in concentration, held the earphones for a moment and firmly announced that the sound was better, very much better (the idea of re-adjusting it to every sixteenth impulse had been his, so he had known it would be). Dyrsin nodded with an ambiguous grin. Bulatov shouted across the room that they should get together with the code experts and readjust to a basis of thirty-two. Two obliging electricians, nearly pulling the earphones apart as each listened with one ear, agreed with joyful exuberance that the sound was indeed clearer.

Bobynin went on measuring the oscillogram without looking up.

The black hands of the big electric clock on the wall jumped to half past ten. Soon, in all the laboratories except Number Seven work would stop, secret periodicals would be locked up, prisoners would go to bed and free workers hurry to the bus stop, where not many buses would pull up at this late hour.

Ilya Khorobrov came from Vyatka, from the most God-forsaken corner of it, near Kay, whence the kingdom of GULAG, bigger than France, stretches across thousands of square miles of forest and marsh. He had seen and understood more than most, but the need to conceal his thoughts, to repress his sense of justice, had etched deep lines round his mouth and given him a disagreeable expression and a stoop.

During the first elections held after the war, he had given vent to his feelings and on his ballot paper had applied an obscene epithet to the Genius of Geniuses himself.

That was the time when, because of the shortage of labour, houses were left in ruins and fields remained unsown. Nevertheless, several detectives were kept busy for a month, studying the handwriting of every voter in the district, and Khorobrov was caught. He went to a camp, naïvely happy at the thought that there, at least, he could speak his mind. But camp life was not as he expected. The authorities were showered with informers' reports, and Khorobrov was silenced.

The sensible thing for him to do now was to immerse himself in work and ensure, if not his release, at least an untroubled existence. But nausea at injustice, even when he was not personally involved, had overwhelmed him to such a degree that he had lost all wish to live.

Going behind the shelves, he bent over Potapov's desk and said softly:

'Time to knock off. It's Saturday.'

Potapov, who had just fitted a pale pink catch to the transparent red plastic cigarette case, leaned back, and admired it:

'Think the colours are all right?'

Getting neither praise nor disapproval, he looked up, like a granny, over the top of his steel-framed spectacles and said:

'Why tease the dragon? Time is on our side. Yakonov will go, and im-me-diately we'll vanish into thin air.'

He had a trick of dividing the important word in a sentence into syllables and emphasizing it by mimicry.

Meanwhile Rubin had come in. He had been in a lyrical mood all evening and his greatest wish now, at eleven at night, when work was nearly over, was to go to bed and read Hemingway. However, he assumed an air of lively interest in the new qualities of the circuit and insisted that Markushev should do the reading because his high voice, with its basic tone of 160 cycles, would transmit least well; this, of course, demonstrated Rubin's expertise. Putting on the earphones, he ordered Markushev to read now louder, now softer, to repeat sentences he, Rubin, had invented in order to check certain combinations of sounds—phrases with which everyone in Mavrino was familiar. Finally, he announced that an overall improvement was noticeable, that the vowels transmitted remarkably well, the labials rather less so, that he was worried by the sound *zh*, that the combination of the consonants *vsp*, so characteristic of the Slav languages, came over deplorably, and further work on these would be necessary.

Rubin's recognition of the improvement was greeted by a joyful outburst. But Bobynin looked up from his oscillogram and ironically, in his deep bass, remarked:

'Nonsense! One step forward, one step back. It's no good guessing. What we need is a method.'

Embarrassed by his direct, implacable stare, everyone fell silent.

Behind the shelves, Potapov was sticking the pink catch on to the cigarette case. He had survived the three years he had spent in a German POW camp, thanks to his extraordinary skill in making attractive lighters, cigarette cases and holders out of rubbish, and without tools of any sort.

No one seemed to be in a hurry to knock off. And this on the eve of a Sunday—once a day of rest for the prisoners, now a working day like any other.

Khorobrov straightened his back. Putting the secret files on the desk for Potapov to hand in, he came out from behind the shelves and walked unhurriedly to the door, avoiding the crowd round the clipper.

Mamurin glared at his back and called after him:

'Why aren't you listening? And where do you think you're going?'

Khorobrov slowly turned and with a crooked smile, replied deliberately:

'I would prefer not to mention it, but since you insist— I am about to go to the lavatory. If I make a good job of it there, I'll go on to my room and to bed.'

The stunned silence that followed was broken by a guffaw from Bobynin—who had hardly ever been heard to laugh.

This was a mutiny! Mamurin made a step as though about to strike Khorobrov, and asked in a shrill voice:

'What d'you mean? Everybody's working and you're going to bed?'

Hardly able to control himself, his hand already on the door, Khorobrov answered:

'Yes, to bed. In accordance with the Constitution, I've worked my twelve hours—and that's enough!' He was about to explode and say something irreparable, but at this moment the door opened and the Duty Officer said to Yakonov:

'There's an urgent call for you from Moscow.'

Yakonov got up quickly and went out in front of Khorobrov.

Potapov put out his desk light, transferred his and Khorobrov's secret papers to Bulatov's desk and limped slowly to the door. (He was lame in his right leg owing to a motorcycle accident he had had before the war.)

Yakonov's call was from Deputy Minister Sevastyanov who ordered him to be at the Ministry by midnight.

Yakonov returned to his office where he had left Verenyov and Nerzhin. He dismissed Nerzhin, offered a lift in his car to Verenyov, got into his coat and put on his gloves; then he went back to his desk and found the note: 'Transfer for Nerzhin', and added:

'Khorobrov too.'

CHAPTER TWELVE

When Nerzhin—vaguely sensing that what he had done was irreparable but not yet realizing it fully—returned to the Acoustics Laboratory, Rubin was gone. The others were still there. Valentin, tinkering with a panel on which there were dozens of radio valves, turning his lively eyes on him.

'Take it easy, young man!' he said, holding up his hand like a policeman stopping a car. 'Why is there no current in my third stage? Can you tell me that?' Then he remembered: 'Oh yes, what was it all about? *Qu'est-ce qui s'est passé?*'

'Mind your own business,' said Nerzhin sullenly. He could scarcely admit to this high priest of his own science that he had just given up mathematics.

'If you're in trouble, listen to dance music.' His thoughts already elsewhere, he called out: 'Vadka! Plug in the oscilloscope.'

As he went to his desk Nerzhin noticed that Simochka was very nervous. She looked at him, her thin brows quivering.

'Where's Rubin?' he asked her.

'Colonel Yakonov wanted him in Number Seven as well,'

75

she answered loudly, and still more loudly, so that everyone could hear, said: 'Let's check my reading of the new word-lists. We still have half an hour.'

Simochka acted as one of the readers in speech tests, and, like all the others, her reading had to be checked from time to time to make sure that her diction came up to the required standard of clarity.

'How can we do that when there's such a noise?'

'Well—let's go into the booth.' She threw a meaningful look at Nerzhin, took a list of words written in black ink on drawing paper and went into the booth.

Nerzhin followed her. He shut the thick outer door, locked it, squeezed through the small second inner one, shut it and pulled the blind down. Simochka flung her arms round his neck and standing on tiptoe kissed him on the lips.

He lifted her off the floor—there was so little space that her shoes banged against the wall—sat down on the only chair in front of the microphone and sat her on his knees.

'Why did Anton send for you? What happened?'

'Is the amplifier turned off? We don't want this to go out over the loudspeaker.'

'Was it something bad?'

'Why do you think it was something bad?'

'I just felt it the moment they rang. And now I see in your face, Gleb Vikentich.'

'How many times have I told you to call me just Gleb?'

'But if I find it hard to?'

'But if I want you to?'

'Was it bad?'

He felt the warmth of her body on his knees and of her cheek pressed against his. It was a sensation not often experienced by a prisoner. He had not been so close to a woman for many years.

Simochka was astonishingly light: it was as though her bones were full of air and she were made of wax. She seemed ridiculously weightless, like a bird that looks bigger because of its feathers.

'Yes, little one—it seems I'll be leaving soon.'

She twisted round in his arms and pressed her hands against his temples, letting fall her scarf from her shoulders.

'Where to?'

'What do you mean, where to? Back to the bottomless pit I came from, like everybody else here—back to the camps.'

'My darling, why?'

Nerzhin looked closely, uncomprehendingly, into the wide-open eyes of this plain girl whose love he had so unexpectedly won. His fate affected her more than it did him.

'I could have stayed,' he said cheerlessly, 'But in another laboratory. So we wouldn't have been together, anyway.'

She clung to him with her whole body, kissed him and asked him if he loved her.

Why, after that first kiss, had he not made love to her? Why had he taken pity on her and spared her for the sake of her possible future happiness? She wasn't likely to find a decent husband; she'd give herself to the first man who came along. She had flung herself into his arms and clung to him, eager and frightened. Why should he hold back and deny her? Soon he would be back in a camp where there wouldn't be another chance like this.

Very moved, he said:

'I'm sorry to leave like this. I'd like to be able to think of . . . I mean . . . leave you with a child.'

She hid her face, embarrassed, and when he tried to raise her head, she resisted him.

'Don't hide your face. . . . Lift your head up. Why don't you say something? Don't you want that?'

She looked up and, from somewhere deep within herself, said:

'I'll wait for you! You have five years to go, haven't you? I'll wait five years for you. And when they let you out . . . you'll come back to me?'

He had said nothing of the sort. She was talking as though he were unmarried. She was determined to get a husband—the poor girl with her long nose!

Gleb's wife was in Moscow. But it was like saying she lived on Mars.

Apart from Simochka here on his knee and his wife out there on Mars, he had to think of the notes hidden in his desk—the materials for a work on the post-Lenin period, to which he had given so much time and thought.

If he was sent back to a camp all these notes would be destroyed.

He ought to tell a lie, say he would come back to her—people always made that sort of promise. Then he'd be able to give her his notes to keep for him.

But she was looking at him with so much hope that he couldn't bring himself to lie even for this purpose.

He evaded her eyes, pulled down her blouse and kissed her bony little shoulders.

Then he said hesitantly:

'You once asked me what I'm so busy writing.'

'Yes, Gleb, what are you writing?' Simochka asked eagerly, calling him Gleb for the first time.

If she had not interrupted him and shown such curiosity, he would probably have told her about it. But she was so impatient that he was put on his guard. He had lived too long in a world where everything was mined and fitted with booby traps.

These trusting, loving eyes might very well be working for the Security Officer.

Come to think of it, how had it all begun? It was she who had first placed her cheek against his. It could be a trap.

'It's only history,' he said. 'Something about the time of Peter the Great. But it means a great deal to me. I shall go on with it until Yakonov throws me out. But where can I leave it then?'

Suspiciously, his eyes probed hers.

She smiled calmly:

'Need you ask? Give it to me. I'll keep it. Go on writing, darling.' Then, angling for something that was of real concern to her, she asked: 'Tell me, is your wife very beautiful?'

The intercom which connected the booth with the laboratory rang. Simochka picked it up, but held it away from her mouth and pressed the button so that she could be heard at the other end of the line. Sitting there blushing and dishevelled, she began to read the word list in a toneless, measured voice. 'Hop, stop, shop. Yes? What do you say, Valentin, a double-diode-triode? We don't have a 6G7 but I think we have a 6G2. I'll finish the word list and come out. Hoot, moot, shoot.' She switched the intercom off and brushed her head lightly against Gleb's: 'I must go. It's becoming obvious. Let me go. Please. . . .'

But she didn't sound as though she meant it.

He held her to him and pressed her whole body even more tightly to his:

'You're not going! I want . . . I . . .'

'Don't! They're waiting for me. I have to close the lab.'

'I want you!'

He kissed her.

'Not today.'

'When?'

She looked at him submissively:

'On Monday. I'll be on duty again. Come here during the dinner break. We'll be alone for a whole hour. If only that crazy Valentin doesn't come here to work.'

While Gleb unlocked and opened the door Simochka managed to straighten her clothes and comb her hair. She went out first, looking cold and aloof.

CHAPTER THIRTEEN

'I'm going to heave my shoe at that blue light one of these days. It gets on my nerves.'

'You'll miss.'

'At five yards? How could I? I bet you tomorrow's stewed fruit I'll hit it.'

'You took your shoes off on the lower bunk. That's an extra yard.'

'All right, at six yards. What'll they think of next, the bastards! Anything to make our lives a misery. I can feel it pressing on my eyeballs all night.'

'What, the light?'

'Yes, the light. Light exerts pressure, as Lebedev discovered. Aristip Ivanich, are you asleep? Do me a favour —hand me up one of my shoes.'

'Certainly, Vyacheslav Petrovich, but tell me first what you've got against blue light.'

'For one thing it has a short-wave length and therefore more quanta. And those quanta hit me right in the eyes.'

'Blue light is nice and soft, it reminds me of the ikon lamp my mother used to light at night when I was little.'

'His mother's got blue epaulettes![1] Here we go again! I keep on saying how can you let people have real democracy? I've never been in a cell where there wasn't an endless argument about every silly question from washing the mess cans to sweeping the floor. Freedom would be the ruin of people. I'm afraid you can only teach them the truth with a big stick.'

'All right, but an ikon lamp would be just right here. It used to be the altar.'

'Not the altar, the space above it. They've built an extra floor over the altar.'

'Dmitry Alexandrovich, what the hell are you doing? Opening a window in December! Stop it!'

'Gentlemen, oxygen makes us immortal. There are twenty-four of us in here, and it's neither freezing nor blowing outside. I'm propping it up with one volume of Ehrenburg.'

'Make it two! It's stifling up here!'

'Are you putting him sideways or longways?'

'Longways, of course. He fits in beautifully.'

'It's enough to drive you crazy! Where's my winter jacket?'

'I'd send all these fresh-air fiends to Oi-Makoi. If they had to work twelve hours a day in the open at sixty below they'd gladly crawl into a pig-sty just to get out of the cold.'

'I'm not against oxygen in principle, but why does it always have to be so cold? I like my oxygen warm.'

'What the hell's going on here? Why is it so dark? Why have they put the lights out so soon?'

'Where do you think you are, Valentin? You can't go wandering around till one in the morning. What do you need light for at midnight?'

'The place is full of smoke again. Why do you all smoke like that? Damn it, you can't breathe in here! And the tea's gone cold too.'

'Where's Lev?'

'Isn't he in his bed?'

'There's a pile of books on his bed, but he's not there.'

'Well, he must be by the lavatory.'

'What do you mean: by the lavatory?'

[1] MVD personnel wear blue epaulettes.

'They've put a white bulb over the door there and the wall is warm from the kitchen. He's probably reading a book. I'm going out there for a wash. Want me to tell him anything?'

'. . . Well then, so she put some bedclothes on the floor for me and made up the bed for herself. She was really hot stuff, I'm telling you.'

'For God's sake, over there! Talk about anything except women. With all the meat they give us to eat here, it's antisocial to talk about women.'

'Don't talk at all! It was lights out long ago.'

'Yes, it was—and I thought I heard the radio somewhere signing off with the anthem.'

'Don't worry—you'll go to sleep when you want to.'

'I was in Africa in the war—with Rommel. The bad thing was the heat, and there was never enough water.'

'In the Arctic Ocean there's a place called Makhotkin Island. Makhotkin was an airman and they named this island after him, but now he's in prison for anti-Soviet propaganda.'

'Mikhail Kuzmich, what are you rolling around for like that?'

'Can't I turn over if I want to?'

'You can, but every time you turn over down there it makes a terrific noise up here.'

'The trouble with you, Ivan Ivanovich, is that you were never in a camp. They sleep four to a bunk there, and if one turns over it's hell for the other three, and if the fellow on the bottom bunk put up a curtain and went to work on a girl-friend, it was like a storm at sea. But it took more than that to stop us sleeping.'

'. . . Grigory Borisovich, when did they first put you in a special prison?'

'. . . I'm thinking of putting in a pentode there and a small rheostat.'

'. . . He was an independent, methodical sort of person. When he took his shoes off at night he didn't leave them on the floor, he put them under his head. . . .'

'In those days it didn't pay to leave anything on the floor!'

'I was in Auschwitz. The terrible thing was: they took people straight from the station to the gas-chamber, with a band playing.'

'The fishing was great, and so was the hunting. In autumn you could go out for an hour and come back with all the pheasants in the world. There was wild boar in the bulrushes down by the water, and the fields were teeming with hare.'

'They first set up a special prison in 1930 after the trial of the "Industrial Party"—they wanted to see how scientists and technicians would work in prison. So the chief scientist in the first special prison was Ramzin. The experiment worked out very well. In normal conditions you could never have two top engineers or scientists on the same project—one would always oust the other in the fight over who was to get all the credit and the Stalin Prize. That's why all ordinary research teams consist of a colourless group around one brilliant head. But in prison it's another thing. There's no question of money or fame for anyone. It's all share and share alike. You can have a dozen academic lions living together peacefully in one den, because they've nowhere else to go. They soon get bored just playing chess or sitting around smoking. So they set about inventing something. No end of original work has been done like that. This is the whole point of the special prison.'

'. . . Have you heard? Bobynin has been taken off somewhere.'

'Where did they take him to, Valentin?'

'How did it happen?'

'The Junior Lieutenant came in and told him to put on his overcoat and cap.'

'Did he have to take his things?'

'No.'

'He must have been called in by the top brass.'

'By Oskolupov?'

'Oskolupov would have come over himself, so guess again.'

'The tea's gone cold, God damn it.'

'Valentin, you're always clicking your spoon on your glass after lights-out and I'm sick of it.'

'How do you expect me to dissolve my sugar?'

'In silence.'

'Only cosmic disasters take place in silence—sound is not transmitted in outer space. If a new star should blow up right behind us we wouldn't even hear it. Ruska, your blanket's falling off, why don't you pull it up? Are you asleep? Do you know that our sun is a new star, and that the earth is doomed to perish in the near future?'

'I don't want to hear it. I'm young and I want to live.'

'Ha, ha, how commonplace! He wants to live. *C'est le mot!* This tea *is* cold!'

'Valentin, where did they take Bobynin?'

'How should I know. Maybe to Stalin.'

'And what would you do, Valentin, if they took you to Stalin?'

'If they took me? I'd tell him all our complaints from a to z.'

'Such as——?'

'Well, all of them, all of them. *Par excellence*—why do we have to live without women? It restricts our creative potential.'

'Pryanchikov, shut up! Everyone's been asleep for ages. What are you yelling about?'

'Suppose I don't want to sleep.'

'Who's smoking? Put those cigarettes away. The Junior Lieutenant is coming.'

'What's that bastard doing here? Careful you don't trip, Lieutenant, you might hurt yourself.'

'Pryanchikov!'

'What?'

'Where are you? Are you asleep?'

'Yes, I'm asleep.'

'Get dressed, come on, get dressed, and put on your overcoat and cap!'

'Shall I take my things?'

'No. There's a car waiting, hurry up.'

'Am I going with Bobynin?'

'He's gone already. There's another one for you.'

'What kind of a car, Lieutenant, a Black Maria?'

'Get a move on. No, it's a Pobeda.'

'Who wants to see me?'

'Come on, Pryanchikov, why do I have to explain everything to you? I don't know myself. Hurry up.'

'Valentin, tell them everything.'

'Ask them about visits! Aren't Section 58 prisoners supposed to get visits once a year?'

'Ask them about exercise.'

'And letters.'

'And clothing.'

'Up the workers! See you later.'

'Lieutenant! Where is Pryanchikov?'

'He's coming, Comrade Major! Here he is!'

'Let them have it straight, Valentin, don't be shy.'

'The bastards are very busy tonight.'

'What's it all about?'

'There's never been anything like this before.'

'Maybe war's broken out and they're taking them off to be shot?'

'Don't be a fool! Think they'd do it in ones and twos? If there was a war they'd shoot us all down together or put plague germs in our food.'

'All right, fellows, let's get some sleep! We'll hear all about it tomorrow.'

. . . 'I remember how Boris Sergeyevich Stechkin used to have to go and see Beria—in 1939 and 1940—*he* never came back empty-handed. Either the head of the prison would be sacked or we'd get more time for exercise. Stechkin could never stand all the bribery and corruption, and the differences in ration—eggs and cream for academicians, forty grams of butter for professors, and only half that much for the rest. He was a good man, Boris Sergeyevich—heaven help him ——'

'Is he dead?'

'No, they let him out. And he got a Stalin Prize.'

CHAPTER FOURTEEN

The weary, measured voice of Adamson, who was serving his second sentence after a first one also spent in special prisons, fell silent. A few people went on telling their stories in whispers. Someone was snoring loudly and at times sounded as though he were about to explode.

The blue bulb set in the round arch above the four-panel doors cast its dim light on a dozen two-decker bunks arranged fan-wise in the big semicircular room. This room, undoubtedly the only one of its kind in Moscow, was a good twelve yards in diameter. Above was a spacious dome which tapered, like a tent, towards the base of a hexagonal tower, and in the dome were five handsome Norman windows. These were barred but not boarded over, and in the daytime one could see across the main road to an untended, forest-like park. On summer evenings the prisoners could hear girls from the Moscow suburbs singing songs which roused and unsettled their spirits.

Nerzhin, on his upper bunk by the middle window, couldn't sleep and didn't even try. Potapov, in his, had long been sleeping the sweet sleep of a hard-working man. His neighbour on the top bunk to the left, the round-faced vacuum-tube specialist nicknamed 'Zemelya', was sprawled on the bed in a trustful posture and wheezing slightly. The bunk on his right had been moved up close to his own, and was occupied by one of the youngest prisoners, Ruska Doronin, who was tossing and turning. Pryanchikov's bunk was under Zemelya's, but he was not in his bed.

Now, when he could at last reflect on the conversation in Yakonov's office, Nerzhin understood everything more clearly. His refusal to join the cryptographic group was not a mere incident in his professional career but a turning-point in his life. It was certain to result, and perhaps very soon, in a long and gruelling journey to Siberia or to the Arctic, where he would either die or survive only after a hard struggle with death.

He wanted to think about this sudden break in his life. What had he managed to achieve during his three-years breathing space in the special prison? Had he been able to steel himself enough to face the ordeal of being thrown back into the abyss of the camps?

It so happened that the next day Gleb would be thirty-one years old. (He had no heart to tell this to his friends, of course.) Was this to be the middle of his life, the end of it, or only the beginning?

He was confused and found it difficult to look at his life from the calm prospect of eternity. For one thing he kept

85

thinking rather weakly that it was not too late to go back on his refusal to join the cryptography unit. He also brooded bitterly on the fact that a visit from his wife had been constantly put off during the last eleven months, and he wondered whether now she would be allowed to come before he was sent away.

And finally there were the promptings of his other self—the tough, resourceful side of him which had been born long ago, when, as a youngster, he had had to queue for bread during the First Five Year Plan. This tenacious inner self was already cheerfully figuring out what he should do when he was searched on leaving Mavrino, at the reception centre in Butyrki, and again at Krasnaya Presnya—how he would hide pieces of pencil lead in his padded jacket, how he might manage to take with him the working clothes issued in the special prison—every stitch of extra clothing was precious to a prisoner doing hard labour in the camps—and how he would prove that the aluminium teaspoon he had managed to keep during his year of prison was his own and not stolen from Mavrino, where the spoons looked almost exactly the same.

He was tempted to get up and start his preparations here and now by the light of the blue bulb, rearranging all his possessions and finding secret places for those that had to be hidden.

Meanwhile Ruska Doronin kept tossing and turning in bed. First he would lie on his stomach with his head under the pillow and pull the blanket up from his feet. Next he would fling himself over on his back, and throw the blanket off, exposing the white top sheet and the lower one which was not so white. (After every bath they were allowed to change one of their sheets, but now, in December, the prison had come to the end of its year's supply of soap and visits to the baths had been suspended.) Suddenly he sat up in bed and propped himself up, his pillow against the back of the iron bedstead. On a corner of the mattress he opened a volume of Mommsen's *History of Ancient Rome*. Noticing that Nerzhin was staring straight at the lamp and not sleeping, Ruska asked in a hoarse whisper:

'Gleb! Have you got a cigarette?'

Ruska normally didn't smoke. Nerzhin reached into the pocket of his overalls which were hung on the back of the bunk, and pulled out two cigarettes. They each lit up.

Ruska smoked with concentration, not turning towards Nerzhin. His fair hair fell over his forehead and even in the deathly light of the blue lamp, his face was handsome; his expression was always changing—at times he seemed innocent and boyish, at others he had a look of sublime cunning.

'Use this,' said Nerzhin, handing him an empty Belomor packet. They both dropped their ashes into it.

Ruska had come to Mavrino last summer and Nerzhin had taken an instant liking to him; he aroused his protective instinct.

But it turned out that even though Ruska was only twenty-three (and they had given him the maximum sentence of twenty-five years) he was quite capable of looking after himself. In the course of a short but hectic life, his character and his outlook on the world had been formed less by his studies at the universities of Moscow and Leningrad (he had spent a fortnight at each) than by his two years of living on false papers after an all-Union warrant had been issued for his arrest (he had told Gleb about this in strict confidence) and now by the two years he had spent in prison. In no time at all he had mastered the jungle laws of the forced-labour camps and was always on his guard—he spoke freely only to a few close friends and put on an air of childish simplicity with everyone else. Full of energy, he tried to make the best use of his time—reading was one of his ways of spending it.

Tired of the confused, trivial thoughts passing through his mind, and still wide awake, Gleb whispered:

'I say—how's your theory of cycles going?'

They had recently talked about it and Ruska was looking in Mommsen for more evidence to back it up.

He turned round but looked blank, his forehead wrinkled apparently with the effort of trying to understand the question.

'I said: how is the theory of cyclical change?'

Ruska sighed and the strained look left his face, together with the restless thought which had absorbed him while he was smoking. He slipped down on one elbow, put the dead butt into the empty packet which Nerzhin held out to him and said listlessly:

'I'm fed up with the lot—books and theories.'

Again they were silent. Nerzhin was going to turn over and try to sleep when suddenly Ruska laughed and began to whisper, gradually getting carried away and speaking faster and faster:

'History is so monotonous it makes you sick to read it. The more decent and honest a man is the worse he gets treated by his compatriots. The Roman consul Spurius Cassius Viscellinus wanted to give land to the common people, and the common people sent him to his death. Spurius Melius wanted to give bread to the hungry and he was executed because they said he was trying to get himself made Emperor. The consul Marcus Manlius, who woke up at the cackling of those famous geese and saved the Capitol, was executed as a traitor. Hannibal was exiled by Carthage, they confiscated his property and levelled his house to the ground, though we should never have heard of the place without him. It all sounds so familiar. They put Gnaius Nevius in fetters to stop his writing plays in which he said what he thought. And the Aetolians proclaimed an amnesty to lure *emigrés* back and then put them to death. Even the Romans discovered it was more economical to feed a slave than to starve him, but that was afterwards forgotten. History is a farce from beginning to end. It's not even a matter of truth or error. There are no signposts to anywhere, and there's nowhere to go.'

In the lifeless blue light the sight of his young lips quivering with despair was particularly upsetting.

Nerzhin himself had put these ideas into Ruska's head, but now when Ruska threw them back at him, he felt he should protest. With his older friends Gleb talked as though nothing were holy, but he felt some responsibility for this youngster.

'Let me tell you one thing,' he said very softly, leaning closer to Ruska's ear. 'This kind of scepticism, agnosticism, pessimism—whatever you call it—it all sounds very clever and ruthless, but you must understand that by its very nature it dooms us to futility. It's not a guide to action, and people can't just stand off, so they must have a set of positive beliefs to show them the way.'

'Even if they land in a swamp? Anything just to keep going, you mean?' Ruska asked angrily.

'Well, yes . . . damn it all!' said Gleb, a little unsure of himself. 'Look, I think scepticism is very important—it's a way of getting at people with one-track minds. But it can never give a man the feeling that he's got firm ground under his feet. And perhaps it's what we need—firm ground under our feet.'

'Give me another cigarette,' said Ruska. He began to smoke nervously. 'You know it's a good thing the MGB didn't give me the chance to study. I'd have taken a degree and perhaps even, like an idiot, gone and made a career as a scholar or written a great big book: done the umpteenth study of earthly Novgorod, or of Caesar's war with the Helvetians. Think of all the civilizations there are in the world! And all the languages and countries! And all the clever people writing clever books. What fool is going to read them all? What was that you quoted? Something like, "Nothing has been invented by great minds that does not appear insubstantial to even greater ones"? Was that it?'

'There you go! Soon you'll have nothing to hang on to and no purpose in life. It's all very well to doubt, it's even a good thing. But shouldn't you have something to love as well?'

'Yes, yes, something to love!' Ruska took him up in a triumphant, hoarse whisper. 'But not history or theory—you can only love a woman!' He leaned over to Nerzhin's bunk and grasped him by the elbow. 'What have they really taken away from us, tell me? The right to go to party meetings or to buy state bonds? The one way the Big Chief could really hurt us was to deprive us of women. And that's what he's done. For twenty-five years! The Bastard! Who can imagine,' he struck his chest with his fist, 'what women mean to a prisoner?'

'You'll go crazy, if you carry on like that,' said Nerzhin, trying to defend himself, but he suddenly felt hot all over at the thought of Simochka and what she had promised for Monday evening. 'Get all that out of your head,' he said. 'You'll just go out of your mind. What's that damn thing

the Freudians talk about? Sublimation. Put all your energy
into other things. Go in for philosophy—then you won't need
bread or water, or women.'

'I'm out of my mind already. I won't sleep till morning.
I want a woman! Everyone needs a woman. I want to feel
one in my arms. I want to . . . God damn it!' Ruska dropped
his burning cigarette on the blanket without noticing it and,
turning away abruptly, flopped down on his stomach and
jerked the blanket up over his head.

Nerzhin grabbed the cigarette as it was rolling off the
bunk on to Potapov below, and put it out. . . . He had less
than two days to go before he saw Simochka. He began to
think in detail how everything would be the day after tomorrow, then with a shudder he put this excruciatingly sweet
thought out of his mind—he felt it clouding his reason. He
bent over Ruska:

'Ruska, how about you? Have you got someone?'

'Yes! I have!' Ruska groaned in agony, lying on his back
tightly clutching the pillow to him. He breathed into it,
and the pillow returned the warmth of his own youth, condemned to spend itself in the bitter sterility of bringing to a
white heat his young, caged body which begged for release
and found none. He wanted to believe that he had a girl,
but he had nothing at all to go on—not even a kiss, or a
promise. There had been nothing more than a look of sympathy on a girl's face as she had listened to him, earlier that
evening, telling his story. And for the first time, seeing himself mirrored in the girl's eyes, Ruska felt there was something heroic and out of the ordinary about his life. There
was nothing between them yet, but he felt something had
happened that gave him the right to say he had a girl.

'Who is she?' Gleb asked.

Raising the blanket just a little Ruska answered from the
darkness:

'Shhh—Clara——'

'Clara? The prosecutor's daughter?'

CHAPTER FIFTEEN

The Head of Section O-I was coming to the end of his report to the Minister, Abakumov.

Tall, his black hair combed straight back, and wearing the epaulettes of a colonel-general, Abakumov sat with his elbows leaning magisterially on his large desk. Large but not fat, he knew how important it was to keep in trim and even played an occasional game of tennis. It was clear from his eyes that he was no fool; they were the roving eyes of a suspicious, quick-witted man. Where necessary he corrected the Head of Section, who busily noted down his remarks.

Abakumov's office was spacious. It had a marble fireplace which was not used—a relic of earlier days—and a tall console-mirror. The high ceiling with its ornate stucco mouldings and its chandelier was painted with romping cupids and nymphs (the Minister had left it as it was except that he had ordered all the green parts to be painted over, because this was a colour he loathed). Neither the balcony door, nor the big windows looking out on to the square were ever opened. There was a fine grandfather clock; on the mantelpiece a smaller, chiming clock with a figurine; and on the wall an electric railway-station clock. They all showed different times, but Abakumov always knew the right time because he had two gold watches as well, one on his hairy wrist and another in his pocket.

The offices in this building grew in size with the rank of their occupants, as did the desks and the velvet-covered conference tables; but the greatest status-symbol of all was the size of the portraits of the Great Generalissimo. Even in the offices of low-grade interrogators he was much larger than life, but in Abakumov's office the Greatest Strategist in History was painted on a canvas fifteen feet high—a realistic portrait showing him full length from his boots to the crown of his marshal's cap, gorgeous with all his orders and decorations. In fact he never wore these honours, many of which he had awarded to himself, or had received from foreign presidents and potentates. The Yugoslav decorations had been carefully painted out.

Yet as though this fifteen-foot painting was inadequate, and because he needed inspiration from the Policeman's Best Friend even when his eyes were lowered, Abakumov also kept a small portrait of Stalin on his desk.

On another wall, with plenty of space around it, was a square portrait of a somewhat bland-looking man with a pince-nez. This was Abakumov's immediate superior, Beria.

As soon as the Head of Section O-I left, three other people entered the room: Deputy Minister Sevastyanov, Major-General Oskolupov, head of the Section for Special Equipment, and Colonel Yakonov, Chief Engineer of the same section; in strict order of seniority and with every mark of special respect for the man behind the desk, they advanced in single file along the dead centre of the patterned carpet. Only Sevastyanov's footsteps could be heard.

A lean old man with short-cropped hair in several shades of grey, dressed in a grey suit, Sevastyanov was the only civilian among the ten deputy ministers who served under Abakumov. He had nothing to do with either Operations or Investigations, being concerned only with communications and technical matters. He was thus less liable to be a target of the Minister's wrath, and hence more relaxed in his presence than the others were. He immediately took a seat in a large leather armchair in front of Abakumov's desk.

Oskolupov, the next in line, was thus revealed to the Minister's gaze; Yakonov stood behind him as if trying to conceal the amplitude of his figure.

Abakumov looked at Oskolupov, whom he had only seen two or three times before, and thought there was something rather likeable about the man. Oskolupov, too, was on the corpulent side. His neck bulged out at the collar of his tunic, and he almost had a double chin when, as now, it was pulled back out of deference. He had the rugged, straightforward, honest face of a man of action, without a trace of the foxy look of a conceited intellectual.

Peering up over Oskolupov's shoulder at Yakonov, Abakumov asked curtly:

'Who are you?'

'Me?' Oskolupov bent forward, distressed at the thought that he had not been recognized.

'Me?' Yakonov now moved into view. He was straining

92

to hold in his stomach, which defied all his efforts to keep it from expanding; his big blue eyes were quite vacant as he introduced himself.

'You're the one I mean,' the Minister said with a nod. 'You're handling the Mavrino project, aren't you? All right, sit down.'

They both sat down.

The Minister picked up a paper-knife made of dark red plastic, scratched himself behind the ear with it, and said:

'Well, now—how long have you been pulling the wool over my eyes? Two years? Weren't you supposed to take only fifteen months? When will the phones be ready?' He added threateningly: 'And don't give me any lies. I don't like lies.'

This was the very question for which these three high-ranking liars had prepared themselves when they learned that they were all three being summoned together. As they had agreed, Oskolupov spoke first. Straining forward, his shoulders squared, and looking keenly into the eyes of the all-powerful Minister, he said:

'Comrade Minister! Comrade Colonel-General! Let me assure you that the personnel of the Section will spare no effort . . .'

Abakumov expressed surprise:

'Where do you think we are? At a public meeting? What am I supposed to do with your "efforts"—wrap them around my backside? I'm asking you to give me a date.'

And he took up his gold-tipped fountain pen, holding it expectantly over his desk diary.

At that moment, as agreed, Yakonov spoke up, making it clear by the subdued tone of his voice that he was speaking not as an administrator but as a specialist:

'Comrade Minister, in a frequency range of up to 2,400 cycles, given an average transmission level of zero point nine . . .'

'Cycles, cycles! Zero point nine cycles—that's all I ever get out of you! Zero point my arse! I want that telephone —two complete units. When will I have it? Well?' He swept the three men with his gaze.

Now it was Sevastyanov's turn to speak. Slowly, running his hand through his short grey-white hair, he said:

'Please let us know what you have in mind, Viktor Semyonovich. Two-way conversations, when we still don't have a foolproof way of encoding them . . .'

'Who the hell d'you think you're talking to? What's all this about encoding?' The Minister looked at him sharply.

Fifteen years ago, long before Abakumov himself or anyone else could have imagined him becoming a minister, and when as a strapping, athletic young man he had worked as a messenger for the NKVD, he had managed perfectly well on his few years of primary schooling. He had acquired all the further education he needed by learning judo and training in the gymnasiums of the Dynamo Sports Club.

Later, in those years when there was a rapidly increasing demand for interrogators and personnel was constantly being replaced, Abakumov was found to have a flair for the work —his long arms were a great asset when it came to 'working over' people under questioning. This was the beginning of a great career. In seven years he had risen to be head of the counter-intelligence agency SMERSH, and now he was a Minister. Not once in all his long ascent to the top had he ever felt at a disadvantage through lack of education— even in his present exalted position he managed to keep abreast of things well enough not to be fooled by his subordinates.

He was now about to lose his temper and was raising his cobblestone of a fist over the desk, when the door suddenly opened. Without knocking, in came a short, cherubic little man with fresh pink cheeks. This was Mikhail Dmitriyevich Ryumin. He was known throughout the Ministry as 'Mike', but there were not many who called him this to his face.

Moving as silently as a cat, he came up to the three seated men, gave them a swift glance of his bright, innocent-looking eyes and shook hands with Sevastyanov, who rose from his seat. Then he walked round to one end of Abakumov's desk, bent down close to the Minister and stroking the edge of the desk with his small pudgy hands, he said in his purring voice:

'Listen, Viktor Semyonovich. If we're going to take on this new job, we ought to turn it over to Sevastyanov. After all, what do we pay them for? Surely they can identify a voice from a magnetic tape? If they can't do it, get rid of them.'

And he smiled as sweetly as if he were treating a little girl to a chocolate. He gazed benevolently round at the three representatives of the Section. For years Ryumin had held the obscure job of chief accountant with the Consumers' Co-operative of Archangel Province. Pink-cheeked and plump, with thin, peevish lips, he did his best to make life a misery for his book-keepers. He was always sucking acid drops which he would offer to the warehouseman; he used diplomatic language with the drivers, behaved rudely to the delivery men and was most punctilious in laying papers on the Chairman's desk for signature.

During the war he had been assigned to the Navy and made an interrogator in the Security Section. He liked the work, and before long he had fabricated a case against a completely innocent war correspondent serving with the Northern Fleet. It was, however, such a crude and blatant frame-up that the Prosecutor's office, which normally did not interfere in the work of the security forces, reported the matter to Abakumov. So the little SMERSH interrogator from the Northern Fleet was called in to give an account of himself. Thinking his last moment had come, he stepped timidly into Abakumov's office. He came out an hour later looking important—he had been appointed to the central staff of SMERSH as a senior interrogator for special cases. From there on his star had been in the ascendant.

'I'll get rid of them all right, Mikhail Dmitriyevich, believe me. By the time I've finished with them they'll wish they'd never been born,' said Abakumov looking grimly at all three.

They lowered their eyes guiltily. 'But,' Abakumov continued, 'I don't quite see what you want; how can you identify an unknown person from his voice on the telephone?'

'I'll give them the tape of the conversation. Let them play around with it and see if it matches up with any known voice.'

'But have you made any arrests yet?'

'Of course,' Ryumin smiled sweetly. 'We picked up four people near the Arbat metro station.' However, a slight shadow crossed his face. For all his outward confidence, he knew that they had not been quick enough and that they had not got the man they were looking for. But the people they had arrested would not be released. In fact they might have to pin the case on one of them just to be able to close it. There was a hint of irritation in Ryumin's insinuating voice:

'I could get half the Ministry of Foreign Affairs on tape for them, if you like. But there's no need for that. All we need are the six or seven people in the Ministry who could have known about it.'

'Well, get them all, the swine! What are you waiting for?' Abakumov demanded indignantly. 'Seven people! It's a big country—they won't be missed!'

'Can't be done, I'm afraid, Viktor Semyonovich,' Ryumin objected. 'You can't do that in the Foreign Ministry—the people in the embassies would smell a rat and the fellow we're looking for could cover up his tracks. In this case we've just got to find out who it was and as quickly as possible.'

'Hmm,' Abakumov said slowly. 'So it's a matter of comparing tapes. Well, I suppose that's something we'll have to learn how to do some day. Sevastyanov, can you do it?'

'I still don't understand what it's all about, Viktor Semyonovich.'

'There's nothing to understand. It's very simple. Some bastard—it must have been a diplomat, or he wouldn't have had the information—made a telephone call to some professor today—what's his name . . .'

'Dobroumov,' said Ryumin.

'Yes, Dobroumov. A professor of medicine. Well, this Dobroumov was recently in France on an official visit, and while he was there the son of a bitch said he'd send them a new drug he's made, as part of an exchange of information. It didn't occur to the bastard that he's giving secrets away. Well, we wanted him to go ahead and actually hand the stuff over, and then we'd have caught him in the act and made a big political case to show what comes of showing too much interest in foreigners. But this skunk telephones the professor and tells him not to give them the drug. We'll pick up the professor and fix him anyway, but it just won't be the same thing. Well, what about it? If you can find out who it was, you'll have earned a medal.'

Sevastyanov looked past Oskolupov at Yakonov, who met his glance and slightly raised his eyebrows. What he meant to convey was that this was something quite new for which there were no established procedures, and that they had enough trouble as it was. Sevastyanov at once understood the significance of Yakonov's glance and he mentally prepared himself to start deliberately confusing the whole issue.

But Oskolupov's mind was working on a different tack. As Head of the Section, he didn't want to be a dummy, a mere figurehead. His appointment to this position had filled him with a sense of his own importance and he fully believed that he understood all the problems and could solve them better than anyone else—otherwise, he felt, he would never have been given the job. And although as a boy he had not even completed primary school, he was convinced that none of his subordinates understood the work better than he did—except, of course, for little matters of detail. During a recent holiday at a luxury resort he had worn civilian clothes and had told people that he was a professor of electronics. He had met a famous writer who was fascinated by him, kept jotting down notes and declared that he would base a portrait of a modern scientist on him. After this Oskolupov felt that he really was a scientist.

Now he took the bit between his teeth:

'Comrade Minister! We can do it!'

Sevastyanov looked at him aghast:

'Where? In which laboratory?'

'In the telephone laboratory at Mavrino, of course. The conversation was by telephone, wasn't it?'

'But Mavrino has another and more important job in hand.'

'What if it has? We'll bring in more staff. There are three hundred already—surely we can get more?'

And he gazed at the Minister with a look of determination.

Without quite smiling, Abakumov's expression betrayed his liking for the General. This was the way Abakumov himself had behaved when he had been on the make—always quick to make mincemeat of anyone to order. One can't help liking a junior who follows in one's footsteps.

'Good for you,' he said. 'That's the way to talk: the

interests of the state come first and the rest can wait. Right?'

'Exactly, Comrade Minister! Exactly, Colonel-General!'

Ryumin was neither surprised by, nor even particularly appreciative of Oskolupov's selfless dedication. Looking blankly at Sevastyanov he said: 'You will be briefed tomorrow morning.'

He exchanged glances with Abakumov and silently went out.

The Minister picked at his teeth with his finger, trying to get at a piece of meat stuck there since dinner.

'Right—when is it going to be ready? You keep making these promises: the 1st of August, then the 7th of November, then the New Year. Well, when will it be?'

He fixed his eyes on Yakonov, putting him in the position of having to reply for all three.

Yakonov seemed to be bothered by the position of his neck. He moved it a little to the right, then a little to the left, glanced up at the Minister with his cold blue eyes, and looked down again.

Yakonov knew that he was very clever and that even cleverer people than he, their minds busy with nothing else for fourteen hours a day and without a single day's holiday in the whole year, were also sweating away at the wretched apparatus—not to mention the part played by outside research of the kind published in the non-classified journals. Yakonov was also keenly aware of the thousands of difficulties already overcome or still looming with which his engineers were beset. Now, in six days' time, the very last deadline they had been able to wring from this uniformed hunk of flesh would run out. They had been forced to set completely unrealistic schedules. The great Patron of Science himself had insisted that this ten-year job must be done in one year.

Beforehand, in Sevastyanov's office, they had agreed to ask for another ten days against a promise to have two prototypes of the new telephone ready by the 10th of January. Sevastyanov had insisted on this, and Oskolupov had agreed. They figured that by then they would be able to deliver a model which, though still not in complete working order, would at least have a nice coat of paint. And then, while the thing was being tested to see whether the scrambling technique was foolproof, it would be possible to gain a little more time for putting the finishing touches to it.

Yakonov, however, knew that inanimate objects have no respect for human deadlines and that even by the 10th of January the telephone would not transmit human speech intelligibly. And Yakonov could then expect the same fate as Mamurin. The Boss would call Beria and ask him: 'What fool made this machine? *Get rid* of him!' At best Yakonov would become another 'Man in the Iron Mask', and perhaps an ordinary prisoner again.

As he sat under the Minister's gaze, feeling the noose tightening around his neck, Yakonov overcame his craven fear and said, hoarsely, as involuntarily as a man gasping for air:

'Give us one more month! One more month! Till the 1st of February!'

He looked at Abakumov with beseeching eyes, almost like a dog.

Clever people are sometimes unfair to others like them. Abakumov was cleverer than Yakonov thought, but through long disuse the Minister's sharp mind was of little service to him. Since throughout his career attention to duty had stood him in better stead than thought, Abakumov was not in the habit of exerting his brain.

He knew that neither six days nor a month would make any difference, and in his opinion this trio of liars—Sevastyanov, Oskolupov and Yakonov—had brought all this on themselves. If it was so difficult, then why, when they took on the job twenty-three months before, had they promised to do it in one year? Why hadn't they asked for three? (He had by now forgotten how mercilessly he had pressed them from the beginning.) If only they had held out against him for more time at the start, he in his turn would have held out against Stalin and got them an extra year, which could then have been spun out into two, but they had so long stood in fear and trembling before higher authority that not one of them, then or now, would have had the courage to stand up to it.

Abakumov himself followed the usual practice of keeping some margin in hand and in agreeing time limits with Stalin, he always added a couple of extra months as a reserve. And he had done so in this case too, promising Stalin to deliver one model of the new telephone by the 1st of March. So if the worst came to the worst, he actually could give them one more month—as long as this was final.

Picking up his fountain pen again, he said:

'What kind of a month do you mean? An honest-to-God month, or are you lying again?'

'Just a month! Not a day more!' Oskolupov said beaming, delighted by this happy turn of events, and looking as if he could hardly wait to go straight back to Mavrino and personally take up a soldering iron.

Abakumov scribbled a note in his desk calendar.

'Very well. Let's say the 21st of January—the anniversary of Lenin's death, and you'll all get the Stalin Prize. Will you make it, Sevastyanov?'

'Yes! We will!'

'Oskolupov! I'll skin you alive if you let me down! Will you make it?'

'Yes, Comrade General. There's nothing left to do except . . . .'

'And you, Yakonov? You know the score, don't you? Will it be ready on time?'

Still managing to keep up his courage, Yakonov stood his ground:

'In one month! By the 1st of February!'

'And if it's not ready by the 1st? Think what you're saying, Colonel. You're lying, aren't you?'

Of course Yakonov was lying. And of course he should have asked for two months. But he'd already burned his boats.

'It will be, Comrade General,' he promised sadly.

'Well, just remember, I didn't make you say it. I can forgive anything except deception! You can go.'

Greatly relieved, they filed out again, one after the other, lowering their eyes before the fifteen-foot portrait of Stalin.

What they did not know was that the Minister had set a trap for them.

As soon as they had left another visitor was ushered in:

'Engineer Pryanchikov.'

CHAPTER SIXTEEN

That night, after Yakonov had been called to the Ministry by Sevastyanov on Abakumov's orders, two telephone messages fifteen minutes apart were sent to Mavrino, summoning Bobynin and Pryanchikov to the Ministry too. This was kept secret from Sevastyanov and his subordinates. The two prisoners were taken to the Ministry in separate cars and made to wait in separate rooms to eliminate any chance of collusion between them.

Pryanchikov was, of course, hardly likely to do anything so underhand; he was so unnaturally candid that many of his more practical-minded contemporaries regarded it as a sign of mental abnormality. In the prison they talked of him as being 'out of phase'. Now in particular he was even less capable of deception than usual, thanks to the profound emotional shock caused by the glimpses of Moscow at night that flashed past the windows of the car. After the drab suburbs surrounding Mavrino, the impact of the gleaming main road, the cheerful bustle in front of a railway station and the neon-lit shop-fronts was all the more violent. Pryanchikov forgot the driver and the two plain-clothes guards. Staring fixedly through the window he felt he was breathing not air but fire. Never having even been driven through Moscow in daytime, he was now the first prisoner from Mavrino to see Moscow by night.

At the Sretenka Gate the car was held up, first by a crowd coming out of a cinema, then by traffic lights. Like millions of other prisoners he had often had the feeling that life 'outside' must have come to a halt; that there were no men left; that all those lonely women must be in mourning for their frustrated love. Yet here, dotted with smart hats and fur coats, was a cheerful, well-fed crowd, and through the cold air, even through the bodywork of the car Pryanchikov's keyed-up faculties sensed the perfume of women passing by as a series of physical blows. As he caught the sounds of their laughter and snatches of muffled talk, he felt like ramming his head through the safety-glass window and shouting to them that he was young, starved of love and jailed for nothing at all. After the monastic seclusion of prison this was magic, a glimpse of the good life which had always eluded him—at first because as a student he had been too poor, later because he had scarcely known any existence outside prisoner-of-war camps and jail.

In the Ministry waiting-room Pryanchikov was still so overwhelmed by his impressions that he failed to notice even the tables and chairs.

A sleek young lieutenant-colonel asked him to follow him. With his thin neck and wrists, his delicate build, narrow shoulders and slim legs, Pryanchikov had never looked so frail as when he entered the large office into which his escort ushered him. It was so big that he did not even notice that it was an office—the office of the man in gold epaulettes seated at the far end. Nor did he notice the fifteen-foot-high portrait of Stalin. His eyes could see nothing but women. As though drunk, he had no idea why he was in this big room nor what it was. The sense of unreality was only increased by his sudden memory of the unfinished glass of cold tea which he had left behind in that semicircular room, still lit by a blue lamp even though the war had been over for five years.

He set off across the lavish carpet, a carpet so soft and with such a deep pile that he felt like rolling in it. Huge windows filled the right-hand side of the room; on the left was a mirror reaching from floor to ceiling.

There are some things in life which only men behind bars really appreciate: for a man only granted the occasional use of a scrap of mirror smaller than the palm of his own hand, a look into a full-length mirror is a great event. As though magnetized by it, Pryanchikov stopped beside the mirror. He stepped closer, revelling in the sight of his own clean, fresh face. He straightened his tie, smoothed the collar of his blue shirt, then backed slowly away, admiring himself from every angle. He glided, almost pirouetted in front of the mirror, then advanced again for a close look. Despite his rather shapeless blue denims he thought he looked distinctly neat and dapper. Much cheered by this discovery, he moved on—not to the serious matter which was the reason for his visit, but simply to go on inspecting the room.

The all-powerful Minister, the man with the power to imprison half the world, the man before whom generals and marshals paled, stared curiously at this frail, blue-clad prisoner. Although he had arrested and condemned millions, it was a long time since the Minister had seen one of them at close quarters. Pryanchikov came mincing up to the Minister and gave him a puzzled look as though surprised to find him there.

'Your name is . . .'—Abakumov looked down at a piece of paper—'Pryanchikov—right?'

'Yes,' said Pryanchikov vacantly, 'it is.'

'And you are the senior engineer of the team working on . . .'—again he checked with his notes—'. . . the artificial speech device, aren't you?'

'Artificial speech device?' Pryanchikov winced. 'Nobody ever calls it that. It was given that clumsy name to make it sound as if we weren't copying a foreign invention. We use the English word "scrambler".'

'Anyway, you are the senior engineer on the project.'

'I suppose so. What of it?' said Pryanchikov warily.

'Sit down.'

Gratefully Pryanchikov sat down, hitching up the neatly creased trouser-legs of his denims.

'I want you to answer my questions with complete frankness and without worrying about any repercussions from your immediate superiors. Tell me honestly—when will the scrambler be ready? In a month? Two months? Don't be afraid to tell me what you really think.'

'The scrambler? Ready in two months? You're joking!' Pryanchikov gave a loud boyish laugh, of the kind never before heard within these walls, threw himself back in the soft leather chair and clasped his hands in mock horror. 'What are you talking about? You obviously have no idea what this job involves. Let me show you.'

He leaped out of the well-sprung armchair towards Abakumov's desk.

'Have you got a scrap of paper? Yes.'

He tore a blank page from the notepad on the Minister's

desk, seized his blood-red pen and started drawing a rough sketch of a sinusoid complex. Such was the childlike innocence of this eccentric that Abakumov was quite unperturbed; tolerating this invasion of his desk, he watched Pryanchikov in silence.

'The point is that the human voice consists of a number of harmonics.' Pryanchikov nearly choked from his urgent desire to explain it as quickly as possible. 'And the idea of the scrambler is that it reproduces the voice artificially. . . . Damn! How on earth do you manage to write with a pen like this? . . . Reproduces the voice artificially by assembling if not all the harmonics then at least the basic ones, each of which is transmitted by a separate set of impulses. Now you must know the Cartesian system of rectangular co-ordinates—every schoolboy does—but do you know about Fourier's Series?'

'Just a moment.' Abakumov succeeded in checking the flow. 'Just tell me one thing: when will it be ready? When?'

'Ready? Well . . . I haven't given it much thought.' Pryanchikov had now forgotten his impressions of Moscow at night; the fascination of his work had taken over and he found it hard to stop. 'The problem is much simpler, of course, if you're prepared to accept a poorer quality of voice reproduction. Then the number of constituent harmonics . . .'

'When will it be ready? By the 1st of March? The 1st of April?'

'God, by April? . . . Without the cryptographers we could be ready in four, maybe five months, no sooner. But we still don't know what effect the encoding and decoding will have on the speech-quality. It might make it much worse, so it's impossible to forecast.' He tugged at Abakumov's sleeve for emphasis. 'Let me explain, then you'll realize that the job is bound to suffer if we have to work under pressure. . . .'

Hypnotized by the meaningless squiggles of the drawing, Abakumov had already pressed a button on his desk. The sleek lieutenant-colonel reappeared and motioned Pryanchikov to leave.

Confused, with his mouth half open, Pryanchikov did as he was told. He was upset most of all by being interrupted in the midst of his explanation. Then on his way out he realized with a start where he was. He had almost reached the door when he remembered that the other prisoners had asked him to complain about their many grievances. He swung round and started back again.

'Look, I almost forgot to tell you . . .'

But the lieutenant-colonel barred his way and pushed him firmly towards the door. The man behind the desk had ceased listening to him. Pryanchikov's mind, filled as it now was with electronics, had perversely forgotten all the wrongs and abuses of prison life except one. He shouted from the doorway:

'By the way, about our tea—there's never any hot water after work late at night, so we can't make tea!'

'Tea?' echoed the man at the desk, who suddenly reminded Pryanchikov of a general. 'All right. We'll see to it.'

CHAPTER SEVENTEEN

It was then Bobynin's turn. He wore the same blue denims, but was a large man with red hair cropped in labour-camp fashion.

He showed about as much interest in the furnishings of the office as if it were a place he came into a hundred times a day. He strode in, sat down without a word in one of the comfortable armchairs near the Minister's desk and elaborately blew his nose into the off-white handkerchief that he had washed himself during his last bath.

Abakumov, who had found Pryanchikov slightly disconcerting but too scatter-brained to be taken seriously, was relieved to see how down-to-earth Bobynin looked. He did not shout at him to stand up, but assuming that he could not distinguish badges of rank and had failed to grasp the significance of the suite of ante-rooms through which he had been led, he enquired mildly:

'Why did you sit down without permission?'

Bobynin, with barely a glance at the Minister and still cleaning his nose with his handkerchief, said airily:

'Well, you see, there's an old Chinese proverb: never walk if you can stand still, never stand if you can sit—but lying down is best of all.'

'Have you any idea who I might be?'

Leaning comfortably on the arms of his chair Bobynin now inspected Abakumov and ventured idly:

'Well, you look a bit like Field-Marshal Goering to me.'

'Like who?'

'Marshal Goering. I remember him visiting an aircraft factory near Halle when I was working there. All the generals were scared stiff of him, but I just turned my back on him. He gave me one look and walked on.'

Something distantly akin to a smile passed across Abakumov's face, but at once turned into a scowl at the unheard-of insolence of this prisoner.

Wincing at the thought, he asked:

'What do you mean? Don't you see any difference between us?'

'Between you and him? Or between you and me?' Bobynin's voice rang like metal on metal. 'I can see the difference between you and me: you need me, but I don't need you.'

Abakumov could put thunder in his voice and knew how to frighten people with it, but in this case he felt it would be ineffectual and undignified. He could see that this prisoner was a tough nut, so he merely said:

'Listen, don't go too far just because I choose to be polite to you. . . .'

'If you were rude to me I wouldn't talk to you at all. You can shout at your colonels and your generals as much as you like because they've got plenty to lose.'

'We can deal with your sort too if we have to.'

'No you can't.' Bobynin's piercing eyes flashed with hatred. 'I've got nothing, see? Nothing! You can't touch my wife and child—they were killed by a bomb. My parents are dead. I own nothing in the world except a handkerchief. These denims and this underwear—which hasn't even got any buttons'—he bared his chest to show what he meant—'is government issue. You took my freedom away a long time ago and you can't give it back to me because you haven't got it yourself. I'm forty-two years old. You gave me twenty-five years. I've done hard labour, I know what it is to have a number instead of a name, to be handcuffed, to be guarded by dogs, to work in a punitive brigade—what more can you do to me? Take me off this special project? You'd be the loser. I need a smoke.'

Abakumov opened a box of special 'Troika' cigarettes and pushed it towards Bobynin:

'Have some of these.'

'Thanks, I prefer my own. Anything else makes me cough.' He took a 'Belomor' from his home-made case. 'You can tell old You-know-who—up there—that you only have power over people so long as you don't take *everything* away from them. But when you've robbed a man of *everything* he's no longer in your power—he's free again.'

Bobynin said no more, absorbed in smoking. He was enjoying baiting the Minister and lounging in this comfortable armchair. He only regretted having refused those luxury cigarettes just to produce an effect.

Abakumov looked down at a sheet of paper.

'Bobynin, are you the engineer in charge of the "speech-clipper" project?'

'Yes.'

'Please tell me exactly when it will be ready for use.'

Bobynin arched his dark, bushy eyebrows.

'What's all this about? Couldn't you find anybody senior to me to tell you that?'

'I want *you* to tell me. Will it be ready by February?'

'February? Are you serious? If you want a rush job and no end of trouble with it afterwards—well, you can have it in six months or so. But if you want it to be totally secure—I've no idea. Maybe a year.'

Abakumov was appalled. He recalled the angry, impatient twitching of the Boss's moustache and he felt sick at the thought of the promises that he had given on Sevastyanov's advice. He had the terrible sinking feeling of a man who goes to a doctor with a cold only to be told that he has cancer of the larynx.

The Minister rested his head on both his hands and said dejectedly:

'Bobynin—please—think what you're saying. Tell me —what can be done to speed things up?'

'Speed it up? Can't be done.'

'But why not? Give me the reasons. Whose fault is it? Don't be afraid to tell me. Name the culprits whatever their rank. I'll sack the lot!'

Bobynin leaned back and stared up at the ceiling where the

plaster nymphs of the old 'Rossiya' insurance company were still disporting themselves.

'But that means that the project will have taken two and a half to three years,' said the Minister indignantly. 'And it was scheduled to take a *year*!'

Bobynin exploded.

'What d'you mean—scheduled? What d'you think science is—a magic wand that you just have to wave to get what you want? Supposing the problem's been put in the wrong terms or new factors crop up? You and your schedule! It never occurs to you, does it, that it's no good issuing orders unless the men on the job have peace of mind, enough to eat and freedom? And then there's this atmosphere of suspicion. We had to shift a small lathe from one place to another. I don't know whether it was our fault or not, but it somehow got damaged. It would have cost thirty roubles to repair. The lathe was a piece of junk, anyway—it was about a hundred years old, no motor, driven by an overhead belt. And because it got broken the Security Officer, Major Shikin, gave us hell for two weeks, questioning everybody to see whether he couldn't double someone's sentence for sabotage. There are two of these Security Officers; they're both parasites, and all they do is get on our nerves. They have nothing better to do than make out endless reports and they're always picking on people—what the hell do you need them for? Everybody knows that we're making secret telephone equipment for Stalin and that Stalin wants results—yet even on a job like this you can't get us the right equipment: we don't have the proper condensers, the valves are the wrong type or there aren't enough oscillographs. It's miserable! It's a disgrace—and you ask me who's to blame. Ever thought about the poor devils who have to do all the work? They slave away for twelve or sixteen hours a day—yet only the senior engineers get a proper meat ration and the rest are lucky if they find a bone in their soup. Why don't you let the fifty-eighters[1] have visits from their relatives? By rights

[1] 'Fifty-eighters'—those convicted under Article 58 of the RSFSR Penal Code, a catch-all statute designed by Stalin to validate the imprisonment of anyone guilty or suspected of activity deemed to be anti-Soviet.

it should be once a month—but you only allow it once a year! What d'you think that does to people's morale? Maybe you don't have enough Black Marias to take us? Maybe you can't afford to pay the guards overtime? Rules and regulations —that's all you can think about. We used to be allowed out into the grounds all day on Sundays—now that's been stopped. What's the point—to get more work out of us? Like hell you will. You won't improve results by keeping us cooped up. Come to that, why did you have to drag me here at this time of night? What's wrong with daytime? I've got to work tomorrow. I need sleep.'

Bobynin sat bolt upright, a big, angry man.

Abakumov was breathing heavily, leaning hard against the desk. It was twenty-five minutes past one. In an hour's time, at half past two, the Minister was due to go and report to Stalin at his house out at Kuntsevo.

If this man was right, Abakumov was in trouble.

Stalin was merciless.

As he dismissed Bobynin he remembered that trio of liars at the Special Equipment Section; a blind fury swept over him and he rang for the three men.

CHAPTER EIGHTEEN

The room was small and low, with no windows but two doors. Despite the lack of windows the air was fresh and sweet, a special engineer being responsible for its circulation and chemical purity. Much of the room was taken up by a low, well-worn couch with chintz cushions. On the wall above it were twin lamps shaded in pale pink glass.

Lying on the couch was the man whose image, more than any other human likeness in history, had been graven in stone, painted in oils, in water-colour, in gouache and in sepia, drawn in charcoal, chalk and brick-dust, patterned in gravel, seashells, glazed tiles, grains of wheat and soya beans, carved in ivory, grown in grass, woven in carpets, registered on celluloid and outlined in the sky by aircraft.

Now, however, he was simply lying with his feet slightly drawn up; they were shod in Caucasian knee-boots so soft and tight that they looked more like gaiters. He wore a military tunic with four large pockets, two on the breast and two at the sides—a comfortable old one from the collection of grey, khaki, black and white tunics which he had been accustomed to wear since Civil War days and which he had only changed for a marshal's uniform after Stalingrad.

The name of this man was for ever headlined in the world's newspapers, intoned by thousands of announcers in hundreds of languages, declaimed by orators, piped by childish voices, chanted in benediction by priests; the name of this man was frozen on the dying lips of prisoners of war, and on the swollen, toothless gums of men in labour camps and jails. His name had been lent to countless cities and squares, streets and avenues, schools, hospitals, mountain ranges, ship canals, factories, mines, state farms, collective farms, battleships, icebreakers, fishing boats, cobbler's shops and crêches—to which would have been added, if a certain group of Moscow journalists had their way, the Volga and the moon.

But he was just a little old man with a wizened fold of skin on his neck (which was never shown on portraits), breath that smelled of Turkish pipe-tobacco, and thick clammy fingers which left their mark on books. He had felt unwell today and the day before. Although the air was warm he felt a chill on his back and shoulders and had covered them with a brown camel-hair shawl.

He had nothing much to do and was enjoying himself by leafing through a small book in a hard brown cover. He admired the photographs, to which he kept returning, and read snatches of the text which he knew almost by heart. The advantage of this book was its pocket size—it could go with people wherever they went. It had two hundred and fifty pages but was printed in widely spaced, bold type so that even the old and the barely literate could read it without strain. Its cover was embossed in gold: *Joseph Vissarionovich Stalin—A Short Biography*.

The plain, straightforward phrases had an irresistible and soothing effect on the human heart: Strategist of genius . . . wise foresight . . . mighty will . . . iron determination . . . Lenin's virtual deputy from 1918 onwards. (Well, wasn't he? . . .) The revolution's greatest military leader found the front in chaos and confusion . . . Frunze's operational plan was based on Stalin's orders . . . (so it was . . .). It was our good fortune that in the difficult years of the War for the Fatherland we were led by a wise and tested Leader— The Great Stalin (yes, they were lucky). Everybody knows the devastating force of Stalin's logic, the crystal clarity of his mind . . . (without false modesty he had to admit it was true) . . . his love for the people . . . his great concern for human beings . . . his dislike of pomp . . . his astounding modesty (very true, that bit about modesty).

Excellent. And they say it's selling well, too. The second edition had run into five million copies, but that was not enough for a country of this size. There was still room for a third edition of ten or twelve million. It should be sold direct in factories, schools and collective farms.

He felt a touch of nausea. He put the book aside, took a peeled *feijoa* from the little round table and bit into it. As he sucked it his nausea went away, leaving a pleasant taste in his mouth with a faint tang of iodine.

Although he was afraid to admit it, he had noticed that his health was getting worse every month. He was suffering from lapses of memory and attacks of nausea. There was no real pain, but for hours on end he felt horribly weak and had to keep to his couch. Even sleep was no relief: he woke up as stale, jaded and sluggish as when he had gone to bed and he found movement difficult. In the Caucasus at seventy a man was in his prime—he could climb mountains, ride horses and chase women. And he had once been so healthy! He so much wanted to live to be ninety, but something was going wrong. For a year now he had not enjoyed his one great pleasure in life—good food. Orange juice made his tongue smart, caviar tasted like putty, and even the fiery Georgian *harcho*, which his doctors forbade him to eat, had lost its savour. Gone, too, was his keen palate for wine; drink only gave him a dull headache. And the thought of a woman had become repulsive.

Now that he had decided to live to ninety, Stalin reflected gloomily that this would give him no personal pleasure and that he would just have to suffer another twenty years for the sake of mankind.

One doctor had warned him . . . but hadn't the man later

been shot? When Moscow's leading doctors applied their stethoscopes to him their hands trembled. They never prescribed injections since he had refused to have them—only electro-therapy and 'as much fruit as possible.' You didn't have to tell a Georgian to eat fruit!

Half closing his eyes, he took another bite.

In Moscow the great celebrations of his seventieth birthday had ended three days ago.

Traicho Kostov had been done to death on the evening of the 20th, so the real festivities had only begun the next day with a solemn gathering in the Bolshoi Theatre at which Mao Tse-tung, La Pasionaria and other comrades had spoken in his honour. After this there was a great banquet for everybody, then a more intimate banquet. They had drunk vintage Spanish wines. He had had to keep his wits about him as he drank, to watch for any hint of treachery in those faces flushed with drink. Then he and Beria had sat alone drinking Caucasian wine and singing Georgian songs. On the 22nd there had been a huge reception for the foreign diplomats. On the 23rd he had seen himself in part two of Virta's film *The Battle of Stalingrad* and on the stage in Vishnevsky's *Unforgettable 1919*.

Although tiring, these works had pleased him very much. (Stalin Prizes for both of them!) A much truer appreciation of the part he had played in the Civil War, not to mention his role in the War for the Fatherland, was emerging. It was now remembered the many occasions on which he had had to advise and restrain the over-trusting, impetuous Lenin. And they were very good, those words that Vishnevsky had put into his mouth: 'Every worker has the right to speak his mind!—one day we'll write that into the constitution.' This showed that even while defending Petrograd against the White armies, he was already thinking about the democracy of the future. In those days, of course, they had called it 'the dictatorship of the proletariat'—but no matter, it was great stuff and true to life.

And it had been very clever of Virta to put in that scene with the Friend. Even though Stalin had never been able to keep any such close, devoted friend, because people had always been so insincere and two-faced (and come to think of it, he had never really had a friend like that in all his life), but how good it would have been to have had a true and selfless friend like the one in the film, to whom he could confide those innermost thoughts that came to him at night.

But the main thing was that the ordinary people loved their Leader, really loved and understood him. This was obvious from the newspapers, the cinema and that exhibition of birthday presents. It was a joy to think that his birthday had been such a great event for the whole people. All those greetings!—greetings from government offices, greetings from institutions, greetings from factories, greetings from private citizens! There were so many that *Pravda* had asked permission to publish two columns of them daily. That meant they would run for several years, but there was no harm in that.

There had been more presents than could be housed in the ten showrooms of the Museum of the Revolution. To allow the people of Moscow to see them unhindered during the day, Stalin had gone to view them at night. The skills of thousands upon thousands of craftsmen, the best that the earth could offer was displayed before him—yet even here he felt listless and indifferent. What use were all these gifts to him? They very soon bored him. And then a recollection of something unpleasant came over him in the museum but, as often happened nowadays, it remained vague, he could not grasp it and he was left with nothing more than a sense of unease. He had walked round three of the rooms without stopping, until he came to a large television set inscribed with the words 'To the great Stalin from the men of the Security Service' (it was the largest Soviet television set ever made and only one model had been produced—at Mavrino). He had looked at it for a moment, turned around and left.

So this great event had gone by, leaving him with nothing but a feeling of emptiness. He was racked and tormented by an indefinable something that had weighed on him since his visit to the museum.

It was true that the people loved him, but they were still riddled with faults. How was he to put them right?

Communism would have come about so much sooner if it had not been for . . . if it had not been for all those soulless bureaucrats. If it had not been for all those swollen-headed Party bigwigs. If it had not been for weaknesses in organizing and enlightening the masses. The failure to educate Party members properly. The slow pace of construction. The bottlenecks in industry. The output of shoddy goods. The bad planning. The resistance to technical change. The unwillingness of youth to go out and work in the backwoods. The wastage of grain during harvest. The embezzlement. The pilfering. The swindling. Sabotage in the labour camps. Leniency by the police. Corruption in housing. The rampant black market. The hoarding. The young people getting out of hand. The grumblers. Snide insinuations from the writers, the pernicious influence of certain films.

No, there was still a lot wrong with the people.

Whose fault was the retreat in 'forty-one? The people were told to stand and die—why didn't they? Who had retreated? The people had retreated!

As he recalled 1941 Stalin was inevitably reminded of his own lapse—his hasty and needless departure from Moscow in October. Of course, nobody would call it running away; Stalin had left behind responsible men and had given them firm instructions to defend the capital to the last drop of blood. But unfortunately these very men had wavered—so he had had to come back himself and take over.

Later on he ordered the imprisonment of anybody who mentioned the panic of the 16th of October 1941; but he had punished himself too, by taking the salute at the 7th of November parade that year. It had been one of the most terrible moments of his life, like the time when he had fallen through the ice during his exile in Siberia—but as then, despair had given him strength. It had been no joke, taking a military parade with the enemy at the gates. . . .

But then it wasn't easy to be the greatest man alive. . . .

Enervated from lying down too long, Stalin surrendered to a dispiriting train of thought. His tired mind kept wandering. He lay with his eyes half closed and the most disjointed recollections from his long, long life passed through his head. For some reason he remembered nothing good, only the bad things, things that rankled. When he thought of Gori, his birthplace, it was not for its pleasant green hills, the banks of its winding rivers, but for all the ugly things which had kept him away from the place for ever. When he thought of 1917 he remembered how Lenin had arrived in Petersburg in April and with such self-assurance had completely reversed the policy so that everyone had laughed at Stalin for having wanted to expand legal Party activity and live in peace with the Provisional Government. They were always laughing at him, yet at the same time always landing him with the difficult and thankless jobs. Why had they sent *him* to the St Peter and St Paul fortress on the 6th of July to persuade the sailors to surrender the fortress to Kerensky and retreat to Kronstadt? Because if they had sent Zinoviev the sailors would have stoned him to death. Because it had to be someone who could talk their language. . . . When he remembered 1920, it was Tukhachevsky swearing and shouting that he would have taken Warsaw if it hadn't been for Stalin. He had paid for that jibe. . . .

No, he had been unlucky all his life. There had always been someone getting in the way. No sooner had he got rid of one, than another had come along.

There came four gentle knocks at the door—if knock was the right word: it was rather as though the person outside had softly pawed the door like a dog. Stalin turned a switch by the couch and a safety-catch clicked as the door was opened by remote control. There was no curtain over the doorway (Stalin hated curtains or anything behind which people might hide) and the bare door opened just enough to admit a dog; but the head that appeared was in the upper half of the doorway and belonged to the still young-looking but already balding Poskryobyshev with his permanent expression of total fidelity and devotion.

Seeing the Boss lying there half covered with a camel-hair shawl, he was alarmed by his appearance. Avoiding a direct question about his health (there was a tacit assumption that Stalin was always quite well) Poskryobyshev said softly:

'You asked Abakumov to come at half past two. Do you still want to see him?'

Stalin unbuttoned the flap of his breast pocket and pulled out a watch on a chain (like all people of his age he could not bear wristwatches).

It was not yet two o'clock.

He was in no mood to get up, change and go to his study, but he mustn't let people get out of hand either: you only had to slacken the reins a bit and they'd think he was losing his grip.

'We'll see,' Stalin answered wearily and blinked. 'I'm not sure.'

'Let him come. He'll wait!'

Poskryobyshev nodded—three times to be on the safe side. (He found that to play the good schoolboy strengthened his position.) He paused for a moment, then enquired solicitously: 'Will there be anything else?'

Stalin looked sadly at this creature whom unfortunately he could not treat as a friend either, because he was far too much of an underling.

'That's all for now, Sasha,' he muttered through his moustache.

Poskryobyshev nodded again, withdrew his head and firmly shut the door.

Stalin reset the safety-catch by remote control and holding his shawl, turned over.

Then, on a little table, lower even than the couch, he noticed a cheaply produced book in a red and black paper cover and he suddenly remembered what it was that had so much weighed on him, that had ruined his birthday celebrations, and that still nagged him now—Tito! This man was still in his way and he was not yet rid of him.

How could they have been so mistaken about this snake in the grass? Those were great days in 'thirty-six and 'thirty-seven, when they had chopped off so many heads—yet they had let Tito go!

With a groan Stalin let his legs down from the couch, sat up and clutched his head, its slightly reddish hair already turning grey and thinning. He smarted with the utter humiliation of it. Like the hero of legend, Stalin had spent his life cutting off the heads of the Hydra. If the bodies of all his victims had been piled up they would have made more than one Mount Elbruz—yet he had stumbled on a molehill—Tito!

Joseph Stalin had met his match in Joseph Broz-Tito. . . .

The fact that Kerensky was still alive somewhere had never worried Stalin. He would not have cared if Nicholas II or Kolchak had come back from the grave—he had nothing against them personally: they had been avowed enemies, they had never had the impertinence to offer their own brand of a new and better socialism.

Better socialism! . . . In other words different from Stalin's! The little guttersnipe! How could you have socialism *without* Stalin?

It wasn't as if Tito would succeed—nothing would come of it. Stalin looked on Tito in the way that an old country doctor with a lifetime's experience of rough and ready kitchen-table surgery regards a young girl just out of medical school.

Three times now they had had to produce new editions of Lenin's collected works and twice re-edit Marx and Engels. Everybody who had argued, all those people mentioned in the notes to the earlier editions who had wanted to build socialism differently, were long since dead. And now when even from the wastes of Siberia there was not a murmur of doubt or criticism to be heard—out crawls this creature Tito and his clever stooge Kardelj, telling you that you should have done it differently!

Stalin suddenly became aware that his heart was beating violently; he could scarcely see and he felt a barely controllable urge to twitch all over. He drew a deep breath, ran his hand over his face and moustache. This would never do. He must not let Tito rob him of all peace of mind, put him off his food and stop him sleeping altogether.

His sight improved a little and he again noticed the little black and red book. The book itself was not to blame, of course. Stalin reached for it eagerly, put some pillows behind him and lay back again for a while.

The book was Reynaud de Jouvenelle's *Tito—the Traitors' Marshal* which had been published in a dozen European languages in millions of copies—how lucky that the author's name made him seem uninvolved in the quarrel, an objective Frenchman, and with an aristocratic-sounding name to boot. Stalin had read the book carefully a few days before, but like all books that pleased him, he kept it at his side. To think of all the millions of people whose eyes it would open to this vain, conceited, cruel, cowardly, vile, hypocritical, despicable tyrant! This sickening traitor! This unspeakable ignoramus! Even some Western Communists had been taken in by him, like that old fool André Marty. He would have to be kicked out of the Party for supporting Tito.

He turned over the pages. There—how could anybody call Tito a hero after reading this? Twice he had tried to surrender to the Germans from cowardice but his Chief of Staff, Jovanovič, had forced him to remain as Commander-in-Chief! One of the best, Jovanovič—but they had killed him. And then there was Petricevič—'murdered for his devotion to Stalin'. Noble Petricevič! Someone always managed to kill off the good people and it was left to him, Stalin, to deal with the bad ones.

It was all there in this book—how Tito must have been a British agent, how proud he had been of his underwear embroidered with the royal emblem, how physically repulsive he was, like Goering, how his fingers dripped with diamond rings, how he covered himself with medals (what miserable vanity in a man totally devoid of military genius!).

What an honest, objective book. But wasn't Tito impotent too? He ought to have mentioned that.

'The Yugoslav Communist Party is run by murderers and spies.' 'Tito only became Party leader because he was recommended by Bela Kun and Traicho Kostov.'

Kostov! Stalin felt stung by the very name. He was seized by rage and he lashed out with his boot as though kicking Traicho in the face—and his grey eyelids twitched with a sense of justice done. So much for Kostov, the dirty swine!

It was amazing how clearly you could see, after the event, what those scoundrels had been up to. The way they had disguised themselves! He had fixed Kun in 'thirty-seven, but it was a mere ten days since Kostov had slandered a bench of socialist judges. To think of all the trials Stalin had successfully organized, the number of enemies he had forced to grovel and confess to the vilest crimes—and now look how they had bungled the Kostov trial. They had been made to look complete fools. What a low trick to play— deceiving his experienced interrogators by grovelling to them and then denying it all at the public hearing! In front of the foreign press, too! What a way for a Party man to behave! What an example to the proletariat! He had to die, anyway, so he might at least have died in a way that did the Party some good!

Stalin threw the book away. Enough of this lying coward—there was work to be done. As the father of his country he must keep vigil while the rest slept peacefully in their beds.

He got up and stooping slightly walked over to another door, not the one at which Poskryobyshev had knocked—and opened it. Locking it behind him, he shuffled down a low, narrow, winding passage. Like his room, it had no windows, but a skylight. He passed mirrors set at an angle which enabled him to see into the ante-room. He walked through into his bedroom, equally low, cramped and windowless and equipped with air-conditioning. There was armour plating between the solid oak panelling and the stonework of the wall.

With a tiny key from a chain on his belt Stalin unlocked the metal cover of a decanter, poured himself a glass of his favourite cordial, drank it and locked the decanter again.

He walked over to the mirror. His eyes stared back at him with that sharp, stern and incorruptible gaze at which many a minister had quailed. It was a plain, bluff soldierly look.

He rang for his Georgian orderly to come and dress him.

However routine the occasion he insisted on dressing the part of the man of destiny.

With his iron will . . . his unshakeable resolution. . . .

CHAPTER NINETEEN

Stalin's most creative hours were the hours of darkness.

In the mornings his suspicious mind only ticked over slowly; he would glumly sack people, cut budgets and merge whole ministries, two or three at a time. At night, on the other hand, his mind, now supple and ingenious, would consider ways of splitting ministries up and devise new names for them, he would approve new expenditure and confirm new appointments.

All his best ideas came to him between midnight and

four o'clock in the morning—how to welsh on the state lottery, for instance, by paying premium winners in new bonds instead of cash; how to introduce prison sentences for absenteeism; how to lengthen the working day and the working week; how to stop people changing jobs; how to frame new laws on forced labour and the death penalty; how to abolish the Third International; how to deport whole peoples to Siberia.

The deportation of whole peoples had been an important theoretical innovation and a bold experiment, to which there had been no alternative. No one could deny that he had always been the Party's leading expert on the question of national minorities.

He had a great many other remarkable measures to his credit as well, but lately he had nevertheless sensed a weak spot in this great edifice and an important new decree was maturing in his mind. He had clamped down on everything— all movement had been stopped, the ebb and flow of human beings had been halted, everybody, all two hundred million of them, knew their place—everybody, that was, except for the young people who were drifting away from the land and into the cities.

In general the situation on the collective farms was very good, as he had seen from the film *Kuban Cossacks* and from Babayevsky's novel *The Knight of the Golden Star*. The film-makers and the novelist had actually been to the collective farms—they were only showing what they had seen and they had shown that all was well. Stalin himself, too, had talked to collective farmers at various congresses.

But as befitted such a shrewd statesman, Stalin was never complacent. He forced himself to take a more penetrating view that went beyond impressions gained from films or books. One of the provincial Party secretaries (later shot, if he remembered rightly) had let slip that the trouble with the collective farms was that only the old people, who had been enrolled in the collectives in the early 'thirties, worked with a will; the young ones (of course, only a few irresponsible individuals) tried to wangle identity papers as soon as they left school and headed for the towns. When Stalin heard this he had begun to brood on it.

It was a lot of nonsense, of course, giving them all secondary education and sending all these cooks' sons to university. This had all been Lenin's fault, though it was still too early to say so aloud. 'Any cook should be able to run the country.' . . . What had Lenin actually meant by this? Did he mean they should take a day off every week to work in the local Soviet? A cook is a cook and his job is to get the dinner ready, whereas telling other people what to do is a highly skilled business; it can only be done by specially selected and trained personnel who have been toughened by years of experience, while in turn the control of this personnel could only be entrusted to one pair of hands—the practised hands of the Leader.

It should be laid down in the rules for collective farms that just as the land belongs to a farm in perpetuity, so all persons born on that land are automatically members of the collective farm. This should be drafted in such a way as to sound like a privilege, and only the local Soviet should have the right to release anyone from membership. A propaganda campaign should be launched at once and there should be articles in the newspapers with headlines like 'The Collective Farms must belong to the Younger Generation!' or 'A Vital Step in Transforming the Countryside!'—but, of course, Soviet journalists didn't need telling how to phrase it.

He seemed to remember that one of the Right Oppositionists (there had never been any such thing as 'Right Opposition', but it had suited Stalin to lump a number of his enemies together and deal with them all at one blow) had warned that this problem would arise. Why was it that the people he liquidated had always managed to be right about something? Despite himself Stalin was swayed by their ideas and he kept a wary ear cocked for their voices from beyond the grave.

This decree was urgent, as were other equally important ones that were taking shape in his mind, but today as he entered his study Stalin felt the need to turn his mind to higher things.

Now that he was entering his eighth decade it would be wrong of him to procrastinate. His immortality was, of course, assured; yet Stalin could not help thinking that although people called him the wisest of the wise, they had still not given him his full due. Their enthusiasm, he felt, was superficial and they did not truly appreciate the extent of his genius. He had lately been obsessed with the idea of making one more major contribution to learning, of leaving his indelible stamp on something else besides philosophy or history. Naturally it would have been easy for him to do this in biology, but he had left biology to Lysenko, that honest, enterprising man of the people. He would have found mathematics or even physics more tempting; he could not help feeling envious when he read those passages in *The Dialectic of Nature* about zero and minus one squared. But despite long sessions with Kiselyov's *Algebra* or Sokolov's *Advanced Physics*, he had found nothing to inspire him.

However, the recent case of Professor Chikobava of Tiflis University had given him an idea, although in the admittedly very different field of linguistics. This Chikobava had come out with what was, at first sight, the anti-Marxist heresy that language is not part of the 'superstructure' but is something in its own right, that language is neither bourgeois nor proletarian but simply national in character, and he had openly dared to take issue with none other than Marr himself. Since both Chikobava and Marr were Georgians the attack had been answered in the Tiflis University '*Journal*', a drab unbound copy of which, with its ornate Georgian lettering, was now lying on Stalin's desk. Some disciples of Marr had already answered the presumptuous Chikobava in terms that could only result in a knock on the door in the early hours of the morning. It had already been hinted that Chikobava was an agent of American imperialism.

Nothing would have saved him had not Stalin picked up the telephone and given orders to leave him alone. He not only spared Chikobava's life but decided to immortalize the professor's home-spun remarks by developing them into a brilliant work of his own composition.

It would, of course, have made a bigger splash to have refuted that counter-revolutionary theory of Relativity, or wave mechanics, but he was so busy with affairs of state that there just hadn't been the time. Linguistics was just another name for grammar, and Stalin had always thought of grammar as of much the same order of difficulty as mathematics.

It should read very well and vividly, he thought to himself as he sat down and began to write: 'Whatever national language of the Soviet Union we may take—Russian, Ukrainian, Byelorussian, Uzbek, Kazakh, Georgian, Armenian, Estonian, Latvian, Lithuanian, Moldavian, Tartar, Azerbaijani, Bashkir, Turkmen . . . (hell, he was finding it more and more difficult to stop himself from reeling off great lists like this. But on the other hand, why not? It impressed the reader and made it harder for him to answer back) . . . it is obvious. . . .' H'm. Here he had better put in something that was obvious.

But what was obvious? Nothing was obvious . . . it was all very hard going.

Now according to Marx economics was the 'basis', all the rest was 'superstructure'. And there was nothing else in between. But Stalin had learned from experience that you didn't get very far without something in between. There were, for instance, neutral countries (although not neutral people, of course). But suppose in the 'twenties he had said at a Party conference 'He who is not with us is not necessarily against us'? They would have kicked him off the platform, and out of the Party, too. Ah well, that's dialectics for you.

The same applied in this case. While reading Chikobava's article Stalin had been struck by a thought which had never occurred to him before: if language belongs to the superstructure, why doesn't it change with each new stage of social development? If it doesn't belong to the superstructure, then what is it? Part of the basis? A mode of production? But the mode of production is made up of productive forces and productive relations. You could scarcely call language a *relation*, could you? So was it a productive force? But productive forces consist of the instruments of production, the means of production and people. And although people talk languages, languages are not people. Hell, how did one sort that one out?

He would have liked to have said that language was an instrument of production like, for instance, a lathe, or a railway or the post office. After all, it was a form of communication;

but if he were to claim that language was an instrument of production, people would laugh at him—though not in this country, of course.

There was no one to advise him—he was alone in the world, like all great philosophers. If only Kant or Spinoza were still alive, or anyone of that calibre, even if they were bourgeois. . . . Should he ring up Beria, perhaps? Useless. Beria knew nothing about Philosophy.

Perhaps if he phrased it very cautiously . . . like this: 'In this respect language, while different in principle from the superstructure, does not, however, differ from instruments of production such as machines, which are as neutral in class terms as language is.'

'Neutral in class terms'! He wouldn't have got away with that in the old days, either. . . .

Putting a full stop, he linked his hands behind his head, yawned and stretched. He had only written one sentence and already he was tired.

Stalin got up and walked the length of the small study, his favourite place for working at night. He went up to a little window that was glazed with two layers of yellowish bullet-proof glass divided by air under high pressure. Outside was a little, walled garden into which the gardener was admitted only in the mornings and then under guard. For most of the time it was deserted.

Now it was full of a mist that hid both the world and the universe beyond. That half of the universe which was within him was orderly and manageable. It was the other half, so-called objective reality, which lurked out there in the mist. Here, within his armour-plated study, Stalin was not afraid of that other half; he felt he had the power to twist and bend it as he wished. It was only when he had to venture out into that objective reality—to attend a banquet in the Hall of Columns, for instance, when he must cross on his own two feet that frightening gap behind his car and the door, walk up the stairs and through that excessively large ante-chamber, past the fawning but much too numerous crowd—only then did he feel faint, completely unprotected and uncertain what to do with his hands, which had long ceased to be capable of defence. So he folded them on his stomach and smiled. Everybody thought that the All-Powerful was smiling graciously at them, but in fact it was a smile of bewilderment. . . .

He himself had called space the basic condition for the existence of matter. Yet having made himself master of one sixth of the world's dry land, he had begun to fear space. What he liked about his study was its very *lack* of space . . .

Again there came that gentle pawing at the door. Stalin pressed the button to unlock the door, which opened to reveal Poskryobyshev's head and face with its expression of a clown who enjoyed punishment.

In a near-whisper he asked gently:

'Shall I send Abakumov home or would you like him to wait a little longer?'

Ah yes, Abakumov. Stalin had been so completely immersed in his writing that he had quite forgotten about him.

He yawned. He was tired of it. The creative spark which had briefly flared up was extinguished, and that last sentence was no good.

'All right, send him in.'

He reached for another decanter with a metal lid, opened it with the key on his belt and drank a glassful.

He could never let up.

CHAPTER TWENTY

So far from calling him 'Alexander' to his face, hardly anyone even dared in private to refer to Poskryobyshev by anything other than his full name. 'Poskryobyshev rang' meant 'the Boss has given orders'. Alexander Poskryobyshev had held the post of chief of Stalin's personal secretariat for over fifteen years. That was a very long time, and anyone who did not know him well might justifiably have wondered how he had managed to keep his head on his shoulders for so long. The secret was simple: this ex-veterinary surgeon from Penza had the soul of an officer's batman, and it was this which had made him so secure in his job. Even after being made a lieutenant-general, a member of the Central Committee and head of a special department for keeping a check on members of the Central Committee, he still behaved like a lackey towards the Boss. Giggling sycophantically he would clink glasses with him in a toast to his native village of Sopliki. With his sixth sense Stalin realized that Poskryobyshev was totally devoid of hostility and he had no misgivings about him. His name, derived from the Russian word 'to scrape', suited him well: at his conception the Fates had somehow failed to scrape together those qualities which go to make a complete human being.

But when he dealt with subordinates this dim-looking, balding courtier became vastly important. When telephoning his juniors he took so little trouble to speak distinctly that the other person almost had to put his ear right into the receiver to catch what he was saying. It was occasionally permissible to joke with him about trivialities, but no one ever dared to ask 'How are things "up there" today?' (Even Stalin's own daughter was never allow to know how 'things' were; whenever she rang him up the only answers she got were that he was 'aroused' or 'not aroused', according to whether his footsteps could be heard.)

Today Poskryobyshev said to Abakumov:

'Stalin is working. He may call you in, and he may not. He says you're to wait.'

He took Abakumov's briefcase, led him into the waiting-room and disappeared.

Even Abakumov had not dared to ask the question which was uppermost in his mind: what sort of a mood is the Boss in today? Heart thumping, he sat alone in the waiting-room.

Whenever he went to see Stalin this strapping, powerful, decisive man experienced the same degree of terror which people had felt at the height of the purges whenever they heard footsteps on the staircase at night. The fear made his ears first turn ice-cold then flush with burning heat, and every time this happened Abakumov's terror was increased at the thought that the redness of his ears might arouse the Boss's suspicion. The slightest thing made Stalin suspicious. He hated it, for instance, if anyone in his presence put their hand into their inside pocket. For this reason Abakumov always transferred his three fountain pens, used for note-taking, from his inside pocket to his outside breast pocket.

The day-to-day running of the Ministry of State Security

was in the hands of Beria, from whom Abakumov received most of his orders. But once a month the Autocrat himself liked to have personal contact with the person to whom he had entrusted the security of his realm. These interviews, which lasted about an hour, were a heavy price to pay for all the might and power with which Abakumov was invested. He was only able to enjoy life in between interviews. When the time for another one came, fear seized him, his ears froze, he handed over his briefcase to Poskryobyshev without knowing whether he would ever get it back again and as he waited outside the study he bowed his ox-like head, never sure whether it would still be on his shoulders in an hour's time.

The terrible thing about Stalin was that if you made a mistake with him, it was like mishandling a detonator—it was the last mistake of your life. Stalin was terrible because he never listened to excuses. He never even accused you; the only sign was a malignant gleam from his yellow, tigerish eyes and a slight puckering of his lower eyelids. Inwardly he had already passed sentence without the victim even being aware of it: he would be allowed to leave, he would be arrested the same night and by morning he would be shot.

Worst of all was his silence and that puckering of his lower eyelids. . . . If Stalin poked you with something heavy or sharp, if he trod on your toe, spat at you or blew hot ash out of his pipe into your face, this meant that his anger was only temporary and would pass. Even if Stalin swore or used the foulest language Abakumov was inwardly relieved: this meant that the Boss still felt that his Minister could be made to mend his ways and could remain in favour. By now, of course, Abakumov realized that his ambition had carried him rather too far: lower down the ladder life was safer, and Stalin was always pleasanter in his dealings with his more distant subordinates; but once a person had advanced so far into the circle close to Stalin there was no way back.

The only prospect was death. One's own. Or . . .

Whenever Abakumov stood face to face with Stalin he was always dogged by the fear of being in some way shown up.

In particular he lived in permanent terror that Stalin

would learn the story of how he had made himself a small fortune in Germany. At the end of the war Abakumov had been the head of SMERSH, in charge of counter-intelligence on all the fighting fronts. It was a brief, splendid period in which people had been in a position to do very well for themselves without any fear of being caught. In order to increase the force of the final knock-out blow against Germany, Stalin borrowed Hitler's method of allowing the troops in the front line to send parcels home. This was based on Stalin's personal insight into the soldiers' mentality, on what he would have felt if he had been in their place. Fighting for one's country, he reasoned, was all very well, fighting for Stalin was better still; but in order to induce the soldiery to risk their lives at the most thankless time of all—nearly at the end of the war—would it not be better to give them a powerful and material incentive by allowing them to send home booty? Men in the ranks could send home ten pounds in weight per month, officers twenty pounds and generals a hundredweight. (This grading by rank was quite fair, because a soldier's pack ought not to be weighed down while he is on the march, whereas a general always had his car). But SMERSH, the counter-intelligence organization, was in an incomparably better position than even the generals. It was out of range of enemy shell-fire, it was never bombed by enemy aircraft. It was always to be found in that zone immediately behind the front line which was just far enough in the rear to be safe from bombardment, yet far enough forward to discourage any visits from the auditors of the Ministry of Finance. Its officers were enveloped in a cloud of secrecy. No one dared investigate what was in those sealed freight cars, what they were removing from that requisitioned estate, what that building was that SMERSH had ringed with sentries. Trucks, trains and aircraft were used to carry back booty for officers of SMERSH. A lieutenant who knew the ropes could make off with a haul worth thousands, a colonel could lay his hands on hundreds of thousands, while the value of Abakumov's loot ran into millions.

It was true that he could not imagine a situation, such as losing his job, in which his gold would be of the slightest use to him, even if it were all in a Swiss bank. No amount of worldly goods would bring a minister back to life once he had lost his head. But it was simply beyond Abakumov's powers to stand by and watch his underlings making their fortunes while taking nothing for himself. So he sent detachment after detachment out hunting. He had even been unable to resist two trunkfuls of men's braces. He looted compulsively.

Unfortunately this hoard of the Nibelungs could not be converted into usable wealth and instead became for Abakumov a constant source of fear. None of those who were in the know would have dared to inform on the mighty Abakumov, but there was always the possibility of something unforeseen giving him away. The stuff was useless to him, and now there was no way of getting rid of it without revealing his misdeeds . . .

. . . He had arrived at half past two in the morning, yet it was now ten minutes to four and he was still pacing up and down the waiting-room, clutching his thick, new notepad and feeling sick with fear. His ears were beginning to burn. Most of all he would have liked Stalin to become so absorbed in work that he had no time to see him; Abakumov was afraid of serious trouble over the scrambler. He had no idea how he was going to talk himself out of the situation.

Then the heavy door opened half-way. Poskryobyshev entered softly, almost on tiptoe, and he beckoned in silence. Abakumov moved forward, trying to shorten his usual long, swaggering stride. He squeezed his carcase through the next door, which was also half open, without opening it any further, grasping it by the polished bronze handle to hold it in place. As he came in he said:

'Good evening, Marshal. May I come in?'

He had made the mistake of not clearing his throat in time and this made his voice sound hoarse and insufficiently subservient.

Stalin was writing at his desk, wearing a tunic with gold buttons and several rows of medal ribbons but no epaulettes. He finished the sentence he was writing before raising his head and glancing at Abakumov with a sinister, owl-like stare. He said nothing.

This was a very bad sign.

Still he said nothing and began writing again.

Abakumov shut the door behind him, but did not dare to take another step without a nod or a gesture of invitation. He stood at attention, leaning slightly forward with a polite smile on his fleshy lips. His ears were aflame.

Abakumov had been in both the Boss's studies—the official daytime study and this little one that he used for night work. The large daytime study on the upper floor was bright and sunny, with ordinary windows. There on the long bookshelves the whole of human thought stood on parade, bound in bright covers. On the spacious walls hung the Leader's favourite pictures—pictures of himself. In one he was seen wearing the winter uniform of the Generalissimo, in another the summer dress of a marshal. There were sofas, armchairs and numerous ordinary chairs, used for receiving foreign delegations and for conferences. It was there, too, that Stalin had himself photographed.

His night-time study, however, hugged the ground; it was devoid of pictures or ornaments and its windows were very small. Four modest bookcases lined the walls; a desk stood in the middle of the room. The only other things in the room were a radiogram in one corner, a record-rack beside it. At night Stalin liked playing records of his old speeches.

Abakumov bent forward enquiringly and waited.

Stalin continued to write with that special concentration and seriousness which is appropriate when every word becomes history the very moment it flows from the pen. Almost the only light in the room was the beam from his desk lamp on to his paper; the concealed wall-lighting was very dim. Stalin occasionally stopped writing to lean back, to glance aside or on to the floor, to glare at Abakumov as though listening to something—although there was not a sound in the room.

What was it that lent such authority to his manner, that gave such significance to his every movement? Surely young Joseph Djugashvili had moved his hands and fingers in just the same way, had raised his eyebrows like this, had looked like this? But in those days no one had been frightened of his look, no one had tried to divine the terrible import of his movements. It was only after a certain number of heads had rolled that people began to interpret certain of the Leader's movements as hints, warnings, threats or commands. When Stalin noticed how others were observing him, he started to watch himself until he too found that he could detect menacing signals in his own gestures and looks; then he began purposely to cultivate them, which made their effect on other people even greater.

Finally, Stalin gave Abakumov one of his grimmest looks and jabbed his pipe-stem in the direction of a chair.

Abakumov gave a start of delight, trotted forward and sat down, though only on the edge of the chair, the more easily to leap to his feet again.

'Well?' said Stalin, looking down at his papers.

The moment had come. The secret was to grasp the conversational initiative and keep it at all costs. Abakumov coughed, cleared his throat and launched forth into a rapid, almost ecstatic monologue. (He always cursed himself afterwards for his garrulous eagerness in Stalin's presence and for the rash promises he made him, but somehow it always happened that when Stalin was gruff with him Abakumov was all the less able to control himself and his promises grew wilder and wilder.)

One of the most attractive features of Abakumov's reports, and the main reason why Stalin liked them, was his invariable discovery of some sinister, widely ramified group of spies and traitors. Abakumov never presented a report without describing how some such gang (a new one each time) had been put out of action. For today he had prepared a story about a hostile group in the Frunze Military Academy and he would make sure that his detailed account of it took up a very long time.

He began, however, by describing his successful efforts (he had no idea whether they really were being successful or not) to arrange for the removal of Tito. He said that a time-bomb would be placed on board Tito's yacht before it set out for the island of Brioni.

Stalin looked up, put his cold pipe into his mouth and took a couple of puffs. This was the only movement he made and he showed no sign of interest, but Abakumov, who had managed to acquire a certain insight into Stalin's behaviour, sensed that he had touched the right spot.

'But what about Ranković?' asked Stalin. Of course, of course! They must find out when the whole clique—Ranković, Kardelj and Moshe Pijade—could all be blown to bits simultaneously. According to their calculations, this ought to occur no later than the spring. (Of course the crew of the yacht would perish in the explosion too, but details like that were no concern of Abakumov's, and Stalin, the Sailors' Best Friend, showed no curiosity on this score.)

But what was he thinking about as he sucked his cold pipe and stared expressionlessly at the Minister past his bulbous, hooked nose? He was obviously not thinking that the Party of which he was the leader had begun by renouncing acts of terrorism against individuals. Nor that he himself had never had any qualms about employing terror as a means of getting to the top. As he sucked his pipe and looked at this hulking, pink-faced rascal with the burning ears, Stalin's thoughts were following the line they always took at the sight of his zealous, unscrupulous, fawning subordinates.

At moments like this his first thought was always: how far can I trust him? And his second thought was whether the moment had come to get rid of him. Stalin knew perfectly well that Abakumov had amassed a fortune in 1945, but he stayed his hand and refrained from punishing him. Stalin was glad that Abakumov was that sort of man. Greedy people were much easier to manipulate. Stalin had learned to be wariest of people who were indifferent to worldly goods, people like Bukharin. He could not understand their motivation and found it hard to manage them.

However, even though he could read Abakumov like a book, he did not trust the man. Distrust of people was the dominating characteristic of Joseph Djugashvili; it was his only philosophy of life. He had not trusted his own mother; neither had he trusted God, before whom as a young man he had bowed down in His temple. He had not trusted his fellow Party members, especially those with the gift of eloquence. He had not trusted his comrades in exile. He did not trust the peasants to sow their grain and harvest the wheat unless he forced them to do it and watched over them. He did not trust the workers to work unless he laid down their production targets. He did not trust the intellectuals to help the cause rather than to harm it. He did not trust the soldiers and the generals to fight without penal battalions and field security squads. He had never trusted his relatives, his wives or his mistresses. He had not even trusted his children. And how right he had been!

In all his long, suspicion-ridden life he had only trusted one man. That man had shown the whole world that he knew his own mind, knew whom it was expedient to like and whom to hate; and he had always known when to turn round and offer the hand of friendship to those who had been his enemies.

This man, whom Stalin had trusted, was Adolf Hitler.

Stalin had looked on with approval and malicious delight as Hitler had overrun Poland, France and Belgium, as his bombers had darkened the sky over England. Molotov had come back from Berlin thoroughly frightened; agents reported that Hitler was transferring his forces eastward; Hess flew to England, and Churchill had warned Stalin of an attack. Every jackdaw in the woods of Byelorussia and on the poplars of Galicia had shrieked war. Every peasant woman in every market-place in Russia had prophesied war day in and day out. Only Stalin had remained unperturbed.

He had trusted Hitler . . .

That trust had very nearly cost him his own life. All the more reason never again to trust anyone . . .

Abakumov was sick to death of all this morbid suspiciousness, but dared not say so. He was tired of fooling around with the laborious business of getting that idiot Petro Popivoda to write articles denouncing Tito. Abakumov had all those fine fellows lined up to go and do the job, and instead of Stalin fussing about their security clearance he ought simply to see them and form his own judgment of them. As things stood now, it was impossible to say whether the operation would be a success or not. Abakumov hated being forced to use these ham-handed methods.

But he knew his Boss. It was fatal to work for him at full capacity; instead, one had to find the golden mean: while Stalin would not tolerate failure, he also hated it if people were too efficient. He saw in this a threat to his own absolute superiority in everything. Nobody else was allowed to achieve perfection.

So Abakumov—and he was not the only one—while appearing to strain at his harness, was actually only working at half pressure. Just as King Midas turned everything he touched into gold, so Stalin's touch turned everything into mediocrity.

Today, however, Abakumov had the impression that as his report progressed Stalin's expression grew brighter. Having described the planned assassination of Tito in great detail, the Minister quickly turned to his reports on the Frunze Academy, the Theological Academy and so on; he even tried to avoid looking at the telephone on Stalin's desk for fear of putting the Leader in mind of it. But he could see that Stalin was straining to remember something, and fervently hoped he was not thinking of the scrambler. Stalin gathered his forehead into thick folds, twitched his large nose and fixed his piercing stare on Abakumov (the Minister tried to look as honest and innocent as possible)—but the passing thought had obviously slipped out of his grasp again. The frown on his grey forehead gave way to a look of perplexity.

Stalin sighed, filled his pipe and lit it.

'Ah, yes,' he recalled at the first puff, although this was only a fleeting recollection and not the main thought that had just occurred to him: 'What about Gomulka—has he been arrested?'

In Poland Gomulka had recently been dismissed from all his posts and was now heading straight for the abyss.

'Yes, he's been arrested,' Abakumov confirmed, slightly rising from his seat in sheer relief. (He had already told Stalin about Gomulka's arrest.) Arresting people was the easiest of his department's jobs.

Stalin pressed a button on his desk to increase the light. The wall lamps were switched on and the room became very bright. Stalin rose from his seat and began to walk up and down, puffing at his pipe. Abakumov recognized this as a sign that the audience was at an end and that the Boss would now start dictating instructions. He opened a large notepad on his knees, took out a fountain pen and prepared to write. (The Leader liked people to note down what he had to say.)

But Stalin walked to the radiogram and back, still smoking his pipe and not saying a word, as though he had completely forgotten about Abakumov. His grey pock-marked face scowled in an agonizing effort to recollect. As he passed by Abakumov in profile the Minister noticed that the Leader's shoulders had grown slightly hunched, which made him look even shorter and smaller. And although Abakumov normally suppressed such thoughts in case some secret mechanism in the wall might read them, it occurred to him that the Old Man had less than ten years to live. The sooner the better, Abakumov thought—life, he felt, would then become bearable, even enjoyable, for him and his colleagues at the top.

Stalin was again suffering from a lapse of memory. His mind was refusing to obey him. On his way into the study from the bedroom he had made a mental note of the question he was to ask Abakumov—and now he had forgotten it. Helpless, he was unable even to frown or rack his brain in order to remember.

Suddenly he jerked up his head, stared at the top of the wall facing him—and remembered. It was not, however, what he should have remembered but something which he had failed to recall two nights ago in the Museum of the Revolution and which he had merely sensed as an unpleasant feeling.

. . . It had happened in 1937: on the twentieth anniversary of the revolution, when so much, as he saw it, had changed in the interpretation of the history of the revolution, he decided to make a personal visit to the Museum to see whether they had made any blunders. Standing in the doorway of one of the rooms—the one which now contained the huge television set—with eyes that were as though suddenly opened he had seen, high up on the opposite wall, two large portraits of Zhelyabov and Sofia Perovskaya, the two Populist terrorists who had assassinated Alexander II. Their expressions were open and fearless, their looks indomitable and they seemed to shout to each person entering the room: 'Kill the tyrant!'

As though transfixed by two arrows, his vocal chords paralysed by the glance of these two revolutionary idealists, Stalin had turned away, made a hoarse sound, coughed and pointed a shaking finger at the two portraits.

They had immediately been taken down, and at the same time the shattered remains of the carriage in which Alexander

135

II had been riding at the moment of his assassination—this was the earliest revolutionary relic—were removed from the Kshesinskaya Palace in Leningrad.

It was then that Stalin had started having apartments and retreats built for himself in different places. It was then that he had lost his taste for life in the crowded city and had moved out, ending up in this villa near Moscow, this cramped study next to the quarters of his bodyguard.

The more people he destroyed the more he was oppressed by fear for his own life. His brain was constantly at work devising improvements in the arrangements for his security, such as the rule that members of the guard were assigned to duty only an hour beforehand and that the guard must be composed of soldiers taken from different barracks: they thus met for the first time in the guardroom, were never together for more than twenty-four hours and had no chance of plotting. The villa he had built himself was like a maze and it was surrounded by three walls, none of whose gates faced each other. He also had several bedrooms and he only gave instructions about which bed was to be made up just before he retired for the night.

He regarded none of these elaborate measures as a sign of cowardice, but only of good sense. The fact was that the safety of his person was crucial to human history, even though other people might not see it this way, and so that these measures did not seem too conspicuous he ordered all the *lesser* leaders both in the capital and the provinces to follow his example. They were forbidden even to go to the lavatory without a guard and they were only allowed to travel in a cortège of three cars, indistinguishable in appearance. . . .

Now, suddenly affected by that memory of the portraits in the Museum he paused in the middle of the room, turned to Abakumov and said, waving his pipe-stem in the air:

'And what are you doing about security for Party officials?'

The look in his eyes became ominous and hostile as he put his head on one side.

With his notepad open Abakumov half rose from his chair (he did not stand up fully, knowing that Stalin liked people to sit still) and began to talk eagerly on this unexpected topic. This always happened at these meetings and Stalin took the slightest hesitation as a sign of ill intent.

'Marshal!' Abakumov's voice trembled as if his feelings had been hurt. 'But that is what we are for, that is the purpose of the Ministry to ensure that you, Marshal, can work and think in peace and guide the destinies of the country.'

(Although Stalin had asked about the 'security of Party officials', Abakumov knew perfectly well that he was referring to himself alone.)

'But not a day goes by without my carrying out all kinds of checks and making arrests.'

Still standing there like a raven with his head on one side, Stalin looked at him sharply.

'Tell me,' he said thoughtfully. 'Do we still have cases involving charges of terrorism?'

Abakumov heaved a bitter sigh.

'I would be glad if I could tell you that there were no more such cases. But there are. We come across them in all sorts of stinking holes.'

Stalin closed one eye; the other one registered pleasure.

'That's good,' he nodded. 'So you're doing your stuff.'

'But of course . . .' Abakumov could not bear to sit in the presence of the Leader when he was standing. and he rose slightly from his chair without fully straightening his legs. 'We don't allow these cases to reach the stage of actual preparations—we nip them in the bud, while it's still only a matter of intent. We get them on Article 19.'

'Good, good,' Stalin said reassuringly and motioned Abakumov to sit. (He could do without this great carcase towering over him.) 'So you think there are still malcontents among the people?'

Abakumov sighed again and replied with an air of regret:

'Yes, Marshal. There is still a certain percentage. . . .'

(He wasn't such a fool as to say there were none; otherwise what was the point of Abakumov and his whole organization?)

'You're quite right,' Stalin said warmly. 'I see you know

your job. Some people say there are no more malcontents, that everybody who votes for us at elections is happy. What d'you say to that?' Stalin smirked. 'Political blindness, that's what it is. The enemy's biding his time; just because he votes for us it doesn't mean he's happy. About five per cent would you say? Or eight, perhaps. . . .?'

(Stalin was particularly proud of his shrewdness, of his ability to take a critical view and to see through flattery.)

'Yes,' Abakumov said with conviction. 'That's just it. About five per cent. Or seven.'

Stalin went back to his desk and walked round it.

'My trouble is,' said Abakumov, who had now regained his courage, his ears had cooled off again—'that I'm never satisfied with what I've done.'

Stalin knocked his pipe against an ashtray.

'And what about the mood of the young people?'

His questions were like knives and if you cut yourself on one it was the end. If Abakumov had said the mood of the young was good, it would have been 'political blindness'. If he had said it was bad that would mean he 'had no faith in the future'.

Abakumov spread his hands, but decided to say nothing.

Without waiting for a reply Stalin said emphatically, tapping his pipe:

'More attention must be paid to the young people. We must be particularly strict with young people who go wrong.'

Abakumov hastily began taking notes.

Stalin was intrigued by the idea, his eyes shone with their tigerish gleam. He refilled his pipe, lit it and again started to pace the room, saying excitedly:

'You must keep a sharper eye on the mood of the students. Root them out—not singly, but in whole groups. And give them the maximum penalty allowed by law—twenty-five years, not ten. Ten years isn't prison—it's a holiday. Ten years is all right for schoolboys, but once they start to grow whiskers, give 'em twenty-five. They're young enough. They'll survive.'

Abakumov noted it all down. The first links in a long chain were being forged.

'And we must stop turning political prisons into rest-homes. Beria was telling me that people still get food parcels in political prisons.'

'We'll put a stop to that,' Abakumov exclaimed in a pained voice, writing it all down. 'That was our mistake, Marshal. You must forgive us!'

(That really was a blunder. He should have known better.)

Stalin stood opposite Abakumov with his legs apart.

'How many times do I have to tell you? It's time you understood. . . .'

There was no anger in his voice. His eyes expressed his confidence that Abakumov would grasp his point.

Abakumov could not remember a time when Stalin had spoken to him with such frank good nature. His feeling of terror vanished and his brain started functioning like that of a normal person in normal circumstances. It now seemed a suitable moment to unburden himself about one of the problems of his job which had long been rankling with him. With a gleam in his eye Abakumov said:

'We do understand, Marshal! We,' (he spoke collectively for the whole Ministry) 'realize what's required: the class struggle must be intensified! In that case, don't you see how much more difficult our job is now that the death penalty has been abolished? For two and a half years we've been at our wit's end because we can't officially account for the people we have to shoot, so there has to be two versions of every sentence passed. And then there's no legal way of accounting for the executioner's salaries, either, which makes a complete mess of our book-keeping system. What's more, without the threat of the death penalty there's no effective deterrent to use against troublemakers in the labour camps. We *need* the death penalty, Marshal—give it back to us!'

Abakumov made his plea in all sincerity, placing his outstretched hand on his heart and gazing expectantly into the swarthy face of his Leader.

With a slight twitch of his bristly moustache, Stalin almost smiled.

'I know,' he said, gently and understandingly. 'I've been thinking about it.'

It was amazing. He knew about everything, he thought

of everything even before you asked him. With divine prescience he anticipated a man's every thought.

'One of these days you shall have the death penalty back again,' he said pensively, staring ahead as though looking into the distant future. 'It will be a useful disciplinary measure.'

He had indeed thought about it. For two years now he had bitterly regretted giving way to his momentary impulse to show off to the West. In abolishing the death penalty he had betrayed his own principles—he had believed that people might not be totally corrupt and treacherous. His entire career as a statesman and military leader had been founded on the conviction that nothing—demotion, persecution, despatch to a lunatic asylum, life imprisonment, deportation—was adequate punishment for a person once he was an avowed enemy: nothing, that is, except death—the one utterly reliable, final punishment. And whenever the lower lids of Stalin's eyes began to pucker, there was only one verdict in those eyes: death. Any lesser penalty simply did not exist in his scale of values.

As Stalin switched his gaze from the bright prospect of the future back to Abakumov, his eyes narrowed cunningly:

'Aren't you afraid, though, that you might be one of the first to be shot?'

Spoken like a mute unstressed cadence, the word 'shot' was scarcely audible, a hint so obvious that it wanted no articulation. But it made Abakumov's blood turn to ice. Stalin was standing only a little more than an arm's length away from him and watching his Minister intently to see how he took this joke. At a loss whether to sit or stand, Abakumov half rose to his feet, his knees quivering with strain as he did so.

'Marshal, I . . . if I deserve it . . . if you have to . . .'

Stalin gave him a hard, penetrating stare. He was quietly considering the thought that had inevitably crossed his mind about Abakumov—hadn't the time perhaps come to get rid of him? Stalin was well aware of when to make use of that most ancient of devices for winning popularity: first lash the executioners into a fury of activity, then disown them at the critical moment and punish them for an excess of zeal. He had often done this before and it had never failed. The day was bound to come when Abakumov, too, would have to suffer the same fate.

'Correct!' said Stalin, with a smile of approval as though rewarding Abakumov for his presence of mind. 'When you deserve it, we'll shoot you.'

Obedient to a gesture from his Leader, Abakumov sat down again.

Stalin reflected for a moment, then with a warmth that the Minister had never yet heard in his voice, he said:

'There will soon be plenty of work for you to do, Abakumov . . . We shall take the same measures that we took in thirty-seven. Before a great war there has to be a great purge.'

'But Marshal,' Abakumov protested, greatly daring, 'aren't we putting enough people in prison already?'

'You don't call *this* putting people in prison, do you?' Stalin brushed the idea aside with playful irony. 'Just wait until we really get started—then you'll see. And when it comes to war we'll force the pace even harder. That means more power to the security service. Budgets, salaries—I won't stint you!'

Calmly, Stalin dismissed him:

'That's all for now.'

Abakumov was not sure whether he was walking or floating as he returned through the ante-room to retrieve his brief-case from Poskryobyshev. As if it were not enough that he could breathe freely again for another month, did he not sense the start of a new era in his relations with the Boss? He had admittedly been threatened with the firing squad, but that, after all, had only been a joke.

CHAPTER TWENTY-ONE

The Immortal One, his imagination aroused, paced firmly up and down his study. It was as if music were rising to a crescendo within his mind, as if some huge brass band were playing a march for him.

Malcontents? So what—there always had been malcontents and always would be. However, a rapid mental survey of world history was enough to remind him that people eventually forgave and forgot bad times, or even remembered them as having been good. A whole people could be just like Queen Anne in Shakespeare's *Richard III*, their anger is short-lived, their will is not steadfast and their memory is weak, and they would always gladly submit to the man who came out on top. He just had to live to be ninety—because his battles were not yet over, his great edifice incomplete, the times uncertain, and there was no one to take his place.

There was still a last world war to be fought and won. These Western Social Democrats had to be smoked out of their holes and finished off like rabbits—not to speak of all the other vermin around the world that had to be exterminated. Then, of course, there were all those economic problems, such as raising the productivity of labour. Only he knew the way to happiness; he had to lead people to it and shove their noses into it, like making a blind puppy drink milk.

But what then?

Bonaparte, now—he had the right idea. He didn't worry when the Jacobins yelped at him, he just proclaimed himself emperor and that was that. There was nothing wrong with the word 'emperor'—it only meant 'commander' or 'chief'! He rather liked the sound of it—'Emperor of the Planet'! 'Emperor of the World!' It was still quite in keeping with world Communism. Back and forth he paced and the bands played.

Perhaps they might find a way, some drug perhaps, to make him immortal if nobody else? But no, they'd be too late. Yet how could he leave the human race to its fate? And to think of the people he was leaving it to! What a mess they would make of things.

Oh well, there it was. Soon, though, engineering techniques would be more advanced and he would have bigger and better monuments built. Monumental propaganda, you might call it. He would have one put on top of Mount Kazbek and another on Elbruz so his head would always be above the clouds. Then he could die, as the Greatest of the Great, without equal in the history of the world.

Suddenly he stopped.

Yes, but suppose . . . of course he had no equals, but suppose—up there, above the clouds . . .?

He started to pace again, but more slowly now.

This was the one vague doubt that occasionally crossed Stalin's mind, though really there was no room for doubt in the matter. There were proofs for everything and all the rest of the claptrap had long been refuted. There was proof that matter could neither be created nor destroyed; there was proof that life probably began in warm seas; there was proof that the existence of Christ was unprovable; there was proof that faith-healing, visions, prophecies, telepathy and such like were so many old wives' tales.

The texture of our mind and spirit, of our likes and habits, is formed in our early years, not in later life. Those childhood memories that never leave us had recently much revived in Stalin's mind. Until he was nineteen he had been brought up on the Old and New Testaments, the Lives of the Saints and church history. He had served at the altar, had sung in the choir and had been particularly fond of Strokin's setting of *Nunc dimittis*. He could still give a faultless rendering of it. And how often during his years of church school and seminary he had kissed the ikons and gazed into the enigmatic eyes of the saints.

Even in the biography published for his seventieth birthday he had seen to it that they included the photograph as he was when he left the church school—little Joseph Djugashvili in his grey cassock with its tight round collar; the lack-lustre oval of his boyish face, as though worn with too much prayer; the long hair of one destined for the priesthood, austerely parted, anointed with holy oil and grown down to the ears. Only the eyes and the taut brows revealed this youthful aspirant as one who might one day become an archbishop.

On Stalin's orders Abakadze, the inspector of church schools who had expelled young Djugashvili from the seminary, had been left to live out his days in peace.

When Stalin had come to the microphone on the 3rd of July 1941, his parched throat strangled by fear and maudlin self-pity (there is no heart quite incapable of pity), it was no accident that he had blurted out the phrase 'brothers and sisters'. It would never have occurred to Lenin, nor to any of the others, to make such a slip of the tongue; but Stalin had lapsed willy-nilly into the language of his schooldays.

It could well be that he had also said a silent prayer in those July days, just as an atheist might cross himself when the bombs began to fall. In recent years he had been very gratified at being mentioned in the church's prayers as the 'Leader Elect of God', and this was why he had maintained the cathedral and monastery at Zagorsk from Kremlin funds. No prime minister of a foreign power was ever received by Stalin in the manner he reserved for his tame, infirm old Patriarch. He always went to meet him at the outer doors and led him in by the arm. He was now thinking vaguely about finding a little estate somewhere, a country seat, that he could present to the Patriarch, just as people had once made bequests to the church for the repose of their souls.

Stalin had noticed in himself a certain attraction not only to the Orthodox Church but also to other forms and features of the old order—that order from which he himself had sprung and which for the past forty years it had been his function to destroy. In the 'thirties he had resurrected for political reasons the forgotten word 'motherland', which had been out of use for fifteen years and which had an almost shameful ring. But as time went by he had actually grown very fond of the words 'Russia' and 'motherland'. He had also taken a great liking to the Russian people—this people which had never betrayed him, which had gone through thick and thin for him—famine, war, labour camps; whatever the difficulties, they had calmly endured them all without a murmur. After the victory over Germany he had been quite sincere when he had praised the Russian people for being so clear-headed, so steadfast . . . and so long-suffering.

Stalin had more and more come to wish that he too might be accepted as a Russian. He even liked the sound of words reminiscent of the old days and had brought some of them back, such as the old titles of officers' ranks. He had renamed the All-Union Central Executive Committee as the 'Supreme Soviet' (what a good word that was—'supreme'). In the same way he had decreed that officers should have batmen again, that boys and girls should be taught separately, that the girls should wear pinafores in school and that their parents should pay school fees. He had also ordained that Soviet people, like all Christian folk, should have their day of rest on Sunday and not on any old day of the week; he had even re-introduced the sanctity of legal marriage, as under the Tsar, although in his time he had suffered under this. Who cared what Engels had to say on this subject?

It had been here, in front of a mirror in this very study, that he had first tried a pair of old Russian epaulettes on his tunic and had felt a thrill of pleasure as he did so. When he came to think of it there was nothing shameful, either, about the imperial crown, that highest mark of distinction. After all, it was part of a stable order which had endured for three hundred years—where was the harm in borrowing some of its best features?

He had also brooded about other things from the past— Port Arthur, for instance. At the time, when he had been an exile on the run in Siberia, he had naturally welcomed the Russian defeat, but after the victory over Japan in 1945 he had really meant it when he had said that Russians of the older generation, like himself, had felt the surrender of Port Arthur as a terrible blow to their pride.

Ah yes, those Russians of the older generation! Stalin sometimes thought it was no accident that it was he who had won the leadership of this country and the hearts of its people, and not one of those loud-mouthed quibblers with their little pointed beards—upstarts with no roots in the country and nothing constructive to offer.

He had them all here on his bookshelves. They were silent now—shot, ground into the soil of Siberia, poisoned, burned, killed in car accidents, driven to suicide. Confiscated, anathematized, relegated to apocryphal status, their works were all lined up on these shelves. Every night they held out their pages to him, wagged their little beards, wrung their hands, spat at him, harangued him hoarsely: 'We told you so!' 'This wasn't the way to do it!' That's all they were any good at—picking holes. Stalin had gathered them all together here—they helped him to work himself into a suitable angry mood at night when taking decisions.

The invisible orchestra, to whose beat he had been pacing up and down, faltered and trailed away. His legs were aching from the waist down and almost failed him, as they were lately prone to do.

The master of half the world in his Generalissimo's tunic, with his low receding forehead, walked slowly past the shelves and ran his claw-like hands over the ranks of his enemies.

As he turned away from the last bookshelf, he noticed the telephone on his desk, and that something which had been eluding him all evening flickered across his mind again like the top of a snake's tail. There was something he had meant to ask Abakumov. . . . Was it about Gomulka's arrest?

Ah, no! Now he remembered. He shuffled over to the desk, picked up a pen and wrote in his diary: 'Scrambler.' They had told him that they had the best people working on it, that there was no lack of equipment or enthusiasm, that the schedules would be met—so why wasn't it ready? That swine Abakumov had had the nerve to sit here for a whole hour and not say a word about it!

They were all like that, in all the ministries—every one of them was trying to hoodwink their Leader. How could he possibly trust them? He had no choice but to work at nights.

He suddenly staggered into a chair—not his armchair but a smaller one near the desk. He felt as though some weight was forcing the left half of his head downwards. He lost hold of his train of thought and stared with blurred gaze round the room, unable to make out whether the walls were near or far.

He was an old man without any friends. Nobody loved him, he believed in nothing and he wanted nothing. He no longer even had any need of his daughter, once his favourite but now only admitted on rare holidays. Helpless fear overcame him as he sensed the dwindling memory, the failing mind. Loneliness crept over him like a paralysis.

Death had already laid its hand on him, but he would not believe it.

CHAPTER TWENTY-TWO

When Colonel Yakonov left the Ministry by the front entrance on Dzerzhinsky Street and went round the black marble prow of the building, passing under the colonnade into Furkasovsky Street, he failed to recognize his own car at first and nearly opened the door of someone else's.

It had been very foggy all night. The snow which had tried to fall during the evening had melted at once and than stopped. Now, just before dawn the fog lay on the ground and the melted snow was thinly covered by a film of ice. It was getting colder, and although it was almost 5 a.m. the sky was still pitch-black.

A student passed Yakonov (the boy had been standing with his girl all night in a doorway) and looked enviously at him as he got into the car. The student sighed, wondering whether he would ever have a car himself. Not only had he never taken his girl out in one, but the only time he had driven anywhere was in the back of a truck going out to harvest on a collective farm. He little knew that Yakonov was more to be pitied than envied.

'Home?' the driver asked.

Yakonov held his pocket-watch in the palm of his hand, but was unable to take in what time it told.

'Home?' the driver repeated.

Yakonov stared at him wildly.

'What? No.'

'To Mavrino?' the driver asked in surprise. Even though he had been waiting in a sheepskin coat and hood, he felt frozen stiff and in need of sleep.

'No,' said Yakonov, putting his hand just above where his heart was.

The driver turned and looked at his boss's face in the faint light of a street lamp which was coming through the misted window, Yakonov was a changed man. His soft lips, usually tightly pressed in calm disdain, were now trembling helplessly.

He still stared blankly at the watch held in his palm.

Although the driver had been waiting in a furious temper since midnight, swearing foul oaths into his sheepskin collar and remembering all the Colonel's misdeeds for the past two years, he asked no more questions but just drove off at random, his ill-temper forgotten.

By now it was very early morning. There were still a few cars in the deserted streets of the capital, but there were no policemen, no pedestrians and no thieves on the prowl. Soon the trolley-buses would start running.

The driver kept glancing back at the Colonel, waiting for him to decide where to go. He had already driven out to the Myasnitsky Gate, along Sretensky and Rozhdestvensky Boulevards to Trubny Square and from there into Neglinnaya Street; he could hardly keep on like this till morning.

Yakonov was looking straight ahead in a fixed, vacant stare.

He lived on Bolshaya Serpukhovka. The driver, thinking that the sight of the streets near his house might prompt him to return home, decided to cross the river. He went down Okhotny Ryad, turned at the Manège, and drove on across the bleak expanse of Red Square.

The crenellated walls of the Kremlin and the tops of the spruces growing by them were touched with frost. The asphalt was grey and slippery. The fog swirled under the car wheels as though trying to escape into the ground.

They passed within a few hundred yards of this heavily guarded wall. Behind it they might well have imagined the Greatest Man on Earth coming to the end of his night's work. But they went by without giving him a thought.

As they drove down past St Basil's Cathedral and turned left on to the Moscow River embankment, the driver stopped the car and asked:

'Wouldn't you like to go home, Comrade Colonel?'

That was where he should have been going. Perhaps his remaining nights at home were fewer than the fingers on his hands. But like a dog that goes off to die by itself, Yakonov now wanted to keep away from his family.

The car stopped. Gathering up his thick leather coat-tails as he got out, he said to the driver:

'You go on home and get some sleep. I'll walk the rest of the way.'

His voice was so sad that he might have been saying good-bye for ever.

A swirling blanket of mist covered the Moscow River up to the parapets of the embankment. His coat unbuttoned, his military fur hat slightly askew, hardly keeping his feet, Yakonov set off along the pavement.

The driver wanted to call him back or drive alongside him slowly, but then he reckoned that people of his boss's rank could probably be trusted not to drown themselves, so he turned the car round and drove off.

For a long time Yakonov walked along an unbroken stretch of the embankment with a wooden fence always on his left and the river on his right. He walked in the middle of the roadway, staring unblinkingly at the distant street lamps, and after a while he realized that this gloomy stroll in utter solitude was giving him a kind of simple pleasure that he had not experienced for a long time.

That second interview with Abakumov had been a total disaster. It had been pandemonium, with Abakumov raging like a mad beast. He had charged at them like a bull, chased them round the office, cursed and sworn in the foulest language, had spat at them, and with a punch to Yakonov's face that was deliberately meant to cause pain, had hit him on his fleshy nose and drawn blood.

He had threatened to demote Sevastyanov to the rank of lieutenant and have him sent to the Arctic as second-in-command of a labour camp, to send Oskolupov as an ordinary warder back to Butyrki Prison, where he had begun his career in 1925, to have Yakonov arrested for concealment and repeated sabotage and sent in prison-blue denims to join Bobynin in Number Seven, where he would be made to work on the speech clipper with his own two hands.

After all this Abakumov had calmed down slightly and had given them a last chance—until the 21st of January.

The large, tastelessly furnished office had swum and lurched before Yakonov's eyes and he had tried to stop his nose bleeding with a handkerchief. Standing helplessly in front of Abakumov he had thought of his two children aged eight and nine and his wife Varya, with whom he spent only one hour in the twenty-four and for whose sake alone he bowed and scraped, fought and bullied for the remaining twenty-three.

His wife was all the dearer to him for their having married late—he had been thirty-six and had only just come back from the place to which Abakumov with his iron fist was threatening to consign him again. Afterwards, Sevastyanov took Oskolupov and Yakonov to his office and said that he would see both of them behind bars before he would let himself be sent to serve as a lieutenant in the Arctic. Finally, Oskolupov took Yakonov to his office and told him that he had always felt there was an obvious link between Yakonov's previous spell in prison and his current acts of sabotage . . .

Yakonov now came to a high concrete bridge which spanned the Moscow River to his right. Instead of taking the steps up to the top, he walked under it through the tunnel where the policeman on guard was walking up and down. He gave a long suspicious look at this strange, drunk-looking man in pince-nez and the tall fur hat of a colonel.

This was the place where the old Yauza River flowed into the Moscow River. Still blind to his surroundings, Yakonov crossed the short bridge over the Yauza.

They had started the usual murderous game and it was approaching its climax. Yakonov knew all there was to know about this kind of lunatic scramble—it was more than flesh and blood could bear to be hopelessly caught up in impossible, grotesque, crippling schedules. You were trapped and held in a deadly grip. The system crushed you, driving you harder and faster all the time, demanding more and more, setting inhuman time-limits. This was why buildings and bridges collapsed, why crops rotted in the fields or never came up at all. But until it dawned on someone that people were only human, there was no way out of this vicious circle for those involved, except by falling ill, getting caught in a machine or having some other kind of accident—then they could live in hospital or in a sanatorium while it all blew over.

Until now, as soon as it had been clear that a project was obviously heading for disaster due to haste, Yakonov had always managed to get out in good time into something else which was quieter, or was still only in embryo.

This time, though, he could see there was no escape. There was no hope of completing the clipper device in such a short time; there was no other job to which he could transfer and it was too late to fall ill.

He leaned over the parapet of the embankment and looked down. Through a gap in the fog that covered the ice Yakonov could see immediately below him a black hole, like a festering winter sore. The black abyss of his past opened up before him and beckoned again.

Yakonov regarded those six years in prison as a ghastly lapse, something obscene and sickening, the greatest catastrophe of his life. He had been sentenced in 1932 when he was a young radio engineer who had twice been abroad on official trips. These trips, in fact, had been his undoing. He had been one of the first to be put into one of the special prisons which were then being set up on Dante's principle of the 'First Circle'. How he longed to forget the whole thing, how he wished that other people would forget it too and that the whole memory of it could be obliterated. He avoided people who had known him as a prisoner and who reminded him of that wretched time in his life.

He swung away from the parapet, crossed over the roadway and walked up on to higher ground. Skirting a long fence round a building-site, he came on to a well-trodden path where it was less slippery underfoot.

Only the central files of the MGB had records to show that even some of its officers were former prisoners. Besides Yakonov there were two other ex-prisoners on the staff at Mavrino. He was careful to avoid them, trying never to talk with them except when duty required it and never staying alone with them in a room so as not to arouse suspicion.

One of them was Knyazhitsky, a seventy-year-old professor of chemistry who had been a favourite pupil of Mendeleyev. He had served his full sentence of ten years, after which, in recognition of his great contribution to science, he had been sent to Mavrino as a free worker, but three years after the war he too had been laid low by the whiplash of Stalin's directive on internal security. He had been rung up one day and called to the Ministry, and had never come back. Yakonov would never forget how Knyazhitsky had walked down the red-carpeted staircase at Mavrino with his silvery head shaking, not knowing why he had been summoned for 'half an hour', while behind his back at the top of the same staircase Shikin, the Security Officer, was already removing the professor's photograph from the notice board, prising it away with his penknife.

The other one, Altynov, had no great reputation as a scientist, but was simply very good at his job. After his first stretch in prison he had become reserved, suspicious and as canny as all ex-convicts. As soon as the internal security directive had begun to cast its net over Moscow, Altynov had craftily got himself admitted to hospital as a heart patient. He had played the part so convincingly and for such a long time that by now the doctors had given him up and his friends, reconciled to the fact that his poor heart was failing after so many years of strain, no longer even bothered to nod their heads sadly.

Yakonov, who like them had for the past year been a marked man as an ex-prisoner, was now open to a charge of sabotage.

The abyss was beckoning.

Yakonov trudged up the path across the vacant site, unaware of his surroundings and not even noticing that he was climbing a slope. At last he had to stop because he was out of breath and his feet hurt from stumbling over the uneven ground.

Then from this vantage point he looked round in the first conscious attempt to discover where he was. In the hour since he had left the car the night scene had changed out of all recognition. It had got colder as morning came on, and the mist had faded away. Although there was no snow there was a hint of white frost on the ground underfoot —on the heaps of brick, rubble and broken glass, on the nearby ramshackle wooden shed or watchman's hut and on the fence surrounding the still empty building site down below.

On this sloping piece of ground, so oddly neglected near the centre of the city, he now noticed a set of white steps going upwards. There were about seven of them and then a gap followed by more steps, or so it appeared.

The sight of these white steps on the hillside stirred a vague memory. Puzzled, he climbed up them and crossed the intervening cinder-covered patch until he came to the second flight of steps. These led to a building which loomed above him in the darkness. It was a building of curious shape which had the air of a ruin, yet of something that had somehow remained oddly intact.

Was it a bombed-out building? Surely there were none left in Moscow. So what had caused this havoc?

The two flights of steps had been divided from each other by some flagstones. Fragments of them now lay all over the steps, making it difficult to walk, and the steps went up to the building in short flights reminiscent of the entrance to a church. They led to a broad iron door which was shut fast and had a knee-high pile of rubble in front of it.

A memory went through Yakonov like a knife. He looked round. He could see the river, picked out by strings of lamps, winding below him in a strangely familiar curve under the bridge and on to the Kremlin.

But what had happened to the bell-tower? It was gone. Or were these piles of stone all that were left of it?

Yakonov felt a prickling in his eyes and he shut them tight. He sat down on a heap of stones beside the steps.

Twenty-two years ago he had stood on this spot with a girl called Agnia.

CHAPTER TWENTY-THREE

He spoke the name—Agnia—and his jaded senses were quickened by a breath of the forgotten past.

He had been twenty-six, she twenty-one.

There was something other-worldly about the girl. It was her misfortune to be too sensitive and fastidious. When she talked her eyebrows and nostrils would sometimes quiver so much that she seemed about to take wing. No one had ever spoken to Yakonov with such severity nor reproached him so much for doing what seemed the most ordinary things— things which to his astonishment, she regarded as base and despicable. Yet strangely enough the more she found fault with him, the fonder he became of her.

He had to take care when arguing with her as she was

rather frail. Walking uphill, running, even talking too much wore her out, and she was easily offended. Yet she was strong enough to spend whole days walking alone in the woods. Unlike most town girls who walk in the country, however, she never took a book with her, as a book would only have distracted her. She just liked to walk or sit, learning the secrets of the woods. Whenever Yakonov went with her he was struck by how observant she was—she could tell him why the trunk of a birch tree was bent to the ground and point out how the grass changed colour in the evening. He never noticed such things—a tree was just a tree, grass was green and he enjoyed the fresh air. She had no time for Turgenev's famous descriptions of nature, which she found painfully superficial.

She and Yakonov had spent the summer of 1927 together in the country. They had stayed in *dachas* near to each other and everybody assumed that they were engaged.

In fact this was by no means so.

Agnia was neither pretty nor plain. Her expression was always changing: her smile could be quite captivating, but at other times she would pull a long face that was anything but attractive. She was taller than average but thin and delicate, and her step was so light that she seemed to walk without touching the ground. Although Yakonov was already quite experienced and liked women with rather more flesh on their bones, Agnia's attraction lay somewhere else than in her body. As he got to know her better he persuaded himself that she also attracted him physically and that she would fill out.

But although she enjoyed his company during those long summer days, walking with him many miles into the green woods, lying side by side with him on the grass, she was always very reluctant to let him hold her hand and would draw away from him and ask him: 'Must you?' It was not that she was shy in front of other people—when they came back to their *dachas* in the evening she meekly walked arm in arm with him for the sake of his male vanity.

Having made up his mind that he loved her, Yakonov one day went down on his knees as they were sitting in the woods and told her so. 'It's so sad,' said Agnia despondently.

'I don't know what to say. I feel nothing at all for you and this makes life unbearable for me. You're so wonderful and so clever I ought to be delighted—instead, I don't want to go on living. . . .'

She said this, yet every morning she watched his face anxiously for any sign of a change in his feelings towards her. Once she said: 'There are lots of girls in Moscow. In the autumn you'll meet someone beautiful and you won't love me any more.'

She let him embrace her and even kiss her, but her lips and her hands were lifeless. 'It's terrible!' she sighed. 'I always thought love would be like fire coming down from heaven. You love me, I couldn't want anyone better—yet I don't feel happy, all I want is to die.'

There was something childlike and innocent about her. The idea of making love frightened her and in a faint voice she would ask him: 'Do we have to?' And Yakonov eagerly assured her: 'Of course it's not the main thing—it's just a way of expressing our feelings for each other!' Then for the first time her lips had timidly responded to his kiss and she said: 'Thank you, my dear. Life wouldn't make any sense otherwise, would it? I think I'm beginning to love you. I promise I'll try to.'

Early one evening that autumn, as they were walking in the streets near Taganka Square, Agnia had said in her quiet voice that was so suited to the country but was drowned by the noise of the city:

'Shall I show you one of the most beautiful places in Moscow?'

She had taken him up to the railings round a small red and white brick church, whose apse backed on to a winding little street with no name. There was not much room inside the railings—a path just wide enough for the priest and deacon walking side by side to lead the Easter procession round the church. Through the little barrel windows the altar candles and the coloured ikon-lamps glowed gently. Outside in a corner of the churchyard grew an old oak tree, taller than the church; its branches were already turning yellow and it stretched itself protectively over the dome and the street, making the church seem even smaller.

'This is the church of St John the Baptist,' said Agnia. 'But it's not the most beautiful place in Moscow.'

'Wait.'

She led him through the little gate. Yellow and orange oak-leaves lay scattered on the churchyard and flagstones. Almost in the shadow of the oak tree there was an ancient onion-domed bell-tower, which together with the tiny church-warden's house shaded the churchyard from the rays of the setting sun. Between the wide-open double iron doors of the north portico was an old beggar woman bowing and crossing herself to the rich golden chant of evensong.

' "And glorious was that church in its beauty and magnificence . . ." ' Agnia whispered, pressing her shoulder close to his.

'What century is it?'

'Why do you have to know the century? What does it matter? Isn't it lovely, anyway?'

'Yes, of course it is, but . . .'

'Look!' She freed her arm from his and holding him by the wrist quickly pulled him towards the main door, out of the shadow and into the flood of light from the setting sun. Here she sat down on a low stone parapet beside the church-yard gate.

Yakonov gasped. As though bursting free of the cramped city, they had come out on to a high spur that commanded a great sweeping view. Interrupted only by the parapet, the white stone steps cascaded down hill to the Moscow River in a long sequence of flights broken by little terraces. The river burned in the sun. To the left was spread out the old merchant quarter of Moscow, it's window-panes flashing in the yellow light; almost in front of them the black chimney-stacks of the Moscow Power Station smoked against the sunset; below at their feet the glittering Yauza River flowed into the Moscow River. To its right stretched the long Reformatory building, beyond it the fretted silhouette of the Kremlin and further still the five red-gold domes of the church of Christ the Saviour blazed in the sunlight.

Amid all this golden flood of light Agnia gazed with half-closed eyes towards the sun, whose rays seemed to have transmuted her yellow shawl into gold.

'Ah, Moscow!' Yakonov said with feeling.

'How well the Russians chose the places to build their churches and monasteries!' Agnia said with a quiver in her voice. 'I remember when I went down the Volga and the Oka, it was just the same there—they were always built in the most superb places.'

'Ah, Moscow!' Yakonov repeated.

'But it's vanishing, Anton,' Agnia whispered. 'Moscow is vanishing.'

'What d'you mean—vanishing? Nonsense.'

'This church is bound to come down,' she insisted.

'How do you know?' he asked indignantly. 'They're sure to leave it alone, it's a historical monument.' He looked up at the little domed bell-tower, where the oak tree thrust its branches through the openwork of the belfry, almost touching the bells.

'They're certain to pull it down,' Agnia predicted with confidence, as she sat motionless in her shawl lit by the yellow light.

Far from Agnia having been taught to believe in God, in the days when everyone was supposed to go to church her mother and her grandmother had never done so; they had never observed the fasts, never gone to communion, sneered at priests and never missed a chance to make fun of a religion which had so easily come to terms with serfdom. Agnia's mother and grandmother and her aunts had their own staunch creed, which was always to side with the underdog, with anybody who was oppressed, persecuted or harried by the authorities. All the revolutionaries in Moscow knew her grandmother, because she sheltered and helped them as much as she could. Her daughters kept up the tradition and gave refuge in their homes to members of the underground, both Socialist-Revolutionaries and Social-Democrats. Little Agnia was always taught to side with the quarry against the hunter; and when she grew up, to the astonishment of her elders, this principle led her to side with the Church, because it was now the Church which was being persecuted.

Whether because she had come to believe in God or was merely forcing herself to believe, she maintained that it would be cowardly to spurn the Church now, and she horrified her mother and grandmother by starting to go to church services and found herself drawn into the spirit of them.

'What makes you think the Church is being persecuted?' Yakonov protested. 'Nobody stops them ringing their bells, baking their communion bread, holding their Easter processions—as long as they keep out of civic affairs and education.'

'Of course they're persecuted,' Agnia protested, in her usual low voice. 'If people are allowed to say and write what they like about the Church without it being able to answer back, if church valuables are confiscated and priests banished —isn't that persecution?'

'Have you seen any priests being banished?'

'That's not the sort of thing you see on the street.'

'And what if it is being persecuted?' Yakonov challenged her. 'What are ten years, when the Church was the persecutor for ten centuries?'

'That was before my time.' Agnia shrugged her thin shoulders. 'I only know what has happened in my own lifetime.'

'But you must know your history! Ignorance is no excuse. Has it ever occurred to you how the Russian Church managed to survive two hundred and forty years under the Tartar yoke?'

'Because its faith was so strong, I suppose,' she hazarded, 'and because Orthodoxy was a greater spiritual force than Mohammedanism.' It was a question rather than a statement.

Yakonov smiled condescendingly:

'You ought to know better than that. Do you think this country of ours was ever really Christian at heart? Do you think in the thousand years of its existence it has ever really forgiven its oppressors? Or loved its enemies? The Church survived because after the Tartar invasion the Metropolitan Cyril was the first Russian to go and pay homage to the Tartar Khan and beg guarantees for the safety of the clergy. So it was Tartar armed force that the Russian clergy used to protect their lands, their serfs and their ritual. In his way the Metropolitan Cyril was right; he was a realist. And why not? That's how to stay on top.'

When Agnia was under attack she never argued, but simply stared perplexedly at Yakonov.

'So do you see what they're built on, all these beautiful, well-sited churches of yours?' Yakonov went on relentlessly. 'On the bones of all those heretics and nonconformists who were burned or flogged to death! And you waste your pity on the Church because it's persecuted!'

He sat down beside her on the parapet, its stonework warm from the sun: 'And you're altogether unfair on the Bolsheviks. You haven't even taken the trouble to read their books. They have the greatest concern for culture. They're against any kind of oppression and they believe in the power of reason. But the main thing is they stand for equality! Just think: complete and absolute equality for everybody. Nobody will have any privileges based on income or position. What could be more attractive than a society like that? Isn't it worth some sacrifice?'

(Aside from its attractiveness, Yakonov's social origins were such that he had every reason to conform to the new society as quickly and as skilfully as possible, before it was too late.)

'And you're only spoiling your chances of going to the university by putting on this act. What do you expect to achieve by this sort of protest?'

'What can a woman ever achieve?' She tossed her head and one of her thin plaits swung over her shoulder and the other on to her breast. (Plaits were out of fashion then, all the women bobbed their hair, but she plaited hers just to be different even though it did not suit her.) 'All women do is stop men from doing great things. Even women like Natasha Rostov in *War and Peace*. I can't stand her.'

'Why not?'

'Because she wouldn't let Pierre Bezukhov join the Decembrists!' Her weak voice trailed away again.

Agnia was quite unpredictable.

Her fine-spun yellow shawl had slipped from her shoulders down to her elbows and looked like a pair of translucent golden wings.

With his two hands Yakonov gently clasped her elbow, as though frightened of breaking it.

'Would you have let him go?'

'Yes,' she said simply.

He was not, as it happened, planning any great deeds

for which he might need her blessing. He was leading a very busy life, he liked his work and he had a promising future.

Some worshippers arriving late for the service passed them · on the way up from the embankment, crossing themselves as they approached the open church doors. As they entered the churchyard the men took off their caps. There were far fewer men than women and no young people at all.

'Aren't you afraid of being seen near a church?'

Without her intending it, Agnia's remark sounded sarcastic. In those days it was already getting risky to be seen near a church, and Yakonov felt a little too conspicuous here.

'Be careful, Agnia,' he said, beginning to get annoyed. 'You must learn how to read the signs of the times. Anyone who can't will be left hopelessly behind. You only feel drawn to the Church because it panders to your morbid fear of life. It really is time you pulled yourself together and took an interest in what's going on around you.'

Agnia looked dejected. The hand with his ring on it hung lifelessly down. She looked bonier and thinner than ever.

'Yes,' she agreed in a low voice. 'There are times when I am very conscious of how hard it is for me to live. I'm one of those people who are out of place in this world. . . .'

This was too much for him. She seemed to be doing her best to put him off. He felt less and less inclined to keep his promise to marry her.

She gave him a searching, unsmiling look.

'And she's not even pretty,' thought Yakonov.

'I'm sure you're going to be famous, successful and have all the things you want,' she said sadly. 'But will you be happy, Anton? . . . You must beware, too. If we get too interested in what's going on around us, we lose . . . we lose . . . how can I put it . . .' She rubbed the tips of two fingers together, groping for the right word, the effort of searching for it reflected in her anguished smile. 'When a bell stops ringing and the chimes fade away, you can't bring them back—and the music is gone for ever. Do you see what I mean?'

She nevertheless persuaded him to go into the church. Supported by massive pillars, the building was surrounded by a gallery pierced with small windows latticed in the old Russian style. A low arcade supported the central nave.

Through the windows of the drum that held the dome the golden light of the setting sun flooded in and played over the top of the ikon screen and the mosaic image of the Lord of Hosts.

The congregation was sparse. Agnia placed a slender candle on a large brass stand and stood piously, unobtrusively, crossing herself, her hands folded on her breast and looking straight ahead with a rapt expression. The diffused sunlight and the deep yellow gleam of the candles restored life and warmth to Agnia's cheeks.

It was two days before Lady Day and they were reading a long collect in honour of the Mother of God. It was highly elaborate in style, an endless passionate eulogy of the Virgin Mary, and for the first time Yakonov appreciated the ecstatic poetry of prayer. This invocation had been composed not by some dull ecclesiastical pedant, but by a great nameless poet, immured in a monastery and moved not by a man's short-lived lust for a woman but by the rapture of sublime love . . .

Yakonov came back to the present. He was sitting in his leather coat, now all dirty, on a pile of jagged rubble by the entrance to the church of St John the Baptist.

Sure enough, the little domed bell-tower had been wantonly destroyed and the steps leading down to the river had been smashed. It was hard to believe that these few square yards of Moscow had been the setting both for that sunlit evening and for this bleak December dawn. But there was the same sweeping view and there was the same winding river between its twin rows of street lamps . . .

. . . Soon after that he had gone abroad on official business. When he came back he was told to write, or rather to sign, for that was what it amounted to, a newspaper article about the rottenness of Western society, morals and culture, about the dire state of intellectual life in the West and about the impossibility of progress in Western science. It was not exactly the whole truth, but then it wasn't exactly a lie either. The facts were there, but they were not the only facts. If he had hesitated, Yakonov would only have aroused suspicion and earned a black mark. Anyway, what harm could it possibly do to anybody?

The article was duly published.

Agnia sent him back his ring by post; tied to it by a thread was a slip of paper with the words: 'To the Metropolitan Cyril.'

He felt relieved.

He got up and standing on tiptoe peered through one of the little latticed windows and looked inside. There was a dank smell of mortar and decay. He could dimly see that the interior, too, was littered with piles of broken stone and rubbish.

Yakonov turned away from the window and feeling his heart beginning to beat slower he leaned against the side of the rusty iron door, which had not been opened for many years.

The thought of Abakumov's threat weighed on him like a block of ice.

Yakonov was clearly at the height of his career. He held high rank in a Ministry that wielded absolute power. He was intelligent, gifted and known as such. A loving wife waited for him at home, his two rosy-cheeked children asleep in their cots. He lived in style in a comfortable, old-fashioned apartment block. His monthly salary ran into thousands, he only had to lift a telephone to call for his personal car. Yet here he was propped against a stone wall and wanting to die. He felt such despair that he could move neither hand nor foot.

It was getting light.

There was something fine and clean about the frosty air. A thick velvet rime encrusted the huge stump of the oak tree, the eaves of the derelict church, the ornate lattice-work of its windows, the cables looping down to a nearby house and, lower still, the edge of the fence that ringed the site of a future skyscraper.

CHAPTER TWENTY-FOUR

Day was breaking.

A thick, rich hoar-frost feathered the posts of the fences, the score of intertwined strands, the thousand stars of the barbed wire, the sloping roof of the watch-tower and the tall grass in the wilderness outside the compound.

Clear-eyed, Dmitry Sologdin gazed at the miracle and rejoiced in it as he stood by the trestle for sawing firewood. He wore a camp jacket over his blue denims, his head was bare, his hair showing its first streaks of grey. He was a slave, he had no rights. He had served twelve years but, because of his second sentence, the end of his punishment was not in sight. His wife had wasted her youth waiting for him. Now, out of fear of losing her job, as she had lost so many others, she had lied to her employers, telling them she had no husband, and had stopped writing. She had been pregnant when he was arrested and he had never seen his only son. He had survived the forests of Chardynsk, the mines of Vorkuta,[1] the torture by sleeplessness, the draining of his strength and desiccation of his body through two interrogations, one of six months, the other of twelve. All he owned was a pair of quilted trousers, stored away in expectation of worse times to come. He was paid thirty roubles a month, and not even that in cash. His hours in the fresh air were fixed and rationed by the prison authorities.

But his soul was at peace. His eye had the brightness of youth. Chest bared to the frost, he breathed deeply, as though inhaling the fullness of life.

His muscles, limp and dry as string at the end of the interrogation, had filled out and craved exercise. This was why he had volunteered for the unpaid daily work of cutting firewood for the prison kitchen.

But the axe and saw were dreaded weapons in the hands of a prisoner, and the authorities had been reluctant and slow to agree. Paid to suspect even the most innocent actions, and perhaps judging others by their own standards, they refused

[1] A large concentration camp area in the far north.

to believe that a man could choose to work for nothing. For a long time, Sologdin was suspected of planning an escape or an armed rising. A guard was posted five feet away, to watch his every movement while keeping out of range of the axe. There were men to spare for such dangerous jobs and the assignment of a full-time guard to watch over a single prisoner did not seem extravagant to officials, trained in the ways of GULAG. The one who raised difficulties (thereby intensifying the suspicion against him) was Sologdin himself. He refused to work under special guard. For some time the supply of firewood was interrupted (the governor couldn't force the prisoners to chop wood: Mavrino was not a camp, the inmates had their brainwork to do, and were not under his jurisdiction). The real trouble was that the planners and accountants had failed to make provision for this work. The free women workers employed in the kitchen refused to do it: they were paid only to cook. The administration tried to foist it on to the guards in their off-duty hours when they would otherwise have been playing dominoes in the guardroom. The guards were all healthy young men, chosen for their toughness. But in their years of service they had forgotten how to work. They were soon doubled up with back-ache, and they missed their dominoes. The kitchen was always short of firewood. In the end, the governor gave in and allowed Sologdin and those of his friends who joined him (usually Nerzhin or Rubin) to work without special supervision. Not that they were unwatched: the man on the watch-tower could see them like the back of his hand, and the Duty Officers were told to keep an eye on them from around the corner.

As the darkness scattered and the fading lamplight merged with the light of day, there appeared from behind the corner of a building the bulky figure of Spiridon, the handyman, in his quilted jacket, and the cap with huge earflaps which he alone was privileged to wear. Spiridon Yegorov was a prisoner, but under the orders of the head of research, not of the prison governor, so it was only for the sake of peace that he sharpened the prison saw and axe. As he drew closer, Sologdin could see the saw, which had been missing from its place, in Spiridon's hands.

Spiridon was allowed to walk about the compound (the whole of it within range of machine-guns) without a guard at any time between reveille and lights out. In making this bold decision, the authorities had been influenced by the fact that he was blind in one eye and had only thirty per cent vision left in the other. The compound was made up of several connecting yards, and covered five acres, so three handy-men had been allowed for in the budget, but Spiridon unwittingly did the work of all three and considered himself lucky. The great thing was that he could eat his fill—at least three pounds a day of the unrationed black bread, and the other prisoners gave him some of their *kasha*. It was a change from his three years in Sevuralsk Camp—three winters of timber-felling and three springs nursing thousands of logs as they floated down the river in rafts—and Spiridon had visibly put on weight and grown flabby.

'Hey! Spiridon!' Sologdin shouted impatiently.

'Coming! What is it?'

Spiridon's mobile face, with its reddish skin and greyish red eyebrows and moustache, wore, as it often did, an obliging expression. What Sologdin didn't know was that an excessively obliging look on Spiridon's face signified derision.

'What d'you mean—what is it? That saw won't cut.'

'I wonder why.' Spiridon was surprised. 'I remember now, you've complained about it all winter. Well now, let's try.'

Holding the saw by one end, he handed Sologdin the other.

They began to saw. The saw jumped out of its groove a couple of times as though it couldn't settle, then bit into the wood and cut smoothly.

'You're holding it too tight,' said Spiridon. 'Hold it lightly, with three fingers, like a pen, and let it go where it wants, smoothly. . . . That's right. Don't jerk as you pull it towards you. . . .'

Each of the two men felt superior to the other—Sologdin because he knew all about the theory of mechanics, the resistance of metals and many other learned things, Spiridon because everything he touched obeyed him. Each patronized the other—Sologdin openly, Spiridon secretly.

Even when cutting through the centre of the thick pine log, the saw never once caught but swung smoothly to and fro, spitting yellowish sawdust on to the trousers of the two men's denims.

Sologdin laughed.

'You're a wonder, Spiridon! You fooled me. I didn't realize you'd set and sharpened the saw yesterday.'

Looking pleased, Spiridon muttered in time to the saw:

'She chews and chews, she never swallows, she gives to others. . . .'

Without waiting to saw clean through the log, he leaned his weight on it and broke it in two.

'I never sharpened anything.' He turned the saw, showing Sologdin the cutting edge. 'Look at the teeth. They're just the same now as they were yesterday.'

Sologdin looked. He could indeed see that they had not been freshly sharpened. Yet that devil must have done something to them!

'Well, come on, Spiridon! One more log.'

Spiridon held his side. 'I'm tired. All the work my grandfathers left unfinished, they've piled on to me. Anyway, your friends will be coming soon.'

But there was no sign of them.

By now it was light. The frosty morning had broken in full majesty. The frost shone even on the drainpipes, and all over the ground, while in the distance its grey strands decorated the crowns of the lime trees in the prisoners' small exercise yard.

'Tell me, how did you get into Mavrino?' asked Sologdin, looking curiously at the handy-man.

It was just that he had no one else to talk to. In all his years in camp, Sologdin had mixed only with educated people, never expecting to get anything worth while from contact with the uneducated.

'Funny, isn't it,' said Spiridon. 'All you learned folk they've scraped together in this place—and me under the same yoke. You see, they'd put me down as a glass-blower. Well, it's true I was a glass-blower once—a master glass-blower at our factory in Bryansk. But that was a long time ago, I haven't got the eyesight for it now, and the work I did then was nothing like what they do here—they need a fancy kind of glass-blower like Ivan. We never had anyone of the sort at our factory. They just picked me because I was down as a glass-blower and when they saw I was no use, they'd have sent me back. But thanks to Colonel Yakonov, I was kept on as a handy-man.'

From the direction of the exercise yard and the low detached building which housed the prison staff, came Nerzhin, his denims left undone, a jacket flung over his shoulders, and a prison towel, so short it was almost square, hanging round his neck.

'Hullo,' he said brusquely. Undressing on the way, he pulled off his denims and under-vest.

Sologdin stared at him. 'Are you crazy? Where do you see snow?'

'There.' He climbed on to the low roof of an outhouse. It was covered with a light, virgin layer of something that was half frost half snow. Picking up handfuls, he rubbed it vigorously over his chest, back and sides. All through winter he rubbed himself down to the waist with snow, unless the guards happened to be looking and stopped him.

'You're steaming!' Spiridon shook his head.

'Still no letter, Spiridon?' asked Nerzhin.

'Yes, it's come.'

'Why didn't you bring it for me to read out to you? Is everything all right?'

'The letter's there, but I can't get it. The Snake has it.'

'Mishin? He won't give it to you?' Nerzhin stopped rubbing himself.

'He put me on the list, but just when he'd hung it up Colonel Yakonov wanted the attic cleared. By the time I was through, the Snake wasn't seeing anybody else. It won't be till Monday now.'

'The swine!' Nerzhin scowled.

'It's not for the likes of me to judge,' Spiridon said with a glance at Sologdin whom he didn't know very well. 'I'll be off.'

His earflaps swinging comically, like a dog's ears, he made off in the direction of the guard-house, where no other prisoner was allowed.

Remembering at the last moment, Sologdin called after him:

'Spiridon! Where's the axe?'

'The Duty Officer will bring it,' Spiridon shouted back, disappearing.

'Well,' said Nerzhin, rubbing himself dry with his scrap of turkish towelling. 'Yakonov isn't pleased with me. He says

167

I treat Number Seven like a poor relation. Apart from that, last night he wanted me to join the cryptographers and I refused.'

Sologdin cocked his head and grinned. Between his faintly greying, neatly trimmed moustache and beard flashed a row of strong white teeth, untouched by decay but thinned out by ill-treatment in camp.

'You're acting like a *bard*, not a *reckoner*.'

Nerzhin was not surprised. It was one of Sologdin's eccentricities to talk in what he called the Language of Maximum Clarity, without using 'bird words', i.e. words of foreign origin. It was hard to tell if this were a game or if he took it seriously, but he went out of his way to avoid even such words as 'engineer' and 'metal', finding Russian substitutes which were sometimes clumsy, sometimes apt. He stuck to it even in discussing his work with the bosses, and made them wait while he was looking for a word.

No one anxious to keep in with the authorities, to get a better job or higher rations, could have done this. But Sologdin had no such ambition: he kept out of their way and he scorned their favours.

Thus he established his reputation among prisoners as a determined and incorrigible eccentric.

He had many other eccentricities as well: his insistence, while sleeping under the window, on keeping it open all through winter, however cold the nights; his self-imposed task of cutting firewood, in which Nerzhin and Rubin had joined him; above all, his knack of putting forward the wildest, the most irrational views on every possible subject (such as that prostitution is morally commendable, or that, in his quarrel with Pushkin, D'Anthès had been in the right) and sticking to them, his young blue eyes and young but sparse teeth flashing, as he argued hotly and occasionally with success. Impossible to pin him down, you could never properly make out whether he was joking or serious. Challenged with being absurd, he roared with laughter: 'What dull lives you lead, gentlemen! We can't all think alike and be cut to the same pattern. Think what would happen. We'd stop arguing or swopping ideas. What a deadly bore!'

The reason he gave for saying 'gentlemen' instead of 'comrades' was that, having been away for twelve years, he had forgotten what it was like outside.

Still half naked, Nerzhin finished drying himself and said glumly:

'Lev is right, I'm a very poor sceptic. I just can't be detached about things.'

He pulled on his vest, which was too small for him, and thrust his arms into the sleeves of his denims.

Sologdin leaned back against the trestle and crossed his arms theatrically.

'A very good thing too, my friend. Sooner or later you had to give up your "all-embracing doubt" ' ('scepticism' in the Language of Maximum Clarity). 'You're no longer a boy.' (Nerzhin was the younger by five years.) 'Time to sort yourself out, to understand the part of good and evil in human life. Where could you do this better than in prison?'

But Nerzhin would not be drawn on the eternal problem of good and evil. Hanging the damp little towel like a muffler round his neck and putting on his jacket and old army cap—it was parting at the seams—he sighed.

'All we know is that we don't know anything.'

He picked up the saw and handed one end to Sologdin.

They had cooled off and set about their task with a will. The saw spat brown powdered bark and cut into the wood—not as easily as when Spiridon held it but smoothly all the same. The two men were used to working together and tolerated each other's mistakes. They worked in silence and with that especial zeal and enjoyment that go with a job unforced by compulsion or need.

Only when they came to their fourth log did Sologdin, flushed scarlet, mutter, 'Look out for the knots,' and when they had finished, Nerzhin replied: 'Yes, that was a knotty bastard.'

With each stroke of the saw, sweet-smelling sawdust, now white, now yellow, poured on to their trousers and shoes. The rhythmic strokes gave peace and a new direction to their thoughts.

Nerzhin, who had got up in a bad mood, was now thinking that the shock of his first year in camp had confused him, but his whole outlook had changed since then. This time he would not compete for a soft job or shy away from ordinary camp labour. With his deeper knowledge of life, he would go out unhurriedly each morning to roll-call, his jacket smeared with cement or oil, and keep on steadily throughout the drudgery of the twelve-hour day, and so throughout the remaining five years of his sentence. Five years weren't ten. You could survive five years.

He also thought of Sologdin who had passed on to him some of his leisurely attitude to life; it was Sologdin who had first prompted him to reflect that prison was not only a curse but also a blessing.

Pulling gently on the saw, he could never have guessed that his partner, as he pulled the saw in his turn, was thinking that prison was an unmitigated curse and that he must, at last, somehow break out of it.

Sologdin was thinking of his great success, the success in his work, which promised him freedom—a success he had secretly achieved over the past months and particularly during the last few weeks. He would hear the verdict on it after breakfast, but he had no doubt of what it would be. With pride he was thinking of his brain, exhausted by so many years of interrogations, camps, hunger, shortage of potassium, yet capable, when it came to the test, of coping with an exceptionally difficult problem. His vitality was at its height, as often happens with men at forty—especially if surplus energy has not been spent on having children but mysteriously transformed into mental energy.

He was also thinking of Nerzhin who was bound soon to be sent away from Mavrino, now that he had spoken so rashly to Yakonov.

Meanwhile they sawed away, they were hot, their faces flushed, their jackets flung aside and the pile of short logs growing into a mound, but there was still no axe.

'Haven't we done enough?' asked Nerzhin. 'We've cut more than we can chop.'

'All right, let's have a rest,' Sologdin agreed, putting down the saw with a twang of its bending blade.

They took off their caps and hung them on the trestle. Steam rose from their hair—Sologdin's thick, Nerzhin's thin. They breathed deeply, as though airing the stalest corners of their being.

'But if they send you off to camp,' Sologdin asked, 'what about that thing you're writing?'

'What about it? After all, it's not easy here either. By keeping so much as a single note, I take an equal risk of dying in a punishment cell here as there. I have no access to a public library and I don't suppose they'll let me near an original source as long as I live. If you mean just paper to write on, I'll always find birch or pine bark in the *taiga*. And I've got an advantage no spy can make me lose: what I've been through, and seen others go through, should give me a good idea of what history is about, don't you think so?'

'Marvellous!' gasped Sologdin. 'In that primordial sphere in which thought develops. . . .'

'Sphere is a bird word,' Nerzhin reminded him.

'Sorry. . . . In that first rounded space in which thought grows,' he held up his head and his hand, 'its originality and strength are what determines the success of the action that follows from it. And like a growing tree, it bears fruit only if it develops naturally. Books and other people's ideas are shears that snip its life. First, have your own idea. After that, you can compare it with what it says in a book. You have matured enormously. I had no idea.'

It was getting cold. Sologdin put on his cap. So did Nerzhin. He was flattered, but tried not to feel smug.

Sologdin was in full spate.

'Now that you may be leaving any day, I must tell you my own rule of life. You might find it useful. Of course I'm very hampered by being tongue-tied and stupid. . . .'

That was Sologdin all over. A flash of brilliance was always preceded by a fit of self-deprecation.

'That's right. You've no memory, you are weak and mis-guided . . .' Nerzhin prompted him.

'Exactly, exactly. . . .' He grinned, baring long white oval teeth. 'That's why, conscious of my many faults, I've spent many years in prison working out these rules. They're like an iron hoop that keeps the will together. A bird's-eye view of the approach to work.' ('Method', Nerzhin automatically translated from the Language of Maximum to that of Seeming Clarity.) 'It's a way to unity—the unity of aim, worker and work.'

They put on their jackets.

The brighter daylight showed it would soon be time for roll-call. Far away, under the vault of the magically whitened lime trees, the prisoners were at their morning exercise. Among the bent or upright figures the tall, thin, erect one of the fifty-year-old artist, Kondrashov-Ivanov stood out. They saw Lev Rubin trying to come and join them but the guard prevented him : it was too late.

'Look at Lev, all steamed up!'

They laughed.

'So if you like, I'll tell you a bit every morning.'

'Of course. Go ahead.'

'Well, how to face difficulties, for instance.'

'Not lose heart?'

'More than that.'

Lev was looking past Nerzhin at the low, dense thickets in the compound, furred all over with frost and touched uncertainly with pink from the eastern sky—the sun was hesitating whether to come out or not. Sologdin's face, compact, lean, with a short, fair curly beard and moustache, had something in it of ancient Russia—a throwback to the face of Alexander Nevsky.

'How to meet difficulties. . . . In exploring new ground, difficulties must be seen as buried treasure. In general, the greater they are, the more valuable. Not so much if they arise from your struggle with yourself. But if they come from the increased resistance of the object—that's splendid!' Something like a pink dawn flashed across his reddened face, like a reflection of difficulties as splendid as the sun. 'The most rewarding way of research is that of the greatest possible resistance from outside and least possible from within. Failure must be seen as the need for further effort and toughening of the will. And the more effort has been put in already, the more joy there is in meeting obstruction : it means that the pick has struck the iron casket which contains the treasure. And the value of overcoming increased difficulties is the greater because failure has made you grow proportionately to their size.'

'Good. I like that!' said Nerzhin from his pile of logs.

The tints of dawn had faded on the bushes and were extinguished by thick grey clouds.

As though taking his eyes away from a book, Sologdin looked absently down at Nerzhin.

'Now listen to the rule of the last inch. The realm of the last inch. The job is almost finished, the goal almost attained, everything possible seems to have been achieved, every difficulty overcome—and yet the quality is just not there. The work needs more finish, perhaps further research. In that moment of weariness and self-satisfaction, the temptation is greatest to give up, not to strive for the peak of quality. That's the realm of the last inch—here the work is very, very complex but it's also particularly valuable because it's done with the most perfect means. The rule of the last inch is simply this—not to leave it undone. And not to put it off —because otherwise your mind loses touch with that realm. And not to mind how much time you spend on it, because the aim is not to finish the job quickly but to reach perfection.'

'Good, good,' whispered Nerzhin.

In a completely different, rough, amused voice, Sologdin called out:

'What happened, Junior Lieutenant? This isn't like you! Where have you been with that axe? Now we won't have time to chop the wood.'

A moon-faced boy, the Duty Officer, Junior Lieutenant Nadelashin had recently been promoted from the rank of sergeant. The prisoners liked him and had nicknamed him Junior.

Puffing and mincing up with comical small steps, he handed Sologdin the axe and said earnestly with an apologetic smile:

'Oh no, please, Sologdin. There's no wood in the kitchen, they can't cook lunch. You can't imagine the amount of work I've got apart from you.'

'Wha-at?' Nerzhin guffawed. 'Work, did you say? Do you call what you do work?'

Nadelashin turned to him. Frowning, he quoted from memory:

' "Work is the overcoming of resistance." When I walk fast I overcome the resistance of air. That's work, too.' He tried to keep his face blank, but it split into a smile as

Nerzhin's and Sologdin's laughter rang out on the frosty air. 'So please chop some.'

Turning, he trotted off in the direction of the staff building, where Sologdin caught sight of the trim, military figure of the prison governor, Lieutenant-Colonel Klimentyev.

'Do my eyes deceive me, Gleb, or is that Klimentiades?' (That year there was a lot of talk in the newspapers about Greek political prisoners who, from their cells, sent telegrams complaining of their ill-treatment to foreign parliaments and to UNO. The Mavrino prisoners, who usually couldn't send so much as postcards even to their wives, took to giving Greek forms to the names of the prison officials—Mishinopoulos, Klimentiades, Shikinidi.) 'What's he doing here on Sunday?'

'Didn't you know? Six people are going on visits.'

Thinking of this, Nerzhin, who had cheered up while they were sawing, was again flooded with misery. It was a year since his last visit and eight months since he had applied for another—his application had neither been granted nor turned down. He knew one of the reasons. To spare his wife, who was doing a post-graduate course at the university, he wrote to her 'post-restante' instead of giving the address of her student hostel. But the prison authorities wanted this address and refused to forward his letters without it. Thanks to his intense inner life, Nerzhin was free from envy: neither the better pay nor the higher rations of other, more deserving prisoners troubled his peace of mind. But his sense of justice was outraged by the thought that while some of them were allowed visits every two months, his sad, thin, vulnerable wife broke her heart wandering about under the fortress walls of prisons—the idea of it tortured him.

Besides, today was his birthday.

'They are, are they . . .?' said Sologdin with equal envy. 'Stool pigeons go once a month. And I'll never see my Nina. . . .'

(He never used the expression 'until the end of my sentence', because it was given him to realize that a term need have no end.)

He watched Klimentyev stop to talk to Nadelashin and go into the staff building.

'Listen,' he said suddenly. 'Your wife knows mine. If

they let you see her, try to get her to give Nina a message
—just say this: "He loves her, he believes in her, he hasn't
lost hope." '

'What are you talking about, you know they've refused,'
said Nerzhin crossly, taking aim with his axe at a piece of
pine wood.

'Look!'

Nerzhin looked round. The lieutenant was walking towards
him, beckoning from the distance. Dropping the axe, stumbling against the trestle—the saw, propped against it, fell
down with a sharp twang—Nerzhin ran like a boy.

Sologdin watched as the lieutenant took him into the
staff building, then he set a log carefully on end and, swinging
the axe, brought it down with such force that it not only
split the wood but buried itself in the ground.

After all, the axe was government issue.

CHAPTER TWENTY-FIVE

The textbook definition of work, as quoted by Junior Lieutenant Nadelashin, really did apply to his job. Although it
took him only twelve hours out of every forty-eight, it was
highly responsible and involved a lot of bustle and running
up and down stairs.

He had been particularly busy the night before. Hardly had
he taken over at 9 p.m., counted the prisoners and made
sure that all two hundred and eighty-one of them were present
and correct, posted the sentries (on the landing, in the corridor of the staff building, and a patrol under the windows
of the special prison), and started feeding and allocating
beds to the newcomers, when he was summoned by the
Security Officer, Major Mishin.

Nadelashin was not only exceptional among jailors (or,
as they are now called, 'prison workers'), he was unusual
among his compatriots. In a country where every other
person has been through a camp or army course of swearing
and where foul language is used not only by drunks in front
of children (and by children at their childish games) or by
passengers boarding a suburban bus, but sometimes in a

heart to heart talk (especially with an interrogator), Nadelashin was incapable of obscene language and even of using
such words as 'bastard' and 'hell'. His strongest expression
of annoyance was 'damn you', and even this he rarely said
aloud.

Having said 'damn you' to himself, he hurried off to see
the major.

Major Mishin, very unfairly described by Bobynin as a
parasite, was an unhealthily fat, purple-faced man; circumstances having kept him late at work that Saturday, he gave
Nadelashin a special job:

   (a) to see whether the Germans and Latvians had
started their Christmas celebrations;
   (b) list all who were taking part;
   (c) check personally, and by warders sent to look every
ten minutes, whether they were drinking wine or digging
escape tunnels, what they were talking about among themselves and, above all, whether they were making anti-
Soviet propaganda;
   (d) if possible, uncover some breach of prison regulations and stop this disgusting outbreak of religious
mania.

Nadelashin wasn't told to 'stop it', only to stop 'if possible'.
Quiet Christmas celebrations were not actually forbidden,
but they were unbearable to Comrade Mishin.

The lieutenant, his face impassive as a winter moon, reminded the major that neither he nor, still less, his men knew
German or Latvian (they didn't even all know Russian).

Mishin recollected that, in all his four years as guard
commander in a camp for German prisoners of war, he had
learned only three words—'Halt!' 'Zurück!' 'Weg!'—and cut
the briefing short.

Nadelashin gave a clumsy salute (his training had included
very little drill) and went off to assign the new arrivals to
their cells and bunks in accordance with the list handed him
by the major. (Mishin attached great importance to the cen-
trally planned distribution of prisoners in their cells, where
he planted his spies at regular intervals. He knew that people
didn't talk as openly amidst the bustle of daytime work as

176

at night before they went to sleep, and that talk was particularly ill-tempered when they woke up in the morning,
so that bedside spying was especially rewarding.)

Pretending to check the electric light bulbs, Nadelashin
duly went once into every cell where Christmas was being
celebrated, sent the guard in once, and listed everyone present.
Then he was again summoned by Mishin and handed him the
list. Mishin was particularly interested in the fact that Rubin
was with the Germans. He entered it in his file.

After that it was time to change the warders and settle
a quarrel between two of them as to which had previously
been on duty longest and how much time he was owed by the
other.

Next came lights-out. Nadelashin had an argument about
hot water with Pryanchikov, made a round of the cells,
turned the white lights out and the blue ones on, and was
once more summoned by Mishin, still at his post (he had a
sick wife and didn't feel like going home to listen to her
whining). Mishin sat in his armchair but kept Nadelashin
on his feet while he questioned him about Rubin: who did
he go about with, and had he on any occasion during the past
week spoken slightingly of the administration or voiced any
demands on behalf of the other prisoners.

Nadelashin had a special position among his brother officers
of the guard. He was often and severely told off. His innate
kindliness had for a long time been a disadvantage to him in
the security service. Had he not adapted himself he would
long since have been thrown out or even sent for trial. He
was never rude to prisoners, he addressed them with a
transparently good-natured smile, he was as lenient as possible
over details of discipline. As a result they liked him, never
crossed him or complained about him, and spoke freely in
his presence. Nadelashin was observant, literate, a good
listener and, to assist his memory, put everything down in a
special notebook; the contents of this little book he afterwards reported to the authorities, thereby making up for his
many shortcomings.

Taking out his notebook, he told the major that on the
7th of December the prisoners, back from their midday exercise, were walking in a crowd down the corridor with Nadelashin behind them. They were grumbling because tomorrow

was Sunday but the authorities had refused to let them take the day off, and Rubin said: 'When will you people realize that you won't get any pity from those rats?'

' "Rats"—is that what he said?' Mishin's face lit up.

'That's what he said,' Nadelashin confirmed, moon-faced and smiling gently.

Mishin reopened the file and made an entry, as well as ordering Nadelashin to write a formal report.

Major Mishin hated Rubin and was collecting evidence against him.

Soon after coming to Mavrino, he had heard that Rubin, a former Party member, boasted right and left of being a Communist at heart, even though in prison. He called him in for a chat about life in general and collaboration in particular. But they failed to reach an understanding. Mishin put the question in the form prescribed at briefing sessions:

'If you are a Soviet man you will work for us.

'If you won't work for us, you are not a Soviet man.

'If you are not Soviet, you are anti-Soviet and deserve an additional sentence.'

But Rubin asked: 'Would I have to write reports in pencil or in ink?'—'Better in ink,' Mishin advised—'Well, I've proved my loyalty to the Soviet régime in blood, so I don't have to prove it in ink as well.'

Thus from the start he showed what a hypocrite and double-dealer he was.

Mishin summoned him once again, but Rubin excused himself on the obviously false pretext that, since he was in prison, he was evidently regarded as politically unreliable, and so long as this was so, he could not collaborate with the head of Security.

Ever since, Mishin had been carefully picking up everything he could find to use against him.

The major was still talking to the lieutenant when an official from the Ministry of State Security arrived by car to fetch Bobynin. Delighted with this chance to further his career, Mishin rushed out without his overcoat, stood beside the car, urged the official to come in and get warm, drew attention to the fact that he worked at night, hustled and confused Nadelashin, and even asked Bobynin (who had deliberately put on his labour camp jacket instead of the perfectly good coat issued him at Mavrino) whether he would be warm enough.

As soon as Bobynin had left, another car came for Pryanchikov—still more reason for the major not to go home. To fill in time while he waited to see who else might be summoned and how long Bobynin and Pryanchikov were kept, he went to see how the warders were spending their time off (they were playing dominoes) and questioned them on Party history (he was responsible for their political education). The warders, technically on duty but usually asleep at this time and at the moment anxious to get back to their game, answered unwillingly. Their answers were deplorable: not only were they confused as to why it had been right for the Bolsheviks to break with the Mensheviks after the 2nd Party Congress and join up with them again after the 4th, but they also said Plekhanov had been the tsarist minister who had had the workers shot in Petersburg on the 9th of January 1905. Nadelashin was told off for letting his shift get out of hand.

At this point Bobynin and Pryanchikov returned together by car and, refusing to tell the major anything, went off to bed. Worried as well as disappointed, Mishin took the car to go home (the last bus had left).

Having cursed the major, the warders would have gone to sleep and Nadelashin taken a nap—but an agitated telephone call came from the officer in charge of the sentries who manned the watch-towers.

From the south-west tower a man had been seen clearly beside the woodshed in the yard; he had crept towards the barbed wire but, frightened by a shout from the guard, had run away and vanished in the shadows.

Although convinced that the guard had been seeing things, and that all the prisoners were safe behind their new steel doors and ancient walls four feet thick, Nadelashin was obliged to act on the officer's report and to report in his turn. He roused his men and with the aid of flashlights conducted a tour of the vast yard. Then he made his own tour of the cells. Fumbling in the faint blue light but unwilling to provoke complaints by switching on the white, he knocked himself hard against somebody's bed, but finally, having shone his flashlight on each sleeping prisoner's head, established that all two hundred and eighty-one were there.

He went to the prison office and, in the round, clear hand expressive of his limpid soul, wrote a report to the prison governor, Lieutenant-Colonel Klimentyev.

By then it was morning, time to inspect the kitchen and sound reveille.

This was how the lieutenant spent his night and he was truly justified in telling Nerzhin that he earned his keep.

Nadelashin was well over thirty, though his fresh, clean-shaven face made him look younger. His father and grand-father had been tailors—not fashionable but skilful, with a middle-class clientele, and readily accepting orders to turn a suit, alter reach-me-downs for younger children, or mend while the customer waited. They intended the boy to follow them in their profession. Ever since his childhood, this light, pleasant work had appealed to him and he trained for it by watching his elders and helping them. But the NEP[1] ended. His father paid a year's tax for his licence as a private trader. Two days later he was assessed a second time for the same year and paid up again. Within two more days he was shamelessly assessed for the third time and the amount was tripled. He tore up his licence, took his sign-board down and joined a co-operative. Soon afterwards his son was conscripted into the army. From it he joined the security forces and later became a warder.

His career was undistinguished. In fourteen years he was twice or three times overtaken by younger men, some of whom were now captains, while he had only been com-missioned a month ago.

He understood much more than he could say aloud. He understood, for instance, that many of the prisoners, deprived though they were of human rights, were human beings of a higher order than himself. And having the normal human capacity to identify himself with others, he failed to see these men as the villains they were made out to be at his political education class.

Even better than the definition of work in the physics course

[1] NEP—New Economic Policy (1921-1928) permitted a degree of private enterprise trading.

180

he had taken at evening classes, he remembered every bend of the corridors of the Lubyanka and the inside of each of its one hundred and ten cells. The Lubyanka rule was to move the warders every two hours from one part of the corridor to another (a precaution against their getting to know their prisoners and being influenced or bribed by them, although the warders had no complaints about their pay). The warder was supposed to look through every peep-hole at least once every three minutes. Nadelashin had an exceptional memory for faces and it seemed to him that he remembered all the prisoners—from famous politicians to simple ex-army officers like Nerzhin—who had passed through the Lubyanka between 1935 and 1947 when he was transferred to Mavrino. He felt he could recognize any of them in the street, whatever they might be wearing—except that they were never likely to be met in the street, because there was no way back from *that* world into *this* one. Only here in Mavrino had he come across a few of his former charges—but of course without giving any sign of recognition. He remembered them growing stiff from lack of sleep in the blinding glare of the three-foot-square 'boxes', using a thread to cut their daily slice of four hundred grams of damp black bread, reading the beautiful old books of which the prison library had so many, walking in single file to the wash-room, clasping their hands behind their back when they were summoned for interrogation, relaxing and talking in the last half hour before lights-out, and sleeping in the bright light on winter nights, arms outside the covers and wrapped in towels against the cold—according to the rules, anyone who kept his arms under the blanket had to be woken up and made to take them out.

Best of all he liked listening to all those bearded academicians, priests, generals, old Bolsheviks and comical foreigners as they talked and argued among themselves. It was his duty to listen, but he also did it for pleasure. Sometimes he wished he could hear a story from start to finish—how a man had lived and what he was in prison for—but he was always being called away in the middle. It amazed him that during the grim months in which their lives were broken and their fate decided, these people found the courage to talk about almost anything except their suffering—Italian painters, the habits of bees, wolf-hunting, or the fact that somewhere, somebody called Corbusier was building houses—houses which were not even for them.

One day he overheard a conversation which fascinated him. He was sitting at the back of a Black Maria, taking two prisoners from the Lubyanka to the 'Sukhanov Villa'—a sinister prison on the outskirts of Moscow. Few returned from it to the Lubyanka, and many left it only for the madhouse or the grave. Nadelashin had not worked there himself, but he had heard that even the food was used as a sophisticated means of torture: instead of the ordinary coarse, indigestible prison fare, the prisoners were put on a delicate, appetizing convalescent-home diet; the torture consisted in the size of the portions—half a saucer of bouillon, an eighth of a cutlet, two shreds of roast potato. It was not nourishment but a reminder of what they had lost. This was much more depressing than the usual bowl of watery soup and helped to drive them out of their minds.

For some reason the two prisoners were not in separate compartments, but locked up together in the back of the Black Maria. Nadelashin missed the beginning of the conversation because of the noise of the motor. Then something went wrong with the engine and the driver got out to see to it while the officer sat in the cab. It was then he heard their quiet voices through the grating in the back door. They were cursing the government and the Tsar, but not the government of the day and not Stalin—they were cursing Tsar Peter the Great! What had he done to them? Yet there they were, cursing him up and down! One of the two objected, among other things, to his having deprived the Russians of their national dress, thereby depriving them of a part of their national identity. He listed the traditional clothes, knowledgeably and in detail—what they looked like and on what occasions they were worn—and he assured his companion that it was not too late to revive some of them, combining them in a dignified and tasteful way with contemporary fashions, which would be much better than blindly copying Paris. The other prisoner made a joke—they could still joke!—about two people needed for this: a brilliant tailor to design them, and a fashionable singer who would wear the clothes and be photographed in them, after which the whole of Russia would take them up.

Nadelashin was all the more interested because tailoring was still his secret hobby. After his duty in the prison corridor with its crazy, feverish atmosphere, he was calmed by the rustling cloth, the soft pliant folds and the innocuousness of the work.

He made clothes for his children, dresses for his wife, suits for himself. But he kept it a secret.

It was thought to be no work for a soldier.

CHAPTER TWENTY-SIX

Lieutenant-Colonel Klimentyev's hair was pitch-black, with a metallic sheen, parted in the middle, and smooth as though moulded to his head. He had sleek handlebar moustaches. He was slim and, at forty-five, held himself like a trim young soldier. He never smiled when he was on duty, and this added to his swarthy, morose appearance.

It was Sunday, but he had arrived even earlier than usual. Cutting across the yard at the busiest time of the prisoners' morning walk, he glanced round with half an eye and noticed some irregularities but, mindful of his rank, said nothing; stopping only to tell Nadelashin to parade prisoner Nerzhin and to report in person before bringing him in, he went into the staff building. He had noticed among other things that on seeing him some prisoners hurried past, others fell behind or turned aside—anything to avoid meeting him and having to say good morning. He observed this coldly and without taking offence. He knew the reason was not so much their genuine contempt for his job as embarrassment before their comrades and fear of appearing subservient. Most of these men, when he summoned them to his office one by one, were amiable and some even ingratiating. People behind bars were of various sorts, some worth more, some less, as he had long since realized. He respected their right to be proud and stood unshakeably on his own right to be severe. A born soldier, he believed that the order he enforced was not a degrading system of bullying but the rational discipline of an army.

He unlocked his office. The room was hot and smelt unpleasantly stuffy from the scorched paint of the radiators. He opened the window, took off his coat and, corseted in his tunic, sat down at his desk and surveyed its surface. The calendar still showed Saturday and had a note on it:

'Christmas tree?'

From this uncluttered office, with no equipment other than a steel safe for the office files, half a dozen chairs, a telephone and a buzzer, the Colonel successfully conducted the outward lives of two hundred and eighty-one prisoners and ran a staff of fifty warders.

Although it was Sunday (he would take a weekday off instead) and he was half an hour ahead of time, the colonel was no less composed and level-headed than usual.

Junior Lieutenant Nadelashin stood before him timidly, with two round red blotches on his cheeks. The colonel scared the wits out of him, even though he had never harmed Nadelashin by entering any of his countless mistakes in the record. Comical, round-faced, anything but soldierly, the lieutenant tried in vain to stand to attention.

He reported that the night had been quiet; there had been no infringements of discipline, but two unusual incidents had occurred. One he had described in his written report (he put this on the edge of the desk but it immediately slipped off and, gliding in an intricate arc, landed under a distant chair; Nadelashin dived after it, brought it back and replaced it on the desk); the other was that prisoners Bobynin and Pryanchikov had been summoned by the Ministry of State Security.

Klimentyev frowned and asked for details of the prisoners' departure and return. It was, of course, an unpleasant, even an alarming piece of news. As governor of this special prison, he was for ever sitting on a volcano—always under the Minister's very nose. Mavrino was not some remote forest camp where the man in charge could keep court jesters and a harem, and pass his own sentences like a feudal lord. Here one had to do things legally, stick to the instructions, never show a spark of temper or of mercy. But then Klimentyev was just the man for the job. He did not believe that Bobynin or Pryanchikov could have found anything illegal in his actions to complain about last night. And his long experience of the service had taught him not to be afraid of being slandered by prisoners: one was much more likely to be slandered by a colleague.

He ran through Nadelashin's report of the other 'incident' and saw at once that there was nothing to it. Nadelashin was literate, and you could always rely on his common sense: that was why he kept him.

But his inefficiency! The colonel reprimanded him. He reminded him of all that had gone wrong on his previous tour of duty. The morning shift was two minutes late going out to work. Several of the beds were untidy and Nadelashin had lacked the necessary firmness to recall the offending prisoners from work and order them to make them up again. He had been told all this at the time, but it was like water off a duck's back! And what about the prisoners' walk this morning? Young Doronin had been standing at the very edge of the exercise yard, staring at the space beyond the compound, near the greenhouses, just where the ground was broken and crossed by a gully—most convenient for anyone attempting to escape. And this same Doronin was serving a twenty-five-year sentence for forging identity papers, and had been on the all-Union wanted list for two years! Yet not one of the warders had told him to move on, and to keep moving in a circle. And where had Gerasimovich been going? Away from the others, behind the big lime trees, in the direction of the machine-shop! And what was in Gerasimovich's record? Second sentence under Section 58, sub-sections 1A to 19, i.e. treason by intent. He hadn't actually committed treason, but neither had he been able to prove that, when he went to Leningrad at the beginning of the war, it was not to await the Germans. Did Nadelashin have to be reminded that prisoners must be studied all the time, both by direct observation and from the records? And what did Nadelashin look like himself? His tunic all rucked up (Nadelashin pulled it down), the star on his cap crooked (Nadelashin put it straight), and saluting like an old woman! No wonder prisoners didn't make their beds properly when he was on duty. Unmade beds today, mutiny and a strike tomorrow.

Finally, the colonel gave him his orders (the warders

assigned to prisoners going on visits to assemble for briefing in Room 3; prisoner Nerzhin to be left waiting in the corridor) and dismissed him.

Nadelashin left the room in a cold sweat. Every time he was told off, he was genuinely upset by the justice of the reprimand and resolved never to disobey his instructions again. But back on duty, he was once more at the mercy of dozens of prisoners, all pulling him this way and that, each wanting his little bit of freedom, and he could not refuse them, and always hoped it would pass unnoticed.

Klimentyev picked up his pen and crossed off the note 'Christmas tree?' on the calendar. He had made up his mind the night before.

There had never been a Christmas tree in a special prison: he could remember no such miracle. But the prisoners—more than once, and including the most reliable among them—had insistently begged to have one this year. In the end, he had asked himself: well, why not? No harm could come of it—there was no danger of fire, they were all expert electricians. On the other hand, it was most important that on New Year's Eve, when all the free workers were off duty and enjoying themselves in Moscow, the prisoners should have a little relaxation as well. He knew that the eve of a holiday was always a bad time for them, that there was a risk of someone being driven to do something foolish or desperate. So last night he had rung up and talked it over with the Prison Administration, to which he was directly responsible. The prison regulations forbade musical instruments, but there was nothing they could find in it about Christmas trees, so while they hadn't actually agreed, they had not definitely refused permission either. The colonel's long and irreproachable record made him confident and firm of purpose. Before the evening was out, on the escalator in the metro on his way home, he decided: very well, they shall have their Christmas tree.

And, as he boarded the train, he thought with pleasure that he was after all, essentially, an intelligent, practical man, not a rubber stamp; he was even kind, but the prisoners would never see it, just as they would never know who had been against their having a Christmas tree and who it was who had decided that they should have one.

For some reason, he felt so happy about his decision that he did not hurry and shove his way into the carriage with the other Muscovites around him but got in last, just as the pneumatic doors were sliding shut; without trying to grab a seat, he took hold of the handrail and stood looking at his virile, vaguely shimmering image in the plate-glass window, behind which the blackness of the tunnel and the cable in its endless tubing went rushing past. After a while, he shifted his gaze to a young woman who sat near him. She was carefully but inexpensively dressed in a black artificial Persian lamb coat and hat, and held a tightly packed briefcase on her knees. He thought she had a nice face but looked tired and, for a young woman, took unusually little interest in her surroundings.

Just then she glanced in his direction, and their eyes met for as long as the uninterested eyes of strangers in a train usually do. But in that moment, a wariness sprang into hers, as of a troubled uncertainty. Klimentyev, with his professional memory for faces, immediately recognized her, and was too late to prevent a flash of recognition in his eyes. She noticed this and it evidently confirmed her guess.

She was the wife of prisoner Nerzhin. Klimentyev had seen her when she had visited her husband at the Taganka Prison.

She frowned and looked away, then glanced back at him. By then, he was staring at the tunnel but noticed out of the corner of his eyes that she was looking at him, and she at once resolutely got up and moved closer, so that he was forced to turn to her again.

She had got up resolutely but, now that she was standing, all her resolution left her. She lost the confident air of an independent young woman travelling on the underground, and it looked as though, with her heavy briefcase, she had got up to give the colonel her place. Hers was the fate of all political prisoners' wives, who, wherever they went, to whomever they appealed, once their unfortunate marriage was known, seemed to bear the stigma of their husbands' shame, as though they shared for all to see the burden of guilt of those villains to whom they had once rashly entrusted their lives. In the long run these women began really to feel guilty, as their husbands certainly did not.

Standing near enough to be heard above the noise of the train, the woman said:

'Forgive me, Comrade Lieutenant-Colonel—I'm not mistaken?—I think you are my husband's . . . commanding officer?'

In his years of service as a prison officer, many women of all kinds had got up and stood before him, and he saw nothing strange in their timid, diffident air. But, although she had put her question so carefully, here, in the underground, in public—the pleading figure in front of him somehow looked indecent.

'Why did you get up? Sit down, sit down,' he muttered embarrassed, pulling her by the sleeve to get her to sit down.

'No, no, that doesn't matter in the least.' She held him with her insistent, almost fanatical eyes. 'Please tell me, why is it that for a whole year I have not been able to vi . . . to see him? When will it be possible, can you tell me?'

Their meeting was as much a coincidence as it would be to hit a grain of sand with another grain of sand from a distance of forty feet. The week before, permission had come from the MGB Prison Administration for prisoner Nerzhin, among others, to see his wife at the Lefort Prison on Sunday, the 25th of December 1949. But a note was attached, saying that to send notice of the meeting to his wife 'poste restante', as the prisoner requested, was forbidden.

Nerzhin was called in and asked for his wife's address. He said he didn't know. Trained by the prison regulations never to tell prisoners the truth, Klimentyev did not expect prisoners to be truthful either. Obviously, Nerzhin knew; he refused to tell for the same reason as the Administration refused to send the notice 'poste restante': wives were notified by postcard. On it was written: 'You are permitted to see your husband at such-and-such a prison.' Not only did the MGB file the wife's address, it tried to reduce the number of women willing to receive such postcards—by letting their neighbours know that they were wives of 'enemies of the people', by flushing them out, isolating them, surrounding them with hostility. That was what the wives were afraid of. Nerzhin's wife lived under her maiden name. Obviously, she must be hiding from the MGB. Klimentyev had explained that, in the circumstances, there could be no meeting, and he had not sent the notice.

But now this woman, drawing to herself the silent attention of the other passengers, stood in this humiliating attitude before him.

'Letters can't be sent "poste restante",' he said just loud enough for her to hear over the rattle of the train. 'You must give your address.'

'But I'm moving!' Her expression changed at once. 'I'm leaving very soon. I haven't got a permanent address at the moment.' He knew she was lying.

Klimentyev thought of getting out at the next station and if she followed him, explaining to her in the entrance hall where there were fewer people that he couldn't speak to her except officially.

But the wife of the enemy of the people seemed to have forgotten her irredeemable crime. She was searching his face, her eyes dry, hot, demanding, obsessed. Klimentyev was amazed by their expression—what power could make this woman cling so stubbornly, so desperately to a man she wouldn't see for years and who was destroying her whole life?

'It's very, very urgent for me,' she insisted, noticing his hesitation.

Klimentyev thought of the paper lying in the prison safe. An amendment to the directive on internal security, it dealt a new blow to relatives who avoided giving their addresses. Major Mishin proposed to make the announcement to the prisoners on Monday. This woman, unless she saw her husband tomorrow, and unless she revealed her address, would never see him again. But if he told her now—the postcard had not been sent, there was nothing about it in the files —she could go to the Lefort Prison tomorrow as though on the off-chance.

The train was slowing down.

All these thoughts raced through Klimentyev's head. He knew that prisoners were their own worst enemies. He knew that the worst enemy of every woman was that woman herself. People could not keep quiet! It had happened to him before: he had foolishly permitted something which was forbidden by the rules, and no one would have been any the wiser if the very people who had benefited by his kindness had not themselves let the cat out of the bag!

He must not give in.

Yet as the many-coloured marble of the station walls flickered past the window and the noise of the slowing train died down, he said:

'You may see your husband. Come tomorrow morning at ten . . .' He didn't say 'to the Lefort Prison' because the passengers, hurrying to the exit were all around him, but—'You know the Lefort Rampart?'

'I know, I know,' she nodded happily.

Her eyes, dry a moment ago, were full of tears.

Avoiding the tears, the gratitude and suchlike nonsense, Klimentyev got out and took the next train.

He was surprised and annoyed at what he had just said.

Lieutenant-Colonel Klimentyev had left Nerzhin waiting in the corridor because Nerzhin was an impudent prisoner who always stuck up for his rights.

His calculation proved right: after cooling his heels for a long time, Nerzhin not only lost all hope of seeing his wife but, accustomed to trouble of every sort, had expected some new misfortune.

He was therefore dumbfounded by the news. The prisoners' exacting moral code, which he himself preached, enjoined upon him to show not the slightest sign of joy or even satisfaction but merely to ask phlegmatically what time he should be ready and leave the room. But the news was so sudden, his joy so great, that he beamed all over his face at the colonel and thanked him from his heart.

The colonel's face was a mask.

He went straight off to brief the warders for the trip to Lefort.

The briefing consisted of a number of points: he stressed the dangers of the occasion; impressed upon the warders the incorrigible wickedness of the prisoners in their charge and the fact that their sole aim was to take advantage of today's meeting to hand over the state secrets in their possession, through their wives, to the United States (the warders knew nothing of the nature of the scientific research being done at Mavrino and were, therefore, easily filled with superstitious dread at the idea that any scrap of paper from within its walls might cause the destruction of their country). Next, he listed the more likely hiding-places in the prisoners' clothes and shoes (actually an hour before the meeting, the prisoners were issued with special clothes for show), and of the methods of detecting them. There followed questions and answers to test whether the technique of search had been thoroughly mastered; and finally examples were quoted of the sort of turn the conversation might take, and how to listen to it intelligently and cut it short should any subject other than purely private and domestic matters be broached.

The colonel knew the regulations and liked order.

CHAPTER TWENTY-SEVEN

Nearly knocking Nadelashin off his feet in the dark corridor, Nerzhin ran to the prisoners' sleeping quarters. The square of turkish towelling still hung from his neck under his padded jacket.

Such is human resilience that, in a flash, he had become a new man. Only five minutes ago, when he stood in the passage waiting to be called in, all thirty years of his life had appeared to him as an absurd and disastrous chain of misfortunes which he had not the strength to shake off. The worst had been his early call-up so soon after his marriage, and later his long years of prison and separation from his wife. He knew that their love was doomed to be trampled under-foot.

But now he was to see her at noon—and his thirty-year-old life suddenly appeared to him in a new light: it was a life taut as a bowstring; a life meaningful in all its happenings, large and small; a life striding from one bold success to another—and in which his war service, his arrest, his separation from his wife, were all, most unexpectedly, steps towards the goal. It was only outwardly that he appeared ill-fated—secretly, he found happiness in his very misfortune. He drank from it as from a spring. Here, in prison, he was discovering people and events he could not have heard of anywhere else on earth—certainly not in the well-fed comfort and seclusion of his home. From his youth up, he had been more afraid of getting stuck in the mud of the commonplace than of anything else. As the proverb goes: 'You don't drown in the sea, you drown in a puddle.'

And his wife—he knew he would return to her. After all, the spiritual bond between them was unbroken. And he was seeing her today! On his birthday! The day after his conversation with Yakonov! They would never allow her to visit him again, but what mattered was today. His thoughts flashed through his head like fiery arrows. He must not forget . . . he must tell her this . . . and that . . . and so much else as well!

He ran into the semicircular room where the prisoners were milling noisily around, some coming back from breakfast, others only now going off to wash, while Valentin Pryanchikov, his blanket thrown off, sat on his bed in his underclothes, laughing and gesticulating as he described his interview last night with the bigwig who had turned out to be the Minister himself! Nerzhin had to listen to all this too. It was one of those rare moments in life: his heart sang, he felt as though his chest were bursting, and a hundred years were not enough for all he wanted to achieve and to set right. But he mustn't miss his breakfast—breakfast wasn't something a prisoner could count on as a daily gift of the gods. Anyway, Valentin's story was coming to its inglorious end. He was collectively condemned as a miserable sod for not having told Abakumov about the prisoners' needs. Now he was struggling and squealing as five self-appointed executioners pulled his trousers off and chased him round the room, hitting him with their belts and scalding him with spoonfuls of tea.

Drinking his morning tea in bed—his bunk was the one below Nerzhin's and across the central gangway from Pryanchikov's now empty one—Potapov watched the fun and laughed until he cried, wiping his eyes behind his spectacles. He had made his bed before reveille, giving it the regulation shape of a neat rectangle. His slice of bread was very thinly buttered—he sent all his wages to his 'old woman', never buying anything from the prison shop. (An expert, irreplaceable in his job and in good standing with the authorities, he was well paid by prison standards: a hundred and fifty roubles a month or a third of a charwoman's wage 'outside'.)

Taking off his quilted jacket and throwing it up on his unmade bunk, Nerzhin said good morning to Potapov and, without waiting for a reply ran off to breakfast.

Potapov was the engineer who had confessed under interrogation (and had signed the confession and stuck to it in court) to having sold the Germans (and for next to nothing at that) the pride of Stalin's Five Year Plans, the Dnieper Dam—though admittedly after it had been blown up. For this horrific, unimaginable crime, the court had, in its mercy, given him only ten years and a further five of loss of rights—'ten and five on the horns' in prison slang.

No one who had known him as a young man, and least of all Potapov himself, could have imagined him at forty, condemned for a political crime. His friends had nicknamed him 'The Robot'. He lived for his work, even the three-day public holidays bored him and, in all his life, he had taken leave only once, for his honeymoon : it was hard to replace him and he willingly stayed. He scarcely noticed such trifles as shortages of sugar, vegetables, bread : he punched another hole in his belt, pulled it tighter and got on with the only thing in the world that mattered—high voltage transmission. Apart from enjoying their jokes, he was only very dimly aware of the existence of those other people who were not working on high voltages. As for those who only wagged their tongues and did nothing with their hands, he did not regard them as people at all. He had held the post of chief engineer in charge of instrumentation at the Dnieper Dam, and there he had met his wife and her life and his were fed to the insatiable bonfire of those days.

In 1941 they were building another power station; Potapov had been exempted from military service. But when they heard that the one on the Dnieper, the work of their youth, had been blown up, he said to his wife :

'I'll have to go, Katia.'

And she replied :

'Yes, my dear, you go.'

So he went, with his thick spectacles, his twisted belt, his crumpled tunic and his holster empty : he was an officer, but in the second year of that all-out war there was still a shortage of officers' small arms. In the heat of July and the smoke of the burning crops, he was captured near Kastornaya. He escaped but was recaptured before he could reach the Soviet lines. He escaped again but was caught in open country by an enemy parachute drop (all three times he was empty-handed).

He went through the cannibal camps of Novograd-Volynsk and Czestochowa, where the prisoners ate grass, tree bark and their dead comrades. The Germans suddenly removed him from this camp, and took him to Berlin, and there a man ('a polite bastard'), who spoke excellent Russian, asked him if he really was Potapov, the famous engineer from the Dnieper Dam Power Station. Could he prove it by drawing—well, say, a diagram of the system for switching on the Dnieper Dam generator? As the diagram had already been widely published, Potapov had no hesitation in complying. Later, he was to tell the Soviet prosecutor all about it himself—though he needn't have said a word.

It was this that the indictment described as his 'betrayal of the secrets of the Dnieper Dam Power Station'.

What did not get into the indictment was the sequel to the story. Having established Potapov's identity, the unknown Russian made him an offer: if he would sign a voluntary declaration of his willingness to work on the reconstruction of the power station, he would at once be released from camp, supplied with ration cards and money, and restored to his beloved work.

At the tempting offer, Potapov's wrinkled face darkened thoughtfully. Without shouting his indignation, or beating his breast, or in any way staking his claim to immortality as a posthumous Hero of the Soviet Union, he said in his quiet voice with its southern accent:

'But you see, I signed my oath of allegiance. If I were now to sign this, it would be in conflict with that, wouldn't it?'

'I respect your convictions,' said the unknown Russian, and sent him back to the camp.

In this mild and undramatic manner, Potapov chose almost certain death in preference to a comfortable life.

Not holding this against him, the Soviet court gave him only ten years.

Markushev, who had signed a similar declaration and did in fact work for the Germans, also got ten years.

That was Stalin's hall-mark, his style—that splendid disregard of differences, that levelling of friends and enemies that made him a unique figure in the whole of human history.

Another thing for which the Soviet court did not condemn Potapov was that in 1945—still in his broken spectacles tied with string but this time with a tommy-gun in his hand —he rode into Berlin on the back of a Red Army tank; this was how Potapov got off so easily, with only 'ten and five on the horns'.

Nerzhin returned from breakfast, took off his boots, climbed up on to his top bunk and started his daily acrobatic feat: making his bed without a wrinkle while standing on it. But as soon as he moved his pillow, he found under it a transparent dark-red cigarette-case filled with a single layer of twelve Belomar cigarettes and, wound in and out of them, a strip of paper with two lines in draughtsman's lettering:

> *Thus he killed ten years,*
> *Spending his prime in idleness.'*

There could be no mistake. In the whole of the prison, only Potapov combined a gift for craftsmanship of this sort with the habit of quoting from the volume of *Eugene Onegin* he had carried about with him ever since he left school.

'Andrey,' Nerzhin hung his head over the side of the bunk.

Potapov had finished his tea and was reading a newspaper. 'Yes?'

'Is this your handiwork?'

'How should I know?' He was trying not to smile. 'You found it, did you?'

'Andrey! It's a dream!'

The crafty, friendly creases on Potapov's face deepened and spread. Straightening his glasses, he said:

'. . . I was sharing a cell in the Lubyanka with Count Esterházy—he and I carrying the slops bucket out in turn, you understand, and me teaching him Russian from the

"Prison Regulations" on the wall—I made him a birthday present of three buttons made of bread (they'd cut every one of his off) and he swore to me that not even from the Habsburgs had he ever had a more timely gift.'

On the voice classification chart, Potapov's voice was described as 'hollow and slightly cracked'.

Still hanging over the side of his bunk, Nerzhin looked warmly into Potapov's rough-hewn face. Wearing his spectacles, he looked no older than his forty-five years, and tough at that. But without them, the deep, dark cavities of his eyes were almost those of a corpse.

'But you embarrass me, Andrey. I can never give you anything like that, I haven't got your hands. . . . How on earth did you remember it was my birthday?'

'Never mind. What other memorable dates have we got left?'

They sighed.

'Like some tea?' Potapov offered. 'I've got my special brew.'

'No time, Andrey. I'm off on a visit.'

'That's good!' Potapov brightened up. 'Your old woman?'

'Yes.'

'Good for you! Only stop breathing down my neck.'

'Don't interfere with my human rights! . . . What's in the paper?' It was more than three years since Potapov and Nerzhin had met in a Butyrki cell, more overcrowded than usual, humming with anxious talk, and half dark even in July. Here, the most unlikely paths crossed. Newcomers from Europe passed through the cell, and tough young Russian prisoners of war who had just exchanged German captivity for prison at home, and battered and branded inmates of camps, in transit from the caverns of GULAG to the oasis of a special prison. Coming into the room, Nerzhin got flat down on his belly and wriggled into the pitch-black space under the plank beds (they were so low that you could not get under them on all fours) and, even before his eyes were used to the darkness, called cheerfully from his lair on the dirty cement floor:

'Who's the last one in?'

A cracked and hollow voice replied:

'I am. You're next.'

After that, day after day, as other prisoners were removed, to be sent off to camps, the two of them moved under the bunks 'from the bucket to the window' and, in their third week, back from the window to the bucket but, this time, on top of the first tier of bunks, and still later, back to the window again. This was how their friendship was cemented, in spite of their difference of age, background and interests.

There, in the long, brooding months after his trial, Potapov admitted to Nerzhin that never in his born days would he have taken the slightest interest in politics if politics hadn't come up and hit him first. Not that he was sorry he had refused the offer of German bread and lost three years starving in a German camp. And he was as convinced as ever that it was not for foreigners to pass judgment on our internal troubles.

But a spark of doubt had kindled in him and was smouldering on. Try as he would, he could not see why a man who had helped to build the Dnieper Dam was in jail for nothing.

CHAPTER TWENTY-EIGHT

Roll-call was at five to nine. This operation took hours in the camps—the prisoners stood in the cold or were chased from place to place while the guards counted and checked and counted again, by ones or fives or hundreds or brigades—but here in the special prison it was quick and painless. Two Duty Officers—the one going off duty and the relief—came in while the prisoners were having their tea; the prisoners stood up (some didn't) and the new Duty Officer, frowning with concentration, counted heads; then announcements were made and complaints unwillingly heard.

The Duty Officer for the day, Senior Lieutenant Shusterman, was tall and dark; his face was not exactly gloomy but, as befitted a highly trained prison officer, totally devoid of all human expression. Like Nadelashin, he had been sent from the Lubyanka to tighten up the discipline at Mavrino. Several prisoners remembered them from their Lubyanka days. As sergeants, they had at one time acted as escorts, that is to say, taken charge of the prisoner while he stood facing the wall, and led him up the famous worn steps to the landing half-way between the fifth and sixth floors (there, a passage connected the main building with the interrogation block and every prisoner for the past thirty years and more had walked that passage—Cadets, SR's, Anarchists, Monarchists, Octobrists, Mensheviks, Bolsheviks, Savinkov, Yakubovich, Kutepov, Ramzin, Shulgin, Bukharin, Rykov, Tukhachevsky, Professor Pletnyov, Academician Vavilov, Field-Marshal Paulus, General Krasnov, world-famous scientists and half-fledged poets, first the criminals themselves, then their wives, then their daughters after them). At an equally famous desk every prisoner signed the thick Register of Destinies, writing his name through a slot in a tin plate (so that he shouldn't see the other signatures); then he was escorted up another flight of steps—where, as in a circus during the *salto mortale*, there were nets to catch him if he jumped off— and along the endless corridors of the Ministry, hot from the electric lights and cold from the gold glitter of colonels' epaulettes.

But however overwhelmed by his first despair, the prisoner quickly noticed the difference between the two: Shusterman, darting glances like gloomy lightning from under his thick eyebrows, dug his claws into the prisoner's arm and dragged him choking up the stairs, while Nadelashin, with his moon face rather like a eunuch's, walked at a distance of a couple of feet, never touched the prisoner and always told him politely which way to turn.

Nadelashin announced that prisoners who were going out on visits should report at the staff building at ten. Somebody asked him if there was to be a film show that day. Nadelashin said no. Over the faint mutter of discontent, Khorobrov said loudly:

'And a good thing too. We can do without shit like *Kuban Cossacks*.'

Shusterman looked up sharply to see who had spoken and in doing so lost count and had to start again.

'That goes down into your file,' someone said in the silence.

'To hell with them.' Khorobrov's mouth twitched with anger. 'There are so many things in my file, there's no room for any more.'

Adamson, an engineer in big square spectacles, said from the next bunk:

'We've asked for a Christmas tree, Lieutenant. Are we going to get it?'

'You are.' Nadelashin was plainly delighted to give the news. 'We'll put it here, in this very room.'

'Then can we start making decorations?' Ruska Doronin shouted happily. He sat cross-legged, like a Turk, on his top bunk, knotting his tie in front of a mirror he had propped up on his pillow. In five minutes he would see Clara—she had just crossed the yard, he had watched her from the window.

'We'll have to see about that. There are no instructions.'

'What d'you want instructions for?'

'What's a Christmas tree without decorations?'

'We'll make them!'

'Calm down, boy. What about our hot water?'

'Is the Minister going to do something about it?'

The room was agog with excitement about the Christmas tree. The Duty Officers had turned to go when Khorobrov shouted after them, his harsh voice, with its Vyatka accent, rising above the din:

'And tell them we'll have it for the Orthodox Christmas, the 7th of January. A Christmas tree is for Christmas, not for the New Year.'

They pretended not to hear and left the room. Everyone was talking at once. But Khorobrov hadn't finished what he wanted to say to the officers and sat talking to himself in silence, his lips moving and his face twitching. He had never kept Christmas or Easter but began observing them in prison out of contrariness. There were at least no extra searches or fatigues to mark the religious holidays.

Adamson finished his tea, wiped the steam off his glasses in their plastic frames, and asked him:

'Aren't you forgetting the prisoner's second commandment: *Never lose your temper.*'

Khorobrov gave him a nasty look.

'That commandment is out of date, it was your wretched lot invented it. You kept quiet and a lot of good it did you —they finished you all off.'

This was unfair. Men who had been arrested with Adam-

199

son's lot had organized the strikes in Vorguta, but this was not the moment to explain to Khorobrov. The commandment had been invented by subsequent 'lots'.

Adamson shrugged his shoulders. 'You'll make trouble and they'll send you to one of the camps.'

'And that, Grigory Borisovich, is exactly what I want. To hell with them. At least I'll be in good company. There might even be no informers.'

Late for everything as usual—he had not even had his tea yet—Rubin, his beard unkempt, stood beside Potapov's and Nerzhin's double-tiered bunk, addressing the top one in a friendly voice:

'Happy birthday to you, my young Montaigne, my idiot boy . . .'

'I'm very touched Lev, but you shouldn't . . .'

Nerzhin was kneeling on his bunk, holding a blotter. Obviously the result of a prisoner's private industry, it was the finest quality in the world—since prisoners have no need to hurry. Neatly tucked away inside the dark-red calico cover, were pockets, fastenings, press-studs and packets of best-quality paper 'liberated' in Germany. All the work had, of course, been done in government time.

'. . . besides, there's hardly anything they'll let you write in a special prison except stool pigeon's reports . . .'

'. . . and I wish,' Rubin made a comical face, his thick lips pushed out like a trumpet, 'that your sceptical and eclectic brain may be illuminated by the truth.'

'What kind of truth? Can anyone tell what the truth is?' Nerzhin sighed. His face, rejuvenated by the bustle of preparation for the meeting with his wife, fell back into its ashen folds; the chestnut hair flopped on either side.

On the bunk above Pryanchikov's, a stout, balding, elderly engineer was using his last seconds of leisure to read the newspaper he had taken from Potapov. Holding it spread out wide, he read it at arm's length, occasionally moving his lips, or frowning; when the bell went in the corridor, he crumpled it up and said with annoyance:

'What the hell is all this rubbish about world domination? They go on and on about it.'

From another top bunk, across the room, a hairy giant,

Dvoyetyosov, swung his big clumsy legs over the side and said in a deep bass:

'Don't you want to dominate the world, Zemelya? Aren't you ambitious?'

'Me?' Zemelya sounded surprised as though he had taken the question seriously. 'No-o-o-o!' His face split into a grin. 'What would I do with it?' He grunted and climbed down.

'Well, if that's the case, let's go and work,' Dvoyetyosov decided and jumped to the floor, landing his enormous bulk with a loud thump.

The bell rang for a long time. It called the prisoners to their Sunday work. It told them that roll-call was over and the 'Heavenly Gate' open, through which they milled in a crowd and up the stairs to the laboratories.

Most of them were on their way out. Doronin had run on ahead. Sologdin, who had shut the window for them to get up and have tea, now closed it half-way, wedging it with a volume of Ehrenburg, and hurried into the passage to catch Professor Chelnov as he came out of the 'professors' cell'. Rubin who, as on all other mornings, had managed to get nothing done in time, shoved his uneaten food and unfinished tea into his locker (something overturned inside it) and wrestled to get his lumpy, hopelessly untidy bed sufficiently tidy not to be made to come back from work and do it again.

Nerzhin was looking at his 'fancy dress'. Once upon a time the prisoners had been allowed to wear their own good suits and overcoats and to go visiting in them. They had since been put into denims for the convenience of the warders (so that the men on the watch-towers could tell them easily from the free workers, and know whom to shoot). Now, when they went out, they were made to change into used suits and shirts—as likely as not, once the property of other prisoners, confiscated after their arrest. Some people enjoyed seeing themselves well dressed if only for a few short hours, others would have preferred to do without the grisly business of getting into dead men's suits, but the authorities flatly refused to let them go in their denims—for fear that their families might get a bad impression of life in prisons, and as no one had the heart to give up the chance of a visit, everyone changed.

The semicircular room was nearly empty. There remained twelve sets of double-tiered beds, welded together by their iron frames and made up as in a hospital—sheets turned back over the blankets and left to gather the dust and get grubbier and grubbier. None but an official and a male mind could have thought of such a system—not even the inventor's wife would have applied it at home—but it was enforced by the regulations of the prison Health Inspector.

No one felt like breaking the peaceful silence, so rare in this room. The four people left in it were Nerzhin, who was changing, Khorobrov, Adamson and a bald draughtsman.

The draughtsman was one of those timid prisoners who, even after years in prison, fail to acquire a prisoner's brashness. He would never have had the nerve to stay away from work even on a Sunday, but today he was feeling ill and had taken care to get a doctor's certificate, so now he sat on his bed, his socks, thread and a home-made darning egg beside him, and was trying with furrowed brow to make up his mind where to start.

Adamson, who had served his full sentence of ten years (not to mention six of exile before that) and had been re-arrested and condemned to another ten, didn't actually refuse to work on Sundays but avoided doing so. There had been a time, in his Komsomol days, when wild horses wouldn't have dragged him away from work on a Sunday, but in those far-off days voluntary Sunday work was regarded as a special measure to put the economy on its feet—a year or two and all would be well, every garden would burst into blossom. But now he was one of the few at Mavrino who had served those terrible full ten years and was still there, and who knew that they were not a myth, an aberration of the court, a bad joke, a mistake to be put right by the first general amnesty (all newcomers believed in a general amnesty)—they were a full ten or twelve or fifteen murderous years of a man's life. He had learned to begrudge every physical movement, to make the most of every moment of rest; he knew that the best way to spend a Sunday was lying on one's bed in one's underclothes. Unhurriedly he removed the book Sologdin had used to keep the window open and closed it, took off his denims, got under the blanket, tucked it round him, rubbed his glasses with a special piece of chamois-leather, straightened the pillow and produced from under the mattress a fat little book in a home-made paper wrapper.

By contrast, Khorobrov was bored and restless. Mulling over his dismal thoughts, he lay fully dressed on top of his blanket, his feet on the bedrail. He was by nature inclined to brood long and painfully over things that other people managed easily to shake off. On the well-known principle of voluntary labour, every Saturday, without even being asked, all the prisoners at Mavrino were put down as having volunteered to work on Sunday and the list was sent across to prison HQ. Had it been a genuine choice, Khorobrov would have signed up every week and spent the day happily at his desk. But because the whole thing was a mockery, a blatant piece of bullying, he felt bound to lie down, idle and bored, locked up in the prison block.

The one dream of every inmate of a labour camp is to spend Sunday in bed in a warm, closed room. But in a place like Mavrino it's not the prisoner's back that aches.

There was nothing in the world to do. He had read all the papers there were the day before. A pile of opened and unopened library books lay on the locker by his bed, but Khorobrov didn't feel like reading them. He had tried the current best-seller *Far from Us* but it had turned his stomach. It was an empty shell, a stuffed corpse. The book was a story about the kind of work done by prisoners in camps, but it never mentioned the name of a camp and the prisoners were not prisoners, kept on prison rations and thrown into punishment cells—they were happy young members of the Komsomol, well-fed, well-shod and bursting with enthusiasm. The experienced reader could sense that the author knew, had seen, had known the truth—perhaps he had even been a security officer in a camp—and the reader would know he was cold-bloodedly lying.[1]

There was also a volume of the selected writings of Galakhov, whose literary reputation was at its height. Thinking that he might be different—there must be something to him—

---

[1] With the title slightly disguised, this refers to a hack novel called *Far from Moscow* by Vasily Azhayev published in 1948. It describes the heroic feat of building an oil pipeline in Siberia, but never mentions that it was done by prison labour.

Khorobrov started it but stopped reading with the same feeling of being mocked as he got from the list of Sunday volunteers. Even Galakhov, who could write so prettily about love, had been stricken with mental paralysis and was going down the drain with the ever-swelling crowd of writers who wrote, if not for children, then for morons who had seen and knew nothing of life and were only too delighted to be amused with any rubbish.

Everything that really moves the human heart was absent from their books. Without the war, they could only have been professional stooges. The war had opened up to them a world of simple, human feeling anyone could understand. But even their war heroes were Hamlets torn by impossible, unbelievable conflicts—like the boy in the Komsomol who wrecks dozens of trains behind the enemy lines but belongs to no organized cell and is therefore night and day in torment about whether he can really be a member of the Komsomol, since he isn't paying his membership dues.

The remaining book on the locker was a volume of *American Tales* by 'progressive' writers. Khorobrov had no means of checking how true they were to life, but he was struck by the selection—every single story contained some abomination about America. It was hard to see how there could be one American left who hadn't either emigrated or hanged himself.

There was nothing to read.

Khorobrov thought of lighting a cigarette. He took one out and rolled it between his fingers. Tightly packed, it rustled in the silence. He felt like smoking it here and now, without getting up, without leaving the room. Prisoners who smoke know that the most satisfying cigarette is the one you smoke lying flat, on your own bunk,—the leisurely cigarette you smoke as you gaze at the ceiling and at the passing pictures of your vanished past and your hopeless future.

But the bald draughtsman was not a smoker and disliked the smell of tobacco, while Adamson, who did smoke, held the misguided theory that a room should have fresh air. Firm in the belief that freedom starts with respect for other people's rights, Khorobrov sighed, got up and went to the door. On his way he noticed the thick little book Adamson was reading; he realized at once that there was no such book in the prison library and that therefore it had come from outside, whence no one bothers to bring a bad book.

He did not, however, lose his head and ask, as a greenhorn would have done, 'What are you reading?' or 'Where did you get it?' (the answer could have been heard by Nerzhin or the draughtsman); instead, he came close up to Adamson and said softly:

'Could I look at the title page?'

'All right,' Adamson said reluctantly.

Khorobrov looked at the title, *The Count of Monte Cristo*, and gave a whistle.

'Grigory,' he pleaded. 'Have you promised it to anyone? Could you lend it to me? . . .'

Adamson took off his spectacles and looked thoughtful.

'Let me see. Will you give me a haircut today?'

The prisoners disliked the visiting Stakhanovite barber. Their own master barbers cut their hair to any style and took their time over it—they had plenty of time to spare.

'Who shall we get the scissors from?'

'I'll ask Zyablik.'

'All right.'

'Good. There's a section up to page 128 that comes out. I'll let you have it soon.'

Seeing that Adamson was already at page 110 Khorobrov went out into the passage to smoke in a completely different, brighter mood.

Nerzhin was feeling more and more elated at the thought of seeing his wife. Wherever she was—presumably at the students' hostel at Stromynka—she too must be feeling nervous and excited. He was sure to forget everything he wanted to tell her, he must make a list, destroy the paper (he couldn't take it with him) and keep remembering those eight points—eight of them: that he might be sent away, that after Prison there might be exile, that . . .

He hurried to the store-room to press his false shirt-front. This was an invention of Ruska Doronin's, which had since been adopted by many other prisoners. It was a scrap of white calico (unknown to the store-keeper, a sheet had been cut into thirty-two), with a collar and tapes at the back sewn on to tie it with. Just big enough to cover the prison number stamped on the shirt and showing at the neck of the denims, it was easy to wash, could be worn on weekdays as well as Sundays and made a prisoner feel he needn't be ashamed in front of the free workers.

Sitting on the stairs, Nerzhin struggled in vain to give a gloss to his shoes by rubbing them with a borrowed piece of dry, crumbling shoe polish (special shoes were not issued, as the prisoner would keep his feet out of sight, under the table).

By the time he came back to shave (razors—even cutthroats—were allowed at Mavrino, so unpredictable were the rules), Khorobrov was deep in his book. The draughtsman's mending had overflowed from his bed to the floor where he sat cutting, patching and making pencil marks, while Adamson had moved his head sideways on the pillow and was instructing him:

'Darning, to be any good, must be done conscientiously. God save us from a formalistic approach. Don't hurry, do it carefully stitch by stitch and go over it twice. A common mistake is to use the broken stitches round the edges of the hole. You should cut all round it—no cheeseparing. Have you ever heard of Berkalov?'

'Who? Berkalov? No.'

'Haven't you really? Berkalov was an old artillery engineer, he invented that BO3—a wonderful gun, fantastic velocity. Well, he too was sitting in a special prison one Sunday, darning his socks. The wireless was on and the announcer said: "Berkalov, Lieutenant-General, Stalin Prize, First Class." And Berkalov had only been a major-general before his arrest! Imagine! Well, he finished his darning and started frying pancakes on a forbidden hot-plate. The warder came in, confiscated the hot-plate and went to report him to the governor—three days in the punishment cell. Just then the governor bursts in and says, "Berkalov! Get your things, you're going to the Kremlin, Kalinin has sent for you!"'

'Where else could it happen but in Russia?'

CHAPTER TWENTY-NINE

A familiar figure in many prison research establishments, Professor Chelnov, an old mathematician arrested seventeen years ago and who, when he had to fill in a form, put down his nationality not as 'Russian' but as 'Prisoner', had applied his mind to many inventions, from the direct flow boiler to the jet engine, and had put his heart and soul into several of them.

He claimed, however, that the expression 'To put one's soul into something' should be used sparingly, and that only prisoners were sure of having immortal souls, whereas a man living in the vain bustle of the world outside might well not have one. At Mavrino, Professor Chelnov was the only prisoner who did not have to wear denims (permission had had to be obtained from Abakumov himself). The reason for this privilege was chiefly that Chelnov was only temporarily at Mavrino: a former Corresponding Member of the Academy of Sciences and Director of the Institute of Mathematics, he was kept at the disposal of Beria and sent to whichever special prison had the most urgent problem to solve. As soon as he had solved it in principle and laid down the basic approach, he was moved on.

But Professor Chelnov had not taken advantage of his free choice in the matter of clothes as an ordinary vain person would do. He wore a cheap suit—the colours of the jacket and trousers didn't even match, he wore felt boots and on his head, with its very few remaining grey hairs, he pulled a knitted cap such as a skier or a girl might wear. The most striking feature of his appearance was an eccentric woollen rug wrapped twice round his shoulders, rather like a woman's thick shawl.

The cap and shawl, however, were worn in such a way that instead of making him a figure of fun they added to the majesty of his presence. His long, oval face, sharp profile and masterful manner in addressing the prison authorities, as well as that pale blue light in the faded eyes that

207

goes only with an abstract mind, all made him look strangely like a Descartes or a Renaissance mathematician.

He had been sent to Mavrino to work out the mathematical principles for a foolproof scrambler—a device of which the automatic rotation switched banks of relays on and off, thereby confusing the order in which electrical impulses were sent out and so distorting the sound of human speech over the telephone that not even a hundred monitors equipped with a hundred similar devices would have the slightest chance of unscrambling the conversation.

The actual blue-prints for this device were being prepared in the Design Office, where everybody was working on it except Sologdin.

As soon as he was transferred to Mavrino from one of the labour camps on the River Inta in Siberia, Sologdin announced to all concerned that his mind had been so affected by chronic undernourishment that he was only fit to work in an auxiliary capacity. He could afford to play this bold hand because he had not done manual labour at the Inta Camp but had worked as an engineer, and was therefore not afraid of being sent back there.

He was not sent away—as he might have been—but kept on probation. Instead of being involved with the main project, with its hurry, tension and nervous strain, he thus found himself in a quiet backwater. This meant that he had no status, but at least he was left alone, the supervision was lax, he had plenty of free time and began—secretly, in the evenings—to work independently on a design for the scrambler.

He believed that a great idea can only be generated by a single, enlightened mind.

Indeed, in the past half year he had found a solution which had eluded ten engineers; they had been specially assigned to the job but were continually pressed and harried. Two days ago—still unofficially—he had submitted his design to Professor Chelnov; and now, climbing the stairs with the crowd of prisoners, he respectfully took the professor by the arm and awaited his verdict.

But Chelnov never worked when he was supposed to be resting.

As they covered the short distance down the corridors and up the stairs, not a word did he drop of the judgment so avidly awaited by Sologdin: instead, he told him with a smile about his morning walk with Rubin. After he had been stopped from joining the woodcutters, Rubin had recited a poem he had composed on a biblical subject. Here and there the metre was a little lame, but there was a certain freshness about the rhymes and on the whole it had to be admitted that the poem wasn't bad. It was a ballad about how, for forty years, Moses led the Jews through the wilderness amidst privations, thirst and hunger and how the people furiously protested and rebelled, but they were wrong, and Moses, who knew that in the end they would come to the promised land, was right. There was no doubt that Rubin felt strongly on the subject and had put a special meaning into his poem.

Chelnov's reactions had been to draw his attention to the geography of the region: from the Nile to Jerusalem was three hundred miles at most, so that, even resting on the Sabbath, they could easily have covered the distance in three weeks! Wasn't it therefore to be supposed that for the rest of the forty years Moses had not so much led them as misled them?

The free worker on duty outside Yakonov's office handed Chelnov the key to his room. Only the Man in the Iron Mask enjoyed a similar privilege. No other prisoner was allowed to spend even a moment in his work-room without a free worker to watch him, for it was a principle of security that he would use any such moment to break into the steel safe with his pencil and photograph the secret documents inside with a camera concealed in his trouser button.

But Chelnov worked in a room in which there was nothing but a cupboard and two plain chairs. So it was decided (naturally, after due consultation with the Ministry) to allow the professor the use of his own key. Ever since that day the room had been a source of perpetual worry to the Security Officer, Major Shikin. At night, when the prisoners were safely locked away behind their double steel doors, this highly paid officer, with no fixed hours of work, would go into the professor's room, tap the walls, dance up and down on the floor-boards and peer into the dusty space between the wall and the cupboard, feeling in his bones that no good would come of this exception to the rules.

But getting the key was not all. Past the first four or five doors along the corridor on the second floor, there was a check-point. It consisted of a locker and a chair. A charwoman sat on the chair—not an ordinary charwoman who sweeps floors and boils water for tea (there were others to do that) but one with a special function: to check passes to the Top Secret Section. The passes—weekly, permanent or for one visit only—were printed by the Ministry's own press to a design by Major Shikin (the idea itself of making the dead-end of the corridor top secret had also been his).

Check-point duty was exacting: few people passed through and it was strictly forbidden to knit socks—both by the regulations on the wall and repeatedly by the major in person. So the charwomen (two of whom divided the twenty-four hours between them) struggled desperately to keep awake. The check-point was also a great nuisance to Colonel Yakonov who was pestered all day long to sign passes.

But there the check-point was. And to meet the expense of the charwomen's wages, only one handy-man (Spiridon) was kept instead of the three provided for in the budget.

Although the woman on duty that morning was the one who let Chelnov through every day, and Chelnov knew perfectly well that her name was Maria Ivanovna, she started up and said:

'Your passes.'

Chelnov produced his cardboard one and Sologdin his paper slip.

After the check-point there were two more doors; then the boarded-up back entrance to the private quarters of the Man in the Iron Mask. After that came Chelnov's office.

This was a cosy little room with a single window looking out on the prisoners' small exercise yard and the grove of century-old lime trees. Abundant frost still covered their high crowns.

A dull white sky cast its light upon the earth.

To the left of the lime trees, beyond the compound, stood a two-storied timber house with a boat-shaped roof, grey with age but now as white as the trees, where the owner of Mavrino had lived while his new stone house was being built. Beyond it were the low roofs of the small village, then a rolling field, and further still, along the line of the railway, bright silver puffs of engine smoke showed clearly in the dull white morning, although the engine itself and the carriages could barely be seen.

But Sologdin hardly noticed the view. Refusing a chair, he leaned against the window-frame and stood, tall, graceful, feeling his strong young legs under him and devouring the roll of papers on Chelnov's desk with his eyes.

Chelnov sat down in his hard armchair with its tall straight back, adjusted the rug round his shoulders, opened his notebook at a page of notes, picked up a long pencil sharpened to a point like a spearhead and looked severely at Sologdin. Immediately, the bantering tone of their conversation of a few moments ago changed abruptly.

Sologdin listened to what seemed to him like the beating of great wings in the small room. Chelnov spoke for less than two minutes, but so concisely that there was no time to draw breath between one idea and another.

Chelnov had done more than Sologdin had asked. He had worked out a preliminary estimate of the theoretical and mathematical possibilities of Sologdin's design. It promised a result not far from the one required—at any rate until the switch could be made to fully electronic equipment. It was still, however, essential:

(a) to work out how the device could be made insensitive to low-energy impulses;
(b) to ensure maximum flywheel momentum.

'And then'—his eyes beamed at Sologdin—'don't forget: your encoding system is based on the random principle, that's good—but randomness, once adopted and stabilized, itself becomes a system. It would be still more effective to evolve a solution by which the randomness is subject to random change.'

He folded his sheet of notes in two and paused thoughtfully.

As for Sologdin, he had closed his eyes as though against a bright light, and stood, unseeing.

He had felt a thrill at Chelnov's first words. Now he pressed his side and shoulder hard against the window-frame as if, in his joy, he might quite easily soar to the ceiling.

. . . What good had he been, what had he achieved before his arrest? An engineer? More of a kid, one who thought of nothing but his good looks and who, in fact, was jailed for five years by a jealous rival.

Then came Butyrki, Krasnaya Presnya, the North-Urals Camp, Ivdel Camp, Kargopol Camp . . .

There was the camp interrogation prison in a cave hollowed out of the mountain.

And there was Camp Security Officer, Lieutenant Kamyshan, who for eleven months groomed him for his second sentence—ten years more. In deciding on how many second sentences to hand out, Kamyshan didn't worry about the number allocated by the Administration—he went after all those whose first sentences were short, or who were held by 'special order' for the duration of the war only. Nor did he rack his brains for long over the charge. Someone said to someone else that the Hermitage had sold a painting to the West—each got ten years.

And there was a woman mixed up in it again—a nurse, a prisoner, on whose account Kamyshan, a handsome, fresh-faced Casanova, was jealous of Sologdin. (He had reason to be jealous. To this day, Sologdin remembered her with such physical pleasure that he only half regretted paying for her with a second term of imprisonment.)

Kamyshan enjoyed hitting people with a stick across the lips, so that their teeth came tumbling out with their blood. On days when he rode into the camp (he had a good seat on a horse) he used the handle of his whip.

It was wartime. Even outside, everything was rationed. As for the camp . . . And the cave . . . conditions were indescribable.

Sologdin had not signed anything—he had learned that from his interrogation before his first sentence. But he was sentenced all the same, and for a longer term—ten years. He was taken straight from the courtroom to the hospital. He was dying. Bread, gruel, soup, nothing was any good to his doomed body. There came the day when they rolled him on to a stretcher and brought him to the morgue, to crack his skull with a big wooden mallet before hauling him off to the cemetery. Just then he moved.

That was where he had come from and—such is the recuperative power of life—through years of work in the quiet of the technicians' hut at Inta, he had risen to be—what? How had it happened? Who was the man to whom this Descartes in his knitted cap was saying all those flattering things?

Chelnov folded his page of notes in four, then in eight.

'So you see, there's still a lot to be done. But your solution is the best that will come up. It will get you your freedom. And the cancellation of your sentence.'

He smiled at a private joke—a smile as sharp and thin as his face.

He was smiling at himself. He who, at various times and in various special prisons had achieved far more than Sologdin would achieve now, had not the slightest prospect of freedom or of a pardon—in fact there was no verdict to cancel: one day he had said of the Wise Father that he was a filthy snake, and for seventeen years he had sat in prison without trial, without sentence, without hope.

With a flash of his blue eyes, Sologdin drew himself up and said a little pompously:

'Vladimir Yerastovich! You have given me strength and confidence. I cannot find words to thank you. I shall always be in your debt!'

But an absent-minded smile was already playing on his lips.

Giving him back his roll of drawings, Chelnov remembered something else:

'But I'm afraid I let you down. You asked me not to show this to Yakonov, but he happened to come in while I was out of the room, and of course unrolled it, and realized at once what it was. I had to give away your name.'

The smile left Sologdin's lips. He frowned.

'Is it so important to you?' Chelnov's features altered very slightly to express his astonishment. 'Why? A day sooner, a day later....'

Sologdin himself didn't quite know why. He lowered his eyes. Wasn't it about time to take the drawing to Yakonov?

'How shall I put it. . . . Isn't there perhaps a certain moral ambiguity? . . . It's not as if it were a bridge, or a crane or a lathe. Our assignment is not for something of

213

great importance to industry—it's more like making a gadget for the boss. And when I think of this particular "customer" picking up the receiver we'll make for him. . . . Well, anyway, so far I've been working on it just . . . to test my strength. For myself.'

He looked up.

'For myself.' Chelnov knew all about this kind of work. As a rule it was research of the highest order.

'But . . . in the circumstances . . . Is this a luxury you can afford?'

His gaze was calm and distant.

Sologdin smiled. 'Forgive me,' he pulled himself together. 'I was only thinking aloud. Please don't blame yourself for anything. I'm infinitely grateful.'

He gave Chelnov's frail, thin hand a respectful clasp and left with his roll under his arm.

He had entered the room a moment ago as a supplicant, but free of responsibilities.

Now he was leaving it, burdened with the weight of victory. He was no longer master of his time, of his intentions or of his work.

Chelnov closed his eyes and, without leaning back, sat for a long time, erect, thin-faced, in his knitted wool cap.

CHAPTER THIRTY

Still inwardly rejoicing, Sologdin flung open the door with unnecessary force and strode into the design office, but instead of the crowd he had expected to find in this large room with its constant buzz of voices, he saw only one substantial figure of a woman near the window.

'Alone, Larisa?' Sologdin asked in surprise. He walked briskly across the room.

Larisa Yemina, a draughtswoman of about thirty, turned round from her drawing-board by the window and smiled over her shoulder at Sologdin as he approached.

'Dmitry? Oh, good. I thought I'd be here by myself all day, and that would have been so boring.'

There was something faintly suggestive in the way she

214

said this, and Sologdin's attention sharpened. With a swift glance over her large figure in its bright-green knitted skirt and jacket, he marched past her, went to his desk without a word and at once, before sitting down, made a small tick on a sheet of pink paper. Then almost turning his back on Yemina, he pinned a drawing to his board.

The design office was a large sunny room on the third floor with three big windows facing south. In addition to some ordinary office desks there were a dozen-odd drawing-boards, some set up almost vertically, some tilted, some horizontal. Sologdin's drawing-board was near the far window, where Yemina also sat. His board, fixed in a vertical position, was so placed as to shield Sologdin completely from the prison staff and from the door, but to allow the light to fall directly on the drawings pinned to it.

Finally Sologdin grunted:

'Why is no one here?'

'I thought you would know that,' she replied sweetly.

Jerking his head towards her he said sarcastically:

'I only know where the four wretched prisoners are who work in this room. One has been called to a meeting. Hugo has a free day because it's the Latvian Christmas. I am here, and Ivan has been given permission to darn his socks, of which in the past year he has managed to accumulate twelve pairs. Now you tell me—where are the sixteen free workers, who are supposed to be so much superior to us?'

He was in profile to Yemina and she could plainly see the amused smile between his trim little moustache and his neat goatee, and the sight thrilled her.

'Didn't you know that our major came to an arrangement with Yakonov last night, so today the design office has a free day? Just my luck to be on duty.'

'A free day?' Sologdin frowned. 'What for?'

'What for? Because it's Sunday.'

'Since when has Sunday been a free day?'

'Well, the Major said we had no urgent work at the moment.'

Sologdin turned sharply towards Yemina.

'No urgent work?' he exclaimed, almost in anger. 'Really? No urgent work, indeed!' A tremor of impatience flickered across Sologdin's lips. 'Suppose I arrange things so that as from tomorrow *all sixteen* of you have to sit here copying night and day? How would you like that, eh?' Out of malicious delight he almost shouted the words 'all sixteen'.

Undismayed by the prospect of being made to copy night and day, Yemina retained the equanimity which so matched her ample charms. So far today she had not even removed the sheet of tracing paper which covered her slightly tilted drawing-board. Comfortably leaning her elbows on it (the tight-fitting sleeves of her knitted jacket greatly emphasized the fleshiness of her arms) and rocking almost imperceptibly backwards and forwards she fixed Sologdin with her amiable, wide-eyed stare:

'God forbid! You wouldn't do anything so unkind, would you?'

With a cold look Sologdin asked:

'How can you use the word "God"? Isn't your husband in the MGB? What would he say if he heard you?'

'Oh, he wouldn't mind,' said Yemina in surprise. 'We bake Easter cakes at Easter, too. What of it?'

'Easter cakes? You don't!'

'We do!'

From where he stood Sologdin looked down on Yemina. She was wearing a knitted suit of bold, vivid green, its tight skirt and jacket showing off her well-covered body. The jacket was unbuttoned, the collar of a white lawn blouse outside it.

Sologdin made a tick on the pink sheet of paper and said with hostility:

'But didn't you say your husband was a lieutenant-colonel?'

'What if he is? As far as he's concerned, my mother and I don't know any better—to him we're just a couple of peasant women,' said Yemina with a disarming smile. Her thick ash-blond braids were coiled round her head like a splendid coronet. When she smiled she really did look like a peasant woman, or rather like an actress playing a peasant woman.

Without replying Sologdin sat down sideways at his desk, so as to avoid seeing Yemina. Frowning, he began to study a drawing.

Sologdin was still under the spell of Professor Chelnov's praise. He felt buoyantly happy and did not want to spoil the mood. His brainchild's lack of sensitivity to low-energy impulses and the question of the correct amount of flywheel inertia Sologdin knew intuitively to be problems which could be solved, although he would naturally have to double-check all his calculations. But Chelnov's parting remark about the problem of random selection disturbed him. This had not implied that there was anything basically wrong with his approach, merely that he was still far from the ideal. At the same time he sensed vaguely that somewhere in his work there was a tiny missing factor which both he and Chelnov had failed to detect. It was vital to make the most of this sabbath calm in order to find out what that missing factor was and put it right. Only then could he show his work to Yakonov and use it to earn his release.

For this reason he determined to stop himself thinking about Yemina and return to the train of thought started in his mind by Professor Chelnov. Yemina had been sitting next to him for six months now but somehow they had never talked to each other for long, and they had never before been alone together in a room as they were now, although Sologdin used occasionally to tease her when he allowed himself a five-minute break from work. Professionally merely his assistant, socially his superior—since he was nothing more than an educated helot—Larisa amused him, though he found the constant sight of her generous body distracting.

Sologdin looked at his drawing and Yemina, still rocking gently back and forth on her elbows, looked back at him. Suddenly she asked in a loud voice:

'Who darns *your* socks, Dmitry?'

Sologdin's eyebrows rose.

'My socks?' He went on looking at his drawing. 'Ivan wears socks because he's still a new boy. He hasn't done three years yet. Socks are just a hangover from what we call . . .'—here he faltered, as he was obliged to use a non-Russian word—'er. capitalism. I don't wear socks.' He made a tick on a white sheet of paper.

'What do you wear, then?'

'You are going too far, Larisa.' Sologdin could not help smiling. 'I wear the pride of our national costume—foot-cloths.'

He said the words with relish.

'But I thought . . . only soldiers wore them.'

'Apart from soldiers there are two sorts of people who wear them—prisoners and peasants.'

'But even foot-cloths need washing and mending.'

'Wrong again. Who bothers to wash foot-cloths? We just wear them for a year without washing them and then throw them out and get issued with new ones.'

'Really? Seriously?' Yemina looked almost frightened.

Sologdin gave a carefree, boyish laugh.

'Well, some people do, anyway. Besides, how can I afford socks? How much do you earn as a draughtswoman working for the MGB?'

'Fifteen hundred a month.'

'There you are!' Sologdin exclaimed triumphantly. 'Fifteen hundred! And I, an engineer, get thirty miserable roubles a month. There's not much left out of that to spend on socks, believe me.'

Sologdin's eyes shone, and although it was not she who was the cause of his high spirits, Yemina blushed.

Larisa's husband was, in plain language, a boor. He had long since treated his family as nothing better than a cushion, while his wife regarded him as a piece of furniture. When he came home from work he would dine long and well, then sleep for a while. Later, sucking his teeth, he would read the newspapers and twiddle the knobs of his radio. Occasionally he would sell it and buy a more up-to-date one. The only thing that made him excited—even passionate—was a football match. Because of his job he naturally supported the MVD team, Dynamo. In everything else he was so dim, so boring that he left Larisa completely cold, and the rest of the men she knew were not much better—they could do nothing but talk shop, play cards, drink themselves purple in the face and then paw her and slobber all over her.

She found Sologdin—brisk, intelligent, witty, with his unpredictable shifts from seriousness to irony—very attractive, although he did nothing to encourage her and obviously didn't care about the effect he had on her.

He turned back to his drawing. Larisa went on looking at his face; she stared at his moustache, his little beard, his moist lips. She wanted to be pricked and rubbed by his beard.

'Dmitry,' she again broke into his silence, 'am I disturbing you?'

'Yes, a little,' replied Sologdin. That missing factor demanded deep, undisturbed thought, but this woman was annoying him. Sologdin swung round from the drawing to his desk, thereby turning to face Yemina, and began shuffling some papers.

He could hear the faint tick of her wrist-watch.

A group of people passed down the corridor, talking in subdued voices. From Number Seven next door came the sound of Mamurin's slightly lisping voice saying: 'When are we going to get that transformer back?' and Markushev's irritated retort: 'You shouldn't have given it to them!'

Larisa put her hands in front of her, clasped them, rested her chin on them and from this position aimed a melting stare at Sologdin.

He read on.

'All day long, every day,' she said in a reverent near-whisper, 'you work so hard, even in prison. You're an extraordinary man, Dmitry.'

'What if I am in prison? I've been in prison since I was twenty-five and by the time I get out I shall be forty-two. Not that I ever shall get out, though. They're bound to increase my sentence. And the prime of my life will have been spent in prison camps. It goes against my pride to knuckle under altogether.'

'You're so methodical!'

'I spent seven years of my sentence on rotten prison soup, which meant doing mental work without sugar or phosphorous. This forced me to follow a very strict routine. In prison or out, it makes no difference. A man has to school himself to develop unshakeable will-power and subordinate it to his reason.'

With her carefully manicured index finger, its round little nail painted raspberry-red, Yemina went on aimlessly and unsuccessfully smoothing down the wrinkled corner of the sheet of protective tracing-paper. With her head almost completely lowered on her clasped hands so that the plaited crown of her thick braids was turning towards him, she said thoughtfully:

'I owe you an apology, Dmitry. . . .'

'What for?'

'Once when I was standing at your desk I looked down and saw that you were writing a letter. . . . Well, you know how it can happen, quite by chance. . . . And then another time . . .'

'You took another peep—quite by chance?'

'. . . I saw you were still writing a letter and it seemed to be the same one.'

'So you could tell it was the same one, could you? And there was a third time, wasn't there?'

'Yes, there was.'

'I see. If this goes on, Larisa, I shall have to dispense with your services as a draughtswoman. Pity, because you don't draw badly.'

'But that was a long time ago. Since then you've stopped writing.'

'So I suppose you at once reported me to Major Shikinidi?'

'Why do you call him "Shikinidi"?'

'Well, Shikin. Did you report me?'

'How could you think that!'

'I don't have to think. It's true, isn't it, that Major Shikin told you to inform on me? He told you to watch what I did, what I said, even what I thought, didn't he?' Sologdin picked up his pencil and made another tick on the white sheet. 'He did tell you, didn't he? Be honest.'

'Yes . . . he did . . .'

'And how many unfavourable reports have you written?'

'But I couldn't do such a thing, Dmitry! And against *you* of all people. On the contrary, I have always been extremely complimentary about you.'

'H'm. Well, for the moment we'll take you at your word. But my warning still stands. It was obviously a harmless piece of purely feminine curiosity and I will satisfy it for you. It was in September. I spent nearly five days in succession writing a letter to my wife.'

'That's what I wanted to ask you. Have you got a wife? Is she waiting for you? Do you always write her such long letters?'

'I have a wife,' Sologdin replied slowly and reflectively, 'but somehow it's as if she had ceased to exist. I can't even manage to write to her any longer. When I did write to her my letters weren't long—I merely spent so long polishing and rewriting them. Letter-writing is a very difficult art. We often write letters much too carelessly and then we're surprised when people grow away from us. My wife hasn't seen me for years but she felt I was there. Letters have been the only link, my only means of keeping her for twelve years.'

Yemina jerked forward, sliding her elbows right up to the edge of Sologdin's desk and clasping her blushing face in her hands.

'Are you sure you can keep her? And *why* try to keep her, Dmitry, *why*? Twelve years have gone by and you've another five more to serve—seventeen altogether. You're stealing the best years of her life! Why do it? Let her live!'

In a measured voice Sologdin said:

'There is a special race of women, Larisa. They are the kind who waited for their Viking husbands to return, they are like Isolde, their faithfulness was as true and as bright as a gem. Life has been so easy for you that women like that are quite outside your ken. . . .'

'Let her live!' Larisa repeated. 'And live *yourself* while you can.'

She was no longer the *grande dame* who sailed majestically along the corridors and stairways of the prison; now, she was straining over Sologdin's desk, breathing hard and audibly. Her flushed face made her look even more like a peasant woman than ever.

Sologdin glanced at her and put another tick on the pink sheet.

'And another thing, Dmitry—for weeks I've been longing to know why you make those ticks, then cross them out a few days later. What does it mean?'

'I'm afraid you're prying again.' He picked up the white sheet. 'I make these ticks every time I use a foreign word without any real need. The total number of ticks show how far I am from my goal. When I used the word "capitalism" just now, for instance, instead of "the rule of usuary", or when in the heat of the moment I was too lazy to use "tale-bearing" instead of "informing", I gave myself two ticks.'

'And what about the pink sheet?'

'So you've noticed I keep a pink sheet too, have you?'

'You tick it more often than the white sheet. Does that also show how far you are from your goal?'

'Yes, it does,' said Sologdin abruptly. 'I use the pink sheet to give myself penalty marks and then I punish myself according to how many there are.'

'Penalty marks? What for?' she asked quietly.

'Have you noticed *when* I make these ticks?'

There was not a sound in the room and Larisa replied softly in a voice that was no more than a sigh:

'Yes, I have.'

Sologdin blushed and reluctantly confessed:

'I put a tick on the pink sheet every time your closeness becomes too much to bear, every time I . . . want you.'

Larisa's cheeks, ears and neck flushed scarlet. She did not move from the edge of his desk and looked him boldly in the eyes.

Sologdin was furious.

'Now I shall have to put down three marks at once—look! One for the brazen look you're giving me and the fact that I like it, two because your blouse isn't buttoned properly and I can see your breasts and three because I want to kiss your neck!'

'Well, kiss it,' she said, now quite mesmerized.

'You must be crazy! Get out, leave me alone!'

She recoiled from Sologdin's desk and jumped up. Her chair fell back with a crash.

He turned away towards his drawing-board. The obsession which he had tried to exorcize by chopping wood every morning was now overwhelming him, and he stared unseeingly at the drawing-board. Suddenly he felt her ample breast touch his shoulder.

'Larisa!' he said sternly, turning his head round towards her. In doing so he found himself face to face with her.

'What?' she breathed.

'Let me, I'm . . . I'm going to lock the door,' he said.

Without moving aside she answered:

'Yes, lock it.'

CHAPTER THIRTY-ONE

Like everyone else, none of the free workers in the prison felt in the mood to work on Sundays. Without the usual rush-hour crowds on the bus the journey to work was comparatively leisurely, and they would spend it calculating how to sit around until six in the evening without really working. This Sunday, though, seemed even busier than a weekday. At about ten in the morning three very long, sleek cars drove up to the main gates. The sentry at the guardhouse saluted. The cars went through the gates, past Spiridon the red-haired handy-man, staring at them as he leaned on his broom, along the driveways cleared of snow and up to the main entrance of the prison. Several high-ranking officers, epaulettes flashing with gold, got out of the three cars. Without waiting to be met the party at once strode up to Yakonov's office on the third floor, so fast that no one had time to take a proper look at them. In some of the laboratories a rumour got round that the Minister himself, Abakumov, had come with eight generals, while in others people just worked calmly on, unaware of the impending thunderstorm.

The rumour was half true—only it was Sevastyanov the Deputy Minister who had come, with four generals. But something unprecedented had happened: Colonel Yakonov was not at work yet. Slamming the drawer of his desk in which he was surreptitiously reading a book the frightened Duty Officer rang Yakonov's flat and then reported to the Deputy Minister that Colonel Yakonov was at home following a heart attack, but that he was dressing and would soon be on his way. Meanwhile Yakonov's deputy, Major Roitman, a thin man whose uniform tunic was nipped in at the waist, adjusted his ill-fitting Sam Browne belt, tripped over the carpet (he was very short-sighted), hurried away from the Acoustics Laboratory and reported to his superiors. He was hurrying not only because regulations decreed that he should, but also in order to defend the interests of the opposition movement within the prison, which he headed. As a rule, Yakonov always tried to prevent Roitman from talking to representatives of higher authority. Already aware of the reason why Pryanchikov had been called out to the Ministry in the middle of the night, Roitman hastened to try and mend the situation and convince this high-ranking deputation that the situation with the scrambler was not as hopeless, as say, with the speech-clipper. Although he was only thirty, Roitman had already won a Stalin Prize and he had shown no hesitation in committing his laboratory to the exciting but hazardous work that came directly under the aegis of the All-Highest.

Of the dozen-odd visitors who began to listen to him, only two had a vague idea of the technical side of the matter and the rest merely tried to look dignified. Mamurin, pale and stammering with fury, was called for by Oskolupov and managed to arrive shortly after Roitman, in time to defend the clipper and announce that it was *almost* ready to be released. Soon afterwards Yakonov himself arrived, with hollow, staring eyes and a face so pale it was almost blue, and sank into a chair by the wall. The talk gradually lost all coherence, until there was such confusion that no one could see any way of saving the entire project from certain doom. What was more, as ill-luck would have it, the two men who were respectively the heart and the conscience of the place—the Security Officer, Major Shikin, and the Party Representative, Comrade Stepanov—had succumbed to a perfectly natural weakness not to come to work that Sunday, not to preside over the prison as they did on weekdays—a step all the more pardonable when one remembers that if Party educational work is being done properly, the presence of the actual leaders at the place of work is by no means essential. Alarm and awareness of his sudden responsibility seized the Duty Officer. At great personal risk he left his telephone, ran round the laboratories and whispered the news of the arrival of these important visitors to the men in charge so that they would be on the alert. Being very excited, however, and in a hurry to get back to his telephones he paid no attention to the locked door of the design office. He also failed to call on the Vacuum Laboratory, where Clara Makarygin was on duty alone and all the rest of the free staff were absent. In their turn the heads of laboratories said nothing aloud—they could hardly order their staffs to look busy just because a party of high-ups had arrived—but they went round all the desks and warned each individual in an embarrassed whisper.

The whole prison sat and waited for the generals to appear. After holding a consultation, some of the important visitors stayed in Yakonov's office and others went to Number Seven. Only Sevastyanov and Major Roitman went down to Acoustics. In order to dodge this new chore, Yakonov had proposed the Acoustics Laboratory as a convenient place to carry out Ryumin's instructions.

'How do you think you can identify this man?' Sevastyanov asked Roitman on the way. Roitman had been unable to give it any real thought, because he had only heard of the assignment five minutes ago; Oskolupov had done all the thinking for him the previous night, when he had gaily taken on this commitment. However, in those five short minutes Roitman had managed to concoct a plausible reply:

'Well, you see,' he said, addressing the Deputy Minister by his name and patronymic without a hint of servility, 'we have a device for reproducing visible speech—VISP for short —which turns out what are called "voice-prints" and one of our men by the name of Rubin can read these voice-prints.'

'A prisoner?'

'Yes. He was an assistant professor of philology. Recently I've had him busy looking for individual speech characteristics in voice-prints. And I hope that when we translate that telephone conversation into voice-prints and then compare it with the voice-prints of the suspects . . .'

'H'm . . . we shall have to clear this philologist with Abakumov,' said Sevastyanov, shaking his head.

'For security reasons?'

'Yes.'

Meanwhile although everyone in the Acoustics Laboratory knew that the chiefs had arrived, they still found it impossible to overcome the deadening inertia of idleness, so they put up a front, idly rummaging in drawers full of radio valves, flicking through diagrams in magazines and yawning out of the window. Of the free workers, the girls had drifted into a little group and were gossiping in whispers, until Roitman's assistant dispersed them. Fortunately for her,

Simochka was not on duty—she had a free day in return for an extra day's work and was thus spared the anguish of seeing Nerzhin dressed up and beaming in anticipation of a visit from the woman who had more right to him than she had.

Nerzhin felt in a birthday mood; he had already wandered into Acoustics for the third time without having any reason to be there, from sheer nervousness while waiting for the long overdue Black Maria. He had not sat in his own chair but on the window-sill, pleasurably inhaling the smoke from a 'Belomor' and listening to Rubin. Because Rubin regarded Professor Chelnov as an unsuitable audience for his poem about Moses, he was now reading it, quietly but intently, to Nerzhin. Rubin was no poet. He had never been much good at rhyming or handling metre, but he occasionally managed to knock out some verse which meant something and which had the ring of sincerity. Just now Rubin very much wanted Nerzhin to compliment him on his poem about Moses.

Rubin could not live without friends. He suffocated without them. He found loneliness so intolerable that he could not even allow an idea to mature before hastening to share every half-baked notion with someone else as soon as it crossed his mind. All his life he had never lacked friends, but in prison it seemed to be his fate that his friends did not share his outlook, while those who did were not his friends.

Nobody in Acoustics was doing any work except for the unfailingly cheerful and industrious Pryanchikov, who had managed to banish his memories of night-life in Moscow and of his grotesque visit to the Ministry. He was thinking about a new improvement in a circuit and crooning to himself.

Just then Sevastyanov and Roitman came in. Roitman was saying:

'In these voice-prints speech is measured simultaneously in three dimensions: in frequency—across the tape, in time—along the tape, and in volume—by the density of the trace. By this means each sound is recorded as a unique shape that can be easily identified. Whatever has been said can be read off the tape. Here . . .'—he led Sevastyanov towards the far end of the laboratory—'. . . is the VISP apparatus. It was designed in our laboratory' (Roitman had already forgotten the extent to which the design had been borrowed) 'and this . . .'—he carefully steered the Deputy Minister towards the window—'. . . is Assistant Professor Rubin, our philologist, the only person in the Soviet Union who can read visible speech.'

Rubin silently rose and bowed.

Rubin and Nerzhin had already caught the word 'voice-print' when Roitman had spoken it coming through the door and they had pricked up their ears: their work, which so far most people had regarded as a joke, was about to emerge into the light of day. During the forty-five seconds that it took Roitman to bring Sevastyanov to Rubin, with the sharpness of perception and quick reactions peculiar to prisoners Nerzhin and Rubin had already grasped that there was to be a demonstration of Rubin's ability to read voice-prints, that only one of the regular speakers could read a sentence into the microphone—and that the only one of these in the room was Nerzhin. Both realized, too, that although Rubin really could read voice-prints, he might easily make a mistake during a test—and this he could not afford to do, because it would mean relegation from the special prison back to the hell of the camps. They conveyed all this to each other in one meaningful exchange of looks.

Rubin whispered:

'If they pick on you to read a sentence, say: "Voice-prints enable deaf people to talk on the telephone." '

Nerzhin whispered:

'If I have to read a sentence chosen by him you'll genuinely have to decipher the sounds. If I smooth back my hair, you're getting it right—if I straighten my tie, you're wrong.'

In his hesitant, carefully modulated voice, which even to someone who could not see him would have branded him as an intellectual, Roitman went on:

'And now Rubin will show you what he can do. One of the speakers—let's say Nerzhin here—will read out a sentence inside the soundproof booth, the VISP will record it and Rubin will try and decipher it.'

Standing a pace away from the Deputy Minister, Nerzhin gave him a convict's insolent stare.

'Would you like to make up a sentence?' he asked dourly.

'No, no,' replied Sevastyanov politely, avoiding his look. 'Make up a sentence of your own.'

Nerzhin obediently took a sheet of paper, thought a moment and then, as though inspired, wrote something. In the ensuing silence he handed it to Sevastyanov in such a way that neither Roitman nor anyone else could read it: 'Voice-prints enable deaf people to talk on the telephone.'

'Is that really so?' Sevastyanov asked in amazement.

'Yes.'

'Read it, please.'

The VISP began to hum.

Nerzhin went into the booth thinking how shabby its sackcloth covering looked (thanks to the eternal shortage of proper materials) and locked the soundproof door. The mechanism went noisily into action and a wet six-foot length of tape, mottled with what looked like a number of ink blobs and smudgy stains, was delivered on to Rubin's desk.

The whole laboratory stopped 'working' and watched tensely. Roitman was visibly nervous. Nerzhin came out of the booth and observed Rubin impassively from a distance. Everyone was standing up except Rubin, who was seated, his bald head gleaming. To spare the visitors' impatience he made no secret of his arcane skill but at once began making marks on the wet tape with his usual blunt grease-pencil.

'Certain sounds, you see, can be identified without any difficulty, such as accented or open vowels. In the first word there is the diphthong "oi" preceded by a voiced consonant "v"; this could not be the unvoiced equivalent of the same consonant, which is "f". The diphthong appears to be followed by an "s", but this could also be a softened "c" followed by an "e". There is a similar sound at the end of the second word, though if this were preceded by a liquid consonant, such as "n", the final sound could be a double consonant, in this case probably "ts". The second word begins with an unvoiced labial plosive and the likelihood is that it is a "p", followed by a rather faint velar consonant and a clear, short open vowel "i". Thus the first two phonemes seem to constitute the words "voice-prints". Now the next word ends in the voiced labial plosive "b" separated from a velar consonant, either "l" or "r", by the indeterminate vowel sound usually represented in spelling by the unaccented letter "e". Therefore the ending of this third word could be spelt "ble" or "bre", although it is more likely to be "ble" because the "l" sound has a lower frequency than the velar "r". The three sounds preceding it are the open vowel "e", the liquid consonant "n" and the long accented "a". Putting these together we get the word "enable". Now the first sound of the next word could be a "d" or a "t". . . . I'll just find out which it is. . . . Antonina, did you borrow my magnifying glass just now? Could I have it back for a moment, please?'

The magnifying glass was quite unnecessary, as the VISP produced a very broad trace, but it was done, in good prison tradition, as a pure piece of eyewash and Nerzhin laughed to himself as he absentmindedly smoothed down his already immaculate hair. Rubin glanced up at him and took the magnifying-glass. The tension mounted, as no one else knew whether Rubin was reading the trace correctly. Astounded, Sevastyanov whispered:

'It's amazing . . . amazing.'

No one noticed when Senior Lieutenant Shusterman entered the room on tiptoe. He had no right to come in here, so he stopped near the door. Having signalled to Nerzhin to leave the room at once, Shusterman did not follow him out but waited for an opportunity to tell Rubin to go too. He intended to order Rubin to remake his bunk in the regulation manner, a form of harassment of which he was particularly fond.

Meanwhile Rubin had deciphered the word 'deaf' and was working on the fifth word. Roitman was beaming, not only because he was sharing in the triumph but because he was genuinely pleased by any successful piece of work.

Just then Rubin happened to look up and met Shusterman's scowling glare. He realized very well why Shusterman was there and his malicious glance replied, 'Go and make it yourself!'

'The last phrase is "on the telephone". This is a combination we encounter so often that I can recognize it at once. And that's it.'

'Astounding,' said Sevastyanov. 'Forgive me, what is your name?'

'Lev Rubin.'

'Well now, Rubin, tell me—can you distinguish the peculiarities of *individual* voices on these voice-prints?'

'We call that the "individual speech type". Yes. In fact we are working on that in our research at this moment.'

'Excellent! I think we may have a *very* interesting problem for you to solve.'

Shusterman tiptoed out.

CHAPTER THIRTY-TWO

The Black Maria which was due to take the prisoners to their visits had had engine trouble and there had been a delay while telephone calls went back and forth and instructions were given. At about eleven o'clock, when Nerzhin was called out of the Acoustics Laboratory to be 'frisked', the six others who were going on visits were already there. Some were still being searched, others had already gone through it and were waiting around in various attitudes—one slumped over the big table, some pacing the room beyond the barrier. At the barrier itself, near the wall, stood Lieutenant-Colonel Klimentyev, all spit and polish, as stiff and neat as a regular soldier waiting to go on parade. His sleek black moustache and his black hair smelled of eau-dé-cologne. Hands clasped behind his back, he stood looking completely detached; but the very fact that he was there forced the guards to conduct the search properly.

At the barrier Nerzhin was met by the outstretched arms of one of the toughest of the warders, Krasnogubenky, who immediately asked:

'What's in your pockets?'

Nerzhin had long since outgrown that obsequious eagerness which novice prisoners adopted when faced by guards and escorts. He did not bother to reply or hasten to turn out the pockets of the unfamiliar tweed suit. He looked lazily at Krasnogubenky and barely raised his arms from his sides to enable the guard to search his pockets. After five years in prison and innumerable searches of this kind Nerzhin did not feel, as a newcomer would have done, that an injury was being done to him, that dirty fingers were fumbling at his bruised heart. Nothing done to his body could cloud his mood of rising euphoria.

Krasnogubenky opened the cigarette case which Potapov had just given him, squinted down the mouthpieces of all the cigarettes to see if anything was hidden there, poked around among the matches in case they concealed anything and checked the seams of his handkerchief for any contraband sewn into them. He found nothing else in the pockets. Then, feeling between Nerzhin's shirt and his unbuttoned jacket he ran his hands over Nerzhin's entire body to discover whether there was anything concealed under his shirt or between the shirt and the shirt-front. Then he squatted down and with a tight two-handed grip he felt his way up one leg and down the other. As Krasnogubenky went down on his heels Nerzhin had a good view of the engraver pacing nervously up and down, and he guessed why he was so upset. While in prison the engraver had discovered a talent for writing short stories and he wrote about his experiences in prisoner-of-war camps in Germany, about encounters in jail, about court-rooms. He had already smuggled out one or two of these stories through his wife, but who was there for her to show them to once they were outside? In prison or out, they had to be hidden. It was hopeless to try and take out the least scrap of paper with anything written on it. But one old man, a friend of the family, had read them and had told him via his wife that even Chekhov had seldom achieved such mastery. This comment had greatly encouraged the engraver.

For today's visit he had written another short story, in his view a brilliant piece of work; but just as the search began he lost his nerve at the sight of Krasnogubenky and, turning aside, he swallowed the ball of tracing paper on which he had written the short story in microscopic hand-writing. Now he felt torn by remorse at having eaten his story—he might have been able to smuggle it through after all.

Krasnogubenky said to Nerzhin:

'Take your shoes off.'

Nerzhin raised his foot on to a stool, unlaced his shoe and flicked it off his foot without looking where it landed. In so doing he revealed a sock with a large hole. Krasnogubenky picked up the shoe, felt inside it and bent the sole. With the same imperturbable expression, as though this

231

were his everyday behaviour, Nerzhin flicked off the second shoe to reveal another sock with a hole in it. Because the socks had such big holes Krasnogubenky did not suspect that there was anything hidden in them and did not ask for them to be taken off.

Nerzhin put his shoes on again and Krasnogubenky lit a cigarette.

Klimentyev had winced when Nerzhin had kicked off his shoes; it was a deliberate insult to the warder. If the officers did not back up the warders, the prisoners would soon be defying other members of the staff too. Again Klimentyev regretted having shown leniency and almost made up his mind to find an excuse to cancel Nerzhin's visit: this insolent prisoner was not only unashamed of his convict status, but even seemed strangely to enjoy it.

'Pay attention!' he rapped out. Seven prisoners and seven warders turned towards him. 'You know the rules, I suppose? You may not give anything to your relatives or take anything from them. Parcels may only be handed over through me. When talking you will not mention the following subjects: work, working conditions, living conditions, daily routine or the location of the prison. No surnames may be mentioned. About yourselves you may only say that you are well and need nothing.'

'Then what can we talk about?' shouted a voice. 'Politics?'

The question was so patently absurd that Klimentyev did not even bother to reply.

'Talk about your crime,' one of the prisoners grimly proposed, 'and how you repent.'

'Judicial proceedings are secret, so you may not discuss them either,' said Klimentyev imperturbably, rejecting the suggestion. 'You can ask about your family or your children. Now there is one new rule: from now on handshaking and kissing is forbidden.'

Nerzhin, who was completely unaffected both by the search and by the clumsy rules, which he knew how to circumvent, saw red at the mention of the ban on kissing.

'We only see each other once a year . . .' he shouted hoarsely at Klimentyev, who turned expectantly in Nerzhin's direction hoping that the prisoner would compromise himself by a further outburst. Nerzhin could almost hear Klimentyev roar: 'Visit cancelled!'

So he choked back the words.

His visit, which had been announced at the last minute, appeared to be outside his legal entitlement, and therefore easily cancelled. . . . Whenever anyone tried to speak the truth or demand justice, he was always prevented by some consideration such as this. Nerzhin mastered his fury, as a prisoner must.

Encountering no further rebellion, Klimentyev added dispassionately:

'If there is a kiss, a handshake or any other violation, the visit will be terminated at once.'

'But my wife doesn't know about this rule! She will kiss me!' the engraver burst out.

'Your relatives will have been warned.' Klimentyev had foreseen the objection.

'There's never been a rule like this before.'

'Well, there is now.'

(Fools! Why did they make so much fuss? As if he had personally invented the new rule instead of merely repeating his instructions.)

'How long does the visit last?'

'If my mother comes too, will they let her in?'

'The visit lasts for thirty minutes. I shall only admit the one person named on the application.'

'What about my five-year-old daughter?'

'Children up to fifteen are admitted with adults.'

'And if they're sixteen?'

'Not admitted. Any more questions? Proceed to the bus. Outside!'

For some odd reason they were not taken in a Black Maria as usual recently, but in a small-size blue city bus.

The bus stood in front of the staff building. The warders, who were new, and dressed in plain-clothes with velour hats, had their hands in their pockets (holding pistols); they mounted the bus first and took seats in three of the corners. Two of them looked like retired prize-fighters or ex-gangsters. They wore very good overcoats.

The early morning hoar-frost was going, but although the

coldest days of winter were over, the thaw had not yet come.

The seven prisoners entered the bus by its only door and sat down, followed by four uniformed warders. The driver slammed the door and revved up.

Lieutenant-Colonel Klimentyev got into his car.

CHAPTER THIRTY-THREE

That noon Yakonov was not to be found in the plushy silence and gleaming comfort of his office—he was in Number Seven, busy 'marrying-up' the clipper and the scrambler. The idea of combining these two devices had been conceived that morning by the ambitious Markushev, and had been widely approved, although everyone who supported it did so for a special reason of his own. Its only opponents were Bobynin, Pryanchikov and Roitman, but nobody listened to them.

Instead, Yakonov's office was occupied by Sevastyanov (who had already telephoned Abakumov), General Bulbanyuk, a prison officer called Lieutenant Smolosidov and Rubin.

Lieutenant Smolosidov was not an easy man to like. Even on the assumption that every person has some redeeming feature, it would have been hard to find anything good in his cast-iron, unsmiling glance, the sullen, ugly set of his thick lips. He had a very lowly job in one of the laboratories, where he hardly ranked much above a radio fitter and for which he was paid less than two thousand roubles a month, the same as the most junior female employee, although he made up for it by robbing Mavrino of the equivalent of a thousand a month in scarce radio parts and selling them on the black market; everyone knew, however, that Smolosidov's job and income were more considerable than they seemed.

The free workers in the prison, even his friends who played volley ball with him, were afraid of him. His face, in which he could never be induced to show the faintest glimmer of genuine feeling, was terrifying; equally terrifying was the special trust placed in him by higher authority. Nobody knew where he lived, or whether indeed he had a home or family. His colleagues never invited him home and he never spent

234

any of his off-duty time with them. His past, too, was a closed book, except for the three medal ribbons on his chest and the boast he had once let slip that during the war a certain famous marshal had not spoken a word that he, Smolosidov, did not overhear. When asked what he meant, he had replied that he had been the marshal's radio operator.

As soon as the question arose as to who was to be put in charge of the recorder with the tape sent from the Maximum Security Registry, General Bulbanyuk at once named Smolosidov.

At this moment Smolosidov was setting up the tape-recorder on a small varnished table and General Bulbanyuk, whose head was like a huge overgrown potato with excrescences that were his nose and ears, was saying:

'You, Rubin, are a prisoner. But you were once a Communist, and you may be one again.'

Rubin wanted to shout that he still was a Communist, but it was beneath his dignity to argue about this with Bulbanyuk.

'Well now, the authorities have seen fit to place a certain trust in you. You are about to hear a state secret on this tape-recorder. We hope you will help us to track down this criminal, this accomplice of outright traitors who want to give away important scientific discoveries to foreigners. I need scarcely say that any attempt to reveal . . .'

'Of course,' Rubin interrupted him; his greatest fear was that he might not be allowed to go on working with the tape. His own career having long ceased to concern him, Rubin lived only for the higher cause of humanity. Even before he had heard the tape he already felt strongly involved in it.

Smolosidov switched on the tape-recorder.

Rubin stared into the coloured fabric which covered the loudspeaker, as though it might reveal the enemy's face. When Rubin stared so intently his face looked drawn and cruel: no one could expect any mercy from a man with a face like that.

In the hushed office they now heard, through a faint crackle, a conversation between an agitated man and a slightly obtuse lady with an old-fashioned accent.

With every sentence the fierce look gradually disappeared from Rubin's face and gave way to one of puzzlement. This was not at all what he had expected, but something quite preposterous. . . .

The tape came to an end.

They were all waiting for Rubin to say something, but he was completely at a loss.

He needed a little time to think, and without so many people staring at him. He relit his cigarette and said:

'Let's have it again.'

Smolosidov switched the tape-recorder to 'Rewind'.

Rubin hopefully watched his bluish fingers—perhaps he might make a mistake and switch to 'Record' instead of 'Playback', then the whole tape would be erased without trace, and Rubin would be spared the need to pronounce on it.

As Rubin smoked he chewed and crushed the cardboard mouthpiece of his cigarette.

No one spoke.

Smolosidov did not make a mistake, but pressed the correct button. Again they could hear the young man's nervous, almost desperate voice and the old lady's reluctant, grumpy replies. Instead of visualizing the criminal Rubin kept seeing this woman—he could just imagine her with elaborately tinted hair, or a wig perhaps.

He put his hands over his face. The worst of it was that no one in his right mind could regard a medical discovery as a state secret, because medicine that asked a sick man his nationality was not medicine; and on purely human grounds Rubin couldn't help liking this man who had been brave enough to telephone a flat under surveillance, probably without realizing what a risk he was taking.

But objectively, although this man had imagined he was doing good, he was in fact working against the forces of progress. If it was considered part of the vital interests of the state to claim that all scientific discoveries had been pioneered in Russia, then anyone who thought differently was objectively standing in the way of progress and must be swept aside.

Perhaps, too, there was more to this conversation than there appeared to be: the frightened way in which the man had repeated the word 'foreigners' and had spoken of handing over 'something'. Perhaps it wasn't a 'drug' at all—perhaps 'drug' was a code-word for something else. Such things had been known to happen: that signal to the sailors of the Baltic Fleet to join the armed uprising in 1917, for instance, when the words 'Send Articles of War' had meant 'Send ships and landing-party' . . .

The tape came to an end again. As Rubin took his hands away from his face and looked at the sullen Smolosidov and at Bulbanyuk's empty, pompous features, he found them both so repulsive that he had to turn away; yet in this very minor juncture in history it was these two who were objectively the embodiment of progress.

He must rise above his personal feelings. It had been thugs like these two, only from the army's political section, who had put Rubin into prison because he was too clever and too honest for them. And again it had been thugs like this, only from the army legal department, who for four years had rejected appeal after appeal in which Rubin had pleaded his innocence.

But he must rise above his personal misfortune, and although these two deserved to have a hand-grenade thrown at them right here in this room, it was not them to whom Rubin owed allegiance but to his country, to its principles, its flag.

Rubin ground out his cigarette butt and dropped it into the ashtray. Trying to keep his eyes on Sevastyanov, who looked decent enough, he said:

'All right, we'll have a try.' He shuddered and gave a deep sigh, as though drawing breath after a steep climb. 'But I can't identify the person unless you have some suspects. Obviously you can't record the voices of everybody in Moscow. Do you have any voices that I can check it against?'

'We picked up four right beside the telephone booth,' Bulbanyuk hastened to assure him, 'but it's not likely to be one of them. It could have been one of five people in the Ministry of Foreign Affairs. I have written down their names without showing their ranks or what posts they hold, so that you won't hesitate to say who you think it is.'

He handed him a piece of paper from a notebook. It had the following list:

1. Petrov.
2. Syagovity.
3. Volodin.
4. Shchevronok.
5. Zavarzin.

Rubin read it and was going to keep it, but Sevastyanov stopped him sharply. 'No! Smolosidov will keep the list.'

Rubin gave it back. He was more amused than offended by this precaution. Those five names were already branded into his mind. With his trained linguist's memory Rubin had instantly made a mental note of them, and even of the etymology of some of them.

'Please get me tapes of all five talking on the telephone.'

'You shall have them tomorrow.'

Rubin thought for a moment.

'And another thing—give me a note of their ages.' He nodded towards the tape-recorder. 'I shall need that tape all the time, beginning from today.'

'Lieutenant Smolosidov will be in charge of it. You will both be given a separate room in the Top Secret Section.'

'They're getting the room ready now,' said Smolosidov.

Experience had taught Rubin to avoid the dangerous word 'when?', so as not to be asked the same question. He knew that there was enough work here for a week or even two, but if he had asked by when it was needed, they would inevitably say 'tomorrow morning'. So instead he asked:

'Who else can I talk to about this job?'

Sevastyanov exchanged glances with Bulbanyuk and replied:

'Only to Major Roitman, Major-General Oskolupov and to the Minister himself.'

'Do you still remember my warning?' asked Bulbanyuk. 'Or shall I repeat it?'

Rubin stood up without asking permission and screwing up his eyes, looked at the General as though he had difficulty in seeing him.

'I must go and think,' he said to no one in particular.

They made no objection to his leaving the room.

Deep in thought Rubin left the office, went past the Duty

Officer and without looking at anyone walked down the staircase with its red carpet.

He must get Gleb Nerzhin on to this new project. How could he work without being able to discuss it with someone? It was going to be a very tough job, as they had only just started research on classifying and defining voice-types.

As a scholar he felt the first thrill of a new challenge. This was really something quite new—tracing a criminal by his voice-print. So far there had been only fingerprints, a science which had taken a long time to develop. Now there was to be a new technique of 'voice-printing' and it had to be invented in a matter of days.

CHAPTER THIRTY-FOUR

Nerzhin took a window-seat and leaning back on the soft upholstery, enjoyed the gently swaying motion of the bus. Beside him sat Illarion Gerasimovich the optics expert, a short narrow-shouldered man whose markedly intellectual features, right down to the pince-nez, made him look exactly like a spy on a propaganda poster.

'You know, I thought I could stand anything,' Nerzhin said quietly to him. 'I'm quite happy to sit with my bare backside on the snow, I don't mind being cooped up in a prison train with twenty-five people to a compartment, I can even stand the sight of the guards smashing our suitcases. But when they trample on the one live feeling that's left to me—my love for my wife, I just can't take it. To see her for half an hour a year and not be allowed to kiss her! They make you pay for these visits.'

Gerasimovich brought his sparse eyebrows together in a frown. They gave him a doleful air even when he was just poring over diagrams.

'I imagine,' he replied, 'that there is only one way to become immune, and that is to kill all affection and give up all desires.'

Gerasimovich had only been in Mavrino for a few months and Nerzhin had not yet had time to get to know him well, but he had taken a great liking to him.

239

They spoke no more. Being taken to a visit was too great an event in a prisoner's life. The time had come to revive tender feelings usually dormant and forgotten in their living tomb, to summon up memories which had no place in their everyday life, to gather the thoughts and emotions of the past year and many more, ready to fuse them all into those brief minutes of reunion.

The bus stopped at the Mavrino guard-house. A sergeant on duty climbed up the steps, put his head through the door of the bus and twice made a silent count of the prisoners in the party (the chief warder had already signed out seven prisoners). Then he crawled under the bus to make sure no one was clinging on to the chassis, although the Devil himself would have found it impossible to hang on there for more than a minute. Only when the sergeant had returned to the guard-house was the first and then the second gate opened. The bus crossed the magic boundary and with a cheerful hum of tyres sped past the woods along the frost-covered road.

It was due to the top-secret nature of Mavrino that prisoners were driven to another place for their visits. Their relatives were not supposed to know the present whereabouts of these living dead, whether they were being brought in from some place a hundred miles away or from the Kremlin, from the airport or the other world. They were only allowed to see well-fed, well-dressed men with white hands who were no longer very talkative, who smiled sadly and assured them all was well and that they had all they wanted.

These meetings were rather like those scenes depicted on ancient Greek steles, showing both the deceased and the living people who had erected the monument to him. The steles always had a thin line dividing the other world from this. The living looked fondly at the dead, while the dead man looked towards Hades with eyes that were neither happy nor sad but somehow blank—the look of someone who knew too much.

As the bus went up a slight rise Nerzhin looked round for a rare glimpse of the building in which they lived and worked. It was made of dark-red brick, surmounted by a round rust-coloured dome above their handsome semicircular room; above it rose a hexagonal tower. On the south side, which contained the Acoustics Laboratory, Number Seven, the Design Office and Yakonov's office, there were long even rows of permanently shut windows, dull and featureless. Local people and Sunday trippers from Moscow who came out here to the woods would never have guessed at the tangle of broken careers, dashed hopes and thwarted emotion concealed behind the walls of that lonely old house. The whole place was permeated with the spirit of secrecy. People in one room knew nothing of those in the next, close neighbours were ignorant of each other. And then there were the girls. Even the Security Officers did not know everything about the girls—those twenty-two foolish, unthinking women allowed into that grim building as free workers, just as they themselves were unaware (this only heaven and at a later stage, history, could know) that all twenty-two of them had braved the threat hanging over them and flouted the instructions which were constantly being dinned into them, and carried on furtive love affairs or took pity on prisoners and passed messages to their families.

Opening his dark-red cigarette case, Gleb began smoking with that particular pleasure that one gets from a cigarette at moments which are out of the ordinary, and although the thought of Nadya filled his mind at the moment, his body, revelling in the novelty of the journey only wanted it to go on and on. . . . If only time would stop and the bus would just go on and on down this snow-covered road marked with black tyre-tracks, alongside the park with the branches of its trees thick with white hoar-frost, past occasional children. Nerzhin had not heard children's voices since before the war—this was a sound that soldiers and prisoners never heard.

Nadya and Gleb had spent only one year together, in a constant flurry as it was their last year at the university. They had spent it working and taking their final exams. Immediately afterwards war had broken out.

And now other people had these funny little toddlers that were running around. But not Nadya and Gleb. . . .

One little boy started to cross the road, and the driver swerved sharply to avoid him. Frightened, the child stopped and put his hand in its blue mitten to his flushed face. Nerzhin had not given a thought to children for years, but now he suddenly realized that Stalin had robbed him and Nadya of their children. By the time he came out of prison and they were together again, his wife would be nearly forty. This was getting rather late for having a baby.

Dozens more brightly clad children were skating on a pond.

The bus turned into some narrow streets and began to bounce over cobblestones.

Descriptions of prison life tend to overdo the horror of it. Surely it is more frightening when there are no actual horrors; what is terrifying is the unchanging routine year after year. The horror is in forgetting that your life—the only life you have—is destroyed; in your willingness to forgive even some ugly swine of a warder, in being obsessed with grabbing a big hunk of bread in the prison mess or getting a decent set of underwear when they take you to the bathhouse.

This is something that cannot be imagined; it has to be experienced. All the poems and ballads about prison are sheer romanticism; no one need have been in prison to write that sort of stuff. The feel of prison only comes from having been inside for long, long years on end. . . .

In one of her letters Nadya had said: 'When you come back . . .' But the horror was that there was no going back. To *return* was impossible. After four years in the army and a ten-year prison sentence there would probably not be a single cell of his body which was the same. Although the man who came back would have the same surname as her husband, he would be a different person and she would realize that her one and only, for whom she had waited fourteen lonely years, was not this man at all—he no longer existed.

If they fell in love with each other all over again in their new, second life, well and good . . . but suppose they did not? . . .

The streets of the city's outskirts were already passing by the windows. In the confinement of prison it seemed to them from the glow in the night sky that Moscow was a blaze of dazzling light. But here there were just rows of peeling one- and two-storey houses badly in need of repair, with sagging wooden fences. They had probably not been touched since the war as all effort had been put to other ends. What must it be like in the provinces, out in Ryazan or Ruzaevka? What was the state of the houses there?

The bus swung into a broad, busy square in front of one of the stations and drove through the swarming tramcars, trolley buses, cars and people. The police had bright new red and blue uniforms, which Nerzhin had never seen before. . . .

He could not understand how Nadya could have waited so long for him. How could she move among those bustling, insatiable crowds, constantly feeling men's eyes on her—and not waver in her love for him? Gleb imagined that if it had been the other way round—if she were imprisoned and he were free—he would not have held out for as much as a year. Before, he would never have believed his frail little wife to be capable of such rocklike constancy and for a long time he had doubted her, but now he had a feeling that Nadya did not find waiting too difficult.

After six months under arrest he had been allowed to write his first letter to his wife. He had written it from the Krasnaya Presnya transit prison with the stub of a pencil on a torn piece of wrapping paper folded into a triangle:

'My darling,
    You've waited for me through four years of war—don't curse me but it was all for nothing, because you must now wait for ten more years. I shall always remember our year together when we were so happy. But from now on you must be free. There's no reason why your life should be ruined too. Marry someone else.'

But Nadya simply interpreted this letter to mean that he no longer loved her and she wondered how he could possibly think of giving her up to someone else. Even during the war she had managed to make her way to the front line, to the Dnieper bridgehead where he was serving. She had obtained a fake army warrant and had arrived in a man's military tunic that was too big for her, having run the gauntlet of searches and interrogations by Field Security. She had arrived in the hope of being able to stay with her husband till the end of the war, or to die with him if he were killed.

During a lull in the fighting, when the grass had time to

243

grow again in the bridgehead, they snatched back a few brief days of the happiness stolen from them. But the Soviet armies roused themselves and went over to the offensive and Nadya had to go home again, wearing the same ill-fitting tunic and travelling on the same faked travel warrant. A lorry took her down a forest track and for a long, long time she waved back at him. . . .

People were clustered in untidy queues round the bus-stops. Whenever a trolley bus drove up some kept in line, others tried to elbow their way forward. Somewhere on the Sadovy Boulevard their bus, temptingly half-empty, halted at a red traffic light a little beyond a bus-stop and a man frantically chased after it, jumped on to the step, hammered on the door and shouted:

'Do you go to the Arbat? Arbat? . . .'

'Get off! Get off!' A warder waved him away.

'Hop in, we'll take you there!' shouted the glass-blower Ivan, and gave a loud guffaw. (Ivan was a minor offender who was allowed a visit once a month.)

All the other prisoners laughed too. The man could not understand what sort of a bus this was and why he was not allowed to board it. But he was used to things not being allowed and jumped off. Half a dozen other would-be passengers dispersed.

The blue bus turned left along Sadovy Boulevard. This meant that they were not going to Butyrki as usual. They must be going to Taganka instead.

. . . If Nerzhin had not been born in Russia, or if he had not been born when he was, or if he had been a different sort of person he would never have been separated from his wife and he would have spent his life peacefully solving differential equations.

There is a passage in Victor Hugo's *Ninety-Three* where Dantenac is sitting on a dune, from which he can see several church towers at once. All of them are in a great commotion, with every bell ringing the tocsin; but the sound is being carried away from him by a high wind and he can hear nothing at all. In the same way, since boyhood Nerzhin had possessed the strange gift of being able to hear all those mute signals of alarm—the living tocsin of groans, shrieks, shouts and the wailing of the doomed that is for ever borne away out of earshot by a relentless wind. Gleb had managed to grow up without reading any of the usual boys' books, but he had been twelve when he had opened the huge pages of *Izvestiya*, with which he could have covered himself from head to foot, and had read about a trial of some engineers accused of sabotage. The young Gleb did not believe a word of it; he did not know why, he could not give a rational explanation for it, but he saw quite clearly that it was all a pack of lies. Several of his friends' fathers were engineers and he simply could not imagine people like that sabotaging things; their job was building things.

At thirteen and fourteen Gleb did not run out to play after he had done his homework but sat down to read the newspapers. He knew the names and positions of all the Party leaders, all the commanders of the Red Army, all the Soviet ambassadors abroad and all the foreign ambassadors in Moscow. He read all the speeches at Party congresses, all the memoirs of old Bolsheviks and the successive histories of the Party—of which there had been several, all different. In the fourth class at school they were already being told about the rudiments of political economy, and in the fifth grade they had a civics lesson nearly every day. Somebody gave him Lenin's *To the Memory of Herzen* and he read it avidly.

Either because his young mind was still fresh or because he read other things besides newspapers, he could clearly detect the falsity in all the inordinate, gushing praise of one man, always that one man. If he was so perfect, did that mean that everybody else was no good? This seemed so unlikely to Gleb that he could not bring himself to share in the general enthusiasm.

Gleb had been only in the tenth class at school when he pushed his way to the newspaper kiosk one December morning and read that Kirov had been murdered, and he suddenly felt, in a flash, that the murderer was none other than Stalin—because only Stalin stood to gain by it. In the midst of the jostling crowd of grown-ups, who did not understand this simple truth, he felt desperately lonely.

Soon dozens, then hundreds of old Bolsheviks, the men who had made the Revolution and whose lives were identified with it, began disappearing into oblivion: some of them, without waiting to be arrested, took poison in their city apartments, others hanged themselves in their country villas; but most of them just let themselves be arrested and inexplicably confessed in court, heaping abuse on themselves at inordinate length and saying they had worked for every intelligence service in the world. It was so excessive, so crude, so farfetched that you had to be stone-deaf not to hear the sound of the lies. Surely people could hear them? Yet Russian writers, who dared to speak of themselves as the heirs of Pushkin and Tolstoy, lauded the tyrant with cloying panegyrics, and Russian composers, trained at the great Moscow Conservatoire, vied with each other to lay their sycophantic hymns of praise at his feet.

Throughout his youth Gleb Nerzhin had heard the furious clangour of the silent tocsin, and he had vowed that he would get at the truth and make sense of all this. Strolling in the Moscow streets at night, when it would have been more normal to have been thinking about girls, Gleb dreamed of the day when it would all be clear to him and when perhaps he might see what it was like behind those high walls where all the victims, to a man, had slandered themselves before going to their death. Did the answer to the riddle lie behind those walls? At that time he knew neither the name of the main prison nor that our wishes always come true provided they are strong enough.

Years later his wish was granted, although it was neither easy nor pleasant. He had been arrested and brought to that very prison, where he had met a few survivors of the great purges; they were not surprised at how much he had pieced together but were able to add a hundred times more.

His wish had been granted, but it had meant the sacrifice of his career, his freedom, his family life. . . . Once the mind is possessed by a single great passion, everything else is ruthlessly excluded—there is no room for it. . . .

. . . The bus rattled over the bridge across the Yauza and along an endless succession of mean, winding streets.

Nerzhin shook himself and said:

'This isn't the way to the Taganka. Where are they taking us? I don't get it.'

Gerasimovich, who had been brooding on his own thoughts, said:

'We must be going to Lefort.'

Some gates were opened for the bus, which drove into the backyard of a two-storey annexe to the high prison building and stopped. Waiting for them in a doorway was the young-looking Lieutenant-Colonel Klimentyev. He wore neither hat nor coat. It was not, in fact, very cold; it was just a gloomy winter's day under a heavily overcast sky, but there was no wind.

At a signal from Klimentyev the warders got out of the bus and lined up, except for two who as before stayed watching at the back of the bus, pistols in pockets; the prisoners, without being allowed so much as a glimpse of the main prison building, where hustled inside behind the lieutenant-colonel. They found themselves in a long narrow corridor with seven open doors. Klimentyev walked on ahead and rattled off his orders, as though in battle:

'Gerasimovich—in here; Lukashenko—in there; Nerzhin —third door, over there. . .'

The prisoners turned off one by one, and in the same fashion Klimentyev put in a warder with each of them. Nerzhin got one of the gangsters in disguise. The little rooms were all identical, and were normally used for interrogation. The windows, which gave little enough light anyway, were barred; there was a chair and table for the interrogator by the window and a smaller table and stool for the prisoner. Nerzhin placed the interrogator's chair nearer to the door for his wife, and for himself took the uncomfortable little stool with a crack in it that threatened to make it painful to sit on. He had once gone through six months of interrogation sitting on a stool like this at just such a wretched little table.

Through the open door Nerzhin heard the click of a woman's heels down the passage, and then came the sound of her dear voice:

'In here?'

She came in.

CHAPTER THIRTY-FIVE

When Nadya had left Gleb at the front, driving away in a battered lorry that had bumped over exposed pine roots and skidded on the sandy ground, while Gleb had stood on the forest track which grew longer, darker and narrower until it swallowed him up, no one could have known that their separation, far from ending with the war, was only really beginning.

Waiting for a husband to come back from the war is always hard, but it is hardest of all in the last few months before it ends—shrapnel and bullets take no account of how long a man has been in the fighting line.

It was now that Gleb's letters stopped coming. Nadya went out and watched for the postman every day. She wrote to her husband, to his friends and to his commanding officers—all were as silent as though they were under a spell.

Not an evening went by in the spring of 1945 without an artillery salute to celebrate the capture of one city after another—Königsberg, Breslau, Frankfurt-on-Oder, Berlin, Prague.

But still no letters. For her the world seemed dark and she could not even work. But she mustn't let herself go! If he were still alive and came back he would scold her for having wasted her time, so she wore herself out working all day long to prepare for a higher degree in chemistry. She also studied foreign languages and dialectical materialism. It was only at night that she wept.

Then suddenly the War Ministry stopped paying her allowance as an officer's wife. This could only mean that he had been killed.

Immediately after that the four-year war came to an end, and the delirious streets swarmed with people mad with joy. Some people fired pistols in the air and all the loudspeakers in the Soviet Union blared victory marches over the ravaged and hungry country.

She was not told that he had been killed, but only that he was missing. The human mind never accepts the irrevocable; so she began to hope against hope that he might have been sent on a special intelligence mission. Their generation, reared on suspicion and secrecy was quick to imagine mysteries where there were none.

That summer was swelteringly hot in the south of Russia, but the sun did not shine for Nadya. She just went on with her studies, fearing his displeasure when he returned; but when four months had gone by since the end of the war, the time had come to admit that the man for whose love she had suffered such agonies of separation was no longer alive. Then came the tattered note folded into a triangle from Krasnaya Presnya saying that she would not see him for another ten years.

Not all her friends could understand why she immediately brightened and became so cheerful on learning that her husband was in prison. She was no longer alone now! What a joy that his sentence was only ten years, not fifteen or twenty-five. No one comes back from the grave, but people did return from forced labour. Free now of the terrible sense of guilt at having survived him, she felt a surge of new strength in the knowledge that he was not dead. Now there was only a noose round her neck and a weight on her shoulders. He was in Moscow, so naturally she must go there and try to save him. (She believed that to be near him was enough to save him.)

But the hard part was getting there. Posterity can never have any conception of what travelling was like in those days, especially travelling to Moscow. To begin with (as in the 'thirties) a person had to show reason for not staying where he was and furnish documents proving that he had official grounds for being a burden on public transport. Having done that, he would get a permit entitling him to spend days on end queueing at railway stations, where he would have to sleep on floors slimy with filth unless he was prepared to slip a furtive bribe through the back door of the booking office. Nadya's pretext for travel was something almost unheard of—that she was being considered for post-graduate work at Moscow University. After paying three times the proper fare she went to Moscow by aeroplane, clutching a briefcase full of textbooks and a pair of felt boots for her husband to wear in Siberia.

She then had one of those extraordinary runs of good luck, when the angels intervene and everything succeeds. The best graduate school in the country accepted this unknown little woman from the provinces, although she had no name, no money, no contacts and no one to pull strings for her. . . . But this turned out to be far easier than getting permission to visit her husband in Krasnaya Presnya. No visits were allowed. The whole prison system was overstrained—the volume of new prisoners being brought in from the West was beyond belief. But once, as she had been standing beside a wooden guard-house waiting for a reply to all her unsuccessful applications, Nadya saw a party of prisoners being led out of the unpainted wooden gate of the prison to work on the wharfs of the Moscow River, and in a happy flash of intuition she guessed that Gleb was among them. There were two hundred of them, and they were all midway between shedding their ordinary clothes and adapting to the dingy prison dress. Each one still wore some memento of the past: an army peaked cap with its coloured arm-of-service band but no chinstrap and no badge; patent leather boots that had still not been bartered for food or taken away by criminal prisoners; or a tattered silk shirt. They all had shaven heads which they shielded from the hot summer sun as best they could; all their faces had a growth of beard and they were all thin, some of them walking skeletons.

Nadya had no need to scan their faces; she at once sensed that Gleb was there. And then she saw him. He was walking along with an open neck, in his serge army tunic whose cuffs still bore his artillery officer's red piping, and on his chest there were the unfaded marks where his medals had been. Like all of them he held his hands behind his back. He did not look either at the sunlit view from the hill, which should have been so inviting to a prisoner, or at the women standing on either side with packages (they were not allowed letters in the transit prison, so he did not know that Nadya was in Moscow). Although just as sallow and emaciated as the others, he was smiling and listening keenly and with evident approval to what his neighbour, a tall, grey-bearded old man, was saying.

Nadya ran alongside the column shouting her husband's name, but her voice was drowned by what the old man was saying and by the furious barking of the guard dogs. Gasping for breath, she ran on just to feast her eyes on his face. How sorry she felt for him, rotting away all those months in a dark, stinking cell. What bliss to see him here beside her. How proud she was that he still held his head up. And how hurt she felt that he seemed so cheerful —he must have forgotten her. And for the first time she felt sorry for herself, that he had done her an injury, that *she* was the victim, not he.

All this passed through her mind in a moment. Then the escort shouted at her, the trained killer dogs pawed the air, strained at their leashes and barked, their eyes bloodshot. Nadya was chased away. The columns had to close ranks to enter a narrow street going downhill and there was no room to walk alongside. The guards who were bringing up the rear kept a long distance between themselves and the column, and although Nadya followed them she could not catch up with the men, who reached the bottom of the hill and disappeared behind a high fence.

Late in the evening and at night, so that the local inhabitants could not see anything, trains of cattle-trucks were shunted up to the transit prison. With lamps bobbing up and down and dogs yelping, with shouts, curses and blows, the escort guards packed the prisoners into cars, forty at a time, and took them off in their thousands to camps in Pechora, Inta, Vorkuta, Sovietskaya Gavan, Norilsk, Irkutsk, Chita, Krasnoyarsk, Novosibirsk, Central Asia, Karaganda, Jeskazgan, at Lake Balkhash, on the River Irtysh, at Tobolsk, the Urals, Saratov, Vyatka, Vologda, Perm, Solvychegodsk, Rybinsk, Potma, Sukhobezvodninsk and many other lesser camps that were nameless. Smaller groups of a hundred or two at a time were taken in trucks to places near Moscow such as Seryebranny Bor, Khimki and Dmitrov, and to other locations in Moscow itself where, behind tall wooden fences wreathed in barbed wire, the new Moscow was being built. . . .

Fate was again unexpectedly kind to Nadya: Gleb was not taken off to the Arctic or somewhere like that, but put in a small work camp in Moscow itself whose inmates were employed in building an apartment house for high officials of the MVD—a crescent-shaped building at Kaluga Gate.

When at last she was granted permission to visit him, Nadya was quite beside herself and rushed to see him there with a feeling that he was already half free.

Kaluga Street was a broad, busy thoroughfare, with a steady flow of limousines, occasionally with diplomatic number plates. Buses and trolley-buses stopped by the railings at the end of Neskuchny Park where the camp guardhouse stood, looking like an ordinary building site office; high up on the unfinished structure were people working in dirty, torn clothing—but all building workers look like that and no passers-by would have guessed that they were prisoners.

Those who did guess held their tongues.

It was a time when money did not go very far and food was expensive. Nadya went short of food and sold off her possessions to buy things for her husband. Her packages were always passed on to him, but she was not often allowed to visit him. This was because Gleb did not always do his full quota of work. When she was allowed to see him he was unrecognizable. As happens with proud people, misfortune had had a good effect on him. He had become gentler, he kissed his wife's hand, he watched for the light in her eyes and he felt as though he were no longer in prison. Life in a prison camp, which is far more ruthless than life among cannibals or rats, had taken its toll, but he had by conscious effort reached a point at which he was no longer sorry for himself and could obstinately repeat to her in all sincerity:

'My dear, you don't know what you're letting yourself in for. You will wait for me for a year, maybe three years, perhaps even five, but the nearer it gets to the end the harder it will be for you to stick it out. The last years will be the worst. We haven't any children, so don't waste the best years of your life—leave me and marry someone else.'

Nadya shook her head sadly:

'Are you looking for an excuse to get rid of me?'

The prisoners lived in an unfinished wing of the same apartment house that they were building. As they got off the trolley-bus, women bringing parcels for their husbands could see over the top of the fence where their menfolk were crowding around two or three windows of their quarters.

Sometimes they would also catch a glimpse of women prisoners among the men. Once one of these women embraced her 'camp husband' and shouted across the fence to his lawful wife:

'Keep away, you whore! Hand over that parcel and don't come back again! If I see you at the guard-house once more I'll scratch your eyes out!'

At that time preparations for the first post-war elections to the Supreme Soviet were actively under way. Although the political prisoners were good workers there was some reluctance to keep them in Moscow, because of possible trouble with them at a time when, for political reasons, security arrangements had to be as inconspicuous as possible. Some of the prisoners would have to be sent away in order to cow the others. There were already ugly rumours among the prisoners that they would soon be shipped off to the far North. Those who had potatoes baked them for the journey.

To protect the voters from undesirable influences, all visits to the Moscow prison camps were stopped prior to the election. In a parcel Nadya had sent Gleb a towel into which she had sewn a note:

'Beloved, however many years go by and however many storms we have to weather' (Nadya often expressed herself in rather exalted language) 'I shall be faithful to you as long as I live. They say that you "politicals" are being transferred. You will be far away, for many long years we shall not be able to see each other or even steal a look at each other through the barbed wire. If it helps to make that grim life out there any easier for you, I don't mind if you go with other women, if you're unfaithful to me. You have my permission, my dear, in fact I insist on it. Anything to keep your spirits up! I'm not afraid, I know you'll come back to me, won't you?'

CHAPTER THIRTY-SIX

Before she had got to know as much as a tenth part of Moscow, Nadya was well versed in that sad geography—the location of the city's prisons. They were, she discovered, evenly distributed round the city as a matter of policy so that in any part of Moscow you were never far from jail. What with taking parcels, making enquiries or visiting, Nadya learned the difference between the Greater Lubyanka (which took prisoners from everywhere) and the Lesser Lubyanka (which served the Moscow region only); she learned that there are detention cells at every railway station; she had several times been to the Butyrki and Taganka jails, and, although it was not shown on their destination boards, she knew which trams went to Lefort and which to Krasnaya Presnya. She even lived near one of them, the so-called 'Sailors' Rest' which had been wrecked in 1917, then restored and made more secure.

After Gleb had been brought back from a remote prison camp to Moscow, this time to an extraordinary special prison where they were well fed and employed on scientific work, Nadya again saw her husband at rare intervals. But the wives were not allowed to know where it was that their husbands were being kept, and for these infrequent visits the men were driven into various Moscow prisons. The most cheerful place for visits was the Taganka, where there were no 'politicals', only criminals, and conditions were quite lax. The meetings took place in the warders' recreation room where the warders amused themselves by playing the accordion; the prisoners were driven there along a quiet street in an open bus, so that even before the official beginning of the visit the wives waiting on the pavement could embrace their husbands. They could linger there, talk about subjects forbidden by regulations and even pass things from hand to hand. The meeting itself was very informal, as they were allowed to sit side by side and there was only one warder to listen in to four couples.

Butyrki was also a relatively free-and-easy prison,

although the wives found it more depressing. After the Luby-anka, it was a great relief for prisoners coming to Butyrki to discover how much easier the discipline was there: you were not blinded by the electric light in the transfer cells, you could walk along the corridors without holding your hands behind your back, you could talk aloud in the cells, peep under the window-screens, lie on your plank bed and even sleep under it in the daytime. And there were other little comforts at Butyrki—you could put your hands under the bedclothes, they let you keep your spectacles at night, they allowed matches in the cells, they did not empty the tobacco out of every cigarette and when you got a loaf of bread in a parcel they only cut it into four instead of slicing it into little pieces. But the wives were unaware of all these indulgences. All they saw was a castellated wall as high as four men, stretching the whole length of a block, the iron gates set between massive concrete pillars—gates that were not like ordinary gates, but which slowly opened and closed by mechanical means to swallow or regurgitate a Black Maria. When the women were admitted for a visit they were led through openings in six-foot-thick masonry and between twenty-foot-high walls that skirted the sinister Pugachov Tower. For ordinary prisoners the visit was conducted through a double set of bars, with a warder walking up and down between them as though he were in a cage himself. Prisoners of a higher category, such as those from special prisons, could speak to their visitors across a wide table divided under-neath by a solid partition which prevented any contact or signalling with the legs, while a warder sat at the end of the table like an unsleeping statue and listened to every word that was said. But the most depressing thing about Butyrki was that their husbands seemed to emerge straight from the very depths of the prison; they would come up from behind those thick, damp walls for half an hour, smiling wanly and assuring their wives that they were fine and needed nothing, then vanish again.

Today, for the first time, the visit was in Lefort Prison. The gate warder put a tick against Nadya's name on a list and pointed towards a long, single-storey building.

Several women were already waiting in the room, which was completely bare except for two long benches and a table, on which the women had put their wickerwork baskets and shopping bags crammed with food for their husbands. Although the inmates of Mavrino, such as Gleb, always had enough to eat, Nadya felt ashamed that on this one occasion in the year she had been unable to bring her husband anything more than a little pastry. She had baked the pastry out of the remains of her white flour, sugar and butter, by getting up early when everybody else in her hostel was still asleep. She had not had time to go shopping for jam or cakes, and she was in any case short of money until the next instalment of her university grant was paid. The visit also happened to coincide with her husband's birthday, and she had no present to give him. She would have liked to have given him a good book; but even this had become impossible since her last visit, when Nadya had brought him a volume of Yesenin's poetry. It had taken a miracle to acquire this book, and it was identical with the copy which Gleb had taken to the war with him and which had vanished when he was arrested. Alluding to this, Nadya had written on the title page:

'All that is lost shall be returned to you.'

In her presence, however, Lieutenant-Colonel Klimentyev had torn out the title page with its inscription and handed it back, saying that no 'written matter' could be included in the prisoners' parcels, but must be submitted separately through the censorship. When Gleb heard about this he ground his teeth and begged her not to try sending him any more books. . . .

Around the table there sat four women, one of them a young girl with a three-year-old daughter. All were strangers to Nadya. She said good morning, the other women replied and turned back to continue their animated conversation. On a short bench against the opposite wall there sat a woman of about thirty-five or forty in a very worn fur coat and a grey knitted headscarf, whose wool had lost all its fleeciness and now consisted of no more than a stringy knitted web. She had crossed her legs, linked her hands round one knee and was staring intently at the floor in front of her. Her whole attitude expressed a dislike of being touched or of talking to anyone. There was nothing in her hands or nearby that resembled a parcel.

The women were prepared to accept Nadya into their company, but she preferred not to join them as she wanted to keep her thoughts to herself on this special occasion. She approached the solitary woman and asked her if she might sit beside her, as the bench was too short to allow her to sit further away. The woman raised her eyes. They were completely colourless. They looked straight through Nadya without a sign of having understood her question.

Nadya sat down and thrust her hands into her sleeves. Tilting her head to rest one cheek on her imitation Persian lamb coat-collar, she too withdrew into her private world. For the present she wanted to shut everything out of her mind except Gleb. She would think of what they were going to say to each other and of that timeless entity which was made up not just of him and of her, but of the two of them together, and which we usually call by that overworked word 'love'. But she found it impossible to isolate herself and could not help overhearing the conversation at the table. The women were describing what their husbands got to eat —what they gave them for breakfast, what they gave them for supper—and how often they had their underwear washed in prison. How on earth did they know all this, she wondered? Surely they didn't waste the precious minutes of their visits discussing things like that? Then they listed, in pounds and ounces, exactly what foods and how much of each they had brought in their parcels. It was a pure instance of that dogged wifely concern, that instinct which makes a family what it is and which keeps the human race going. Nadya, however, did not see it like that; to her it was merely degrading and pathetic to squander those priceless moments on such trivia. Surely these women's time would be better spent reflecting on the people who had had the effrontery to imprison their husbands? If they did that, then perhaps their menfolk might not be behind bars at all and would not need food parcels!

A seventh woman, with greying hair, arrived late and out of breath. Nadya recognized her from a previous visit. Married to the engraver, she had been his first wife whom he had later remarried. She was quite ready to tell her story: she

had always adored her husband and regarded him as a very
clever man; but he had complained about her psychological
complexes and had left her and their child to go and live
with another woman, a redhead, with whom he had lived for
three years until the war had come and he had been conscripted. He had been taken prisoner early in the war but
had lived in Germany as a free man and there too, alas, he
had had his little distractions. When he was released from
captivity he had been arrested at the frontier and sentenced
to ten years. He had sent a message from Butyrki to his redhead that he was in prison and wanted food parcels, but
she had said: 'Better unfaithful to me than a traitor to his
country—I could have forgiven him that!' So he had turned
with entreaty to his first wife, who had brought him parcels
and gone to visit him—and now he was begging her forgiveness and swearing to love her for ever. Nadya recalled how,
in telling her story, the engraver's wife had said bitterly that
if your husband was in prison, the best way to make sure
he appreciated you properly when he came out was to be unfaithful to him. Otherwise he would think there must be
something the matter with you, because no one had wanted
you while he had been gone.

The new arrival at once turned the conversation at the
table into a different channel. She began describing all the
trouble she had had consulting lawyers at the legal aid office
in Nikolskaya Street. This had long been known as the best
one of its kind, yet the lawyers that she consulted charged
their clients thousands of roubles, spent most of their time
dining out on the proceeds and neglected their clients' affairs.
When asked, the lawyers confidentially justified the need for
such high fees by saying that they did not keep it all for
themselves but had to share it with others. There was no
way of checking on them. It was quite likely that they never
shared the fees with anybody, but they always hinted portentously that many others beside themselves had a finger in
the pie and that all these people had to be kept happy.
When faced with the concrete wall of the law these women
were as helpless as when they stood outside the twenty-foot-
high ramparts of Butyrki Prison; lacking wings to fly over,
they could do nothing but prostrate themselves in front of
anyone who seemed to offer a way through. The official pro-

ceedings which went on behind that wall were like the mysterious revolutions of some great machine, and just occasionally, despite a prisoner's obvious guilt and despite the utter disparity between accuser and accused, by a sheer miracle this machine might, like a lottery, throw out a winning ticket. So these women paid their lawyers—not because they expected to draw a winning ticket, but just to be able to dream that they might.

The engraver's wife believed implicitly that she would ultimately be successful. She had, it appeared, scraped together forty thousand roubles by selling the lease of her room and begging from relatives, and she had spent every kopeck of it on lawyers' fees. She had changed lawyers three times; they had submitted three petitions for clemency and five appeals and several officials had promised to give her case sympathetic consideration. She knew by name all the regular prosecuting attorneys of the three main offices of the Public Prosecutor's department, she practically lived in the waiting-rooms of the Supreme Court and the Supreme Soviet. Like all trusting people, especially women, she exaggerated the significance of every hopeful-sounding remark and of every glance that was anything less than hostile.

'The thing to do is to keep writing—to keep writing to *everybody*,' she insisted, and by so saying she encouraged other women to follow her example. 'Our husbands are suffering. No one is ever released without an effort. Keep writing!'

This woman's story, too, had the effect of upsetting and annoying Nadya. Listening to the engraver's ageing wife, the other women could not help thinking that she was being so much cleverer and more energetic than all the rest of them and that after so much effort she was bound to get her husband out of prison. Then came self-reproach—'And what have I been doing? Why couldn't I have done what she has done? Why haven't I been such a loyal wife?'

Nadya had only once taken legal aid. The lawyer had helped her to submit one petition and she had only paid him two thousand five hundred roubles—obviously too little, because he had taken offence and ignored her case.

'Yes,' she said in a quiet voice, almost to herself, 'I wonder —have we done everything we could? Are our consciences clear?'

The women round the table were talking so loudly that they did not hear her, but the woman alongside her on the bench turned her head sharply as though Nadya had kicked her or insulted her.

'What *can* we do?' she rapped out fiercely. 'She's talking rubbish. A political prisoner is not a criminal, he's an *enemy*! If you were to spend a million roubles you couldn't get a political prisoner reprieved!'

Her face was lined, her voice rang with the purity of intense suffering. Nadya's heart warmed towards this woman, who was considerably older than herself. In a tone of voice that carried an implied apology for speaking in such high-flown terms, she said:

'I meant that we don't sacrifice ourselves to the limit. . . . The wives of the Decembrists didn't spare themselves, you know, they gave up everything and went to Siberia with their husbands. . . . Perhaps it's too much to expect to get one's husband released, but might one not be able to arrange for his sentence to be commuted to exile if one tried hard enough? If I were given the choice I'd rather he were exiled to any place—to the tundra, to the Arctic Circle, to somewhere where the sun never shines—provided I could go with him. I would give up everything. . . .'

The woman's face, wrapped in a grey headscarf, was as austere as a nun's. Looking at Nadya with astonishment and respect she said:

'Do you still feel strong enough to go to Siberia? How lucky you are. I have no strength left to do anything. I really believe that if any man was kind enough to propose to me, no matter how old he was, I'd marry him.'

Nadya shuddered:

'How could you abandon your husband . . . when he's behind bars?'

The woman clutched Nadya by the sleeve of her coat and said:

'A hundred or more years ago, my dear, it was easy enough to be a loving, faithful wife. I don't think the wives of the Decembrists did anything really brave. Were they pestered with prying questionnaires whenever they tried to get a job? Did they have to hide the fact that they were married as though it were an infectious disease, simply to avoid losing

260

their jobs, simply in order not to lose their only income of five hundred roubles a month? Did they have to share a flat where everyone turned their backs on them? Did they have to hear other people's whispering that they were traitors to their country every time they went to the communal tap for water? Did their own mothers and sisters advise them to be sensible and get a divorce? No, they most certainly did not! They basked in the approval of the best people in society! With their gracious help, poets turned their deeds into legends. When they drove off to Siberia in their expensive private carriages, they didn't have to worry about losing their Moscow residence permit which gave them the right to nine miserable square yards of accommodation, did they? They didn't have to bother about trifling little matters like getting a black mark on their employment card, did they? Or where to store their furniture, or how to buy a saucepan, or that there was no bread in the shops . . .! It's all very fine to say you'd go to Siberia . . . you obviously haven't been waiting for long!'

Her voice was nearly breaking. Nadya's eyes filled with tears to hear the woman's passionate tirade.

'My husband will soon have been in prison for five years,' she said in self-justification. 'And then there was the war. . . .'

'That doesn't count!' said the woman forcibly. 'Everybody had to wait during the war, that was easy enough. You could actually *talk* about it openly and read each other's letters! But it's a different matter when you have to wait and you daren't even tell anybody, believe me.'

She stopped, realizing that Nadya needed no telling.

It was half past eleven. At last in came Lieutenant-Colonel Klimentyev, accompanied by a fat, surly-looking sergeant-major, who began examining the parcels. He slit open each packet of biscuits and broke every pie in half. He also broke Nadya's pastry, looking to see whether a note, some money or poison had been baked into it. Klimentyev took away their visitors' passes, wrote their names in a large book, then snapped to attention and barked out:

'Pay attention! You know the regulations. The visit lasts thirty minutes. Nothing may be handed over to the prisoner. The prisoner may not be asked questions about his work, his living conditions or his daily routine. Any infringe-

261

ment of these regulations is a criminal offence. Furthermore, as from today's visit handshaking or kissing is prohibited. Infringement of this rule will result in immediate cancellation of the visit.'

The women meekly said nothing.

'Gerasimovich, Natalya!' Klimentyev called out the first name.

Nadya's companion stood up, clumped across the floor in her pre-war felt boots and went out into the corridor.

CHAPTER THIRTY-SEVEN

Though she had cried a little while waiting, Nadya felt light at heart when at last she went in.

As she appeared in the doorway, Nerzhin got up to meet her and he was smiling. His smile lasted only for as long as it took them to step closer to each other, but it made her feel jubilant: it meant that he loved her as much as ever and had not changed towards her.

The bull-necked individual in the soft grey suit, who looked like a retired gangster, went up to the small table and stood between them in the narrow room, preventing them from touching.

'Oh come on, can't I take her by the hand!' Nerzhin said angrily.

'It's against the rules,' the warder answered, lowering his heavy jaw just enough to let the words through.

Nadya smiled vacantly and signalled her husband not to argue. She sat down in the armchair put there for her. In places bits of stuffing were sticking out from the leather upholstery. Several generations of interrogators had sat in this armchair and sent hundreds of people to their graves before being despatched there themselves.

'Well, happy birthday!' she said, trying to seem cheerful.

'Thank you.'

'Such a coincidence—that it should be today.'

'Must be my lucky star. . . .'

It took some time for them to get used to speaking to each other again.

Nadya did her best to ignore the irksome presence of the warder watching them. Nerzhin tried to sit in such a way that the rickety stool did not hurt him.

The little table that had stood between generations of prisoners and their interrogators now stood between husband and wife.

'In case I forget—I've brought you something to eat—you remember those pastries that mother makes? I'm sorry there's nothing else.'

'Silly, you shouldn't have bothered. We have everything we need.'

'But you don't have pastry, do you? You told me not to bring any more books. Are you reading Yesenin?'

Nerzhin's face darkened. It was more than a month now since he had been reported to Shikin for having the Yesenin book and Shikin had confiscated it on the grounds that it was banned work.

'I'm reading it.' (What was the point of going into details, when they had only half an hour?)

Although it was not at all warm in the room—there was hardly any heating—Nadya unbuttoned her coat collar and opened it. She wanted to show her husband not only her new fur coat—on which he made no comment—but also her new blouse. She also hoped that the orange colour of the blouse would brighten her face, which she thought must look grey in this dim light.

In one long, roving glance Nerzhin cast his eyes over his wife—her face, her neck and the opening at her bosom. Nadya was roused by this look of his—it was the most important moment in the whole visit—and she made a movement as though to go towards him.

'You have a new blouse. Let me get a better view of it.'

'And what about my fur coat?' She made a sulky face.

'What about it?'

'It's new.'

'So it is.' Gleb at last caught on. 'A new fur coat.' And he ran his eyes over the black curls, not knowing that it was Astrakhan, real or artificial—he was the last man in the world to be able to tell a five-hundred-rouble coat from one costing five-thousand roubles.

Now she threw the coat back. He saw her neck, as it
263

always had been, finely moulded like a young girl's, and her narrow shoulders which he had loved to fondle when he embraced her, and, beneath the folds of her blouse, her breasts which had lost their fullness in the course of these years.

The sight of these pathetically flat breasts cancelled out a fleeting sense of grievance at the thought of her buying new clothes and making new friends, and it was borne in on him that her life, too, had been crushed under the wheels of the grey prison van.

'You're very thin,' he said with sympathy. 'You should eat more. Can't you eat better?'

'You don't think I'm pretty any more?' said the look in her eyes.

'You're just as wonderful as ever!' he signalled back mutely.

(Though words like this were not forbidden by the lieutenant-colonel, it was impossible to say them aloud in front of a stranger.)

'I do eat well,' she lied. 'It's just that I have such a busy life, and I'm always so harassed.'

'How is that? Tell me about it.'

'No, you tell me about yourself first.'

'What is there to tell you?' Nerzhin said, smiling. 'I'm all right.'

'Well, you see——' she began hesitantly.

The warder stood a foot and a half from the table; he was squat like a bulldog and watched them with the supercilious air of a stone lion guarding the entrance to a public building.

They had to find a way of speaking that would be above his head, an allusive language of obscure references. They relied on their greater intelligence, of which they felt comfortably aware, to guide them.

'Is the suit yours?' she asked.

Nerzhin made a wry face and shook his head.

'Mine? Only for three hours. It's like a Potemkin village. Don't let the Sphinx bother you.'

'I can't help it,' she said, pouting a little coyly, like a child, certain now that he still liked her looks.

'We get used to looking at the funny side of it.'

Nadya remembered her conversation with the Gerasimovich woman and sighed:

'But we don't.'

Nerzhin tried to touch her knees with his own, but a bar under the table, intended to prevent prisoners from stretching their legs during interrogation, made even this impossible. The table wobbled. Putting his elbows on it and leaning closer to his wife, Nerzhin said with annoyance:

'That's how it is—obstacles everywhere.'

'Are you mine? Mine?' he asked her with his eyes.

'I am still the same. I haven't changed, believe me,' her shining grey eyes answered back at him.

'And what obstacles do you have? Tell me. Have you dropped your graduate work?'

'No.'

'So you've presented your thesis?'

'No.'

'How come?'

'Well, it's like this——' She began to speak very quickly, alarmed that so much of their time had already gone by. 'No one has presented a thesis in the last three years. They just keep giving people extensions. For instance, one student spent two years writing on "Problems of Public Catering", but she was told to change her subject——'

(Oh, why did she have to talk about that? It was all so trivial.)

'—My own thesis is ready and typed out, but I'm still having to make various changes——'

(Because of the current campaign against 'Western influences; but how could she go into all that here?)

'—and then I have to get photocopies made, and it still has to be bound. It's all very complicated.'

'But are they paying you your grant?'

'No.'

'What are you living on then?'

'My own earnings.'

'So you're working? Where?'

'In the university.'

'What doing?'

'Well, you see, it's only a sort of vague temporary job.

265

I'm only hanging on by the skin of my teeth. It's the same in the hostel, too. In fact I——'

She glanced at the warder. What she wanted to say was that the police should have cancelled her permit to live at the hostel in Stromynka, but that, by some oversight, they had renewed it for a further six months. The error might come to light any day. All the more reason for not mentioning it in front of an MVD sergeant.

So, instead, she said: 'I got permission for this visit today because . . . Well, it happened like this——'

(But it would take more than half an hour to tell the story.)

'Wait, tell me that later. What I meant was: are there any obstacles on account of *me*?'

'Immense ones, darling. They are giving me—— they want me to work on a *special subject*—— I am trying not to accept it.'

'What do you mean by *special subject*?'

She sighed helplessly and glanced again at the warder, who had pricked up his ears and looked as if he was about to bark or snap at her; he stood there glowering into their faces, less than three feet away.

Nadya spread out her hands in a gesture of helplessness. How could she explain that even in the university almost all work was classified as secret, and that any such employment involved a new, still more rigorous security check on her husband, her husband's relatives and the relatives of their relatives. If she were to say that her husband had been sentenced under Article 58, she would not only be refused work at the university but forbidden to present her thesis as well. If she lied and said her husband was missing in action, she would still have to give his surname, and all they had to do was check it in the MVD files, upon which she would be tried for making a false statement. There was yet a third possibility, but under Nerzhin's watchful gaze Nadya hastily put it out of her mind and began to talk brightly about something quite different:

'You know, I've joined an amateur musical group at the university. They send me all the time to play at concerts. Not long ago I played in the Hall of Columns on the same evening as Jacob Zak——'

Gleb smiled and nodded, clearly incredulous.

'—Well, it was a trade union evening, and so it happened quite by accident, but there he was . . . and you know, it was funny—I had my best dress on, but they wouldn't let me perform in it. They rang up a theatre, and got me another one, a wonderful thing that went right down to the ankles.'

'And they took it away again afterwards?'

'Oh yes. You know the other girls call me a fool for wasting my time on music. But I tell them: "It's better to be wasting your time on some*thing* like this than to run around with some*one*——" '

Nerzhin looked at her gratefully, and then said with concern:

'But just a minute, tell me about that special subject——'

Nadya lowered her eyes.

'I 'wanted to say—only you won't take it to heart, will you? . . . you once said we ought to get divorced——' She said it very quietly.

(This was the third possibility—one which would give her a chance to live again. Of course she would not put herself down as 'divorced' because she would then be asked the surname of her former husband, his present address, the names and addresses of all his relatives, and even their years of birth and occupations. Instead she would simply write: 'Unmarried.')

Yes, there was a time when he had insisted on this. But now he was startled. Only at this moment did he notice that her wedding ring, which she had always worn, was not on her finger.

'Yes, of course,' he agreed, with every appearance of alacrity.

'Then you won't be against it . . . if . . . I have to . . . do it?' With a great effort she looked at him. Her eyes were very wide. The fine pinpoints of her grey pupils were alight with a plea for forgiveness and understanding. 'It would be . . . *pseudo*,' she added, breathing the word rather than speaking it.

'Good girl. You should have done it long ago!' Nerzhin agreed in a voice of firm conviction, though he didn't feel it, and he decided not to begin puzzling about the meaning of it until she had left.

'Maybe I won't have to,' she said in a tone of entreaty, pulling her coat over her shoulders again. She suddenly looked tired and worn. 'I just wanted to have your agreement, in case of need. Maybe it won't arise.'

'No, you should. You're quite right,' Nerzhin said without feeling, his thoughts now shifting to the main thing he had been going to tell her. 'Please,' he went on, 'don't bank too much on my being released when my sentence is up.'

Nerzhin himself fully expected that he would have to serve a second term and spend the rest of his life in prison—it had happened to many of his comrades. This was not something he could put in a letter and he had to mention it now.

A look of alarm appeared on Nadya's face.

'A sentence is an elastic thing,' he explained, speaking fast and swallowing the ends of his words, to make it hard for the warder to follow. 'It can stretch on for ever. History is full of examples. And even if it should miraculously come to an end, don't imagine you and I will be able to go back home, to our old life. One thing you must understand and never forget: they don't sell tickets to the past. How I regret, for instance, that I never learned how to make shoes. That's a trade which would really come in handy in some God-forsaken place in Siberia, in Krasnoyarsk or down on the Angara. That's the only sort of life to prepare for. Who needs Euler's mathematical formulae out there?'

He had got away with it: the retired gangster didn't move a muscle but only blinked in his effort to keep pace with the swift flow of Nerzhin's words.

But Nerzhin had forgotten, or rather had never understood —none of them did—that ordinary earthbound mortals cannot scale such icy peaks all at once. He did not know that even now, as in the beginning, Nadya still punctiliously ticked off the remaining days and weeks of his sentence. For him it was a cold, glaring infinity, but for her it was only 264 weeks and 61 months—slightly more than five years—already much less time than had gone by since he first went to the war.

As Nerzhin spoke, the alarm on Nadya's face turned to horror.

'No, no!' she cried out. 'Don't say that, darling!' (She had forgotten about the warder and was no longer ashamed to show her feelings.) 'Don't take my hopes away! I don't want to believe it! It simply can't be! Or did you think I would really leave you?'

Her upper lip trembled, her face was contorted and her eyes were filled with utter devotion.

'I believe you, I believe you, Nadya!' he said in a changed voice. 'I know what you meant.'

She fell silent and sank back in her chair.

The swarthy, dapper Klimentyev was standing in the doorway, eyeing the three people with their heads so close together. He called the warder in a low voice.

The retired gangster, as loth to move as a man in the middle of eating his favourite pudding, went over to the lieutenant-colonel. Still within easy earshot, they exchanged only a couple of words, but this was long enough for Nerzhin to ask Nadya under his breath:

'Do you know Sologdin's wife?'

Used to meeting emergencies in conversation, Nadya swiftly replied:

'Yes.'

'And her address?'

'Yes.'

'They aren't letting him have visits, tell her that he——'
The gangster returned.

'—loves her, believes in her and hasn't lost hope!' Gleb finished the sentence in a very clear voice.

'Loves her, believes in her and hasn't lost hope,' Nadya repeated with a sigh, and looked closely at her husband. She somehow saw him in a new light now.

'It suits you,' she said sadly.

'What does?'

'Everything. All this. Being here,' she said, disguising her meaning with inflexions of her voice which the warder could not catch.

This glimpse of a new side to Gleb was not something which brought him any closer to her.

She, too, had put off pondering the meaning of all he said until later, until after the visit; she did not know what conclusions she would then draw, but she was already instinctively looking for the weaknesses, the infirmities, the pleas for help which would give her good cause to devote the

269

rest of her life to him, even waiting a further ten years and then going out to join him in Siberia.

But he was smiling with that same self-confidence he had shown at Krasnaya Presnya. He was always self-sufficient, and never needed anyone's sympathy. He even seemed to be comfortable sitting on the hard little stool, and he looked around the room eagerly, apparently culling interesting observations even here. He looked healthy and his eyes sparkled. Did he really need a woman's loyalty?

But this thought had not yet taken shape in her mind, and Nerzhin had no idea that she was on the verge of thinking it.

'Your time's up!' Klimentyev said in the doorway.

'Already?' Nadya asked in surprise.

Nerzhin frowned, trying to remember the most important thing he had meant to tell her during their meeting.

'Oh, by the way, don't be surprised if I'm sent away from here, a long way away, and if letters stop entirely.'

'Can they do that? Where to?' Nadya cried out.

(Oh, why did he have to wait till now to tell her this?)

'God alone knows,' he said, shrugging his shoulders, with a meaningful stress on the word 'God'.

'Don't tell me you've started believing in God?'

(They hadn't really talked about anything!)

He smiled:

'Like Pascal, Newton, Einstein . . .'

'You know you're not supposed to mention people's names!' the warder barked. 'Come on now, your time's up.'

They both stood up together, and now that there was no longer any risk of having the visit broken off, Nerzhin embraced Nadya across the small table, kissed her on the cheek and clung to the soft lips he had completely forgotten. He had no hope of being in Moscow next year to kiss them again. His voice quivered with tenderness:

'Let's do what's best for you. I——'

He did not finish.

They looked into each other's eyes.

'What's this!' the warder bellowed and pulled Nerzhin back by the shoulder. 'I'm taking away your visit!'

Nerzhin tore himself free.

'Go ahead and take it away, and to hell with you,' Nerzhin muttered.

Nadya backed towards the door and with the fingers of her ringless hand she waved good-bye to her husband.

Then she disappeared into the corridor.

CHAPTER THIRTY-EIGHT

Gerasimovich and his wife kissed.

He was short—the same height as his wife, as it appeared when he stood next to her.

The warder was an easy-going, simple-hearted youth who did not mind at all if they kissed. He was even embarrassed to be in their way and would have stood with his face to the wall for the whole half hour, if it was up to him, but Klimentyev had ordered that all the doors be left open so he could personally keep a watch on the warders from the corridor.

Actually, Klimentyev himself would have had nothing against the prisoners kissing their wives, as he saw no danger to state secrets in this kind of contact. But he had to be careful of the warders and prisoners, some of whom were informers, in case he himself were denounced.

Gerasimovich and his wife kissed, but they felt no thrill, as they would have done in their younger years. Snatched from fate, under the noses of the authorities, it was an insipid kiss, without taste or smell—the sort of pallid kiss one might exchange with a dead person in a dream.

They sat down, separated by the table.

This rough little table with its top of warped plywood had a story richer than many human lives. Over the years countless men and women had sat here, breaking down in sobs, quaking in terror, struggling desperately to keep awake, speaking proud, angry words or signing craven denunciations against their closest friends. They were not usually allowed pencils or pens—except to write out statements in their own hand—but, in doing so, some prisoners had managed to leave marks on the warped surface of the desk, strange wavy or barbed scrawls, which seemed in a mysterious way to record the convolutions of the unconscious mind.

Gerasimovich looked at his wife.

His first thought was how dowdy she had become. Her eyes were sunken. There were wrinkles around her eyes and lips. The skin of her face was flabby, and she seemed to have stopped caring for it. Her coat was pre-war and had long needed at least to be turned. The fur on the collar had gone thin and worn, and her headscarf was very ancient indeed—he seemed to remember their buying it long ago in Komsomolsk-on-Amur with a clothing coupon; and she had later worn it in Leningrad when she went to fetch water from the Little Neva.

Gerasimovich tried to suppress the mean thought, which leapt up within him, that his wife was no longer very pretty. No other woman in the world was so much part of him, or was so closely intertwined with all his memories. No young girl, however pretty and fresh, but whose brief experience of life was a closed book to him, could ever mean more to him than his wife.

Natasha had not been quite eighteen when they first met in Leningrad at a party to see in New Year's Day, 1930. In six days time that would be twenty years ago.

Natasha was just nineteen when he had been arrested the first time—for sabotage.

Gerasimovich had started out on his career at a period when the word 'engineer' was still almost synonymous with the word 'wrecker', and it was common practice to suspect all engineers of being saboteurs. Because of short-sightedness, Gerasimovich, then a very recent graduate, wore a pince-nez which made him look exactly like the intellectual pictured on spy posters during the 'thirties. In those days, he used to nod to all and sundry, saying 'Sorry' in the meekest of voices as though hoping to placate them. At meetings he kept total silence and sat quiet as a mouse. He had no idea how much this annoyed everyone.

However, it was so difficult to make a case against him that even by stretching things to the utmost they could not give him more than three years. Then, when he arrived at the Amur River to serve his sentence, he was not kept under guard. His fiancée was allowed to join him and they married out there.

All the time they dreamed of the day when they would return to Leningrad. When it at last came, in 1935, vast numbers of people were already being sent in the opposite direction. . . .

Natasha was also looking closely at her husband. She remembered how she had seen his face change in those days —the lips had become hard, the eyes had turned cold, sometimes even glinting cruelly behind his pince-nez. He had stopped apologizing to people for his existence. He was never allowed to forget his past and was always being thrown out of jobs or given menial work unsuited to a person of his education. They had been forced to keep on the move all the time and found it very hard to earn a living. They had lost a baby daughter, and then a son. Eventually, in sheer despair, they had decided to go back to Leningrad, and they had arrived there in June 1941 of all times. . . .

Life was now harder than ever, and they were dogged by his past, but for one only at home in a laboratory, he had taken well to manual labour and thrived on it. He got through the autumn digging trenches and with the first snow he became a grave-digger.

In the besieged city nothing was in more demand, and more remunerative, than this gruesome profession. To bury their dead properly, people were quite ready to part with a little of their beggarly bread-ration.

One shuddered to eat such bread, but Gerasimovich thought how little pity people had wasted on him and Natasha, so why should they show pity?

They managed to survive. But even before the end of the blockade, Illarion was arrested for *intent* to betray his country. A lot of people were arrested on these grounds in Leningrad —since the city was not occupied by the enemy, an ordinary charge of treason made little sense.

Oddly enough, as she now looked carefully at her husband, Natasha could see no traces of those difficult years. His eyes had a bright, bland look behind his gleaming pince-nez. His cheeks were not sunken. He had no wrinkles. His suit was of good quality and his necktie was carefully knotted.

One could well have thought that she was the prisoner, not he.

Her first unkind thought was that he must be living very well indeed in the special prison, where he was left in peace to get on with his research, and never bothered his head about all her sufferings.

But she suppressed this wicked thought and asked in a weak voice:

'Well, how are things with you?'

(As though she could think of nothing better to say, after twelve months of waiting and all those nights thinking about him in her cold, lonely bed.)

And Gerasimovich, mentally surveying the years of forced labour in Siberia, with its stunting effect on the mind, and thinking of all the comforts of a special prison, replied:

'Not so bad.'

They had only half an hour, and the seconds passed quickly, like grains of sand trickling through the neck of an hourglass. Dozens of urgent questions crowded Natasha's mind, but all she asked was:

'When did you find out about the visit?'

'Day before yesterday. And you?'

'Tuesday. The lieutenant-colonel asked me just now whether I wasn't your sister.'

'Because we have the same patronymic?'

'Yes.'

When they had become engaged, and later when they lived on the Amur, everyone took them for brother and sister. They had the kind of happy affinity, both inwardly and outwardly, which makes a couple more than husband and wife.

'How are things at work?' he enquired.

'Why do you ask?' she said anxiously. 'Do you know?'

'What do you mean?'

He knew certain things, but he wasn't sure what was in her mind.

He knew, for instance, that the wives of prisoners were always being harassed. But how could he know that last Wednesday his wife had lost her job because she was married to him? Having received only three days ago a notice granting permission for this visit, she had not yet begun to look for new work. She had waited for their meeting, as though by some miracle it might give illumination, showing her what to do.

But how could he advise her? He had been in prison for too long and knew nothing of the world outside.

The great decision she had to make was whether to divorce him or not.

As the minutes slipped by in this drab, poorly heated room, with its dim light from the barred window, her hopes of a miracle were fading.

She realized that in this meagre half hour she could not give her husband any idea of her loneliness and suffering, and that he had a life of his own, which had taken a quite different course from hers. So why should she upset him with her worries, if they meant nothing to him anyway?

The warder turned to the wall and began to study the plaster.

'Tell me about yourself,' said Gerasimovich, holding his wife's hand across the table. In his eyes she saw the same glow of tenderness which he had shown her during the most cruel months of the blockade in Leningrad.

'Is there any chance of a reduction in your sentence, Illarion?'

What she meant was: would the amount of work he did be credited in his favour? In the camp on the Amur River every full working day had counted as two days of one's sentence.

He shook his head:

'Not a hope! They've never done that here, as you well know. If you invent something big—then they free you sooner. But the trouble is that the research we're doing here,' and he glanced at the warder's back, 'is—well, very objectionable——'

He could not have put it more plainly.

He took his wife's hand and caressed it lightly with his cheek.

In frozen wartime Leningrad he had not flinched at the thought of taking bread for a burial from someone who might himself have to be buried the next day. But he could never do anything like that now . . .

'Are you sad all alone? Are you very sad?' he asked still tenderly rubbing his cheek against her hand.

'Was she sad?' he asked! Now the visit was nearly over, she felt sick at heart. She would soon have to go out into the bleak streets feeling none the better for this meeting, and utterly alone. Everything was too pointless and futile for words. Her dreary humdrum life enveloped her like grey cotton wool.

'Natasha!' He stroked her hands. 'If you count it up, I haven't got much more to go now—only three years. Only three——'

'Only three!' She stopped him angrily, feeling her voice tremble, and losing control of it. 'Only three? *Only*, you say! You could get out straight away, but the research is "very objectionable" is it? You're among friends and you're doing the work you like. Nobody pushes you around, but I've been sacked, I've got nothing to live on. I won't get a job anywhere. I can't go on! I'm at the end of my tether. I won't last another month! I might as well die. The neighbours treat me like dirt—they've thrown my trunk out of the hall and pulled down a shelf I put on the wall. They know I daren't say a word, because they can have me thrown out of Moscow! I've stopped going to see my sisters and my aunt Zhenya —they all jeer at me and they say they've never heard of such a fool. They keep telling me to divorce you and remarry. When is all this going to end? Just look at me! I'm thirty-seven years old. In three years I'll be an old woman. I come home and I don't make myself dinner; I don't clean the room—I haven't the heart. I just flop down on the couch and lie there like a log. I beg you, my darling, please do something to get out earlier. You're so clever, invent something for them. You must save me!'

She had not meant to say any of this, but it was all too much for her. Shaking with sobs and kissing her husband's hand, she let her head fall against the rough, warped little table, which had seen many such tears.

'Please calm yourself,' the warder said sheepishly, glancing at the open door.

Gerasimovich's face froze. This unseemly weeping could be heard all down the corridor. The lieutenant-colonel stood grimly in the doorway, glaring at the woman's back, and shut the door.

The regulations did not explicitly forbid the shedding of tears, but, if one went by the spirit of the law, they clearly could not be permitted.

CHAPTER THIRTY-NINE

'Nothing could be simpler. You make a solution of chloride of lime and brush it on the identity card, just like that. All you have to know is how long to leave it and when to wash it off.'

'And then what?'

'It dries and you've got a clean, brand-new card, all you have to do is write in the name you want: like Sidorov or Petrushin, born in such-and-such a village.'

'And you never got caught?'

'Caught—for that? Clara Petrovna—or rather—would you mind if I . . .'

'What?'

'—call you Clara—while there's nobody around?'

'Go ahead.'

'Well, you see, Clara, I got arrested the first time because I was an innocent kid. But the second time it was a very different story. There was a general warrant out for me—and at a time when things were really tough—from the end of 'forty-five to the end of 'forty-seven. That meant I had to forge not only my identity card, with my residence permit in it, but also a work permit, ration coupons and so forth. And on top of it all I scrounged extra bread coupons and made my living by selling them.'

'But that's very bad.'

'Who says it was good? I didn't invent the system. I was forced to do it.'

'But you could have just worked.'

'"Just working" doesn't get you very far. No one ever did well from honest labour. And what job could I have done? They didn't give me a chance to learn a trade or a profession. Well, anyway—I didn't exactly get caught, but I made mistakes. In the Crimea, I got to know a girl who worked in the police there. Don't think there was anything between us—she just took a liking to me and told me about those funny serial numbers on identity papers: if you were in German-occupied territory during the war they gave you a special code number.'

'But you weren't in occupied territory!'

'I know I wasn't, but, remember, it was somebody else's identity card. So I had to buy myself a new one.'

'Where?'

'Clara! You say you've lived in Tashkent and know the Tezik market, and you ask me where! I was going to buy myself an Order of the Red Banner too, but the fellow wanted two thousand roubles; I only had one thousand eight hundred, but he was stubborn, and stuck out for two thousand.'

'But what did you want a medal for?'

'What does anybody want a medal for? Very simple— I just wanted to show off a bit, and make out I was a war hero. Of course, if I had a brain like yours——'

'What do you mean: a brain like mine?'

'Well, you're so cool-headed and sensible, and you look intelligent.'

'Oh, come on!'

'It's true. All my life I've dreamed of meeting a sensible girl like you.'

'Why?'

'Because I'm so scatter-brained. I need someone to keep me out of trouble.'

'Now, please, go on with your story.'

'Where was I? Oh yes, when I got out of the Lubyanka I was so happy that my head was spinning. But there was a little voice inside me saying: it's too good to be true, because they never really let anyone go. Someone told me in the cell: guilty or not, they always give you ten years hard labour, and the gag for another five.'

'What does that mean: "the gag"?'

'My God, what ignorance! And you a prosecutor's daughter! Aren't you interested in what your old man does? "The gag" means you're deprived of civil rights. You can't vote or stand for office!'

'Wait a minute, someone's coming,' Clara interrupted.

'Don't worry, it's only Zemelya. Just stay where you are —no need to move away from me. Take this folder here and pretend to be reading it. That's right. . . .'

'And so I reckoned they only let me out to keep tabs on me —to see which of my old pals I'd meet, and whether I'd go to see the Americans at their *dacha* again. I knew they'd never give me any peace and soon put me back inside again. So I fooled them! I said good-bye to my mother and left home at night. I went straight to the fellow who got me into the business of forging papers. For two years they hunted all over the country for me, but I kept moving around under false names—I went to Central Asia, Issyk-Kul, the Crimea, Moldavia, Armenia, Vladivostok. Then I suddenly felt home-sick and wanted to see my mother. I didn't dare go back home to Moscow, so I went not far away, to Zagorsk, and got a job as a labourer there in a factory and my mother came out to see me on Sundays. But after a few weeks there, I overslept one day and came late to work. So I was had up for trial.'

'And did they find out who you were?'

'Good God, no! They had no idea who I was and gave me three months under my false name. So there I was in a labour camp and the same old warrant out for me all over the country: 'Rostislav Doronin: Blue eyes, straight nose, red hair, birthmark on left shoulder.' I bet it cost them a pretty penny, that search. I did my three months, got my papers from the Camp Commandant and cleared off down to the Caucasus as fast as I could go.'

'And kept on the move again?'

'What do you think?'

'Then how——?'

'How did I get caught again? Well, you see, I decided I'd like to go back to university. . . .'

'Ah, I'm glad to see you at least wanted to lead an honest life. It's a very good thing to study. It's so worth while.'

'I'm afraid, Clara, it's not always so worth while. I thought about it all later on in prison. What sort of an education can you get from a professor who's scared stiff of losing his job? In an arts subject at any rate. You did science, didn't you?'

'Yes, but I was in an arts faculty for a while too.'

'And dropped it, I bet. Tell me about it later. Now, if I'd had any sense, and a little more patience, I'd have scouted round till I found someone to sell me his school-leaving certificate. It wouldn't have been hard to get one. I should have known better, but I thought to myself: surely they won't have traced me right back to my school? So I dug out my old certificate and applied to the university —but to Leningrad this time, in the geography department.'

'But in Moscow you did history.'

'I'd grown to like geography after all my wandering around. I had a hell of an interesting time seeing all those different kinds of landscape—mountains, valleys, forests, subtropics. And so many different kinds of people. Well, what do you think happened? I hadn't been at the university a week when they grabbed me! So there I was, back in jail. Only now they gave me twenty-four years and packed me off to the *tundra*, where I'd never been before—to do my fieldwork.'

'How can you laugh about it like that?'

'What's the use of crying? If I cried about everything, Clara, I wouldn't have enough tears. And I wasn't the only one. They sent me up to Vorkuta with a lot of other fellows to dig coal! Vorkuta's run on forced labour. So is the whole of the north. It's like Thomas More's dream come true.'

'Whose dream? I'm so ignorant, I feel ashamed sometimes.'

'Thomas More, the old geezer who wrote *Utopia*. He had the decency to admit there'd always be menial jobs that nobody wants to do. He thought about this and found the answer: even in a socialist society there'd be law-breakers and they should be made to do all the hard manual labour. In other words, there's nothing new about labour camps— they were thought up by Thomas More!'

'I can't take it all in. What a way to live these days— roving around all over the place on forged papers. I've never met anyone like you before.'

'But I'm not really like that, Clara! You know what Marx said: environment determines consciousness. I was a good boy, always did what my mother told me and read all the right books. My heart always sank into my boots at the mere sight of a policeman. Then gradually you learn better. What was I to do? Sit there like a rabbit till they picked me up a second time?'

'I don't know what you could have done, but what a way to live! It must feel awful to be a pariah like that, an outcast always on the run.'

'Well, sometimes it is awful, but there are other times when you don't feel so bad about it. When I think of some of the things I've seen—like the fellow in that market in Tashkent openly selling brand-new medals complete with blank citation certificates. Who was the crooked swine he got them from? See what I mean? I'm all for an honest life, Clara, but I think the same rules should apply to everyone—to everyone, get me?'

'But if everyone waits for the next person, things will never change. Everyone should——'

'Everyone should, but not everyone does. Listen, Clara, let me put it quite plainly. Why did we have a Revolution? To do away with inequality! What were the Russian people sick and tired off? Privilege! Some were dressed in rags and others in sable coats; some went on foot and others rode in carriages; some slaved away in factories while others ate themselves sick in restaurants. Right?'

'Of course.'

'Very well, then. In that case, why are people still so keen on privilege? And how can you talk about me? I was just a kid—I could only go by what I saw grown-ups doing— and it was really something, believe me! In the small town in Kazakhstan where I worked for a while do you think the wives of the local bigwigs ever went to the ordinary shops? Never! I remember once being sent to the house of the local Party Secretary to deliver a crate of macaroni. A whole crate —it had never been opened. You can bet this wasn't the first time—or the last!'

'I know, it's awful! That's always made me sick—do you believe me?'

'Of course I believe you. I'd sooner believe a human being than a book published in a million copies. Privilege spreads like the plague. Once people are allowed to buy in special shops, they'll never go anywhere else. Once they start being treated in special clinics, they'll never want anything else. Once they have their own cars, they'll never travel any other way. And if there's any swank place "for members only"—people will break their necks to get in.'

'Yes, I know, and it's awful.'

'Any bastard who can build a fence round himself is bound to do it. When he was a kid, maybe, he thought it was all right to climb a rich man's fence and steal his apples; now he puts up a great big fence of his own to keep everyone out, and he doesn't see why he shouldn't.'

'Rostislav——'

'Just call me Ruska, what the hell!'

'I can't do that.'

'In that case I'm going. There's the bell for lunch. I'm Ruska to everyone else, why not to you?'

'Well, all right, Ruska. . . . I'm not an utter fool, you know. I can think for myself, too. We've got to fight against all this—but not your way.'

'I haven't even started yet. All I'm saying is: you can't have equality unless it's the same for everyone, damn it! Oh, I'm sorry, I didn't mean to talk like that! It's just that they din all these beautiful words in your ears when you're a kid at school, and then you find you can't move an inch without pulling strings or giving bribes. So we all grow up to be crooks. You can't be squeamish if you want to get by.'

'No, you mustn't say that! There are lots of good things about this country. You are overdoing it. Don't talk like that! You've been through a great deal and had an awful time, but it's a poor philosophy to say you can't be squeamish if you want to get by. You mustn't say such things!'

At this moment Zemelya shouted over:

'Ruska! The lunch bell has rung, didn't you hear?'

'All right, Zemelya, run along, I'm just coming. . . . Listen, Clara: There's nothing I'd like better than to live a different life—I swear it. I've thought about it a lot. But I need a friend, a girl with some common sense who could help me to plan my life properly. Whether it's all right to say this to you, I don't know.'

'Yes, it's all right.'

'How easy for you to say that! But it's not all right, of course—with your background. You're from a different world altogether.'

'Don't think I've had such an easy time either. I understand.'

'You've been looking at me so nicely today—and yesterday as well—that I want to tell you everything about myself, as if you were my closest friend. I know I seem like any other prisoner but I . . . God, if only I could tell you what a knife-edge I'm on now! It's enough to give any normal person a heart attack. I'll talk about that later. But let me tell you this: I have the energy of a volcano in me, Clara. A twenty-five-year sentence means nothing to me—I could get out of this place any time. Only this morning I figured an easy way of doing it. The day I hear from some girl that she's waiting for me to come and marry her, I'll be out in three months with brand-new papers that nobody could pick holes in. I'd take her off to Chita, to Odessa or to Veliki Ustyug! And we'd start a new life. We'd be free—and live like decent, sensible people should live.'

'I can just imagine it!'

'You know how those characters in Chekhov always talk about life in twenty, thirty or two hundred years time? Or about doing an honest day's work in a brickyard and coming home dog-tired in the evening? What ridiculous dreams they had! But I'm not joking. I couldn't be more serious. Honestly—all I want is to study and to work. But not all by myself, Clara! How quiet it is, with nobody in the room. Would you like to go to Veliki Ustyug? It's a very ancient city. I've never been there yet.'

'What an extraordinary person you are.'

'I looked for her in Leningrad University, but little did I know where I'd find her.'

'Who?'

'Clara, I'd be like wax in a woman's hands. She could make anything she liked out of me—the world's greatest swindler, or card-sharper, or the leading authority on Etruscan vases or cosmic rays. Would you like that?'

'But you'd forge your diploma, wouldn't you?'

'No, I'd really do it. I'll be whatever you say. All I need is that head of yours—whenever you come into the laboratory, you have that way of turning it so slowly to look at me.'

CHAPTER FORTY

Pyotr Makarygin, a major-general by rank and a lawyer by training, had a long record of service as State Prosecuting Attorney in 'special' cases, that is to say cases whose subject-matter made them unsuitable for public hearing and were therefore dealt with *in camera*. Although not exactly a famous prosecutor he was very sound at his job and unwaveringly firm in the execution of his duties.

He had three daughters, all by his first wife. He had met her during the Civil War and she had died giving birth to Clara. The three girls had been brought up by their step-mother who had succeeded in being what is known as a good mother to them. His daughters' names were Danera, Datoma and Clara. As was the fashion in those days, Danera stood for DAughter of the New ERA and Datoma stood for DAughter of the TOiling MAsses. Clara was just Clara, and no one in the family could remember whether her name was supposed to mean anything. The girls had been born at two-year intervals. The middle one, Datoma, finished school in 1940 and managed to outstrip Danera somewhat by getting married a month before her in the spring of 1941. She was a slim girl with blonde curls down to her shoulders and loved it when her fiancé took her dancing at the Metropole. Her father disapproved of her marrying so young, but he had to give his consent. His son-in-law was an extremely eligible young man—a brilliant graduate of the Diplomatic School with powerful connections, the son of a famous father who had been killed in the Civil War. His name was Inno-kenty Volodin.

While the eldest daughter Danera lay stretched out on a divan reading the whole of the world's literature from Homer to Claude Farrère, her mother pulled strings at school to cover up her poor marks in mathematics. After school, and without any help from her father, Danera became a student actress at the Institute of Cinematography, where in her second year she married a well-known director;

evacuated with him to Alma-Ata she played the heroine's part in his film, then divorced him for professional reasons, contracted a liaison with a married man, a general in the army supply services, and set off with him for the field of battle—or to be more exact, for the Third Echelon, that best of all possible war zones, out of range of enemy shells and shielded from the horrors of war on the home front. There she met a war correspondent called Galakhov, who was just coming into fashion as a writer, and toured the front line with him, gathering heroic copy for his newspaper. She relinquished the general to his former wife and went back to Moscow with her writer. Since then Galakhov had prospered, Danera held a literary salon and enjoyed a reputation as one of the most intelligent women in Moscow.

So for eight years now Clara was the only daughter left at home.

Clara was never spoken of as beautiful, and rarely called pretty, but she had a face that was open and honest, with a hint of obstinacy suggested by the rather firm, angular cast of her forehead. There was firmness, too, in the unhurried way she moved her arms. She seldom laughed, spoke little and preferred to listen.

When Clara was in the ninth grade at school everything seemed to happen at once—both her sisters got married, the war broke out, she and her stepmother were evacuated to Tashkent (her father sent them there only three days after the German invasion) and her father was ordered into the army legal department as Chief Prosecutor at a divisional headquarters. They spent three years in Tashkent living in the house of one of her father's old friends, who was the local Deputy Chief Prosecuting Attorney. Living quietly in their second-floor apartment near the officer's mess of the local District Headquarters, they were shielded by the blinds on the windows both from the Central Asian heat and from the squalor of wartime Tashkent. For every one man called away from that city for army service, ten newcomers came in, and although every one of them had convincing documentary proof that duty required him to be in Tashkent and not in the front line, Clara had an uncontrollable feeling of being awash in a foul sewer.

Inexorably that law took its effect which decrees that

although no one goes to fight of their own free will, all the best and warmest-hearted men found their way to the battle-front and there, by the same process of selection, most of them perished. Three thousand miles to the west all was devotion, heroism and courage, while here it seemed to Clara that all of life's more unattractive aspects predominated.

Clara finished school in Tashkent, and the family began arguing about her future career. She had no leaning towards anything in particular, and no clear idea of what she wanted to do in life. It was Danera who made the choice for her; in her letters and on her farewell visit before leaving for the front she insisted that Clara should study literature at the university, although she had already found out at school that literature bored her: Gorky was regarded as sound, but he was such a bore; Mayakovsky was equally sound, yet somehow so clumsy; Saltykov-Shchedrin was so progressive, yet impossible to read for pleasure; then there was Turgenev —nice, but rather a fuddy-duddy with his old-fashioned aristocratic ideals, while Goncharov was studied for the light he threw on the beginnings of Russian capitalism, and Tolstoy spoiled himself as a writer by playing the peasant patriarch. (Their teacher had advised them not to read Tolstoy's novels, because they were very long and would only confuse the clear ideas which they had learned from reading critical studies about him.) And then there had been a brisk round-up of a whole heap of absolute unknowns like Stepnyak-Kravchinsky, Dostoyevsky and Sukhovo-Kobylin, who were, it seemed, so unimportant that one did not even have to learn the titles of their books. One writer alone —Pushkin—shone like the sun through all those years of dull names, dates and facts.

The teaching of literature in school had consisted entirely of forcible instruction in the meaning of these writers' works, their political attitudes and the ways in which they responded to the pressure of the laws of class struggle; then when the pre-revolutionary writers had been exhausted, it was the turn of Soviet Russian literature and the writings of the non-Russian fraternal peoples of the USSR, who were ground through the mill of Marxist analysis. To the very end of it all Clara and her school-friends never did manage to discover just why so much attention had to be paid to these writers: they were not, it appeared, particularly intelligent (the commentators and critics, and above all the Party leaders were all much cleverer), they often went wrong, made mistakes that would have been obvious to any schoolboy, came under bad influences—and yet one still had to write essays about them and woe to anyone who made a spelling mistake or put a comma in the wrong place. Was it surprising that young people left school with nothing but loathing for these monstrous taskmasters?

For Danera literature had somehow been different—it had been fun; and she assured Clara that at university it would be fun for her too. Yet it was not. The lectures were all about Old Slavonic philology and medieval chronicles; the courses on mythology and comparative literature were incomprehensible, while the talk in the seminars was always about Communist writers like Louis Aragon and Howard Fast, or dear old Gorky and his influence on Uzbek literature. Sitting through the lectures and seminars (although she soon gave the seminars up) Clara was always expecting to be given some brilliant insight into life—about wartime Tashkent, for example.

The brother of one of Clara's classmates had been run over and killed by a goods wagon when he and some friends had tried to steal a box of bread from a moving train. . . . One day, in one of the university corridors, Clara had thrown away a half-eaten sandwich into the dustbin, and at once a student of her year who also belonged to the Louis Aragon seminar, with only the clumsiest attempt to conceal what he was doing, fished her sandwich out of the rubbish and put it into his pocket. Another girl student once took Clara along with her to give her advice on what to buy in the famous Tezik bazaar—the biggest flea-market in all Central Asia, if not the whole Soviet Union. For the length of two blocks the street seethed with people and there was an unusually large number of men crippled in the war—men limping on crutches, men waving the stumps of arms, legless men pulling themselves along on little makeshift trolleys; men selling things, begging, threatening. Clara gave them what she could, her heart breaking. Further on it became more and more crowded, until it was almost impossible to shoulder one's way through the clusters of hard-faced black marketeers. No one showed the least surprise at the prices here or regarded them as anything but normal, although they ran into thousands of roubles and were completely out of proportion to most people's earnings. The shops in town were empty, but here you could buy whatever you wanted: there was everything—food, clothing, even American chewing gum, revolvers, or books on black and white magic.

But at the university not a word was said about this side of life; indeed, they seemed totally ignorant of it. From the way they taught literature there it appeared that the world was made up of everything except what you could see around you with your own two eyes.

Depressed at the thought that in five years time she too would end up by standing in front of a class, telling little girls to read boring books and pedantically correcting their spelling and punctuation, Clara began to spend most of her time playing tennis at the excellent local tennis club. So the long, hot autumn passed happily by. Then in winter came trouble—she fell ill. She was ill for a whole year. She lay in bed first in hospital, then at home, then in hospital, then back at home again. She was treated by specialists, given intravenous and intramuscular injections and transfusions, and examined by yet more specialists.

Throughout this time, when first her life and then her future health hung in the balance, all those nights lying awake in the dark, through all those days shuffling despondent and alone around hospital corridors, when the sights and smells grew utterly intolerable, Clara had little else to do but think. By the end of that year she found in herself the desire and the inner resources to cope with the complex realities of life— a life which made everything she had been taught at the university seem like so much idle, trivial chatter.

She did not go back to the faculty of literature. By the time she was convalescing the Germans were in retreat and the front line had advanced as far west as Byelorussia. All the evacuees started going home, and the Makarygins returned to Moscow.

It was strange, but amid the bright lights, the noise and

traffic it was as though all her thoughts about life, which had been so clear during the days of her illness, had become muddled and had faded away. Clara even found it hard to make up her mind on such a simple matter as what subject she should study now. She only knew that she wanted to do something where they *did* things rather than talked, so she opted for one of the technological faculties; and since she wanted nothing to do with nasty, big, dirty machines, she landed up in Electronics.

Lacking proper advice, she found after a while that she had again made the wrong choice, but she admitted this to no one, determined to work hard and finish the course. Besides, she was not the only one of her intake to have chosen her subject at random. In grabbing at the golden opportunity of a higher education, so many of her generation switched faculties with abandon: if they failed to get into the Institute of Aviation, they would sign on in Veterinary Surgery; if they were turned down by Chemical Engineering, they became palaeontologists instead.

When the war was over Clara's father was kept very busy in Europe, and was not demobilized until the autumn of 1945. He was immediately allocated a five-roomed flat in the new MVD housing project at the Kaluga Gate, and soon after his return he took his wife and daughter to inspect their new home.

The car drove up to the end of the railings that surrounded Neskuchny Park and stopped short of the bridge over the Ring Road. It was a warm October morning of an extended Indian summer. Mother and daughter wore dresses that rustled beneath their light raincoats, while Clara's father displayed a chestful of medals under his unbuttoned general's overcoat.

The Kaluga Gate block of flats was crescent-shaped, with one wing on Bolshaya Kaluga Street, the other on the Ring Road. The whole thing was eight storeys high, with plans for a sixteen-storey tower-block, where the tenants could sunbathe on the roof which would be topped by a forty-foot-high statue of a peasant woman. The building was still surrounded by woods and on the side facing the street and the square the brickwork was not even finished. However, as a result of pressure from above the builders had already finished a second portion, consisting of all the flats on one staircase, and had handed it over to the MVD.

As always on busy streets, the building site was surrounded by a solid wooden fence; somehow the passers-by managed not to notice the multiple rows of barbed wire fixed to the top of the fence and the hideous guard-towers above it, while the people living across the street had grown so used to them that they did not notice these features either.

The general's family crossed the square and walked around the building to where the barbed wire had already been taken down and the finished section had been fenced off from the 'work zone'. They were met at the main entrance by an amiable foreman; there was also a sentry on the door, but Clara paid him no attention. Everything was ready—the paint was dry on the banisters, the door-handles had been polished, numbers had been screwed to the front doors, the windows had been cleaned and only a shabbily dressed woman, her face invisible as she knelt down, was swabbing the steps of the staircase.

'Hey, you!' the foreman shouted curtly. The woman stopped her washing. Moving aside to leave room to pass her in single file, she did not raise her head from her bucket and floor-cloth.

The general walked past.

The foreman walked past.

Rustling her flounced, perfumed skirt and almost brushing the charwoman's face with it, the general's wife walked past. Perhaps goaded by the sight and smell of the skirt, the woman raised her head from her low kneeling position and looked up to see if there were any more of 'them'. Clara was transfixed by her look of burning contempt. Spattered with drops of dirty water, the woman had the sensitive face of an intellectual. Apart from the sense of shame which we all feel whenever we have to walk past a woman washing a floor, at the sight of this ragged skirt and this quilted jerkin with its stuffing coming out Clara felt an infinitely more intense stab of both shame and fear. She froze. Opening her handbag, she made as if to empty it and give everything in it to this woman—but she could not.

'Well, hurry up!' said the woman angrily.

Clutching the hem of her fashionable dress and wine-red coat, pressing herself against the banister and feeling a coward, Clara ran upstairs.

Inside the flat there was no need to have the floors washed —they were parquet.

They liked the flat. Clara's stepmother gave the foreman some instructions about the finishing touches and was particularly annoyed because the parquet squeaked in one of the rooms. The foreman tested a few of the blocks of wood by bouncing on them and promised to have it put right.

'Who are the people building this place and doing all the work?' Clara asked bluntly.

The foreman smiled and said nothing. Her father answered: 'Prisoners, that's who!'

On their way back the woman was gone and the sentry was no longer on duty outside.

A few days later they moved into the flat.

Four years had now passed since then, but Clara had been unable to forget that woman. She would only go upstairs by the lift, and if she happened to walk she would always press herself superstitiously against the banister at that spot on the staircase, as though afraid of treading on a woman swabbing the floor. It was irrational, but compulsive.

Clara's father found that in the four years of war his daughter had changed completely. In the past he had thought of his elder daughters as amusing but frivolous; Clara had seemed likely to be the thoughtful, serious kind. She had turned out to be thoroughly wrong-headed; although thoughtful, her mind worked on quite impossible lines. She picked up all kinds of dangerously harmful stories which she enjoyed recounting at the dinner-table; the stories themselves, in fact, were not so disturbing as the way she had of generalizing from any incident, however *untypical* it might be of Soviet life. Once, after listening to one of her stories, the old general had banged his fist down on his plate and stalked out, leaving his meal unfinished on the table.

Year after year the unanswered questions piled up in Clara's mind, and there was no one she could talk to about them.

Then one day, walking downstairs with her brother-in-law, she had been unable to stop herself from gripping his sleeve at the step where she always had to avoid the invisible woman. Her brother-in-law Innokenty noticed this and asked what the matter was. Clara stammered something, afraid he might think she was insane. And then she let loose all her pent-up thoughts.

Although normally a rather dandified, supercilious creature, Innokenty did not laugh now as he listened to all she had to say. Clasping her two arms he said, his eyes shining:

'Clara—I do believe you're beginning to see the light!'

Afraid to spoil that joyous moment of frank confidence, not moving from the step where it had happened, Clara put her hands in their open-work gloves on Innokenty's shoulders and bombarded him with all the questions that had so long been waiting to be spoken.

Innokenty did not reply at once. Dropping his normally bantering air, he simply stood looking at his sister-in-law, then he suddenly said:

'I only want to ask you one question, Clara. Why were you only a little girl before the war? You would have made me such a perfect wife. . . .'

Clara blushed, stamped her foot and took her hands away.

They went on down.

Later, she forced Innokenty to start answering her questions.

That conversation had taken place the previous summer, just about the time when Clara had been successfully filling in forms to apply for a job. Her social origins were irreproachable, she had been born at the right time, she had grown up in prosperity free of any of the sins which can blight the record of Soviet citizens. Her clearance having gone through, she walked past the guard-house and into the mysterious world of Mavrino.

CHAPTER FORTY-ONE

Together with all the other new girls from the Electronics Institute, Clara had also sat through the awesome briefing given by the swarthy Major Shikin—the briefing from which they had learned how they would be working among hirelings of world imperialism.

Clara had been assigned to the Vacuum Laboratory, where electronic tubes were made to order in vast quantities for the other laboratories. The tubes were first made in a small glass-blowing shop, and then brought to the Vacuum Laboratory, a big dark-room facing north, where they were emptied of air by three noisy vacuum pumps. These divided the room in half, like a partition, and even in daytime the electric lights were never switched off here. The floor was covered with stone slabs and there was always an echoing sound of people's footsteps or of chairs being moved. There was a prisoner in constant attendance at each pump, and there were two or three others sitting at desks. The only two free workers here were a girl called Tamara, and the head of the laboratory who wore a captain's uniform.

Clara had been introduced to this man in Yakonov's office. He was a stout, elderly Jew and had a certain air of resignation about him. Adding nothing to Shikin's warning about the perils ahead, he motioned her to follow him, and as they went down a stairway he said:

'Of course, you don't know anything and can't do anything, I suppose? In a professional sense, I mean.'

To this Clara gave a mumbled reply. As if she weren't terrified enough already there was now the fear of being shown up and made fun of for her ignorance.

She entered the laboratory, where the monsters in blue denims had their being, and felt as though she was walking into a cage full of wild animals.

And indeed, the three prisoners making vacuum tubes had very much the air of caged animals as they stalked up and down in front of their pumps. Because of an urgent order they had not been given any sleep for two nights running. One of them, an unshaven and bedraggled man of about forty with a bald patch—beamed all over his face at her:

'Aha, reinforcements!'

Her fears vanished. It was said with such disarming simplicity that Clara would have smiled back at him, had she not been as good as most girls are at controlling her features.

The youngest of the three, who was working the smallest of the pumps, also stopped. He was very young and had a gay, slightly mischievous face with large, innocent eyes. He looked at Clara like someone taken completely by surprise.

The oldest of them, Dvoyetyosov, whose enormous pump at the far end of the room made a particularly loud noise, was a tall, awkward man who, for all his scrawniness, had a large, bulging stomach. He looked contemptuously at Clara and went behind a cupboard, as if to avoid the sight of such an abomination.

Clara learned later that he was like this with all the free workers, and that whenever any member of the prison staff came into the room he always deliberately turned on some particularly loud machine, so they had to shout to make themselves heard. He never bothered about his appearance and would come in with a trouser button hanging by a thread, or with a hole at the back. Or he would scratch himself under his denims, while there were girls in the room, and say:

'It's a free country, isn't it?—so why should I worry?'

The prisoner who had spoken first was known by the others, including the younger ones, simply by his nickname, Zemelya, and he didn't mind this at all. He had what people call a sunny disposition, and was always grinning from ear to ear. As she got to know him better in the weeks to come, Clara noticed that he never seemed to worry about anything whether it was the loss of a pencil or the ruin of his whole life. Nothing ever made him angry and he feared no one. He was a born engineer, though what he really knew about was aeroplane engines, and he had been brought to Mavrino by mistake. But he had settled down here and was in no hurry to go elsewhere, rightly considering that he was better off where he was.

In the evening when the pumps were shut down, Zemelya loved to listen to what people had to say, or to talk himself:

'I used to be able to get breakfast for five kopecks. Come to that, you could buy anything you wanted. There were people shoving stuff at you all over the place,' he smiled broadly. 'And no one sold trash either—it would have been thrown in their faces. Then we had real boots in those days. They were made to last ten years—fifteen if you kept them in good repair. The leather on the uppers wasn't cut like it is now, it went right round under the welt.' He grinned and screwed up his eyes as if he was looking up at the warm sun. 'Or take the railways, for example: you could come to the station a minute before the train left, buy your ticket and hop in—there was always plenty of room. Life was very simple, very simple indeed. . . .'

Whenever there was talk like this, Dvoyetyosov, the older man, always came waddling out of his dark corner, where his writing desk was safely concealed from the prying eyes of the prison staff. He would stand in the middle of the room, his hands shoved in his pockets, his bulging eyes squinting over the glasses on the end of his nose:

'What are you talking about, Zemelya? What do you remember, I'd like to know?'

'I do remember a little,' Zemelya said, with an apologetic smile.

'Too bad,' Dvoyetyosov said, shaking his head. 'Better forget it. Stick to your pump.'

He stood there a little longer, foolishly peering over the top of his glasses. Then he shuffled back to his corner.

Clara's duties had turned out to be simple: taking turns with Tamara, she was supposed to be in attendance from morning till six in the evening one day, and then all afternoon till eleven at night the next day. The captain was always there during the day in case he was wanted by his superiors, but since he had given up all hope of promotion, he never came in the evening. The girls' principal task was just to be there and keep an eye on the prisoners. Apart from this, 'to give them practice', the captain assigned them small jobs of a non-urgent kind. Clara saw Tamara only a couple of hours each day. Tamara had worked at Mavrino for over a year now and seemed on fairly close terms with the prisoners. Clara even suspected that she was bringing in books on the sly for one of them. What was more,

Tamara went to a class, here on the premises, at which the free workers were taught English by prisoners (the advantage, of course, was that it cost nothing). Tamara had quickly allayed Clara's fears that these people were capable of anything terrible.

Before long, Clara got into a conversation with one of the prisoners herself—not, it was true, a political prisoner, but an ordinary one, of whom there were very few at Mavrino. This was the glass-blower, Ivan, who was, to his misfortune, a great master of his art. His wife's old mother had said of him that he was a glorious workman, and an even more glorious drunkard. He earned a great deal of money, spent the greater part of it on drink, was always beating his wife and setting upon his neighbours. But none of this would have mattered if he had not fallen foul of the MGB. He had been summoned to an interview with an important-looking official in civilian clothes who had offered him a job at three thousand roubles a month. At the time Ivan worked at a place where the standard rate was less, but where he earned more by doing piecework. Forgetting where he was, he rashly asked for four thousand. The official went up another two hundred, but Ivan stuck to his guns, and he was shown out. The next payday he came home drunk as usual and started to make a racket in the courtyard of the tenement house where he lived. This time the police, who previously could never be reached on these occasions, came at once in force and hauled him off. He was tried the very next day, and given a year. After the trial they took him to the same official who told him that he was being sent to do the job offered him before—but without pay now. If these conditions did not suit him, he could always go and mine coal in the Arctic.

So Ivan now sat in prison blowing cathode-ray tubes of all shapes and sizes. His one-year sentence was nearly up, but as a convicted prisoner he was now liable to deportation from Moscow and he was therefore begging to be kept on as a free worker, even at a wage of only one thousand five hundred roubles.

Though no one else in Mavrino was much impressed by this artless tale with its happy ending—there were people here who had met the Pope or Albert Einstein—Clara was

296

shaken to the core by it. It brought home to her that, as Ivan said, 'They can do just what they want.'

Her hitherto quite untroubled mind was suddenly assailed by qualms: suppose some of these people in blue denims had done nothing at all? If that was so, then might not her father at one time or another have sentenced an innocent man?

Not long after this she had been to the Maly Theatre with Alyosha Lansky, a young man who was taking her out at the time.

They were playing Gorky's *Vassa Zheleznova*, but it was a very dreary performance. The theatre was less than half full, and this seemed to put the actors off their stroke. They came on stage bored, like people arriving for work at an office, brightening up only when the time came to leave. It was almost a disgrace to play to such an empty theatre. The whole thing seemed like a silly game unworthy of grown people, and even the acting of the amazingly natural Pashennaya was ruined by the staleness of the occasion. One felt that if a member of the audience had said quietly in the hushed theatre, as in an ordinary room: 'Stop making fools of yourselves!' the performance would simply have disintegrated. The cast's embarrassment spread to the audience, so that everybody felt they were taking part in something shameful and avoided looking at each other. People were just as subdued in the intervals as during the performances. Couples strolled quietly up and down the foyer, talking in whispers.

As Clara and Alyosha walked around like this during the first interval, Alyosha stood up for Gorky and the theatre, reserving his strictures for 'Peoples' Artist' Kharov, who today was obviously just walking through his part. He was even harder on the Ministry of Culture which, with its bureaucratic approach, had undermined the confidence of the Soviet playgoer in 'our realist theatre'.

Alyosha had a regular, oval face and the good complexion of a sportsman. His eyes had a calm and intelligent look which they owed to the many books he had read in his twenty-seven years. The holder of a graduate degree in literature, a member of the Union of Soviet Writers and a successful critic enjoying the benign protection of Galakhov, Alyosha spent less time writing himself than keeping others out of print.

In the second interval Clara said she would like to stay in their box. The boxes next to them were empty and there was no one in the stalls below.

'I know why I'm bored with Ostrovsky and Gorky,' she said, 'it's this constant harping on the evils of money and the horrors of family life in days gone by—young women being married off to old men, and all that kind of thing. It's just fighting shadows—all this was fifty or a hundred years ago, but we're still supposed to get worked up about it. You never see plays about what's going on now.'

'Such as, for example?' Alyosha looked intrigued and smiled at her. He realized he had not been wrong about her: though you could not have told from her looks, life was never dull with this girl. 'Such as?' he repeated.

Trying not to be too indiscreet (it was a state secret, after all) nor to reveal the extent of her sympathy with them, Clara told him she was working with political prisoners, who had been described to her as hirelings of imperialism, but who on closer acquaintance had turned out to be quite different. What really worried her and what she wanted Alyosha to tell her was: could some of them be innocent?

He listened carefully and replied calmly:

'Yes, of course. That's inevitable under any penal system.'

'But, Alyosha! That means "they" can do just what they want! How terrible!'

Alyosha placed his pink, long-fingered hand caressingly on Clara's clenched fist, which was resting on the red plush of the edge of the box.

'No,' he said in a mild, but emphatic voice. 'Who do you mean by "they"? Nobody can do just what they want. Only history does what it wants. That sometimes seems appalling to people like you and me, but, Clara, you have to face the fact that there is a law of big numbers. The bigger the scope of some historical development, the greater the probability of particular errors, whether in tactics, or in the field of law, ideology, economics and so forth. We can grasp the overall process, the general trend of events, but the vital thing is to see that it's both inevitable and necessary. Yes, some people get hurt, of course—often through no fault of their own. Think of all those killed in the war. Or all those people who died so meaninglessly in the Ashkhabad earthquake last year. And what about road accidents? As the traffic grows, more and more people will get killed. The wise thing is to accept all this as a fact of life.'

But Clara angrily tossed back her head.

'Fact of life!' she exclaimed, in a whisper—the bell had already rung twice and people were coming back to their seats—'The law of big numbers ought to be tried out on you! It all sounds so nice and easy when you talk like that, but don't you see that things aren't always the way you write?'

'You mean we're just hypocritical?' Alyosha asked, a little on his guard now. He loved to argue.

'No, I don't say that.' The bell rang a third time and the lights began to dim. With a woman's love of having the last word, she quickly whispered into his ear: 'I know you mean what you say, but you're so frightened someone might upset your tidy system of ideas that you avoid people who think differently. You pick up these ideas by talking with people of your own kind, or from reading their books. "Resonance" —they call it in physics'—the curtain now began to rise and she hurried to finish: 'You all start off with the same stock of ideas and egg each other on until they seem tremendously . . .'

She broke off, now annoyed at herself for this senseless outburst, which spoiled the whole third act for both of them.

This was a pity, because the play finally managed to pick up, thanks to Royek entering into the spirit of her role as Vassa's younger daughter. Pashennaya, too, recovered her usual marvellous form.

Clara had perhaps herself failed to realize that she was concerned not so much by the fate of innocent victims in general as by that of the youngest of the three prisoners who worked the vacuum pumps—the boy with the blue eyes and dark-golden bloom on his cheeks who looked even younger than his twenty-three years. From their first meeting he had feasted his eyes on her, showing his sheer joy in a way that Clara had never known among her Moscow admirers. It had, of course, not occurred to her that the men she knew outside prison had a choice of women prettier than she, while Ruska had come from a camp where for two years he had not seen a woman, so that Clara—as

Tamara had been at first—was a source of unfailing wonder.

Yet Ruska had other concerns apart from his delight in Clara's company. In the seclusion of the dimly lit laboratory, he lived a rich, hectic life of his own: he was always surreptitiously making something, secretly studying English in working hours, or phoning his friends in other laboratories and rushing out to meet them in the corridor. He was always dashing about and seemed perpetually engrossed in something of extraordinary interest to him.

At the same time he by no means neglected his personal appearance. He wore a brightly coloured tie and always seemed to be wearing an immaculate white shirt under his denims. Clara did not know that it was only a shirt-front which Ruska had made himself by tearing a strip off a prison bedsheet.

The young men Clara met outside prison were already well launched on their careers and their whole demeanour, as well as their dress and conversation, was calculated to make them look dignified. But in Ruska's company she felt young and wanted to let herself go. As she secretly observed him, she felt more and more drawn to him, and could not believe that either he or the good-natured Zemelya were in fact the dangerous criminals Major Shikin had said they were. She was particularly curious about Ruska—what heinous crime he was supposed to have committed and how long his sentence was. She could see that he was not married, but could not bring herself to ask about the other things she wanted to know, in case such questions would painfully remind him of a dreadful past he wished to put behind him.

After two more months, Clara had got quite used to all of them and they often talked in her presence about small matters unconnected with their work. Ruska was always on the look-out for a chance to spend a little time alone with her in the laboratory during her evening duty, or when the other prisoners were at dinner. He would come in on the pretext of having left something behind, or of wanting to get on with his work while it was quiet.

When Ruska came to see her like this, Clara forgot all Major Shikin's warnings.

Their conversation on the previous evening had been so

intense that it had swept away the barriers between them, like a flood of water breaking through a dam.

It turned out that there was nothing so reprehensible about his past—he had been robbed of his freedom for no good reason, and now he craved for a chance to study and try all the things he had not been able to do in his short life.

He had lived with his mother in a village near Moscow. Just about the time he had finished school some Americans from the Embassy had rented a house near by. Ruska and his comrades had been careless enough—curiosity had got the better of them—to go fishing a couple of times with these Americans. At the time, it didn't seem to matter. But shortly after Ruska entered Moscow University that September, he was arrested. He was picked up secretly, in the street, so that for a long time his mother had no idea what had become of him. He explained to Clara that they always tried to arrest people like this to prevent them hiding anything or giving anyone a secret password or sign. They put him in the Lubyanka (which Clara had not even heard of until she came to Mavrino). His interrogators wanted to know what instructions he had received from the American intelligence service, and how he was supposed to pass information to them. As Ruska himself said, he was just a kid and, completely baffled by it all, he could only cry. Then suddenly, a miracle happened: he was let free from that place which no one ever left. . . .

That was in 1945: and it was this point he had reached in his story the day before.

Clara could hardly sleep that night. The next day, in defiance of all the rules, she had openly sat down next to Ruska, near the small, throbbing vacuum pump, and continued her conversation with him.

By the lunch break they were fast friends, like two children, taking turns to bite the same big apple. They could not understand why it had taken so many months for them to start talking to each other like this, and now there was hardly time for all they wanted to say. In his impatience to speak, Ruska sometimes interrupted her by putting his hand on hers, and she saw nothing wrong in this. After everyone had gone out to lunch, leaving them alone, the touching of their shoulders or hands at once took on a different meaning. Clara saw his bright blue eyes gazing at her in adoration.

'Clara,' he said in a choking voice, 'who knows when we will be sitting like this again? It's all like a miracle for me. I can't believe it.' He pressed and fondled her hands. 'Clara, perhaps my whole life will be spent in prison. Give me something to remember this moment by. Let me kiss you once—just once!'

Clara felt like a goddess who had appeared before a prisoner languishing in a dungeon. This was no ordinary, commonplace kiss. Ruska pulled her to him and kissed violently. She responded in kind.

He wanted to kiss her again, but Clara broke free—she was shaken and her head was spinning.

'Please go,' she said. He got up and stood before her, a little unsteady on his feet.

'Go now!' Clara begged.

He hesitated, but then did as she said. At the doorway he turned round, looked at her beseechingly and stumbled from the room.

Soon everyone returned from the lunch break.

Clara did not dare look up at Ruska, or at anyone else. She was tingling all over—certainly not from shame, but if this was happiness, it was most unsettling.

She heard someone say that the prisoners were going to be allowed to decorate a New Year's tree.

She sat still for three hours; only her fingers moved as she plaited a little basket from bright plastic-covered wires, a gift to go under the New Year's tree.

And the glass-blower, Ivan, returned from his visit, blew two funny little glass hobgoblins who appeared to be armed with rifles. Then he made a little cage out of glass rods, and inside it, on a silvery thread, he hung a glass moon which tinkled sadly.

CHAPTER FORTY-TWO

A dense grey blanket of low cloud had covered the sky over Moscow for half the day, and it was not very cold. Just before supper, when the seven prisoners stepped out of the blue bus on to the exercise yard at Mavrino, the first few impatient snowflakes began falling. One of them, a little star in the shape of a regular hexagon, fell on to the sleeve of Nerzhin's faded old army greatcoat. He stopped in the middle of the little yard and gulped the air deeply.

Senior Lieutenant Shusterman appeared and told him to go inside, as it was not an exercise period. This annoyed him. He did not just want to stay outside; he actively did not want to go indoors. He did not want to have to tell anyone about his visit, share it with anybody or seek anyone's sympathy: not to have to talk, not to have to listen. He just wanted to be alone and slowly to digest all the emotional nourishment that he had brought back from the visit before it dissolved and became a mere memory. But as in every prison camp, one can never be alone.

As he entered the building (prisoners had their own special entrance—wooden steps leading down to a passage in the basement) Nerzhin stopped and reflected where to go. Soon an idea came to him, and he started to walk up a back staircase which was hardly ever used. Pushing his way past a heap of broken chairs he set off up to the third-floor landing.

This landing had been converted into a studio for a prisoner called Kondrashov-Ivanov, who was an artist. He had nothing directly to do with the work done at Mavrino, but was kept there rather as landowners once kept talented serfs. The halls and passages of the main building had spacious walls which needed decorating with pictures. The private apartments of the Deputy Minister, Sevastyanov, and of some of his close colleagues, were less vast but more numerous; all the more pressing, therefore, was the need to adorn them with pictures that were large, beautiful and free of cost. Admittedly

Kondrashov-Ivanov's efforts to fulfil these aesthetic demands were unsatisfactory: although the pictures he painted were certainly large and cost nothing, they were *not* beautiful. When his patrons came to inspect his collection they tried in vain to explain to him how to draw and what colours to use, and so with a sigh they took what there was. Still, these pictures were always improved when they were put into gilt frames.

Passing on his way up a large completed picture that had been commissioned for the main entrance hall—*A. S. Popov demonstrating the first wireless telegraphy apparatus to Admiral Makarov*—Nerzhin turned the corner at the top of the stairs and before catching sight of the artist he saw high up on the wall straight in front of him a six-foot-high picture called *The Ravaged Oak*. Although it too was finished none of the artist's patrons wanted it. The picture was of a lone oak tree, which by some mysterious force was growing on the outcrop of a bare cliff-face. A dangerous pathway led up the precipice towards the tree, carrying the eye of the viewer with it. The tree was gnarled and bent by the hurricanes which blew there. The stormy sky behind the tree was a sky where the clouds never parted, the sun never shone. Disfigured by unceasing combat with the winds which constantly tried to uproot it from the cliff, this obstinate, angular tree with its broken, claw-like, twisted branches, had never given up the struggle and clung on to its precarious patch of ground over the abyss.

Along the walls of the staircase hung other and lesser canvases, whilst a few more were fixed to easels. Light came from two windows—one facing north, the other west. The window of the Man in the Iron Mask, with its bars and pink curtains, gave on to this landing, which was the nearest it got to the light of day. There was nothing else, not even a chair. The only seat was a log of wood. Although the staircase was unheated and the place was permanently damp and cold, Kondrashov-Ivanov's quilted jerkin lay on the floor and he himself, arms and legs sticking comically out of his shrunken denims, stood tall, motionless and erect apparently impervious to the cold. A large pair of spectacles, which made his expression look tougher and more severe than it really was, rested on his ears and nose with a firmness that withstood the constant jerky movements of Kondrashov's body. His gaze was fixed on one point and he held brush and palette in his hands that dangled at his side.

Hearing Nerzhin's furtive tread, he turned. Their eyes met, each still gazing with his own thoughts. The artist did not welcome visitors, as he needed to be alone and in silence, but when he saw who it was he was delighted. With total lack of hypocrisy, with a rapture that if it had not been his usual manner would have been almost fulsome, he exclaimed:

'Gleb Nerzhin! Come in, come in!'

He gestured hospitably with his brush and palette.

Generosity is a two-edged virtue for an artist—it nourishes his imagination but has a fatal effect on his routine.

Nerzhin hesitated shyly on the last step but one. Almost in a whisper, as though there were a third person whom he was afraid to wake up, he said:

'I don't want to disturb you. I came to see if I could . . . if you'd mind if I could just . . . sit down . . . without talking. . . .'

'But of course you can!' said the artist, also in a low voice, and nodded. He probably remembered, or saw from the look in Nerzhin's eyes, that he had been on a visit. Kondrashov stepped back as though bowing himself out, and pointed his brush towards the small log.

Gathering up the long skirts of his greatcoat, which he had managed to keep intact throughout his spell in prison, Nerzhin sat down on the log, leaned back against the banister railings and although he was longing for a smoke, refrained from lighting a cigarette.

The artist turned back to stare at the same spot on the picture.

There was silence.

Nerzhin basked in a faint and not unpleasant sense of emotional stimulation. He wanted to put his lips to the fingertips that had touched his wife's hands, neck and hair as they had said good-bye. . . . A man can live for years deprived of his birthright. All that remain are his reason (if he has any) and his convictions (if he is mature enough to have acquired them), and on top of it all—self-sacrifice and concern for the greater good of society. He becomes, in short, the Athenian idea, the very model of human-kind; but not a complete person.

The love of women, of which one is deprived, seems literally to outweigh everything else. Simple words like 'Do you love me?'—'Yes, I do. Do you love me?' said with looks alone or with lips moving in silence can fill one's very being with their joyous sound.

What a pity that he had not made up his mind to kiss her at the very beginning of the visit. Now, that kiss was gone for ever. His wife's lips had looked different, they seemed to have weakened and forgotten how to kiss. How weary she had been, what a hunted look there had been in her eyes when she had talked of divorce. Why not get legally divorced, though? To Gleb one piece of officially stamped paper was as meaningless as another; but as one who had endured a great deal in his lifetime, he knew that events and things have their own inexorable logic. In their everyday actions people never dream of what totally contradictory results such actions may have. Nadya would be the same; she would get a divorce in order to avoid the persecution inseparable from being a political prisoner's wife and having done so, before she knew where she was, she would have married again. Somehow, as he had watched her give a last wave of her ringless hand he had felt a stab of premonition that they were saying good-bye to each other for the last time. . . .

After sitting for a long while in silence Nerzhin came to his senses with a jerk, conscious that the last remnants of happiness from his visit had been banished by the grimly realistic trend that his thoughts had taken. Their effect, however, had been to bring his mind into equilibrium again and he began to revert to his customary prison self.

'You like it here,' she had said, meaning 'in prison'.

There was some truth in it. Sometimes he did not regret his five years in jail at all; they had acquired their own kind of validity. Where else but in prison could one get to know people so well, where else could one reflect so well on oneself? It might well be that his unique, preordained consignment to prison had saved him from countless youthful mistakes, from countless false steps. As Spiridon used to say: 'Sometimes it's the Devil himself who takes care of us.'

Or take this artist, so innocent that he was virtually invulnerable to the gibes of fortune—how much or how little had he lost by being imprisoned? Exhibitions? He would never have had the initiative to arrange for his works to be exhibited and if he had painted for fifty years not one of his pictures would have been hung in any decent gallery. Money? He would never have earned anything from his paintings, nor did he in prison. Admirers of his work? He has here just as many as he is likely to have had 'outside'. A studio? When he was a free man he never had as much space as he now has on this chilly landing. He used to live and paint in the same tiny, narrow space, more like a passage than a room. To have room to work he used to pile his chairs on top of each other, his mattress would slide on to the floor and visitors would ask him whether he was packing up to move house. He had one table and whenever he set up a still life on it he and his wife had to eat off chairs until the picture was finished. During the war oil and paint were unobtainable, so he used sunflower-seed oil from his food ration to mix his colours. To get a ration card he had to work, so he was sent to a Chemical Warfare Battalion to paint portraits of the soldiers who did best in military and political training. Ten of these portraits were commissioned, but he had a strong preference for one of his sitters, a girl, whom he exhausted by making her pose for hours on end. Worse, he failed completely to paint the sort of portrait that Headquarters required, and no one else had ever shown the least interest in buying the picture, which he entitled *Moscow 1941*.

Yet that portrait had caught the very spirit of 1941. It was of a girl dressed in a protective anti-gas suit. Her hair, not so much red as coppery-auburn, streamed out from under her forage cap and enveloped her head in a swirling aureole. Her head was thrown back, she was staring wildly in front of her at something horrible and unforgettable, and her eyes were filled with tears of anger. There was nothing feeble or girlish about her figure. Ready for action, her hands gripped the sling of her gas-mask satchel and the blackish-grey anti-gas suit with its harsh angular folds and the silvery sheen of its crinkled surface made her look like a knight in armour. This tough little girl from Kaluga had a look that was a mixture of bravery and cruelty; although she was quite pretty, Kondrashov-Ivanov had really shown her as he saw her—as Joan of Arc. The portrait was very close in spirit to a wartime recruiting poster with its caption of 'We shall never forget or forgive!' Yet no one liked this picture, no one bought it, it was never exhibited and his angry, vengeful madonna stood for years in his tiny room, turned to the wall, and was still there on the day of his arrest.

It so happened that a certain unrecognized and unpublished author once wrote a novel and invited a couple of dozen friends to hear him read it aloud—something in the nature of a gathering at a nineteenth-century literary salon. But that novel cost every member of its audience a twenty-five-year sentence of corrective labour. Among them had been Kondrashov-Ivanov, the great-grandson of the Decembrist Kondrashov who had been sentenced to twenty years exile for his part in the uprising, and who had acquired fame from the touching devotion of a French governess who loved him so much that she had joined him in Siberia.

Admittedly Kondrashov-Ivanov was not sent to a camp in Siberia, but went straight from the special tribunal to Mavrino where Sevastyanov arranged that he should paint pictures at the rate of one a month. For the past year Kondrashov had painted the pictures which now adorned the walls of Mavrino and other places. What could be better? Being a man of fifty, with a twenty-five-year sentence ahead of him that first tranquil year of prison had flown by; he treasured it, in case he might never have a year like it again. He was oblivious to the prison food, to prison clothes and roll-calls.

He painted several pictures in quick succession, often leaving a canvas unfinished and coming back to it later. He brought none of them to that stage which a master of his art regards as perfection. He was not indeed aware that such a stage existed. He abandoned each canvas at the moment when he ceased to feel there was something special about it, the moment when his eye began to take the picture for granted; he abandoned them whenever he found that they could only be marginally improved, that in fact he was spoiling them and not improving them at all.

When he abandoned a picture he turned it to the wall and

covered it up. Once they were put away, he cut himself off from his pictures; but when he picked them up again and looked at them before handing them over for ever, unpaid for, to hang in surroundings of vulgar luxury, the artist felt a thrill of excitement as he parted with them. Even if nobody ever saw them again, *he* had painted them! . . .

Fully awake again, Nerzhin now began to inspect Kondrashov's latest picture, *Autumn Stream*, or as the artist called it, *Largo in A minor*, a composition based on the four-to-five ratio of the Egyptian square. The picture was dominated by a stream at the moment just before it froze. It was impossible to tell which way it was flowing, because being just about to ice over it was scarcely flowing at all. The shadows were hinted at by brown shading, being the colour of the dead leaves lying on the bed of the stream. The left bank stuck out in a promontory, the right bank curved away. Blobs of the first snowfall lay on both banks, yellowish-brown grass thrusting up on the melted patches between them. Two clumps of willow grew by the water's edge, an ethereal smoky-grey, wet with melting snow. Yet this was not the main point of the picture; it was rather its dense background of a forest of blackish olive-coloured fir trees, amid whose front rank there flamed the rebellious crimson autumn foliage of a birch tree. Its solitary blaze of colour made the regiment of conifers seem all the more solid and grim as they thrust their spiked tops into the sky. The sky was a confusion of dappled streaks, so bleak that the setting sun, too weak to drive its rays through the murk, seemed smothered by it. But the heart of the picture was not here either; it was in the chill water of the stream as it stood waiting for the grip of the ice. It had consistency and depth. It was leaden yet translucent and it was very, very cold. By its power to absorb the change in temperature it held in itself the balance between autumn and winter and perhaps some other, less intangible balance.

This was the picture at which the artist was now staring.

There is a law that governs all artistic creation, of which Kondrashov had long been aware, which he tried to resist but to which time after time he feebly submitted. This law said that no previous work of his carried any weight, that it could not be counted to the artist's credit. The focal point of all his past experience was always the canvas on which he was working at the time; for him the work in hand was the ultimate expression of his intellect and skill, the first real test of his gifts. But he was so often disappointed. All of his previous works had disappointed him but each time he forgot the despair, so here he was working on something else, and it was again his first work—only *now* was he really finding out how to paint! And again he was in despair, convinced that it was a failure, that his whole life had been wasted and that he was totally devoid of talent.

For instance, this water he was painting—it had consistency, it was cold, it was deep and still; it was all these things but it did not convey the ultimate unity of all things in nature. Kondrashov, a man of intense feeling, never found in himself that wholeness which he perceived in nature and to which he paid homage; that gift of awareness, serenity and oneness. The question was—did his painting of water convey that sublime serenity or not? He went through agonies of despair wondering whether it did.

'You know,' Nerzhin said slowly. 'I do believe I'm beginning to see your point—all these landscapes of yours are Russia.'

'Not the Caucasus?' Kondrashov-Ivanov spun round; his spectacles did not budge, as though they were glued to his face. Athough this point was not Kondrashov's chief concern, it was nevertheless of importance to him. Many people came away baffled by Kondrashov's landscapes, which they found not so much Russian as Caucasian—too grand, too majestic to be Russian.

'You could certainly find places like that in Russia,' Nerzhin said with growing certainty. He stood up from the log and walked around, examining *Strange Morning* and other landscapes.

'Of course you could!' said the artist excitedly. 'Not only could you find them in Russia (if we weren't in prison I could take you to places just like this near Moscow) but you could *not* find them in the Caucasus. The trouble is that everyone has been taken in by Levitan. Thanks to him we've come to think of our Russian countryside as poor, humble and pleasant in a modest sort of way But if Russia were really

310

like that, how would you explain our religious fanatics who burnt themselves alive? How would you explain the revolt of the *streltsy* against Peter the Great? How would you explain Peter himself, the Decembrists, the terrorists like those who assassinated Alexander II?'

'Or Zhelyabov, or Lenin!' Nerzhin took him up enthusiastically. 'Yes, you're right!'

Kondrashov had no need of urging; he was in full flood. His spectacles flashed as he jerked his head round.

'This Russia of ours is not as tame as it looks! It will not submit! It has never meekly accepted the Tartar yoke! It fights back!'

'I see what you mean,' Nerzhin nodded. 'Take this ravaged oak of yours—how can people say it's Caucasian? But think what they can do to us, every one of us, even here in this most enlightened of the prisons. . . .' He gestured helplessly. 'Not to mention the camps—why there they don't just undermine our dignity: they make us give up the last remnants of our conscience in exchange for 200 grams of black bread.'

Kondrashov-Ivanov appeared to straighten up further, to stretch himself to his full, considerable height.

'Never! Never!' he cried, looking onwards and upwards like Egmont as he was being led to the block. 'No prison camp should ever destroy a man's dignity!'

Nerzhin said with a wry grin:

'Perhaps it shouldn't—but it does. You haven't been in a prison camp, so you can't judge. You don't know the way they grind our bones to powder in those camps. People go there as themselves but when they come out again—*if* they come out again—they are so different that they are unrecognizable. Environment determines consciousness, as we all know.'

'No!' Kondrashov-Ivanov spread out his long arms as though about to grapple with the whole world. 'No, no, no! That would mean utter degradation! What would be the point of living? Tell me, then—why are lovers faithful to each other when they're parted? Environment after all, should make them be unfaithful to each other. And why are people *different*, even though they are thrown together in *identical* conditions—in the same prison camp, for instance?'

Nerzhin was calmly convinced that his own hard-won

experience was superior to the fantastic imaginings of this eternal idealist, but he could not help admiring the strength of his conviction. Kondrashov went on:

'Man is invested from birth with a certain . . . essence. It is as it were the nucleus of his personality, his ego. The only question is—which determines which? Is man formed by life or does he, if he has a strong enough personality, shape life around him?' He suddenly lowered his voice and bent down towards Nerzhin, who had settled down again on the log: '. . . because he has something against which to measure himself. Because he can look at an image of perfection, which at rare moments manifests itself to his inward ego.'

Kondrashov was bending low over Nerzhin in a conspiratorial whisper, his spectacles flashing with anticipation, he asked him:

'Shall I *show* you what I mean?'

The argument was about to end as it always does when one crosses swords with an artist: they have their own special logic.

'Yes, of course, please show me!'

Without fully straightening up, Kondrashov shuffled furtively over to a corner, pulled out a small canvas nailed to a stretcher and brought it over, holding its back towards Nerzhin.

'Do you know who Parsifal was?' he enquired hoarsely.

'Wasn't he something to do with Lohengrin?'

'His father. The guardian of the Holy Grail.'

'There's an opera by Wagner about it, isn't there?'

'The moment which I have shown here isn't in Wagner nor in von Eschenbach, either. It is an idea of my own. It is what a man might experience when he suddenly glimpses the image of perfection . . .'

Kondrashov closed his eyes, compressed his lips and bit them. He was preparing himself. Nerzhin wondered why the picture he was about to see was so small. The artist opened his eyes:

'This is only a sketch. A sketch for the greatest picture of my life. I shall probably never paint it. It is the moment when Parsifal first sees the castle . . . of the Holy . . . . Grail!'

He turned round to put the sketch on an easel in front of

Nerzhin, staring at it all the while. He raised the back of his hand to his eyes as though shielding them from the light coming from the picture. As he stepped further and further back the better to take in his vision of it he tripped on the top step of the staircase and nearly fell. In shape the picture was twice as high as it was long. It showed a wedge-shaped ravine dividing two mountain crags. Above them both to right and left, could just be seen the outermost trees of a forest—a dense, primeval forest. Some creeping ferns, some ugly, menacing prehensile thickets clung to the very edge, and even to the overhanging face of the rock. Above and to the left a pale grey horse was coming out of the forest, ridden by a man in helmet and cape. Unafraid of the abyss the horse had raised its foreleg before taking the final step, prepared at its rider's command to gather itself and jump over—a leap that was well within its power. But the rider was not looking at the chasm that faced the horse. Dazed, wondering, he was looking into the middle distance, where the upper reaches of the sky were suffused with an orange-gold radiance which might have been from the sun or from something else even more brilliant hidden from view by a castle. Its walls and turrets growing out of the ledges of the mountainside, visible also from below through the gap between the crags, between the ferns and trees, rising to a needle-point at the top of the picture—indistinct in outline, as though woven from gently shimmering clouds, yet still vaguely discernible in all the details of its unearthly perfection, enveloped in a shining and lilac-coloured aureole— stood the castle of the Holy Grail.

CHAPTER FORTY-THREE

Except for the plump Gustav with his pink ears, Doronin was the youngest prisoner in Mavrino, and his face was still spotted with adolescent pimples. His good nature, skill and dexterity endeared him to everyone. On the few occasions when the prison authorities allowed brief games of volleyball, Ruska threw himself into it body and soul. If the men at the net let the ball through he would dive from the base line to return it, even at the cost of losing the skin off his knees. Everyone also liked him for his nickname, Ruska ('Ginger'), which seemed appropriate when, after two months at Mavrino he again grew a head of curly red hair which had been shaved off in the camp.

He had been brought from Vorkuta because he was listed in the MVD records as a lathe-operator, but in Mavrino he was soon revealed as a fake and had to be replaced by someone who really knew the job. He was saved from being sent back to camp by Dvoyetyosov, who put him to work on the smallest of the vacuum pumps. Ruska soon picked up the knack. For him Mavrino was like a rest-home, and he desperately wanted to stay. He had had a grim life in Vorkuta, though he now talked with light-hearted bravado about how he had nearly died in the mines, and had played the old prisoner's trick of faking a high temperature by putting stones under his armpits. When they tried to catch him out by using two thermometers, he found stones of equal size so that both thermometers never showed a difference of more than a tenth of a degree.

But in reminiscing cheerfully about his past—a past which would haunt him for the twenty-five years of his sentence, Ruska told very few people, and then only in secret, of his great feat in evading a nation-wide search for two years.

There had, however, been little to distinguish Ruska from the ordinary run of Mavrino inmates until a certain event which had taken place one day that September. With the air of a conspirator, he had gone round to twenty of the most influential prisoners—those who constituted a kind of public opinion—and told each of them with great excitement that he had just been recruited as an informer by Major Shikin and that he had agreed with the intention of exploiting his position for the common good.

Though Ruska's dossier abounded with notes of his five aliases and all kinds of code-marks and symbols indicating that he was dangerous, prone to escape and must be moved only in handcuffs, Major Shikin, bent on enlarging his network of informers, had decided that Ruska, being young, unstable and very eager to stay in Mavrino, would certainly prove reliable.

Ruska had been called to Shikin's office in secret—this was done by first summoning people to the main prison office—and had spent three hours with him. During this time, as he listened to Shikin's tedious rigmarole, Ruska's sharp eyes took in just about everything: the major's large head with hair grown grey in a lifetime of sifting and filing secret denunciations, his swarthy face, his tiny hands, his schoolboy's shoes, the marble writing set and the silk window blinds; and though he was sitting over five feet away, Ruska also contrived to read, upside-down, the headings on files and papers under the glass on Shikin's desk, noting which documents Shikin clearly kept in the safe, and which he locked away in his desk.

Yet, now and again, Ruska gazed with his innocent blue eyes straight into the major's and nodded agreement. The brain behind those guileless blue eyes was teeming with desperate schemes, but Shikin, used to the drearisome conformity of human beings, would never have guessed.

Ruska knew only too well that Shikin might indeed send him back to Vorkuta, if he refused to comply.

Like the rest of his generation, Ruska had been taught to believe that 'pity' and 'kindness' were concepts to be despised or derided and that the word 'conscience' was only part of the cant used by priests. At the same time they were told that informing was not only a patriotic duty but a service to the person one denounced and an activity conducive to the well-being of society in general. Ruska had not entirely swallowed this, but it had had some effect, and the question now uppermost in his mind was not whether informing was an evil thing in itself, but what the consequences might be. From what he had seen of life and heard in many a violent argument among prisoners he could even envisage that the day might come when the archives would be opened and all those Shikins would be covered with ignominy in public trials.

So he reckoned that in the long run it might be as dangerous to co-operate with Shikin as in the short run it would be to refuse.

But beyond these considerations, Ruska liked to gamble for high stakes. Peering at the intriguing papers under the glass on Shikin's desk, he thrilled at the thought of what games he could play. He was growing restive in the confined comfort of the special prison.

So, after enquiring for the sake of plausibility how much he would be paid, he agreed with a great show of eagerness.

When Ruska had left, Shikin congratulated himself on his psychological insight, paced back and forth in his office and rubbed his small hands: an enthusiast like this promised to yield a rich harvest of information. Meanwhile Ruska, no less pleased than Shikin, was making the rounds of all the prisoners who could be trusted, telling them he had agreed to become an informer just for fun—and also to study the Security Officers' methods and expose the real spies among them. . . .

Even the older prisoners could not recall anyone ever having owned up to such a thing. Mistrustfully they asked Ruska why he was risking his neck by bragging about it, and his reply was:

'When the whole of this gang is put on trial, you'll testify in my favour.'

Each of the twenty prisoners he had taken into his confidence told one or two more, yet no one went to denounce Ruska to Shikin. About fifty people were thus shown to be above suspicion.

The prison was agog with this story for quite a time. Everybody believed Ruska and continued to do so. But, as always, the situation had its own particular logic. Shikin kept demanding results and Ruska had to give him something. He went around to all his confidants and complained:

'Gentlemen! You can imagine how many reports Shikin gets if I've only been at it a month and he's already plaguing the life out of me. Give me a break and let me have something.'

Some brushed him off, but others gave a few tidbits. Everybody agreed that they should do in a certain lady who worked in Mavrino only out of greed, to add to the thousands of roubles already brought home by her husband. She treated the prisoners like dirt, and freely gave it as her opinion that they should all be shot. Though she said this only among the other free workers, it soon reached the ears of the prisoners. She had got one of them into trouble for having an affair with a girl, and another for making a suitcase out of prison materials. Ruska slandered her unmercifully, reporting that she mailed letters for prisoners and stole condensers from the laboratories. And though Ruska provided not a shred of evidence, and despite the protests of the woman's husband, who was an MVD colonel, the power of the secret denunciation in our country is such that the lady was dismissed and she left in tears.

Occasionally Ruska informed on fellow-prisoners too, but only over quite innocuous matters, and he took care to warn them beforehand. But later he stopped warning them and said nothing. Nor did they bother to ask him questions: they all sensed only too well that he was still reporting on them—but now about things he would not have cared to admit.

So Ruska suffered the usual fate of double-dealers: as before, no one gave his game away but they all began to avoid him. He wasn't able to make up for his membership of the stool-pigeon's confraternity by telling them how Shikin kept under the glass on his desk a special schedule showing when informers could drop into his office without being summoned: knowing these times it would have been possible to show up all the agents in their midst.

Nerzhin, who liked Ruska and was impressed by his intrigues, did not suspect that it was Ruska who had informed on him for having the book of Yesenin's verse. Ruska had no idea that the loss of this book would cause Nerzhin such distress. He had reasoned that, since it would immediately be established that the book was Nerzhin's own, it would not in fact be taken from him, and Shikin would merely be rather amused by Ruska's suggestion that the book Nerzhin was hiding in his suitcase had probably been smuggled in to him by one of the girls.

With the salty-sweet taste of Clara's kiss still on his lips, Ruska had gone outside into the grounds. The snow on the lime trees looked to him like blossom, and the air seemed as warm as in spring. In his two years on the run, when all his thoughts had been set on keeping out of the hands of his pursuers, he had had no time for women. He had gone to prison a virgin, and at night this weighed on him heavily.

Outside, he was reminded by the sight of the long, low, staff building of the spectacle he was going to stage the following day, during the lunch period, and about which it was now time to spread the word—he had not been able to do so earlier for fear of jeopardizing it. And buoyed up by Clara's adoration of him—it trebled his confidence in his own cleverness—he looked around and, seeing Rubin and Nerzhin at the far end of the exercise ground, by a lime tree with a double trunk, strode briskly over towards them. His cap had got pushed back so that part of his curly hair was rashly exposed to the mild air.

As he came up, Rubin had his back to him, while Nerzhin was facing him. Their conversation was obviously about something important: Nerzhin looked gloomy and very earnest. As Ruska approached, Nerzhin didn't move a muscle —there was not the slightest change in the look on his face or in the inflexion of his voice, nor did he give any sign that he had even seen Ruska—but the words he now spoke clearly had nothing to do with what he had just been talking about:

'As a rule, if a composer writes too much I'm always against him. For example, Mozart turned out forty-one symphonies. Only a hack could have done that much, couldn't he?'

No, they did not trust him. These words were, of course, a blind, and though there was nothing in them to tell Rubin that someone was coming, he turned around. Seeing Ruska, he said:

'Listen here, child. What do you think—is genius compatible with wickedness?'

Ruska looked at Rubin with no hint of pretence. His face shone with innocence and mischief.

'I don't think so, Lev, but for some time everyone has been avoiding me as if I was a combination of both. Gentlemen, I've come to make a proposal to you: how would you like it, if to-morrow during the lunch break, I betray all the Judases to you at the very moment they receive their thirty pieces of silver?'

'How can you do that?'

'Well, you know the general principle of a just society, that every labourer is worthy of his hire? Tomorrow each

Judas will be receiving his piece of silver for the third quarter of the year.'

Nerzhin expressed mock indignation: 'What mismanagement! It's already the fourth quarter and they're only paying for the third? Why such a delay?'

'A lot of people have to approve and sign the pay list,' Ruska explained in an apologetic tone. 'I'll be getting mine, too.'

'Why are they paying *you* for the third quarter?' Rubin asked in surprise. 'You only started half-way through the quarter, didn't you?'

'So what? It's a bonus for good work!' said Ruska, looking at them with a disarming smile.

'Do they pay you in cash?'

'God forbid! We get a money order from a fictitious person to be credited to our account. They asked me whose name they should send it in. "Would you like it from Ivan Ivanovich Ivanov?" they asked, but that sounds so hackneyed, it really jarred on me and I said: "Can't you have it sent from Klava Kudvyavtseva?" It's always nice to think there's a woman looking after you.'

'And how much do you get per quarter?'

'That's the funniest part of all! According to the pay list, every informer gets 150 roubles a quarter, but for appearance's sake it has to be sent by money order. Now, on 150 roubles the Post Office deducts a fee of three roubles. Since the security people are too greedy to make this up out of their own pocket and can't be bothered to suggest a raise of three roubles for their informers, and since no normal person would ever send such an odd sum by mail, these missing three roubles are the mark of Judas. Tomorrow during the lunch break you might all gather around near the office and try to take a peek at the money orders of anybody who comes out of Mishin's office. We ought to get to know our stool-pigeons, don't you think, gentlemen?'

CHAPTER FORTY-FOUR

At that same moment when the first sparse snowflakes broke
loose from the sky and began falling on to the dingy streets,
their cobblestones swept clear by car tyres of the last remnants of the past days' snow, the girl graduate students of
Room 418 in the Stromynka students hostel were engaged
in their usual Sunday afternoon pursuits.

Room 418's wide square window, divided into nine panes,
looked out on to the Sailors' Rest Prison. The room was
a long rectangle stretching from window to door, with a row
of three beds along each wall, separated by wickerwork
bookcases and bedside lockers. In the middle of the room,
leaving only a narrow space between them and the beds, were
two adjacent tables. The one nearest the window was the
'work' table, piled with books, notebooks, drawings and
heaps of typewritten pages, at one corner of which Olga, a
short blonde girl, had settled down to read some typescript;
the other was the communal table, at which Musa was
writing a letter and Ludmila was sitting in front of a mirror
taking her hair out of curl-papers. There was some space
between the last beds and the door, with enough room on
one side for some coat-hooks, on the other a washbasin
screened off by a little curtain (the girls were supposed
to wash at the end of the corridor, but they found the
washplace bleak, cold and too far away).

On the bed nearest to the washbasin lay Erica, a Hungarian girl, reading a book. She was wearing a dressing-gown
known to the room as 'the Brazilian flag'. She had other
fanciful dressing-gowns, which the girls loved, but whenever
she went out she dressed with great restraint, almost as if
afraid of drawing attention to herself. She had acquired the
habit when she had been a member of the Hungarian Communist underground movement.

The next bed, Ludmila's, was unmade (she had only just
got up) and the blankets and sheets hung down to the floor,
but a freshly ironed blue silk dress and a pair of stockings

were carefully draped over the pillow and bed-head. Ludmila herself was sitting at the table, loudly describing to no one in particular the story of how she was being courted by some Spanish poet who had been brought out of Spain as a boy at the end of the Civil War. She described the restaurant in great detail—what the band was like, what they had eaten and what they had drunk.

Resting her chin on her little round fists and trying not to listen to Ludmila, Olga was reading. She might have told her to shut up, but as Olga's dead mother used to say, 'Nobody likes a scold.' People had already tried stopping Ludmila from talking, but it only made her worse. She was not, in fact, a graduate student; she had already graduated from an institute of applied economics and had come to Moscow to train as a teacher of political economy, although coming as she did from a family where there was no shortage of money, she seemed to have enrolled in her course more for amusement than for anything else. What sickened Olga most of all about Ludmila's stories was this constant obsession with pleasure, with a side of life which demanded large amounts of money, spare time, an empty head and the belief, fundamental to Ludmila's character, that going out with men and relations with men in general, was not only the most important thing in life but the only thing. Olga, on the other hand, was firmly convinced that for their ill-fated generation of women (she had been born in 1923) it was out of the question to base one's life on that assumption. Accepting Ludmila's point of view meant tying your life to the thinnest of threads and daily expecting to see it broken or to discover that it had never been fastened to anything solid after all. Olga herself, however, had her own shimmering spider's web, which was swaying enticingly in front of her. That very evening Olga was going to a concert with a man she liked very much. The spider's web was there, she could even grasp it with both hands if she wanted to, but she was frightened by the thought of pulling too hard—it might break . . . So Olga had not yet begun ironing in preparation for the evening but instead was reading. She was just finishing—not from necessity but for pleasure—a smudgy second carbon copy of a report on excavations made during the past autumn in Novgorod, after Olga had left.

She had taken up archaeology late in her university career, just before her fifth year; she felt that even as a historian there must be some way of working with one's hands. Since then she had never regretted switching to archaeology: that summer she had experienced the thrill of personally unearthing a twelfth-century document—a letter written on birch-bark. This scrap, which she regarded as 'her' document, only contained a few words—a husband writing to tell his wife to send Sasha with two horses to such-and-such a place at such-and-such a time—but to Olga these few lines which she had dug up were like a clarion call from the past, of greater significance than the high-flown language of the old Russian chronicles. That a Novgorod housewife of the twelfth century should be literate meant that she must have been a most unusual woman. What a city that must have been! Who was Sasha—her son? a servant? What had the horses looked like that she gave into Sasha's charge to take away? . . . This simple domestic note made Olga so intensely anxious to know more about ancient Novgorod that she found it hard to restrain her imagination. Sometimes, even when she was working in a library, she would close her eyes and imagine that it was a winter's evening, not snowing and not too cold, and that she was driving in a sleigh on the road from Tver. Even from afar she could see a mass of lights and she herself was a woman of ancient Novgorod, her heart thumping with joy because she was going home after a long absence to this free city, her beloved, noisy, unique city with its half a million inhabitants. . . .

Ludmila, however, regarded the external trappings of her love affairs as the most thrilling aspect of it all. Even after three months of married life back home in Voronezh and her various subsequent liaisons with other men, Ludmila had always regretted that the days of her virginity had passed away too quickly. From the very start, therefore, of her acquaintance with this Spanish poet she had taken to acting the part of a chaste maid, trembling and ashamed at the least touch of shoulder or elbow and when the poet, his emotions deeply aroused, had begged her to give him her *first* kiss she had trembled so much, torn between excitement and despair, that she had inspired the poet to write a whole poem of twenty-four lines. Unfortunately, it had not been in Russian.

Musa, an excessively fat girl whose coarse features and spectacles made her look older than her thirty years, was too polite to interrupt Ludmila's irritating and offensive chatter, although she was trying to write a letter to her very elderly parents, who lived in a faraway provincial town. Her father and mother still loved each other like two newlyweds and every morning on his way to work her father would continually look round until he turned the corner and wave to her mother who would wave back to him through the open window. Their daughter loved them with equal devotion and there was no one in the world closer to her than her ageing parents. It was not only her habit to write them frequent and detailed letters about her doings, it was her pleasure. This time, however, she was in a frantic state. Two days ago, on Friday evening, something had happened which had overshadowed her tireless daily stint of work on Turgenev, an occupation which was her substitute for everything else in life. She had a disgusting feeling as though she had been smeared in something dirty and obscene which she could never either wipe off, hide or show to anyone, and that to go on living like this was impossible.

That Friday evening, back from the library and planning to go to bed early, she had been called into the hostel office and told to go into an adjoining room. Sitting there were two men in plain-clothes who began by being very polite, introducing themselves as Nikolai Ivanovich and Sergei Ivanovich. Unconcerned by the lateness of the time of day, they had kept her for an hour, then two, then three. At first they questioned her on the people she lived with, then on those she worked with (although they naturally knew all this as well as she did). They talked to her at length about patriotism, about how it was the duty of a member of a learned profession not to shut themselves up in an ivory tower but to put all their abilities at the service of society. All this was true enough and Musa could find nothing objectionable in it. Then the two men had suggested that she should 'help' them, by meeting one of them at certain agreed times in this office, or at the Party reading-room, or in one of the university club-rooms, where she would have to answer various questions or tell them what she had been able to observe.

Then began the most protracted and terrible part of the whole interview. Their manner became more and more rude and they shouted at her things like: 'Stop being so obstinate! We're not a foreign intelligence agency trying to recruit you!' 'She'd be as much use to a foreign spy-ring as a fifth leg on a horse! . . .' At this point they threatened quite openly that if she did not do as they said she would not be allowed to present her thesis (she was in the final stage of her work, which had to be finished by June, and her thesis was almost ready) and her career would be ruined, because the country had no need of people who refused to behave like responsible citizens. This frightened her very much; she quite believed that they might easily have her expelled from the university. It was then that one of them took out a pistol and as they passed it back and forth between them it was aimed, as though casually, at Musa. The effect on her of the pistol was, however, the exact opposite of that intended. She ceased being frightened, because the thought of being shot alarmed her less than the prospect of being dismissed from the university with an adverse report. At one o'clock in the morning they had let her go, giving her till Tuesday to think it over—till this coming Tuesday the 27th of December—and had made her sign a promise to keep the subject of her interview strictly secret. They had assured her that they knew about *everything* that went on and if she discussed this talk with anyone, her signature on this document meant that she would be arrested and sent for trial.

By what unhappy chance had they picked on her? Now with a feeling of being doomed to wait until Tuesday, unable to work, she recalled the times, only a few days ago, when she had thought of nothing but Turgenev, when there had been nothing to make her life an agony and she, fool that she was, had not realized how happy she had been. . . .

'. . . so I said to him—you Spaniards are always so concerned with a person's honour. Don't you see that if you were to kiss me on the lips I should be dishonoured?' Beneath her blonde hair Ludmila's attractive but rather hard face mimicked the despair of a girl who has been dishonoured.

Olga sighed noisily and put down her archaeological report. She wanted to snap at Ludmila, but restrained herself. At moments like this her chin, as charmingly rounded as were her whole face and her wrists, took on a cast of firmness. Frowning, she stood up in silence and stretched out (she was so short that she could hardly reach) to switch on the iron at the adaptor in its lamp socket, from which it had not been unplugged since Ludmila had finished ironing. (At Stromynka electric irons and boiling-rings were strictly forbidden; the hostel wardens were always on the lookout for adaptors and none of the rooms were provided with sockets.)

Meanwhile the slender Erica was reading the *Selected Works* of Galakhov. This book opened up for her a world of high-minded people, a bright and beautiful world where all troubles were overcome with ease. Galakhov's heroes never thought twice about serving their country or sacrificing their lives. Erica was amazed by their strength of character and single-mindedness. She had to admit that when she had belonged to the underground in Admiral Horthy's Hungary she could never have experienced such remorse over not paying her Komsomol membership dues as did Galakhov's young Communist while he was blowing up trains behind the enemy lines.

Putting down the book and rolling over on to her side she joined in to listen to Ludmila's story. Here in Room 418 she had come to hear of the most extraordinary things: how an engineer had turned down an exciting job on a construction site in Siberia and had preferred to stay in Moscow selling beer; how someone else had won their doctorate but still could not get a job. (Erica's eyes had widened—'Surely there aren't any unemployed in the Soviet Union?') To get a Moscow residence permit, it appeared, someone's palm had to be well greased. 'Of course that's only a temporary problem, isn't it?' Erica had said.

Ludmila finished the story about her poet by saying that if he did marry her, she had no alternative but to give a physically convincing performance of being a virgin and she started to describe how she proposed to do this on her wedding night.

A wrinkle of pain flicked across Musa's forehead. Unable to restrain herself any longer she banged on the table and said:

'But that's rubbish! Think of all the women in literature who suffered rather than . . .'

'They were fools, that's all!' Ludmila replied gaily, pleased that someone was listening to her. 'Because they thought it couldn't be done. . . . But it's so easy!'

Olga removed the blanket from the end of the communal table and tested the iron. Her new greyish-brown coat and skirt meant everything to her. She lived on *kasha* and potatoes (since the beginning of the war she could not remember a time when she had had enough to eat) and if she could ever avoid paying forty kopecks for her trolley-bus fare she did so, but this suit of hers was a good one, there was nothing about it to feel ashamed of. . . . She would probably have minded less about burning herself with the iron than scorching her suit.

Ludmila, however, doubted whether she would marry this poet:

'He's not a member of the Union of Soviet Writers, he writes all his stuff in Spanish and how on earth he expects to earn a living at it I simply can't imagine!'

Erica was so amazed that she swung her feet on to the floor.

'What?' she enquired. 'Do you . . . do people in the Soviet Union marry for *money*?'

'You'll find out when you've been here long enough,' said Ludmila, shaking her head as she looked into a mirror. She had taken out all her curl-papers and her head was a mass of fair curls. One of them alone would have been enough to ensnare the heart of a young poet.

'Girls, I've come to the conclusion that . . .' Erica began, then noticing that Musa was looking down at the floor beside her with an odd expression she screamed and swung her legs back on to the bed.

'Has it gone?' she cried, her face distorted.

326

The girls laughed. There was nothing there.

Occasionally in the daytime, though they were bolder at night, horrible Russian rats would run squeaking, their little feet pattering, across the floor of Room 418. In all her years of fighting Horthy in the underground movement Erica had never been as frightened as she was now by the thought that these rats might jump up on to her bed and run all over her. With her friends there to laugh at her she was not so frightened in the daytime, but at night she wrapped herself, head and all, in the blankets and swore that if she survived till morning she would leave the hostel. Nadya, who was doing her thesis in chemistry, brought some poison, which they applied liberally around the room, but this only kept them down for a while and before long they were back again. Two weeks ago Erica had made up her mind. Scooping water out of the bucket one morning she had fished out a drowned baby rat in her mug. Shaking with disgust as she remembered the look of quizzical concentration on its little pointed face, Erica went that same day to the Hungarian Embassy and begged to be moved into a single apartment. The Embassy sent a request to the Ministry of Foreign Affairs of the USSR, the Ministry of Foreign Affairs passed it to the Ministry of Higher Education, the Ministry of Higher Education passed it to the Rector of the University who in turn handed it to his Administrative Department. The Administrative Department replied that there were no single apartments available at present and that they had never had a complaint about rats in Stromynka before. The correspondence went back and forth again, while the Embassy still held out a hope that they would find Erica an apartment.

She now sat, clasping her knees to her chest, wrapped in her Brazilian flag like an exotic bird.

'Oh, girls, girls,' she said in a pathetic sing-song. 'I like you all so much, I wouldn't leave you for anything if it weren't for the rats!'

This was only partly true. Although she did like the girls, Erica had found that there was not one of them to whom she could talk about the deep anxiety she felt for the fate of her poor Hungary. Since the trial of Laszlo Rajk strange things had been happening in Hungary. Rumours had leaked out that Communists, fellow-members with her of the underground movement, were being arrested. A nephew of Rajk, also studying at Moscow University, and some other Hungarian students with him, had been recalled to Hungary and no one had heard a word from them since.

There was a knock at the door (it was the agreed signal meaning 'Don't hide the iron, it's one of us'). Musa stood up and, limping slightly from her premature rheumatism in one knee, unlatched the door. In bustled Dasha, a brisk girl with a large, slightly crooked mouth.

'Hello, girls,' she said laughing, but without forgetting to replace the latch. 'Just wrenched myself away from a fate worse than death. Guess who with!'

'Are you so well off for boy-friends?' Ludmila asked in surprise as she rummaged in her suitcase. The university had still not fully recovered from the war; there was only a handful of men among the post-graduates and these few were all somehow inadequate.

'Wait!' Entering into the spirit of the game Olga flung her arms forward and stared hypnotically at Dasha, first having stood the iron on its end. 'Jaws?'

('Jaws' was a doctoral candidate who had twice failed in Dialectical and Historical Materialism and had been dismissed from the graduate school as invincibly stupid.)

'The Waiter!' cried Dasha, taking her fur hat with ear-flaps off from her dark, tightly curled hair. She stood by the door, slowly removing her cheap overcoat with its goatskin collar which she had been able to buy three years before with her clothing coupons in the university shop.

'Oh, him!'

'I was riding in a tram and he got on,' said Dasha, laughing, 'and he recognized me at once. "Which stop are you going to?" Well, what could I do? We got off together. "Do you still work in the same bath-house? I went there often enough but you were never there." '

'You should have said . . .' Olga gasped, almost speechless from Dasha's infectious laughter, 'you should have said . . . you should have said . . .' Quite unable to finish her suggestion she collapsed, roaring with laughter, on to her bed.

'What waiter? What bath-house?' Erica managed to put in.

'You should have said . . .' Olga spluttered, but was seized by another paroxysm of laughter. She stretched out her hands and tried to convey by waving her fingers what she could not say aloud.

Ludmila began laughing too, as did the mystified Erica, and even Musa's stern, plain face broke into a smile. She took off her spectacles and wiped them.

'He asked me where I was going and whether I knew anybody at the student hostel,' said Dasha, choking with laughter, 'so I said . . . the janitress was a friend of mine . . . and she was knitting . . . some mittens for me!!'

'Mittens?!'

'Yes!'

'Please tell me—who's this waiter?' begged Erica.

Olga, who choked easily when she laughed, had to be patted on the back. She laughed not only because she was young but also because she had a theory that laughter is good both for the person who laughs and for the person who hears it and that only someone who can laugh heartily is fit to live.

They calmed down. The iron grew hot waiting to be used. Olga started dexterously splashing water on her jacket and carefully held a white cloth over it. Dasha took off her overcoat. Her tight grey sweater and plain, belted skirt showed off her slender, well-proportioned figure which never sagged after a long day bent over her work. Turning back her brightly coloured counterpane she carefully perched on the edge of her bed. It was adorned with almost ritual neatness—the bolster and pillows carefully fluffed up, a lace pillowslip, and embroidered napkins displayed on the wall behind. She explained to Erica:

'It was last autumn, when it was still quite warm, before you came here . . . the question was—how to find a boy-friend? Who is there to introduce you to one? So Ludmila advised me to go for a walk in Sokolniki Park—alone! A girl doesn't have a chance when you go in twos and threes.'

'It never fails,' said Ludmila. She was carefully removing

a stain from the toe of her shoe. 'There's something odd about a girl by herself. Men seem drawn to her.'

'So I went,' Dasha went on, only she no longer sounded cheerful. 'I walked around, sat down, looked at the trees. And sure enough a man soon came and sat beside me. Nothing special to look at. He turned out to be a waiter, working in a snack-bar. And where did I work? he asked . . . I felt too ashamed to say I was a graduate student. An educated woman scares a man off . . .'

'Oh come, don't say that! The idea's too depressing . . .' Olga put in crossly.

In the decimated and ruined world left after the iron hulk of war had been hauled away, when instead of all the men of their own age or men five, ten or fifteen years older than they there were only gravestones, she could not possibly have spoiled her chance of a night out by admitting that she was one of those despised 'educated women'.

'. . . So I said I was a cashier at some public baths. He insisted on knowing which baths and which shift I worked. I had a job getting away from him. . . .'

All Dasha's animation was gone, her dark eyes staring miserably in front of her. She had worked all day long in the Lenin Library, then eaten an inadequate, nasty meal in the dining hall and was now coming back to the depressing prospect of a long, empty Sunday evening. Once, in the senior classes of her large, roomy, timber-built school in the country she had enjoyed her education. She had been thrilled when she was allowed a residence permit in Moscow in order to study at the university. But she was not getting any younger now, she had been at school and university for a total of eighteen years and she was getting fed up with constantly studying until her head ached. And what was it all for? How would it help her to experience the simple joy of having a baby, when there was no one to father it?

As the room fell silent Dasha, with a thoughtful expression, came out with her favourite saying:

'No, girls, life isn't like it is in books.'

There was a man in Dasha's life, an agronomist at the collective farm near her home in the country, who was writing to her and asking her to marry him. Soon, though, she would take her degree and the whole village would be asking why she had bothered to study so much when she was just going to end up by marrying this man. After all, any farm girl could do the same. . . . On the other hand, Dasha felt that even with her degree she would never fit into the sort of world she would have liked to be in—she lacked that ease of manner, which the brazen Ludmila had. With an envious glance at Ludmila, Dasha said:

'I should wash your feet if I were you, my dear.'

Ludmila inspected herself.

'Do you think so?'

To do this she would have to heat some water on the boiling-ring (which was also kept hidden) and the adaptor was in use with the iron. Dasha felt a need to busy herself with something as a cure for her unhappiness, and she remembered that she had bought some new underwear which had been the wrong size, but which she had snapped up while it was available. She took it out and began to alter it to fit her.

Now the only break in the general silence was the faint creak of the table as Olga ironed, and Musa could really concentrate on her letter again. But it was no good—it sounded wrong. She re-read her last few sentences, changed a word, tidied up a few indistinct letters . . . but it was still no good. Her letter contained lies and her parents would sense it at once. They would realize that something was worrying their daughter, that something unpleasant had happened—but that she wouldn't say outright what it was. What could make her tell lies for the first time in her life? If there had been no one else in the room Musa would have groaned, or wept aloud and it might have helped a little. Instead she threw down her pen and put her head in her hands, hiding her face from the others. This was it—the most crucial decision of her life and no one to ask for advice, no one who could help her. On Tuesday she would have to face those two men again, those two slick professional manipulators. This, she felt, must be what it is like when a shell splinter enters your body—a metallic chunk of alien matter that feels much bigger than it really is. How good it would be *not* to have that steel fragment lodged in your chest. There was no removing it now; there was no hope, because these men never gave up and never left you alone. But she could not give in either. How could she write about the elements of Hamlet and Don Quixote in the human character, knowing all the time that she was an informer, that she had an agent's cover-name—some carefully nondescript pseudonym like 'Sweetheart' or 'Rover', a name suitable for a dog—and that she had to supply information on these girls, or on her professor. . . .

Screwing up her eyes, Musa tried unobtrusively to brush away the tears.

Olga had finished ironing her skirt, and now it was the turn of her pale fawn blouse with the bright pink buttons.

'Where's Nadya?' asked Dasha.

Nobody answered. Nobody knew.

As she sat over her sewing, Dasha had a sudden impulse to talk about Nadya and she went on:

'How long do you think she can keep it up? He was posted as missing but the war's been over for five years now. Don't you think she ought to make a complete break and start living again?'

'Oh, stop it!' Musa cried in anguish, clasping her head in her hands. The wide sleeves of her grey check dress slid down to her elbows, baring her flabby white arms. 'It's because she really loves him! True love lasts beyond the grave!'

Olga twisted her moist, slightly puffy lips and said,

'Beyond the grave? Aren't you getting a bit metaphysical, Musa?'

'During the war,' Erica put in, 'many men were sent far away, overseas even. Maybe he's over there and still alive.'

'Yes, it's possible,' Olga agreed. 'She may still be hoping for that. But Nadya, you know . . . she's one of these people who thrives on sorrow—her own, that is. There'd be something missing from her life if she didn't have something to be miserable about.'

Pausing in her needlework, Dasha waited until they had all had their say and slowly rubbed the point of her needle back and forth along a seam as though she were sharpening it. When she had started this conversation she knew that she had something to say which was going to surprise them all.

'Listen,' she said portentously, 'what Nadya tells us is all

332

a pack of lies. She doesn't think her husband's dead and she's not hoping that one day he may turn up. She knows perfectly well that her husband is alive, and what's more she knows *where* he is.'

'How do you know?' the girls interrupted her in a confused babble.

Dasha gazed triumphantly round. Her room-mates had long since nicknamed her 'the detective' because of her rare perspicacity.

'By using my ears. Has she ever talked about him as if he were dead? No, she hasn't. She even tries not to say "he *was*", but somehow manages without either "was" or "is". If he really were missing, don't you think there might be the odd occasion when she'd think of him as being dead?'

'In that case what has become of him?'

'What!' cried Dasha, laying her work aside altogether. 'Can't you guess?'

They could not.

'He's alive, but he's left her! And she's too ashamed to admit it! It's so humiliating. So she made up the story that he's "missing".'

'Yes, I believe that,' said Ludmila in agreement as she splashed about behind the screen.

'You mean she's sacrificing herself for his sake!' Musa exclaimed. 'She feels she must keep quiet about it and not marry again!'

'Good for you, Dasha, I'm sure you're right,' said Ludmila, leaping out from behind the screen wearing only her slip. Bare-legged, she looked even slimmer and taller. 'She was so miserable about it that she invented this pious act about being faithful to a dead man's memory. Far from sacrificing herself she's really dying for someone to make a pass at her, but nobody *wants* her. If one of us walks down the street every man turns round and stares, but no one would want her even if she threw herself at them.'

And Ludmila vanished behind the screen again.

'But not everybody expects to be stared at in the street,' Olga objected. 'One ought to be above that sort of thing.'

Ludmila laughed aloud. 'It's easy enough to say that when you're one of those who *do* get stared at in the street.'

'Still, Shchagov comes to see her.' said Erica.

'Comes to see her! That's nothing,' scoffed Ludmila, invisible. 'What counts is getting him hooked.'

'What does "hooked" mean?' Erica asked innocently.

Everybody laughed.

'You may say that,' Dasha persisted, 'but suppose she was still hoping to get her husband back from the other woman?'

The secret knock came at the door.

Everybody stopped talking and Dasha opened the latch. With her shuffling walk and haggard face Nadya entered, looking just as if she were doing her best to confirm all the unkindest things that Ludmila had been saying about her. Strangely she did not even say something like 'Well, here I am,' or 'Hello, girls?' She simply hung up her coat and walked over to her bed. At this moment the hardest thing of all for her would have been to make small-talk.

Erica went on reading. Olga switched on the ceiling light and finished her ironing.

No one could find anything to say. To cover up the awkward silence. Dasha picked up her sewing again and drawled, as though finishing something she had been saying:

'Life isn't like it is in books. . . .'

CHAPTER FORTY-FIVE

After her visit to Gleb, Nadya wanted only to be with other women in the same plight and all she felt in the mood to talk about was their menfolk behind bars. She went straight from Lefort all the way across Moscow to Sologdin's wife in Krasnaya Presnya: she had to pass on the solemn message that had been entrusted to her.

But Nadya did not find her at home—for the simple reason that Sunday was the only day Sologdin's wife had for all the week's errands, both for herself and her son. Nadya could not leave a note with the neighbours either: Sologdin's wife had told her, and she could well believe it, that her neighbours were unfriendly and spied on her.

Nadya had walked quickly up the steep, dark stairs,

looking forward to talking with this woman who shared her secret grief. She came down again feeling not just disappointed, but almost distraught. And as images slowly appear on blank paper in the photographer's dark-room, all the gloomy thoughts and forebodings which had come to her in prison now took shape and began to weigh on her mind.

There was no doubt about it: he had said she should not be surprised if they sent him away from Moscow and his letters stopped. What on earth would she do then, without even these annual visits to look forward to?

And hadn't he used some peculiar phrase about God? Prison was breaking his spirit, and making an idealist or a mystic of him. He would come back a changed man and she wouldn't know him any more.

But the worst thing had been his saying, almost threateningly: 'Don't bank too much on my being released when my sentence is up . . . a sentence is an elastic thing.' She had cried out that she couldn't believe it, that it was unthinkable. But now, as the hours went by and she travelled all the way back across Moscow, from Krasnaya Presnya to the hostel in Stromynka, she was at the mercy of these anxious thoughts. If Gleb's prison term would never end, what was the use of waiting, and why go on living?

She got back to the hostel too late to eat in the canteen —a little thing which was now really the last straw for her. She also thought of how she had been fined ten roubles a couple of days ago, for jumping off a bus at the wrong end. That was a lot of money for her these days.

As she arrived at the hostel, a pleasant, light snow was starting to fall. Outside stood a small boy, his cap pulled down over his eyes, selling loose cigarettes. Nadya went up to him and bought two.

'What about a match?' she said, speaking to herself rather than to the boy.

'Here you are, lady! Help yourself!' The boy handed her a box of matches. 'We don't charge for matches.'

Not stopping to worry what people might think, Nadya lit the cigarette, but clumsily, with the second match, so that it caught only on one side. She handed back the box and, still reluctant to go inside, began walking slowly up and down. Smoking was not yet a habit with her, but this was by no means her first cigarette.

The hot smoke burned her mouth, and made her feel queasy —this eased her anguish a little.

When she had smoked half the cigarette, Nadya threw it away and went upstairs to Room 418.

She walked past Ludmila's unmade bed, repelled by the sight of it, and lay down wearily on her own, wanting only to be left alone.

There, side by side, on the 'work' table were the four typed copies of her thesis. She thought of her endless trouble with it: all those diagrams and photocopies, the two revisions she had had to make—and now it had come back for a third! It was also hopelessly overdue, and the extra time she had obtained was against the rules.

Then she thought of the secret, special project which would bring her money and a little peace, if she could get on to it. But to do so, she would have to fill out that terrible eight-page questionnaire, and submit it to the Personnel Section by next Tuesday.

If she gave honest answers to all their questions, she would be expelled from the university by the end of the week—and then from the hostel, and from Moscow itself.

Or else she could get a divorce right away.

Gleb hadn't really been of much help.

She felt such an agony of mind, and so confused, that she could think of no way out.

Erica made her bed as best she could: as this sort of thing had always been done for her by servants, she was not very good at it. Then she put on some rouge and went off to Lenin's Library.

Musa was trying to read, but she could not concentrate. She saw that Nadya was lying so still because of utter dejection, and she kept glancing at her anxiously, but didn't like to ask her anything.

Dasha, who couldn't bear to be idle, had started some ironing. 'I heard today,' she said, 'that they're going to give us twice as much money for books this year.'

Olga got all excited and said: 'You're joking!'

336

'That's what the dean was saying.'

'Just a minute. How much would that be?' Olga's face lit up with a zeal shown only by people who are not used to money and not really greedy for it. 'Twice three hundred is six hundred. Twice seventy is one hundred and forty, twice five is—heavens!' she shouted, clapping her hands. 'Seven hundred and fifty! Now that's something!'

'Now you can buy yourself a complete Solovyov!' said Dasha.

'I don't know about that,' said Olga with a smile. 'I could also get myself a dress in cerise crêpe georgette. Can you imagine?' She picked up the edge of her skirt. 'With double pleats.'

Olga was still short of many things, and she had only begun to take an interest in clothes again this last year, after her mother's death. She now had no one left in her family—in the space of a single week in 1942 she and her mother had received official notices that both her father and her brother had been killed. Shortly after this her mother had fallen seriously ill, and Olga had had to give up her studies during her first year at the history faculty, and she had only been able to start again a year later as an external student. At nights she had worked as a relief nurse in a hospital and looked after things at home during the day. To get firewood, she had to go out into the woods and saw timber, and the only way to provide the milk needed for her sick mother was by exchanging her bread ration for it.

Looking at her pleasant, chubby face—she was now twenty-six—one would never have guessed any of this.

She believed that people should get over their troubles as best they could and keep them to themselves.

For this reason she was vexed by Nadya sitting there on the opposite bed, her face set in an expression of suffering which upset everyone in the room, and she said,

'What's wrong with you, Nadya? You were cheerful enough when you left this morning.'

The words were sympathetic in themselves, but they conveyed her irritation.

Nadya watched Olga fasten a red, flower-shaped brooch to the lapel of her jacket, and put on perfume.

The perfume seemed to envelope Olga in an invisible

cloud of happiness, but in Nadya's nostrils it reeked of lost hopes.

Her face as strained as ever, and speaking with great effort, Nadya said:

'Am I being a nuisance? Am I getting on your nerves?'

There was no reproach in the words themselves, only in the way they were said.

Olga straightened up, pursed her lips and stuck her chin out. The two women looked at each other across the table piled with Nadya's thesis.

'Look here, Nadya,' Olga said, in a very precise tone. 'I don't want to hurt your feelings, but as our mutual friend Aristotle said, man is a social animal. It's all right to share our joys; but we have no right to spread gloom and despondency.'

Nadya sat on her bed in a hunched posture that made her look much older.

'Do you have any idea,' she replied, in a low, lifeless voice, 'of how wretched a person can feel?'

'Of course I do. I know you're feeling wretched. But you mustn't work yourself up into a state and think you're the only one in the whole world to suffer. There are others who may have gone through much more than you. You should bear that in mind.'

She refrained from asking why it was worse to have a husband missing—a husband could be replaced—than to lose a mother, father and brother, who could never be replaced.

She stood there a little longer, very erect, looking sternly at Nadya.

Nadya knew what Olga was thinking, but she couldn't accept the argument. It was true that there is nothing more final than death. But a person dies only once, and when you've got over the shock, his death gradually recedes into the past and your grief doesn't last for ever—so there's nothing to stop you pinning a red brooch to your lapel, putting on perfume and going out to meet a boy-friend.

But Nadya's sorrow would never be mended and would always be with her—in the present and future, as it had been in the past. There was no getting away from it, however much she fought it or clutched at straws.

338

To put her case to Olga she would have had to tell her the truth. But this would have been dangerous.

So she gave up and blamed it all on her work. Nodding towards her thesis, she said:

'Well, I'm sorry, I'm completely worn out. I don't have the strength to revise it again. How many times can you revise a thing?'

As soon as it appeared that Nadya was not making out her troubles to be worse than anyone else's, Olga relented:

'Oh, you have to weed out the foreigners, do you? Well, you're not the only one. Don't let that get you down.'

Weeding out the foreigners' meant going through the thesis throwing out every reference to a foreigner: 'As Lowe has shown' for instance, would have to read, 'As scientists have shown'; 'As Langmuir has demonstrated' would become 'As has been demonstrated'. On the other hand, if a Russian, or a russified Dane or German had done anything at all to distinguish himself, then you had to give his full name and duly bring out his great patriotism and immortal services to science.

'No. I got rid of the foreigners long ago. Now I have to throw out Academician B. and the whole of his theory. I'd built the entire thesis around it. And now it turns out that he . . .'

Academician B. had now been hurled into the same abyss as Nadya's husband.

'Don't take it to heart so much!' Olga urged her. 'At least they're going to let you revise it. It could have been worse. Musa was telling us . . .'

But Musa did not hear her. She was buried in her book now, oblivious to the surroundings.

'. . . Musa was saying that there was a girl in the literature faculty who presented her thesis on Zweig four years ago, and was made an assistant professor on the strength of it. Suddenly they discovered that three times in the thesis she had described Stefan Zweig as "a cosmopolitan"—as though it was a good thing! So they called her in to the Faculty Board, and took her degree away. Wasn't that awful!'

'You chemists have nothing to complain of, Nadya,' said Dasha. 'What about us in Politics? What do you think we should do—hang ourselves? No we just carry on as best we can. Look how I've been saved by Stuzhaila-Olyabishkin, for instance.'

As everybody knew, this was Dasha's third attempt at a thesis. Her first subject had been 'Problems of Public Catering under Socialism'. Twenty years ago this had been a perfectly straightforward topic: then, every schoolgirl, including Dasha, knew that the ordinary home kitchen was on its way out, and that the housewife of the future, liberated from domestic drudgery, would get her meals from public catering establishments to be known as 'cooking factories'. But over the years the subject had become obscure and even hazardous. All that could now be said for certain was that nobody ate in a public canteen—this was true of Dasha herself—except out of dire necessity.

There were effective only two forms of public catering: the restaurants, which were, however, a poor embodiment of socialist principles, and all the grubby little booths which sold nothing but vodka. The 'cooking factories', too, still existed in theory, because the Great Leader had been too busy for the last twenty years to make any new pronouncement on the subject of catering. It was, therefore, dangerous for lesser persons to express any thoughts they might have. Dasha worried over the thesis for a long time, until finally her professor gave her a new subject; but he was ill-advised enough to suggest: 'Trade in Consumers' Goods under Socialism.' There turned out to be very little material on this theme. In every major speech and party directive there was a reference to the need, and even desirability of producing consumer goods. In practice, however, compared to steel and petroleum products, consumer goods were on the scarce side, and whether light industry would develop or wither away, even the Faculty Board did not know, so they wisely rejected this subject too.

Then some kind person at last came to her rescue and suggested: 'The Russian Nineteenth-Century Political Economist Stuzhaila-Olyabishkin.' Dasha managed to get this accepted.

Laughing, Olga said: 'You might at least have found a picture of him by now—you owe him so much!'

'But the trouble is I can't find one.'

'That's sheer ingratitude!' Olga thought she might cheer Nadya up like this, but she only succeeded in conveying her own elation at the thought of her evening out.

'I'd have found one and hung it over my bed. I can just imagine him: a venerable old fogey of a landlord who hankers after higher things—I can see him eating his enormous breakfast and then sitting in his dressing-gown at the window in his God-forsaken provincial hole (like in *Eugene Onegin*—"where the storms of history passed him by"), watching a peasant girl feeding the pigs, and brooding about the wealth of nations. Then in the evenings he would play cards.' Olga burst out laughing.

Meantime Ludmila had put on her light blue dress, which had been lying spread out fanwise across her unmade bed (the sight of this again made Nadya wince), and was now standing in front of the mirror, refreshing the mascara on her eyebrows and eyelashes, and then carefully making up her lips into a rose-bud.

Suddenly Musa spoke up in her natural-seeming tone of voice—as though everybody had just been waiting for her to say something:

'Have you ever noticed what makes the characters of Russian literature different from those in Western literature? In the West they have no time for anything except their careers, money and fame. But in Russia they don't even need food and drink—all they want is justice. Don't they?'

And she buried herself in her book again.

Ludmila had put on her galoshes and was reaching for her fur coat, when Nadya nodded towards her bed, and said with disgust:

'Are you going to leave that filthy mess for us to tidy up again?'

'Please leave it alone!' Ludmila said angrily, her eyes flashing. 'Don't you ever dare touch my bed again!' Her voice rose to a scream. 'And don't preach at me!'

'It's time you understood!' Nadya burst out, letting out all her pent-up feelings. 'It's an insult to us—as though we'd nothing better to think about than your evening's entertainment!'

'You're jealous, aren't you? Not having much luck yourself, are you?'

Olga had opened her mouth to join in the attack on Ludmila, but she took Nadya's reference to 'evening's entertainment' as a dig at herself as well (and anyway, these evenings out were not as much fun as some people might think). 'There's nothing to be jealous of!' Nadya shouted back, in a hollow, broken voice.

'If you missed your vocation,' Ludmila shouted even louder, sensing victory, 'and came here instead of going into a nunnery, then just keep quiet in your corner, and stop acting like a mother-in-law. It makes me sick. You old maid!'

'Ludmila, how dare you!' Olga screamed.

'Well, why does she stick her nose into everyone else's business? She's an old maid, a failure!'

Now Dasha joined in, aggressively trying to make a point, and Musa roused herself too, waved her book at Ludmila and screamed:

'What a cheap, vulgar thing to say!'

All five of them were shouting discordantly, none listening to the other.

Quite at a loss by now, ashamed of her outburst and her unrestrained sobs, Nadya, still wearing her best for the prison visit, threw herself down on her bed and covered her head with the pillow.

Ludmila powdered her face again, straightened the wavy blonde hair falling over the collar of her squirrel coat, pulled the veil on her hat down just below her eyes, and, not making her bed, but throwing her blanket over it as a concession, left the room.

The others called to Nadya, but she made no movement. Dasha took Nadya's shoes off and covered up her legs with a blanket.

Someone knocked at the door and Olga rushed out into the hall. A moment later she came back like the wind, tucked her curls up under her hat, slipped into a dark blue coat trimmed with yellow fur and sallied forth again, as though she were walking on air—but also with the light of battle in her eye.

So it was that Room 418 sent out into the world, one after the other, two beautiful, elegantly dressed and seductive young

342

women, thereby losing what gaiety it had, and becoming even gloomier.

Moscow was an enormous city, but there was nowhere at all to go. . . .

Musa had stopped reading; she took off her glasses and hid her face in her large hands.

Dasha said:

'Olga's a fool. He'll play around with her and then drop her. They say he has another girl somewhere. And maybe a child, too.'

Musa looked up and said:

'But Olga isn't tied to him. If he's the wrong sort, she can always leave him.'

'What do you mean, not tied to him!' Dasha scoffed. 'Of course she is——'

'Oh, you always know everything! How can you know that?' Musa was indignant.

'Well, she spends the night at his place.'

'Oh, that doesn't mean anything! That doesn't prove anything at all,' said Musa.

'But it's the only way nowadays, otherwise you can't keep them at all.'

The two girls were silent, each thinking her own thoughts.

The snow outside was falling more heavily, and it was already dark.

The water gurgled quietly in the radiator under the window.

The thought of having to spend their Sunday evening in this miserable hole was unbearable.

Dasha thought of that waiter she had thrown over. He was a fine sturdy fellow. Why had she got rid of him like that? He could have taken her to some club away from the centre of Moscow, where no one from the university ever went.

'Musa, let's go to the cinema!' Dasha said.

'What's on?'

'*The Indian Tomb*, it's a foreign film.'

'Oh, that's terrible commercial trash!'

'But it's playing right here in the building!'

Musa did not answer.

'We'll die of boredom here, come on!'

'I'm not going,' said Musa. 'Find some work to do.'

Suddenly the electric light dimmed. Only a thin red filament glowed feebly in the bulb.

'That's the limit!' Dasha groaned. 'You could hang yourself in a place like this!'

Musa sat there like a statue.

Nadya still lay motionless on her bed.

'Musa, let's go to the cinema.'

There was a knock at the door.

Dasha looked out into the hall, and shouted over her shoulder:

'Nadya! Shchagov is here! Are you going to get up?'

CHAPTER FORTY-SIX

Nadya had lain sobbing for a long time, biting her blanket to make herself stop. Her face grew wet and salty with weeping, which she muffled by pulling the pillows over her head. She would have been glad to leave the room and go out until late at night, but in all this great city of Moscow there was nowhere for her to go.

It was not the first time in this hostel that she had been jeered at for being a crabbed old maid, an unkindness that was all the more hurtful for being unjust. Yet who could have failed to be affected by five years of having to tell lies, of wearing a perpetual mask that made her face longer and her voice harsher. It was hardly surprising if the judgments that they passed on her were so callous; perhaps she really had turned into an intolerable old maid?

It was so hard to take a balanced view of oneself. Unlike at home where you could always get away with a fit of temper, in the hostel, in the company of your equals you always tended to see yourself in a bad light.

Apart from Gleb there was no one at all to understand her; and now even Gleb couldn't understand. He had told her nothing, given her no advice that might have helped her to go on living. Instead he had told her that there might never be an end to their separation. . . . With a series of swift, sure blows her husband had smashed everything with which she had fortified herself day after day, with which she had bolstered her faith, her hopes, her self-sufficiency. If there really was to be no end to his prison sentence, then she was no longer any use to him. . . . Oh God, oh God . . .

Nadya lay prone on her bed. With eyes open and unmoving she stared through the gap between the pillow and the sheet at the patch of wall in front of her, half consciously aware that there was something odd about the lightning. It seemed to be very dark, yet she could still make out the blisters on the familiar, rough ochre-washed wall.

Suddenly, through the pillow, Nadya heard a special knock on the plywood panel of the door—twelve pattering taps in three groups of four, like a bouncing pea. And even before Dasha said: 'Nadya, it's Shchagov. Are you going to get up?' Nadya had already pulled the pillow away from her head, jumped on to the floor in her stockings, straightened her twisted skirt and combed her hair, her feet groping for her slippers. In the dim, gloomy light shed by the lamp on half current, Musa saw how Nadya was hurrying and stepped aside. Dasha flew to Ludmila's bed, quickly pulled up the bedclothes and tidied her scattered belongings away.

The visitor was admitted.

Shchagov came in wearing his old army greatcoat thrown over his shoulders. A tall man, there was still a soldierly air about him: he could bend down, but not stoop. His movements were economical and precise.

'Good evening, young ladies,' he said in his condescending way. 'I've come to find out how you're passing the time in the dark, so that I can follow suit. Personally I'm dying of boredom.'

(What a relief—it was so dark that he could not see how puffy her eyes were from crying.)

'So you wouldn't have come at all if the current hadn't been turned down, I suppose?' said Dasha in the coy tone she unconsciously adopted whenever she talked to an unmarried man.

'Never. In bright light women's faces are devoid of charm. You can see their evil looks and envious glances' (Nadya shuddered, as though he had been in the room earlier), 'their premature wrinkles and their overdone make-up. If I were a woman I would pass a law that only allowed the electric light to burn at half strength. Then they'd all get married in no time.'

Dasha gave Shchagov a stern look. He always talked like this and she did not like his rather artificial turns of phrase. . . . She also found him insincere.

'May I sit down?'

'Please do,' said Nadya in the calm voice of a good hostess that showed no trace of her recent tiredness, sorrow and tears. Unlike Dasha she admired his self-possession, his low, steady and slightly drawling voice. Everything about him suggested calm, and she liked his wit.

'Well, since you may not invite me a second time, I hasten to take my seat. What are you young creatures up to?'

Nadya was silent. She found it difficult to talk to him because she had quarrelled with him two days before and with a sudden unpremeditated gesture which had implied a degree of intimacy between them which did not really exist, she had hit him on the back with her briefcase and run away. It had been stupid and childish and now she felt relieved that other people were in the room.

It was Dasha who replied.

'We were going out to the cinema—by ourselves.'

'What's on?'

'*The Indian Tomb.*'

'Ah, you must see that. A nurse I know said "there's lots of shooting and lots of people get killed—in fact, it's a marvellous film".'

Shchagov settled himself comfortably at the communal table.

'What's the matter with you all? I expected to find you having an orgy and instead it's more like a wake. Having trouble with your parents? Or are you upset by the latest decision made by the Party committee? I didn't think it affected you, though.'

'What decision?' said Nadya quietly.

'What decision? A probe into the social backgrounds of students to see whether their parents really are what they say they are. What about you, Musa? Have you been hiding anything? It opens up all sorts of possibilities. Somebody may have confided in someone else, perhaps, or talked in their

346

sleep, or read another person's letter—you know the sort of thing.'

(Nadya's heart sank. More prying and snooping. It sickened her. How could one escape from it all?)

'How despicable!' said Musa.

'Don't tell me *that* depresses you too? Well then, shall I tell you a very funny story about the secret ballot at the Engineering Faculty board yesterday . . .?'

Shchagov told his story to them all, but his eyes were watching Nadya. He had long been wondering what it was that Nadya wanted from him. Her intentions were becoming more and more obvious each time they met. Either she stood behind him when he was playing chess with someone or she would beg him to play with her and teach her the gambits. (At least chess helped her to make the time pass.) Sometimes she would ask him to come and hear her play at a concert—a natural human urge to perform in front of a sympathetic audience. Or she might find that she had a 'spare' ticket to the cinema and would invite him. (Just to go out somewhere with a man for an evening's worth of illusion. . . .) Then on his birthday she had given him a present of a notebook, but she had done it clumsily by pushing it into his coat pocket and trying to run away. Why behave like that? Why run away? (From sheer embarrassment. . . .) He had caught up with her and in trying to return the present had put his arms round her and she had not immediately tried to pull herself away but had let him hold her. (Nadya had not felt a man's embrace for so long, and it's suddenness and force had paralysed her.)

What had she meant by playfully hitting him with her briefcase? Shchagov was as reserved with her as he was with everyone. But was this lonely woman perhaps signalling for help! If so, who could be so firm and unbending as to refuse it to her? So Shchagov had left his own room, No. 142, and gone to No. 418, certain that he would find Nadya there yet beginning to be worried by what might happen between them. . . .

Although they laughed at his story about the faculty board, it was only out of politeness.

'Well, are we going to have some proper light or not?' Musa exclaimed impatiently.

'I see you don't think my stories are a bit funny. Especially Nadya. To me she looks gloomier than a thundercloud. And I know why. She was fined ten roubles yesterday and she resents it.'

Nadya's reaction to his joke was to seize her handbag, wrench open the catch and pull something out of it at random which she hysterically tore up, throwing the pieces on to the table in front of Shchagov.

'Musa—for the last time, are you coming?' said Dasha in an agonized voice, reaching for her coat.

'Coming,' Musa said glumly, and strode over to the coat-hooks.

Shchagov and Nadya looked round as the two women went out. When they had gone, a terrible feeling of shame and embarrassment came over Nadya. Shchagov examined the pieces of torn paper. They were the rustling fragments of a ten-rouble note. . . .

He stood up, letting his greatcoat fall into the chair, squeezed past the bookshelf and walked over to where Nadya was standing between the work-table and her bed. Standing a great deal taller than her, he took her small hands in his big ones.

'Nadya,' he said, feeling the excitement rise in him as he spoke, 'forgive me. I feel very guilty. . . .'

She stood without moving, her heart thumping, feeling weak. The strange thought flashed through her mind that here at least there was no warder to thrust his ox-like head towards them. That they could say what they liked and leave each other when they felt like it, not when they were told. Very close to hers she could see his firm, honest face, both halves of which were identical.

He loosened his fingers from hers and ran them along her forearm over the muslin of her blouse.

'Nadya,' he said again very softly. (Here was someone whose advice she could ask about the special job she was being offered, someone to whom she could unburden herself. . . .)

'Let me go,' Nadya answered in a voice both weary and reluctant.

She had begun it, yet now it was she who was asking him to let her go.

'What am I to think about you, Nadya?' he asked, sliding his hands along her blouse from her elbows to her shoulders, feeling the warmth and softness of her arms.

'What d'you mean—think about me?' she countered indistinctly, making no effort to free herself from his hands. His reply was to grasp her by the shoulders and pull her towards him. The dim light concealed the sudden colouring of her face, and she pushed herself from him with her hands against his chest.

'Let me go! How could you think that . . .'

She shook her head angrily and a lock of her hair fell over her face, covering one eye.

'God knows what I'm supposed to think,' he muttered angrily, letting her go and walking past her to the window.

The water in the radiator gurgled gently.

With shaking hands Nadya straightened her hair. Breathing audibly, his hands shaking too, Shchagov lit a cigarette. What *did* the woman want?

'Do you know,' he asked jerkily, 'how dry hay burns?'

'Yes,' she replied apathetically, 'it flares up and then there's nothing left but a handful of ashes.'

'That's right—it flares up,' he stressed. 'So why do you keep throwing fire on dry hay?'

(Was that what she was doing? . . . How could he so misunderstand her? She had simply wanted someone to like her, even if only now and again.)

'Let's go out somewhere,' she demanded.

'We're not going anywhere. We're staying here.'

He was smoking in his usual unruffled way again, the cardboard mouthpiece stuck slightly askew between his strong lips, a habit which Nadya liked.

'No, please, let's go somewhere,' she insisted.

'Here or nowhere,' he snapped mercilessly. 'I must warn you—I'm engaged to marry a girl. That's why I can't promise you anything. And . . . I don't want anyone to see us in town together.'

CHAPTER FORTY-SEVEN

What had made Nadya and Shchagov friends was the fact that neither of them was from Moscow. The natives of the city Nadya met at the university put on a poisonous air of superiority: 'Muscovite patriotism,' as they called it. However well she did in her work for her professor, they thought Nadya a second-rate person—even more so than most other provincials because she was so bad at hiding her feelings.

Shchagov was a provincial too, but he had forged ahead in Moscow as easily as an icebreaker through water. Once, in the library, she had seen a young graduate student trying to snub Shchagov. Arrogantly, cocking his head, the student had asked: 'And where might you hail from?'

Shchagov, who was taller, had given the student a slow, pitying look and said, rocking back and forth a little on his heels: 'You were never there. From a province called The Front. A village called Foxhole.'

It has long been observed that our life is lived at a very uneven level of intensity. Everyone has his special time of life when he manifests himself most fully, feels most profoundly himself and produces the greatest effect on himself and on others. And anything that happens afterwards, however outwardly significant, is always a decline by comparison. What we remember and glory in, going over it again and again, for ever ringing the changes on it, is always some episode or experience that can never be repeated. For some, this may even be in childhood, and such people remain children for the rest of their lives; for others it is first love—these are the people who spread the myth that love comes only once. But whatever it was—a time of great wealth, fame or power—anyone who has experienced such things will never stop talking about them, mumbling even with the toothless gums of old age about their departed glory. If the greatest time in Nerzhin's life had been prison, for Shchagov it had been the war.

Shchagov had really been through the mill. He had been

called up in the first month, and was not demobilized until 1946. There was not a day during the whole of these four years when he didn't wonder whether he would live till evening. He never had any safe staff jobs and he left the front only to go into hospital. He was in the great retreat from Kiev in 1941, and then in 1942 from the Don. Although things got better after that, he found himself on the retreat again in 1943—and even in 1944, near Kovel. In roadside ditches, in flooded trenches, in the ruins of gutted houses he learned the value of a tin of soup, an hour of quiet, the meaning of true comradeship, the meaning of life itself.

It would be many, many years before Shchagov got over his wartime experience. There were still only two categories of people for him: those who had been soldiers and those who had not. Even in the great city of Moscow, where memories were short, he kept to his belief that only the word 'soldier' was a guarantee of true friendship and sincerity. Experience had taught him not to trust anyone who had not been tested in battle.

By the end of the war Shchagov had no family to go back to, and the house he once lived in had been totally destroyed by a bomb. He had nothing except the clothes on his back, a suitcase full of German loot and the twelve months' full pay given to all demobilized officers as a gratuity by way of easing their return to civilian life.

When he came back from the war Shchagov, like many others, was stunned by what he found. For a while returned soldiers like himself were better people than they had been before: they had been purified by the nearness of death and were, hence, all the more struck by the changes at home—changes which had gradually come about far behind the front lines. They were appalled by the callous, often totally unscrupulous, way in which people treated each other, by the gulf between helpless poverty and insolent wealth.

And the hell of it was that the ex-soldiers everywhere, walking the streets and riding in the metro, were all dressed differently now and no longer recognized each other. And they somehow accepted the new state of affairs, forgetting the code of behaviour which had bound them together at the front.

There was much food for thought in all this, but Shchagov asked no questions. He was not one of those insatiable souls who are always thirsting after righteousness. He understood very well that everything always went along just as it did, and that there was no stopping it. All that was up to you was whether you jumped on the bandwagon or not. It was clear now that a general's daughter, solely by virtue of her birth, was bound to have an easy life, and would not set foot in a factory. Similarly, nobody who had ever been a party official, however minor and even if he'd been demoted, would be found soiling his hands with manual labour. Production plans were not carried out by those who designed them —any more than those who gave orders to attack actually charged into battle themselves.

In fact, there was nothing new about all this, but it cut Shchagov to the quick that after all his long footslogging service in the war, he could not take for granted his right to a place in the life he had fought so hard to defend. Now he had to prove his right all over again—this time without bullets or hand grenades, but in a bloodless battle with officialdom to get it formally approved, signed and sealed. And it all had to be endured with a smile.

Shchagov had been in such a hurry to get to the front in 1941 that he had not taken his degree, so that now, after the war, he had to complete his studies for this before going on to a doctorate. He had specialized in theoretical mechanics, and it had been his intention, even before the war, to make a career of it. It had been easier then. But now he found that science—any kind of science—was getting too popular: salaries for qualified people had gone up.

He gathered his strength for yet another long haul, and one by one he sold off his German souvenirs in the market.

He did not go in for fashionable clothes, but defiantly continued to wear what he had been demobilized in: his army breeches and boots, a tunic made of English wool, still with its four ribbons and two wound-stripes. All this carefully-preserved aura of the front reminded Nadya very much of Gleb.

Sensitive as she was to any reminder of her own inadequacy, Nadya felt like a little girl in the presence of Shchagov with his tremendous experience of life, and it was no wonder that she had gone to him with some of her problems—but even to him she had persistently lied about Gleb, saying only that he was missing.

Nadya had got involved with him almost without noticing —that ticket to the cinema, their joking tussle over the note-book—and now that Shchagov had come tonight, even while he was still only teasing Dasha, she had realized at once that he had come to see her, and that something was going to happen.

A minute before, she had been crying her heart out over her ruined life. But after she had torn up the ten-rouble note she had felt a surge of new strength and readiness to face life again. She had been aware of no inconsistency in this.

But Shchagov, overcoming the strong feelings aroused by his brief flirtation with her, had recovered his usual composure and clearly given her to understand that there could be no question of his marrying her.

After hearing about his fiancée, Nadya walked unsteadily round the room for a while, then came over and stood at the window next to him, and silently drew on the pane with her finger.

He was sorry for her. He wanted to break the silence and tell her quite simply, with a kind of bluntness he had long ago abandoned, that as a poor graduate student, with neither connections nor prospects, she could not possibly help him to get all the things he felt he had a right to. He wanted to explain to her that though his fiancée lived a life of luxury, she had not been spoilt by it. She had a fine flat in an exclusive building reserved for the élite. It had a porter and carpets on the stairs—not something you saw very often nowadays. But the main thing was that all his problems would be solved at one go, in a way that couldn't be more satisfactory.

But he kept these thoughts to himself.

And Nadya, leaning her forehead against the glass and staring out into the night, at last said glumly:

'Wonderful. You have a fiancée. And I have a husband.'

Shchagov looked at her in astonishment.

'A husband? Where is he? I thought he was missing?'

'No, he's not missing,' Nadya almost whispered.

(How rashly she was giving herself away!)

'You think he's still alive?'

'I saw him—today.'

(Now she had given herself away completely, but let him at least see that she was not just a stupid girl throwing herself at him!)

Shchagov was quick to see the meaning of what she had just said. He did not think, as a woman might have, that Nadya had simply been thrown over by her husband. He knew that 'missing in action' almost always meant 'displaced person', and that anyone in this category who came back again was generally sent straight to prison.

He took Nadya's elbow.

'Is he in prison?'

'Yes.'

'Well, well, well,' Shchagov said, greatly relieved. He thought a minute, then quickly went out of the room.

Nadya was so overcome with shame and hopelessness that she had not caught the change in his voice.

It was a good thing that he'd gone, and she was glad that she had unburdened herself: she was now all alone again with her sorrows, but at least she could be honest about them.

There was only a very faint glow from the lamp filament.

Barely able to move her legs, she walked across the room, found the second cigarette in her coat pocket, got a match and lit it. There was a strange satisfaction in the bitter taste.

She was not used to smoking, and it made her cough.

She saw Shchagov's overcoat lying in a shapeless heap on one of the chairs.

What a hurry he'd been in—and so scared he'd forgotten his overcoat.

It was very quiet; the radio in the next room was playing Liszt's 'Étude in C Minor'.

She had played it once when she was young, but she hadn't really understood it then. Though her fingers had played the notes, the word '*disperato*' had meant nothing to her in those days.

Leaning her forehead against the middle pane of the window, she reached out and touched the other cold panes

with the palms of her hands, standing like someone cruci-
fied on the black cross of the window.

There had been just this one tiny warm spot in her life—
and now it was gone.

It took her only a minute or two to resign herself to the
loss, and she was her husband's wife again.

She stared out into the darkness, trying to make out the
chimney of the Sailors' Rest Prison. '*Disperato!*' It was the
impotent desperation of someone trying to rise to their knees,
but always falling back again. That high, urgent A-sharp was
the frantic cry of a woman, a cry of utter defeat.

She could see a long row of street lights stretching away
into the darkness, as though into the future—a future for
which she had no will to live.

The Étude ended, and a voice announced the time: 6 p.m.

Nadya had forgotten all about Shchagov, when suddenly
he came back in without knocking.

He had a bottle and two small glasses with him.

'Well, soldier's wife!' he said cheerfully. 'Don't lose heart!
Here take a glass. If you've got a good head on your shoulders, you'll be all right. Let's drink to the resurrection of the
dead!'

CHAPTER FORTY-EIGHT

At six o'clock on a Sunday evening even the prisoners at
Mavrino retired to rest until the next morning. There was
no way of avoiding this annoying break in the prisoners'
work, because on Sundays the free workers only came on
duty for one shift. It was a tradition which the officers in
charge made no effort to change because none of them wanted
to work on Sunday evenings either. Only Mamurin, The
Man in the Iron Mask, disliked these idle evenings when the
free employees had left and all the prisoners (who were also
human beings in a sense) had been locked in their rooms;
he was then left alone to pace the empty prison corridors,
past doors sealed with lead or sealing wax, or to measure
the length of his cell between the washbasin, the cupboard

355

and the bed. Mamurin had tried to arrange for Number Seven to work on Sunday evening, but he had been unable to overcome the conservatism of the prison staff who did not want to double the guards inside the building.

As a result two hundred and eighty-one prisoners, in defiance of all reasonable argument and of the letter of the prison labour code, spent Sunday evening brazenly doing nothing.

This 'rest' was such that anyone unfamiliar with it might have thought it was a diabolical form of torture. Because it was dark outside and special vigilance was needed on Sundays the prison officers could not allow the time to be spent in walking outdoors or watching a cinema show in the yard. After a year-long correspondence with higher authority it was also decided that musical instruments such as accordions, guitars, balalaikas and mouth-organs were forbidden in the prison since their combined volume might contribute to undermining the stone foundations (the Security Officers, through their informers, were constantly trying to find out whether the prisoners had any home-made flutes or penny whistles, and anyone caught playing on the comb was summoned to the governor's office and a reprimand was entered in his file). Under the circumstances there could be no question of allowing the prisoners to have radio sets or even the most battered gramophones.

The prisoners could, it was true, make use of the prison library. But the Mavrino administration had no funds to buy books or bookshelves. All that happened was that Rubin was nominated prison librarian (he had asked for the job himself in the hope of laying his hands on some good books), and one day he was given a medley of a hundred-odd tattered volumes in which books like Turgenev's *Mumu*, Stasov's *Letters* and Mommsen's *History of Rome* were all mixed together, and was ordered to circulate them among the prisoners. The inmates had either read all these books long ago or did not want them, and instead asked the free workers to get them reading matter—this gave the Security Officers a perfect excuse for conducting searches.

For their recreation the prisoners had the run of ten rooms on two floors, the upper and lower corridors, a narrow wooden staircase linking the two floors and a lavatory under the staircase. Recreation consisted in allowing the prisoners to lie on their bunks as much as they liked (even to sleep, if they could amid so much noise), to walk up and down their rooms or even from room to room wearing nothing but their underwear if they liked, to smoke freely in the corridors, to argue about politics in front of the informers and to use the lavatory without let or hindrance. (Anyone who has done a long stretch in prison and has had to relieve himself twice a day to order can judge the full value of this blissful sort of freedom.) The real value of the 'recreation' was that the time was your own and not the state's. For that reason these recreation periods were genuinely restful.

They began when the heavy iron doors were locked from the outside, after which no one opened them, no one went outside and none of the prisoners was sent for or harassed. During those few short hours not a sound, not a word, not a glimpse of the outside world could penetrate inside or trouble anyone's peace of mind. They felt at rest because the entire outside world—the universe with all its stars, this planet with all its continents, the capitals of the world with all their glitter and pomp—had all vanished into oblivion, transformed into a black ocean, virtually invisible beyond the barred windows and the dim yellow glow of the lights round the perimeter.

Brightly lit within by the MGB's inexhaustible supply of electric current, the two-storeyed building of what had once been the estate chapel, its walls the thickness of four and a half bricks, sailed aimlessly and serenely through that black ocean of human destinies and human folly, casting faint streaks of light from its portholes in its wake. In that night between Sunday and Monday the moon might split in two, a new mountain range might be thrown up in the steppes of the Ukraine, Japan might be swallowed up by the sea or a new flood might begin, but the prisoners locked up in their ark would hear nothing about it until morning roll-call. Nor, too, could they be troubled by telegrams from relatives, tiresome phone calls, a baby catching diphtheria or arrest by night.

The men floating in this ark were detached and their thoughts could wander unfettered. They were not hungry and not full. They were not happy and therefore not disturbed

357

by the prospect of forfeiting happiness. Their heads were not full of trivial worries about their jobs, office intrigue or anxieties about promotion, their shoulders unbowed by cares about housing, fuel, food and clothing for their children. Love, man's age-old source of pleasure and suffering, was powerless to touch them with its agony or its expectation. Their terms of imprisonment were so long that none of them had started to think of the time when they would be released. Men of outstanding intellect, education and experience, who were normally too devoted to their families to have enough of themselves to spare for friendship, were here wholly given over to their friends. From this ark, serenely ploughing its way through the darkness, it was easy for them to survey, as from a great height, the whole tortuous, errant flow of history; yet at the same time, like people completely immersed in it, they could see every pebble in its depths.

On these Sunday evenings the physical, material world never intruded. A spirit of manly friendship and philosophy hovered over the sail-shaped vault of the ceiling. Was this, perhaps, that state of bliss which all the philosophers of antiquity tried in vain to define and describe?

CHAPTER FORTY-NINE

In the semicircular room on the second floor, under the high-vaulted ceiling over the altar, the atmosphere was particularly lively and the imagination could easily run riot.

By six in the evening, all twenty-five men who lived in this room had gathered there together. Some, sloughing their hated prison skins, got undressed as quickly as possible, and flopped down in their underwear on the lower bunks or scrambled like monkeys to the upper ones. Others just threw themselves on their beds without taking off their denims. One man was standing on a top bunk, waving his arms and shouting to a friend across the room, but others just quietly settled in and took stock of things, anticipating the pleasure of the free hours ahead, uncertain how best to begin making the most of them.

Among the latter was Isaac Kagan, the short, dark, shaggy 'director of the accumulator room', as he was called. For him it was always particularly good to come into this bright, spacious room after the dark, badly ventilated basement where he worked like a mole fourteen hours a day. But he was glad even of this, saying that in a labour camp he would have been dead long ago. He was not one of those people who were always prating about how much better they had lived in the camps than out of them.

Before his arrest Isaac Kagan, who had done a course in engineering but never taken his degree, had been in charge of stores in a factory. He had tried to live his own life and keep out of harm's way during these heroic times. He calculated that as an inconspicuous storekeeper he was more likely to be left in peace and do reasonably well for himself. Indeed, he was passionately concerned about one thing only in the privacy of his isolated life: how to make money. He had no interest whatsoever in politics and only tried to observe the laws of his religion, keeping the sabbath even in the storeroom. However, for reasons best known to themselves, the MGB decided to enlist Kagan as an informer and they began to pester him, inviting him to secret rendezvous with them and so forth. Kagan was sickened by the very idea but he had neither the courage nor the straightforwardness (who did?) to tell them to their faces what he thought of their vile proposal, and he just stalled for all he was worth, fidgeting in his chair and mumbling incomprehensibly, yet never actually coming to the point of signing an agreement to work for them. It was not that he would have been incapable of informing: he would have had no compunction at all in denouncing someone who had personally done him wrong, but it would have sickened him to inform on people who had been kind to him or even on people about whom he had no particular feelings.

His obstinacy earned him a black mark with the MGB and they just bided their time, waiting for a chance to get their own back. It came with a—perhaps prearranged—conversation in Kagan's storeroom: one man grumbled about the quality of the tools, others about supplies and planning in general. Kagan said nothing at all and just went on writing out invoices with his indelible pencil. Word of this conversation soon reached the MGB—if they had not known about it beforehand—and all those who had taken part in it denounced each other. Every one of them got ten years under Article 58, Section 10 ('propaganda and agitation against the Soviet Union'). Kagan was brought together with the others five times and confronted with their evidence but none of it showed that he had said a single word. If Article 58 had been less comprehensive, they would theoretically have had to let him go, but the MGB had recourse to Section 12 under which persons could be prosecuted for failing to inform the authorities of offences covered in other sections of Article 58. So Kagan also got ten years.

He had managed to have himself transferred to Mavrino from a labour camp, thanks to his extraordinary ingenuity. At a difficult moment, when he was about to be thrown out of his comfortable job as an orderly in one of the prison huts and sent to fell trees with the rest, he had written a letter addressed to the Chairman of the Council of Ministers, Comrade Stalin, saying that, if given the opportunity by the Government, he would undertake to devise a radio control system for torpedo boats.

The ploy worked. No one would have shed a tear if Kagan had appealed for mercy on humanitarian grounds, but his offer to invent something of great military importance earned him an immediate transfer to Moscow. He was taken to Mavrino, and seen by various officials in MGB uniforms who were eager that he should at once start giving practical effect to his bold ideas. But, feasting now on the white bread and butter of the special prison, Kagan was in no hurry. With perfect composure he said that, since he was not himself a specialist on torpedoes, he would naturally require the services of someone who knew all about them. It took them two months to find another prisoner with expert knowledge of torpedoes, whereupon Kagan made the reasonable point that, not being himself a marine engineer, he would naturally require special assistance in this field too. After another two months they found him a prisoner who could help him out on the engineering side. At this point Kagan sighed and said that radio wasn't exactly his line either. There were plenty of radio engineers at Mavrino already and one of them was detailed to work for Kagan, who now gathered his team together and said quite imperturbably, in a tone of voice which made it impossible to suspect that he might be pulling anybody's leg: 'Well, friends—now that you have all been brought together like this, you will be quite capable, by your combined efforts, of designing a form of radio control for torpedo boats, and it's not for me to interfere and give advice to people who know their business as well as you do.' Then, lo and behold, the three specialists were sent off to another special prison working for the navy, while Kagan stayed on in Mavrino (where everyone had meanwhile got used to him) as the man who looked after the accumulator room.

At the moment Kagan was pestering Rubin, but at a respectable distance so that Rubin, who was lying on his bunk, could not kick at him.

'Lev,' he said in his thick, rather indistinct and slow manner, 'you are clearly losing your sense of social responsibility. The masses are craving for entertainment. Only you can provide it—and here you are with your nose stuck in a book.'

'Go to hell,' Rubin said. He had turned over on his stomach to read, and still fully dressed in his denims, he had covered his shoulders with the warm, quilted jacket brought with him from the labour camp. The window between him and Sologdin had been propped open with a volume of Mayakovsky to give a draft of fresh air which had a pleasant tang of snow about it.

'No, seriously, Lev!' Kagan persisted. 'Everyone is dying to hear your version of "The Crow and the Fox" again—it was really very good.'

'And who went telling tales about me afterwards? I bet it was you,' Rubin snapped back at him.

The previous Sunday evening, to amuse the others, Rubin had recited a parody of Krylov's fable, 'The Crow and the Fox', full of camp slang and off-colour expressions. He had been made to repeat it five times and as a mark of appreciation the prisoners had hoisted him up on their shoulders, but on Monday Major Mishin had called him in and proceeded to make a case against him for 'corrupting the morals of enemies of the people'. Statements had been taken from witnesses, Rubin was made to produce the manuscript of the parody and write out an explanatory note.

Today after lunch, Rubin had worked for two hours in the new room set aside for him. From the tape of the telephone conversation he had picked out speech peculiarities typical of the person they were trying to identify, had fed them into the visible speech apparatus, and hung up the wet strips to dry. He had arrived at some preliminary conclusions, but he felt no inspiration for the work as he observed Smolosidov putting a seal on the door when they left the room. After this, he had returned to the semicircular room with the other prisoners—they were like a herd of cattle going home to the village.

As always, under his pillow, under his mattress, under his bunk and in the locker where he also kept food, there were half a dozen or so of the most interesting books he had received in parcels—interesting, that is, to him alone, which was why they had not been pilfered: dictionaries of Chinese, Latvian, Hungarian and Sanscrit, Capek's *War with the Newts*, a collection of stories by some extremely progressive Japanese writers, Hemingway's *For Whom the Bell Tolls* in the English original (they had stopped translating him because he was no longer progressive) two monographs on the Encyclopedists; *Joseph Fouché* by Stefan Zweig in German, and a novel by Upton Sinclair which had never been translated into Russian. Rubin needed the dictionaries because for two years he had been at work on a grandiose project, in the spirit of Engels and Nikolai Marr—to show that all words in all languages derive from the roots for 'hand' and 'work'; he had no idea that the night before the Greatest Linguist of all Times had raised the blade of his ideological guillotine over Marr's head.

The number of absolutely essential books in the world was beyond belief, and Rubin was so anxious to read them all that he could never find time to write one of his own. Just now he was all set to read on till long after midnight, forgetting about the long working day that would begin in the morning. But Rubin's love of argument and holding forth was also especially intense at night, and he needed very little encouragement to display his gifts before his fellow-prisoners. There were those among them who did not trust Rubin, regarding him as an informer because of his avowedly orthodox views; but there was no one who did not enjoy his clever improvisations.

His slang rendering of 'The Crow and the Fox' had been such a success that many other people in the room followed Kagan's example and loudly clamoured for him to put on some new act. And when Rubin sat up, gloomy and bearded, and clambered out of his lower bunk as though it were a cave, every prisoner dropped what he was doing and prepared to listen. Only Dvoyetyosov, on his upper bunk, went on clipping his toenails, letting the parings fly all over the place; and Adamson, lying under his blanket, continued to read without turning round. Prisoners from other rooms crowded in the doorway, among them the Tartar Amantai Bulatov in horn-rimmed glasses, who shouted 'Please! Please!' in a rasping voice.

Rubin had no wish at all to entertain a crowd which included some people who were scornful of his dearest beliefs and he knew, too, that a new performance by him would only bring more trouble next day when he would again be hauled out for questioning by Shikin or Mishin. But Rubin was one of those proverbial people who would sacrifice anything for a good story and, putting on a frown, he looked solemnly around and said in the quiet which followed:

'Comrades! I am staggered by your frivolity. How can we indulge in such things while we have so many criminals in our midst—brazen criminals who have still not been exposed? No society can flourish without a fair system of justice. I think we should begin our evening with a small trial. As a curtain-raiser.'

'Hear, hear!'

'Who are we going to try?'

'Anybody! Who cares?' other voices cried out.

'A very good idea!' said Sologdin, encouragingly, settling down more comfortably. Today, as never before, he felt he had earned his evening's rest, and he wanted to be entertained in original fashion.

Kagan, feeling that the fun he had initiated was now threatening to get out of hand, prudently backed away and sat down on his bunk.

'You will learn who we are going to try in the course of the proceedings themselves,' explained Rubin, who had not yet decided who it should be. 'If you don't mind, I will be the prosecutor, inasmuch as this is an office which has always aroused very special feelings in me.' (Everyone at Mavrino knew that Rubin had been dealt with by prosecutors who seemed to have a personal grudge against him and that for the past five years he had vainly been trying to appeal to the Military Prosecutor-General.) 'Gleb! You be the judge and pick three jurymen—impartial, objective and all that —in other words, ready to obey your slightest whim.'

Nerzhin, kicking off his shoes on to the floor, sat up in his bunk. As the day went on the state of mind engendered by his meeting with Nadya had begun to give way to his usual feeling of identification with the familiar world of prison, and it was easy for him to respond to Rubin's invitation. He moved to the edge of his bunk, put his legs through the wooden bars there and said from this vantage-point, as though speaking from the bench in court:

'Well, come up here, anybody who wants to be a jury-man!'

All the many prisoners in the room were keen enough to hear the trial, but, whether out of prudence or fear of making fools of themselves, none of them appeared anxious to serve on the 'jury'. On his upper bunk next to Nerzhin's, Zemelya lay re-reading the morning newspaper. Nerzhin snatched at it:

'That's enough reading for one day! If you're not careful you'll get ideas above your station. Sit up and come on the jury.'

There was applause from below.

'Come on, Zemelya, come on!'

Zemelya was a soft-hearted soul who could never say no. Smiling awkwardly, he hung his balding head through the bars and said:

'It's a great honour to be chosen by the people! But I don't know anything about law. I'm not really up to it.'

Everybody laughed and to shouts of 'We're not up to it either!' Zemelya was 'elected' by acclaim.

On Nerzhin's other side lay Ruska Doronin. He had

undressed and was entirely hidden under his blanket with a pillow over his head to hide his face which was flushed with happiness. He did not want to hear or see, or be seen himself. He was only there in body; his mind and his heart were with Clara, who was now on her way home. Just before leaving she had finished making the little wire basket for the New Year's tree and had secretly given it to Ruska. He was now holding it under the blanket and kissing it.

Seeing that it was useless to bother him, Nerzhin looked around for a second candidate.

'Amantai! Amantai!' he shouted to Bulatov. 'Come and join the jury.'

Bulatov's spectacles glinted roguishly.

'I would, but there's no room left up there! I'll stay down here and be the court usher.'

Khorobrov who had already managed to give a haircut to Adamson and a couple of others, and was now attending to a new 'customer' (the man was sitting stripped to the waist so that he would not have trouble with all the hairs in his underwear afterwards) shouted out from the middle of the room:

'Why do you need another juryman? Isn't the verdict already fixed? Just get on with the job!'

'You're right,' said Nerzhin. 'We can do without any more jurymen. Who needs the parasites, anyway? But where is the accused? Bring in the accused! Pray silence for the court!'

He knocked his long cigarette holder on the bunk and conversation ceased.

'Let's begin the trial!' voices demanded. Some of the prisoners were sitting and others were standing.

From his place in the bunk below Nerzhin, Potapov intoned in a mournful voice:

'Even were I to rise up to Heaven, Thou art there. Even were I to descend into hell, Thou art there. Yeah, even were I to make my abode in the depths of the sea, there too would Thy right hand reach me!' (Potapov was old enough to have done divinity in his pre-revolutionary high school and with the well-disciplined mind of an engineer he had remembered the text of the Orthodox catechism.)

There was now a loud clinking of a spoon stirring sugar in a glass—this came from the bunk under Zemelya's.

'Valentin!' Nerzhin said grimly. 'How many times have you been told not to clink your spoon?'

'Put him on trial!' Bulatov yelled, and several willing pairs of hands dragged Pryanchikov out of the half-darkness of the lower bunk into the centre of the room.

'Cut it out!' said Pryanchikov, struggling violently. 'I'm sick of prosecutors and trials! Who has any right to sit in judgment? What a joke! I despise you!' he shouted at Nerzhin.

By the time Nerzhin had assembled his court, Rubin already had everything worked out. His dark-brown eyes shone with pleasure at his own inventiveness. With a broad sweep of his hand he ordered Pryanchikov's release:

'Let him go! With his passion for universal justice Valentin will make the perfect stooge defence counsel. Give him a chair!'

In any play-acting of this kind there is always a tricky moment when it either becomes vulgar and offensive or else suddenly takes wing. Rubin, who had thrown a blanket over his shoulder like a gown, climbed up on a locker in his stockinged feet and began to address the 'judge':

'State Counsellor of Justice! The accused has so far evaded arrest and the court will therefore try him *in absentia*. I ask you to begin.'

Among the crowd in the doorway was the ginger-whiskered handy-man, Spiridon. The expression on his intelligent, wrinkled face with its flabby cheeks was—rather engagingly —both stern and genial at the same time. He was looking on with knitted brows.

Behind Spiridon, with his long, delicate and slightly waxy face, and a woollen cap on his head, stood Professor Chelnov.

Nerzhin announced in a grating voice:

'Attention, comrades! I hereby declare this session of the Mavrino military tribunal to be open. We are hearing the case of——'

'Prince Igor, son of Svyatoslav,' Rubin prompted him.

Seizing on the idea, Nerzhin pretended to read in a monotonous nasal voice:

'We are hearing the case of Igor, son of Svyatoslav, Prince of Novgorod-Seversky and Putivl, year of birth approximately —damn it, why approximately? Since none of the relevant documents are before the court, the Prosecutor will proceed to read the indictment without more ado.'

CHAPTER FIFTY

Rubin began his speech with such ease and fluency that he might have been reading from a sheet of paper—he had been tried four times and had all the legal phraseology at his finger-tips:

'In the matter of case number five billion, three million, six hundred and fifty one thousand eight hundred and seventy four, to wit the State *versus* Igor, son of Svyatoslav. The Accused is hereby indicted by the state security authorities. An investigation has shown that the said Igor son of Svyatoslav, holding high command in the glorious Russian army with the rank of prince has proved to be a base traitor to his country, his treason consisting in the fact that he did voluntarily surrender to the sworn enemy of our people, the Polovtsian Khan Konchak; and furthermore did cause to surrender his son Vladimir as well as his brother and his nephew and the whole of his army with all the weapons and equipment in his charge.

'His treachery was further evident in that allowing himself to be misled by an eclipse of the sun staged as an act of provocation by the forces of clerical reaction, he failed to carry out a proper campaign of political education among his troops.

'Although the Accused himself has so far evaded apprehension by the officers of the court, nevertheless a witness, namely, Borodin, Alexander, musician, will give incontrovertible evidence to show that the Accused not only commenced battle in unfavourable meteorological and tactical conditions but that he and his progeny did also conduct themselves in captivity in a manner unbecoming to their rank. The material conditions under which they were maintained in their alleged captivity show that they were the recipients of every possible favour on the part of Khan Konchak; objectively this was tantamount to accepting a reward from the Polovtsians for the treacherous surrender of the troops under their command.

'A statement taken from the witness Borodin shows, for example, that in captivity Prince Igor was given a choice of horses in addition to his own:

> ' "*Take any horse thou wilt.*"
> (*Summary of Evidence*, Vol. I, sheet 233)

At the same time Konchak said to Prince Igor:

> ' "*Thou deemst thyself a captive here*
> *Yet art thou not less captive than a guest?*"
> (idem, Vol. I, sheet 281)

and further:

> ' "*What captive lives like this, forsooth?*"
> (idem, Vol. I, sheet 300)

The Polovtsian Khan was cynically outspoken about his relations with the traitor:

> ' "*For thy boldness and thy mettle*
> *I have come to like thee, Prince.*"
> (idem. Vol. III, sheet 5)

Further careful investigation has shown that this shameless association had existed long before the battle on the River Kayala.

> ' "*Thou wert ever dear to me.*"
> (idem, sheet 14, evidence of Borodin)

and moreover:

> ' "*I fain would be thy ally, not thy foe,*
> *Thy trusted friend and kinsman . . .*"
> (idem.)

Such is the objective proof that the Accused was an active accomplice of the Khan Konchak and is a Polovtsian agent and spy of long standing.

'On the basis of the foregoing Igor, son of Svyatoslav, born 1161, native of the town of Kiev, Russian, no Party affiliation, no previous convictions, citizen of the USSR, formerly army commander with the rank of prince is hereby charged:

'That he committed high treason against his Country, aggravated by sabotage, espionage and criminal association with the Polovtsian Khan over a period of many years; that is to say, is accused of offences under Article 58 (Section 1), 58 (Section 6), 58 (Section 9) and 68 (Section 11) of the Criminal Code of the Russian Soviet Federated Socialist Republic.

'To the above charges Igor, son of Svyatoslav, has pleaded guilty.

'In virtue of Article 208 of the Code of Criminal Procedure of the RSFSR the State Prosecutor has been instructed to commit the Accused to trial on the present indictment.'

Rubin paused for breath and looked round triumphantly at the other prisoners. He was so carried away by his imagination that there was now no stopping him and he was egged on by the guffaws coming from the bunks and the doorway. He had already gone much farther than he would have liked in the presence of several informers and one or two other ill-disposed people.

Spiridon, with his rank growth of coarse, reddish-grey hair sprouting untidily over his forehead, ears and neck, had not laughed once. He sat looking on glumly. He had never heard of this prince of the olden days who had been taken prisoner, but the familiar court atmosphere and the cocksure self-confidence of the Prosecutor brought back to him all that he had been through himself and he sensed how unfair all the Prosecutor's arguments were and what a raw deal the poor devil of a prince was getting.

'The Accused being absent and there being no cause to examine the witnesses,' Nerzhin announced in the same measured, nasal tones, 'we shall proceed to hear the arguments of counsel. I again call on the Prosecution.'

He looked sideways at Zemelya.

'Of course, of course,' the 'juryman' nodded with the usual complaisance.

'Comrade judges,' Rubin began his sombre peroration. 'There is little for me to add by way of comment to this series of fearful charges, to this tangle of sordid crimes that has been unravelled before your eyes. Firstly, I should like to contest in the strongest possible terms the widely held and despicable misconception that a wounded man is morally entitled to surrender. Our view is radically different, comrades! In any case, are we sure that he was wounded? What proof can there be, seven hundred and sixty-five years after the event? Where is the relevant certificate signed by the chief medical officer? The court has seen no such document, comrade judges! . . .'

Amantai Bulatov took off his spectacles. Without them his normally bright, cheerful eyes took on a wistful look. He, Pryanchikov and Potapov and many of the others gathered here had all been imprisoned for 'treason', on the grounds that they had 'voluntarily' surrendered to the Germans.

'Furthermore,' boomed the Prosecutor, 'I should like to emphasize the revolting nature of the Accused's behaviour in the Polovtsian camp. Instead of showing concern for his country, Prince Igor thinks only of his wife. His words are:

> ' "*Thou art alone, my dearest one,*
> *Thou art alone. . . .*"

'If we analyse his motive, this outburst of his is understandable, because Yaroslavna was his second wife, a young woman and as such probably not to be trusted, but objectively we can see that Prince Igor was simply concerned with saving his own skin! And again I put it to you—for whom did the Polovtsians perform their dances? For him! Meanwhile his vile offspring has sexual intercourse with the Khan's daughter, despite the fact that Soviet citizens are categorically forbidden to enter into wedlock with foreign nationals! What is more, this took place at a moment of extreme tension in Soviet-Polovtsian relations when . . .'

'Excuse me,' the shaggy-haired Kagan interrupted him from his bunk, 'how does the Prosecutor know that Russia was under Soviet rule at the time?'

'Usher! Remove this hireling of a foreign power!' Nerzhin thumped the table, but before Bulatov could move, Rubin adroitly parried the attack.

'With the court's permission, I should like to answer that question. A dialectical analysis of the text provides us with convincing proof that this was so. I refer to the line:

'"*The red banners waved over Putivl.*"

'Surely this is clear enough? The noble Prince Vladimir Galitsky, commandant of the Putivl military district, summons the people's militia, to defend their native city—and what is Prince Igor doing all this time? Gazing at the naked legs of the Polovtsian maidens! I think we would all agree that this would be a most delightful way of passing the time: That being so, why didn't Prince Igor accept the Khan's offer of "any one of these beauties"? Who of us can believe that a man would voluntarily refuse the offer of a woman? Here, in fact, we have the ultimate in cynicism which reveals the irrefutable guilt of the accused—I refer to his so-called escape from captivity and his "voluntary" return to his country! Who could believe that a man who has been offered "gold and any horse thou wilt" would abandon all that and voluntarily return home? How could he possibly do a thing like that?'

It was just this sort of question which had been put to returning Russian prisoners of war. Spiridon, for instance, had been asked: 'Why should you want to come home if you hadn't been recruited as a foreign spy?'

'There can surely be only one explanation: Prince Igor was recruited by the Polovtsian intelligence service and sent back to undermine the Kievan state! Comrade judges! Like all of you, I am boiling with indignation! In the name of common decency I demand that he be hanged like a dog! However, since capital punishment has been abolished—sentence him instead to twenty-five years hard labour plus five years deprivation of civil rights! Furthermore, I suggest that at the court's discretion the opera *Prince Igor* be banned from the stage as a totally amoral work likely to promote a mood of treachery among our young people! The witness in this case, Borodin, should be held criminally responsible and placed in custody. The two former aristocrats, Rimsky and Korsakov, should also be held responsible, since if they had not completed this disastrous opera it would never have reached the stage. That is all I have to say.' Rubin slid ponderously down from the locker-top, greatly upset by his own speech.

No one laughed.

Without waiting to be invited Pryanchikov rose from his chair. Slightly embarrassed, he said quietly amid complete silence:

'*Tant pis,* gentlemen, *tant pis.* Is this the Stone Age or the twentieth century? What does treason mean any longer? This is the age of nuclear fission, of transistors, of computers! Who nowadays has the right to sit in judgment on his fellow man? Who has the right to deprive another of his freedom?'

'I beg your pardon—is this a speech for the defence?' Professor Chelnov enquired politely, drawing everyone's attention.'First of all, on behalf of the Prosecution, I should like to add a few facts omitted by my learned colleague. . . .'

'Of course, of course,' said Nerzhin encouragingly. 'We are always in favour of the prosecution and biased against the defence. If necessary we are prepared to break any of the rules of judicial procedure. Proceed!'

Professor Chelnov's lips twisted into a faint smile. He spoke in a low voice, and he was only audible because he was listened to with such deference. His pale eyes seemed to look past his audience, as though the pages of ancient chronicles were unfolding before him. The pointed top of his woollen cap gave his face a keen, wary look.

'I wish to point out,' said this professor of mathematics, 'that Prince Igor should have been shown up long before his appointment as army commander—on completion, in fact, of his first security clearance questionnaire. His mother was a Polovtsian, daughter of a Polovtsian prince. Half Polovtsian by blood, Prince Igor was for years an ally of the Polovtsians. He was therefore already Konchak's "ally . . . trusted friend and kinsman" before the campaign took place! When defeated by the grandsons of Vladimir Monomakh in 1180, Igor and Khan Konchak had escaped in the same boat! Later, Svyatoslav and Rurik Rostislavich invited Igor to take part in a joint all-Russian campaign against the Polovtsians, but Igor refused on the pretext that the terrain was icebound.

'Perhaps it was then, and for that reason, that Konchak's daughter Svoboda was betrothed to Igor's son Vladimir? Finally, in the year in question at this trial, 1185, who was it who helped Igor to escape from capture? A Polovtsian! A Polovtsian called Ovlur, whom Igor later raised to the nobility. And then Konchak's daughter bore Igor a grandson . . . for concealing these facts I submit that responsibility must be laid on the author of the libretto, and on Stasov, the music critic, who failed to point out the treasonable implications of Borodin's opera, and finally on Count Musin-Pushkin, for his obvious complicity in the burning of the only manuscript of the ancient Lay of Igor's Raid, on which the opera is based. Clearly someone who stood to gain by it was responsible for trying to confuse the issue.'

Chelnov stepped back as a sign that he had finished, the same faint smile still on his lips.

There was silence.

'Who's going to defend the Accused? The man must be defended, after all!' objected Isaac Kagan.

'He doesn't need a defence!' shouted Dvoyetyosov. 'Just say he's guilty and put him up against a wall!'

Sologdin frowned. Rubin's speech had been extremely funny and he greatly respected Chelnov's erudition, but Prince Igor was after all one of the glorious figures of Russian history, the very flower of the great age of chivalry, and therefore it was improper to use his name, even indirectly, as a butt of derision, Sologdin felt a sense of resentment.

'No, I don't care what you say, I shall speak in his defence,' said Kagan boldly, looking craftily round at the audience. 'Comrade judges! As Defence Counsel, I fully concur with all the remarks made by the Prosecutor.' He spoke in a slurred, drawling voice. 'My conscience prompts me to say that Prince Igor should not only be hung but quartered as well. It is true that capital punishment has been banned from our humane statute-books for three years, and we have been obliged to substitute other penalties. But I cannot understand why the Prosecutor is so suspiciously soft-hearted?

(I suggest that it is time the Prosecutor himself should be investigated.) Why has he only proposed twenty-five years forced labour? There is, after all, another punishment in our judicial code which is only slightly different from capital punishment and which is far more terrible than twenty-five years forced labour.'

Kagan paused for effect.

'What punishment is that?' the audience shouted impatiently. Speaking even more slowly than before, looking even more innocent he replied:

'Article 20, Section "A".'

With all their prison experience, none of the men present had ever heard of such an article. This was real finesse!

'What does it say?' A barrage of obscene suggestions came from all sides. 'Cut off his . . .?'

'Almost, almost,' said Kagan imperturbably. 'It amounts to spiritual castration. Article 20, Section "A" sentences a man to be declared an enemy of the working people and to be expelled beyond the territorial limits of the USSR! Let him rot there in the West! That's all I have to say.'

And the little man, holding his shaggy head to one side, went modestly back to his bunk.

A roar of laughter shook the room.

'What? What?' roared Khorobrov, gasping for breath, his customer writhing as the clippers jerked. 'Expulsion? Is there such a punishment?'

'Increase his sentence! Increase his sentence!' they all shouted. Spiridon smiled the cunning smile of a peasant.

Everybody started talking at once and the gathering broke up.

Rubin was lying on his stomach again trying to concentrate on his Mongolian dictionary. Cursing himself for his stupid exhibitionism, he felt nothing but shame for the part he had played.

CHAPTER FIFTY-ONE

Adamson, lying with his shoulder and cheek pressed to his raised pillow, had just gone on reading *The Count of Monte Cristo*. He was not one to be amused by a mock trial and he lay with his back to what was going on in the room; only when Chelnov was speaking did he turn his head slightly —some of this had been new to him.

In twenty years of exile, prison, solitary confinement, labour camps and places like Mavrino, Adamson, who had once been a forceful and sensitive public speaker, had become unfeeling and indifferent to his own sufferings and those of people around him.

The trial which had just been staged in the room was about the fate of prisoners of war: that is, about all the Soviet soldiers first ineptly led by their generals into captivity and then callously abandoned by Stalin to die of hunger in German camps. The survivors, on returning to Russia at the end of the war, had been sent straight to the labour camps and thus provided the main new contingent of forced labour in 1945 and 1946. Adamson recognized in theory the tragedy of what had happened to them, but they were only one of many categories of prisoners, and by no means the most remarkable. They were interesting mainly because they had seen something of life abroad, and were, therefore, as Potapov joked, 'living false witnesses', but they were none the less a dreary, pathetic lot—helpless victims of war rather than men who had voluntarily chosen to stake their lives for political reasons.

Every new influx of prisoners sent to the camps by the MVD had its own history, and its own heroes—in this the successive waves were like new generations and there was a corresponding lack of understanding between them.

Thus, it seemed to Adamson that none of these people in the room was remotely comparable to those giants like himself who at the end of the 'twenties had chosen deportation to Siberia rather than retract what they had said at

Party meetings—this was all they had to do to continue leading a life of relative comfort—and it was up to each of them to decide for himself. They had all refused to accept anything that distorted or dishonoured the Revolution and were ready to sacrifice their lives to make it pure again. But now there was this young generation who, thirty years after the October Revolution, came to prison swearing obscenely, like peasants, and saying things for which, during the Civil War, they would have been shot.

For these reasons, though he had no particular quarrel with any of the ex-prisoners of war, Adamson did not recognize the species as a whole.

Furthermore, as he kept on telling himself (he had long since lost interest in prisoners' arguments, life stories and eye-witness tales. He had lost whatever curiosity he might have felt in his young days about anything said by his fellow-prisoners, and he had also long ago become utterly bored by the work he was given to do. Since his family did not live in Moscow he was not allowed visits and therefore felt quite out of touch with them—the letters which reached him in Mavrino had to go through censorship and were inevitably lifeless and uninformative. He did not waste his time on newspapers—their contents were immediately clear to him from a glance at the headlines. He had no opportunity to listen to music programmes for more than an hour a day, and he could not stand the spoken word on the radio, any more than he could read books which were full of lies. And though somewhere deep inside him he maintained a lively and indeed acutely sensitive interest in the world and in the fate of the doctrine on the altar of which he had offered up his life, outwardly he had trained himself to be totally contemptuous of everything around him. This was why Adamson, who had managed to survive all these years without being shot or otherwise done to death, now read for preference not books which might give inspiration but only books which amused him and helped make his endless sentence seem a little shorter.

They had certainly not read *Monte Cristo* out on the Yenisei in 1929. He could remember that time when they had organized a meeting in the remote village of Doshchany on the River Angara—they had to travel there three hundred

376

miles by sledge to meet other exiles, who had come from even remoter places, and under the pretext of a New Year's party, they had held a conference on the international situation and the state of affairs in the Soviet Union. The temperature had dropped to more than 50° centigrade below zero. There was very little heat from the small iron stove in the corner of the large Siberian log-cabin which had been given to the exiles only because the usual tiled stove was broken beyond repair. The walls of the cabin were frozen through, and in the quiet of the night the logs of which they were made sometimes cracked like rifle shots.

The conference was opened by Satanevich with a report on Party policy in the countryside. He took off his cap, thus freeing his dangling black forelock, but kept on his sheepskin coat with the English phrase book which always stuck out of the pocket. ('Know your enemy,' he would explain.) He was one of those who always liked to be the leader, and he was later shot, it seems, during a strike in Vorkuta. Unfortunately, during the earnest discussion of his and other reports the unity of this pathetic gathering of exiles disintegrated. There were as many different opinions as there were people present and the conference wearily finished its business in the early hours of the morning without being able to agree on a resolution.

Afterwards, having decorated the rough splintered table with pine twigs, they ate and drank from the standard cups and plates supplied to political exiles. The thawing sprigs smelled of snow and resin and pricked the hands. Drinking toasts in home-distilled vodka, they swore solemnly never to capitulate or sign the recantations demanded of them.

Then they sang hallowed revolutionary songs such as *Warszawianka*, *Over the World Our Banner Flies* and *The Black Baron*, and after that went on arguing about anything that occurred to them.

Rosa, a worker from the Kharkhov Tobacco Factory, was sitting on a feather bolster which she had brought all the way from the Ukraine to Siberia and of which she was very proud. Chain-smoking, she contemptuously tossed back her bobbed curls and said: 'I can't stand the intelligentsia! They're so finicky and complicated—it really makes me sick.

Human nature is much simpler than the pre-Revolutionary writers make out. What we must do is free mankind from all this sophistication!'

Somehow they got on to the subject of whether women should wear jewellery or not. One of the group, Patrushev, who before his arrest had been a prosecutor in Odessa and whose fiancée, it so happened, had recently come out to join him in Siberia, was indignant: 'Why do you want the society of the future to be so austere? Why shouldn't I dream of a time when every girl can wear pearls and every man can put a tiara on the head of his beloved?' This had caused an uproar and the others had answered back furiously with quotations from Marx, Plekhanov, Campanella and Feuerbach.

How easily it had been to speak in those days of the 'society of the future'!

The sun rose on the first day of the New Year, 1930, and they all went out to admire it. It was a bracing frosty morning and columns of smoke rising straight up from nearby huts were as pink as the sky itself. On the white expanses of the Angara peasant women were driving their cattle to drink at a hole in the ice round which a screen of pine branches had been built. There was no sign of either men or horses: they had all been sent away to fell timber.

Twenty years had gone by since then, and all those toasts they had drunk and oaths they had taken no longer made any sense and had faded from memory. Those of them who had subsequently capitulated had been shot as well as those who had not. Only Adamson, a lone survivor preserved in the sheltered conditions of special prisons like Mavrino, kept a memory and understanding of those years—they were nurtured in his head, like a tree growing unseen in a hothouse.
. . .

Adamson was thinking of all this and staring vacantly at his book when Nerzhin came and sat down on the edge of his bunk.

They had first got to know each other three years ago in Butyrki, where they had shared a cell with Potapov. Adamson was then coming to the end of his first ten-year sentence, and he deeply impressed the other prisoners in the cell with his aloof air of authority and his deep-rooted scepticism about everybody's prospects—though he himself secretly cherished the insane idea that he might soon be able to return to his family.

After Butyrki, Nerzhin and Adamson had lost sight of each other for a time. By some extraordinary fluke, Adamson had indeed been released—but only for as long as it took his family to move and settle in Sterlitamak, in Bashkiria, where the police had agreed to give Adamson a residence permit. As soon as his family had moved, he had been arrested once more and during the interrogation they asked him only one thing: had he been deported in 1929, lived in Siberia till 1934 and then spent the following years in prison? Having established that this was the case and that he had already served his sentence in full and more besides, the Special Tribunal had forthwith given him another ten years. But the people in charge of the special prisons had learned from the central MVD files that this man who had once worked for them was now in an ordinary prison and they at once had him transferred. So Adamson had been brought to Mavrino where, as was bound to happen to him in any prison or camp, he had immediately met old friends, including Nerzhin and Potapov. And when they had all three stood and smoked a cigarette on the prison staircase Adamson felt that he had not really lived in freedom for a whole year, or seen his family, or given his wife another daughter, but that it had all been a cruel dream, and that the only unchanging reality in the world was prison.

Now Nerzhin had come to invite Adamson to a small party that was going to be given in honour of his birthday. Adamson belatedly wished Nerzhin many happy returns and, peering at him through his glasses, asked who would be there. He was not at all pleased at the idea of putting on his denims and going to some kind of birthday party, instead of just continuing to lie blissfully in his underwear, reading his book. The worst of it was that he knew he would have a miserable time—there was bound to be a political argument which, as usual, would be futile and unrewarding, and in which he would inevitably get involved. But he had to keep out of things like this, because he found it just as repugnant to reveal his innermost beliefs, held at the cost of so much humiliation, to these 'young' prisoners as it would have been to display his wife naked to them.

Nerzhin told him who else would be there. The only prisoner in Mavrino to whom Adamson felt really close was Rubin, but now he had the unpleasant task of reprimanding him for today's disgraceful performance, which had been unworthy of a true Communist. As for Sologdin and Pryanchikov who would also be there—Adamson had no time for them at all.

But it couldn't be helped—he had to accept. Nerzhin told him that the party would begin between Potapov's and Pryanchikov's bunks in half an hour, as soon as Potapov had finished the sweet he was making.

As they talked, Nerzhin saw what Adamson was reading and he said:

'I once read *Monte Cristo* in prison too, but I didn't get to the end of it. I noticed that though Dumas tried to build up a feeling of horror, the Château d'If comes out as a nice old-fashioned sort of place. Of course, as you might expect from someone who'd never been in prison, Dumas says nothing about such charming details as how they dealt with the prisoners' slops. But it's not hard to see why it was so easy for Dantes to escape. No wonder his tunnel wasn't discovered if his cell was never searched for years on end and the warders were never changed—all experience tells us that prison warders must be changed every two hours to make sure they keep each other up to scratch. At the Château d'If days went by without anyone coming into the cells and looking around. They didn't even have peep-holes in the doors. The place was really more like a seaside resort than a prison. They even left a metal bowl in the cell, so Dantes had something to dig through the floor with. Then, to crown it all, they were fools enough to put him in a sack in the morgue without first running a red-hot iron or a bayonet through him. Dumas should have paid more attention to detail instead of piling on the agony the way he does.'

Nerzhin never read a book just for amusement. He always saw either an ally or an enemy in the author and delivered cut-and-dried judgments, which he expected other people to share.

Adamson knew this boring habit of his and he listened to him without raising his head from the pillow, looking at him calmly through his square spectacles.

'All right,' he said. 'I'll come.' And stretching out more comfortably, he went on reading.

CHAPTER FIFTY-TWO

Nerzhin went to help Potapov prepare the sweet. After years of hunger as a prisoner of war in Germany and then in the Soviet prisons, Potapov had come to the conclusion that the consumption of food was a natural process that not only had nothing shameful or contemptible about it but was highly pleasurable and essential to human existence.

Being one of those engineers who are as clever with their hands as they are with their head, he soon became a remarkably fine cook. In the German prisoner-of-war camp he had learned how to bake an orange tart out of nothing but potato peelings, and in his days in the special prison he had specialized in making sweets and brought it to a fine art.

Having pushed two bedside lockers together in the space between his bed and Pryanchikov's he was now busily at work over them in the agreeable half-light created by the shadows cast by the upper bunks. Because the room was semicircular, the beds were laid out radially and the gap between them was narrow at the foot then widened out towards the window. Potapov was also making full use of the huge, deep window-sill, and jars of jam, plastic containers and metal bowls were disposed all around. With hieratic solemnity Potapov was beating up a mixture of cocoa and two eggs (a present from Rubin, who received constant food parcels from home and always shared them out) into some nameless concoction. As Nerzhin wandered up, Potapov muttered to him to find some more glasses, as there were not enough. One was the cap of a thermos flask, two were laboratory beakers and two more Potapov had stuck together out of greaseproof paper, rather like ice-cream tubs.

Nerzhin suggested using a couple of shaving mugs, which he promised to rinse out carefully in hot water.

There was a relaxed atmosphere in the room. Some of the inmates were sitting on the beds of friends who were lying down and talking to them, others were reading, exchanging occasional remarks, while still others lay silent and inactive, hands behind their heads, staring unblinkingly at the white ceiling. The talk merged into a general hum of many voices.

Zemelya was sprawled comfortably on his upper bunk stripped down to his pants (it was pretty warm on top) stroking his hairy chest. As he smiled his invariably kindly smile he was talking to Mish, a Mordvin, lying two bunks further away.

'If you really want to know, it all started with half-kopecks.'

'Why half-kopecks?'

'Back in 'twenty-six, 'twenty-seven—you were only a boy then—a little notice-board used to hang over every cashier's desk: "Change given in half-kopecks". And there really was such a coin. The cashiers would always hand them out without a murmur. It was still the NEP in those days, and it was peacetime too.'

'Weren't there any wars?'

'Of course not! That was before all the wars started—there was *real* peace in those days. Under the NEP, you know, we only worked a six-hour day, not like now. And we seemed to manage all right. And if they kept you for fifteen minutes after hours, they'd start paying you overtime. Then what d'you think was the first thing to go? The half-kopeck! That's when everything started going downhill. Next thing all the copper coins disappeared. Then in 'thirty the silver went too, so there wasn't any small change at all. Do what you like, they wouldn't give you any. Nothing's been right since then. As there weren't any small coins you could only count in roubles. Even the beggars gave up asking for a kopeck—"God bless you—give us a rouble"—they'd say. At work they never bothered to pay you the kopecks they owed you—no good asking even, they just laughed at you for niggling. Fools! Half-kopecks meant showing some consideration for people, but when they refuse to give you

382

sixty kopecks change out of a rouble that's just daylight robbery. If we'd worried more about that half-kopeck then we might not be in the mess we are now.'

On the other side of the room, also on an upper bunk, a prisoner turned aside from reading to say to a neighbour: 'God, the tsarist government was stupid! Listen to this, Sasha: there was a girl revolutionary who went on a hunger strike for a week to make the prison governor apologize to her and he did, the fool. Try and make the governor of Krasnaya Presnya apologize to you and see what happens!'

'Nowadays they would force-feed her through a tube after three days and they'd double her sentence for bad behaviour. Where did you read that?'

'In a book by Gorky.'

Dvoyetyosov, who was lying on a nearby bed, roused himself at that and growled threateningly:

'Who's reading Gorky?'

'I am.'

'What the hell for?'

'Listen to what he says about the Nizhni Novgorod prison, for instance. You could put a ladder up against the wall and climb over, and nobody would stop you—can you imagine it? And Gorky said that the warders' pistols were so rusty they could only use them for knocking nails into the wall. Interesting, isn't it?'

Underneath him on the lower bunk the usual prison argument was in progress over when was the best time to go to prison. The question assumed that no one could avoid being imprisoned at some time or other. (Prisoners are generally inclined to exaggerate the number of people 'inside'; when the actual prison population was no more than twelve or fifteen million, for instance, they were convinced that there were no more men left outside.) They were discussing whether it was better to be in prison as a young man or later on in life. In these arguments some, generally the younger ones, cheerfully maintained that the best time is when you're young: it gives you a chance to learn what life is about, what things are worth living for and what are not, and they reckoned that by the time a man is thirty-five, having done his ten years' hard, he can set about living on the right lines.

When an older man goes to prison, on the other hand, he

is apt to tear his hair with remorse at having messed up his life, at having done nothing but make one mistake after another and now it is too late to put them right. Others (generally older men) contend with equal force that if an older man is sent to prison it is like quietly retiring on a pension or going into a monastery, that he had the best out of life while he was in his prime (when prisoners reminisce, "the best" usually comes down to women, good clothes, plenty to eat and plenty to drink); and no camp can screw much work out of an old man, whereas a young man is squeezed so dry by prison work that afterwards he doesn't even want a woman any more.

And so they argued on, in the way that prisoners always argue—some felt better for it, others felt embittered, but whatever the outcome, not a flicker of the truth arose from all their arguments and their graphic examples. Sunday evenings invariably ended with a feeling that prison was a good thing, but when they got up on Monday morning it was only too plain that any time was a bad time to be in prison.

Yet even this was not wholly true. . . .

The discussion about the best time of one's life to be imprisoned was not, however, one of those arguments which inflamed the participants; it was one which rather tended to soothe them, to spread an air of philosophic resignation, and it never led to any outbursts of violence.

Thomas Hobbes once said that an axiom such as, 'The sum of the angles of a triangle is equal to a hundred and eighty degrees' could only lead to bloodshed if it threatened someone's interests.

But Hobbes knew nothing of the prison mentality. On the bed nearest the door, one of those arguments was in progress which was liable to end in a fight, or even bloodshed, although no one's interests were involved. A prisoner who was an electrician had been joined for the evening by his friend who was a lathe operator and somehow the subject had turned to the town of Sestroretsk, then to the kind of stoves that people in Sestroretsk use to heat their houses. The lathe operator had spent a winter in Sestroretsk and knew all about the local stoves. The electrician had never been there himself but his brother-in-law was a skilled stove-builder who had plied his trade in Sestroretsk and his description of the stoves there was the exact opposite. Their quarrel, which had begun as an ordinary argument, had already reached the point where their voices were shaking with anger and personal insults were being exchanged. Shouting louder than anybody else in the room, each was in the galling position of being unable to prove beyond doubt that he was right and they had tried in vain to find an umpire among the others. Suddenly they remembered that Spiridon knew all about stoves and would at any rate, be able to tell one or the other that there were no stoves like that to be found in Sestroretsk or anywhere else. To everyone's relief the two men marched out of the room to see Spiridon.

In the heat of the argument, however, they forgot to shut the door behind them and in from the passage came the sound of another equally overwrought argument over which date marked the exact half-way mark in the twentieth century—the 1st of January 1950, or the 1st of January 1951. The argument had obviously been going on for a long time and had got stuck on the question of the year of Christ's birth.

The doors slammed shut. The ear-splitting noise stopped, the room was quiet again and Khorobrov could be heard saying to the bald draughtsman on the bunk above him: 'When our people make the first flight to the moon, they'll hold a meeting round the launching-pad before they start. The crew of the rocket will promise to be economical with fuel, to beat the record for outer space, not to stop the space-ship for repairs on the way and to make nothing less than a perfect landing. Of the three members of the crew, one will be the commissar. He'll spend the whole trip giving the pilot and the navigator political lectures on the importance of interplanetary flight and he will pester them to give him facts and figures for his propaganda bulletin.'

This was overheard by Pryanchikov, who was just crossing the room with soap and towel. Skipping over to Khorobrov and frowning mysteriously he said:

'Don't worry, Ilya. It won't be like that.'

'What will it be like, then?'

Pryanchikov put his finger dramatically to his lips, then said:

'The first ones to fly to the moon will be the Americans!'

He burst into peals of child-like laughter and scampered off.

The engraver was sitting on Sologdin's bed, where they were carrying on an absorbing discussion about women. The engraver was forty, and although his face was still young his hair was almost completely grey, which made him very good-looking. He was in excellent form that night. It was true that he had made a mistake that morning by screwing up his short story into a ball and swallowing it, when it had turned out that he might have been able to smuggle it through the search and pass it to his wife. But during the visit he had learned that over the past months his wife had shown his previous stories to several trustworthy people and they had all been thrilled by them. Naturally praise that came from friends and relatives might be exaggerated and biased, but hell—whose opinion was unbiased, anyway? In any case, whether his stories were good or bad, the engraver had preserved something of the truth for posterity—a cry from the heart about Stalin's treatment of millions of returned prisoners of war. He was filled with pride and happiness at the thought of it and firmly determined to go on writing his short stories. The visit that morning had been altogether successful—his devoted wife was still waiting for him, she had been working hard to have him released and was expecting her efforts soon to produce some positive results.

As an outlet for his exaltation he had embarked on a long talk with Sologdin, in his eyes an intelligent but otherwise very average person, who had no such bright hopes of release.

Sologdin was lying stretched out on his bed with some worthless book open on his chest and looked at the engraver, his eyes twinkling. With his slightly curly blond beard, his clear eyes, tall brow and the clean-cut features of a Kievan warrior, Sologdin was unnaturally, almost indecently handsome. Today he too was in a triumphant mood. His heart sang with joy at having overcome the problems of his scrambling device. His release was now only a matter of a year (or rather it would be when he had made up his mind to hand the scrambler to Yakonov). A brilliant career might be awaiting him after his release. Besides, today his body no longer ached for a woman as it usually did, but felt appeased. Despite his penalty marks on the sheet of pink paper, despite his resistance to Larisa, Sologdin now admitted, as he lay that evening stretched out on his bed, that this was what he had been wanting from her all the time.

And as an outlet for his exaltation he amused himself by lazily following the twists and turns of the uninteresting story told by this intelligent but otherwise very average person, the engraver, who did not have Sologdin's bright hopes of release.

Sologdin always insisted to everybody that he had a very poor memory, limited abilities and a total lack of will-power. But one could infer what he *really* thought about himself, not by what he said but by the way he listened to other people. He listened to them in a way which implied that merely by doing so, he was doing them a favour and was only concealing the fact out of politeness.

The engraver began by describing his two wives in Russia, then he talked about his life in Germany and the charming German girls whose favours he had enjoyed. He drew a comparison between Russian and German women which was new to Sologdin. In his view, having lived with both, he preferred German women. He found Russian women too independent, too demanding. Their relentless gaze never ceased to probe and analyse the man they loved until they discovered his weaknesses—lack of consideration, perhaps, or lack of courage. As a wife or mistress a Russian woman, you felt, behaved as your equal, whereas a German girl bent herself like a sapling in the hands of her lover. She regarded him as a god, treated him as the most precious and most important person in the world, abandoned herself entirely to his mercy, dreamed only of how to please him— and because of this his German women had made the engraver feel all the more virile and masterful.

Rubin unthinkingly went out into the corridor for a smoke, but there, as everywhere else in Mavrino, he found that people were always baiting him. Backing out of some pointless argument, he hurriedly returned to his books, but someone on a lower bunk grabbed him by the trouser-leg as he passed, and asked him: 'Hey, Rubin! Is it true that in China informers' letters can be posted without a stamp?'

Rubin pulled himself free and passed on, but another prisoner, an engineer, leaned down from a top bunk, grabbed him by the collar of his denims and started delivering a harangue which he felt he owed him from a previous argument: 'Look—the essential thing is to remould people's consciences so that they only take pride in what they do with their own two hands and feel ashamed at being overseers or bosses or windbags of that sort. If the day ever comes when a family thinks it a disgrace for their daughter to marry a bureaucrat—that's what I'd call socialism and I wouldn't mind living under it!'

Rubin pulled his collar free, dashed to his bunk and flung himself down among his dictionaries.

CHAPTER FIFTY-THREE

There were seven men round the table which consisted of three lockers of different heights—they had been pushed together and covered with a piece of bright green paper of German manufacture. Sologdin and Rubin sat with Potapov on his bunk; Adamson and Kondrashov had joined Pryanchikov on his, and Nerzhin, as the guest of honour, sat on the broad window-sill at the end of the table. Above them Zemelya was already asleep, and the occupants of the other adjacent bunks were not around. This space between the two double bunks was cut off from the rest of the room, almost like a compartment in a sleeping-car.

The fancy pastry made by Nadya—an unheard-of luxury in Mavrino—had been placed in a plastic bowl in the middle of the table: there was absurdly little of it for seven men. There were also plain biscuits—some of them smeared with Potapov's concoction and therefore referred to as cakes. Then there was a glutinous substance made by boiling an unopened can of condensed milk. Finally, behind Nerzhin's back, concealed in a large opaque jar, was the enticing liquid for which the makeshift cups had been provided—a little alcohol, obtained from the prisoners in the Chemical Laboratory in exchange for a piece of high-class insulating material, had been diluted with water in the proportion of four to one, and then coloured with cocoa. The resulting brown liquid was not very potent, but it was eagerly awaited.

'Now then, gentlemen,' Sologdin said, leaning back theatrically, his eyes flashing even in the half-darkness of the 'compartment'. 'Let each of us think back to the last time he sat down to a banquet.'

'I did yesterday—with the Germans,' grunted Rubin, who couldn't stand sentiment.

Assuming that Sologdin always addressed people as 'gentlemen' because his mind had suffered in twelve years in prison, and that this also explained the many other oddities in his way of thinking, Rubin always tried to keep his temper with him, however wild some of the things he said.

'No, gentlemen,' Sologdin said. 'I mean a *real* banquet and all that goes with it—a heavy, brocaded tablecloth, liquor and wine in cut glass decanters and, of course, well-dressed women.'

Sologdin's intention was to whet their appetites by first lingering over past memories like this, but Potapov cast an eye over his guests with the jealous, appraising glance of a good host, and interrupted in his usual gruff manner:

'Unless you want to be caught with this stuff, we'd better proceed to the serious business of the evening.'

He signalled to Nerzhin to fill their cups.

While the liquor was being poured out they were all silent and none of them could help, after all, recalling past occasions.

'It was a long time ago,' Nerzhin sighed.

'I'm not sure I even remember!' Potapov said, shaking himself. He had always been so overwhelmed with work before the war that he was not sure whether the wedding reception he now vaguely remembered had been his own or someone else's.

'I can tell you the last time it happened to me,' said Pryanchikov with relish. '*Avec plaisir!* in 1945 in Paris I . . .'

'Just a minute, Valentin,' Potapov stopped him, 'first we must have a toast.'

'To our guest of honour!' Kondrashov-Ivanov proposed in

a voice louder than necessary, sitting even more upright than before. 'And may there be . . .'

But before the company could reach for their cups Nerzhin stood up in the little space by the window and said quietly:

'My friends, excuse me if I depart from the usual practice.'

He had to pause for breath because he was so moved by the warm feelings which showed in those six pairs of eyes.

'To be fair,' he resumed, '—our lives aren't as bad as all that. Think how fortunate we are to be sitting here round this table, able to exchange ideas without fear or concealment. We couldn't have done that when we were free, could we?'

'No, and as a matter of fact, we were seldom free for very long,' Adamson said with a wry smile. Not counting his childhood, he had spent less than half his life outside prison.

'Friends!' Nerzhin went on, carried away by his own eloquence. 'I am thirty-one years old. Over these years my life has had its ups and downs, and if it continues on its sinusoidal curve then I may still have my hollow triumphs and moments of imagined greatness; but, I swear I will never forget the real human greatness that I have come to know only in prison! I am proud that such a choice company as this has come together today on the modest occasion of my birthday. Even if it sounds a little high-flown, let's drink a toast to the friendship which thrives between prison walls!'

Paper cups silently touched those of glass and plastic, and they drank the brown liquor slowly, rolling it round their tongues.

'It has something!' said Rubin approvingly. 'Bravo, Potapov!'

'Yes, it has,' Sologdin agreed. He was in a mood to praise everything today.

Nerzhin laughed:

'It's a most unusual event when Lev and Dmitry agree about something! I can't remember it ever happening before.'

'But, Gleb,' Sologdin said, 'don't you remember that time at New Year's when Lev and I agreed that a wife who has been unfaithful cannot be forgiven, but that a husband can be?'

Adamson put on a blasé smile:

'What man wouldn't agree with that?'

'This fine specimen,' said Rubin, pointing at Nerzhin, 'maintained on that occasion that a woman can be forgiven too, that there's no difference.'

'Did you say that?' Kondrashov asked quickly.

'What a fool!' Pryanchikov guffawed. 'How can you compare the two?'

'The way they're built and their function in coitus shows that they're absolutely different!' Sologdin exclaimed.

'It's not my fault if I think as I do,' Nerzhin said. 'It's the way I was brought up—I remember all those red banners fluttering over our heads with the word "equality" in letters of gold! Since then, of course, I've learnt more sense, but I once fondly imagined that if nations and people were equal, then why not men and women too?'

'No one says it's your fault!' Kondrashov said just as quickly. 'Just stick to your guns.'

'We can forgive your talking that sort of nonsense only because of your extreme youth,' Sologdin pronounced. (He was five years older.)

'Gleb is right in principle,' Rubin said a little diffidently. 'I'm all for equality between men and women myself. But the thought of embracing my wife after someone else has! Ugh! It would be biologically impossible for me.'

'But, gentlemen, it's all too absurd for words!' Pryanchikov cried out, only to be interrupted, as usual.

'There's no problem,' Potapov said to Rubin, 'as long as *you* don't embrace anyone but your wife!'

'For goodness sake . . .' Rubin expostulated feebly, muffling his broad smile in his pirate's beard.

Someone noisily opened the door and came in. Potapov and Adamson looked round, but it was not one of the warders.

'*Delenda est Carthago?*' asked Adamson, nodding towards the jar with the liquor.

'The quicker the better. Who wants a stretch in solitary? Gleb, pour out the rest.'

Nerzhin poured what was left into their cups, scrupulously dividing it into equal parts.

391

'Well, will you let us drink your health at last?' Adamson asked.

'No, friends, I want to suggest a different toast. . . . I saw my wife today, and she seemed to me to personify all our wives—tormented, persecuted and living in constant fear. We can stand it because we have no choice, but think what it's like for them! Let's drink to these women who have shackled themselves to . . .'

'Yes, what saints they are!' Kondrashov exclaimed.

They drank.

For a little while no one said anything.

'Look at the snow out there.' Adamson broke the silence. Everyone looked past Nerzhin out of the windows which were all misted over. They could not see the snow itself— only the black reflection of scurrying snowflakes cast on the prison windows by the lamps and searchlights of the perimeter.

Somewhere beyond that thick curtain of snow was Gleb's wife.

'For us even the snow has to be black,' Kondrashov said.

'We have drunk to friendship and love: these are great and timeless things,' said Rubin with approval. 'About love I have never had any doubts. But I must admit that before all my experience of war and prison I didn't have much faith in friends, particularly in the business about laying down your life for them. In the ordinary way of things you just have your family and there's not really much room for friendship, is there?'

'That's what a lot of people think,' Adamson replied. 'You know that song called *Down in the Valley*? It's been popular in Russia for well over a century and even today people are always asking for it to be played on the radio. Now, if you listen to the words, it's a nasty, whining, petty-minded thing:

> ' "*Friends are friends, they say,*
> *Only till the first black day.*" '

'What a revolting thought!' Kondrashov said. 'How could

anyone live a single day, if he believed that? You'd want to hang yourself!'

'It would be better to put it the other way round: only on a black day can you tell who your friends are.'

'Who said that?'

'Merzlyakov.'

'What a dreadful name! Lev, who was Merzlyakov?'

'He was a poet, twenty years older than Pushkin.'

'I suppose you know all about him?'

'Yes—he was a professor at the University of Moscow and he translated Torquato Tasso's *Jerusalem Delivered* into Russian.'

'Tell me, is there anything Lev doesn't know? Apart from higher mathematics.'

'And even simple arithmetic.'

'But he's always using expressions like: "We must find the common denominator"!'

'Gentlemen! Let me give an example of how right Merzlyakov was!' Pryanchikov butted in, almost choking in his eagerness to get a word in, like a child sitting at table with his elders. He was in many ways just as good as the others —he was quick-witted, intelligent and engagingly straightforward. But because he somehow lacked a commanding masculine presence, he looked fifteen years younger than he was and they all treated him like a mere boy. 'Everybody knows you're always betrayed by someone you just think is a friend! That's what I thought about a fellow I escaped from a German camp with, but then at the end of the war he turned me in to our own people.'

'That was a lousy thing to do!' Kondrashov put in.

'It happened like this: quite honestly, I didn't want to come back home. I already had a job in Germany. I had money, and girl-friends.'

Nearly all of them had heard the story before. For Rubin it was all well and good to be friends with the cheerful, likeable Valentin Pryanchikov in Mavrino, but it was also clear to him that what had happened to him in the ('objectively speaking') reactionary Europe of 1945, was not betrayal, but that his friend had simply been performing his patriotic duty by getting Pryanchikov to return home, even against his will.

Adamson dozed behind his rigidly fixed spectacles. He had known there would be some futile talk of this kind. His own feeling was that all those wretched displaced persons just had to be brought back to Russia somehow or other.

Rubin and Nerzhin, having been put through the same mill as the ex-prisoners of war in the first year after the war, felt almost as though they belonged to the same category, and they were utterly tired of hearing stories by people who had been forcibly repatriated from Western Europe. At their end of the table they had therefore got Kondrashov to start talking about art. Rubin did not think much of Kondrashov as an artist, or indeed take him very seriously as a person, since he ignored economic and historical factors. Nevertheless, without his even noticing, he always imbibed a little wisdom from Kondrashov's talk.

For Kondrashov art was not an activity like any other, or a mode of perception, but a way of life—the only possible one. He felt that everything around him—landscapes, objects, the characters of people or shades of colour—all had their own peculiar *resonance*, which he could unerringly identify and place in the tonic scale. Rubin, for example, was C Minor. Similarly, everything had its own colour—whether it was a human voice, a passing mood, a novel or the notes in the tonic scale: C Sharp Major, for instance, was dark blue and gold.

Kondrashov was well known for his passionate likes and dislikes—he was never indifferent about anything and his judgments were absolute. He admired Rembrandt, but saw no good in Raphael. In Russian painting he worshipped Valentin Serov,[1] but loathed the 'Wanderers'.[2] He couldn't stand Chekhov and he was repelled by Tchaikovsky. ('He's so stifling, he takes away hope and life!') But he felt such affinity for Bach's chorales and Beethoven's concertos that he might have composed them himself.

They had now got him on to the subject of whether or not painting should imitate nature.

'Now suppose you want to paint a view of a garden seen

[1] Famous Russian painter (1865-1911).

[2] 'The Wanderers' (*Peredvizhniki*): a late nineteenth-century school of Russian realist painters.

through an open window on a summer morning,' he was saying. His voice was so youthful and vibrant with feeling that, just to hear him, one would have thought it was a young man speaking. 'Even if you do your best to put down everything you see, will it really be *everything*? What about the singing of the birds? And the freshness of the morning? And your own feeling of somehow being cleansed by it all? After all, as you paint, you perceive these things—they are inseparable from what you see. But how can you capture them in the painting so they are not lost for anyone who looks at it? Obviously they must be suggested by your composition, and the colour you use—since you have no other means of conveying them.'

'So you shouldn't simply copy what you see?'

'Of course not! In fact, whenever you do a landscape,' Kondrashov went on excitedly, 'or a portrait, you start by thinking how wonderful your subject is and how great it would be if only you could get it down just as it is! But as the work goes on, you begin to find all sorts of things wrong with whatever you're painting. Parts of it look absurd, or out of keeping with the rest: that's not right, you say, and start painting it the way you think it *ought* to be.' Kondrashov looked at them exultantly.

'But, good God,' Rubin protested, 'where will you end up if you paint things as they *ought* to be? That way you can turn people into angels or devils, or stand them on pedestals. Surely, if you paint a portrait of Potapov here, you should show him as he is.'

'What does that mean: show him as he is?' Kondrashov came back at him. 'Of course there must be some external resemblance in the features, the shape of the eyes, the colour of the hair and so forth. But isn't it rash to believe that we can see and know reality exactly as it is—particularly when it's a question of the spirit? Who can perceive the spirit? But if I look at the person whose portrait I am painting and discern potential qualities of mind or character which he hasn't so far shown in life, why shouldn't I depict them? What's wrong about helping a man to find his higher self?'

'That's pure socialist realism!' said Nerzhin, clapping his hands. 'The Deputy Minister doesn't realize how lucky he is to have you here.'

395

'Why shouldn't I give a man his due and show his true worth?' Kondrashov continued, and his spectacles, firmly clamped on his nose, glinted defiantly in the semi-darkness. 'And I'll tell you something else: perhaps the most important thing about painting portraits, or about communicating with people in any other way, is that you can actually bring out the best in a person by seeing it in him and identifying it.'

'In other words,' Rubin scoffed, 'you don't believe in objectivity in art, or in anything else.'

'No, I'm not objective and I'm proud of it!' Kondrashov said loudly.

'Really now, what do you mean?' Rubin asked in astonishment.

'Just what I say: I'm proud of not being objective!' Kondrashov hurled his words at Rubin, and was only prevented by the bunk over his head from standing up. 'And what about you? You're not objective either, you only think you are—which is much worse! My great advantage over you is that I know I'm not objective and give myself credit for it. It's this that makes me what I am.'

'I'm not objective, you say?' Rubin said, taken aback. 'If I'm not objective, I'd like to know who is!'

'No one is, of course!' Kondrashov said triumphantly. 'No one! No one ever was and no one will ever be! Every act of cognition has an emotional colouring. People think that after long research they may arrive at some truth or other, but don't we always dimly see what we're looking for even before we begin? Then think how often you take a dislike to a book as soon as you've read the first page only to find how right you were when you come to the end of it! Or take your own case: you want to make a comparative study of all the languages in the world, and it may take you forty years, but you're already sure that you can prove that all words derive from the root for "hand". Is that what you call objective?'

Nerzhin, delighted by this, burst out laughing. Rubin laughed too—no one could get angry with this innocent creature!

'Doesn't this sort of thing happen all the time in the social sciences?' Nerzhin said archly.

'If you didn't have some inkling of what you were going

to find,' Rubin replied patiently, 'there could hardly be any progress at all. . . .'

'Progress!' Nerzhin snorted. 'Who wants progress? That's just what I like about art—the fact that there can't be any "progress" in it.'

'Just what I say! For example—in the seventeenth century there was Rembrandt, and he's still with us today, and nobody can improve on him, whereas seventeenth-century technology now looks very crude to us. Or take the great inventions of the 1870s: we now think nothing at all of them, but has there been any advance on *Anna Karenina* which was written at the same time?'

'What you say,' Adamson now intervened, turning away from Pryanchikov, 'could be interpreted quite differently—one could argue that the scientists and inventors have really been doing their stuff all these centuries, and that's why they've made such great advances—while all these art snobs have obviously been wasting their time on tomfoolery. You might even say that they are just parasites who have always . . .'

'Sold themselves!' Sologdin continued for him, seeming very pleased at the idea.

Even such opposites as he and Adamson were capable of a display of unity in some things.

'Well said!' Pryanchikov joined in. 'That's exactly the point I was trying to make last night in the Acoustics Lab!' —he had actually been pleading the case for jazz, but he now had the idea that he'd been saying the same thing as Adamson.

'Perhaps I can make peace between you,' said Potapov, grinning slyly, 'by telling you about the case of a certain electrical engineer and a certain mathematician who were once so concerned about the catastrophic state of their country's literature, that they decided to collaborate on a short story. Unfortunately, it was never put down on paper because neither of them had a pencil at the time.'

'Andrey!' Nerzhin exclaimed, 'do you think you can reconstruct it?'

'Well, I'll do my best, with your help. After all, it was the only work I've ever composed. I ought to be able to remember it.'

397

'What a good idea, gentlemen!' Sologdin said, cheering up and settling in his seat more comfortably. He was very fond of such stories made up in prison.

Potapov went on:

'But you understand, of course—as Lev would be the first to remind us—that no work of art can be appreciated without some knowledge of the conditions in which it arose. . . . But do eat your pastry—it was made specially for you!'

'Now this is the background of the story: in the summer of 1946, in a desperately overcrowded cell in the Butyrki, Gleb and I happened to be next to each other. There we were, lying on those hard wooden benches, almost dead from lack of air and hunger, and with nothing else to do except talk and watch what was going on around us. Then one of us said: "Just suppose . . ."'

'It was you, Andrey, who said that, and it was you who thought of the idea and gave it a title.'

'Well, anyway, we both said: "Just suppose . . ."'

'Oh, come on, get on with it! What was the title?'

'We called it: "The Smile of the Buddha".'

CHAPTER FIFTY-FOUR

The action of this remarkable tale took place in that glorious, blazing hot summer of 19—, when the prisoners, untold numbers of them, wearing nothing but loin-cloths because of the suffocating heat, were languishing behind the dim, shuttered windows of the notorious Butyrki Prison.

How is one to describe that well-appointed edifice? Its origins can be traced back to a barracks built by Catherine the Great. In the harsh reign of the Empress there was no lack of bricks for its fortified walls and vaulted arches. After the death of the enlightened autocrat and friend of Voltaire, this vast pile, which had once echoed to the tramp of grenadiers' boots, lay deserted for many long years. However, with the longed-for advent of 'progress' to our benighted motherland, the august heirs of Her Gracious Majesty saw fit to incarcerate therein both the heretics who threatened the stability of the Throne and those obscurantists who resisted progress.

The mason's chisel and the plasterer's trowel enabled the suites of rooms to be divided up into hundreds of spacious and comfortable cells, while the unrivalled skill of Russia's blacksmiths forged unbendable bars to go over the windows and made the tubular frames of the beds, which were let down at night and pulled up in the daytime. The finest serf craftsmen added their invaluable contribution to the greater glory of Butyrki: weavers wove canvas sacks as mattresses for the bed-frames, plumbers installed a cunning system of pipes to carry away the sewage, tinsmiths wrought capacious slop-buckets complete with handles and lids, carpenters made food-hatches in the doors, glaziers installed peep-holes, locksmiths fitted locks and most recently, in the era of People's Commissar Yezhof, certain master glaziers made special panes of unbreakable dark glass which were placed over the barred windows to prevent the abominable inmates from seeing a patch of blue sky or the last remaining corner of the prison yard visible to them—the erstwhile barracks' chapel, now also converted into prison cells.

For reasons of convenience (it meant that the warders did not have to be of a high educational standard) the men in charge of Butyrki Prison arranged for exactly twenty-five bunks to be fixed to the walls of each cell, so that the arithmetic of counting heads was very simple: a hundred prisoners to every four cells and two hundred prisoners to a corridor.

And so for years this salubrious establishment flourished, evoking neither the censure of public opinion nor complaints from the prisoners. (The rarity of such censure or complaints, both before and after the Revolution, may be judged from their infrequency in the pages of *The Stock Exchange Gazette* and their total absence from *Izvestiya*.)

But then hard times came for the major-general who held the post of governor of Butyrki Prison. From the very first days of the war he was obliged to exceed the statutory limit of twenty-five prisoners per cell and to put in more people than he had beds for. When the excess took on alarming proportions, the bunks were let down permanently, their canvas mattresses removed, a wooden upper bunk was added to each one and the major-general and his colleagues triumphantly filled each cell first with fifty men and later, after the end of the war, with seventy-five. Even this was no problem for the warders, who knew that there were now six hundred men to a corridor, for which they were paid a bonus.

With the prison so full there was no longer any point in supplying the inmates with books, chess or dominoes, because there would not have been enough of such amenities to go round. Gradually the prisoners' bread ration was reduced, fish was replaced by what could have been the flesh of amphibia and hymenoptera, vegetables by something rather like silage. (The terrible Pugachov Tower, where Catherine the Great had kept the great rebel in chains, was now commonly referred to as 'The Silo'.) As a constant flow of prisoners passed through Butyrki, the traditional lore that passed by word of mouth from one generation of convicts to another was lost or garbled, and people forgot or never knew that their predecessors had once lounged on canvas mattresses and had read forbidden books (only because someone had forgotten to remove them from the prison library). When the steaming cauldron of soup (which, for all they knew, might have been made of ichthyosaurus and silage) was carried into the cell, the prisoners sat on their plank-beds, knees drawn up to their chests for lack of space, leaning on their forepaws like a row of keen-eyed mongrel dogs, they watched with bared teeth to see that the wretched gruel was doled out fairly between their bowls. When the bowls had been placed in two rows—'from the slop-bucket to the window' and 'from the window to the radiator'—the seventy-five inhabitants of the upper and lower kennels, almost knocking over each other's bowls with their paws and their tails, shovelled the life-giving gruel into their mouths and for a while their loud gobbling was the only sound to disturb the philosophic calm of the cell.

Everyone was happy and not a word of complaint found its way into the pages of either *Trud*, the trade-union paper, or the *Journal of the Moscow Patriarchate*.

Cell No. 72 was no different from any of the others.

Although it had already been singled out for its doom, the prisoners dozing or muttering curses on its bunks were all unaware of the horrors that awaited them. On the eve of the fateful day, they spent a long time, as usual, making themselves comfortable on the cement floor near the slop-bucket. They lay on their bunks in their underpants fanning themselves for relief from the stifling heat (the cells were never properly ventilated from one year's end to the other), swatted flies and told stories of the happy days they had spent during the war in Norway, Iceland or Greenland. By the special internal timeclock that every prisoner develops by long practice, they knew that it was only five minutes until the duty warder bellowed through their food-hatch: 'Lights out!'

Suddenly the prisoners were shocked to hear the sound of the door being unlocked. It was then flung open to reveal a sprightly young captain in white gloves. He was in a high state of excitement, and was followed by a covey of lieutenants and sergeants. In deathly silence the prisoners were ordered out into the corridor with their belongings. (An instant rumour sprang up among the men that they were being taken away to be shot.) Fifty of them were removed and pushed into neighbouring cells, just in time to grab somewhere to sleep before lights-out. These ones were lucky enough to avoid the awful fate which awaited the other twenty-five. The last thing they saw as they left their beloved Cell No. 72 was some kind of infernal machine that looked like a paint-sprayer being trundled through their door. Then they were ordered to turn left and were marched off. Keys jangling on their belts, the warders snapped their fingers as they went—a signal used by the Butyrki staff to indicate that they were escorting prisoners. They led them through several steel doors and down many staircases into a hall; it was neither the cellar where executions were carried out, nor a torture chamber, but was familiar to every prisoner as the changing-room of the famous Butyrki bath-house. It had a deceptively harmless every-day look about it. The walls, benches and floor were faced with red, green and chocolate-brown tiles. A number of trolleys on rails were pushed noisily out of the fumigation chamber; they were provided with rows of fearsome hooks on which the prisoners hung their lice-ridden clothes. Although this was not their normal bath-night, the prisoners asked no questions (the third prison commandment is: 'Take what you're given'), and jostling one another they each selected one of the scalding hot metal hooks and hung up their shabby, thread-bare clothes—darkened, stained and in places scorched by the heat-sterilization to which they were subjected every ten days—while the infernal attendants, two old women oblivious to the prisoners' revolting male nudity, pushed the trolleys clanging back into the fumigation chamber and slammed the iron door behind them.

So the twenty-five prisoners were locked in the changing-room, each holding only a handkerchief or a substitute made of a piece of torn shirting. Those of them whose emaciated bodies still retained a thin layer of tanned flesh on that modest part of the body with which nature has endowed us with the fortunate ability to sit down, parked themselves on the warm stone benches, which were covered with emerald and reddish-brown tiles. (The Butyrki bathhouse is far superior in the luxury of its appointments to the Sandunovski bath-house,[1] and many foreigners are said to have surrendered themselves into the hands of the Cheka simply in order to enjoy a wash in that bath-house.) Other prisoners, so thin that they could only sit down on something soft, paced up and down the changing-room, making no attempt to hide their genitals, and arguing furiously over the meaning of this unusual treatment.

However, they were kept waiting in the changing-room for so long that the arguments died down, their bodies came out in goose-pimples and their stomachs, accustomed to sleep from ten o'clock onwards every night, started grumbling for lack of sustenance. Majority opinion inclined to agree with the pessimists, who maintained that poisonous gas would be released through gratings in the walls and the floor and they would all soon be dead. Some prisoners were even overtaken by nausea from what they held to be an evident smell of gas.

Then the door opened with a clang and the scene was transformed. Instead of the usual couple of warders in filthy overalls carrying sheep-shears clogged with hair and

[1] Famous public baths.

two pairs of blunt scissors to wrench off the prisoners' toenails, four apprentices wheeled in four barbers' chairs complete with mirrors, eau-de-cologne, brilliantine, nail varnish and even a stock of theatrical wigs. Behind them entered four genuine professional hairdressers, two of whom were Armenians. The barber's shop was set up and instead of being clumsily and painfully shorn, their heads were dusted with pink powder. Lantern jaws were deftly shaved with a featherlight touch, accompanied by a whispered enquiry after the prisoners' comfort. Far from being shorn bare, those who were thin on top were offered wigs. In place of the usual scalping, prisoners who so desired were allowed to keep their incipient beards or side-whiskers. The barbers' apprentices lay prostrate and clipped the prisoners' toenails. Finally, as they walked into the bath-house, instead of having the customary twenty grams of evil smelling liquid soap ladled into their open palms, a sergeant stood at the doorway and made each prisoner sign for a sponge and a whole tablet of bath soap called 'Lilac Fairy'!

Then, as usual, they were locked into the bath-house and allowed to wash themselves to their hearts' content. But the prisoners had other things on their minds besides washing. The arguments raged hotter than the water in the prison boilers. This time victory went to the optimists, who insisted that Stalin and Beria had defected to China, Molotov and Kagonovich had been converted to catholicism, a provisional social-democratic government had been set up in Russia and that elections for a Constituent Assembly were already in progress.

Then with a noise of thunder the bath-house door was opened and the most incredible sights awaited them in the rainbow-tiled changing-room: each man was handed a soft, fluffy towel and . . . a bowlful of porridge, equivalent to six days rations in a labour camp! The prisoners dropped their towels and without the use of spoons or other implements, bolted down the porridge at astounding speed. Even the old major, hardened by years in the prison service, was amazed and ordered them to be given another bowlful apiece, which they also devoured. You'll never guess what came afterwards—potatoes. Not frozen, or rotten, or black potatoes but just ordinary, decent, edible potatoes.

'Impossible!' the audience protested. 'That's going too far!'

'No, it's true.' Admittedly they were the sort of potatoes usually fed to pigs, small and boiled in their skins, and since the prisoners had by then had quite enough they might not have eaten them; but with diabolical cunning they were not doled out in portions—they were simply brought along all together in a bucket. With a wild roar the prisoners fell on the bucket and a minute later it was rattling over the stone floor, empty. Salt was then produced, but who cared about salt?

Meanwhile the naked bodies dried. The old major ordered the prisoners to pick up their towels from the floor and made the following speech:

'Brothers!' he said. 'You are all decent Soviet citizens, only temporarily isolated from society, some for ten years, some for twenty-five, for your trivial misdeeds. Up till now, despite repeated personal instructions from Comrade Stalin, the staff of Butyrki Prison has been guilty of grave errors of administration. Now all that is to be put right.' ('They're going to send us home,' the prisoners decided gleefully.) 'From now on rest-home conditions will prevail.' ('They're keeping us here,' they thought, crestfallen.) 'In addition to the privileges allowed to you before, you are now permitted:

'1. To observe the practices of your religion.
'2. To lie on your bunks day or night.
'3. To leave the cell to go to the lavatory whenever you like.
'4. To write your memoirs.

In addition to all other prohibitions already in force, you are not allowed to:

'1. Blow your nose on prison sheets or curtains.
'2. Ask for a second helping of food.
3. Contradict the prison staff or complain to them when distinguished visitors enter the cells.
'4. Take "Kazbek" brand cigarettes from boxes on the table without being asked.

Anyone who infringes these rules will be given fifteen days' solitary and sent to a camp in Siberia without mail privileges. Understood?'

No sooner had the major finished his speech when there appeared . . . not the squeaking trolleys bringing the prisoners' underwear and grubby jackets—no, the inferno had swallowed up their ragged garments and destroyed them—but four charming young laundresses, eyes downcast and blushing, whose sweet smiles convinced the prisoners that their manly attributes had not entirely deserted them, and began to hand out sets of blue silk underwear. The prisoners were then given poplin shirts, neckties, in discreet colours, bright yellow American boots supplied under Lend-Lease and suits of imitation twill.

Dumbstruck with delight, the prisoners were marched back in double file to Cell No. 72. But ye gods—what a transformation!

Even in the corridor before reaching the cell they crossed a fleecy strip of carpet leading enticingly to the lavatory. As they entered the cell a stream of fresh air wafted over them and glorious sunlight shone straight into their eyes. (The preparations had lasted the whole night and the morning sun was already shining.) Overnight the bars on their window had been painted blue and the shutters had been removed; a large movable mirror had been fastened to the side of the old chapel in the courtyard and a specially detailed warder was constantly adjusting it so that a beam of reflected sunlight always fell on the window of Cell No. 72. The walls of the cell, which only yesterday had been a drab olive green, had been sprayed with bright, glossy oil paint on which artists had put several doves with ribbons in their beaks that bore such inscriptions as 'Peace in our time!' and 'Peace on earth!'

There was no trace of the bug-infested plank beds. Canvas webbing had been stretched across the frames, the bunks had been made up with plump down-filled pillows and from the coyly turned-down corner of the blanket came the white gleam of a sheet. Beside each of the twenty-five bunks stood a bedside locker, the walls carried shelves full of books by Marx, Engels, St Augustine and St Thomas

Aquinas, the table in the centre was covered with a starched table-cloth and on it were ashtrays and an unopened packet of 'Kazbek' cigarettes. (The prison accountants had managed to sanction the cost of all the luxuries conjured up on that magic night with the exception of the packet of 'Kazbek', for which they could devise no proper authorization. The prison governor decided to pay for the cigarettes out of his own pocket and this was why the penalty for filching them was so severe.)

Most remarkable of all, however, was the transformation that had been wrought in the corner where the slop-bucket usually stood. The wall had been scrubbed clean and painted. Up above glowed a large votive lamp in front of an ikon of the Virgin and Child; beside it shone the rich vestments of St Nicholas of Lycia; on a pedestal stood a white statue of the catholic Madonna and in a shallow niche in the wall that had been left there by the builders, lay the Bible, the Koran, the Talmud and a small dark statuette of the Buddha. The Buddha's eyelids were half closed, the corners of his lips drawn back and the weathered bronze made it seem that he was smiling.

Stuffed full of porridge and potato, and overwhelmed by this wealth of new impressions, the prisoners undressed and went to sleep at once. A faint breeze fluttered the net curtains draped over the windows to keep the flies out. A warder stood at the slightly open door to see that nobody stole a 'Kazbek'.

They slept peacefully until noon, when the same extremely agitated captain, wearing white gloves, ran in to announce reveille: the prisoners quickly dressed and tidied their bunks. A little round table with a white cloth was hastily pushed into the cell and piled with copies of magazines like *Ogonyok*, *The USSR Reconstructs* and the American Russian-language magazine called *Amerika*. Two old armchairs in dust covers were wheeled in on squeaking castors—and an unbearable, ominous silence settled on the cell. The captain walked up and down between the bunks with a white stick rapping anyone over the knuckles if they reached for the copy of *Amerika*.

Amid the oppressive silence the prisoners listened. As you know from personal experience, a prisoner's hearing is the most vital of all his senses. His sight is usually restricted by walls, shutters and screens, his sense of smell is blunted by foul aromas, and there is nothing new on which he can exercise his sense of touch. His hearing, on the other hand, develops to a remarkable degree. However far away it may be, every sound is instantly identified; it signals what is going on in the prison and marks the passage of time. They can tell whether the hot water is being brought round, whether they are due for exercise, or whether someone is getting a parcel.

It was their hearing which brought the first inkling of a solution to the mystery. The steel grille near Cell No. 75 clanged and a large number of people entered the corridor. There came sounds of discreet talk and footsteps muffled by the carpets. Then women's voices could be distinguished and the rustle of skirts. At last, outside the very door of No. 72, the governor of Butyrki Jail said invitingly:

'Now I expect Mrs R. would probably like to inspect one of our cells. Which one would she like to see? No. 72 perhaps, as we happen to be here. Open the door, Sergeant.'

Into the cell walked Mrs. R. accompanied by a secretary, an interpreter, two respectable ladies, who looked like Quakers, the prison governor and several more figures in civilian clothes and in MVD uniform. The white-gloved captain stepped aside. The widow of the famous politician, a lady of great shrewdness and progressive views, who had achieved so much in the cause of human rights, Mrs R. had undertaken to pay a visit to America's gallant ally and see for herself how UNRRA aid was being distributed (malicious rumours had spread to America alleging that UNRRA's relief supplies were not reaching the needy people for whom they were intended) and to discover whether freedom of conscience was being restricted in the USSR. She had already met a number of ordinary Soviet citizens (officials disguised in rough workers' overalls for the occasion) who had expressed their gratitude to the UN for its generous and disinterested aid to war-torn Russia. Mrs R. had then insisted on being shown round a prison and her wish had been granted. She sat down in one of the armchairs, her entourage stood round her and she began talking through the interpreter.

The sunlight reflected from the mirror was still streaming

into the cell; the breeze continued to ruffle the mosquito netting.

Mrs R. was delighted that the cell, selected completely at random and visited on the spur of the moment, was so beautifully white-washed and so free of flies; she was also impressed by the fact that although it was a weekday the ikon lamp was lit.

At first the prisoners were shy and did not stir, but when the interpreter translated the distinguished visitor's enquiry as to whether the prisoners refrained from smoking in order to help keep the air so pure, one of the prisoners strolled casually over to the table, unsealed the packet of 'Kazbek', lit a cigarette and handed one to his friend.

The Governor's face darkened.

'We are *fighting* the tobacco menace,' he said meaningfully. 'Tobacco, of course, is a poison.'

Another prisoner sat down at the table and began looking through the magazine *Amerika*, for some reason turning the pages in great haste.

'What are these men being punished for? That gentleman over there, for example, the one reading the magazine?' asked the distinguished visitor.

('That gentleman' had been given ten years for being careless enough to make the acquaintance of an American tourist.)

The governor replied:

'That man was an active collaborator with the Germans. He served in the Gestapo, was personally responsible for burning down a Russian village and, if you will pardon my bluntness, raped three Russian peasant girls. The number of babies that he murdered is countless.'

'Wasn't he sentenced to be hanged?' exclaimed Mrs R.

'No, we hope to reform him . . . he has been sentenced to ten years honest labour.'

The expression on the prisoner's face was agonized, but he said nothing and simply went on reading *Amerika* with feverish haste.

At that moment a Russian Orthodox priest, wearing a large mother-of-pearl pectoral cross, happened to come into the cell. He was clearly making his usual round and looked very embarrassed to find the governor and a party of foreign guests in the cell.

He made a move to go out again, but Mrs R. was pleased by his unassuming behaviour and she asked him to carry on with his duties. The priest then handed a pocket New Testament to a stupefied prisoner, sat down on another prisoner's bunk and said to the man, who was petrified with astonishment:

'Now, my son, last time you asked me to tell you about the Passion of Our Lord Jesus Christ.'

Mrs R. then asked the governor to ask the prisoners in her presence whether they had any complaints to make about the work of the UN.

In a threatening voice the governor said:

'Listen, you lot! Weren't you told to keep your hands off those cigarettes? Do you want a taste of solitary, or what?'

The prisoners, who had so far been as silent as if they had been put under a spell, burst out indignantly:

'There's nothing else to smoke!'

'We're dying for a smoke!'

'We left all our tobacco in our other clothes!'

'We didn't know we weren't supposed to smoke these!'

Observing the prisoners' unfeigned indignation and obviously genuine replies, the distinguished lady was particularly interested to hear their remarks translated:

'They are unanimously protesting against the oppression of the Negroes in the USA and want the question raised in the UN . . .'

Thus a quarter of an hour or so passed in an agreeable exchange of views. Then the duty warder reported to the governor that it was supper-time. The visitor asked them not to be embarrassed by her presence but to serve the food while she was there. The door was flung open and a bevy of pretty young waitresses (none other than the four laundresses in disguise) brought in several large tureens of 'ordinary' chicken-noodle soup and started doling it out on plates. Instantly an impulse of primitive, instinctual behaviour seemed to transform the hitherto well-behaved prisoners. They jumped, boots and all, on to their bunks, hugged their knees to their chest in this strange dog-like posture. They watched, teeth bared, to see that the soup was dished out fairly. The lady visitors were shocked, but the interpreter explained to them that it was a Russian national custom.

It proved impossible to persuade the prisoners to sit up to the table and eat with nickel-plated spoons; instead they produced their worn old wooden spoons. As soon as the priest had said grace and the waitresses had handed round the plates, pointing out that there was a plate on the table for chicken bones, there came a terrible sound of sucking and gulping, followed by the merry crunching of chicken bones, and all the food on the plates vanished. No one made use of the plate for discarded bones.

'Perhaps they are hungry,' suggested the anxious lady guest. 'Perhaps they'd like some more?'

'Anyone want a second helping?' said the governor hoarsely.

No one did, remembering the wise prisoner's axiom: 'If you ask for more, you'll get it—from the prosecutor.'

However, the prisoners gobbled their meatballs and rice with the same incredible speed. There was no fruit salad that day, as it was a weekday.

Convinced of the falsehood of the allegations spread by malicious scandalmongers in the West, Mrs R. and her entourage went out into the corridor, where she said:

'What coarse manners they have and how uneducated these miserable creatures are! One can only hope they learn to behave better after ten years in here. You have a splendid prison here!'

The priest nipped out of the room before he was shut inside. As the visitors left the corridor, the captain in white gloves ran back into the cell and shouted:

'Atten-tion! Line up by two's! Get out in the corridor!'

Noticing that some of the prisoners had failed to understand him, he made himself clear to the stragglers with the help of the toe of his boot. It was at this point that it appeared that one ingenious prisoner had taken the permission to write their memoirs literally and while the others had been asleep he had dashed off two chapters, entitled 'How I was tortured' and 'People I have met in Lefort'. His memoirs were confiscated on the spot and the over-zealous author was hauled off to face a new charge of 'basely slandering the state security forces'.

Once more, to the rattle of keys and snapping of warders' fingers, they were led through the maze of steel doors to the changing-room, gorgeous as ever in malachite green and ruby-red tiles. There they were stripped of everything, including their silk underwear, and subjected to an unusually strict body search, during which one prisoner was found to have concealed a piece of paper in his cheek; it was a page torn from the New Testament which contained the Sermon on the Mount. For this he was slapped on the right cheek and then on the left. Again they signed the list as the sponges and tablets of 'Lilac Fairy' were removed.

In came two warders in dirty overalls, each with a pair of clippers choked with hair and began to shave the prisoners' heads, then their cheeks and temples, using the same implement. Finally, each man got a twenty-gram dollop of stinking *ersatz* soap and they were locked into the bath-house. The prisoners had no alternative but to wash themselves all over again.

With the usual sound of thunder the door was flung open and they filed back into the changing-room. The two old women, ministrants of the inferno, pushed out the squeaking trolleys on which the familiar prison rags hung on rows of hooks.

Glumly they returned to Cell No. 72, where fifty of their comrades already lay on the old lice-infested bunks, burning with curiosity to know what had happened. The windows were shuttered again, the doves had been painted out with olive-green paint and in the corner stood a four-gallon slop-bucket.

And smiling inscrutably, forgotten in his niche, sat the little bronze Buddha. . . .

CHAPTER FIFTY-FIVE

While this story was being told, Shchagov polished his old but still respectable box-calf boots, put on what had once been his dress uniform with its campaign ribbons and the medals he had cleaned and pinned on (alas! uniforms were going sadly out of fashion and he would soon have to enter the highly competitive market for civilian suits and shoes) and drove to the other end of Moscow, to Prosecutor Makarygin's house near the Kaluga Gate, where, thanks to his wartime comrade, Alyosha Lansky, he had been asked to a party.

The party, for young people and relations, was being given to celebrate the award of his second Order of Lenin to Makarygin. As it happened, most of the young people were unrelated to the family and didn't care a damn about the Prosecutor's honours, but the old man was footing the bill so why not have a party! Lisa—the girl whom Shchagov had mentioned to Nadya as his fiancée, although nothing definite had yet been decided or announced—was going to be there, and it was because of her that he had called Alyosha and got himself invited.

Mentally rehearsing his first few sentences to his hosts, he walked up the stairs where Clara was always seeing the woman with the floor-cloth, to the very flat where, four years earlier, the man whose wife he had been on the point of seducing today had crawled on his knees, laying the parquet floor.

Houses, like books, have their special destinies.

He rang the bell. The door was opened by Clara, who did not know him by sight. But each guessed who the other was.

She wore a dull-green wool-crêpe dress with a narrow waist and a flared skirt. Bands of openwork embroidery—also green but shiny—at the neck and wrists gave the impression of bracelets and a necklace.

The narrow hallway was already cluttered up with men's and women's fur coats. Before Clara could tell her guest to take off his, the telephone rang on the wall in the passage.

She lifted the receiver and spoke, waving and pointing with her left hand, to show where he should leave his things.

'Innokenty? . . . Hello! . . . What, you haven't started yet? . . . come at once! . . . What d'you mean, you don't feel like it? . . . You can't do that to Papa! . . . Don't be so lazy . . . Of course you can . . . All right then, I'll call Dottie . . . Dottie!' She shouted into the living-room. 'Your husband's on the phone, come on. Take your coat off.' (Shchagov had already taken off his greatcoat.) 'Take your galoshes off.' (He had come without.) 'Look, he says he won't come, do make him!'

Clara's sister Datoma (married to a diplomat, as Shchagov had been told by Lansky) came out into the passage and took the receiver. She stood between him and the living-room, fragrant in cherry-pink; in no hurry to get by, he looked her over without seeming to do so. Something unusual about her dress (he didn't realize it was the line of the shoulders, curving as nature intended, instead of hideously padded as the fashion required) gave her an exceptional feminine grace. He also noticed that the sleeves were not part of the dress (it was sleeveless) but of a loose jacket she wore on top.

Not one of the three people crowded in the cosy little carpeted hall could for a moment have imagined that the harmless-looking shiny black receiver, that casual conversation about coming to the party concealed a mortal danger, such as may lie in wait for us even in the skull of a dead horse.[1]

From the moment when, that afternoon, Rubin had asked for further records of the telephone conversations of the suspects, the receiver at the Volodin's flat had for the first time been lifted by Volodin himself, and the ribbon on the tape-recorder at the central exchange rustled as it recorded Innokenty Volodin's voice.

He had felt it would be wiser not to use the telephone these days. But his wife had gone out without him and left a message saying that he simply must come to his father-in-law's party tonight.

He had rung up to avoid going.

[1] Reference to a legend about Prince Oleg; told by a wizard that his horse would cause his death he had it killed: later a snake hiding in the skull emerged and he died of its bite.

After his anxious night, it would of course have made things easier for him if today had been a weekday, not a Sunday. He could have judged from various signs whether the arrangements for his posting to Paris were going forward or had been cancelled. But on a Sunday, what is there to tell you whether the holiday quiet is peaceful or threatening?

All through the past twenty-four hours, he had kept thinking that his call had been senseless, almost suicidal—perhaps it had not even been useful. He thought with irritation of that fool, Dobroumov's wife—though of course she wasn't to blame either: the chain of mutual mistrust didn't start or end with her.

There was nothing to show that he had been found out, but a mysterious inborn sense of danger warned him, he felt a growing premonition of disaster—it was because of this that he didn't feel like going to any party.

He was trying to convince his wife, arguing, dragging out his words as people do when they speak of something they would rather not explain—and the various idiosyncracies of his speech went down on to the narrow brown tape, to be turned overnight into the voice-prints on the wet film Rubin would examine on his desk at nine in the morning.

Dottie did not speak to him in the sharp tone she had acquired over the past few months—perhaps touched by his tired voice, she begged him very gently to come, if only for an hour.

Innokenty felt sorry for his wife and gave in.

Yet he kept his hand on the receiver as he replaced it, and stood still, as though something had remained unsaid.

The woman for whom he felt sorry was not the wife he half lived with, the one he meant to leave behind again when he went abroad in a few days, but the teenage girl, still in her last year of school, her fair hair down to her shoulders—the girl with whom he had once begun to discover what life was about. Their passion had flared up and would brook no opposition, they refused even to talk of putting off their wedding for a year. With that instinct which guides us amidst deceptive appearances and trappings, they had truly found each other and would not let go. The marriage was opposed by Innokenty's mother, already seriously ill (but what mother makes no opposition to the marriage of her son?) and by the Prosecutor (but what father lightly gives away a lovely daughter of eighteen?). Both had to give way. The young people married and were so blissfully happy that they were known as a perfect couple to all their friends.

They started their married life in exceptionally favourable circumstances. They belonged to that circle of society where such a thing as walking or taking the Metro is unknown, where even before the war, a journey was made by air in preference to a sleeping-car, where there is never any worry even about furnishing a flat—in each new post, whether in the country near Moscow or in Teheran, on the Syrian sea coast or in Switzerland, there was a furnished house or villa or flat waiting for the newly-weds. Their outlook on life was identical. They held that 'you only live once'. You should therefore take from life everything it can give you, though not, perhaps, children, because children are tyrants—they feed on you, they suck you dry, without making any sacrifice in return, without even being grateful.

Holding such views, they were in perfect harmony with their surroundings, which suited them down to the ground. They did their best to taste of every new exotic fruit; to know the aroma of every rare brandy, and the difference between a Rhine wine, a Corsican wine and all the other wines from all the vineyards of the earth; to wear all the clothes and dance all the dances; to swim off every fashionable beach; to go sailing and play tennis; to sit through two acts of every off-beat play; to leaf through every book that had caused a sensation.

For six of the best years of their lives, each gave the other all that he or she wanted. Most of them were the years when humanity was torn apart, men and women died fighting or buried under the ruins of cities, when grown-up people, driven out of their minds, stole bread rations as small as communion wafers from children. Not a breath of the sorrow of the world fanned the cheeks of Innokenty and Datoma.

After all, you live only once.

But as the Russians were fond of saying in days of old —inscrutable are the ways of the Lord. In their sixth year of marriage, when the guns were silent, the bombers grounded, the scorched and stunted grass shivered into life, and men everywhere remembered that you only live once—it was then that Innokenty experienced towards all the material fruits of the earth—all the things that you can smell, touch, eat, drink and handle—a sense of satiated, stale revulsion.

This feeling alarmed him and he fought it like a disease, waiting for it to pass, but it remained. Worst of all—he couldn't make out what was wrong with him. He had everything, yet he lacked something. Even the amusing people who were his staunchest friends unaccountably failed to please him—one was not too bright, another a bit coarse, a third could think of nothing but himself.

Not only his friends but even the lovely Dottie (as he had long since called her in Western fashion)—the wife with whom he had been so at one—he now saw as distinct and separate from himself.

Now her judgments struck him as too harsh, her voice too self-assured. She acted in a way he felt to be wrong and was adamant in her conviction that she was right.

Their routine 'smart' way of life embarrassed him, but Dottie wouldn't hear of any change. More than that—she who had once moved easily from place to place, with no regret for the things they left behind (there were always better ones awaiting them elsewhere), was now consumed by the greed to possess and to keep for good all the things they had ever had in any of their flats. She took advantage of their two years in Paris to send to Moscow case after cardboard case stuffed with lengths of dress material, dresses, hats, shoes. Innokenty found it distasteful. And had she only now developed—or had he merely never noticed it before—this way of chewing noisily, almost champing, especially when she was eating fruit?

The real trouble was, of course, not with his friends or with Dottie—it was in himself.

For a long time, Innokenty had been known as a confirmed 'epicurean'—people told him he was, and he agreed, without knowing exactly what it meant. One day at home in Moscow, when he had nothing better to do, it occurred to him that it might be amusing to read up what the Master had actually taught. He started going through the three cup-

416

boards his mother had left him, looking for a book on Epicurus he remembered seeing in one of them as a child.

He set about the task of sorting them out with an almost paralysing distaste, a feeling of numbness in all his limbs, of reluctance to bend down, to shift heavy weights, to breathe dust. He was unused to so much effort and it exhausted him. Nevertheless, he forced himself to go on—and together with the special, faintly musty smell of all these long-forgotten things, there came to him a breath of rejuvenating freshness. He did, incidentally, find the book he was looking for and was later to read it, but the important thing he discovered was not in the book but in the letters and the life of the mother he had never before understood, and had been fond of only as a child. Her death had left him almost unmoved and he had not come back from Beirut for the funeral.

His memories of his father were confused with the earliest impressions of his childhood—silver trumpets blaring on a stucco ceiling, stories of soldiers and bivouacs at night. His father was killed near Tambov in 1921, too early for the son to remember him, but from all around him the boy heard endless tales of the prowess of the naval commander who had covered himself with glory during the Civil War. Brought up on his father's legend, Innokenty took great pride in him and in his fight for the common people against the wicked rich, corrupted by wealth. But towards his mother —always concerned for him but always vaguely worried, nostalgic, always surrounded by books and hot-water bottles —he felt superior, as sons usually do, never suspecting that she had any life of her own, apart from himself, his childhood, his needs, never thinking about her being ill and in pain, or her dying at the age of forty-seven.

His parents had lived very little together. Innokenty had never had any reason to ask himself what their short married life had been like, and it would not have entered his head to question his mother.

But now, there it all was in her letters and diaries. Their marriage had been a whirlwind, like everything else in those years. Circumstances flung them together, and circumstances had kept them apart and in the end parted them for good. And his mother had not just been an adjunct to his father, as had always appeared to him—she was a world in herself. He learned, too, that all her life she had loved another man but never succeeded in being with him.

Tied with coloured strips of soft material were batches of letters from her friends and acquaintances—artists, painters, poets who were now forgotten or remembered only with scorn. Old notebooks in blue morocco bindings were filled with entries, some in Russian, some in French, in his mother's peculiar handwriting—as though a small wounded bird had fluttered about, leaving the scratchy, wavering mark of its claw. There were many pages of reminiscences of literary evenings and visits to the theatre. One description went straight to his heart, of a white June night in Petersburg, when his mother, as an enthusiastic teenage girl, went with a crowd, all equally carried away, all crying for joy, as they met the Moscow Arts Theatre troupe at Petersburg station. A breath of that joy touched Innokenty. He knew of no such theatre company today, and if there were one, he could think of no one staying up all night to meet it, except the representatives of the Cultural Department with bouquets ordered on expenses. Certainly no one would weep for joy on such an occasion!

The diaries told him more and more about his mother's mind. There were even pages headed 'Ethical Considerations'.

'Compassion is the spontaneous movement of the virtuous heart.'

Compassion? Innokenty frowned. He had been taught at school that pity is as shameful and degrading for the one who pities as for the one who is pitied.

'Never be sure that you are more right than other people. Respect their opinions even if they are opposed to yours.'

This was pretty old-fashioned! If my view of the world is right, how can I respect those who disagree with me?

He could almost hear his mother's brittle voice as he read: 'What is the most precious thing in the world? It seems to be the consciousness of not participating in injustice. Injustice is stronger than you are, it always was and it always will be, but let it not be committed through you.'

Yes, his mother had been a weak woman, he couldn't see her putting up a fight, the very idea of it was absurd.

If, six years ago, he had opened her diaries, he would not even have noticed this passage. But now he read it slowly and it astonished him. Not that any of it was so extraordinary, and some of the things she said were plainly wrong, but it astonished him all the same. Even the words she and her girl-friends used to express their ideas were old-fashioned: 'Truth, Goodness and Beauty', 'Good and Evil' (all with capitals), 'the ethical imperative'. In the language he spoke and heard around him, words were more concrete and therefore easier to understand: rightmindedness, humaneness, dedication, purposefulness.

But although he was undoubtedly rightminded, humane, dedicated and purposeful (purposefulness was the quality his contemporaries admired most and tried to develop in themselves) yet, sitting on a low stool in front of the open cupboards, he felt he had discovered something that had been missing from his life.

There were albums of old photographs, with their typically sharp focus. Tied in separate batches were theatre programmes from Moscow and Petersburg. There was the daily theatre paper *The Spectator*; and *The Cinema News*—to think that it existed then!—and a thick pile of magazines of every possible variety—the titles alone were enough to make you giddy—*Apollo, the Golden Fleece, The Scales, the World of Art, The Sun of Russia, The Awakening, Pegasus*—illustrated with reproductions of unknown paintings, sculptures (not a trace of them at the Tretyakov Gallery!), photographs of stage sets. Verses by unknown poets. And countless newspaper supplements, and hundreds of names of European writers of whom Innokenty had never heard. And not only writers—here were dozens of publishers, all vanished and forgotten as though the earth had swallowed them up: Gryphon, Briar, Scorpion, Musagetes, Halcyon, Northern Lights, Logos, Prometheus, The Common Good.

For days and nights he sat in front of the open cupboards, breathed their air, and poisoned himself with it—the air of his mother's private world, the world that his father, in a black raincoat with cartridges at his belt, had walked into in those far-off days with a search warrant.

And here was Datoma interrupting him as usual to beg

him to come to some party or other! He gave her a blank stare, frowned, tried to picture to himself the pompous crowd, where everybody would be completely alike, where everybody would spring smartly to his feet to toast Comrade Stalin, and would then consume large quantities of food and drink (without Comrade Stalin), and afterwards play cards. It was all so stupid!

His eyes focused on Datoma, and he begged her to go without him. But it seemed incredible to her that anyone could so turn his back upon life as to fiddle about with old photograph albums in preference to going to a party! Linked as they were with vague but undying memories of his childhood, the discoveries he made among these old, discarded things spoke to Innokenty's heart, but meant nothing to his wife.

His mother got her way: risen from the grave, she took her son away from her daughter-in-law.

What he made of her message, what he understood her to say, was that, just as the essence of food cannot be expressed in terms of calories, so the essence of life is not to be conveyed by a formula, however brilliant.

Once started, he could not stop. Grown sluggish and bored with study during the past few years (his facility in French which had been such an asset in his job had been acquired in childhood from his mother), he now became a voracious reader.

He found that he had to start by learning how to read. All his life he had been protected from forbidden books and had read only those which were thoroughly approved, he had got into the habit of trusting the author blindly, of believing every word. Now that he was reading authors who disagreed with one another, it took him a long time to assert himself, not to be swayed first by one, then by another, then by a third.

He went to Paris, attached to UNESCO, where he read a great deal more in such leisure as his job left him, and there came a moment when he felt at last that he more or less knew where he stood.

It was not that he had made a great many new discoveries for himself—but he had made a few.

His philosophy of life had been that we only live once.

Now there had matured in him the sense of another truth about himself and the world: that we have only one conscience—and that a crippled conscience is as irretrievable as a lost life.

These were the things he was beginning to understand and to ponder when, that Saturday, a few days before he was due to go to Paris again, he had heard, to his misfortune, about the trap set for the trusting Dobroumov. He was by now sophisticated enough to know that it was not just a matter of one gullible professor—a whole campaign would be built up on the professor's case. But Dobroumov himself also mattered to him because he reminded Innokenty of his mother.

For hours, his mind in turmoil, he had paced his office (the colleague with whom he shared it was away on a mission)—swaying, staggering, clutching his head—and in the end he had decided to ring up, even though he knew that Dobroumov's telephone might already be tapped, and that only a handful of people at the Ministry had been let into the secret.

It seemed as though it had all happened very long ago, yet it was only yesterday.

He had spent the whole of today distraught, keeping away from his flat for fear of arrest. Many times in the course of these twenty-four hours he had felt in turn furiously angry, miserably frightened, resigned to his fate and once more terrified. He had not expected, the night before, to be so upset. He had not supposed himself to be so frightened for his own skin.

Now the taxi swept him along Bolshaya Kaluzhskaya Street with its brilliant lights. It was snowing heavily and the windscreen wiper twitched to and fro.

He was thinking of Dottie. By last spring they were so estranged that he had not taken her with him to Rome.

In return, when he came back in August, he heard that he was sharing her with a certain staff officer. She didn't even bother to deny that she had been unfaithful but, with unanswerable feminine logic, put the blame on Innokenty—why had he left her on her own?

Innokenty did not even feel any pain at losing her—he was almost relieved. He did not want revenge, he wasn't jealous, he had simply stopped going to her room and for the past four months he had merely despised her. There could, of course, be no question of a divorce—it would have ruined his career.

Yet now, in these last days before his departure—or his arrest!—he felt like being kind to Dottie. He remembered the good, not the bad things about her.

They would bully and frighten her enough if they arrested him. . . .

Beyond the railings of Neskuchny Park on his right, black tree-trunks flickered past, the branches white under the fresh snowfall.

The thickly falling snow brought calm and forgetfulness.

CHAPTER FIFTY-SIX

The Prosecutor's flat was the envy of the whole of Block No. 2, although the Makarygins themselves found it on the small side. It consisted of two flats knocked into one, had two front doors (one boarded up), two baths, two lavatories, two corridors, two kitchens and five rooms, in the largest of which dinner had been served.

Twenty-five people sat at table, and the two Bashkir maids (the Makarygins', and another, borrowed for the evening from the neighbours) only just managed to get round with the dishes. Their faces, flushed from the kitchen, were grave and concentrated. The Prosecutor's tall, stout, youngish wife watched them with approval.

His first wife—who had been with him through the Civil War, had been good with a machine-gun, wore a leather jacket and lived by the latest Party directive—could never have achieved the comfort and luxury of his present establishment; indeed, if she hadn't died when Clara was born, it is difficult to imagine how she would have coped with today's world at all.

By contrast, his present wife, Alevtina, knew that a family needs to be well fed, that carpets and table linen are important status symbols and that cut glass is a fitting ornament for a dinner party. She had accumulated hers over the years—not for her the shoddy stuff you get nowadays, mass produced by dozens of careless hands, but the kind into which a master craftsman has put something of his soul. Hers was the antique crystal confiscated from convicted persons during the 'twenties and 'thirties and occasionally to be found in the special shops for members of the legal profession. Later, in Latvia, she had added lavishly to her collection; for two years after the war the Prosecutor had worked in Riga, and there, at the second-hand shops and straight from the flea market, she had picked up a good deal in the way of furniture, glass, china and even some silver spoons.

Tonight, in the bright light over the two long tables, the noble crystal flashed many-coloured sparks from all its diamond-cut facets. There was 'ruby' crystal—'golden' (dark red), 'copper' (almost brown) and 'selenium' (shining faintly through with a yellow tint). There was green—deep, thick 'chrome' and 'cadmium' with its golden tinge; and 'cobalt' blue, and milky-white 'opalescent', and 'iridescent' shot through with all the colours of the rainbow, and mock ivory too. There were jugs with double spouts and big glass stoppers and many-tiered *épergnes* with triple cut-glass dishes for fruit, nuts and sweets, rising high above the crowded tables. And, of course, the ordinary lead-glass fluted vases, goblets and glasses for wine and liqueurs. The sets were mixed: hardly one colour or monogram occurred six or a dozen times.

Enhancing all this glitter at the 'grown-ups' table, the Prosecutor's brand-new medal shone on his breast, standing out amidst the older, duller ones he had pinned on for the occasion.

The 'children's' table stretched right across the room. The two tables adjoined but were set at an angle, so that not all the guests could see, much less hear, each other. Conversation had broken up into groups, but from all the voices together rose a happy, confident, crescendo noise bubbling over with the sound of young people's laughter and the clinking of glasses.

The official toasts, duly proposed, had long since been drunk (to Comrade Stalin, to members of the legal profession and to the host—wishing him that his latest decoration should not be his last). By half past ten a score of dishes had been passed round—salty, bitter-sweet, sour, pickled, smoked, lean, fat, frozen, enriched with vitamins—many deserved praise, but people didn't eat them with the same attention and relish as each would have done at home. As usual at a grand dinner party, the cooking was excellent, the quantities excessive, and the guests, crowded and getting in each other's way, made it their business not to eat but to talk amusingly and showed a studied contempt for the food.

True, there were some exceptions. Shchagov, reduced for years to eating in a students' canteen, and Clara's two girl-friends from her Institute, treated the food with reverence though trying to maintain an indifferent air, and a protégée of the Prosecutor's wife, who sat beside her, ate with unconcealed greed. A girlhood friend of Alevtina's, but married to a Party agricultural official in the remote region of Zarechensk, this unfortunate woman would never, with her stupid husband, succeed in Moscow society. She was in Moscow on a shopping expedition. It flattered her hostess that she tasted each dish, praised it, asked for the recipe and openly admired the furniture and everything about the Makarygins' background. On the other hand, the presence of Major-General Slovuta, who had turned up unexpectedly, made Alevtina feel ashamed of her one-time friend, just as she felt ashamed of her husband's old friend, Dushan Radovich. Both had been asked because the party had originally been planned as an informal family affair, but now Slovuta might well think that the Makarygins were in the habit of receiving 'riff-raff' (as Alevtina called anyone who failed to achieve a social position or a well-paid job). This poisoned her evening. She had placed her friend at the opposite end of the table from Slovuta, and kept telling her to keep her voice down.

They were discussing the servant problem and Datoma, who was also concerned by it, joined in (everybody had been emancipated and educated so fast that nobody wanted to help others to cook or wash up or do the laundry). In Zarechensk they had helped a peasant girl to leave her collective farm and in return she worked for them for two years:

after that they got identity papers for her and she could go to Moscow. There were various other arrangements as well: the isolation hospital was supposed to employ two nurses who had never been seen near the place—instead, the money went to pay the wages of a maid each for the head of the hospital and the head of the public health department. Datoma wrinkled her silky forehead: things were so much easier in the country!

Bored at her father's table, her sister Danera—black-eyed, swift and resolute (she never finished her sentences or allowed others to finish theirs)—went to join the younger set. She was dressed in black: the gleaming imported silk covered her body like thin, shiny patent leather, only her alabaster arms emerging from the sheath.

She raised one arm in a challenging salute to Lansky, as she crossed the room:

'Alyosha! Here I come! How about *Unforgettable* 1919? . . .'

With the level smile with which he greeted everyone, Lansky replied:

'I saw it last night.'

'I didn't see you. I looked for you through my opera glasses, I wanted to strike while the iron was hot.'

Sitting beside Clara whose decision he expected tonight, Lansky prepared without much enthusiasm to argue—since an argument with Danera was unavoidable; it was always happening to him, at literary parties, at publishers' offices, at the restaurant of the Writers' Club. Free from the ties imposed by a literary or a Party post, Danera boldly (but within limits) attacked playwrights, stage designers and producers, not sparing even her husband, Nikolai Galakhov. Her daring judgments, added to her daring clothes and her daring past, which was known to all, heightened her charm and pleasantly enlivened the conversation in circles where people's opinions were ruled by expediency. She also attacked reviewers in general, and Alyosha's articles in particular. Smiling and unruffled, he patiently explained to her where she deviated into ideological heresies. He was all the more ready to keep up this joking, friendly running fight because his own position as a writer depended largely upon Galakhov.

425

Unforgettable 1919 was a play by Vishnevsky, allegedly about the Baltic sailors and the revolution in Petrograd but really about Stalin saving Petrograd, the revolution and the country. Timed for the seventieth birthday of the Father of Nations it suggested that, with Stalin there to help and guide him, Lenin had just about managed to cope.

'Don't you see,' Danera said with a dreamy look as she sat down in the chair offered her, across the table from Lansky: 'A play needs to have some exciting idea, something almost challenging and provocative. Take this same Vishnevsky's *Optimistic Tragedy*—you remember the chorus of the two sailors, and the dialogue: "Isn't there too much blood in this play?—No more than in Shakespeare's"—Wasn't that original! But here's another Vishnevsky play and what do we find? Well, of course, it's realistic, it's a memorable portrait of the Leader, it's historically accurate—but that's all. . . .'

'What do you mean?' The young man who had seated her beside him asked sternly. The emblem of the Order of Lenin was pinned carelessly, a little askew, to his lapel. 'What more do you want? I can't think of a more moving portrait of Comrade Stalin. A lot of people in the audience were crying.'

'I had tears in my eyes myself, I'm not talking about that,' Danera put him in his place and turned back to Lansky: 'There's hardly a single name in the play! Look at the characters—four unidentified Party secretaries, seven commanders, four commissars—it sounds like the report of a meeting! And for the umpteenth time, of course, all those sailors—exactly the same rollicking types from one play to the next, whether it's by Belotserkovsky, Lavrenev, Vishnevsky or Sobolev'[1] (she nodded her head in time to the litany, her eyes half closed) 'you know in advance who is good, who is bad, how it will end. . . .'

'And what's wrong with that?' Lansky was surprised. 'Why does it always have to be superficially entertaining and untrue to life? Did our fathers have the slightest doubt of how the Civil War would end? And did we doubt how the last

[1] Belotserkovsky, Lavrenev, Vishnevsky and Sobolev are all Soviet playwrights who have written on naval themes.

war would end, even when the enemy was at the gates of Moscow?'

'And does the playwright doubt how his play will be received? Do explain to me, Alyosha, why is it that every one of our first nights is a success? Never, never does the author have to worry in case it's a flop! Honestly, one of these nights I'll put two fingers in my mouth and give a good loud whistle.'

She demonstrated charmingly how she would do it, but it was clear from the way she put her fingers in her mouth that no whistle would result.

The young man with a solemn manner, sitting next to her, filled her glass but she left it untouched.

'Nothing is simpler,' said Lansky, not at all put out. 'The reason why our plays are not—and can't be—failures is that the author and the public have exactly the same views on art as on life in general. . . .'

'Oh for God's sake, Alyosha!' Danera made a face. 'Keep that for your article. I know it all by heart—that the people aren't interested in the critic's *personal* opinion, that his job is to write the truth and there is only one truth. . . .'

'Exactly!' Lansky smiled serenely. 'My business as a critic is not just to be swayed by my feelings. My duty is to relate my feelings to the problems of society. . . .'

He explained at length, but remembered every now and then to glance at Clara and brush her fingers under the edge of the table, as though to tell her that his attention was all hers and he was waiting for her answer.

Clara could not be jealous of Danera (actually, it was Danera who had first brought Lansky to the house, especially for Clara) but all this literary gossip took him annoyingly away from her. Besides, as Danera crossed her beautiful arms, Clara wished that she too had worn a short-sleeved dress— her own arms were just as good.

But, in general, she felt pleased with her looks tonight, and this moment of annoyance could not upset her mood of extraordinary, heady gaiety. It had been with her all day —she hadn't planned it, it had simply happened that everything turned out right for her. This morning—only this morning! It seemed ages ago—she had had that wonderful, exciting talk with Ruska. And he had kissed her so touchingly. And that little Christmas present she had made for him! By the time she had rushed home, everything was ready for the party—and of course the party itself was really for her. She had loved putting on her new green dress with the inset panels, and had taken it on herself to receive the guests in the hall. At twenty-four, she felt as if she were young for the second time. This, truly, was her day—now, and never again. Had she actually this morning promised Ruska to wait for him? And had she, who so hated being touched, actually allowed Alyosha's hand to linger in hers just now? There had been a coolness between them for the past month, but now, still holding her hand, he had said:

'I don't care what you think of me, Clara—I've booked two seats at the Aurora for New Year's Eve—will you come? I know it's not really our kind of place, but just for fun— will you?'

She had not had time to say no—she had not had time to say anything when fat Zhenka came bursting in, clamouring for some record he couldn't find. After that, they hadn't had a moment alone together, and all evening she had felt that sooner or later they must go on with their conversation.

Zhenka and Clara's two girl-friends—they had all been fellow-students of hers at the Institute—still felt as though they were students when they came to see her; despite the presence of distinguished guests, they behaved rather badly. Zhenka helped himself to the wine and made his neighbour giggle so much that in the end she choked and jumped up, scarlet, shrieking: 'Oh, I can't.' But Alevtina's nephew, a young lieutenant in the security service held on to her and slapped her back to stop her coughing. (Everybody thought he was a Frontier Guard because of the green piping on his uniform and his green cap-band; in fact he lived in Moscow and worked on the trains, checking the passengers' documents.)

Shchagov too had been put at the young people's table and was sitting next to his Lisa. He spoke to her, piled food on to her plate and filled her glass attentively, but did so almost mechanically—he was thinking only of what he saw around him. A polite smile fixed on his face, he was taking in his surroundings—all these lavish furnishings and the people who took them so much for granted. From the generals' epaulettes and the diplomatic gold braid at the far end of the room to the Order of Lenin stuck carelessly into the lapel of the young man next to him (and this was the crowd Shchagov had hoped to impress with his wretched medals!), he could see no one who could have been a fellow soldier of his at the front, no one who had crossed a mine-field, or sprinted desperately across a ploughed field in what was pompously described as an attack. At the start of the evening he had conjured up the faces of his comrades—killed in a field or at the foot of a barn wall, or on assault craft. He had felt like jerking the tablecloth and shouting: 'And you, you bastard, where were you then?'

However, the party had gone on, and Shchagov had drunk pleasantly—not enough to be drunk, but the soles of his feet no longer felt the pressure of his full weight on the floor. And just as the floor seemed to yield a little, so the décor, with its brightness and warmth, seemed to become gentler, more mellow, more welcoming; it no longer shut him out. Shchagov could move about in it—both his mind and his body with the old wounds that had started to nag again and the hollow feeling in the pit of his stomach.

Was it perhaps a sign of age that he was always seeing people either as 'soldiers' or as 'civilians'? Take even the war medals—how much they had cost and how brightly they had shone at the time—yet people were almost too embarrassed to wear them nowadays. You couldn't take someone by the scruff of his neck and shake him and ask him: 'Where were you?' Some people had fought while others had hidden and kept out of the way, but they were all mixed up by now, you couldn't tell them apart. It was a law of nature, of time, of oblivion: 'Glory to the dead, life to the living.'

He alone among all these people knew what comfort and security really meant, and he alone truly deserved them. He had made only his first step into this world, but he had come to stay. Looking round him, Shchagov thought: 'This is my future!'

His young neighbour—the one with the decoration on his lapel and a striped, bright-blue and pale-yellow tie—had blonde hair which, for some reason, was already receding and he had a shifty look in his eye. He was twenty-four but was trying to behave as though he were at least thirty, keeping his hands still and his lower lip firmly under control. Although so young, he was one of the most highly valued secretaries in the office of the Praesidium of the Supreme Soviet. He realized perfectly well that the Prosecutor's wife was anxious to marry Clara off to him, but by now Clara was not much of a catch. In any case, it was wiser to put off marriage until he was older. Danera, now, that was a different matter—Danera radiated something—well, something that made him feel as happy as a schoolboy beside her. It raised him enormously in his own eyes just to flirt with the wife of such a well-known writer—not to mention anything else. At the moment he was giving her all his attention, trying occasionally to touch her as though by chance, and he would have been glad to be on her side in the argument if the conversation hadn't taken such a turn that he had to tell her where she was wrong.

'But that disagrees with what Gorky said! You'll be contradicting Gorky next!' Lansky was holding his own.

'Gorky was the founder of Socialist Realism,' the young man reminded Danera. 'To put his authority in doubt would be as criminal as . . . well . . .'

He couldn't bring himself to make the comparison.

Lansky nodded in grave approval. Danera smiled.

'Mama!' Clara shouted impatiently. 'Couldn't we get up now, at our table? We'll be back for tea.'

The Prosecutor's wife had already been to the kitchen to arrange about tea, and was now on her way back, while her boring friend had got her claws into poor Datoma and was telling her at enormous length all about how the children of the Party activists at Zarechensk were on a special footing, there was any amount of milk for them and they could always get injections of penicillin. The conversation shifted to medicine. Datoma who, in spite of her youth, already had various complaints, always felt nervous when people talked about illness.

Alevtina gave them a look which conveyed that a good social position was the best guarantee of health. All you have to do is ring up a famous specialist, preferably one with a Stalin Prize—he'll write out a prescription and that'll be the end of your worry about your heart attack. Neither she nor her husband were ever afraid of being ill.

Hearing Clara call out, her stepmother said reproachfully:

'You're not a very good hostess, my girl, are you? You should be pressing your guests to eat, not hurrying them away from the table.'

'Oh no, we want to dance, we want to dance!' cried the Frontier Guard.

Zhenka quickly poured himself another glass of wine.

'Let's dance! Let's dance!' other people were shouting.

The young people scattered. From the next room came the powerful sound of the radiogram playing the tango *Autumn Leaves*.

CHAPTER FIFTY-SEVEN

Datoma had gone off to dance. Alevtina's friend was helping to clear up. The only people left at the 'grown-ups'' table were five men: Makarygin himself; his great friend of Civil War days, a Serb, Dushan Radovich, once a professor at the long since abolished Institute of Red Professors; Slovuta, a more recent friend, who had been his fellow-student at the Advanced Course of Legal Studies and was now, like himself, a public prosecutor and a major-general, and the two sons-in-law—Innokenty Volodin in his grey tunic and gold braid (his father-in-law had insisted on his wearing full-dress uniform), and the well-known writer and Stalin Prize winner, Nikolai Galakhov.

Makarygin—he had meant tonight's party to be cosy and informal—had given an official dinner for his colleagues two days earlier, but one of the most senior of them, Slovuta, had only yesterday returned from the Far East (he was a prosecutor in the case of the Japanese officers who had plotted bacteriological warfare); so he had had to be asked for tonight. Unfortunately, Radovich, a most unsuitable guest, had already been invited. Makarygin had not intended to parade him before his official guests—all he had wanted, at this party for young people, was someone of his own age with whom he could relax and talk of old times. He could have put Radovich off, but felt it would be too cowardly. He had insisted instead, on the presence of both his sons-in-law—the diplomat with his gold braid and the writer with his laureate's emblem.

Makarygin was now very much afraid of Radovich putting his foot in it (not that his friend was a fool, but he could be tactless when he lost his temper), so he tried to steer the conversation into safe shallows. After his daughters had left the room, he lowered his booming voice and jokingly complained of Innokenty who had still not given him any grandchildren to comfort his old age.

'Look at them! A nice pair! Think of nothing but themselves! Not a care in the world! Proper wastrels. He calls himself an Epicurean—you can ask him. Isn't that right, Innokenty?—you're a follower of Epicurus?'

It was unthinkable to call a member of the Soviet Communist Party a neo-Kantian or a pseudo-Hegelian, or a subjectivist, an agnostic or—God forbid—a revisionist. But 'Epicurean' sounded harmless enough not to interfere with his standing as an orthodox Marxist.

Even Radovich, who knew every detail of Marx's and Engels' lives, approved.

'Epicurus was all right, he was a materialist. Karl Marx wrote a dissertation about him.'

Radovich was thin, dry and his brown parchment skin seemed to be stretched over his bare bones.

Innokenty suddenly felt much better. Here, in this cheerful room, full of voices, laughter and bright colours, the idea of his arrest seemed too absurd. The last of his fears had gradually been dispelled. He drank and, warming up to the party, looked around him with amusement at all these people who knew nothing of his secret. Makarygin, Slovuta even, who at other times might have aroused his scorn, were now kindly, pleasant companions who shared his secure life.

'Epicurus? Of course! I don't deny it for a moment. But you may be surprised to know that Epicurean is a much misused word. Whenever you want to say that somebody is inordinately greedy, lewd, sensual or just a plain swine, you say he's an Epicurean. No, wait a moment, I'm serious.'

Waving an empty wine-glass in his delicate, slim fingers, he stopped Makarygin from interrupting him. 'In actual fact, Epicurus was just the opposite of what people think. Do you know that one of the three basic evils he said prevented human happiness was "insatiable desire"? How's that for "Epicureanism"? The last thing he meant us to do was go in for orgies. What he says is that a human being really requires very little—that's why his happiness does not depend upon fate. True, he recognized ordinary human pleasure as the highest good, but he added that, as pleasure must always be preceded by a period of unsatisfied desire—therefore of *dis*-pleasure—it's better to refrain from all desires except the very simplest. That was how he proposed to liberate man from the fear of the blows of fate—he was a great optimist, Epicurus!'

'Is that really so?' Galakhov took out a small leather-bound notebook with an ivory propelling pencil. In spite of his great fame, he had a simple manner and could wink or slap a fellow on the back. His hair was already going picturesquely grey around his slightly tanned, broad face.

'Fill it up, fill it up,' Slovuta said to Makarygin, pointing to Innokenty's empty glass. 'Or he'll persuade us to believe anything.'

Makarygin filled the glass, and Innokenty drained it. Now that he had put up such a neat argument for Epicurus's teaching, it struck him for the first time as indeed worth following.

Radovich, too, smiled at Innokenty's unorthodox profession of faith. He never touched spirits (he was not allowed to) and had sat through most of the evening motionless, withdrawn, severe in his plain semi-military field jacket and cheap glasses in plain frames. (Living until recently in Sterlitamak, he had gone about in a Budyonny helmet, as during the Civil War and the NEP—although by now it made people giggle and dogs bark. He would never have got away with it in Moscow—the police might even have stopped him.)

Slovuta had a youngish-looking, flabby face. He slightly patronized Makarygin (he was about to be promoted to lieutenant-general) but was delighted to meet Galakhov and looked forward to saying casually at the party he still meant to go to after this one: 'Galakhov—I've just had a drink with

433

him—was telling me . . .' But, as it happened, this evening Galakhov was silent and reserved, no doubt brooding over his next novel. Deciding there was nothing more to be gained here, Slovuta prepared to leave.

His host pressed him to stay and finally induced him to visit his 'smoker's altar'. He kept in his study a collection of various brands of cigarettes and tobacco, of which he was very proud. He himself usually smoked Bulgarian pipe-tobacco, supplied by friends, and a few cigars in the evening, but he liked to impress his friends by offering a wide choice.

The door of the study was just behind his chair. He opened it and invited Slovuta and his sons-in-law in. But Innokenty and Galakhov got out of staying with the older men on the pretext that they had to go and look after their wives. Makarygin felt offended. He was more nervous than ever that Radovich might be tactless. He turned to him behind Slovuta's back and sternly shook his finger.

Alone in the dining-room, the two brothers-in-law were in no hurry to join their wives. They were at that happy age when they still counted as young but nobody would drag them off to dance, so they could enjoy the pleasure of male talk amidst unfinished bottles and to the sound of far-off music.

As it happened, Galakhov had the week before thought up a new plot—based on a conspiracy between the imperialist powers and the Soviet diplomats' efforts to keep the peace —not for a novel, but for a play, as this would make it easier for him to gloss over circumstances and details of background with which he was unfamiliar. It suited him very well to have an opportunity of interviewing his brother-in-law : he wished to study him as a typical representative of the Soviet foreign service, as well as to pick up information about life in the West, where the play was set but where Galakhov had only been once, for a few days, at a peace congress. He felt uneasy writing about a way of life of which he knew nothing, but with every year he felt more and more that life abroad, or in some remote historical period, or even a fantasy about people on the moon, would be easier

434

to tackle than the reality of Soviet life, so complex and so full of pitfalls for a writer.

The two men talked across the table, leaning forward so that their heads were close together.

'Naturally, it's a writer's privilege to cross-examine.' Innokenty nodded. His eyes had the same sparkle as when he had defended Epicurus.

'Misfortune, rather than privilege, perhaps.' Galakhov's little flat ivory pencil lay ready to hand on the tablecloth.

'Anyway, writers always remind me of prosecutors, except that they get no leave and no rest. Wherever they are, they are always pursuing their enquiry into crime, real or imaginary.'

'You mean they are the voice of conscience?'

'Judging by what some of you write, I would say—not always.'

'Yet it isn't crime we look for in a human being—we look for his qualities, his better side.'

'That's just where you cease to play the part of conscience. So you want to write about diplomats?'

Galakhov smiled. He had a virile smile, in keeping with his broad features, so different from Innokenty's finely drawn ones.

'What I want or don't want. . . . It's not as simple as it sounds in New Year interviews. But what I do want is to collect some material. . . . And I can't just question the first diplomat I meet. I'm lucky to have one in the family.'

'That shows how shrewd you are. To begin with, a stranger would tell you a pack of lies. After all, there are plenty of things we can't talk about.'

They looked into each other's eyes.

'I quite understand. . . . But . . . that side of your activity . . . wouldn't come into it anyway, so it's not my . . .'

'Ah, so you are mainly interested in life at an embassy, our office hours, receptions, presenting our credentials. . . .'

'No, something deeper than that! And—well, how does a Soviet diplomat react inwardly. . . .'

'Oh, that! Yes, I see. I could talk all night about that, if you like. But tell me something first—have you given up the war theme? Exhausted it?'

Galakhov shook his head. 'It's inexhaustible.'

'Yes, it was lucky for you writers, wasn't it? Conflicts, tragedies—where would you have found them otherwise?' Innokenty watched him brightly. The writer frowned.

'The war is a subject very close to my heart.'

'Of course—you have written masterpieces about it. . . .'

'In a way, I think it's my constant theme. I'll come back to it again and again, so long as I live.'

'You don't think it would be better not to?' Innokenty asked very softly, tentatively.

'I must,' Galakhov replied firmly, confidently. 'What war does to a man. . . .'

'Oh, I agree about that,' Innokenty cut in. 'But look at our war books. What are they about? How to take up battle stations, how to shoot to kill, "we'll never forgive and forget", obedience to his commander is the soldier's law. All much better explained in an army manual. Oh, and how hard the poor old general works, pointing his finger at the map.'

Galakhov looked troubled.

Putting his hand on Galakhov's across the table, Innokenty said without mockery:

'Look, do novels really have to be like military textbooks? Or like newspapers? Or like slogans? I know Mayakovsky made it a point of honour not to rise above the level of a daily paper—but then why have literature at all? Aren't writers supposed to teach, to guide? Isn't that what was always thought? And for a country to have a great writer—don't be shocked, I'll whisper it—is like having another government. That's why no régime has ever loved great writers, only minor ones.'

The two brothers-in-law met seldom and did not know each other well. Galakhov said cautiously:

'What you say is only true of bourgeois countries.'

'Of course!' Innokenty agreed lightly. 'Our ways are altogether different. We have a unique literature—created not for readers but for writers.'

'You mean we aren't much read?' Galakhov was capable of agreeing with some very painful criticisms of Soviet literature and of his own books, but not of giving up the hope that he was being read and read widely (just as Lansky felt

436

sure that his articles formed the taste and even the moral character of the nation). 'You are wrong there. We have a bigger public than perhaps we deserve.'

Innokenty shook his head. 'Oh, I didn't mean . . . Hell . . . Our father-in-law kept filling up my glass, now I can't think straight. Listen, Nikolai, believe me, it's not just because you are my brother-in-law, I really do wish you well, there's something I like a lot about you. That's just why at the moment I feel like asking you . . . quite simply . . . have you ever thought about it?—how do you, yourself, see your place in Russian literature? Here you are, you could almost publish your collected works, you're thirty-seven, Pushkin died younger than that. No danger is threatening you. But all the same, who are you? What ideas have you produced to comfort our tormented age? . . . Apart, of course, from the obvious ones you get from Socialist Realism?'

Small creases came and went on Galakhov's forehead, his cheek twitched.

'Yes. . . . You've touched on a sore point. . . .' He stared at the tablecloth. 'Is there any Russian writer who hasn't some time secretly tried on Pushkin's frock-coat? Or Tolstoy's Russian shirt? . . .' He turned his pencil over twice and looked up at Innokenty with total frankness. He felt like saying what he could never say among his literary friends. 'When I was a boy—at the beginning of the five year plans—it seemed to me I'd die of happiness if I ever saw my name under a published poem. That would be the beginning of immortality. . . . But afterwards . . .'

Pushing her way past the empty chairs, Datoma was coming towards them.

'You won't send me away? Are you being terribly highbrow?' Her lips curved in a smile.

Innokenty looked at her curiously. Her fair curls fell to her shoulders, just as nine years ago. Waiting for the men to reply, she stood playing with the ends of her raglan-sleeved jacket. Its cherry pink brought out the pink in her cheeks.

He hadn't seen her like this for a long time. During the past months, she had been asserting her independence, especi-

437

ally the independence of her outlook on life. But now some change in her (or was it a foreboding of their separation?) made her seem gentle and affectionate. And although Innokenty could not forgive her the long months of misunderstanding and estrangement, and although he knew that she could not have changed all at once so completely, he took her hand and made her sit beside him. She sat down with a graceful movement of her still slender body, and clung as close to him as was decent while making it clear to everyone that she loved her husband and was happy with him. It flashed through Innokenty's mind that it might be better for her future if they did not put on this show of domestic bliss but, all the same, he gently stroked her arm in its cherry-pink sleeve.

Galakhov's ivory pencil lay unused.

Leaning his elbows on the table, he looked past Innokenty and his wife at the big window facing the lights of Kaluga Gate. It was impossible for him to talk freely about himself in front of women.

Afterwards . . . Yes, afterwards . . . His full-length poems were published; after a run in Moscow, his plays were produced at hundreds of provincial theatres; young girls copied out his poems and learned them by heart; during the war, national newspapers had readily offered him space in their pages; had tried his hand at sketches, short stories, reviews; finally a novel had won him the Stalin Prize. And what now? He was famous but not immortal.

Sometime, somehow, he didn't know how it had happened, he had become a 'safe' writer—safe, but dull. Plays, stories, the novel—all had died in front of his eyes before he had reached the age of thirty-seven.

But was it really so necessary to chase after immortality? Very few of his fellow-writers thought so. Most of them were more concerned with today, with their position while they were alive. To hell with immortality, they said, isn't it more important to influence the course of life now? And they had influenced it. Their books were printed in astronomical editions, all the libraries had to buy them, they were even boosted in special month-long publicity campaigns.

Of course, there were many true things they couldn't write about. They consoled themselves by thinking that, some day, circumstances would change and they would insist on coming back to these events, showing them in their true light, they would re-write their earlier books. Meanwhile they would write what could be written—that quarter, that eighth, that sixteenth—well, that thirty-second part of the truth—because something was better than nothing.

What depressed Galakhov was that he couldn't think what to write about—with every page it seemed to get more difficult. He tried to work to a timetable, to fight his boredom, his fatigue, his distractions, the temptation to listen for the postman and slip out to have a look at the paper. He tried for months on end not to open a book by Tolstoy, because the infectious Tolstoy manner took over and pseudo-Tolstoy prose flowed like automatic writing from his pen. He made sure that his study was properly aired and heated to just the right temperature, and that there was not a speck of dust on his desk—otherwise he couldn't work.

Every time he started a new book, he felt hopeful, he swore to himself and to his friends that this time nothing and no one would prevent him, he would write a genuine book. He set about it with enthusiasm. But very soon he noticed that he was not alone. Swimming in front of him was the ever clearer image of the one he was writing for and through whose eyes he re-read every paragraph he had just written. And this was not the Reader—brother, friend and contemporary, it was not even the reviewer as such, it was always for some reason one particular, famous reviewer, the reviewer-in-chief —Zhabov.

He could just imagine Zhabov reading his latest book and thundering at him (it had happened before), spreading himself over half a page in the *Literary Gazette*. He would head the article 'Who is Behind this New Trend?' or 'More about some Fashionable Trends in our Literature'. He would not attack the book at once, he would start with some sacrosanct pronouncement by Belinsky or Nekrasov—something that only the blackest villain could quarrel with—and he would subtly twist their words, give them a meaning they were never intended to have—and very soon he would show, with Belinsky or Herzen as his witnesses, that Galakhov's new book showed his vicious, anti-social character and revealed the shaky foundations of his philosophy.

As in paragraph after paragraph Galakhov tried to guess the form Zhabov's attack would take and ensure against it, he soon found himself watering the book down until it was as bland and insipid as all the rest.

Only by the time he was more than half-way through did he realize that, like all the others he had written, the book was an *ersatz*, once again it had not come off. . . .

'You want to know what is typical of a Soviet diplomat. Oh well,' Innokenty was absent-mindedly stroking his wife's hand; his smile had grown less cheerful. 'I don't really have to tell you, do I? The highest principles, the highest standards. Complete dedication to our cause. Deep, personal devotion to Comrade Stalin. Some are good, others not so good at foreign languages. What else? A few are attached to the fleshpots, because, as the saying goes, you only live once—but that's not typical at all.'

CHAPTER FIFTY-EIGHT

Radovich had been a complete failure for a very long time. Since the early 'thirties he had been banned as a lecturer and a writer and his health was bad: a splinter of shell had remained embedded in his chest since the Civil War, he had suffered from ulcers for fifteen years, and every morning for several years past he had had to wash out his stomach by letting a tube down through his gullet—a painful procedure but without it he could not have digested his food and stayed alive.

However, no cloud being without its silver lining, his very illnesses had saved his life. Prominent in Comintern circles in the 'twenties, he had survived the purges only because during the most critical times he was never out of hospital. The same thing had happened last year when all Serbs still in the Soviet Union had either been pressed into the anti-Tito movement or put in prison.

Aware of the precariousness of his position, he made superhuman efforts to control his tongue, to avoid getting too heated in controversial discussions and to live the colourless life of an invalid.

At the moment, he exercised self-control only with the help of Makarygin's collection; set out on a small, oval, ebony table in the study were cigarette papers, a miniature cigarette machine, a selection of pipes on a stand and a large mother-of-pearl ashtray. Beside the table stood a smoker's cabinet made of Karelian birch, with many small drawers (like those for pills in a chemist's shop), each containing a different brand of cigarette—some with, others without cardboard mouthpieces—pipe- and cigarette-tobacco and even snuff. The whole was known as the 'smoker's altar'.

Listening in silence to Slovuta's detailed account of the Japanese officers' crimes against humanity, on which he had delivered his verdict from the investigators' evidence submitted to him, Radovich sniffed voluptuously at the contents of the cabinet, examining, hesitating between the various brands. Smoking was suicide for him, all his doctors had forbidden it, but as he had also been forbidden to eat (he had hardly had any dinner) and drink he was particularly sensitive to the smell and taste of tobacco. He felt that to give up smoking would be to remove his last pleasure in life. *Fumo ergo sum*—I smoke therefore I am—he replied to those who urged him to abstain, as he rolled himself another cigarette packed with coarse *makhorka*—the only tobacco he could afford. Evacuated to Sterlitamak during the war, he had bought leaf tobacco from the old men who grew it in their back gardens, and dried and cut it himself. Unmarried and unemployed, this kept him busy and helped him to think.

Even if he had 'flown off the handle', Radovich would have said nothing very terrible: Marxism was in his flesh and blood and he was orthodox in all his reasoning. But the Stalinist rabble, more intolerant of variations of nuance than of contrasts of colour, would have chopped his head off for the little which divided him from them.

Luckily he managed to keep quiet, and the conversation shifted from war crimes to cigars—about which Slovuta knew nothing, and almost choked himself by carelessly inhaling —then to the fact that with every year the prosecutors, despite their increasing numbers, seemed to have more and more work to do.

'What do the crime statistics say?' Radovich asked, his face impassive in its parchment mask.

The statistics said nothing—they were dumb, invisible and for all anyone knew, non-existent.

'According to the statistics, the number of crimes in our country is diminishing,' said Slovuta who had not seen the statistics but read the newspapers. He added frankly: 'All the same, there are quite enough. It's our heritage from the old régime. People are very spoilt—corrupted by bourgeois ideology.'

The fact that seventy-five per cent of those who came before the courts had grown up after 1917 did not occur to him: he had not read it anywhere.

Makarygin shook his head as though to say he didn't need convincing.

'When Lenin told us that the cultural revolution would be even more difficult than the October Revolution, we could not imagine how it could be so. Now, we realize how far-sighted he was.'

Makarygin's head was round as a ball, and his ears stuck out.

All three men were puffing away, filling the room with smoke.

The style of the furniture was mixed. Makarygin used an antique pedestal desk. The inkstand on it was in the latest fashion, with a nearly two-foot-high model of the Kremlin Spassky Tower, complete with clock and star. The two inkwells (raised like turrets on the Kremlin wall) were dry: it was a long time since the learned lawyer had had anything to write at home (there was always plenty of time at the office) except private letters, for which he used a fountain pen. On the shelves, inside the glazed bookcases from Riga, stood legal codes and manuals; collected volumes of the journal *The Soviet State and the Law* for several years; the *Large Soviet Encyclopaedia* (the 'bad' one, with enemies of the people in it), the new *Large Soviet Encyclopaedia* (still with names of enemies of the people) and the *Small Encyclopaedia* (also full of 'errors' and containing names of enemies).

None of the law books had been opened by Makarygin for a long time because all of them, including the criminal code of 1926, though still valid, were hopelessly outdated by events and had been effectively replaced by a batch of important directives, most of them secret, and known only by code numbers (e.g. 083 or 005, 2748). These directives, which contained the sum total of legal wisdom, were kept in a small file at Makarygin's office. The books on show in the study were for prestige. The only books Makarygin read (at night, or travelling or on holiday) were thrillers which he kept in a cupboard.

A large photo of Stalin in Generalissimo's uniform stood on the desk, and a small bust of Lenin on a shelf.

Pot-bellied, bursting out of his dress uniform, his neck overflowing its high collar, Slovuta looked round him with approval.

'Nice room. Do yourself well. Has your son-in-law got one Stalin Prize or two?'

'Two.'

'And the other's a counsellor?'

'Yes.'

'He's bright, he'll be an ambassador. What about your youngest—found a husband for her yet?'

'Stubborn as a mule, that girl. I've tried, but she won't play. Soon be an old maid.'

'Educated, I suppose? Looking for an engineer?' When Slovuta laughed, his belly and his whole body heaved and shook. 'On eight hundred a month? Marry her to someone in the Security Service, they're the best, you find her one. Well, thanks, old man, for thinking of me, mustn't stay any longer, they're waiting for me—it's nearly eleven. And you, professor, keep well, look after yourself.'

'Good-bye, Comrade General.'

Radovich stood up to shake hands, but Slovuta ignored him and turned to the door. Hurt and scornful, Radovich watched his huge round back as he went off with Makarygin who was seeing him to his car.

Left alone with the books, Radovich made for them at once. He passed his hand along a shelf, hesitated, took out a volume of Plekhanov and was going back to his chair when he picked up another book, in a black and red paper jacket, lying on the desk.

But the book scorched his lifeless, parchment-like fingers. Just published (in a first edition of a million copies), it was called *Tito, the Traitor's Marshal*, by one Reynaud de Jouvenelle.

Scores of vulgar, subservient, lying books had passed through his hands in the last twelve years, but never, it seemed to him, had he come across anything so degrading as this. Running his quick practised reader's eye over the pages, within two minutes he had mentally gutted it—who could want such a book, and what kind of a man was the author, and how much more venom was to be spat undeservedly at Yugoslavia? 'No need,' he read, 'for a detailed study of the motives of Laszlo Rajk's confession: the fact that he confessed proves his guilt.' He flung the book aside, but the words stayed before his eyes.

No, of course!—no need for a detailed study of Rajk's motives! No need for a detailed study of how his torturers beat him, starved him, kept him without sleep, perhaps spread-eagled him on the floor and crushed his genitals with their boots (Adamson, an old prisoner he had made friends with in Sterlitamak, had told him about their methods). 'The fact that he confessed proves his guilt'—the epitome of Stalinist justice!

But Yugoslavia was too raw, too painful a subject for him to touch on with his friend Pyotr. So, when Makarygin came back and, with an involuntary, loving glance at his new medal ('it's not so much the medal, it's knowing that you haven't been forgotten') strolled across the room, Dushan sat quietly doubled up in his armchair, deep in a volume of Plekhanov.

'Well, thanks for not letting fly, Dushan! I was afraid you might, you know.' Makarygin took another cigar and dropped on to the sofa.

'Why ever should I?'

'Why? I don't know.' He clipped the cigar. 'You're always going on about something.' He lit it. 'I noticed that when he was talking about the Japanese, you were bursting to argue.'

Radovich sat up.

'Because it stinks of a put-up job from ten thousand miles away.'

'Are you crazy? This is a Party matter—how can you say such things?'

'Nothing Party about it. The Slovutas aren't the Party. And why have we just discovered now, in 'forty-nine, what the Japanese were planning in 'forty-three? Haven't we held them as prisoners of war since 1945? And in any case—what country makes war without developing its armoury of weapons? Do you believe everything you're told? Do you also believe that colorado beetles were dropped on us from American planes? Well?'

Makarygin's protruding ears reddened.

'I don't see why not, and even if they weren't—politics are like the stage: you have to shout and make up your face, or you don't get across to your audience.'

Parchment to parchment, Dushan's fingers turned the pages of Plekhanov. Smoking in silence, Makarygin groped for something that had just slipped his mind.

Oh yes. Clara! Outwardly all was well with Makarygin's daughters, but for a long time now—especially in the past few weeks—the youngest, his favourite, the one who so reminded him of her mother, had been a worry to him. Every time the three of them dined alone, without guests, instead of being relaxed and cosy, they quarrelled. None of the simple human things—things you could discuss without upsetting your digestion—would Clara talk about. She always brought conversation round to those 'poor things' with whom she worked, and because of whom she had apparently lost all sense of caution and vigilance. She dramatized things, talked about innocent people behind bars, and was even ready to insult her own father, saying it was he who put them there, and then choke with rage and rush off without finishing her meal.

The other day, he had found her in the dining-room—her shoe was on the sideboard, and she was hammering it with a candlestick to fix a loose nail and singing some nonsense that sounded like 'beat the drum'—he could make nothing of the words but the tune struck him as all too familiar. Trying to keep calm, he said:

'Couldn't you think of something more suitable to your occupation than "The Wide World is Full of Tears"? People

445

died with that song on their lips, they sang it on their way to Siberia.'

Whether out of contrariness or for some other reason, she bristled:

'Fancy that! How noble of them! So they went to Siberia! Just like people do now!'

The Prosecutor was staggered by the insolence, the injustice of the comparison. Had she no sense of historical perspective? Controlling himself not to hit her, he snatched the shoe from her hands and sent it clattering to the floor.

'But how *can* you compare the Party of the working class with fascist scum!'

Pig-headed, that's what she was—you could punch her on the head and still not make her cry—she stood on the parquet floor with one shoe on and one off.

'Oh! Come off it, father! You don't belong to the working class. You were a worker once for two years and you've been a prosecutor for thirty. You—a worker! You live off the fat of the land! You even have a chauffeur to drive your own car! Environment determines consciousness—isn't that what your generation taught us?'

'*Social* environment, you idiot! And *social* consciousness!'

'What is that? Some people have mansions and others sheds, some have cars and others have holes in their shoes. What's social about it?'

Her father was choking with the sheer impossibility of conveying the wisdom of the older generation simply and briefly to a silly young fool like her.

'You're stupid. . . . You don't understand anything and you won't learn. . . .'

'Go on then, teach me! Go on! Where does all your salary come from? Why do they pay you thousands of roubles when you don't produce anything?'

'*Accumulated* labour, you fool! Read Marx! Education, special training—that's accumulated labour, you're paid more for it. Why d'you think they pay you eighteen hundred at your research institute?'

At this point, his wife came bursting in on the row, and also turned on Clara—why hadn't she sent for a man and paid him to mend her shoe, what were cobblers for, why spoil the sideboard and the candlestick . . .?

Sitting on the sofa in the study, Makarygin closed his eyes and clearly saw his daughter showering him with clever insults, then picking up her shoe and limping off to her room.

'Dushan, old man!' He sighed wearily. 'What on earth am I to do with my daughter?'

'Which daughter?' Dushan was surprised. He turned a few more pages, reading a word here and there.

Makarygin's chin was almost as broad as his forehead. The width and squareness of his face went well with the stern duties of a public prosecutor, and his bulging ears sat on him like wings on a sphinx. It was strange to see a bewildered expression on such a face.

'How could it have happened, Dushan? Did we imagine, when we were fighting Kolchak, that this is all the gratitude we'd get from our children?'

He described the scene with the shoe.

Radovich took a grubby piece of chamois leather from his pocket and polished his glasses, a tense look on his face.

'There's a nice young fellow lives next door to me—a demobilized officer. He was telling me one day—he always used to share a dug-out with his men. But the colonel and the commissar were always at him: why didn't he have a dug-out made for himself, and why didn't his batman cook him special food? No self-respect! What did he think he had officer's rations for? . . . This boy had been brought up a Leninist like us—he didn't think it right. But, in the end, the colonel gave him a direct order—"Stop being a disgrace to your rank." So the next place they came to after marching all day, he said to the men: "Make me a special dug-out. Get me some furniture." And his commanders praised him. "High time," they said.'

'What are you getting at?' The Prosecutor frowned. Dushan was becoming more and more disagreeable—always needling people, and sour because he'd not got anywhere himself.

'What am I getting at?' Radovich rose, lean and upright. 'The girl is right. We were warned against that sort of thing. We should learn from our enemies.'

'Are you becoming an anarchist?' Makarygin was amazed.

447

'No, Pyotr, I'm appealing to your Communist conscience,' cried Dushan, raising his hand and pointing with a lean first finger. ' "The wide world is full of tears"—remember? Accumulated labour! What about those double salary packets you get every so often? You get paid eight thousand a month or so, don't you? And the charwoman gets two hundred and fifty!'

Makarygin's face was squarer than ever; one cheek twitched.

'You've gone crazy, living in your cave. You've completely lost touch with reality. What am I to do—go tomorrow morning and ask to be paid two hundred and fifty roubles? And what am I going to live on? Anyway, they'd throw me out as a madman! You don't think other people would refuse their pay, or do you?'

Pointing his finger like a lance, Radovich feverishly stressed his words with a thrusting movement: 'We need a drastic cure for all this! We need to purge ourselves of this bourgeois corruption! Pyotr! Look at yourself! What have you become?'

Makarygin defended himself with his open palm.

'Life wouldn't be worth living! What did we fight for? Remember Engels: "equality" doesn't mean reducing everyone to nothing. Our goal is that *all* should prosper.'

'Don't take refuge in Engels. Feuerbach is more in your line: "Your *first* duty is to create *your* own happiness. If you are happy, you'll make others happy too. . . ." '

'Magnificently put!' Makarygin struck his hands together. 'I never knew that. You must show me the passage.'

'Mag-ni-ficent!' Radovich roared through a fit of laughing, or perhaps coughing, that shook his whole frame. 'The ethics of Oscar Wilde's miller! No! It's too good! Nobody who hasn't suffered for twenty years should be allowed to meddle with philosophy!'

'You crazy fanatic! You dried-up old mummy! You prehistoric communist!'

'It hasn't taken *you* long to forget history!' He snatched up from the desk the framed photograph of a woman in a leather jerkin with a rifle slung over her shoulder. 'D'you happen to remember that Lena was in the workers' opposition with Schlyapnikov? Be thankful she died! Or they

448

wouldn't have used you as prosecutor in the Shakhty[1] case . . .'

'Put it down!' Makarygin shouted, his face white. 'You prehistoric dinosaur.'

'No, I'm not! All I want is to go back to Lenin!' He lowered his voice. 'Nobody writes about it here—in Yugoslavia the workers control production. There . . .'

Makarygin smiled disagreeably.

'As a Serb, it's hard for you to be objective. I understand and forgive you. You remember what Marx wrote about "Balkan provincialism"? The Balkans are not the world.'

'But all the same . . .' Radovich exclaimed and broke off. Here was the limit at which even a friendship began in the Red Guards could founder. Beyond it there would be no Pyotr, only the Public Prosecutor.

Extinguished, silent, Radovich shrivelled back into parchment.

'Go on, go on, say it!' Makarygin insisted angrily. 'So your semi-fascist régime in Yugoslavia is true socialism? And ours has degenerated? We've had our Thermidor? It's been said before. We've heard that kind of nonsense long ago, only those who did the talking are dead. Next you'll say that in the struggle with the capitalist world we're doomed to destruction. Is that it?'

'No! No!' Radovich came to life again, with great conviction and the light of prophecy in his eyes. 'Never! The capitalist world is torn by conflicts that are infinitely worse. And as all the members of the Comintern foretold, I too firmly believe that we shall soon witness an armed clash over world markets between England and the United States!'

[1] Shakhty: a town in the Donbass where in 1928 the engineers were accused of sabotage and tried.

CHAPTER FIFTY-NINE

Meanwhile, in the drawing-room, the young people were dancing to a new and very large radiogram; it was the latest model and there were plenty of records—a whole cupboard full, including of course the speeches of the Father of the Peoples, with his slurred diction and his Georgian accent (these were to be found in every respectable house, but neither the Makarygins nor any other normal human being ever listened to them), and songs about him and various other patriotic numbers, such as the Soviet Air Force song (records which would have sounded as inappropriate in these surroundings as Bible stories told in an aristocratic drawing-room). The records put on tonight were imported ones—you couldn't buy them in the shops—they even included some of Leshchenko's *émigré* songs.

In the dimly lit room beyond the drawing-room, Clara switched on the television set. Another feature of the room was a piano, never played from the day it was bought and never without its embroidered runner on the lid. Television had just come in, the screen was about the size of a postcard. Tonight, the picture was blurred and kept fading. As a radio engineer, Clara should have known how to put it right, but she called in Zhenka. Zhenka, although drunk, soon spotted what was wrong (he worked all day on a multi-megawatt jammer) and was just able to deal with the fault before passing out in the bathroom.

The balcony door, half hidden by silk hangings, looked out on to the busy traffic near Kaluga Gate—headlights, green and red traffic lights, red rear lights—all under the gently falling snow.

There was too much furniture for eight couples to dance at the same time, so they took turns for the floor. Among the cheerful faces of the dancers, that of the Frontier Guard stood out by its air of earnest concentration, and Lansky's by his deprecating smile, as though he were apologizing to all those present for being engaged in so frivolous a pastime.

The young man who worked in the Supreme Soviet never left Danera's side until, bored, she sent him off to dance with someone else. One of Clara's fellow-students, a skinny girl with a nice face, had been gazing all the evening at the young official. Mildly flattered—although in general he shunned undistinguished young people—he rewarded her by asking her to dance. It was a fox-trot. After the music had stopped one of the Bashkir maids came round with ices.

The young official took his partner to the balcony door, where two armchairs had been placed side by side; he brought ices to her and praised her dancing. She smiled nervously. The curtains helped to screen them from the room. He looked at her childish neck, at the small breasts under the thin blouse, and clasped her hand encouragingly, as it lay on her knee; suddenly the girl spoke:

'I am glad to meet you here, Vitaly Evgenievich! Do forgive me for pestering you, but I can never reach you at your office.' (Vitaly removed his hand.) 'My father is in a labour camp, he's had a stroke, and his doctor's certificate and my application for his release were sent in over six months ago.' (Vitaly lay back limply in his armchair, twirling his spoon in the ice cream. The girl had quite forgotten hers; an awkward movement sent it flying first on to her dress, where it left a stain, and then on to the floor by the door, where it lay.) 'He's paralysed all down his right side. Another stroke will kill him. He's a doomed man—why keep him in prison?'

She gave a wry smile.

'You know—this isn't very tactful of you. . . . My office number is no secret, ring me up and I'll make an appointment. By the way, under what article of the law was your father charged? Was it fifty-eight?'

'No, no, of course not,' the girl exclaimed with relief. 'I would never have dared to ask you if it were that! No, it was the law of the 7th of August.'

'Makes no difference. There are to be no more releases on health grounds under that law either.'

'But that's dreadful! He'll die in camp! Whatever can be the point of keeping a dying man?'

He looked her straight in the eye.

'If everybody reasoned like that, what would be the point

of making laws?' He gave an amused smile. 'After all, your father was tried and sentenced by a court! Think it out! What does it mean "He'll die in camp"? People die in camp as they do elsewhere. And, if it's time to die, does it make any difference where you die?'

He rose impatiently and left her.

His words had sounded so simple and convincing that no one, however eloquent, could possibly go on arguing.

Unseen by Clara, the tactless girl quietly crossed the room, slipped into the dining-room where the table was being laid for tea, put her things on in the hall and left.

Clara was still fiddling with the television set, but only making the picture worse (Zhenka was coming round in the bathroom).

Passing the dejected girl at the door, Galakhov, Innokenty and Datoma went into the drawing-room. Lansky came towards them.

All of us have a special feeling for those who appreciate us. Lansky greatly appreciated Galakhov's books and expected him to write still better ones; this made Galakhov enjoy collaborating with him and furthering his career.

At the moment, Alyosha was in that special party mood when a man can say something daring and get away with it.

'Admit it, Nikolai Arkadievich,' he beamed at Galakhov. 'In your heart of hearts you are not a writer but—a soldier!' (This was so like Innokenty's question all over again that for a moment Galakhov was startled.)

'Yes, of course, a soldier!' Galakhov agreed with a manly smile.

His eyes narrowed, as he gazed into the distance. Nothing, not even the most glorious day in his career as writer so far, had left him with such a feeling of pride and, above all, of moral cleanliness, as the day when something had made him drive to the headquarters of a battalion which had been almost cut off—and passing through a burst of shell-fire, reach a battered dug-out where, late at night, the four of them—he and the battalion staff—had eaten their supper out of the same mess-tin. Then he had felt at one with those war-seasoned soldiers.

'Then may I introduce the friend with whom I was at the front—Captain Shchagov?'

Shchagov stood up, straight as a lance, not demeaning himself by adopting a respectful expression. His big nose and wide cheeks added to the sturdy frankness of his face.

The famous writer, at his side, with a glance at the ribbons and war medals, took his hand and shook it in friendship.

'Major Galakhov,' he introduced himself, smiling. 'Which front were you on? Sit down and tell me all about it.'

Pushing up against Innokenty and Dottie, they sat down on a low divan covered with a Turkish rug. They wanted to squeeze Lansky in as well, but he made a mysterious sign and vanished. (When two old soldiers get together they need a drink!) Shchagov told Galakhov about his first meeting with Lansky, in Poland, on a wild day—the 5th of September 1944—when our men had broken through to Narev and pressed on across the river—with practically nothing but logs to cross on. Knowing that it would be easy today and too late tomorrow, they pushed on through a corridor less than a mile wide, which the Germans were trying to cut. That night they brought up three hundred tanks from the north and two hundred more from the south.

The moment they started reminiscing about the war, Shchagov forgot the language he spoke all day at the university, and Galakhov dropped the jargon of editorial offices, writers' meetings and, still more, the stilted prose in which books are written; both also lost the polished overtones of the drawing-room, because it is impossible in that bland language to convey the smoky, sweaty life of soldiers at the front. Indeed, after the first five minutes, both felt badly in need of swear-words—which, alas, were unthinkable in these surroundings.

Alyosha joined them with three glasses and what was left of a bottle of brandy. He pulled up a chair, so that he could sit facing the two men, and poured the drinks.

'To friendship between soldiers!' proposed Galakhov.

They drank.

Lansky held the bottle against the light and said reproachfully:

'There's still some left.'

He poured it out.

'To those who never came back!' said Shchagov.

They drank. Lansky looked round guiltily and pushed the empty bottle under the sofa.

They were already slightly drunk and became a little more so now. Lansky told his story of that memorable day: how, as a brand-new war correspondent (two months after taking his degree) he was going to the front for the first time, and the lorry which gave him a lift (it was loaded with anti-tank shells for Shchagov) made a dash under the noses of the Germans from Dlugosedlo to Kabat, through a corridor so narrow that the 'north' Germans were shelling the 'south' Germans and that one of our generals, returning from leave on that very day, skidded in his jeep into the German lines and was never heard of again.

Innokenty, who was listening, asked what it felt like to be so close to death. Carried away, Lansky said that, at such desperate moments, one forgot to be afraid. Shchagov raised an eyebrow:

'You forget it until the first time you're hit. You're not afraid of anything to begin with, and you're afraid of everything after that. The only comfort is that death has nothing to do with you: either you're there and death is somewhere else, or vice versa.'

The radiogram played *Baby, come Back.*

Shchagov's and Lansky's war memories were of no interest to Galakhov, partly because he had not been present at the battle and had never been to Dlugosedlo or Kabat, and partly because unlike such small fry among reporters as Lansky, he had dealt with strategy. He saw battles, not as raging around some rickety little bridge made of rotten planks or in the back-yards of a village, but in their widest context, and with a field marshal's understanding of their objectives. He broke up the conversation:

'Yes, that's war! We go into it all pink and fresh and we come out tempered like steel. . . . Did they sing the "war correspondent's song" on your sector, Alyosha?'

'They certainly did!' He hummed the tune.

'Nera! Nera!' called Galakhov. 'Come and join us. We're going to sing the war correspondents' song.'

454

Danera joined them at once.

'Of course! I was at the front myself!'

Someone stopped the radiogram and the three of them sang, their musical shortcomings redeemed by depth of feeling.

> *'Not a sector from Moscow to Brest*
> *Where our feet haven't roamed in the dust.*
> *With Leica and notebook and some with a gun*
> *We wandered through heat and through cold.'*

Everybody gathered round to listen. Young people stared curiously at the celebrity.

> *'We were hoarse from wind and vodka*
> *But to those who sneered we said:*
> *If you'd run about as much as us*
> *You'd long ago be dead.*

Still with the same fixed smile on his lips, Shchagov, as soon as the song broke out, felt distant and cold, ashamed of his earlier enthusiasm because of those who would never come back—the men who had drunk water from the Dnieper in 'forty-one, and chewed pine-needles in front of Novgorod in 'forty-two. Lanksy was a decent chap and Galakhov a worthy writer, but they knew nothing about what war had really meant. The distance between even the bravest correspondents, those who dashed into the heat of battle (and they were not the majority) and the combatants, was as great as between a prince who ploughs and a peasant at his plough: the journalists were not part of the forces, they were not subject to military law and discipline, no one would charge them with treason if they panicked and ran away. Hence the unbridgeable gap between the mentality of the soldier with his feet rooted in the earth of the front line, with nowhere to go from the face of death, and the winged journalist who, in a day or two, would be back in his Moscow flat.

Innokenty, playing absent-mindedly with his wife's hand, listened, and understood the song in his own way. He knew nothing of the war, but he knew about the privileges our war correspondents had enjoyed. They were not the down-

455

at-heel reporters described in the song, whose lives were of no account and who risked their job if they missed a scoop. Wherever a correspondent turned up with his notebook, he was received like a Party boss. Achievements were inflated, deficiencies concealed. He was treated almost as someone who could issue 'directives'. His success as a reporter depended not on the speed and accuracy of his information but on his having the right point of view and presenting the facts in the right perspective. Given the correct outlook, there was no need for him to rush into the heat of battle, since he could perfectly well express it from a safe-distance at the rear.

Clara, proud at having finally got the television set working again, came out of the darkened room and stood where Lansky could see her. Observing that she was pretty, that she had a good figure, and that on the whole he really did like her, he gave her an engaging smile and sang the last verse, in which the three of them were joined by others. At the final words where there was a faint hiss and the entire flat was plunged into darkness.

'Short circuit,' someone called out, and all the young people laughed. When they stopped laughing, one of them said, jokingly:

'Stop it, Mika! It's not Lucy, it's me.'

They laughed again. Then they all spoke at once and did nothing. Here and there matches were lit, blown out or dropped burning on to the floor.

There was light from the windows. From the corridor, the Bashkir maid informed her mistress:

'The light's still on outside on the stairs.'

'Zhenka! Where's Zhenka! Go and mend it.'

'Zhenka can't come,' a gloomy voice said confidently.

'Then call the electrician!' the Prosecutor's wife said from the dining-room. 'Clara dear, ring them up.'

'Don't ring up, Clara. What d'you want an electrician for? Surely you can fix it yourself.'

'I expect it's the television,' said Clara.

'What is all this nonsense?' the Prosecutor's wife asked grimly, her voice sounding much nearer now. 'Do you want my daughter to be electrocuted? If anybody knows how to do the job, let them get on with it. If not, let's ring up.'

456

There was an uneasy silence. Someone said the fuse box was on the landing. But although so many of the most useful members of society in our scientific age were present—a diplomat, a writer, a critic, a civil servant in an important institution, an actor, a Frontier Guard, a law student—none of them volunteered. The only one to speak up was Shchagov, whose presence so far had appeared superfluous.

'I'll try, if you like. Could you unplug the television, Clara?'

Shchagov went into the corridor, where the giggling maids held a candle for him to work by. Their mistress had praised them, and promised them an extra ten roubles each. They liked working for the Makarygins and hoped by the spring after next to have saved sufficient money to buy some smart enough clothes to marry in town, and never have to go home again.

When the lights came on Clara was nowhere to be seen. Lansky had gently shepherded her into the other corridor, the dead-end one, where they were standing behind a cupboard.

She had agreed to see the New Year in with him at the Aurora. He rejoiced at the thought that this restless, high-spirited girl would become his wife and friendly critic, who would always keep him up to the mark. He bent over her hair and kissed the embroidered cuff of her long sleeve.

Clara, a little breathless, looked down on his bowed head. It was not her fault that the two of them—he and the other—were not one but two. It was not her fault that the time had come when she was compelled by nature's inexorable law to fall to the one who had caught her like a ripe September apple dropping from a tree.

CHAPTER SIXTY

Alone under the vaulted ceiling, burying his face in his hot pillow, imagining it to be Clara's breast, Ruska lay weak with happiness. Half a day had gone by since he had kissed her but he could still not bring himself to sully his lips with speech or food.

'But you can't possibly *wait* for me!' he had said to her. And she had replied: 'Why not? Why shouldn't I?'

'. . . here you are again evading an honest, man-to-man argument,' he heard almost directly below him. 'All you can do is smother me with polysyllables.'

'And who do you think you are—the Mavrino oracle? What makes you think I want to argue with you? How do you know it doesn't bore me as much as trying to convince old Spiridon that the earth moves round the sun? What do I care what he thinks? Let him live out his days in peace!'

'Where else can you argue if not in prison? You'd soon be put inside if you tried anywhere else. It's here you meet the real arguers!—But you'd sooner not? Is that it?'

As though spellbound by their endless disagreements and each unwilling to leave the battle-ground for fear of seeming to admit defeat, Rubin and Sologdin still sat over the remains of the birthday feast. Adamson had gone off long ago to read *Monte Cristo*, and Pryanchikov to look at a copy of last year's *Ogonyok*, which had turned up from somewhere. Potapov, faithfully discharging his duties as host, washed up, pushed the lockers back into place and went to bed with his head under the pillow to keep out the light and noise. Many people in the room were already asleep, others reading or talking quietly—any moment the white light would be switched off and the blue one switched on.

Sologdin lowered his voice and remonstrated gently:

'A proper argument, I'm telling you from experience, should be conducted like a duel. We agree on an umpire—say Gleb, we can call him in a minute. Then we take a sheet of paper and draw a line down the middle. Across the top we write the subject of the debate. Then each puts down his point of view, clearly and briefly, on his side of the paper. To make sure that we choose our words carefully, there is no time-limit.'

'You're crazy,' Rubin said sleepily, his wrinkled eyelids closing. Above the beard, his face looked haggard. 'Are we going to argue all night?'

'On the contrary!' Sologdin cried cheerfully, his eyes bright, 'That's the remarkable thing about a good argument between men. It's only when you talk a lot of hot air that you can go on for weeks. A disagreement on *paper* is sometimes over in ten minutes: you see at once if you are talking about two different things or where you disagree. Then, if it's worth going on, you each write down your arguments in turn. Like a duel: thrust and parry, blow for blow! That way you can't wriggle out, pretend you haven't used this or that expression, substitute different words—as a result, in two or three rounds it's clear who has lost and who has won.'

'And no time limit?'

'No time limit for getting at the truth.'

'And you're sure we won't have to fight with swords as well?'

Sologdin's face darkened.

'I knew it! You start by jumping down my throat. . . .'

'It's my impression that you did! . . .'

'You call me all sorts of names—you've got plenty up your sleeve: "obscurantist", "reactionary", "priests' lackey" —you've got more names than scientific definitions. And then, when I push you into a corner and offer to have an *honest* discussion, you're busy, or you don't feel like it, or you're tired!'

Sologdin was aching to have an argument, as he always was on a Sunday evening which, in his timetable, was set aside for relaxation. Besides, he had had a very successful day.

Rubin really was tired. He had a new, difficult and not very attractive task facing him. Next morning, he would have to start, single-handed, on what amounted to the creation of a whole new science—he must save his energy for that. And there were letters he had long been meaning to write. And his books—the Mongolian, Spanish, Arabic and various other dictionaries, and Capek, and Hemingway, and Upton Sinclair. And all evening—what with the mock trial, and people needling him, and the birthday party—he had been distracted from an important project he was working on.

But he was held fast by the rules of prison debate. He could never afford to be defeated because here, in the special prison, the burden of defending progressive ideas rested on him.

'What can we argue about?' he spread his hands. 'We've said everything we had to say to each other long ago.'

'I leave you the choice!' Sologdin replied with a magnanimous gesture as though conceding the choice of place and weapons.

'All right, I choose—nothing.'

'That's against the rules!'

Rubin tugged irritably at a black wisp of beard. 'What rules? What rules are you talking about? What's this inquisition? Can't you get it into your head that for two people to argue they have to start from some sort of common basis, some basic ideas they can agree on. . . .'

'There you go! That's exactly what you're used to! Arguing only with the like-minded! When it comes to arguing as man to man, you don't know how to do it!'

'But surely you don't think that duelling is still the best way of settling a quarrel?'

'Disprove it!' Sologdin beamed. 'If duels were still fought, who would dare to slander anyone? Who would dare to push the weak to the wall?'

'You and your pugnacious friends would! You think the middle ages, with their stupid arrogant knights, their crusaders, were the peak of civilization!'

'The highest achievement of the human spirit, yes! The triumph of spirit over flesh! The assault on heaven, sword in hand!'

'And what about the slaughter and looting? You're the perfect type of the conquistador—do you know that?'

'You flatter me!' Sologdin bowed smugly.

'Flatter you! It's horrible! Horrible!' To show his horror, Rubin tore at his receding hair with both hands.

'And you are an Old Testament fanatic!' parried Sologdin. 'You have a one-track mind.'

'You see?—What can we argue about? The Slav soul? Or the restoration of ikons?'

'All right,' Sologdin conceded. 'As it's so late I won't insist on tackling the most important questions. But let's try out my duelling method on something neat and elegant—I'll give you several subjects to choose from. Shall we argue about literature—it's your field, not mine.'

'What about it?'

'Well, say—how we are to understand the character of Stavrogin?'

'But there are dozens of critical studies! . . .'

'And not one of them's worth a penny. I've read them all. Stavrogin! Svidrigailov! Kirillov! Nobody understands them. They are as complex, as unpredictable as only people in real life can be. We hardly ever understand a person at first sight, and we never understand them right through. Something unexpected always turns up. That's just where Dostoyevsky is such a genius! And literary critics think they can hold his characters up to the light and see through them. It's comic!'

Rubin made as if to get up (it was the right moment to leave without loss of face); Sologdin went on hurriedly:

'All right. Let's take an ethical theme: the role of pride in human life.'

Rubin shrugged his shoulders with a look of boredom. 'We aren't at school!'

He half rose (he could now leave with honour). Sologdin grabbed his arm: 'Wait! Here's another . . .'

'Stop it!' Rubin shook him off good-humouredly. 'I haven't got time to talk nonsense, and how can I talk to you seriously? You're a barbarian! A caveman! Everything is upside down in your head! You're the only man left on earth who still doesn't believe in the three laws of dialectics. The three laws from which everything else follows!'

Sologdin waved the accusation aside with a pale pink palm. 'How do you know I don't? I do, now.'

'What? You have accepted dialectics?' Rubin pushed out his big, fleshy lips into a trumpet: 'You really have?'

'Yes, and what's more, I've also thought about it. I've been thinking about it every morning for two months, which is more than you have.'

'You've even thought about it! Good boy!' He still held his lips like a trumpet. 'Dare I ask—is it possible that you also accept the practical criterion in epistemology?'

Sologdin frowned.

'You mean knowing how to apply theory to practice? But that's just what practical knowledge is!'

'Oh, well, then—you're a natural-born materialist!' He was still pouting slightly. 'A little primitive, perhaps, but then what is there to argue about?'

461

Sologdin sat up. 'I like that! First we can't argue because we don't agree, and when we do agree there's nothing to argue about! You certainly *will* argue now!'

'Don't you bully me! What about?'

Sologdin had also risen and was waving his hands excitedly.

'I'll tell you what about. I agree to fight under the most favourable conditions for you. I'll beat you with your very own weapons. What we'll argue about is that you don't understand your three great laws! You've learned them like a parrot and never thought them out. I can catch you out every time.'

'Catch me out, then!' Rubin shouted, angry at himself for getting drawn into this contest.

'I will.' Sologdin sat down. 'Take a seat.'

Rubin remained standing, still hoping to get away.

'Let's see, what's the easiest way to start.' Sologdin was enjoying himself. 'These laws show us the *direction* of a development. Is that right?'

'The direction?'

'Yes. Which way it's going, what it's developing . . . progressing to.'

'Naturally.'

'And how do they show it? Where exactly do you see it?' Sologdin questioned him coldly.

'The laws themselves do. They reflect the movement.'

Rubin sat down. They lowered their voices and became more matter-of-fact.

'And which of the three shows the direction?'

'Well, not the first of course. The second. The third, I suppose.'

'Uh-uh. The third, is it? And how do you define it?'

'What?'

'The direction!'

Rubin frowned.

'Look here, do we really have to do all this hair-splitting?'

'That's hair-splitting, is it? You're not familiar with the exact sciences. If a law gives us no numerical correlations and if it doesn't even tell us the direction in which the process is developing, then it doesn't tell us anything. All right. Let's look at it another way. You very often use the words: "negation of negation". But what do they actually mean to you? Can you answer this, for instance: does negation of

462

negation *always* take place in the course of a development, or not always?'

Rubin felt a momentary hesitation. The question was unexpected, this was not the usual way of putting it. But as usual in an argument, he answered before he had had time to see what had held him up.

'Basically, it does. . . . For the most part!'

'There we have it!' Sologdin shouted, satisfied. 'There's your jargon: "basically", "for the most part"! That's the way to snarl things up so that you can never find the ends!' He rushed on as though smiting Saracens right and left. 'Why can't you give me a straight answer: *when* does negation of negation take place and when doesn't it? When is it to be expected and when not?'

Rubin had lost all trace of his weary listlessness, he had pulled himself together and was doing his best to collect his wits for this useless and yet somehow important discussion.

'But what can be the practical importance of knowing "when it can" and "when it can't"?'

'That's marvellous! What's the practical importance of one of the three great laws from which everything else follows! Well, how am I to talk to you?'

'You're putting the cart before the horse. . . .'

'Jargon! All jargon!'

'Yes, you are,' Rubin insisted. 'None of us would dream of trying to analyse a concrete situation simply by applying to it a ready-made dialectical law. That's why we don't have to know "when it can" and "when it can't". . . .'

'Well, now I'll tell you the answer. But you'll say you knew all along, because it's obvious. . . . Now listen: if a thing *can* be brought back to its original state, recover its former quality, by reversing the process of its development, then there is *no* negation of negation. For instance, if a nut is screwed on too tight and you unscrew it—the process is reversed, quantity changes into quality, and there is no negation of negation. But if the original quality *cannot* be recovered, then the process of development *may* involve negation, but only if it admits of repetition. In other words: irreversible changes imply negation only where the negation of that negation itself is possible!

'Ivan is a man, if he's not Ivan he's not a man,' muttered Rubin.

'About the nut. If, when you were screwing it on, you damaged the thread, then, when you unscrew it, it will not go back to its original state—the state of a nut with an undamaged thread. If you want to reproduce that state, you can do it only by throwing the nut into the melting pot, making a hexagonal rod and cutting a new nut.'

'Look here,' Rubin said amicably. 'You don't seriously think you can explain dialectics by what happens to a nut?'

'Why can't I? What better example could there be? There isn't a machine that can hold together without nuts. As you see, each of these three stages is irreversible, it negates the one before it, and the new nut is the negation of the old. Quite simple!' He threw back his head, his pointed little beard thrust out.

'Wait a minute! How have you disproved what I said? You've arrived at exactly the same conclusion—the third law gives you the direction of the development!'

Sologdin put his hand on his breast and bowed.

'If you weren't so quick at putting two and two together, I doubt if I would so much enjoy talking to you. Yes, it does give it. But you must know how to use the law. Do you know how to take it? How not to worship the law blindly but to work with it? For instance, you have just deduced that the third stage really does give the direction. But I ask you: does it always? The answer is: always if you are talking about animate nature—there, you always have birth, growth and death. But not by any means always if you are talking of inanimate things.'

'But it's society we are mainly interested in.'

'Who are "we"? I'm not. I'm an engineer. What society? The only kind I'm interested in is the society of pretty women!' He twirled his moustache and burst out laughing.

'Oh, well,' Rubin said thoughtfully. 'I suppose there may be a grain of sense in all that. But it's mostly verbal diarrhoea. Nothing has been added to the science of dialectics.'

'It's you that have verbal diarrhoea.' Sologdin boiled up again. 'If you deduce everything from these three laws . . .'

'We don't, I tell you!'

'You don't?'

'No.'

'Then what are they for? An ornament or something?'

'Will you listen to me! You've got a head, haven't you? Every decision is based on a concrete analysis of a given situation, got that? All economic teaching is based on the production unit. All social teaching on the analysis of the existing social circumstances.'

'Then what good are they, your three laws?' shouted Sologdin, his voice booming in the quiet room. 'You can do perfectly well without them, can't you?'

'No, of course we can't,' Rubin quickly corrected himself.

'But why not? If you can't deduce anything from them. If they don't even tell you the direction of the movement! Isn't that verbal diarrhoea? If all you have to do is repeat like a parrot: "negation of negation"—then what the hell is the use of them?'

Potapov, who had been trying vainly to shut out the noise, flung his pillow aside and sat up.

'Look here, you two! If you can't sleep, go and talk somewhere else. You might show a little consideration for other people, if only . . .' He pointed at Ruska's top bunk.

This, from the even-tempered Potapov, and now the complete silence in the room, of which they suddenly became aware, and the knowledge that they were surrounded by informers (not that Rubin had anything to fear from shouting his views at the top of his voice), all this would have brought most sober people to their senses.

But Rubin and Sologdin could not stop. This was only the beginning of a very long argument—by no means their first. They realized they must leave the room, but they could neither get out of the clinch nor keep quiet. They could still be heard shouting as they went out, then the door of the passage cut off their voices.

Almost at once, the white light was switched off and the blue came on.

Ruska was awake and lying closest to where they had been arguing, but the thing furthest from his mind was to collect information for a report to the Security Officer. Potapov's unfinished sentence—he had guessed what it meant although he hadn't seen the gesture—filled him with bitterness, coming, as it did, from a man he respected.

465

In his dangerous double game with the Security Officer he had foreseen everything, he had outwitted Shikin over the money orders and was on the eve of creating a public scandal —but he was helpless against the suspicion of his friends. His lonely purpose, just because it was so unusual and secret, exposed him to shame and disgrace. It astounded him that these mature, intelligent, experienced men should lack the generosity of mind to understand him, to know that he was not a traitor.

As always when a man loses the goodwill of others, the one person who still loved him became twice as dear to him.

Clara! She would understand. He would tell her all about it tomorrow, and she would understand.

Wide awake and with no wish to sleep, he tossed and turned on his bunk, thinking of Clara's searching look and working out his escape plan with greater and greater confidence—under the barbed wire, along the gully to the main road and by bus to the centre of Moscow.

There, Clara would help him.

It was harder to find a man among the seven million inhabitants of Moscow than in the whole of the bare and lonely region of Vorkuta. He would hide in Moscow. . . .

CHAPTER SIXTY-ONE

Nerzhin's friendship with the handy-man Spiridon was indulgently referred to by Rubin and Sologdin as an attempt to 'go among the people', in search of the same great homespun truth which had been sought in vain by Gogol, Nekrasov, Herzen, the Slavophiles, the Populists, Dostoyevsky, Leo Tolstoy, and, last but not least, Vasisualy Lokhankin.[1]

Neither Rubin nor Sologdin needed this homespun truth themselves, because each of them already had his own ultimate truth.

Rubin knew perfectly well that 'the people' was an artificial concept, an unjustified generalization, and that every people is divided into *classes*, which even change their

[1] Character in Ilf and Petrov's satire, *The Golden Calf.*

nature in the course of time. To seek the key to an understanding of life among the peasants was quite futile, because only the proletariat was consistently revolutionary in its outlook—the future belong to it and only its collectivism and selflessness could give life a higher meaning.

For Sologdin, on the other hand, 'the people' was just a general term for all those dull, drab, uncouth individuals who were totally absorbed in their joyless, daily round. The great temple of the human spirit could not be built on such foundations. Only outstanding individuals, shining forth like lonely stars in the dark firmament of our existence, could embody the higher meaning of life.

Both he and Rubin were sure than Nerzhin would get over his present mood, and come to think better of it.

In fact, Nerzhin had already been through many extreme phases in the evolution of his ideas.

With its anguished concern for the peasants, Russian nineteenth-century literature had created for him, as for all its other readers, the image of a venerable, grey-haired People which embodies wisdom, moral purity and greatness.

But this had been something remote, existing in books, somewhere in the villages, fields and by-ways of the nineteenth century. When the heavens unfolded on the twentieth century, these places had long ago ceased to exist in Russia.

There was no old Russia, but something called the Soviet Union, in which there was a great city, where Gleb had grown up, enjoying all the benefits which flowed from the cornucopia of science. He had been blessed with a quick intelligence, but he soon found that there were others who were even more intelligent and depressingly more learned than he was. The People at that time still only existed in books, and, as he then saw it, nobody mattered unless he was highly educated and had an all-round knowledge of history, science and art. It seemed obvious to him that unless you were numbered among that élite, you were a miserable failure.

When the war broke out, Nerzhin at first found himself serving in a horse-drawn transport unit. Almost dying with shame at his own clumsiness, he had to chase after the

467

horses to bridle them. He did not know how to ride, how to handle harness or a pitchfork, and whenever he hit a nail with a hammer, it always bent, as if in mockery of his poor workmanship. And the harder things became for Nerzhin, the louder were the guffaws of the scruffy, foul-mouthed, callous and very disagreeable representatives of the People around him.

After this, Nerzhin had been commissioned as an artillery officer. He now regained all his youthful dash, walking around in a smart, tightly belted uniform and flourishing a switch he had cut himself—he had nothing else to carry. He rode jauntily on the running-boards of speeding lorries, swore with gusto as they made difficult river crossings, willingly went into action at any time of day or night, and in any weather, leading his obedient, devoted, proficient (and therefore very agreeable) People into battle. And this small segment of the People, which he somehow felt was all his own, seemed happy to listen to his political lectures about how the People as a whole had risen as one man to defend the Motherland.

Then Nerzhin had been arrested, and very soon, numbed by his first deadly experience of prisons and camps, he was horrified to discover a very different side to the 'élite': in conditions where only courage, strength of character and loyalty to friends made a man and could decide the fate of a comrade, these delicate, sensitive, highly educated persons, with their love of the beautiful, often proved to be craven cowards, very good at finding excuses for their own despicable behaviour and turning into wheedling, two-faced traitors. Nerzhin could only barely see himself as not being like them, and he recoiled from these people among whom he had not long ago thought it honourable to be numbered. He now had nothing but scorn and hatred for those he had once venerated, and he determined to rid himself of his intellectual's sophistication, his genteel and simpering mannerisms. At this time of abysmal defeat, with his life in ruins, Nerzhin came to feel that the only people who mattered were those who ploughed the land and forged the steel, or worked wood and metal with their own hands. He wanted to learn the wisdom of their skilled hands and make their philosophy of life his own. And so he came back full circle to the fashionable idea of the previous century about 'going among the people'.

But, unlike his intellectual forebears of the nineteenth-century nobility, Nerzhin didn't have to put on simple dress and laboriously seek a way to the People—he was thrown down among them in the shabby quilted trousers and jacket of a prisoner and made to do his work-quota side by side with them. He thus lived their life not as a social superior who had deigned to come among them, but as an equal not easily distinguished from them.

If Nerzhin had now learnt to drive a nail home without bending it, or to plane two wooden boards to exactly the same thickness, it was not to prove himself in the eyes of the ordinary people, but to earn his soggy hunk of daily bread. The brutal education of camp life had destroyed yet another of his illusions: he understood that he had reached rock bottom—beyond this there was nothing and nobody—and that the People possessed no advantage, no great, home-spun wisdom. Sitting in the snow with them, on orders from the guards, hiding with them from the foreman in some corner of a building site, carrying bricks in the bitter cold, and drying footcloths with them in the prison huts, Nerzhin saw clearly enough that these people were in no way superior to him. They did not stand up to hunger and thirst any better than he, and they were not less daunted by the grim prospect of ten years in prison. They were no more resourceful in the face of such crises as transfers to another prison or inspections—though they were, if anything, more apt to be taken in by informers. They were also more liable to fall for the blatant lies told by the authorities and they naïvely waited for the amnesty which Stalin never gave them—he would sooner have died. If some brute of a camp officer happened to be in a good mood and smiled at them, they smiled back, and they were much more eager for small material things: for instance, the sour millet cake, occasionally given as an 'extra', or a pair of unsightly prison trousers if they looked a little newer or brighter. Few of them had the sort of beliefs for which they would willingly have sacrificed their lives.

The only solution left, Nerzhin now felt, was simply to be oneself.

Once he had got over this latest delusion (though whether it was his last or not remained to be seen), he felt he had arrived at his own original view of the People. One belonged to the People neither by virtue of speaking the same language as everybody else nor by being among the select few stamped with the hallmark of genius. You were not born into the People, nor did you become part of it through work or education.

It was only character that mattered, and this was something that everybody had to forge for himself, by constant effort over the years.

Only thus could one make onself into a human being and hence be regarded as a tiny part of one's people.

CHAPTER SIXTY-TWO

The moment Spiridon had come to Mavrino, Nerzhin had taken note of this red-haired man with the round head. Until you got to know him well you couldn't tell whether the look on his face was one of deference, or whether he was making fun of you. There were other workers in Mavrino—carpenters, lathe operators and the like—but there was something strikingly 'deep' about Spiridon that marked him off from the others and left no doubt that he was the sort of real representative of the People to whom an intellectual might turn for 'insight'.

But Nerzhin could find no excuse to get to know Spiridon better—they had no particular reason to talk to each other, they did not meet at work, and they lived in different parts of the prison. The small group of workers had their own quarters and they spent their leisure hours separately. In fact, when Nerzhin started dropping in to see him, Spiridon and the people who occupied the bunks near him unanimously decided that Nerzhin must be an informer working for the Security Officers.

Spiridon regarded himself as quite the most humble inmate of Mavrino and he couldn't think why on earth the Security Officers might be after him, but since anyone was fair game to them, he wasn't taking any chances. When-over Nerzhin came in, Spiridon beamed all over his face, made room for him on his bunk and, with a stupid look started talking about something very remote from politics: about how spawning fish could be caught with a spike, or, in quiet waters, caught by the gills with a cleft stick, or simply netted; about how he had stalked elk and brown bears (and how you should beware of a black bear with a white patch on its neck); how you could get rid of snakes with lungwort, and how good clover was for mowing. Then he spun out a long story about how in the 'twenties he had courted his Martha while she was acting in a play at the village club. Her parents had wanted to marry her off to a rich miller, but out of love she had agreed to run away with him, and they had married in secret on St Peter's day.

While he told these tales Spiridon's eyes, which had an unhealthy look and scarcely moved under his thick reddish brows, seemed to be saying: 'Why do you come here, you spy? You won't get anything out of me.' Indeed, a real spy would long ago have given up in despair, and few people would have had enough curiosity to listen to Spiridon's tall stories Sunday after Sunday. But Nerzhin, who was at first rather embarrassed about going to see him like this, was so eager to get a proper understanding here in prison of many things he had not understood before, that week after week he continued to visit Spiridon and, far from being bored by his stories, he found them invigorating. They revived memories of dank early mornings by some river or other, they brought a breath of wind from the fields and took him back to those extraordinary seven years in Russia—the years of NEP. From the first primitive forest settlements of the early Slavs right up to the latest reorganization of the collective farms, these seven years of NEP were without parallel in the history of the Russian countryside. Nerzhin had been just a child in those days, and he was very sorry he had not been born earlier, so that he could have understood what was going on.

Listening as Spiridon spoke in his warm husky voice, Nerzhin never tried to draw him out on politics by asking leading questions. So Spiridon gradually began to trust him and became deeply engrossed himself in all this past history;

he was no longer constantly on his guard, his forehead was less deeply lined and his ruddy face looked more serene.

Because of his poor eyesight Spiridon could not read books in prison, but for Nerzhin's benefit he occasionally used bookish words—generally in the wrong sense—and he once mentioned the name of Yesenin, some of whose verse had once been recited by his wife in those days when she had acted in the village club.

'Yesenin?' Nerzhin said in surprise. 'Really? I have one of his books with me here—he's not so easy to get hold of nowadays.' He had then fetched the small volume—its cover was decorated with a maple-leaf pattern—to show to Spiridon. He was fascinated by the thought that, by some miracle, this semi-literate peasant might understand and appreciate Yesenin. But no miracle took place and Spiridon could only remember having liked two poems. Not a line of either, however, had stayed in his memory.

It was a couple of days after this that Nerzhin had been summoned to Major Shikin and ordered to hand over the volume of Yesenin so that a check could be made on it. Nerzhin had no idea who had informed on him, but because he had lost his book in this way and suffered at the hands of the Security Officer, Spiridon now trusted him completely and even began to call him by his first name. After this they no longer talked in the room, but below the back staircase where they couldn't be overheard.

From then on, over the next five or six Sundays, Spiridon began to talk with the frankness which Nerzhin had hoped for, and he now heard the life story of this Russian peasant who had been seventeen at the time of the Revolution and was over forty when the war with Hitler began.

Spiridon's red head was as round as a pebble—one could almost think that it had been shaped by the angry waves that had washed over him all his life. His father had been killed in the First World War and at the age of fourteen he found himself head of the household. He went out to work in the fields with the old men—the only ones who were left. 'It only took me half a day,' he said, 'to learn how to use a scythe.'

At sixteen he went to work in a glass factory, and he

was soon marching behind the red flag in workers' demonstrations. When he heard that the land was going to be given to the peasants, he went back to his village and took his share. For a year the whole family—his mother and younger brothers and sisters—worked very hard and in the autumn they had all the grain they needed. But after Christmas they were made to give up half of it for the cities, and the requisitioners were never satisfied. After Easter they started calling up everybody over eighteen for service in the Red Army. Spiridon, who was just nineteen, saw no sense in leaving his land and with others like him he went off into the woods, refusing to fight either for the Reds or the Whites, and wanting only to be left in peace. But he and the others were not able to hide out for long in the woods—they fell into the hands of the Whites who occupied the whole region for a while. The Whites wanted to know if there were any Commissars among them. There weren't any, but all the same their leader was shot just to frighten the rest of them, who were now made to put on the cap badges of the White Army, and issued with rifles.

With the Whites things were more or less the same as they had been under the tsar. After Spiridon and his friends had served with them for a while, they were captured by the Reds —to whom, it must be said, they scarcely offered any resistance. The Bolsheviks shot their officers and told them to remove their White cap badges and put on Red armbands instead.

Spiridon stayed with the Reds until the end of the Civil War. He was then in the Polish campaign and, after that, instead of being demobilized, he was kept on in his unit which was now made part of the so-called 'Labour Army'. Soon, however, they were brought to Petrograd—this, he said, was 'in the first week of Lent'—and sent over the frozen Gulf of Finland to capture some fort whose name he didn't remember.[1] Only after this was he allowed to go home.

He got back to his village in the spring and eagerly set to work on the land for which he had fought so hard. Unlike many others he had not utterly lost his bearings because of

[1] This refers to the suppression of the Kronstadt rebellion in March 1921, when Trotsky subdued the dissident naval garrison by attacking across the ice.

the war: he quickly settled down, married and got himself some horses.

Although it was the poor peasants who were the backbone of the new régime, people did not want to stay poor, but to get rich, and the good workers—like Spiridon—were very keen to improve their lot.

A fashionable word in those days was 'intensive cultivator': it was applied to people who farmed their land well, by using their brains, without the help of hired labour.

'A good marriage makes all the difference in life,' Spiridon kept saying, and it was to his wife Martha that he owed what happiness and good fortune he had had in his life. She kept him from drinking and bad company. She bore him three children one after another—two sons and a daughter— but after their birth she remained just as close to him and worked as hard as ever to make a good home for him. She could read and write and she kept abreast of things by reading the magazine *Home Agronomist*. This was how Spiridon became an 'intensive cultivator'.

'Intensive cultivators' were given every encouragement in the shape of loans, seeds and so forth. Spiridon and Martha went from strength to strength, the money piled up and, little knowing that all this well-being would soon be at an end, they began to think about building themselves a house of brick. Spiridon was a respected figure—as a hero of the Civil War (and by now a member of the Party) he was elected to the local Soviet.

Then everything literally went up in smoke—their wooden house burnt down and they barely managed to save the children. All of a sudden they were destitute.

But before long things began to look up again. They had scarcely started to struggle to their feet after the fire when word came from faraway Moscow that the kulaks were to be done away with. All these 'intensive cultivators' who had been encouraged for no good reason were now, with even less reason, denounced as kulaks and hounded out of existence. So Martha and Spiridon were very glad that they had not put up a brick house for themselves.

This was a prime example of the quirks of fate, and of how good sometimes comes of misfortune.

Instead of being sent by the OGPU to die in the tundra, Spiridon found himself made a 'commissar for collectivization' whose job was to herd people into the collective farms. He began to carry an ugly-looking revolver at his hip, evicted people from their houses and sent them off under police guard with nothing except the clothes they were standing up in. He took no account of whether they were kulaks or not, but went by the lists that had been provided.

In this, as in other twists and turns of his life, Spiridon's behaviour was not easily explained or analysed in terms of the Marxist doctrine about class. Nerzhin did not try to probe or reopen any of Spiridon's old wounds, but he could see how he must have been sickened by it all. At this time Spiridon took to drink—it was almost as though he had once owned the whole village, but now felt responsible for letting it go to rack and ruin. He had taken on this job of commissar, but he was no good at it. He was unable to prevent the peasants slaughtering their cattle and joining the collective farm without any livestock at all.

For this Spiridon was stripped of his commissar's rank. But they did not stop at this and, with his hands behind his back and escorted by militiamen with guns (one in front and one behind), he was marched off to jail. His trial was swift (in his own words: 'They never wasted much time on us in those days')—they gave him ten years for 'economic counter-revolution' and packed him off to the White Sea Canal, and when that was finished, to the Moscow-Volga Canal. Here he worked sometimes as a navvy and sometimes as a carpenter. The rations were good, but he worried himself sick all the time about his Martha left with three children to fend for.

Then Spiridon's case was suddenly reviewed. They said he had been guilty not of 'economic counter-revolution' but of what they called 'dereliction of duty' and so, instead of being a 'class enemy' he was promoted to the category of 'class ally'. He was summoned by the camp authorities and told that they were now going to make him a prison warder and gave him a rifle. Though until this moment Spiridon, like any other self-respecting prisoner, had cursed the warders for all he was worth—particularly if they were former prisoners—he now took the rifle and marched his former comrades up and down

475

like any other warder—for the simple reason that this would earn him a reduction of his sentence and forty roubles a month which he could send home to his family.

Before long he was being congratulated by the Camp Commandant on his release. He was given identity papers which enabled him to work in a factory, instead of having to go back to the collective farm. He got a job in a glass factory and soon distinguished himself as one of the best glass-blowers, even getting on to the factory's 'Red Roll of Honour'. He told Martha and the children to come and join him, and started doing all the overtime he could, trying to get them back to the level they had reached at the time of the fire which had destroyed their home years before. They now began to think about a little house of their own, with a garden to grow vegetables, and about education for the children, who were aged fifteen, fourteen and thirteen, when the war broke out. Soon there was fighting very close to the little town of Pochep where they were living.

Listening to Spiridon's story Nerzhin waited, almost with bated breath, to see what would happen next. He had already been thinking that Spiridon must have been one of those who welcomed the Germans, out of spite at having been sent to prison. But not a bit of it. At first he behaved like the model patriot of a Soviet novel: he buried his belongings in the ground and when the factory's equipment was evacuated by rail and the workers were given horses and carts to get away themselves, he put his wife and three children in one of them and set off from Pochep to Kaluga, together with thousands of others.

But as they were approaching Kaluga something went wrong and the column in which they were moving got broken up (there were now only hundreds, not thousands of them). The men were told to report for military service and their families were ordered to proceed by themselves.

When he saw that he was being parted from his family, and evidently not doubting that he was doing the right thing, Spiridon bolted with his family into the forest, waited for the front line to sweep past them, and then, on the same horse and cart (which he now cherished as his own, instead of regarding it with the indifference accorded to state property) took his family all the way back to Pochep.

From there he returned to his native village and took over someone's empty house. The villagers were now told by the Germans that they could help themselves to the land which had formerly belonged to the collective farm and work it on their own account. So Spiridon began to sow and plough without any qualms of conscience, and scarcely bothered his head about how the war was going. He just did his work in the same calm, matter-of-fact way as in those distant years long before the war, when nobody had heard of collective farms.

Then the partisans came to him and told him that this was no time for ploughing, and that he must come away and fight with them. But Spiridon replied that someone had to do the ploughing, and he stayed on his land. Shortly after this, the partisans killed a German despatch-rider right in the middle of the village. They knew what they were doing: the Germans moved in straightaway, evicted everybody from their houses and burned the village to the ground.

And now, not thinking twice about it, Spiridon decided that he must get even with the Germans. He took Martha and the children to her mother and then went straight off to join the partisans. They gave him a tommy-gun and hand-grenades, and with the same skill with which he had worked in the factory and on his land, he shot up German patrols on the railway track, attacked military convoys and helped to blow up bridges. Every so often he went to see his family and he did not have the feeling of being separated from them.

As the Red Army advanced westwards again there was talk about how they would soon come to the end of their life in the forest and be taken on as regular soldiers. Spiridon was even told that he would get a medal for his service with the partisans.

However, when the front line drew near to the village where Martha was now living, the Germans drove all the inhabitants back with them. One of Spiridon's boys came and told him this. And instead of waiting for the Red Army, without word to anyone, Spiridon threw down his tommy-gun and two drums of ammunition, and went off in search of his family. He joined their column, as though he were a civilian himself, and with the same cart, pulled by the same horse as before, set off on the congested road from Pochep to Slutsk. Again he was guided by what he instinctively felt to be the right decision.

By this time Nerzhin could only sit there with his head in his hands. It was all quite beyond him, but since it was none of his business how Spiridon behaved and since he was only, as it were, conducting a social investigation, he again refrained from probing and just said: 'Well, what did you do next?'

Spiridon could, of course, have gone off into the forest again, and indeed he did try it once, but they had an ugly encounter with some bandits, and his daughter had a narrow escape from them. So they decided to go on with the column. In any case, as he now realized when he began to think about it, the Soviet authorities wouldn't believe him, and would not forgive him for having been slow to join the partisans and also for having run away from them. He thus decided he might as well be hanged for a sheep as for a lamb and went on all the way to Slutsk. There they were herded into trains and given rations to last them till they reached the Rhineland. Just before they were put on the train there was a rumour that children would be left behind, and Spiridon began to think of how they could get away. But they took everybody, so he left his horse and cart without a murmur and got on the train with his family. He and his sons were sent to work in a factory near Mainz, and his wife and daughter went to work for a farmer.

In the factory one day, the foreman struck Spiridon's youngest son. Without a moment's thought Spiridon seized an axe and threatened the foreman with it. Under German law he could have been shot. But it did not come to this—the foreman calmed down, went over to Spiridon and said (according to Spiridon): 'I am *Vater* myself, I *verstehe*,' and he didn't report him. A little later Spiridon learned that the foreman had received that very morning official notification of his son's death in action on the Russian front. As he remembered this foreman in the Rhineland, tears came into Spiridon's eyes and he wiped them away with his sleeve: 'After this I can't really feel angry about the Germans. I could even forgive them for burning down my house.'

This was one of the very rare occasions when he felt that

478

his first instinctive reaction might have been wrong. During all the terrible years of his life, during all its cruel ups and downs, this stubborn red-haired peasant had never once paused to reflect at critical moments of decision. In his everyday practice Spiridon refuted many of the fondest ideas of Montaigne and Charron. Despite his horrifying ignorance and lack of understanding of the highest achievements of man and society, his actions and decisions were invariably distinguished by good sense. For example, when he heard that all the dogs in the village were to be shot by the Germans he put a cow's head under the snow for the survivors to feed on. Then, though he had no idea of geography or the German language, when he and his elder son were having a very hard time digging trenches in Alsace—and the Americans were now shooting them up from the air—they both made off without telling anyone and, moving only by night, without being able to read German signs, they made their way across country and straight as the crow flies, they covered the ninety kilometres to the farm near Mainz where his wife was living. There they hid in a dug-out in the garden until the Americans came.

He was untroubled by any vexed philosophical questions about the nature of perception, and he was convinced that his senses served him very well indeed, that he saw, heard and understood everything with unfailing clarity.

In matters of ethics Spiridon was equally matter-of-fact and straightforward. He never slandered anyone, he never bore false witness, he only swore when he had to and he killed only in war. He didn't think any man should fight except for a wife. He could never have brought himself to steal the smallest thing from anyone. It may be, as he himself said, that he had 'played around' with the girls before his marriage, but then didn't Pushkin once say that he was irked most of all by the commandment which says 'Thou shalt not covet thy neighbour's wife'?

Now, at the age of fifty, nearly blind, and evidently doomed to die here in prison, Spiridon did not put on the pious air of a martyr, and showed no signs of despondency or contrition —still less did his imprisonment appear to be having on him the corrective effect which was its avowed purpose—but, from dawn to dusk he went round with his broom, sweeping the prison ground, thus justifying his existence in the eyes of the prison governor and the security officers.

The only thing to which Spiridon was attached was the land.

The only thing he possessed was his family.

High-sounding words like 'motherland', 'religion' and 'socialism', not being current in ordinary everyday conversation, seemed to be completely unknown to Spiridon. His ears were deaf to them and he could never have got his tongue round them.

His motherland was his family.

His religion was his family.

And Socialism was his family too.

As for all the tsars, priests, do-gooders, writers and public speakers, hacks and rabble-rousers, prosecutors and judges, who had in any way impinged on Spiridon in the course of his life, his only retort was silently and angrily to tell them all to go to the devil.

CHAPTER SIXTY-THREE

The steps of the wooden staircase over their heads creaked and shivered from the tread of people going up and down. Sometimes specks of dust and bits of dirt floated down from above, but Spiridon and Nerzhin scarcely noticed. Their hands clasped round their knees, they sat on the unswept floor in their dirty, worn blue denims, the seats of which were hard and shiny. To sit on the bare floor like this was none too comfortable and they leant back a little, resting their shoulders against the sloping, indented underside of the lower steps of the staircase. Their eyes looked straight ahead at the peeling wall of the lavatory.

As always when he was thinking hard, or trying to take something in, Nerzhin smoked one cigarette after another, and he put the crushed butts side by side next to the rotten skirting board at the base of the dirty wall with its crumbling plaster.

Although he also got a ration of Belomar cigarettes Spiridon followed the advice of the German doctors who had restored a little of the sight to one of his eyes, and never smoked at all.

He still felt gratitude and respect for those German doctors. When he had gone completely blind, they had injected something into his spine with a large needle, put some kind of ointment on his eyes and kept them bandaged for a long time. Then they had taken the bandages off in a semi-dark room and ordered him to open his eyes. The world became bright again. The dim night-light at his side looked like the sun to Spiridon and, seeing with his one eye the head of his saviour silhouetted against it, he took his hand and kissed it.

Nerzhin could picture to himself the face of the German eye doctor. Perhaps his usually severe expression had softened for a moment, but what must he have thought of this wild man with red hair from the eastern steppes, whose warm voice and eager thanks, now that he was free of his bandages, were in such contradiction to the barbaric behaviour which had brought him to hospital?

It had happened after the war when Spiridon was living with his family in an American camp for displaced persons. Here he had met somebody from his native village—a man whom he referred to as a 'rascal', because of something he had done when they were setting up the collective farm. He had travelled with this man to Slutsk, but in Germany they had got separated. Now, in order to celebrate their reunion in the displaced persons' camp, the 'rascal' had obtained a bottle of spirits, which cost him nothing. They couldn't read the German label, and the canny, mistrustful Spiridon who had survived so many dangers, but had the devil-may-care streak of all Russians, said: 'All right, let's drink.' Spiridon drank a whole glass of it and his friend finished off the rest at one gulp. Luckily his sons had not been there, otherwise they might have had a nip of it too.

When he came to some time after mid-day, Spiridon was alarmed that it was already so dark; he put his head out of the window, but it wasn't much lighter outside, and he couldn't understand why the top half seemed to be missing from the American staff building over the road, and from the sentry standing in front of it. He thought he wouldn't mention this to Martha, but by the evening he had gone completely blind.

The 'rascal' died.

After the first operation the doctors said he should take things easy for a year and then have another operation—this, they said, would completely restore the sight to his left eye and bring about a fifty per cent improvement in the right one. They were quite positive about this—all he had to do was wait—but Spiridon and his family decided they wanted to go back to Russia.

Nerzhin looked searchingly at Spiridon:

'But,' he asked, 'didn't you have some idea of what to expect when you got back?'

The network of tiny wrinkles round Spiridon's eyes and on his temples puckered as he smiled:

'Of course, I knew they'd take it out on us. It's true they told a great tale in all those leaflets they handed us about letting bygones be bygones: our brothers and sisters would be waiting for us, they said, and the bells would be ringing, and nobody would have to go back to the collective farms if he didn't want. To hear them talk, you could have run home barefoot . . . but I didn't believe those leaflets and I knew I wouldn't be long out of prison.'

His short stubbly whiskers, with a few grey hairs among the red ones, quivered slightly at the memory.

'What I said to Martha was: "They promise us a lake, but suppose it turns out to be no more than a puddle?" She gave me a little pat on the head, and she said: "You ought to get your eyes better first, before we make up our minds. Have that second operation." But then the three children started playing up: "Let's go back home," they said. "Why wait for an operation here? Don't we have eye doctors in Russia? We want to go to a Russian school"—my eldest boy had only two more classes to do in Russia. Then my daughter Vera starts crying her head off: "You don't want me to marry a German, do you?" The poor girl thought she'd never get the husband she wanted in Germany. . . . I said to them: "Children, it's true we've got doctors in Russia, but the thing is—will we ever get to see them?" Then I thought to myself: "I'll be the only one to get into trouble, why should

482

the children suffer? They'll put me in prison, but let the children alone." '

So they started back. At the frontier men and women were separated and sent on in different trains. Spiridon's family, which had managed to keep together throughout the war, was now split up. Nobody bothered to ask them where they came from. His wife and daughter had been sent, without any trial, to the Perm region where his daughter was now working a power-driven saw in a lumber camp. Spiridon and his sons were put behind barbed wire, tried for treason and each given ten years. Spiridon was sent with his younger son to a camp in Solikamsk, where he was able to look after him for a couple of years. But the other son was sent right out to Kolyma in the far east of Siberia.

That's what it was like at home—so much for the good husband his daughter had hoped for, and the boys' education in Russian schools.

The ordeal of interrogation in prison, and then under-nourishment in the camp (he gave half his daily ration to his son) did nothing to improve his eyesight, and his good eye—the left one—had got steadily worse. To have asked for medical help in this remote lumber camp with its vicious struggle for life would have been almost like praying to be taken bodily up to heaven. The wretched little clinic at the camp could not even have advised him where to go for treatment.

Nerzhin was constantly puzzled by the enigma of his new friend. He could not look down on, nor look up to this peasant, who had been so caught up by the events of his time—indeed he now literally sat by his side, shoulder to shoulder. For some time, more and more insistently, Nerzhin had had it on the tip of his tongue to ask Spiridon just one question. It was a question prompted by what he had learned of Spiridon's life, and today it looked as though the time had come to ask it.

Thinking about this complicated life of Spiridon's and the way he had often crossed the line between opposing sides, he wondered whether there wasn't perhaps more to it than a simple urge for self-preservation. Was it all somehow in keeping with the Tolstoyan maxim that nobody in the world is either right or wrong? Could it be that, underlying

483

this almost instinctive behaviour of the red-haired peasant, there was some universal system of philosophical scepticism?

Suppose Nerzhin's social investigation were to lead today, right here under the staircase, to some quite unexpected and fascinating conclusion?

'I feel bad, Gleb,' Spiridon was now saying, rubbing his stubbly cheek hard with a rough, battered hand—it looked as though he was trying to get the skin off. 'It's four months now since I had any letters from home.'

'But you said they had one for you?'

Spiridon looked at him reproachfully—though his eyes were nearly blind, they never had that glassy look of people blind from birth, and there was still a lot of expression in them:

'What good is a letter that's four months old?'

'When they let you have it tomorrow, bring it along and I'll read it for you.'

'I'll be here as fast as my legs can carry me.'

'Perhaps something's got lost in the post? Or perhaps the security people are holding something up? You shouldn't worry so much.'

'How can I help worrying? I'm frightened for my Vera. She's only twenty-one and she's all on her own.'

Nerzhin had seen a photograph of Vera which had been taken that spring. She was a large, buxom girl with big trusting eyes. Her father had brought her safe and sound all through the war. In the forest near Slutsk he had saved her with a hand-grenade from bandits who had wanted to rape her at the age of fifteen.

But what could he do to protect her now he was in prison?

Nerzhin could see in his mind's eye the dense forest round Perm; he could almost hear the power-driven saw chattering like a machine-gun, and the dreadful roar of tractors hauling tree-trunks; he could visualize only too well the lorries with their back wheels bogged down in the swamps and their radiators raised to heaven as though in prayer; the fierce, grimy tractor drivers who could no longer distinguish obscenities from ordinary words—and among them a girl in overalls and trousers which provocatively emphasized her femininity. She would have to sleep together with them by the camp-fires and nobody, as they passed by, would ever miss an opportunity to paw her. Spiridon certainly had every reason to be worried.

Any attempt to reassure him would have been futile. Nerzhin felt that it was better to take his mind off it all by encouraging him to say what he, Nerzhin, was hoping to hear from him—the thing he hoped would give him the needed counter-balance to the outlook of his intellectual friends. Might he now learn what form scepticism had taken in the mind of this simple peasant and thus perhaps be strengthened in his own convictions?

Resting his hand on Spiridon's shoulder and leaning back against the sloping underside of the staircase as before, Nerzhin began to put his question in an oblique, roundabout fashion:

'There's something I keep wanting to ask you, Spiridon, but I don't quite know how to put it. You've been telling me all these things that have happened to you. You've had a very hard life with all kinds of ups and downs, and I suppose there are a great many more like you. All these years you've been thrashing around trying to work things out, haven't you? What I mean is, what's your . . .'—he almost said 'criterion'—'what's your judgment of life in general? For instance, do you think there are people who do wicked things on purpose? Is there anybody who says to himself: " "I'll show everybody what for"? Do you think that's likely? Perhaps everybody wants to do good—or they *think* they want to do good, but since none of us are blameless and we all make mistakes—and some of us are just crazy, anyway—we do all these bad things to each other. We tell ourselves we are doing good, but in fact it all comes out the other way. It's all a bit like that saying of yours—you sow rye and weeds come up.'

Spiridon was looking hard at him, as though suspecting a trap. Nerzhin felt he was not expressing himself very well, but he went on:

'Now, suppose I think you're making a mistake and I want to put you right, and I tell you what I think, but you don't listen and even tell me to shut up? What should I do? Hit you over the head with a stick? That wouldn't be so bad if I really were right, but suppose I only *think* I'm right? After all, things are always changing, aren't they? What I mean is: if you can't always be sure that you're right, should you stick your nose into other people's business? Is there any way for a man to know who is right and who is wrong?'

'I can tell you,' Spiridon said brightening up, and as readily as if he had been asked which of the warders had come on duty that morning. 'I can tell you: wolf-hounds are right and cannibals are wrong.'

'What's that again?' Nerzhin said, taken aback by the simplicity and force of Spiridon's judgment.

'What I said was,' Spiridon repeated with stark conviction, turning his head towards Nerzhin and breathing hotly into his face from under his moustache: 'the wolf-hounds are right and the cannibals wrong.'

CHAPTER SIXTY-FOUR

The fresh-faced young lieutenant with the neat little square moustache under his nose, who had come on guard duty that Sunday evening, had gone round the upper and lower corridors after lights out, sending the prisoners back to their bunks—on Sundays they were always reluctant to go to bed. He would have gone round a second time, but he didn't want to leave the trim young nurse in the prison sick bay. The nurse had a husband in Moscow, who was completely cut off from her during her twenty-four hour spell of duty in this closely guarded prison, and the lieutenant had great hopes for making progress with her tonight, but she kept pushing him away and saying with a giggle: 'Stop playing the fool.'

This was why, instead of going round a second time himself, he sent his sergeant to chase the prisoners back to their sleeping quarters. The sergeant could see that the lieutenant would be staying in the sick bay till morning, and would not, therefore, check up on him. So he did not bother very much about whether the prisoners went to bed or not—partly because he was tired of this dog's life and partly because he knew perfectly well that grown-up people who had to work in the morning would make sure of getting all the sleep they needed.

It was forbidden to switch off the lights in the corridors and on the staircase for fear this might help the prisoners in case of any attempted break-out or mutiny.

Because on this particular evening neither the lieutenant nor the sergeant had bothered to chase them away, Rubin and Sologdin remained standing against the wall in the large main passageway. It was already one o'clock in the morning, but they had forgotten about sleep. They were carrying on one of those fierce, endless disputes with which any Russian celebration is likely to end—if it doesn't end in a fight.

Their attempt to settle their differences on paper had not succeeded; during the last hour or so they had gone over the other two laws of the dialectic and they had invoked the shades of Hegel and Feuerbach. But there was no foothold or resting-place for them on these cold Olympian heights and always they tumbled back into the hot volcanic crater of their own arguments.

'You are a fossil, an ichthyosaurus!' cried Rubin, exasperated. 'How on earth are you going to live in the world outside with wild ideas like that? How can you possibly be accepted into any society?'

'Society?' Sologdin looked quite astonished. 'For as long as I can remember I have been in prison, not in society! I have always had nothing but barbed wire and warders round me. As a matter of plain fact, I'm cut off from the world outside, and shall be for ever, so why should I prepare myself to become part of society . . .?'

Earlier, they had been over the question of whether or not the younger generation was growing up to be better.

'How dare you talk about the younger generation?' Rubin had said angrily. 'I fought with them in the war and went behind the enemy lines with them, but all you know is what you've heard from some loud-mouthed ragamuffin in a transit prison. You were twelve years in the camp, and what did you see of the country before that? The sights of old Moscow? Or maybe you managed to get out to Kolomenskoye on Sundays?'

'The country? How can you judge what's going on in the country?' Sologdin shouted, but he tried to keep his voice down, and it sounded as though he was being throttled. 'You ought to be ashamed of yourself! Think of all those people who came through Butyrki—Gromov, Ivanteyev, Yashin, Blokhin—they told you the sober truth, things that had happened to them personally. But did you listen to them? And what about the people here—Vartapetov and the other man . . .'

'Who? Why should I listen to them? They're blind, they're like wild animals who have hurt their paws. They see the failure of their own lives as a cosmic disaster. They can't see any further than the slop-bucket in their cell!'

They now plunged on, disregarding logic and losing the thread of their arguments. They had forgotten where they were (there was now nobody left in the passageway except two fanatical chess players still sitting over their game and an old metal-worker who smoked like a chimney and was coughing all the time) and were very conspicuous here, gesticulating wildly with flushed faces and thrusting their beards —one large and black and the other neat and fair—into each other's faces.

They were both now concerned with only one thing: how to find the other's weak spot and hit him where it hurt most.

If the substance of which our eyes is made were capable of melting from the heat of the feelings mirrored in them, Sologdin's would have liquefied from the intensity with which he looked at Rubin.

'It's impossible to talk to you! You are quite impervious to reason! You think nothing of confusing black and white! And what I find particularly revolting is that in your heart of hearts you believe that the end justifies the means. But if you were asked to admit this outright, you would deny it. You would deny it—I know you would!'

'Why should I?' Rubin replied icily. 'On the personal plane I don't accept it. But it's a different matter if we are talking about society as a whole. For the first time in the history of mankind we have an aim which is so sublime that we can really say that it justifies the means employed to attain it.'

'Oh, that's what you think, is it?' Seeing a chink in Rubin's armour, Sologdin quickly made a telling thrust with his rapier: 'Now just remember that the higher the aim,

488

the higher your means should be as well. Wicked means destroy the end.'

'Wicked means? Who's using wicked means? Perhaps you have no time for revolutionary means? Perhaps you deny the need for the dictatorship of the proletariat?'

'Don't bring politics into it,' Sologdin said, waggling his forefinger under Rubin's nose like the point of a sword. 'I'm in here under Article 58, but I was never involved in politics and don't want to get involved now. Look at this metal-worker over here—he can hardly read or write, but he's in here under Article 58 too.'

'Just tell me straight.' Rubin tried to pin him down. 'Do you recognize the dictatorship of the proletariat?'

'I never said a word about the rule of the working class. The question I asked you was a moral one: does the end justify the means or does it not? And by your answer you have exposed yourself.'

'I didn't say I believed in it on the personal plane.'

'It makes no difference,' Sologdin exclaimed in his strangled voice. 'Do you mean that if you kill or betray someone, it's a crime, but if the great Leader and Teacher calmly wipes out five or ten million—this is justified and has to be understood in a progressive sense?'

'You can't make comparisons like that. These are two different things!'

'You must be putting it on—you're too intelligent to believe anything so monstrous. No person in his right mind could think like that! You're simply lying!'

'You're the one who's lying. Everything about you is pure affectation—this idiotic "Language of Maximum Clarity", this pose of being a knight in shining armour, and the way you try and look like Alexander Nevsky! It's all bogus, because you're a failure in life! And this wood-cutting stunt is just a sham too.'

'So that's why you've stopped coming to help. You're not so keen when you have to work with your hands instead of your tongue, are you?'

'What do you mean, "stopped"? Just because I haven't been for three days?'

Their argument now went on in a headlong rush. Like

a night express hurtling over empty steppes, past stations, signals and cities, ablaze with light, it plunged on through both the dark and bright places of their minds and occasionally something was thrown into flickering relief or drowned in a thundering roar.

'If you take such a high moral stand, you ought first to look at yourself,' Rubin said indignantly. 'What's *your* attitude to ends and means? On the personal level, I mean. What was your great dream when you first went in for engineering? I bet you wanted to make a million, like Koreiko[1] . . .?'

'And what about you—teaching village kids to inform on their parents. . . .'

They had known one another for two years and they were now exploiting all the confidences they had exchanged in intimate conversation to try and hurt each other as much as possible. They remembered everything and hurled it into each other's faces. The contest was no longer on the level of generalities, but descended lower and lower to a personal level at which they could inflict pain with particular savagery.

'I know who your real friends are,' Sologdin raged, 'Shikin and Mishin. These are your soulmates! I can't understand why you don't admit it openly. Why be so hypocritical?'

'What did you say?' said Rubin, choking. 'You don't mean that seriously do you?'

Sologdin knew very well that Rubin wasn't an informer and never could be, but in his anger he had not been able to resist the temptation to lump him together with the Security Officers.

'At any rate,' he continued, 'it would be quite logical for you to be on their side. If our jailors are working for a just cause, then it's your duty to help them as much as you can. What would be wrong with informing? Not to mention the fact that Shikin would write a good report on you, and your case might be reviewed. . . .'

'You'd better watch out.' Rubin clenched his large fists and raised them. 'You can get hurt for saying things like that.'

'All I said,' Sologdin went on more calmly, 'was that it

[1] Character in Ilf and Petrov's *Golden Calf*.

would be more logical on your part—if the end justifies the means.'

Rubin unclenched his fists and looked at Sologdin with contempt:

'The first thing you've got to have is principles—but you haven't got any. You just talk all this abstract nonsense about Good and Evil. . . .'

But Sologdin didn't take this up and went on making his own point. 'Well, tell me if I'm wrong. Since we're all in prison for good cause—all, that is, except you—then our jailors must be right. Twice a year you write letters asking for a pardon. . . .'

'Nonsense—not a pardon, a review of my case.'

'What's the difference?'

'There's a lot of difference.'

'However often they refuse, you go on begging for it. You refused to argue a while back about the importance of pride, but that's something you could do with. For the sake of nominal freedom you're willing to go down on your hands and knees. You're like a dog on a chain—whoever holds the chain has complete power over you.'

'And aren't you in their power too?' Rubin said furiously. 'Nothing would make you beg too?'

'No!'

'That's because you haven't a chance of getting your freedom. If you had, I bet you'd do a damn sight more than beg, you'd . . .'

'Never!' Sologdin said firmly.

'How high-minded you are! You sneer at the people in Number Seven for working away as they do, but if you could find a way of distinguishing yourself I bet you'd go crawling on your belly.'

'Never!' Sologdin said. He was now shaking with fury.

'But let me tell you,' Rubin gloated, 'that you haven't got the gumption to distinguish yourself. It's just a matter of sour grapes. If you could do something and they called you in, I tell you you'd go crawling on your belly.'

'Just try and prove it.' It was now Sologdin's turn to clench his fists. 'You'd better be careful what you say.'

'I'll prove it all right, if you give me time! Just give me a year, will you?'

'Ten, if you like.'

'I'll catch you out all right, though of course you would be quite capable of being an exception to the dialectical law that everything is in flux and constantly changes.'

'It's only with people like you that everything is in flux and constantly changes. Don't judge others by yourself.'

CHAPTER SIXTY-FIVE

There is nothing predictable about relations between men and women—they have no set course and there are no laws to govern them. They sometimes reach such a dead end that there's nothing to do but sit down and howl: everything that could be said has been said, all arguments have been exhausted. But then, at a chance meeting of eyes, the blank wall may suddenly crumble away, and where all was darkness there is light and an easy path along which two people can walk again—for a short while, at least.

Innokenty had long ago made up his mind that it was all over between Dottie and him, and that in view of her lack of feeling and shallowness it couldn't be otherwise. But he had felt very warm towards her this evening at her father's, where she had behaved so sweetly and he still felt the same as they returned home in their car. It had been a long time since they had so amicably compared notes about an evening spent together and, listening to what she was saying about Clara getting married, he put his arm round her shoulders and took her by the hand. He did this without thinking. It suddenly occurred to him that if she had never been his wife or his mistress, but belonged to someone else, and he had put his arms round her like this, he would have given anything to possess her.

But why, since she was his wife, did this sudden desire seem so outrageous to him?

The terrible and shameful thing about it was that she now roused him so much because of her depravity, because she had been unfaithful to him. The attraction was all the more powerful for being abnormal. It was as though he wanted to prove something by this. But what? And to whom?

492

In their drawing-room, saying good night to him Dottie apologetically rested her head on his chest, kissed him on the neck and lowering her eyes, went into her bedroom. Innokenty went to his study and got undressed. Suddenly he felt that he must go to her.

There was another thing too: the whole evening he had felt shielded from the danger of arrest by the crowd of singing, laughing people and the din of their conversation —it gave him a sense of security. But in the loneliness of his study, he was now again overwhelmed by fear and he needed warmth and protection.

In his tasselled dressing-gown and slippers he stood and hesitated at the door of his wife's bedroom. Still undecided whether to knock or not he pressed lightly on the door with his hand. Dottie had always kept the door locked at night, but it now yielded to his touch.

So he went in without knocking, pulled back the curtain hanging over the door and saw Dottie over in the right-hand corner—she was in bed under her mauve velvet bedspread.

She didn't seem surprised and made no movement.

There was a lamp on the low bedside table which lit up her delicate features, her untidy hair, her shoulders, hands and breasts. Her nightdress was peach coloured with a golden sheen and every fold, the neckline and the lace trimmings, were of the sort that had been cunningly designed to make a woman many times more attractive than she would have been naked.

It was rather warm in the bedroom, but Innokenty was even glad of this, because he felt rather chilly. There was a faint trace of perfume in the air.

He went to the middle of the room where there was a little table covered by a pale grey cloth; he picked up a seashell lying there, and, his head turned away from her, he said moodily:

'I'm surprised at myself. I don't see how there could ever be anything between us again' (Innokenty had never told her that he had been unfaithful to her in Rome, and he didn't think it counted). 'But I suddenly thought I'd come and see you.'

He weighed the seashell nervously in his hand and turned his head to her.

He despised himself.

She moved her head round slightly on the pillow and looked across at him with a look that was both searching and affectionate, though she could hardly have been able to see him very well in the semi-darkness of the room, with only the light from the shaded bedside lamp. She was holding a book in one hand—her arm was dangling over the edge of the bed, looking bare and helpless below the ruffles at the top of the sleeve.

'Why don't you just come and lie down by me?' she suggested gently.

Just lie down? Why not? Even though, as a man, he could never forgive what had happened.

And then it was easier to talk lying down. It was somehow much easier to get out the things you had on your mind if you were lying in each other's arms under a blanket, not sitting in chairs.

So he stepped uncertainly towards her.

She pulled back the blanket and held it up, inviting him into the warmth of the bed.

Not noticing that he had trodden on the book she had dropped on the carpet, Innokenty lay down and was enfolded in the warm depths of the bed.

CHAPTER SIXTY-SIX

At last the whole prison was asleep.

Two hundred and eighty prisoners slept under the blue night lamps, face upwards or their heads buried in their pillows, breathing quietly, snoring hideously or shouting incoherently in their sleep, curled up for warmth or sprawled out because they were too hot. They all dreamed different things: the old men saw their relatives and the young men dreamed of women; some remembered lost possessions, a train journey, a church service or the judges at their trial. But whatever their dreams, they never forgot for one moment, even in their sleep, that they were prisoners and that if they found themselves walking on green grass or in city streets, then it meant they had run away, or been let out by mistake, and there must be a search party after them. They never had that blissful sense of being released from their chains that Longfellow described in his *Dream of a Prisoner*. The shock of their unjust arrest and ten-or twenty-five-year sentence, the barking of dogs, the heavy tread of their guards, the excruciating din of the signal for reveille in the camps—all this had penetrated to the marrow of their bones through every other layer of experience—both secondary and even primary —so much so that, if he were woken by a fire in jail, a sleeping prisoner would first remember where he was and only then rouse himself at the smell of burning.

Mamurin was asleep in his solitary quarters. The off-duty warders were asleep—as were the ones who had taken over from them. The nurse in the sick bay, who had resisted the lieutenant with the square moustache all evening, had at last given in and they were both now asleep on the narrow couch in her office. Finally, the drab little warder by the iron door at the bottom of the prison's main staircase, thinking it unlikely that anybody would now come to check on him (and having obtained no response from the internal telephone) also fell asleep, sitting with his head on the desk in front of him and no longer looking from time to time, as was his duty, through the peep-hole into the lower prison corridor.

Then, having waited with clenched teeth for this very late hour when the prison system had ceased to function, the 281st prisoner softly went out of the semicircular room, his eyes half closed against the bright blue light and crushing underfoot the cigarette butts littered everywhere on the floor. He had pulled on his boots without bothering to wind the usual cloths round his feet and he wore his shabby army greatcoat with nothing else except his underwear. His black beard was unkempt, as was the thinning hair on his head, and he had an agonized look on his face.

He had been unable to sleep, and had now got up to take a walk along the corridor. He had tried this on other occasions —it helped him to calm down and it soothed the stabbing pain at the back of his head and the dull, aching feeling in the region of his liver.

Though all he wanted to do was walk up and down, he took with him by force of habit a couple of books and a blunt pencil. In one of the books he had put his draft manuscript of a 'Proposal for The Establishment of Civic Temples'. He laid all this, together with a tin of tobacco and his pipe, on the long dirty table, and began to pace up and down the corridor, holding his greatcoat round him. He realized that it was equally bad for all prisoners—for those who had been arrested for no reason at all, and even for those who really were opponents of the régime, and had been imprisoned as such. Nevertheless, he felt that his own position here was tragic in the Aristotelian sense. He had been struck down by something that he loved more than anything else. He had been put in prison by unfeeling and indifferent people because of his love for the common cause—a love that was almost unseemly in its intensity. Hence by a tragic contradiction, Rubin found he had to try and stick up for his human dignity, and that of his comrades, in a daily battle with prison officers and warders who were only implementing a law which in itself was absolutely right, just and progressive. Yet these comrades of his were often not real comrades at all and they hurled reproaches at him, cursed and swore at him, almost savaged him, because all they saw was their own personal misfortune and they were blind to the great law by which everything took its inevitable course. And, scornfully ignoring their insults, he had to go on patiently trying to convince them by force of argument that, seen in the wide perspective, everything was proceeding just as it should, industry was flourishing, agriculture was prospering, science and culture were blossoming forth as never before.

All these fellow-prisoners who so violently disagreed with him often pointed to their superior numbers as proof that they, not Rubin, were the true representatives of the People. But everything in him cried out that this was a lie. The People were not in prison, or behind barbed wire. The People were those who had captured Berlin, and had met the Americans on the River Elbe; the People had been demobilized in their millions and returned home to rebuild the Dnieper Dam, to bring the Donbass back to life again, to raise Stalingrad from the ruins. Feeling at one with these millions, Rubin never had a sense of loneliness in his battle against a few score fellow-prisoners.

They often baited him, not out of concern for the truth, but simply to find release for feelings they could not vent on their jailors. They taunted him without caring that all these arguments caused him agony and brought him nearer the grave.

But he had to go on arguing with them. The trouble was that on the 'Mavrino sector of the front', as he called it, there were very few people as qualified as he to stand up for socialism.

He knocked on the peep-hole in the iron door. It was only when he had rapped hard the third time that the sleepy face of the little warder appeared behind the glass.

'I'm feeling ill,' Rubin said, 'I need some medicine. Take me to the sick bay.'

The warder thought a moment and said: 'All right, I'll phone them.'

Rubin continued to walk up and down.

He was altogether a tragic figure.

He had first been to prison at an earlier age than anyone else in Mavrino.

When he was only sixteen, a grown-up cousin whom he hero-worshipped had asked him to hide some printing type. The young Lev had eagerly agreed. But one day it had been seen by a boy who lived next door, who had reported him to the authorities. Rubin, however, did not give his cousin away and made up a story about how he had found the type under the staircase of the apartment block where they lived.

As he now went on walking up and down the corridor, Rubin vividly recalled his solitary cell in the Kharkov central prison to which he had been taken twenty years before.

The prison had been built in the American style—all the cells looked down on a central court with iron catwalks going all the way round, and all the many floors were interconnected by iron stairways. Down below in the middle there was a supervisor directing everything like a traffic policeman, and signalling the warders with flags. The slightest sound echoed round the whole prison. Rubin once heard somebody being dragged down one of the iron staircases. Suddenly the man's deafening screams shook the whole prison:

'Comrades,' he yelled at the top of his voice, 'greetings from the ice-box! Down with Stalin's hangmen!'

He was then beaten—there had been no mistaking that sound of people hitting something soft! They put a gag in his mouth and his screams faltered and died away—but three hundred men in their solitary cells started hammering on their doors and shouting:

'Down with the killers!'

'They're out for the workers' blood again.'

'It's the tsar all over again.'

'Long live Leninism!'

Then, suddenly, in some of the cells frantic voices began to sing:

> *'Arise ye prisoners of starvation.'*

Soon the whole unseen multitude took up the refrain in a great roar:

> *'This is our last*
> *And final struggle.'*

There was no way of telling, but Lev thought that many of them, like himself, must have had tears of emotion in their eyes.

The whole prison was buzzing like a beehive that had been disturbed. The handful of warders with their keys stood frozen on the iron catwalks, aghast at this singing of the immortal anthem of the proletariat . . .

The throbbing pains at the back of his head were getting worse, and so was the discomfort in his right side under the liver.

He knocked on the glass of the peep-hole once more. At his second knock the drowsy face of the warder again appeared. Sliding back the glass he said in a peevish voice:

'I phoned, but there's no reply.'

He wanted to shut the peep-hole again, but Rubin wouldn't let him, holding it with his hand: 'Well, go along there yourself!' he shouted in pain and irritation. 'I'm ill, don't you understand? I can't sleep! Call the nurse!'

'Oh, all right then,' said the warder and shut the peephole.

Rubin again began to walk up and down, just as des-

pairingly as before, pacing the length of the filthy corridor—
the floor of which was covered with cigarette butts and
spittle. Time seemed to stand still.

After the jail in Kharkov which he always remembered
with pride—even though these two weeks of solitary confinement had been a black mark against him ever since and
partly accounted for the severity of his present sentence—his
mind was invaded by other memories which he kept deeply
hidden and at the thought of which he burned with shame.

There was that time he had been summoned to the Party
office in the Kharkov Tractor Works. His feelings about the
Works were those of someone who might almost have helped
to found them. He was on the editorial board of the Works
newspaper, and was always running round urging on the
younger workers to greater efforts, and putting new heart
into the older ones; he made and put up posters extolling the
successes of the Stakhanovites or castigating people responsible for hold-ups and waste.

Then only twenty-two, he had walked into the Party
office wearing his embroidered Ukrainian shirt. He had behaved with the same bluff straightforwardness as when he
had once been to see the First Secretary of the Ukrainian
Central Committee—'Hello, Comrade Postyshev,' he had
said, stretching out his hand. In the same way he now
greeted the forty-year-old woman sitting here with the red
kerchief over her short hair. 'Hello, Comrade Bakhtina!
Did you want to see me?'

'Hello, Comrade Rubin,' she said and shook his hand.
'Sit down.'

He sat down.

There was another man in the room. Wearing a suit, tie
and light-brown shoes, he didn't look like a worker. He sat
by himself leafing through some papers and paid no attention to either of them.

The Party office was as bare and plain as a confessional
booth. The dominant colours were bright red and sober,
workaday black. In a rather constrained and lifeless way the
woman began to talk to Rubin about the sort of factory
business they often earnestly discussed together, but suddenly
she leaned back in her chair and said sternly:

'Comrade Rubin! You must make a clean breast to the Party!'

Rubin was flabbergasted. Hadn't he always served the Party without sparing himself, working night and day for it?

It seemed that this wasn't enough, but what else could they want of him?

Now the other man politely intervened. He addressed Rubin in a formal way that jarred on his proletarian ear. He said that Rubin should give a full and honest account of everything he knew about his married cousin—was it true that he had formerly been active in the organized opposition, and that he was now concealing this from the Party? . . .

He should have answered straight away, but it was difficult under the fixed stare of these two . . .

Rubin had learnt to look at the Revolution through the eyes of this cousin. He knew from him that not everything was such plain sailing as it seemed at May Day parades. In more senses than one the Revolution was like springtime—this meant there was a lot of mud through which they had to wade in search of a good firm way ahead. But it was four years since his cousin had talked like this, and there was now no more squabbling in the Party ranks. The Oppositionists were almost forgotten. Whether one liked it or not, collectivization had been pushed through, and in agriculture, as somebody had said, all the precarious little 'boats' of the peasant farms had been converted into a 'great ocean liner'. The blast furnaces of Magnitogorsk were already sending their smoke skywards and the collectivized land was being ploughed up by tractors made in the four great factories built during the first Five Year Plan. Objectively speaking, all this was to the greater glory of World Revolution, so wasn't it immaterial in whose name all these mighty feats were performed? (And Rubin, in fact, had made himself love the very name of the man in question.) So what was the point in arresting and taking vengeance on people who had earlier been in disagreement?

'I don't know. He was never in the Opposition,' Rubin at last replied, though his reason told him that this romantic schoolboy loyalty would not help, and it was useless to deny the facts.

The Secretary of the Party Committee remonstrated with short incisive gestures: wasn't the Party the most important thing in our lives? How could anyone want to deceive the Party? How could anyone not want to tell the truth to the Party? The Party was not vindictive—the Party was our conscience. He should remember the words of Lenin. . . .

If Rubin had found himself looking down the barrels of ten pistols he would not have been afraid. No threat of prison or of banishment to Solovki[1] would have forced him to tell them what they wanted to hear. But how could he lie to the Party? He could keep nothing back in this black and red confessional booth.

He told them when and where his cousin had been in the Opposition, and what he had done as a member of it.

The woman inquisitor was now silent, but the polite man in the light-brown boots said:

'Now, if I understood you correctly . . .'—and he read the record he had made of Rubin's words. 'Will you please sign —down here.'

Rubin recoiled in horror:

'Who are you? You are not the Party!'

'What do you mean?' the man said, offended. 'I am also a member of the Party. And an official of the GPU.'

Rubin again knocked at the peep-hole. The warder, who had clearly been startled out of his sleep, asked drowsily:

'What are you knocking for? I keep on ringing, but there's no reply.'

Rubin's eyes flashed with anger:

'I asked you to go there yourself! There's something wrong with my heart. I might even die!'

'You won't die,' the guard said in a conciliatory tone and even with a hint of sympathy. 'You'll last out till the morning. I can't just go and leave my post, can I?'

'What harm is there in that?' Rubin shouted.

'None at all, but it's against orders. You were in the army, weren't you?'

Rubin's head was now throbbing so violently that he felt

[1] Solovki: an island in the White Sea whose prison was notorious in the 'twenties and 'thirties.

he really might die any moment. The guard saw the pain on his face and said:

'All right, stop knocking on the glass and get away from the peep-hole, while I run along and see.'

As far as Rubin could tell, he was as good as his word. The pain didn't seem quite as bad now, and he again started pacing the corridor.

The memories that now went through his mind were ones which he would rather have forgotten. To forget them would have healed his pain.

Shortly after his two weeks in the Kharkov prison, to redeem himself in the eyes of the Komsomol and justify his existence both to himself and the proletariat (the only revolutionary class!), Rubin went off with a gun to help collectivize the countryside.

There were times when he had to run for his life, or shoot his way out after being ambushed by angry peasants. But he had thought of this only as an extension of the Civil War.

It had all seemed so much a matter of course—digging up pits where grain had been hidden, seeing to it that none of these peasants could grind flour, bake bread or even draw water from their wells. He would have seen them in hell first—even if they had a dying child—rather than let them bake bread. And soon he was not moved, any more than by a tramcar in the city, at the familiar sight of the forlorn horse and cart going round the numbed villages at dawn, and the cry of the driver, as he knocked on shutters with his whip:

'Any dead here?'

But before long, the cry changed to:

'Anyone alive here?'

All this was imprinted in his mind, as though branded there with a red-hot iron. And sometimes he thought that everything he had suffered—his war wounds, his imprisonment and his ill-health—was punishment for it.

True, he had only got his deserts, but since he now knew what a terrible thing he had done, and would never do it again, and had paid the price, was there no way of purging himself? He would have given anything to be able to say it had never happened. . . .

There is nothing a sleepless night cannot wring from an erring soul in distress. . . .

The warder suddenly opened the peep-hole, this time without Rubin having to knock. He had, after all, plucked up enough courage to leave his post for a moment and go to the duty-room. He had found them all asleep there, with nobody in attendance at the internal telephone. He woke up the sergeant who listened to what he had to say, and told him off for leaving his post; knowing that the nurse was sleeping with the lieutenant, he could scarcely take it on himself to disturb them.

'There's nothing doing,' the warder said through the peep-hole. 'I went to the duty-room and told them, but they say it can't be done. You'll have to wait till morning.'

'I'm dying, I'm dying!' Rubin shouted hoarsely. 'Call the Duty Officer at once. I'll go on hunger strike.'

'Hunger strike? That's nothing to do with me, is it?' the warder replied, reasonably enough. 'You can go on hunger strike at breakfast in the morning. . . . Come on now, get back to bed. I'll phone the sergeant again later.'

What could Rubin do, except try to rise above this kind of thing?

So, fighting the pain and the nausea, he again tried to walk back and forth with the same measured step. He remembered Krylov's fable *The Sabre Blade*. Before his prison days, he had not been particularly struck by it, but now it was different:

> *A sabre blade, once keen and thrusting,*
> *Among a waste of iron rusting,*
> *On market-day was taken out*
> *And sold for nothing to a country lout.*

The peasant had used the sword to cut wood. The sword had become jagged and rusty. Then one day the hedgehog under the bench in the peasant's hut asked the sword:

> *Why, if the sabre blade*
> *Is worth the fuss that's often made,*

>   *What shame to trim the stakes, at rustic*
> *clown's desire,*
> *Or chop the faggots for the fire?'*

How often Rubin had mentally applied the sword's answer
to himself:

> *'In some good soldier's hand, the foe I could*
> *contain,*
> *But here my talent is in vain!*
> *And so for menial tasks my services they claim;*
> *'Tis by compulsion too.*
> *He only is to blame,*
> *Who could not understand, what work I'm*
> *meant to do.'*

CHAPTER SIXTY-SEVEN

Rubin suddenly felt weak at the knees and sat down at the
table, slumping against its hard edge.

For all his violent rejection of Sologdin's arguments he
had to admit—this pained him more than anything—that
there was sometimes a grain of truth in them. It was true,
for instance, that moral standards had declined, particularly
among the younger generation, and that people were losing
their sense of values.

In the old days people had leaned on the Church and
the priests for moral guidance. And even nowadays, what
Polish peasant woman would take any serious step in life
without consulting her priest?

It could be that the country now needed firm moral foundations, even more urgently than the Volga-Don Canal or
the great new dam on the Angara River.

The question was: how to set about creating them? This
was the whole point of the 'Proposal for the Establishment of
Civic Temples', of which Rubin had already made a rough
draft. Now was the time, when he was suffering from insomnia like this, to put the finishing touches to it; then,
when he was next allowed a visitor, he must ask him to

smuggle it out of the prison and have it properly typed for submission to the Party Central Committee. He wouldn't be able to sign it in his own name—the Central Committee would hardly take kindly to advice proffered by a political prisoner. But it couldn't be anonymous either, so it would have to be signed by one of his friends from army days—for a good cause like this Rubin would gladly forgo any glory involved.

In spite of the shooting pains in his head, he filled his pipe with 'Golden Fleece' tobacco and lit up. This was just force of habit—he did not really want to smoke, and was even repelled by the idea. But only then did he start to read his draft.

Sitting in his greatcoat at the rough bare boards of the table covered with breadcrumbs and cigarette ash, he looked through the many pages of this selfless proposal written out in his sprawling handwriting. The air in the unswept corridor was stale and a sleepy prisoner occasionally scurried through on his way to the lavatory.

In the preamble he spoke of the need to raise even higher the moral standards of the population (which, he emphasized, were already very high), to endow revolutionary and other anniversaries with greater significance, and to enhance with solemn ritual such occasions as weddings, the naming of new-born children, the reaching of adulthood and secular funeral services. (The author at this point intimated that these occasions tended to be observed in a perfunctory manner and that for this reason citizens were not always very aware of the family and social ties by which they were bound.)

The solution offered was the establishment all over the country of Civic Temples which should be architecturally imposing and dominate their surroundings.

Subdivided into sections and paragraphs, the memorandum then carefully detailed all the finer points of organization —for instance, the size of the area and the number of people to be served by each Temple; precisely which days in the calendar should be observed by mass meetings, and how long the different types of ritual should last. Marriages were to be preceded by a formal engagement and a public announcement two weeks ahead. It was proposed that youth about to enter adulthood should be brought to the Temples in groups and, in the presence of large numbers of their elders, made to take a special oath and solemnly vow loyalty to their country, obedience to their parents and adherence to a general code of ethics.

The proposal laid particular emphasis on the need to ensure that all these ritual observances should be carried out in a proper setting, that the garments of the Temple ministrants should testify by their magnificence to the purity of mind of those who wore them; that the form of words employed in the various rituals should, by its rhythmic quality, achieve maximum emotional impact; that every possible means should be used to affect the sense organs of visitors to the Temples: by impregnating the air with a special aroma, by choral and other musical performances, by the skilful use of coloured glass, spotlights and tasteful murals calculated to develop the aesthetic sense of the population —not to mention the overall architectural design which should convey a feeling of grandeur and eternity.

Rubin had agonized over every word, picking synonyms with the utmost care. One incautious word and people of shallow intellect might easily conclude that he was simply proposing the reintroduction of Christian temples without Christ. Nothing could have been further from the truth! Persons with a fondness for historical analogy, on the other hand, might well accuse him of trying to bring back Robespierre's cult of the Supreme Being. But this too would be wide of the mark.

In Rubin's view, the most original section of his proposal was the one on these new . . . not priests—ministrants, as he called them. He felt that the success of the whole proposal vitally depended on whether or not it would be possible to establish throughout the country a body of ministrants who, because of their immaculate and selfless personal conduct, would enjoy the affection and confidence of the People. He suggested that the best procedure, the one most likely to maintain high moral standards, would be for the Party authorities to select suitable candidates from all walks of life and train them as full-time ministrants. Once urgent initial needs had been met, it should be possible, as the years went by, gradually to widen the scope and duration of this training programme, and give the ministrants an excellent all-round education which should, he stressed, include the art of oratory and elocution. (Rubin made so bold as to suggest that the art of public speaking had suffered a decline —perhaps because there was no longer any need to exercise persuasion on the people of a country who unconditionally supported their beloved Government without having to be told.)

Such were the author's powers of concentration that he became wholly engrossed in the correction of his manuscript and was able to disregard his pain, if not forget it.

He was not particularly surprised that no one bothered to attend a prisoner who felt very ill at an awkward time of night. He had seen many such cases during his time in prison.

So when the key suddenly rattled in the door, Rubin's first startled thought was that he was about to be discovered doing something not permitted at this unusual hour, and would be made to undergo some tedious punishment. He grabbed his papers, books and tobacco and started to make for his bunk, but it was too late: the squat, coarse-featured sergeant had seen him and was calling him over to the open door.

Rubin at once came back to earth—he again felt how lonely, sick and helpless he was, and remembered all the slights he had to endure.

'Sergeant,' he said, slowly going over to him, 'for three hours I've been trying to get the nurse to see me. I'm going to complain about both you and her to the prison administration of the MGB.'

But the tone of the sergeant's reply was quite amiable: 'There was nothing I could do till now, Rubin—it wasn't my fault. Come along.'

When he had learned that the prisoner kicking up all this fuss was one of the biggest trouble-makers in the place, he had quickly made up his mind to rouse the lieutenant. For a long time there was no answer to his knock, but eventually the nurse put her head round the door and hastily withdrew it. At last the lieutenant himself came out, and frowning, gave the sergeant permission to bring Rubin along to the sick bay.

Rubin put on his greatcoat properly and buttoned it up

to conceal his underwear. The sergeant led him through the basement corridor and they went out into the prison grounds up some steps which were thickly covered with fluffy snow. In the darkness of this quiet picture-book night, with the thick white snowflakes falling round them all the time, Rubin and the sergeant crossed the prison yard, leaving deep footprints in the soft snow. Under this precious sky, now covered by snow clouds which were murky brown from the glow of the prison lights, feeling the innocent, child-like touch of the cold snowflakes on his beard and flushed face, Rubin stopped in his tracks and shut his eyes. He was enveloped by a delicious sense of peace. This powerful sense of being was all the keener for being so short-lived. What happiness it would be if he didn't have to go anywhere and beg for things, if he had no desires at all but could just stand here like this the whole night, as blissfully as the trees there, catching the snowflakes as they came down.

At this moment he heard the long wavering hoot of a train from the railway which passed within less than half a mile of Mavrino—it was that special sound, so lonely and plaintive in the night, which in our later years reminds us of childhood, because when we were children it seemed to hold out so much promise of things to come.

If only he could just stand here for half an hour he would be fully healed in mind and body, and perhaps he would compose a wistful little poem about trains hooting in the night.

Oh, if only he didn't have to go on, walking behind the warder! . . .

But the warder was already looking back with suspicion, fearful perhaps that he might be planning to escape.

So Rubin's legs carried him onwards, to the appointed place.

The nurse looked pink and refreshed by sleep. She was in her white nurse's overall and it was evident that she had nothing on underneath. Any prisoner would have noted this at once—so normally would Rubin—and let his eyes dwell on her figure, but at the moment Rubin had no time for this brazen hussy who had kept him waiting in agony the whole night long.

'Please give me my usual pills and something for insomnia

—only not luminal. I want to get to sleep straight away.'

'We have nothing for insomnia,' she said in a mechanical voice.

'But *please*!' Rubin begged. 'I have to work for the Minister in the morning and I can't get to sleep.'

This reference to the Minister and the thought that Rubin would just stand here and badger her till he got it (she also had a shrewd idea that the lieutenant might shortly come back) prompted her to depart from her usual rule and give him the medicine.

She got some pills from the medicine chest and made Rubin take them here in her presence—in the prison regulations medicines were put in the same category as weapons and it was strictly forbidden to allow prisoners to handle them.

Rubin asked what time it was and, on being told it was half past three, he left the room. Crossing the yard again and looking up fondly at the lime trees bathed in reflected light from the 200- and 500-watt lamps on the perimeter, he took a deep breath of the air with its tang of snow, and bending down, he scooped up a large handful of the gleaming white floss at his feet; he rubbed his neck and face with it and filled his mouth with it.

He felt as though his soul had partaken of the freshness of the world.

CHAPTER SIXTY-EIGHT

The door from the bedroom to the dining-room was ajar and he clearly heard one loud stroke from the large clock on the wall; it took the sound some time to die away.

That meant it was half past something—Adam Roitman didn't know what—and he would have looked at his wristwatch, which was ticking away reassuringly on the bedside table, but he didn't want to disturb his wife by switching on the light. She was sleeping on her side in a remarkably graceful position with her face against his shoulder, and her breast resting in the crook of his arm.

They had been married for five years already, but even in his present half-conscious state, he felt a glow of tenderness because she was here beside him and was sleeping in her own funny way, warming her small feet, which were always cold, between his legs.

Adam had only just woken up after sleeping fitfully. He would have liked to doze off again, but he began to think of the news on the radio that evening, and then of all his troubles at work. This and much else began to run through his mind, forcing his eyes open and inducing the kind of wakefulness that makes it futile even to think of sleep.

The noise of feet shuffling and stamping, and of furniture being moved that had come all evening from the Makarygins' flat above them, had long ago ceased.

In the gap where the curtains didn't quite meet, the faint greyness of the night came through the window.

Lying flat on his back in bed, unable to sleep, Adam Roitman had none of the self-assurance and feeling of superiority given him during the day by his epaulettes of a major in the MGB and the little badge proclaiming him to be a holder of the Stalin Prize. Now, at night, he felt much the same as any other ordinary mortal, and was all too aware that the world was a cruel, overcrowded place, and not easy to live in.

That evening, while the Makarygins' party had been in full swing, Roitman had been visited by an old friend who was Jewish like himself. This friend had come without his wife, in a worried state of mind, and what he had to say was very disturbing.

It wasn't exactly new. It had all begun in the spring with an article denouncing certain theatre critics, and at first people might have thought there was nothing very sinister about the way the real Jewish names of some of the critics were added in brackets after their adopted Russian names. Then the whole business had begun to spread to the writers in general.

Next, a certain minor and very odious newspaper supposedly concerned with literature had poisonously launched a new watch-word: 'cosmopolitan'. And, hey presto, this noble word formerly used to denote the unity of the whole world, this proud title given only to the most universal geniuses, such as Dante, Goethe and Byron, suddenly became mean, crabbed and vicious, and hissed out from the pages of the newspaper in the sense of 'Yid'.

The word had then gone on its way, slithering into secret dossiers, to lurk there coyly until needed.

Scientists and technicians were also feeling the first chilling currents. During the last month or so, after years of smooth and distinguished professional advancement, Roitman had begun to feel the ground give way under him.

Perhaps his memory deceived him, but hadn't he been right in thinking that during the Revolution, and for a long time afterwards, Jews were regarded as more reliable than Russians? In those days, the authorities always probed more deeply into the antecedents of a Russian, demanding to know who his parents were and what the source of his income was before 1917. No such checks had to be made on Jews: they had all been on the side of the Revolution which delivered them from pogroms and the Pale of Settlement.

But now this. . . . Surreptitiously, hiding behind minor figures, Joseph Stalin was taking it upon himself to be the new scourge of the Israelites.

If some class of people was persecuted because they had oppressed others, or were members of a ruling élite, or held certain political views, or because of the company they kept, there was always a rational, or quasi-rational motive for their treatment. Furthermore, any member of such a group belonged to it of his own free will, and didn't have to stay in it. But what could you do about your race?

(Here Roitman thought of an objection to his own argument: people couldn't choose their social origins either, but they were also persecuted for them.)

What hurt Roitman most of all was that he longed only to be just like everybody else and to be accepted. But he wasn't wanted, he was rejected and made to feel he had no business here, that he was a 'Yid'.

Very slowly and solemnly the clock in the dining-room began to strike the hour. At the fourth stroke it was silent. Roitman had been expecting a fifth, and he was glad it was only four. He might still manage to get some sleep.

He moved slightly. His wife murmured something in her sleep and turned over on her other side, but instinctively snuggled up to him with her back. He also turned over, curling round her. Gratefully, she became still again.

Their small son was sleeping very quietly in the dining-room. He never cried or called for them during the night.

They were very proud of him because he was only three and already so clever. Even to the prisoners in the Acoustics Laboratory Roitman was always gleefully describing all the things he got up to, not understanding, with the usual insensitivity of happy people, that his stories only caused pain to men deprived of the joys of fatherhood.

The boy could already chatter away with great fluency, but his pronunciation was still unsettled—in the daytime he talked like his mother, who had the pleasant brogue of the Volga region from which she came, and in the evenings like his father, who had never rid himself of a strong Jewish accent.

If happiness comes to a man at all, its blessings often seem boundless. Love, marriage and then the birth of his son had come to Roitman together with the end of the war and his Stalin Prize. Life had been kind to him during the war as well: he had spent it far away from the front in Bashkiria, where he and his present colleagues at Mavrino had devised the first system for scrambling telephone conversations. This system now seemed very crude, but at the time they had all been awarded Stalin Prizes for it.

They had really worked hard then! But what had happened now to all their pioneering zeal? Where was the inspiration they had felt in those days?

With the insight that comes only in the darkness when you can't sleep and your eyes, not distracted by anything else, are turned inwards, Roitman suddenly understood what had been amiss during recent years. The trouble was, he realized, that he was no longer doing the work himself.

Little by little, he had ceased to do original research himself and begun, instead, to supervise the work of others.

· · ·

As though stung by the thought, he took his hand from his wife, propped his pillow up higher and lay on his back again.

How easy and insidious it was—on a Saturday evening, before going off to spend Sunday at home, already planning a pleasant day with his family, he would say to Pryanchikov:

'Perhaps tomorrow you can think about how to get rid of these non-linear distortions,' and to Rubin: 'Have a look at the article in this American journal that's just come in, and do me an abstract, will you?'

Then on the Monday morning he would come to his office, refreshed by his day off, to find lying on his desk a summary in Russian of the article in the 'Proceedings', and Pryanchikov would tell him how to overcome the latest snags they had encountered, or even report that he had already done so on Sunday.

How very convenient it was. . . .

And the prisoners didn't hold it against him at all. On the contrary, they liked him because he treated them so decently, not behaving like their jailor.

But he no longer had the feeling of doing original work; the pleasures of sudden inspiration and the disappointments of unforeseen setbacks were now equally unknown to him.

Pushing back his blanket, he sat up in bed, clasped his hands on his knees and rested his chin on them.

What in fact had he been doing these last few years? He had spent all his time intriguing, fighting to come out on top in the feuds that went on in Mavrino. He and his friends were doing their utmost to discredit and unseat Yakonov—they resented his illustrious reputation and grand manner, and feared he might land a Stalin Prize, taking all the glory for himself. Exploiting the fact that, because of his past troubles, all Yakonov's efforts to join the Party had failed, the 'young guard' used Party meetings as the forum for their attack on him. They would bring up his progress reports here and then ask him to leave, or even discuss them in his presence (only Party members had the right to vote on them), and these discussions always went against him. At moments Roitman even felt sorry for him, but he could see no other way of dealing with him.

Now everything had gone sour on them. In their campaign against Yakonov the 'young guard' had given no thought to the fact that four out of five of them were Jews, and Yakonov now never tired of repeating on every possible occasion that 'cosmopolitanism' was a direct threat to the Socialist Fatherland.

Yesterday, when the Minister had so disastrously lost his temper, one of the prisoners, Markushev, had afterwards suggested they might consider combining the scrambled and the speech clipper in one system. It was on the whole a ludicrous idea, but it could easily be held up to higher authority as a radical improvement, and Yakonov had immediately ordered the transfer of both the scrambler and Pryanchikov to Number Seven. Roitman had at once rushed over to protest in the presence of Sevastyanov, but Yakonov had said, indulgently patting Roitman on the back like a good friend who was simply a little overwrought:

'Come now, Adam! Surely you don't want the Deputy Minister here to think you are putting your personal interests above those of the Special Equipment Section?'

This was the measure of how desperate things had become. After a slap in the face like this, you daren't even cry. They grabbed you by the throat in broad daylight, and you had to pretend you liked it.

The clock now struck five—he had not heard it strike the half hour.

He no longer wanted to sleep, and by now he was tired of lying in bed.

He slipped out of bed very quickly and put his feet, one after the other, in his slippers. Tiptoeing past a chair that stood in the way, he went up to the window and drew back the silk curtains a little more.

What a lot of snow had fallen!

Right across from the building was the furthest and most neglected corner of Neskuchny Park. He could see the steep, snow-covered sides of the ravine and the fine white pine trees growing there. The window-panes were edged on the outside with fringes of fluffy snow.

But by now it had almost stopped snowing.

Another reason he had not been able to get on with his own research in recent years was that he constantly had to attend meetings and was overwhelmed with paperwork. Every Monday there was the political study group, and on Fridays he had to take a class in electronics; there were Party meetings once a week, and two or three times a month he had to go to evening meetings at the Ministry; there was always a monthly conference on security matters; he had to submit his research plan and progress report once a month, and, as if this weren't enough, he was expected to write a quarterly report on each of the prisoners—this took a whole day. Another thing was that every half hour or so during the working day some members of his staff would come up and ask him to sign an order for something from the stores—no wretched little condenser, or piece of wire or radio valve could be issued without permission from him as head of the laboratory.

If only he could be free of all this bureaucratic nonsense and intrigue! How he would have liked to sit over blueprints, handle a soldering iron again and watch the flickering pulse on the green screen of the oscilloscope. No wonder Pryanchikov could hum his boogie woogie, as though he hadn't a care in the world. What joy it was to be only thirty-one, not having to wear these grim epaulettes or worry about keeping up appearances, but feeling free to make things, and use your imagination, like a school kid.

As he said the words 'like a school kid' to himself, he remembered his own schooldays and his brain recalled, with the merciless clarity of night-time, a deeply buried incident he hadn't thought of for many years.

At the age of twelve, with a Red tie round his neck and his voice trembling with righteous indignation, he had stood up in front of all the Young Pioneers at his school, and denounced an agent of the class enemy, demanding that he be expelled from school and the Young Pioneers. Like Mitya Shtitelman and Misha Luxembourg, who had spoken before and after him, he had accused his classmate Oleg Rozhdestvensky of anti-Semitism, attendance at church and bourgeois origins. They had all three cast withering looks at the boy shaking with fear in front of them.

This was at the end of the 'twenties, when schoolchildren were intensely involved in politics. It was a southern town and about half the boys in Adam's class had been Jewish. Although they were the sons of lawyers, dentists or even small shopkeepers, they all fervently believed themselves to be proletarians.

Oleg, a pale thin boy who was top of the class, never talked about politics and had joined the Pioneers with obvious reluctance. The other boys, in their zeal, suspected he was a secret malcontent. They watched him closely, trying to catch him out. At last he played into their hands by saying: 'Everybody has the right to say anything he thinks.'

'What do you mean: "anything"?' Shtitelman had pounced on him. 'When someone calls me a "dirty Yid", is that all right too?'

Oleg would not back down and he said, stretching out his thin neck: 'Everybody should be able to *say* what he likes.'

This was quite enough to mount a case against Oleg. Two of his friends, Shurik Burikov and Shurik Vorozhbit, came forward to testify that they had seen him go to church with his mother, and that he had once come to school with a little cross round his neck. At one meeting after another twelve-year-old Robespierres got up and in front of the whole school denounced this accomplice of the anti-Semites and dealer in religious opium who, for the last two weeks had been too frightened to eat his food and had still not dared to tell his parents that he had been thrown out of the Pioneers and would soon be expelled from school.

It was not Roitman who had started this affair—he was only brought into it by the others—but even now, in the darkness, his cheeks burned with shame at the vileness of it.

Everything seemed to be closing in on him and there was no way out of his feud with Yakonov, or anything else.

If you wanted to put the world to rights, who should you begin with: yourself, or others? . . .

His head was now so heavy, and he felt so empty inside that he knew he would be able to sleep.

He went back and quietly slipped under the blanket. He must get to sleep before it struck six.

In the morning he would start making great play with their work on voice-prints. He really held a trump card here. If all went well, he might end up with his own research institute. . . .

CHAPTER SIXTY-NINE

Reveille for the prisoners in Mavrino was at seven o'clock in the morning.

But that Monday, long before the usual time, the duty warder came into the room where the workers lived and shook Spiridon by the shoulder. The janitor groaned, opened his eyes and, looking up, saw the warder by the light from the blue lamp.

'Get dressed, the lieutenant wants to see you,' the warder said quietly.

But Spiridon just lay there with his eyes wide open, not budging.

'Do you hear me? The lieutenant wants to see you.'

'What's it all about?' Spiridon asked, still not moving.

'Come on, get up,' the warder said impatiently. 'I don't know what it's about.'

'A-a-a-h.' Spiridon stretched himself, putting his hands behind his head and giving a great yawn. 'Will we ever get any peace? . . . What's the time?'

'Nearly six.'

'Nearly six! . . . All right, I'm coming.'

But he still made no move to get up.

The warder looked at him suspiciously and went out.

Only a corner of Spiridon's pillow was lit by the blue lamp—everything else was shielded from the light by the upper bunk. Spiridon lay motionless, his face partly in light and partly in shadow, with his hands behind his head.

He was sorry to have been woken up out of a dream, and was wondering how it would have ended.

He had been driving along in a cart piled with brushwood and logs. (He had hidden the logs underneath in case he should run into a forester.) The forest looked familiar and he thought he was on his way home to his village, though he couldn't say he'd ever been on this road before. But he saw every detail of it very clearly—as though he still had the use of both eyes—great gnarled roots lying across the road, a tree that had been split by lightning, a clump of young pines and the sandy soil in which the wheels of his cart sank deeply. There was a smell of approaching spring in the air, and he breathed it in greedily. He breathed like this because he was fully aware in his dream of being a prisoner who had been condemned to ten years. He realized he had escaped from prison, that he would have been missed already, and that he must get this firewood home to his wife and daughter before they sent the dogs after him.

But what had made him happiest of all in the dream was the horse. It wasn't just any old horse but the first of the many he had owned, and the one he had liked most: the light roan mare Grivna which he had bought as a three-year-old for his farm after the Civil War. She would have been grey, but the reddish-brown tinge to her coat made her into what they call a 'strawberry roan'. With this horse he had first started to get on his feet, and when he and Martha had run away to marry, he had harnessed Grivna to the cart which took them to their wedding. And now, in his dream, he was happy and surprised to find that Grivna was still alive and in such fine fettle, trotting smartly uphill and not daunted by the hard going over the sandy soil. Grivna had long sensitive grey ears, and by twitching them slightly she conveyed her thoughts to her master, telling him that she knew just what he wanted of her, and that she would not let him down. Even to show her the whip would have been an insult, and Spiridon never took it with him when he drove her.

In his dream he almost wanted to get off the cart and kiss Grivna on the nose to show his joy that she was still so young and would in all likelihood still be there when he came out of prison. But suddenly, as they were coming downhill to cross a stream, Spiridon noticed that the logs on his cart were slipping and might fall off when they forded the stream. Then, with a jolt, he was himself thrown to the ground. It was the warder waking him up.

As he now lay awake in his bunk, he thought not only of Grivna but of the dozens of other horses he had worked with (these he remembered as vividly as people) and all the thousands more he must have seen in his lifetime. He was upset to think how so many had been destroyed without rhyme or reason—starved for lack of oats and hay, worked to death or sold to the Tartars for meat. Spiridon could understand anything that had a reason, but why they had got rid of the horses was beyond him. There had been all this talk about their work being done by tractors, but in the upshot, the women had to do it.

And it wasn't only horses that had been treated like this. Spiridon remembered the time when he had himself cut down the fruit trees in people's orchards so they had no more to lose and were forced to join the collective farm.

'Spiridon!' the warder now shouted loudly from the doorway, waking up two of the others.

'All right, I'm coming, blast your eyes!' Spiridon said sharply, putting his bare feet on the floor. He stumbled over to the radiator to get the puttees he had hung there to dry.

The door closed behind the warder. The metal-worker in the bunk next to Spiridon's asked him: 'Where are you going?'

'His lordship wants me, I have to earn my keep,' he said angrily. Spiridon had never been a lie-a-bed, but in prison he didn't like to get up while it was still dark. The worst thing for a prisoner was being driven out of bed before it was light. In the labour camps of the Far North they got them up at five in the morning—so in Mavrino you had to be grateful for small mercies.

He wound the long soldier's puttees round the bottoms of his padded trousers and over the tops of his boots. Next, he climbed into his blue denims, and put on his black quilted jacket and his high fur hat with the large earflaps. Then, hitching his worn canvas belt round his waist, he set off. The warder opened the iron door for him and he went on his way, unaccompanied, through the basement corridor, where his studded boots clattered on the cement floor, and up the steps into the yard. Though he could see nothing in the semi-darkness, his feet told him straight away how many inches of snow had fallen. The blizzard must have gone on all night. He trudged over towards the staff building where a light was shining. Just as he got there the Duty Officer —the lieutenant with the moustache—came out of the door. When he had left the nurse a little while back, he had found the snow lying thickly on the ground and sent for Spiridon. Sticking both hands in his belt, he said:

'Come on, man. We need all that snow cleared away in the drive. Then make a path between here and the kitchen. After that you can see to the exercise ground. Get a move on now!'

'Get a move on yourself,' Spiridon muttered under his breath, setting off over the virgin snow to get his shovel.

'What did you say?' the lieutenant barked threateningly.

Spiridon looked back at him:

'I said *jawohl*, sir—*jawohl*!' (that's what Spiridon had always answered back to the Germans when they barked at him like this). 'Tell them in the kitchen to save some potatoes for me.'

'All right, now get on with it.'

Spiridon always behaved sensibly, careful not to get on the wrong side of his superiors, but today he was in a very bad mood because it was Monday morning, and he had to start slaving away again even before he was properly awake; he was also full of gloomy forebodings about that letter from home which would be handed to him today. All the wretchedness of his fifty years in this vale of sorrows now welled up inside and choked him.

It had stopped snowing altogether. The lime trees were dead still and white all over—not from yesterday's hoar-frost, which had gone by midday, but from the snow which had fallen in the night. By the dark sky and the stillness of the air Spiridon could tell that this snow wouldn't last long.

At first he worked sullenly, but after the first fifty shovelfuls or so he got in his stride and even cheered up a little. Spiridon was one of those people (his wife was the same) who can forget their troubles by working. So he began to feel better.

Instead of starting with the main drive, as the lieutenant had told him, he did things his own way and first cleared the pathways used by his fellow-prisoners: the one to the kitchen, the one round the exercise ground which he made three times wider than his plywood shovel. The main drive, used only by the bosses, could wait.

He was thinking about his daughter. He and his wife had already lived their lives, and his sons, even though they were behind barbed wire, were men after all—hardship never hurt a young man and could even stand him in good stead later in life. But his daughter was another matter.

Although Spiridon could see nothing with one eye and had only three-tenths of normal vision in the other, he shovelled the snow from the path all the way round the exercise ground in a perfect oval. This he did before it was light, finishing at seven, just in time for two prisoners, Potapov and Khorobrov, who now came up the steps from the basement. They were both so fond of their early morning walk that they had got up and washed before reveille.

Fresh air was rationed, and it was precious.

'I say, Spiridon, have you been up all night?' Khorobrov said, raising the collar of his shabby black overcoat which he had been wearing at the time of his arrest.

'How can you get any sleep, with these devils?' Spiridon replied. But he was no longer as angry as before. During this hour of silent work all his gloomy thought about his jailors had left him and now he felt only the peace of a man stolidly resigned to his sorrows; and without putting it in so many words, he had made up his mind that if his daughter had gone wrong in some way, he would be gentle with her when he wrote back—she would be the one to suffer, after all.

But his anxiety about his daughter—it could have been the effect of the lime trees which were still so hushed at this early hour—soon gave way to smaller concerns: he must see to those two boards which would now be buried under the snow; and he had to fix his broom—the head was coming off the handle. Meanwhile he still had to clear the main drive before the arrival of the free workers and the bosses in their cars. He swung his shovel on his shoulder and went round out of sight to the front of the building.

The spare figure of Sologdin now appeared; with his jacket thrown over his shoulders—he never seemed to feel the cold—he had come out to do his daily stint of chopping firewood. After last night's absurd quarrel with Rubin and all the insults that had been flung at him, he had slept badly for the first time in his two years here; now he needed fresh air, solitude and a chance to collect his thoughts. There was enough wood already sawn to keep him busy for quite a while.

Potapov, hobbling slightly because of an injury to his leg, was walking round slowly with Khorobrov. He was wearing the Red Army greatcoat he had been given at the time of the storming of Berlin. He had gone into the city on a tank with other soldiers taking part in the final assault (he had previously lost his officer's rank by the mere fact of having spent some time in German hands).

Khorobrov was not yet fully awake, but his alert mind was already hard at work. The words he now spoke seemed to circle pointlessly in the dark air and come back like a boomerang to lacerate Khorobrov himself: 'Remember how they used to tell us that the Ford assembly line turns workers into machines and is the most inhuman form of capitalist exploitation? But that was fifteen years ago, and under the name "continuous flow production" the assembly line is now held up as the best and most modern technique known to man! If Stalin thought it necessary to carry out a mass baptism of the Russian people, I am sure he would find a way of presenting it as a new triumph for atheist propaganda.'

Potapov always felt particularly sad in the mornings. This was the only time when he could think about his ruined life, the son growing up without him and his wife left all alone. Later in the day he was completely caught up in his work and had no time to think.

He thought there was too much pique in Khorobrov's words and that one could easily be led astray by them. He therefore continued to walk in silence, hobbling on his bad leg, and trying to breathe as deeply and evenly as he could.

They walked round and round.

More and more prisoners came out to join them—some of them walked alone, others in twos or threes. None of them, for various reasons, were anxious to be overheard and they were careful not to crowd together or pass each other without need.

Dawn was only just beginning to break. The first morning light was slow to pierce the snow clouds covering the sky. Yellow circles of light were still cast on the snow by the lamps of the perimeter.

The newly fallen snow was as soft as ever and did not crunch underfoot; it made the air seem very fresh.

The tall, erect Kondrashov (he had not yet been in a labour camp and wore a felt hat) was walking with his neighbour from the next bunk, the small, frail Gerasimovich, who was wearing a peaked cap, and scarcely came up to Kondrashov's shoulder.

Shattered by yesterday's meeting with his wife, Gerasimovich had spent the rest of the day in bed like a sick man. He had been shaken to the core by his wife's outburst and it had cost him a great effort to come outside at all this morning. Huddling up and shivering in his coat, he had wanted to go straight back inside, but seeing Kondrashov he decided to go round once with him and then he stayed for the rest of the morning walk.

'What?' Kondrashov was saying with astonishment. 'You mean to say you don't know anything about Pavel Korin?' He spoke as though every schoolboy knew about him. 'They say he's done an extraordinary painting called "The Russia that Was"—only nobody's ever seen it. Some people say it's six yards wide and other that it's twelve yards wide. And they also say . . .'

The grey light was growing stronger.

A warder came out shouting that the exercise period was over.

In the basement corridor the prisoners returning fresh from their walk couldn't help jostling the deathly pale dark-bearded Rubin who was trying to get past them. Today he had got up too late either to chop wood (which in any case was unthinkable after his quarrel with Sologdin) or to take his morning walk. He felt sluggish and leaden after his short, drugged sleep, and he craved for oxygen in a way unknown to people who can breathe as much fresh air as they want. He was now desperately anxious to get outside for a gulp of fresh air and a handful of snow to rub on his face.

But the warder, standing at the top of the steps, would not let him by.

So he stood at the bottom of the wooden steps where a a little snow had drifted in and there was a breath of fresh air. He slowly made three circular movements with his arms and breathed in deeply; then he gathered up some snow from the floor, rubbed his face with it and went back.

Spiridon, who had cleared a path for cars right up to the outside gate, now also came back into the prison. He was hungry and cheerful.

In the staff building two lieutenants—the one with the square moustache and his relief, Zhvakun—opened an envelope and together read an order left for them by Major Mishin.

Lieutenant Zhvakun was an uncouth fellow with a broad, expressionless face who during the war had served in the rank of sergeant with the military tribunal of an army division. His job had been to execute its decisions and the work had earned him promotion. He was anxious to keep his position at Mavrino, and not having a very firm grasp of the written word, he read Mishin's order twice to make sure he had it right.

At ten minutes to nine the two lieutenants went round all the rooms to make their check and, following their instructions, Zhvakun read out this announcement to the prisoners:

'Within three days all prisoners must submit to Major Mishin a list of their next of kin giving their surnames, first names and patronymics, nature of the relationship, place of work and home address.

'For the purpose of this list, next of kin are the prisoner's mother, father, legally registered wife, sons and daughters of legally registered marriages. Brothers, sisters, aunts and uncles, nephews and nieces, grandchildren and grandparents do not count as next of kin.

'From the 1st of January prisoners will be allowed to receive letters from, and to be visited only by such next of kin as are shown in their list.

'Furthermore, from the 1st of January, the prisoner's monthly letter may not exceed more than one page in length.'

This was so cruel and pitiless that none of them could at first take it in. For this reason they greeted Zhvakun's announcement neither with despair nor disgust but only with ironical jeers:

'Happy New Year.' 'You want us to inform on our relatives?' 'Why should we do your work for you?' 'What about the handwriting—how small can it be?'

As he counted heads, Zhvakun also tried to remember who had shouted what, so he could report them to the major. They always made trouble, these prisoners, whatever you did: whether it was good or bad . . .

The prisoners went off to work in a bad mood.

Even the old hands were staggered by the callousness of this new regulation. It was cruel in two ways. In the first place it meant that you had to inform on your relatives if you still wanted to keep in touch with them—many of them had managed to stay in their jobs and flats only by concealing the fact that one of their family was in prison. The second thing was the exclusion of unregistered wives and children, as well as brothers, sisters and cousins. After the war, with all the losses caused by bombing, evacuation and famine, many prisoners had been left with no other next of kin. Furthermore, since your arrest was always unexpected and you could never put your affairs in order beforehand, many of them had never managed to register their marriages with the women they considered to be their wives. And now their relationship with these women was no longer officially recognized.

Even the keenest among them felt in no mood for work. When the bell rang, they took their time, dawdling in the corridors, smoking and talking. At their work-places they continued to smoke and talk. Could it be, they wondered, that information about all their relatives was not already kept, neatly entered on cards, in the central files? The naïve and inexperienced were convinced that it was. But the old hands shook their heads knowingly, saying that the filing of data about relatives was quite haphazard—the officials concerned didn't always bother with such small fry, they could not collate all the information on the myriads of forms that came in to them, and the prisons got behind in making returns based on their records of visitors and parcels handed in. For this reason, the old hands concluded, to make up the list demanded by Mishin would be the worst trick anyone could play on his relatives.

The prisoners talked on like this, and none of them felt like working.

This was the beginning of the last week of the year, and those in charge of the research at Mavrino had been aiming to make a heroic effort to meet their commitments under the plan for 1949 (and also under the monthly plan for December), as well as to prepare estimates for the coming year, and for shorter periods in the immediate future (for the first ten days of January and for the month as a whole). The paperwork involved in all this had to be done by the administration, but the real work depended on the prisoners. Their mood today was therefore a matter of considerable importance.

The heads of the research side of Mavrino had not been informed of the devastating announcement made this morning by the prison security authorities in accordance with *their* annual plan.

No one could ever have said that the Ministry of State Security was guided by precepts derived from the Gospels. But in one respect it seemed to owe something to them: the right hand did not know what the left hand was doing.

Major Roitman, whose freshly shaven face showed no trace of the doubts that had beset him during the night, had called a meeting of all the prisoners and free workers in the Acoustics Laboratory to discuss the plans for the remainder of this year, and for the coming one. Roitman's long, intelligent face had thick, pouting lips, like a Negro's. The shoulder belt over his military tunic, which was a trifle too large for his narrow chest, looking singularly out of place. He was trying to put a bold front on things and cheer them all up, but an atmosphere of calamity already pervaded the room—there was a yawning gap in the middle where the scrambling apparatus had stood; Pryanchikov, their brightest star, was no longer with them, and Rubin was now closeted with Smolosidov on the third floor. Roitman himself, moreover, was expected to go up there to join them the moment he had finished here.

Simochka was missing too: she would not come till the evening, when she was due to stand in for someone else. This at least was some relief for Nerzhin, who would not have to make signals and write little notes to her all the time.

During the discussion of the plans, Nerzhin sat back in his well-upholstered chair, his feet resting on the lower rung of the chair in front of him. Most of the time he looked out of the window.

Outside, the wind had begun to blow from the west, evidently making the air warmer. The clouded sky was leaden and the snow had begun to pack down. This was the beginning of another nasty, depressing thaw.

Nerzhin hadn't had enough sleep, the wrinkles on his face stood out sharply in the grey light and the corners of his mouth were drooping. He had the feeling, so familiar to prisoners on a Monday morning, of scarcely having the strength to move or go on living. Through narrowed eyes he gazed vacantly at the dark fence round the prison and at the watch-tower with its guard right opposite the window.

This was what could happen if you had a visit only once a year. Yesterday he had seen his wife and thought he had told her everything of importance, but now there was this business today. When would he ever get a chance of telling her? How on earth could he write asking whether she minded him saying where she worked? After yesterday's meeting it was clear enough that she wouldn't want that. Suppose he tried to explain in a letter that they would have to write the address on the envelope, and that would mean giving her away!

But what was she going to think if he didn't write at all? After the way he had smiled at her yesterday, was he never again to give her a sign of life?

He had a feeling of being in a vice, not a metaphorical one, but one of those huge things you see on a joiner's bench with jaws and a clamp big enough to hold a man's neck—he could feel the jaws tightening and throttling him.

There was no way out. Everything was as bad as it could be.

The well-mannered, short-sighted Roitman peered with gentle eyes through his anastigmatic spectacles and spoke wearily, in a tone of entreaty rather than authority, about plans, plans, plans.

But the seed fell on stony ground.

CHAPTER SEVENTY

A similar meeting had been called in the Design Office. Free workers and prisoners were seated close together round several tables.

Although the windows of this room looked south and it was on the upper floor, the grey morning light was insufficient to work by and the lights had been switched on over several of the drawing-boards. The lieutenant-colonel in charge of the office spoke sitting down, and without much conviction, about the fulfilment of this year's plans, the tasks for the coming year and the need to distinguish themselves with feats of socialist labour. He had included in the plan, though he did not himself believe it was feasible, a promise to complete by the end of the coming year all the blueprints for the new foolproof scrambler, but he presented this item in such a way that his designers were left with some good excuses in case of failure.

Sologdin sat at the back and, bright-eyed, stared past the others at the wall. His complexion was smooth and fresh; no one could have imagined that he had anything on his mind —it looked rather as though he was using the meeting as an excuse to have a little rest.

He was, however, deep in thought. He had only a few hours, or even minutes—he wasn't sure how long—to make a vital decision, and he had to get it right. He had been thinking so hard while he chopped his wood that morning that he had not really been aware of what he was doing. The thoughts flashing disjointedly through his mind were like rays of light scattered by the facets of uncoordinated revolving mirrors in some optical instrument.

He had greeted that morning's announcement with a wry smile. He had seen it coming ages ago and had already ceased all correspondence with his family. This new measure had only confirmed him in his suspicion that things were going to get tighter all the time, and that there would be no question of being released, in the ordinary way, at the end of one's sentence.

What now upset him most of all was that, after last night's absurd argument, Rubin had somehow obtained the right to sit in judgment on him. He could strike Rubin off his list of friends and try to forget him, but it was not so easy to forget his final words. These would remain to taunt him.

The meeting ended and they all went back to their places. Larisa's chair was empty: she had the day off to make up for having worked on Sunday.

As far as Sologdin was concerned, it was just as well: she would have just been a nuisance today.

He stood up and unpinned a dirty sheet of paper from his drawing-board—underneath it was his design for the main section of the scrambler.

Resting his hand on the back of his chair, he stood looking at it for a long time.

The more he gazed at his brainchild, the calmer he felt. The revolving mirrors in his mind began to turn more slowly and in more co-ordinated fashion.

One of the draughtswomen, as always happened every week, was now going round and asking for used sheets of drawing paper which were no longer needed. It was forbidden to tear them up and throw them in the wastepaper basket— they had to be burnt outside in the yard, after a record had been made of the total number.

Sologdin took a very soft thick pencil, casually drew several lines through his diagram and then scribbled all over it.

Next he unpinned it, tore it on one side, put it between two other waste sheets, rolled them all up together and handed them to the woman, saying:

'Here you are, there are three of them.'

Then he sat down at his desk, pretended to consult a technical manual and watched out of the corner of his eye to see what would happen to his three sheets of paper.

The draughtswoman, helped by another one, was counting her haul and making a record.

Sologdin was watching to see whether one of the designers would come over and look through the sheets.

None of them did.

This was clearly a lapse on the part of the Security Officers. They thought it was enough to have these waste sheets burnt. If they had any sense they would set up a super design office where people would do nothing but sit and inspect all the drawings thrown out by the regular design office.

Sologdin had nobody to share his little joke with, so he just grinned to himself under his moustache.

Now, rolling up all the sheets and borrowing a box of matches, the two women went out of the room.

Counting the seconds by rhythmically drawing lines on a piece of paper, Sologdin knew exactly when they would reach the bottom of the stairs, put on their coats and appear in the yard.

Few people in the room could see him behind his raised drawing-board, but he had a good view of one corner of the yard where there was a smoke-blackened brazier to which Spiridon had cleared a path that morning. The snow had in any case packed down by now, and the two women had no trouble walking there in their overshoes.

For a long time they tried in vain to set fire to one of the sheets of paper. At first they lit single matches, and then, it seemed, several at a time, but either the wind put them out, or they broke, or the lighted sulphur flew on to their clothes and they frantically shook it off. By now they could have so few matches left that it looked at though they would be forced to return and borrow another box.

Time was passing and Sologdin might be summoned by Yakonov at any moment.

But then the two women shouted something, beckoned with their hands, and Spiridon came up to them in his fur hat, carrying his broom.

Not to get it singed, he took his hat off and laid it on the snow beside him. Then he thrust both hands with a sheet of paper into the brazier and stuck his head in too; after poking about a while, he pulled his head out and Sologdin saw the paper turn red and burst into flames. Spiridon now quickly began to throw the other sheets of paper on top of it. Flames shot in the air from the brazier and the whole pile began to turn to ash.

Just at this moment somebody called out Sologdin's name. The lieutenant-colonel wanted to see him. Someone had come from the Filtration Laboratory to complain that they were still waiting for a design for two small brackets they had ordered.

The lieutenant-colonel didn't like to bully people and he only said, frowning slightly:

'Listen, Sologdin, it's not really so difficult, is it? It was ordered on Thursday, you know.'

Sologdin stood at attention:

'I'm sorry. I'm just finishing them now—they'll be ready in an hour.'

He hadn't yet begun them, but it wouldn't have done to admit they were only an hour's work.

CHAPTER SEVENTY-ONE

Responsibility for security at Mavrino was divided between Mishin, who looked after the prisoners as such, and Shikin, who was concerned with them from the point of view of their work.

Belonging to different departments and receiving their pay from different sources, Mishin and Shikin did not have to compete with each other. But nor, if it came to that, did they co-operate. This was partly out of laziness, but also because their offices were on different floors of different buildings; it was forbidden to discuss security matters on the phone, and since they were of equal rank, each would have thought it below his dignity to go and see the other. Thus they worked in their separate spheres, never meeting for months on end, though in their quarterly reports they each duly stressed the need for the close co-ordination of all security work at Mavrino.

Major Shikin had once been struck by the title of an article in *Pravda*: 'The profession of his Choice'. The article was actually about a Party propagandist who liked nothing more than to go round explaining things to people—he told workers of the importance of increasing output; he impressed on soldiers how they must be ready to die for their country, and to the population at large he extolled the policies of the Party. But it was the title that had caught Shikin's eye. He was sure that he too had not missed his vocation—no

531

other profession had ever appealed to him in the slightest. He loved his work and it suited him perfectly.

After graduating from a GPU training college, Shikin had gone on to do a special course for interrogators. But he had spent little time in this branch.

He had first worked as a security officer with the transport section of the GPU and then, during the war, he had been head of a military censorship department. After the war he had served as a repatriation officer and then in a camp where returning prisoners of war were vetted and classified. Next he had helped to supervise the deportation of the Black Sea Greeks to Central Asia, after which he had finally landed up as Security Officer in Mavrino.

There was a lot to be said for the profession of Shikin's choice.

For instance, since the Civil War it was no longer dangerous. The success of all operations was ensured by the use of superior force—it was always two or three armed men against one unarmed enemy who would always be caught off his guard, and was sometimes barely awake.

Then, the work was highly paid, and they were entitled to buy in special shops reserved exclusively for their use; they had an option on good flats confiscated from enemies of the People, their pensions were higher than for the military, and the best resort hotels and sanatoria in the country were at their disposal.

Not being bound by fixed production quotas, they were scarcely overworked—though Shikin had been told by friends that in 1937 and 1945 the interrogators had toiled away like slaves. However, never having been involved in anything like this, Shikin did not really believe it.

There were times when he could quietly doze at his desk for months on end. A certain slowness went very well with this kind of work. Added to the natural slowness of a well-fed man, there was the calculated slowness intended to have its effect on a prisoner and make it easier to break him down —for instance, the very deliberate sharpening of one's pencil, the careful choice of pen and paper, the painstaking writing down of all kinds of useless formal details. This leisurely style of work was excellent for the nervous system and made for a longer life.

The routine was also much to Shikin's liking. In effect, it was almost entirely a matter of keeping careful records. For example, any interview conducted by him never just ended there: it always had as its sequel the writing of a report or denunciation, the signing of an undertaking not to make false statements, divulge state secrets, leave one's place of residence until further notice and so forth.

Patience and attention to detail—qualities natural to Shikin—were needed to keep such records in good order, and it was important to maintain a careful filing system so that any paper could be found at a moment's notice. As an officer, Shikin could not himself do the menial work of filing and he was assisted by a special girl-clerk cleared for top-secret work who came from the general prison office for this purpose. She was very tall and couldn't see very well.

But what Shikin liked most of all about his work was that it gave him a sense of power and lent him a certain aura of mystery in the eyes of others.

He was flattered by the respect, even timidity, which he inspired in his colleagues, who, though they also worked for the MGB, were not doing his kind of secret work. All of them—up to and including Colonel Yakonov—could be asked by Shikin to give an account of their activities, but Shikin was answerable to none of them. When, dark-faced under his close-cropped greying hair, and carrying his large briefcase under his arm, he went up the broad carpeted staircase to his office, and the girl lieutenants of the MGB shyly stood aside and hastened to greet him, Shikin felt with particular pride how valuable and special he was.

If Shikin had been told—though he never was—that he was an object of hatred because he maltreated people, he would have been genuinely indignant. He had never found pleasure in any form of cruelty or thought that it was an end in itself. It was true that there were such people: he had seen them on the stage and in films. But they were sadists who loved to torture people, and had lost all human feeling. In any case they were always White Guardists or Fascists. Apart from doing his duty, Shikin was concerned only to prevent people committing wrongful acts or thinking harmful thoughts.

Once, on the main staircase, which was used both by free workers and prisoners, a package containing 150 roubles had been found. It was picked up by two technicians, both of them lieutenants of the MGB, who could neither keep it to themselves nor secretly try to find the owner. The fact that two of them were involved made this impossible and they had to hand the money to Major Shikin.

The finding of money on a staircase used by prisoners (who were strictly forbidden to have any) was a major event affecting the security of the State. But Shikin decided not to make too much of it and simply put up a notice saying:

The person who has lost 150 roubles on the staircase can collect them from Major Shikin at any time.

It was a very considerable sum. But such was the healthy respect inspired by Shikin that the days and weeks passed by without anyone coming to claim the wretched money; the notice grew faded and grubby, a corner was torn off and one day somebody printed on it in blue pencil:

STUFF IT IN YOUR JUMPER YOU DIRTY DOG

The Duty Officer tore down the notice and brought it to the major. For a long time after this, Shikin prowled round the laboratories examining all the pencils and comparing the shades of blue. Shikin had been touched to the quick by this coarse remark, which was really quite unfair. It had never occurred to him to take money that didn't belong to him; his only aim had been to get the owner to come and see him so that he could make an example of him, give him hell for lack of vigilance in front of everybody else and then, naturally, return the money to him.

Even so, he couldn't very well throw it away and two months later he gave it to the gawky, wall-eyed girl who came to file his papers once a week.

Always a model family man till now Shikin, like a fool, had fallen for this filing clerk who at thirty-eight was a little faded, had thick ugly legs and was taller by a head.

He saw something in her that he had never found in anyone else and always counted the days till their next

534

meeting. He became so careless that on one occasion, when he had moved into a room next door while his office was being re-done, they had been heard and even seen by two prisoners, a joiner and a plasterer, who looked through a crack in the wall. The story had got round and among themselves the prisoners had amused themselves hugely at the expense of their good shepherd; they even wanted to write a letter to his wife, but they didn't know the address. So instead they denounced him to his superiors.

But they didn't succeed in getting rid of him. Major-General Oskolupov reprimanded Shikin not for carrying on with his secretary (this was something that reflected on her morality rather than on his) nor for doing so in working hours (Shikin was not, after all bound by a strict work quota), but for having been so careless as to let it become common knowledge among the prisoners.

On Monday the 26th of December (he had given himself Sunday off) Major Shikin came to work a little after nine o'clock—though nobody could have said anything, even if he had arrived only at midday.

On the third floor, opposite Yakonov's office, there was a kind of small lobby which was never lit, and from which two doors led off, one to Shikin's office and the other to the Party Committee room. Both doors were padded with black leather and had no signs on them. This was a very convenient arrangement for Shikin—from the corridor nobody could tell which of the two doors a person had entered.

As he approached his office today, Shikin met the Head of the Party Committee, Stepanov, a gaunt sickly man with dully gleaming spectacles. They shook hands and Stepanov said quietly:

'Comrade Shikin' (he always addressed people formally), 'come in and have a game!'

This was an invitation to play on the Party committee's small billiard table. Shikin sometimes went in for a game with him, but today he had many urgent things to see to and he shook his greying head importantly.

Stepanov sighed and went off to play by himself.

Going into his office, Shikin carefully laid his briefcase on his desk. (All the documents handled by Shikin were

535

secret or top secret and had to be kept in the safe. But since people were less impressed if you went around without a briefcase, he used it to take home office copies of magazines like *Krokodil*—though it would have cost him very little to subscribe to them himself.) He walked along a strip of carpet up to the window, stood there for a moment and went back to the door. His cares seemed to be lying in ambush for him, lurking behind the safe, the cupboard and the sofa—they all seemed to crowd round him now and demand attention.

The things he had to do! . . .

He stroked the top of his short-cropped greying head with the palms of his hands. His first job was to see how his important new scheme was going. The fruit of many months' work, it had at last been formally approved by Yakonov, and explained to the people in the laboratories, but it was not yet in operation. Briefly, it was a new system of keeping a check on the results of research in progress.

After a very thorough study of the security arrangements at Mavrino, Major Shikin had found (and he was very proud of his discovery) that they were by no means foolproof. It was true that fifty safes, each as high as a man, had been requisitioned in Germany, and that each room in Mavrino was equipped with one. Under the supervision of some responsible person, all documents that were secret, or in any way confidential, were locked away during lunch and dinner and overnight, but the fatal weakness here was that only completed work or work in progress was handled like this. Nobody bothered about the rough drafts and notes embodying the first flashes of inspiration and hunches which would eventually grow into next year's research projects—that is, the most promising long-range ideas. It only needed a clever spy who knew something about science to get through the barbed wire into the prison compound, ferret around in a dustbin until he found a piece of blotting paper with some diagrams scribbled on it, and the American intelligence service would be apprised of the whole direction our work was taking.

In his usual conscientious way Shikin had once made Spiridon turn out in his presence all the contents of a dustbin in the yard. He had found two damp pieces of paper stuck together with snow and ashes, on which some diagrams had once clearly been drawn. Shikin had not hesitated to pick up this filthy piece of refuse and deposit it in front of Yakonov on his desk. Yakonov didn't know where to look!

After this there was no more trouble about accepting Shikin's proposal for the introduction of a system of individual work-books. Suitable books had immediately been obtained from the MGB stationery stores; they each contained 200 large pages numbered in sequence, and were to be distributed to everyone except the fitters, lathe operators and the handy-man. Henceforth no one would be allowed to write on anything except the pages of his personal book. Apart from eliminating the danger of drafts scribbled on loose sheets of paper, this innovation was important in another way: it would now be possible to keep a check on the development of people's ideas. Since the date had to be recorded in the workbook every day, Major Shikin would be able to follow the progress of every prisoner—how much he had done on Wednesday and what new thoughts he might have had on Friday. Each of these 250 work-books would be a kind of extension of himself—every prisoner would have a Shikin looking over his shoulder. Cunning and lazy as they were, the prisoners were always trying to shirk whenever they possibly could. Just as the output of workers was checked, it would now be possible, thanks to Major Shikin's inventive mind, to keep tabs on the research of engineers and scientists. (What a pity that Stalin Prizes were never given to Security Officers!)

His first task today was to see whether the books had been distributed and to make sure people had written their names in them.

Another matter Shikin had to attend to today was the completion of the list of prisoners due to be sent back to the camps, and he must find out exactly when transport would be available.

Shikin was also much pre-occupied by a case which he had mounted in grand style, but which was making little progress. This was the case of a lathe which had been damaged while ten prisoners were hauling it from the Number Three laboratory to the machine-tool workshops. His investigation had now been going on for a week and eighty pages of evidence

537

had been taken, but he still could not get at the truth—the prisoners concerned were not new to this kind of thing.

Finally he had to look into the source of a novel by Dickens which, according to a report from Doronin, was being read in the semi circular room, in particular by Adamson. It would be a sheer waste of time to question Adamson —he had already been sentenced to a second term and hence had nothing more to lose. He would have to call in the free workers with whom Adamson had dealings and scare them out of their wits by saying everything was known.

Yes, he really had so much to do—not to mention what his informers might have to tell him.

(He didn't know, for instance, that he would also have to investigate a slanderous skit on Soviet legal procedure which had taken the form of a mock trial of Prince Igor.)

Despairingly, Shikin rubbed his temples and forehead, hoping all these worries would somehow sort themselves out and settle down. While he wondered what to do first, he decided to 'go out among the masses', that is, walk down the corridor in the hope of meeting one of his informers who might indicate by a slight movement of the eyebrows that he had some urgent report which could not wait until his next scheduled visit.

But when he reached the desk of the Duty Officer for his floor, he heard him talking on the telephone about some 'new group'.

What on earth was this? Was it possible for a new group to have been set up on Sunday, in Shikin's absence?

The Duty Officer told him the whole story.

This was appalling! The Deputy Minister and some generals had come to the prison, and Shikin hadn't been there to receive them! He was furious. He had lost a chance of showing the Minister how vigilant he was—he could have warned him against that double-dealer Rubin who should never have been put on such an important project; he could have advised the Deputy Minister that the man was completely deceitful—he talked about his belief in the victory of communism but refused to supply information to the Security Officer! And the brazen way he flaunted that beard, the scoundrel! Who did he think he was—Vasco da Gama? He would make him shave it off.

Shikin set off slowly but purposefully, stepping carefully in his schoolboy shoes, towards Room 21. Actually he would soon fix Rubin. The other day Rubin had handed in a petition to the Supreme Court requesting a review of his case (he did this twice a year). It was up to Shikin to decide whether to send it on with a recommendation or, as on previous occasions, with a damning comment.

The door of Room 21 had no glass panels in it. Shikin gave it a shove, but it was locked. Then he knocked. He heard no movement inside, but all at once the door opened slightly and Smolosidov, with his swarthy face and sinister black forelock, looked out. Seeing Shikin, he stood quite still and didn't open the door any wider.

'Good morning,' Shikin ventured, not used to this kind of reception.

Smolosidov was a cut above Shikin in the 'profession of his choice'. With his bent arms drawn slightly back, hunched slightly like a boxer, he just stood there silently.

'I wonder . . . could I . . .' Shikin floundered, 'come in and introduce myself to your group?'

Smolosidov stepped back half a pace and, continuing to block the way into the room, beckoned to Shikin. Shikin squeezed round the door and looked up where Smolosidov was pointing. On the inside of the door there was a notice saying:

LIST OF PERSONS WHO MAY BE ADMITTED TO ROOM 21

1. Sevastyanov, Deputy Minister of the MGB.
2. Major General Bulbanyuk, Section Chief.
3. Major General Oskolupov, Section Chief.
4. Major Roitman, Engineer in charge of group.
5. Lieutenant Smolosidov.
6. Rubin, prisoner.

Signed: Minister of State Security
Abakumov.

Awe-struck, Shikin retreated into the corridor.

'Could I please . . . see Rubin . . .?' he asked in a whisper.

'No,' Smolosidov replied, also in a whisper.

And he locked the door.

CHAPTER SEVENTY-TWO

At one time the Trade Union organization had meant a great deal in the life of the free workers at Mavrino. But this had come to the ears of a certain very high-ranking comrade (so high-ranking that people hesitated to address him as 'Comrade'), and he had said: 'What do you mean by this? Don't you know that Mavrino is a military establishment? What are they doing with a Trade Union? You should watch your step.' (He never spoiled his underlings by addressing them as 'comrades'.)

The same day the Trade Union branch in Mavrino was closed down.

But Mavrino survived this blow.

The importance of its Party branch, which had always been considerable, now grew immensely, and the Party organization of the Moscow region decided that the Mavrino Party Committee needed a full-time secretary. After looking through a few files submitted by their personnel department, the Bureau of the Regional Party Committee picked their man for the job. His basic data were as follows:

Stepanov (Boris Sergeyevich)—born in 1900, in the village of Lupachi in the Bobrov district; son of poor peasants; served as village militiaman after the Revolution; no professional training; social status: white-collar worker; education: four classes of elementary school and two years in Party school; member of Party since 1921 and engaged in Party work since 1923; no deviations from Party line and no dealings with opposition; no contact with White Army or White Guardist organizations; never engaged in Revolutionary or partisan movements; no residence on German-occupied territory or visits abroad; no knowledge of foreign languages or non-Russian languages of the USSR; has suffered from concussion; awarded order of Red Star and medal 'In commemoration of victory over Germany in Great Patriotic War'.

At the moment when Stepanov was recommended for this

new task he was out in Volokolamsk doing Party propaganda among the peasants who were bringing in the harvest. Whenever the collective farmers had a moment's rest—if they stopped to eat or smoke—he at once called them together and lectured them on the importance of sowing their crops every year and of using only the very best seed, on the desirability of growing more grain than had been sown as seed, and then of harvesting it without loss or pilfering, and delivering it to the State as quickly as possible. Never resting for a moment, he then went and explained to the tractor drivers the need to economize on petrol, to take good care of their equipment and never to let it stand idle; if pressed, he also answered their questions about the poor quality of repairs and the failure to issue them with working clothes.

A general meeting of the Mavrino Party organization warmly accepted the recommendation of the Regional Committee and unanimously elected Stepanov, before they had even set eyes on him, as their full-time secretary. Stepanov was replaced in Volokolamsk by a former official of a co-operative who had been dismissed for negligence. In Mavrino a room was prepared for him next to the Security Officer's, and he took up his duties.

His first act was to take over from his predecessor. Lieutenant Klykachov, who had only been a part-time secretary. The lieutenant was very thin—probably because he was so restless and versatile. Apart from supervising the Decoding Laboratory and the work of research groups concerned with cryptography and statistics, he also conducted a Komsomol study group and contrived to be the leading light of the 'young guard'. Although his superiors thought him exacting and his subordinates regarded him as a busybody, the new Secretary at once suspected that Party affairs in Mavrino must have been very neglected.

So it proved to be.

It took the lieutenant a whole week to hand over to Stepanov. Scarcely leaving the office, Stepanov studied every single document, getting to know each Party member from his file and photograph before making his acquaintance in the flesh. The hand of the new Secretary lay heavy on the lieutenant.

One after the other grave omissions came to light. Apart

from gaps in personal records and the absence of detailed reports on each individual member and candidate member, there had been a basically unsound approach to all the Committee's activities—they had never been properly recorded on paper and thus assumed a rather shadowy quality.

'Who will ever believe it?' Stepanov intoned, holding his hand over his head with a lighted cigarette. 'Who will ever believe you when you say all these things were done?'

He politely explained that all the initiatives mentioned by the lieutenant existed only '*on paper*' (which was his way of saying that he had only the lieutenant's word for them) instead of '*in reality*' (by which he meant: duly entered in the records).

For example: it might be true that some people at Mavrino (not prisoners, of course) had formed a team to play volley-ball during their lunch break, even encroaching on their working time to do so. Very likely they did. But that wasn't the point. The point was that nobody was going to keep a constant check to make sure the ball really bounced back and forth. Why hadn't the volley-ball players been encouraged, after the team had been in existence for a while, to put up something about their achievements on the prison notice board? The lieutenant could later have removed and filed this notice in his records for future reference. There could then never be the slightest doubt in the mind of any inspector that volley-ball had actually been played, and that this activity had proceeded under the guidance of the Party. But as things stood, who was going to take it all on trust?

This was true of everything else as well.

'Words are not words until they are filed'—with this profound remark Stepanov took over the reins of office.

Just as a catholic priest might never be able to believe that anyone could lie in confession, it never occurred to Stepanov that statements officially recorded on paper could be anything less than the truth.

The lieutenant, however, did not argue with Stepanov. Constantly nodding his narrow head on its long slender neck, he put on a look of infinite gratitude, appearing to listen and learn, and agreeing with every word that Stepanov said. Stepanov soon warmed to the lieutenant. He listened attentively as the lieutenant expressed his concern that such an important secret establishment as Mavrino was headed by a man like Colonel Yakonov, whose file showed not only that he had a dubious background but had been, not to put too fine a point on it, an outright enemy. Stepanov shared his extreme apprehension.

Virtually appointing Klykachov his right-hand man, Stepanov told him to drop in whenever he liked and from then on often gave him the benefit of his wisdom.

Klykachov very soon came to know the new Party Secretary better than anyone, and it was he who maliciously dubbed him 'the Pastor'.

Thanks to Klykachov the 'young guard' soon got on quite good terms with the Pastor, as they called him behind his back. They were quick to see the advantages of a Party secretary who was not openly one of their number, but gave the appearance of being impartial.

Stepanov was a great stickler for the law. If you said you were sorry for someone and hoped they would be treated leniently a look of pain would come over his face, and wrinkling his brow—which, because of a receding hair line, looked higher than it was—he hunched his shoulders as though a new burden had fallen on them. But he would pull himself together and speak out against the heretics with passionate conviction. The white reflections of window panes danced in his glasses as he said:

'Comrades, comrades, what's this I hear? How can you say such things? You must always uphold the law. Just remember that. Whatever your own feelings, always uphold the law. This is the only way to help the person for whose sake you might be tempted to bypass it. Always bear in mind that the law is there to serve society and the individual. We frequently fail to recognize this and try, in our blindness, to get round it.'

For his part, Stepanov was pleased that the 'young guard' were so keen on Party meetings as a forum for criticism. He saw in them the core of that 'healthy collective' which he always tried to create at every new place of work. If people did not come forward to denounce the lawbreakers in their midst, if they were silent at meetings, Stepanov rightly considered the situation to be 'unhealthy'. In the eyes of Stepanov (and in the eyes of people higher than he) a collective was healthy only if it was prepared to come down hard on those of its own members who deserved it.

Stepanov had many such firm beliefs which it was now impossible for him to abandon. For instance, in his view no Party meeting was complete unless it ended with the adoption of a thunderous resolution castigating certain individual members of the collective and calling for new feats of labour. He had a particular fondness for 'open' Party meetings, since they were also attended by non-members of the Party, who could be torn to shreds, without being allowed to vote or answer back. Before the resolution was voted, people sometimes asked indignantly:

'What's this supposed to be—a Party meeting or a trial?'

'Just a moment, comrades, just a moment!' Stepanov would splutter. Hastily putting a pill into his mouth with a trembling hand (after his concussion he suffered from fearful headaches if he got excited—this always happened when he felt the truth was at stake) he would stand in the middle of the room so that the large beads of sweat on his balding head could be seen in the glare from the ceiling lights:

'So you are against criticism and self-criticism, are you?' and shaking his fist at the audience, dinning his words into their heads, he went on to explain: 'Self-criticism is the highest motive force of our society, the main stimulus to progress! It is time to understand that when we criticize members of our collective, it is not to put them on trial but to keep everybody on the alert! About this there can be no two opinions, comrades! Of course, there is criticism and criticism. What we need is *helpful* criticism, not criticism of trusted Party members in positions of authority! We must not confuse freedom to criticize with petty bourgeois anarchism!' And going to where the jug of water stood, he swallowed another pill.

The upshot was always the same: the whole healthy collective, including those denounced in it for 'criminal negligence' or 'delay bordering on sabotage', unanimously voted for the resolution.

Stepanov liked the resolutions to be carefully drafted in great detail. He always knew in advance what the sense of the meeting would be, but he was sometimes too busy to write the resolution out in full beforehand. Whenever this happened, after the chairman of the meeting had called on him to read out the draft of the resolution, Stepanov would wipe the sweat from his forehead and say:

'Comrades! I have been very busy and have not had time to supply certain details, names and facts in my draft of the resolution,' or: 'Comrades! I had to go to a committee meeting and I haven't been able to draft the text of our resolution today.' In either event, he would go on to conclude: 'I therefore call on you to pass the resolution in general outline and tomorrow, when I have more time, I will fill in the details.'

The Mavrino collective was so healthy that it passed such resolutions without a murmur, not knowing (and never finding out) on whom it had pronounced its strictures and on whom it had showered its praise.

The position of the new Secretary was much strengthened by the fact that he had no time for intimate personal relationships. Everybody respectfully referred to him by his name and patronymic. Taking this to be his due, he never returned the compliment, and even in the excitement of a game of billiards in the Party office he would shout: 'Try for a corner shot, Comrade Shikin!' (or 'Comrade Klykachov').

Stepanov did not like attempts to appeal to his better nature, and never himself made any such appeals to others. If, therefore, he sensed dissatisfaction with his proposals, or resistance to them, he did not make speeches or argue, but took a large blank sheet of paper, wrote in capitals at the top: 'The Comrades listed below are requested to . . .' and gave the details of what he wanted them to do and the date by which he expected them to do it. Underneath he listed their names in order, with a space for their signatures. He then instructed his secretary to take it round to the comrades concerned who, however much they might fume over this blank, impersonal sheet of paper, had no choice but to sign, and then to do whatever it was.

Doubt or hesitation was unknown to Stepanov. When it was announced on the radio that Yugoslavia was no longer a land of heroes but the home of the Tito clique, he at once explained this change of line with the earnest conviction of one who had himself been contemplating it for many years. If anyone timidly called his intention to a contradiction between yesterday's instructions and today's, to faults in the organization of supplies for Mavrino, to the poor quality of some item of Soviet-made equipment or to difficulties over housing, the Secretary would smile and his eyes would light up behind his glasses:

'Well, it can't be helped, comrades. There must have been a muddle somewhere. But even here we are making progress, you must admit!'

However, even Stepanov was human and had his little foibles. For instance, he liked to be praised by his superiors and he was very flattered when ordinary Party members expressed admiration for his wide experience of Party work. He was pleased by what he felt to be well-deserved compliments.

He also drank vodka—but only if someone treated him, or it was put on the table at mealtimes, and he always complained how bad it was for his health. This was why he never bought any himself and never treated anyone else in return.

These were probably his only faults.

'The young guard' often argued among themselves about the Pastor. Roitman said:

'He is a genie out of an inkwell with the soul of a printed form. People of this sort are inevitable in periods of transition.'

But Klykachov laughed at them:

'Don't you fool yourselves. If any of us fall foul of him he'll grind us in the dirt. He's not as stupid as he looks. He's learnt a thing or two in his fifty years. These resolutions denouncing people—you don't think he brings them in just for fun, do you? No, it's his way of keeping a record of everything that happens here. He's gathering material for any eventuality. If ever there's any investigation he can always show that he had always given good warning about everything well in advance.'

Speaking from better knowledge than the others, Klykachov made Stepanov out to be a sly, underhand schemer whose main concern was to ensure a good future for his three sons. For this he would stop at nothing.

Stepanov indeed had three sons who were always asking him for money. He had sent all three to the university to study history. In theory it was a sound thing to do, but he had failed to reckon with a vast over-production of history teachers. There was no more room for them in any of the schools, technical colleges and training courses in either Moscow or the Moscow region. Before long there were no openings for historians anywhere this side of the Urals. When the first son graduated he was not able to stay in Moscow and support his parents, but had to go right out to Khanty-Mansiisk in Siberia. The second son was being offered a post on the borders of Outer Mongolia, and when the third was qualified he would be very lucky to get anything nearer home than the island of Borneo. Their father was all the more intent on keeping his job, his small house on the outskirts of Moscow and the tiny vegetable garden, which kept him going in sauerkraut and provided enough for the upkeep of two or three pigs. To his wife, a level-headed woman, (though perhaps rather backward politically), pig-keeping was the most important thing in life and a welcome addition to the family budget. That Sunday she had insisted on her husband going to the country with her to buy a new piglet. It was only this expedition—a successful one as it turned out—that had kept him away from work the day before. But he had been so distressed by a certain event on Saturday that all the time he could hardly wait to get back to Mavrino.

He had really had a very nasty shock on the Saturday. It had happened during a conversation with a highly placed official in the Political Section of the Ministry. This official, who despite his heavy responsibilities had a very ample figure, weighing perhaps fifteen stone, looked at the lean, bespectacled Stepanov and asked in a lazy, mellow voice:

'Tell me, Stepanov, what's happening about your Hebrews?'

'About my what?' Stepanov asked, straining to hear properly the second time.

'Your Hebrews,' but seeing the blank look on Stepanov's face, he explained: 'Your Yids, I mean.'

Quite taken off his guard and fearing to repeat this tricky word, the use of which had until recently been punishable by ten years' imprisonment, Stepanov mumbled vaguely:

'Er, yes, we have a few . . .'

'I know, but what are you doing about them?'

But at this moment the phone rang, the official lifted the receiver and never got back to his conversation with Stepanov.

Feeling quite at sea, Stepanov had re-read a great pile of Party directives, circulars and instructions, but they were all insidiously reticent on the Jewish question.

The whole Sunday, as they were going out to buy the piglet, he racked his brain and clutched at his breast in desperation. He must be getting rather slow on the uptake in his old age! But how could he have known? During all his years of Party work he had always taken it for granted that the Jewish comrades were particularly devoted. What a disgrace that a Party worker of his experience had failed to notice the beginning of an important new drive and even found himself indirectly implicated in a subversive intrigue through his connection with this Roitman-Klykachov group.

* * *

Now, on Monday morning, Stepanov had arrived at work in a state of perplexity. After Shikin had declined to play billiards (he had hoped to find something out from him), unnerved by his lack of instructions, Stepanov locked himself in the Party office and for two solid hours frantically knocked the billiard balls round the table, and sometimes on to the floor. The huge medallion on the wall was a silent witness to several brilliant strokes by which two or three balls were sunk in the pockets with a single shot. But the imitation bronze profiles of Marx, Engels, Lenin and Stalin offered no advice as to what he should do to save his 'healthy collective', let alone consolidate it, in these new circumstances.

At last, when he was quite exhausted, the telephone rang and he ran to pick up the receiver.

The voice at the other end said that a car was already on its way to Mavrino with two comrades who would brief him on a new phase in the struggle against alien influences.

His mood was transformed; with a flourish he drove two balls into a pocket and then removed all evidence of his game.

His mood was further improved by the sudden recollection of how well their new pink-eared piglet had eaten its mash yesterday evening and this morning. There was every hope of being able to fatten it up very nicely at little expense.

CHAPTER SEVENTY-THREE

Major Shikin was sitting in Colonel Yakonov's office.

They were talking amicably, as equals, though they actually despised and hated each other.

At meetings Yakonov liked to use the phrase 'We of the Service . . .'. But in Shikin's eyes he was still an enemy of the people who in earlier days had travelled abroad and been imprisoned as a result. True, he had been released and even taken on by the Ministry of State Security. But this did not mean he was innocent! The day would come when Yakonov would be exposed for what he was and arrested again. It would then give Shikin the greatest pleasure to be able to strip off his epaulettes. The earnest major with his short body and large head was irked by the colonel's condescending manner, the lordly self-assurance with which he bore the burdens of his office. Shikin therefore always tried to emphasize his own importance and that of security work—never given its due by the colonel.

He was now suggesting that at the next meeting in the Ministry of security matters, Yakonov should report on the state of affairs at Mavrino and ruthlessly expose all the shortcomings. At the same time he could raise the question of weeding out the work-shy prisoners, and also the question of introducing the new work-books.

Yakonov, though he had dark circles under his eyes and felt wretched after his seizure, was as bland and round-faced as ever and he nodded attentively as he listened to the major. But deep down behind all the walls and ramparts of his mind —where no one, except perhaps his wife, knew what was going on—he was thinking to himself what a repulsive little louse he was, this Major Shikin who had gone grey poring over secret denunciations. Everything he did was idiotic and all his proposals were sheer cretinism.

Yakonov had been given just one month, and not a day more. At the end of that time his head might fall. If only he could throw off the shackles of high office and sit down himself at a drawing-board, and find time to think.

But the very fact that he was sitting in this enormous leather chair had its own dialectic: though responsible for everything he could not personally get to grips with it, only talk on the telephone and sign documents.

Then there was this running battle with Roitman's group which took so much out of him. Petty as it was, he was compelled to go on with it. He was in no position to throw them out of Mavrino, and his only aim was to force them into submission. Their aim, on the other hand, was to get rid of him and they were capable of destroying him.

Shikin was still talking. Yakonov was gazing at a point just to one side of him. In a physical sense, his eyes were open, but they might have been closed—in spirit he was no longer present in the office but had fled to his home, leaving behind only his flabby body dressed in its military tunic.

'My home is my castle!' How wise of the English to have discovered this principle. On your tiny territory you live only by your own laws. You are protected by four walls and a roof from the outside world where you are always under pressure, for ever being pushed around and pestered.

When you come home, you are met at your own front door by your wife, her eyes attentive and shining softly. And then there are your children—so funny and always springing surprises (if they don't yet go to school—so much the better). They amuse and refresh you, when you come in tired of being badgered and hounded. They chatter away in English which they have been taught by your wife. She sits down at the piano and plays a charming waltz by Waldteufel. It may be very short, this time spent with your family during the lunch break and then late at night, but at least you are safe from pompous jacks-in-office and vicious young men who are out to get you.

Yakonov's work involved so much torment, humiliation, inhuman strain and administrative wrangling, that he would gladly have given it up, if only he could; apart from anything else, he was feeling his years and would have liked to keep to the cosy little world of his own home.

This was not to say the outside world didn't interest him —it did, very much. Had there ever been a more absorbing period in world history than the present? For him, international politics was like chess, with hundreds of games going on simultaneously. But he had no wish to take part as a player or, worse still, as a pawn. He just wanted to observe and relish the spectacle, wearing his dressing-gown and sitting in his old rocking-chair among his books.

He was well equipped to sit back and watch the world go by. He knew two foreign languages and could listen to all the news he wanted from abroad. The Ministry distributed Western technical and military periodicals, immediately on receipt, to all the secret research establishments under its control. These publications often had something on politics —the coming global war or the political future of the world. Then, as one who moved in higher circles, Yakonov was always hearing things not reported in the press. Nor did he turn his nose up at books on diplomacy and espionage translated from foreign languages. And besides all this, he had a head on his shoulders and his own well-developed philosophy. His idea of playing chess was simply to follow the match between East and West, trying to guess the future moves.

Whose side was he on? When things were going well at work he was, of course, for the East. But if things were going badly and he was having trouble, he rather tended to the side of the West. Beyond this, however, it was his belief that victory went to those who were strongest and most ruthless. This, alas, was what history was about.

As a young man he had picked up and made his own the current saying: 'People are swine.' The longer he lived, the more this was borne out. And the more he allowed himself to be guided by it, the truer he found it and the easier it was to live. If all people were swine, it followed that you should never work for others, only for yourself. It also meant that there was no point in making sacrifices 'for the common good' and nobody had the right to expect it. It was all beautifully summed up in the saying 'charity begins at home'.

It was therefore wrong of the guardians of political morality to worry about his past. Brooding on the lesson of his own experience, Yakonov had understood that people only went to prison as a result of some miscalculation. Anyone with brains would see the danger coming, wriggle out of it and always manage to stay free. What was the point of a life spent behind bars? If Yakonov had completely turned his back on the prisoners, it was not just for appearance's sake, but because he really felt it. No other work would have brought him seven thousand roubles a month and provided him with four large rooms and a balcony—or at least he wouldn't have had all this so quickly. He had been wronged, and his treatment was often stupid and always cruel—but this was the nature of power, this was how it showed itself.

As Yakonov was thinking these thoughts, Shikin suddenly handed him a list of the prisoners who were due to be transferred back to labour camps the next day. There were sixteen already agreed upon, and Shikin was now happy to add the names of two more who had been noted by Yakonov in his desk diary. But the figure they had agreed on with the Ministry had been twenty, so they would urgently have to 'fill in' by finding two more and give their names to Lieutenant-Colonel Klimentyev by five o'clock at the latest.

But no suitable candidate sprang to mind. The trouble was that the Security Officer always wanted to get rid of the best workers—they were unreliable from his point of view—and keep the idlers and good-for-nothings. This made it difficult for Yakonov and Shikin to agree on who should be sent back to the camps.

Yakonov said:

'Leave the list with me. Let's both give it a little more thought and phone each other later.'

Shikin slowly got up and—he shouldn't have done it, but he couldn't help himself—complained to this unworthy person about the action of the Minister in admitting Rubin and Roitman to Room 21, but denying entrance to both of them—Shikin and Yakonov. Fancy doing this to them on their own premises!

Yakonov raised his brows and at the same time lowered his eyelids completely—for one moment he looked like a blind man who seemed to be saying in dumb show: 'Yes, Major, I am very, very pained, but the light of the sun is too strong for my humble eyes.'

In fact, Yakonov was secretly glad. This new project

552

in Room 21 was a tricky business. Roitman was a hot-head and it might be his undoing.

Shikin left and Yakonov's mind again turned to the most pleasant of the day's business, something he hadn't got round to the day before.

If he could really get ahead with the foolproof scrambler, he would be safe from Abakumov's wrath in a month's time. He rang the drawing office and told them to send Sologdin along with his new design.

A couple of minutes later there was a knock at the door and in came the tall, slender Sologdin with his curly little beard. He was wearing his grubby denims, and he had nothing in his hands.

Yakonov had scarcely even spoken to him before: he never had any need to call Sologdin to his office and whenever he saw him in the drawing office or walking past in the corridor he had no reason to take notice of such a lowly person. But now, squinting down at the list of names and patronymics under the glass on his desk, he looked approvingly at Sologdin with all the cordiality of a hospitable grandee, and said with a broad gesture:

'Do sit down, Dmitry Alexandrovich. I am very pleased to see you.'

Holding his arms stiffly at his side Sologdin came up, bowed silently and remained standing very still and erect.

'So you have been preparing a little surprise for us, have you?' Yakonov purred. 'The other day, Saturday I think, I saw your design for the main section of a foolproof scrambler. . . . Why don't you sit down? . . . I only had a quick look at it and I am most anxious to talk about it in greater detail.'

Sologdin did not flinch under Yakonov's kindly gaze and just stood there, not moving a muscle. Like a dueller waiting for his opponent's shot, he had turned his head slightly and he answered very clearly:

'You are mistaken, Anton Nikolayevich. It is true that I worked on the scrambler to the best of my ability but the result, which you saw, was woefully inadequate, a poor product of my very indifferent skills.'

Yakonov threw himself back in his chair and protested amiably:

'Come, come, my dear fellow! None of your false modesty!

553

I only had a brief glimpse of what you'd done, but I formed a very good impression indeed. And Professor Chelnov, who is a better judge than either of us, was full of praise. I am now going to ask that we shouldn't be disturbed, so bring your drawing and gather your thoughts and we'll go into it all very carefully. Would you like me to call Professor Chelnov as well?'

Yakonov was not just a thick-skinned administrator concerned only with results and output. He was also an engineer whose mind had once teemed with bold ideas and he now looked forward to the subtle pleasure of talking about a project which had involved so much thought and energy. This was the only kind of pleasure he still got from his work. All agog, he smiled entreatingly at Sologdin.

Sologdin was also an engineer, and had been for fourteen years. But for twelve he had been a prisoner.

His throat felt very dry and he had difficulty in getting out his words:

'All the same, Anton Nikolayevich, you are quite mistaken. That was a rough sketch unworthy of your notice.'

Yakonov frowned and said, beginning to lose patience: 'Very well, very well, just let's have a look at it.'

On Yakonov's epaulettes, which were gold with blue edging, there were three stars—three large gold stars in the form of a triangle. Sologdin suddenly thought of Lieutenant Kamyshan, the Security Officer at the prison in the cave. One day, during those months when he had regularly beaten Sologdin, he had appeared wearing three golden stars, only slightly smaller than Yakonov's, in place of his lieutenant's epaulettes.

'The drawing you saw no longer exists,' said Sologdin, and his voice trembled. 'I found that it contained some hopeless flaws and I . . . burnt it.'

The colonel went pale. One could hear his laboured breathing in the ominous silence. Sologdin held his breath.

'How? With your own hands?'

'No, of course not. I handed it in as waste in the usual way.' His voice was hollow and faint—there was no trace of his habitual self-assurance.

'But perhaps it wasn't burnt?' Yakonov moved forward in his chair, looking hopeful.

'It was. I was watching at the window,' came Sologdin's crushing reply.

Gripping the arm of his chair with one hand and seizing a marble paperweight with the other, as though he was going to smash it on Sologdin's skull, the colonel heaved up his large body and leaned over across the table.

With his head thrown back slightly, Sologdin continued to stand there like a blue statue.

Between the two engineers there was no further questions or explanations. An electric current passed between them, locking them together with a charge of unbearable tension.

'I'll destroy you,' threatened the colonel's bloodshot eyes.

'Slap on a third sentence, you swine,' Sologdin's eyes screamed back.

It seemed the tension could only be discharged by a crack of thunder.

But Yakonov, putting his hand over his forehead and eyes, as though blinded by the light, turned away and walked to the window.

Gripping the back of a nearby chair Sologdin, at the limit of his endurance, lowered his eyes.

'A month, one wretched little month and then I'm sunk,' thought Yakonov with fearful clarity.

'I would never survive a third sentence,' Sologdin thought numbly.

Yakonov turned round to face him again.

'How could you? Aren't you an engineer?' was the question in his eyes.

The reply in Sologdin's was blinding:

'Weren't you once a prisoner? You've forgotten what it's like.'

They looked in hatred and fascination at one another, each seeing himself as he might have been. Neither could look away and break the current that passed between them.

Yakonov might now have begun to shout, bang his fist on the table and threaten—Sologdin had prepared for this eventuality too.

But Yakonov took out a clean white handkerchief, mopped his forehead with it and looked closely at Sologdin.

Sologdin continued to stand his ground, still trying not to flinch.

Yakonov rested one hand on the window-sill and with the other he beckoned Sologdin over to him.

Sologdin took three firm steps forward.

Hunching his shoulders a little like an old man Yakonov asked him:

'Sologdin, are you from Moscow?'

'Yes,' Sologdin said, not lowering his eyes.

'Well look over there,' Yakonov continued. 'Do you see that bus stop on the main road?'

It was very clearly visible from the window and Sologdin looked out at it.

'It's half an hour's ride from here to the centre of Moscow,' Yakonov said softly.

Sologdin turned round to look at him again.

Suddenly Yakonov, as though he were falling forward, put his two hands on Sologdin's shoulders.

'Sologdin!' he said in a strained voice, 'in June or July this year you might have been able to get on that bus. But you didn't want it that way. In August you might have been given leave and you could have gone down to the Black Sea. How long is it since you've been in the water, Sologdin? It never happens to prisoners, does it?'

'I wouldn't say that. It does in the lumber camps,' Sologdin contradicted him.

'Fine bathing that is,' said Yakonov, his hands still on Sologdin's shoulders. 'But where you're going, Sologdin, the rivers never thaw. . . . Listen, I don't believe there is any man who doesn't know what's good for him. Why did you burn that drawing?'

Sologdin's blue eyes were just as steady, unyielding and inflexible as before. In their black pupils Yakonov saw his own large head.

How odd it was, this small blue circle with the black spot in the middle, and beyond it the whole unfathomable universe of one man.

'What do you think?' Sologdin parried the question, the fleshy lips between his moustache and little beard curling very slightly.

'I don't understand,' Yakonov said, removing his hands and walking away. 'I don't understand people who want to commit suicide.'

From behind his back he heard Sologdin's voice, now resonant and self-assured again:

'I am too insignificant and unknown, Colonel. I didn't want to give up my chance of freedom for nothing.'

Yakonov, now back at his desk, turned round sharply.

'If I had not burnt the drawing,' Sologdin went on, 'but put it in front of you in its final shape, any one of you could have had me transferred to a camp tomorrow, and put somebody else's signature on my design. It's been known to happen. And, I can tell you, it's not very easy to write complaints from a transit prison: they take away your pencil, won't give you any paper or send your statement to the wrong address. Once you're on your way to a camp you can never get a hearing.'

Yakonov listened almost with admiration—he had liked the man as soon as he came into the room.

'So you would be willing to draw it again?' The words were spoken in desperation and impotence.

'It would take three days for me to do that drawing again,' said Sologdin, his eyes gleaming. 'And in five weeks I could make blue-prints for the whole thing, with complete specifications. Would that suit you?'

'In a month! We need it in a month!' said Yakonov, sliding forward on his elbows over the desk towards Sologdin.

'All right, you can have it in a month,' Sologdin replied coldly.

But now Yakonov was suspicious.

'Wait a minute. Didn't you say that drawing was no good and you had found some basic flaws in it?'

Sologdin laughed openly: 'Lack of phosphorus and oxygen, and the monotony of life sometimes play tricks with me. This occasionally gives me a jaundiced view of things. But at the moment I agree with Professor Chelnov and think it was completely on the right lines.'

Yakonov also smiled. His relief was so great that it even, for some reason, made him yawn. He sat down in his chair, marvelling at Sologdin's self-control and the way in which he had conducted this conversation.

'You were taking a great risk, my dear sir. This could have ended very differently.'

'I don't think so, Anton Nikolayevich. I believe I have sized up the general situation here very well—and your own situation too. Of course you know the French expression "*Sa majesté la chance!*" Fortune doesn't often smile on us, but when it does one must grasp it with both hands.'

Sologdin now talked and behaved with as little restraint as if he had been chopping wood with Nerzhin.

He sat down and continued to grin at Yakonov.

'So what are we going to do?' the colonel asked in a friendly tone.

Sologdin answered as though he was reading from a prepared statement:

'To begin with, I would like to keep Oskolupov out of the picture. He is very fond of signing his name to other people's work. I don't imagine that you would stoop to anything like that, would you?'

Yakonov eagerly shook his head. He was only too glad to keep Oskolupov out of it.

'But I must remind you that nothing at the moment exists on paper. If you set so much store by my design, perhaps you can find a way of talking about me to the Minister himself. Or if that's not possible, to his deputy. I should like him personally to sign an order putting me in charge of the project. With this guarantee I would be ready to begin work. I particularly need the Minister's signature because I would like to establish the work in my group on a rather unusual footing. I disapprove of all this night work and the desperate attempts to catch up on Sunday—its turning people into complete wrecks. They should be as keen to get to work as they would be to go and see a girl-friend.' Sologdin's manner was becoming almost flippant, as if Yakonov and he were childhood friends. 'While they are on this job, I want them to sleep properly and take regular exercise. If any of them want to they should be allowed to saw wood for the kitchen. We ought to think about the kitchen too, don't you think?'

The door to Yakonov's office suddenly flew open. The thin, balding Stepanov, with his dully gleaming spectacles, came in.

'Anton Nikolayevitch,' he said gravely. 'Can I have a word with you? It's very important.'

It was hard to believe that Stepanov had actually addressed someone by his name and patronymic.

'So you'll let me have that order, will you?' said Sologdin, getting up.

The colonel nodded and Sologdin left the room with a light, firm step.

Yakonov did not at first take in what Stepanov was now telling him in such great excitement:

'Comrade Yakonov! Some comrades from the Political Department have just been to see me and given me a real talking-to. I have slipped up very badly, they said, by allowing our Party organization to be penetrated by a group of . . . er—let's call them homeless cosmopolitans. And I have shown political blindness by not standing up for you when they tried to victimize you. We must be fearless in owning up to our mistakes. We must both sit down now and work out a resolution—then I'll call an open meeting and we'll strike hard at these alien influences.'

Yakonov's prospects, which only yesterday had been so gloomy, were improving by leaps and bounds.

CHAPTER SEVENTY-FOUR

Before lunch the Duty Officer, Lieutenant Zhvakun, put up in the main prison corridor a list of people whom Major Mishin wished to see during the lunch break. Ostensibly the only purpose of these lists was to summon prisoners to collect letters or notices about money orders.

In Mavrino the procedure of giving prisoners their letters was invested with a certain amount of mystery. Nothing could have been further from the commonplace business of delivery by a postman wandering from house to house like a tramp. Here letters were handed over behind closed doors by the Security Officer. After he had read it to satisfy himself that it contained no sinful or seditious matter, the Security Officer would make a short speech and give the prisoner his letter with the envelope conspicuously open, thus ensuring that any lingering sense of privacy was destroyed. A letter that had gone through so many hands, and been so closely scanned for incriminating material before being disfigured by the black smudge of the censor's stamp, lost what little personal meaning it ever had and took on the aspect of an official document. (In some special prisons this was understood so well that prisoners were not allowed to keep their letters but only to read them through once—in exceptional cases twice—in the Security Officer's presence. The recipient was then made to sign his letter as an indication that he had read it. If anybody tried to make notes while reading a letter from his wife or mother he was regarded with the same suspicion as if he had attempted to copy a secret military document. Prisoners receiving photographs from home were also only allowed to look at them. After signature they were then filed away in the prisoner's record.)

As soon as Zhvakun put the list up, prisoners began to queue to collect, or send letters: outgoing mail also had to be handed personally to the Security Officer. This system gave Major Mishin an excellent excuse for talking to his informers outside his regular rota of appointments with them. To create confusion and cover up for his spies, he also kept innocent prisoners in his office for longer than was necessary. There was thus a good deal of mutual suspicion in the queue, and sometimes, to keep on the right side of them, people smiled ingratiatingly at prisoners they knew for certain were informing on them.

When the bell rang for lunch, prisoners started running up the basement steps out into the yard. The wind was damp but not cold, and none of them bothered to put on their hats and coats for the short dash across the yard to the staff building.

Because of the new rules about correspondence announced that morning, the queue was unusually long and there was not enough room for the forty or so men crowding the corridor. The sergeant assisting the Duty Officer fussily gave orders with all the vigour of a man in the pink of health. He counted off twenty-five of the prisoners and told the rest to come back during the dinner break. Those allowed to stay he lined up along the walls. He then paced the corridor, keeping order and directing the prisoners one by one past several doors to Major Mishin's office. Here they knocked, received permission to enter and went in. The sergeant kept the queue on the move during the whole lunch break.

Spiridon had begged for his letter earlier in the morning, but Mishin had told him he would have to come for it at the same time as all the others.

But half an hour before lunch Spiridon was called out for questioning by Major Shikin. If Spiridon had told Shikin everything he wanted to know, he would have been let off in good time to go and collect his letter. But he stubbornly refused to answer, and Major Shikin was unwilling to let him go without getting what he wanted. So he continued his questioning during the lunch break—in any case he usually avoided the lunch hour in the free workers' canteen and went later to miss the rush.

First in the queue outside Mishin's office was Dyrsin, a hollow-cheeked engineer from Number Seven, where he did one of the most important jobs. For more than three months he had received no letters. To all his questions Mishin had said there was nothing for him. Mamurin had also refused to make any enquiries on his behalf. Then today he had seen his name on the list and, despite the pain in his chest, had managed to run over to the administration block before anyone else. He had no relatives left except his wife who, like him, had been worn out by ten years of waiting.

The sergeant motioned Dyrsin to go to Mishin's office and his place at the head of the queue was now taken by Ruska Doronin with his fair curly hair. He had a mischievous gleam in his eye. Next to him he saw the Latvian Hugo, one of the people to whom he had told his secret, and he tossed back his hair and whispered to him:

'I'm here to collect my money—the money they owe me.'

'In you go!' the sergeant suddenly ordered Ruska.

He ran towards the major's office and met Dyrsin who was looking sadder than ever.

Out in the yard Dyrsin's friend and workmate, Amantai Bulatov, asked him what had happened. Dyrsin's always unshaven face became even longer:

'I don't know. He said there's a letter, but he wants to see

561

me after the lunch break so he can have a talk with me.'

'They're real bastards!' Bulatov said emphatically and his eyes flashed behind his horn-rimmed glasses. 'I've been telling you for ages now: they're just keeping your letters back. You should refuse to work.'

'They'll only give me a second sentence,' Dyrsin said with a sigh. His shoulders were always hunched and he kept his head down as though he had once been hit very hard from behind.

Bulatov sighed too. It was easier for him to be militant because he still had a very long time to go. The nearer a prisoner comes to the end of his sentence the less inclined he is to take risks, and this was Dyrsin's last year.

The sky was a dull grey all over. It gave no impression of height or of being like a dome over the earth—it was more like a dirty tarpaulin awning. Under the raw, damp wind the snow was settling down and becoming porous and the whiteness of the early morning was touched here and there with brown. Under the feet of the prisoners it formed slippery brown humps.

They were taking their lunch-time walk as usual. No matter how vile the weather the prisoners, starved of air, never refused to go out. After being cooped up inside they even liked this blustery damp wind—it seemed to blow the stale air out of them, and their stale thoughts together with it.

Among them, rushing round frantically, was the engraver. He kept taking some other prisoner by the arm, walking round the exercise ground a couple of times with them and asking their advice. His situation was particularly appalling: he could not, in prison, register his marriage with the woman who was not now regarded as his wife in a legal sense. he was no longer allowed to write to her, and since he had already written his letter for December, he would not be able to tell her what had happened. Everybody sympathized with him. His situation was certainly preposterous. But everybody had too much trouble of their own to worry about other people's.

Kondrashov, tall and erect as a ramrod, was walking round slowly, staring with a fixed gaze over the heads of all the others. A man of strong emotions he was telling Professor Chelnov in a gloomily exalted tone that when human dignity had been so trampled on, it was just asking for humiliation to go on living. Anybody with courage had a simple way out of these never-ending insults to one's pride.

By way of reply Professor Chelnov, in his usual knitted cap and with his shawl round his shoulders, calmly quoted from Boethius' *The Consolation of Philosophy*.

The group who had come to watch for the informers stood huddling together by the doors of the staff building. There was Bulatov whose voice carried all over the yard, Khorobrov, the good-natured Zemelya from the Vacuum Laboratory, his elder colleague Dvoyetyosov, who as a matter of principle always wore the torn jacket he had brought from the labour camp, the restless Pryanchikov who never missed anything, Max who was representing the Germans and somebody else representing the Latvians.

'We must get to know our informers!' Bulatov kept saying, encouraging them all to see it through.

'We know most of them in any case,' said Khorobrov standing in the doorway and running his eyes over the queue. He knew almost for certain which of the men were waiting to collect their Judas money. But of course, only the clumsiest had given themselves away.

Ruska now came back to them in high spirits and could barely refrain from waving his money order over his head. They all gathered round, bent their heads over it and quickly examined it—it was from the mythical Klavdiya Kudryavtseva and was made out for 147 roubles in Doronin's name.

The whole group was seen by Arthur Siromakha, the king of the informers, as he came from his lunch to take his place at the end of the queue. With his fish-like eyes he had looked them over out of habit but he could not yet see any particular significance in them.

Ruska took his money order back from them and went away, as they had agreed beforehand.

The third to go in to the Security Officer was a forty-year-old engineer, a specialist in energetics, who the evening before had got on Rubin's nerves with his schemes for a new kind of socialism, and had then started a childish pillow-fight on the top bunks.

The fourth was Victor Lyubimichev who went in with a quick, light step. He got on well with everybody. When he smiled he showed his large even teeth and disarmingly addressed all the other prisoners, old or young, as 'brother'. His pure-heartedness came out in this simple way of addressing people.

The engineer came out to the door holding a letter. He was so engrossed in it that he didn't at once find the edge of the doorsteps with his foot. Then he wandered away to one side, still seeing nothing, and nobody in the group waiting for the informers wanted to bother him. Without coat or hat, with the wind ruffling his hair which was still untouched by grey despite all he had gone through, he was reading the very first letter from his daughter Ariadna whom he had last seen eight years ago as he left for the front in 1941 (he had been captured by the Germans and had gone straight to prison on being repatriated at the end of the war). Ariadna had then been a fair-haired little girl of six who had clung to him with her arms round his neck. During his days as a prisoner of war, living in huts so thick with typhus lice that they crunched underfoot, and standing in the queue for hours at a time for a ladleful of stinking prison soup, it was the precious memory of fair-haired Ariadna—as though like her namesake she were spinning a thread—which gave him the strength to want to go on living and return. But when he returned to Russia, he went straight to prison and never saw her. She and her mother had been evacuated to Chelyabinsk, where they stayed after the war. His wife had evidently taken up with someone else and couldn't have told Ariadna anything about him until very recently.

In her letter, written in a careful, schoolgirl's handwriting with no crossings out, she said:

Dear Daddy,

I haven't written before because I didn't know where to begin and what to write. The reason is that I haven't seen you for a very long time, and I thought my father was dead. It even feels very funny to have a Daddy all of a sudden.

You ask me how I'm getting on. I'm getting on just

564

like everybody else. You'll be pleased to hear I have just joined the Komsomol. You say I should write and tell you if there's anything I need. Of course, I need lots of things. Right now I am saving up my money for some bootees and to have a spring coat made for myself. Daddy, you ask me to come and visit you. But is there any hurry about this? Coming such a long way to see you wouldn't be much fun, you must admit. When you can, you'll come and see me. I wish you success in your work. Good-bye for now.

I kiss you,

Ariadna

P.S. Have you seen the film *The First Glove*? It is wonderful. I go to all the films.

'Are we going to check up on Lyubimichev?' asked Khorobrov, as they waited for him to come out from the Security Officer.

'Why, for heaven's sake? Lyubimichev's all right,' they all replied.

But Khorobrov had always had an odd feeling about the man, and he had now been in with the Security Officer for a suspiciously long time.

Viktor Lyubimichev had the innocent eyes of a fawn. Nature had given him the supple body of a good sportsman, soldier and lover. Life had plucked him straight from the sportsfield and thrown him into a German prisoner-of-war camp in Bavaria. In this crowded place of death into which the enemy had herded Russian soldiers, but to which the Red Cross, thanks to Stalin, was not admitted, the only people to survive were those who had gone furthest in rejecting the relative and limited concept of good and of conscience— those who could betray their own people by working as interpreters; those who could become camp guards and beat their fellow-countrymen on the head with sticks; those who could bring themselves to steal the bread of the starving by going to work in the kitchens. You could also survive by burying the dead and cleaning the latrines. To anyone who did this the Nazis gave an extra ladleful of soup. Only two people were needed for cleaning the latrines but every day fifty people went out to dig graves. Every day a dozen carts took the dead out to be dumped in the pits prepared for them. By the summer of 1942 even the gravediggers were on their last legs. Viktor Lyubimichev wanted to live with all the craving for life of a body that had as yet known so little of it. He made up his mind that if he had to die, he would be the last, and was trying to get himself taken on as a camp guard. But by a fortunate chance the camp was visited around this time by a man who had been a political officer in the Red Army and now urged the prisoners of war in his nasal voice to fight against the Soviet régime. Some people signed up—among them people who had been in the Komsomol . . . a German field kitchen had been drawn up just outside the camp gates and the volunteers were fed there right on the spot with as much as they could eat. Lyubimichev served in France with the Vlasov[1] army tracking down members of the French resistance in the Vosges, and then fighting against the Allied troops when they crossed the Channel in 1944. In 1945, during the great round-up, he managed to slip through the net and when he came back to Russia he was not at first imprisoned. But his past soon caught up with him, and he was arrested not long after he had married a girl with the same bright eyes and supple young body as his own, and whom he left in the first month of pregnancy. In prison he found a number of Russians who had been in the French resistance movement—the same resistance movement whose members he had helped to hunt down in the Vosges. In Butyrki, playing dominoes and waiting for parcels from their homes, they sat and reminisced about their days in France, where both he and they had fought so hard. They were then all given exactly the same sentence of ten years. Lyubimichev had thus been taught by the whole of his experience that nobody could ever possibly have any 'convictions'—which was just as true of the people who had tried and condemned them.

Quite unsuspecting, with the usual innocent look in his eyes, holding a piece of paper which looked very much like

[1] Vlasov: Soviet General who defected to the Germans and commanded an Army Corps largely composed of renegade Soviet troops recruited from prisoner-of-war camps.

a money order, Viktor not only made no attempt to by-pass the group of 'observers' but went up to them and asked:

'Any of you eaten? What's the second course? Is it worth going along?'

Nodding towards the paper in Viktor's hand, Khorobrov asked:

'Someone sent you a lot of money? Maybe the lunch here isn't good enough for you now?'

'It's nothing at all,' Lyubimichev said casually and made to hide the money order in his pocket. He hadn't bothered to do this earlier, knowing that everybody was a little afraid of him because of his physical strength and wouldn't have dared insist on seeing it. But while he was talking with Khorobrov, Bulatov had bent down, as though for fun, and twisting his head round, read out:

'Hey! One thousand four hundred and seventy roubles. You can afford to turn your nose up at the prison lunch.'

If any other prisoner had done this, Viktor would have given him a friendly punch and hidden the money order away. But he couldn't do this with Bulatov, because Bulatov had promised to wangle him a job in Number Seven and was already seeing to it. This would make life much easier for him and increase his chances of freedom. So he said:

'Where do you see a thousand? Look.'

And everybody saw the exact sum. It was 147 roubles.

'Isn't that strange? Why couldn't they make it 150?' Amantai said, not batting an eyelid. 'Well you'd better run along: it's meat cutlets for the second course.'

But before Lyubimichev could move or Bulatov's voice had died away, Khorobrov, no longer able to contain himself, began to shake with anger. He had forgotten they must control their feelings, keep a smile on their faces and go on catching out the informers. He had forgotten that the main thing was to identify them, and there was no way of getting rid of them. He had himself suffered a great deal from informers and had seen many people destroyed by them. There was nobody he hated more than these underhand traitors. And now this boy, who was young enough to be his son and looked like a Greek god, had turned out to be one of these vile spies, betraying people of his own free will.

'You filthy swine!' said Khorobrov, his lips quivering. 'Is

this the way you're trying to get your sentence cut, over our dead bodies?'

With the alertness of a good boxer Lyubimichev sprang back, raised his fist and said threateningly:

'Watch it, you scum.'

But Bulatov was already pulling Khorobrov away and the huge clumsy Dvoyetyosov in his tattered jacket seized Lyubimichev's raised right hand from behind and gripped it tight.

'Easy now, easy now,' Dvoyetyosov said with a look of derision and with the almost loving gentleness which is possible when all the muscles of the body are fully braced.

Lyubimichev twisted round to face Dvoyetyosov and his innocent fawn's eyes met the short-sighted bulging eyes of this man whose left hand now held his in such a vice.

Lyubimichev didn't raise his free hand. He saw from the look in these owl-like eyes and knew from the grip on his arm that one of them would not come out of this alive.

'Easy now, easy now,' Dvoyetyosov said again. 'The second course is meat cutlets. You don't want to miss them, do you?'

Lyubimichev broke away, and throwing his head back proudly, went to the top of the basement steps. His smooth cheeks were burning. He was already wondering how he could get even with Khorobrov, still unaware of how deeply wounded he was by the accusation. Though he had always thought he knew what life was about, he now found he still had a lot to learn.

He just couldn't understand how they had guessed.

Bulatov followed him with his eyes and said, clutching his head:

'My God, who can you believe after this?'

The whole of this scene had taken place very quietly, with very little movement, and nothing was noticed either by the other prisoners taking their lunch-time walk or by the two guards stationed on the edge of the exercise ground. Only Siromakha, narrowing his weary, lifeless eyes, had watched everything from inside the door at the end of the queue and, remembering Ruska's behaviour, saw the meaning of it all in a flash.

He suddenly came to life and said to the prisoners in front of him:

'I forgot to switch something off in the lab. You wouldn't let me through first, would you?—I won't be long.'

'You're not the only one,' people said and laughed. 'We've heard that one before.' They wouldn't let him by.

'I'll have to go back,' Siromakha then said with a worried look and giving a wide berth to the knot of people round the door he ran to the main building. He raced up to the third floor without stopping to draw breath. But Major Shikin's office was locked from the inside and he couldn't see through the keyhole. This could mean that Shikin was questioning someone, or that he was busy with the lanky girl who came to file his papers. Siromakha drew back helplessly. Every minute informers were being identified and there was nothing he could do!

He should have gone back to the queue, but the instinct of the hunted animal was stronger than his wish to earn a good mark with the major. He was frightened of again going past that angry group at the door—they might pounce on him not for any particular reason, but because they already knew only too well what he was.

Meanwhile a group of people had gathered round Orobintsev, the holder of a doctorate in chemistry, who had come out into the yard after seeing Mishin. He was a small bespectacled man dressed in the expensive fur coat and hat which he had worn before his arrest and of which he had not yet been stripped—he had never passed through a transit prison or camp. Round him were gathered prisoners—they included the bald designer—who were as simple-minded as himself, and he was giving them an interview. It is well known that for the most part people believe only what they want to. And those listening to Orobintsev wanted to believe that the list of relatives they had been asked for was not tantamount to a denunciation but a sensible measure intended to simplify matters. Orobintsev had just handed his list, divided neatly into columns, to Major Mishin and he was now passing on with an air of authority the Security Officer's explanations of certain points, such as: where minors should be entered, and what you should write if your father was in fact your step-father. There was only one point at which Major Mishin had wounded Orobintsev's sensibilities. This was when he had said that he couldn't remember exactly his wife's place of birth, at which Mishin had guffawed loudly and asked:

'Did you find her in a brothel or something?'

These innocents were now listening to Orobintsev, ignoring another group which was gathered round Adamson, sheltering from the wind near the three lime trees.

Enjoying a leisurely smoke after his good lunch Adamson was telling the people round him that there was nothing new about this restriction on correspondence—there had been even worse restrictions in the past and this one wouldn't last for ever, but only until some minister or general was replaced. For this reason they shouldn't take it too badly and should try not to hand in a list if they could avoid it. It might all blow over after a while. Adamson's eyes were narrow and almond-shaped, and when he took off his glasses he looked even more *blasé* about everything around him: the same things happened time and time again, and the far-flung empire of the camps and prisons held no more surprises for him. Adamson had been in prison so long that all his feelings seemed to have been deadened and what for others was a tragedy was to him a mere trifle.

The group waiting for informers round the door, which had now grown in number, had made a new catch. Jeering, they had pulled a money order for 147 roubles out of the pocket of Isaac Kagan. When, before this, they had asked him what he had got from the Security Officer, he denied having received anything, saying that he had been called in by mistake and couldn't understand why. When they took the money order from him by force and began to taunt him with it, far from blushing or hurrying away, Kagan went from one to the other and, catching at their clothes, protested at great length that it was all a mistake, that he would show them a letter from his wife saying she had found herself short of three roubles at the post office and could only send him 147. He even tried to get them to go along with him to the accumulator room where he could show them the letter. Then, shaking his tousled head and not noticing that the scarf had slipped from his neck and was almost dragging on the ground, he explained with great plausibility why he had at first denied receiving the money order. Kagan was by nature very pertinacious. Once he had begun to talk with you there was no getting rid of him except by admitting that he was right and letting him have the last word. Khorobrov, who had the bunk next to him, knew the story of how he had been arrested for refusing to work as an informer and just couldn't find it in himself to be really angry. All he said was:

'Isaac, Isaac, what a swine you are. You once refused thousands to do this sort of thing and now a couple of hundred is enough to buy you.'

Or had they done it by threatening to send him to a camp?

But not in the least put out, Isaac continued to protest and might have convinced them all if they hadn't caught yet another informer, a Latvian this time. This drew attention away from Kagan and he left.

The second shift was called to lunch and the first came out for some air. Nerzhin came up the steps in his greatcoat. He at once caught sight of Ruska Doronin who was standing at the edge of the exercise ground. A glint of triumph in his eyes, Ruska kept looking to see how the hunt for the informers was going and also watched the path to the free workers' exercise ground at the end of which one could just see the bus stop on the main road—very shortly now Clara would be arriving for evening duty and that's where she would get off the bus.

'Well, what do you think of it?' he grinned at Nerzhin and nodded towards the group by the door. 'Have you heard about Lyubimichev?'

Nerzhin went up to him and threw his arm round his shoulders.

'You deserve a medal—but I worry about you.'

'But you haven't seen the half of it yet, just wait till I really get going.'

Nerzhin shook his head, laughed and walked on. He met Pryanchikov who was hurrying to lunch with a broad grin on his face; he had been standing with the rest helping to catch the informers and had grown hoarse swearing at them in his high-pitched voice.

'You've missed all the fun,' he said. 'Where's Rubin?'

'He has an urgent job and didn't go to lunch.'

'What? I thought we only had urgent work in Number Seven. Oh, anyway, to hell with you all.' He ran off.

The next person Nerzhin met was Gerasimovich who was walking with his shabby peaked cap pulled down hard over his eyes and the collar of his short, thin coat turned up. The nods they exchanged were friendly but sad. Gerasimovich, huddling in his coat against the wind, had his hands in his pockets and he looked as frail as a sparrow. But he was like the sparrow in the Russian proverb that has the heart of a cat.

CHAPTER SEVENTY-FIVE

Major Mishin's work, compared with Major Shikin's, had its own peculiar advantages and disadvantages. The best part of it was reading the prisoners' letters and deciding whether to send them or not. The bad side was that he had no say in sending prisoners back to labour camps, withholding payment for their work, deciding how the different categories of prisoners should be fed and when they should be allowed visits by their relatives; nor was he empowered to harass them in matters connected with their work. Mishin had many reasons to envy his rival, Major Shikin, who was always the first to learn of any new developments inside the prison. Mishin's one advantage over him was being able to peep through the curtain on his window at goings-on in the prison grounds—this Shikin was unable to do because of the awkward situation of his window on the third floor. These direct observations of the prisoners in their daily life gave Mishin a certain amount of useful material. From his vantage point he was able to supplement the information he got from his informers by noting which of the prisoners walked together, and whether they were talking seriously or just chatting to pass the time. Then, the next time he handed over a letter to someone, or took one for posting, he liked to astonish the man by asking casually:

'By the way, what were you and Petrov talking about in the lunch break yesterday?'

He was sometimes able to get quite useful pieces of information from prisoners he caught off guard like this.

Today, too, during the lunch break Mishin had asked

the sergeant not to send in any prisoners for a few minutes so he could look out into the yard for a while. But he had seen nothing of the people lying in wait for the informers—they were at the other end of the building.

At three o'clock, when the lunch break was over and the sergeant sent away all those who had come too late, Mishin told him to let Dyrsin come in.

Nature had been unkind to Dyrsin and given him sunken cheeks, high cheekbones, slurred speech and even a peculiar surname. He had gone to his institute from the factory bench, after study in a special workers' night school and had graduated by dint of sheer hard work. He was not without talent, but he could never display it to advantage and all his life people had brow-beaten and snubbed him. In Number Seven he was regarded as fair game by anybody who wanted to exploit him, and because his ten-year sentence, which had been shortened by a few remissions, was now coming to an end, he was particularly afraid of the prison staff. Most of all he was terrified of receiving a second sentence—he had often seen this happen to prisoners in the war years.

The reason for his imprisonment was quite grotesque. At the beginning of the war he had been denounced for 'anti-Soviet propaganda' by his neighbours who wanted—and were subsequently given—his flat. When the investigation showed that he had not been guilty of any such thing, it was then alleged that since he listened to German broadcasts he would have been capable of carrying on 'anti-Soviet propaganda'. He didn't, it was true, actually listen to German broadcasts, but since he was in possession of a radio set despite the ban, he *could* have done so. Finally, although he didn't in fact have a radio set, it was alleged that he could have had one, since he was a radio engineer by training, and hadn't a box containing two valves been found during the search of his flat?

Dyrsin had had more than his fair share of life in the camps during the war years. He knew what it was to eat soggy grain which was meant for horses, and to try and keep alive by mixing flour with snow while the prisoners were actually building their camp in the middle of nowhere. Dyrsin had spent eight years in this way and during this time

573

his two children had died and his wife had become a shrunken old woman. Then it was remembered that he was an engineer and he was brought to Mavrino where he was given real butter with his meals and allowed to send a hundred roubles a month home to his wife.

The reason he was so worried now was that quite unaccountably he had had no letters from her for some time. For all he knew she might be dead.

Major Mishin was sitting with his hands folded on the desk in front of him. All his papers had been cleared away, the lid was on the inkwell, his pen was dry and there was no expression—there never was—on his fat, purplish face. The skin on his forehead was shiny and taut, and quite unmarked by the wrinkles of age or reflection. His cheeks also were very full. His face was like that of an earthenware buddha which had been fired with a glaze of pink and purple. But his eyes were quite dull, expressionless and empty—they had the special vacant stare of arrogance.

Dyrsin, who had been turning over in his mind all the unpleasant possibilities, was quite amazed when Mishin—this had never happened before—asked him to sit down. Pausing for effect in accordance with instructions, the major finally said:

'Now for the last two months you've done nothing but complain. You keep coming here and complaining because there are no letters for you.'

'It's more than three months since I got one, Major,' Dyrsin said timidly.

'All right, three. What's the difference? Has it ever occurred to you what sort of person your wife is?'

Mishin spoke slowly, pronouncing the words very clearly and pausing between sentences.

'. . . what sort of person your wife is? Eh?'

'I . . . don't understand . . .' Dyrsin mumbled.

'What don't you understand? I mean from the political point of view.'

Dyrsin went pale. He thought there was nothing he hadn't suffered, but for this he was quite unprepared. Had his wife written something in a letter for which, now, just before he was due to be released, she might be . . .?

He prayed silently for her (he had learned to pray in the camps).

'She's always whining, and we can do without people like that,' the Major said bluntly. 'And she suffers from some peculiar blindness: she ignores the good things in our life and harps on the bad side.'

'For God's sake, what's happened to her?' Dyrsin exclaimed, wild-eyed.

'What's happened to her?' Mishin spoke even more slowly than usual. 'To her? Nothing. (Dyrsin sighed with relief.) So far!'

With very deliberate movements he took a letter out of the drawer and handed it to Dyrsin.

'Thank you,' said Dyrsin, breathing hard. 'Can I go now?'

'No! You must read it here. I can't let you take a letter like this to your quarters. What would the others think about life outside prison if they see letters like this? Just read it.'

Mishin sat perfectly still, a little purple god, undismayed by the burdens of his office.

Dyrsin took the letter out of its envelope. Though he noticed nothing, a stranger would have been struck by the appearance of the letter—it seemed to convey an impression of the woman who had written it. The paper was rough— it looked almost like wrapping paper—and none of the lines were even, but sloped down to the right, sagging pathetically. The letter was dated September the 18th:

Dear Vanya,

I'm writing this to you but I'm half asleep so it's very hard. When I've finished work I go straight into the garden and dig potatoes with Manya. They are very tiny this year. I didn't go anywhere on holiday—I don't have anything decent to wear, my clothes are all in rags. I wanted to save up some money and come and see you but I couldn't manage it. Nika tried to come and see you but they told her they didn't have anyone of that name and her mother and father were very angry with her for going at all. They said she'd only called attention to herself and now they would watch her as well. Altogether we're on very bad terms with them and they're not even speaking with L.V.

We're in a very bad way. Grandmother's been in bed for three years now. She's all skin and bones and can't seem to die or get better and she's really getting us down. She smells something awful and there are rows going on all the time. I'm not on speaking terms with L.V. Manya's left her husband for good. She's not very well and the children won't behave. When we get home from work it's really terrible. Life is sheer misery and there's no escape. When will we see the end of it?

Well, love and kisses. Good-bye for now.

The letter had no signature.

Mishin waited patiently for Dyrsin to read the letter a couple of times and with a slight movement of his fair eyebrows said:

'I didn't give you this letter when it came. I thought this might be a passing mood and I didn't want your work to suffer. I was waiting for her to write something a little more cheerful, but this is what came last month.'

Dyrsin looked ready to fling himself on the major, but he said nothing and on his gaunt face there was not even reproach, only pain. With trembling fingers he took out the second letter from the unsealed envelope. The lines were just as uneven and straggling as before, but this time the letter had been written on a sheet of paper torn from an exercise book.

October 30th

Dear Vanya,

I expect you're upset because I don't write much, but I get home from work late and nearly every day I have to go out looking for firewood, and by that time it's night and I'm so tired I just go straight to bed. I sleep badly because of Grandma. I get up at five in the morning and have to be at work by eight. Thank goodness it's a warm autumn but I shudder to think of the winter. There's no coal to be had anywhere unless you're important enough or know the right people. I was carrying a load of brushwood on my back the other day, but it fell off

576

and I had to drag it behind me. I just hadn't the strength to pick it up again and I felt like the old woman in the story book carrying firewood. I ruptured myself getting it home. Nika came home for the holidays—she's quite a young lady now and didn't even come to see us. I get into a terrible state when I think of you. You are the only hope I have left. I'll keep on working while I have the strength—I'm just frightened of falling ill like Grandmother. She has lost the use of her legs and she's all swollen up. She can't get in or out of bed by herself. They don't take people like her in the hospitals, it's not worth their while. L.V. and I have to get her out of bed, she wets her bed and there's a terrible smell all the time. It's more than flesh and blood can stand. It's not her fault of course but I just can't go on like this.

You tell us we shouldn't quarrel but we have rows all the time. You should hear the language that L.V. uses. And Manya's always swearing at the children. I wonder if ours would have grown up to be like that? You know I sometimes think it's just as well we lost them. Little Valerik started at school this year and he needs such a lot of things, but there's no money. Though it's true Manya's getting alimony from Paul—the court's making him pay. Well that's all for now. Look after yourself. Love and kisses.

I thought I might get a bit of rest during the holiday but we have to drag ourselves out for the big parade. . . .

Dyrsin sat there aghast. He held his hands to his face as though to wash it.

'Well, have you finished it?' Mishin asked him. 'Have you read it all? Now, you're a grown man with some education. You've been in prison long enough to understand the meaning of a letter like this. During the war people were sent to prison for such things. Everybody looks forward to the big parade on November the 7th, but not her, eh? And what's this about coal? There's coal for everybody, not just for important people—though of course she must take her turn with the rest. I was wondering whether I should give you this letter or not, but then there was another one, just as bad. After giving the matter some thought I've decided this can't go on. You must bring it to an end yourself. You must write her something cheerful to buck her up— you know what I mean, something optimistic. Tell her she has no need to complain and everything will work out in the end. Look, they've come into some money now. Just read this.'

He was handing over the letters in the order in which they had been written, and the third was dated December the 8th.

Dear Vanya,

I have bad news for you. Grandmother died on the 26th November, 1949 at five minutes past twelve in the middle of the day. We didn't have a penny in the house when she died but thank goodness Misha lent us 200 roubles for the coffin. Of course it wasn't much of a funeral—we didn't have a priest or any music. We just took it to the cemetery on a cart and shoved it in the grave as best we could. It's a little quieter at home now, but it seems very empty. I'm not too well myself. At night I sweat so much that the sheets and pillow are all wet. A gypsy woman told me I'll die this winter, and I can't say I'll be sorry. L.V. must have consumption. She coughs all the time and she's spitting blood. She comes home from work in a terrible temper and carries on something awful. Manya and her will be the death of me. And on top of all this four more of my teeth need seeing to, and I've lost two. I ought to get some false ones, but I can't afford it and I'd have to wait ages anyway.

The three months wages you sent me came just in time—we were freezing to death. I'd just got my card —it was No. 4,576—to go to the coal depot but they give you nothing but dust so it's more trouble than it's worth. But with your 300 roubles, and 200 more of Manya's, we had enough to pay a man who knows where to get proper coal and he brought it right to the door. But we haven't enough potatoes to last the winter. You wouldn't believe it, but we hardly got anything from the garden. It's been too dry for anything to grow.

There's nothing but trouble with the children. Valerik's

getting very bad marks at school and Lord knows what he does with himself in the evenings. The headmaster asked Manya to go and see him and wanted to know why she couldn't control her children. Zhenya's only six but he's just as bad as the other and they both use such filthy language. They're just a couple of hooligans, there's no other word for it. All the spare money I have is spent on them but the other day Valerik called me a bitch. To think I have to listen to this kind of thing from the brat. What will they be like when they grow up? In May we should get some of the things Grandmother left but they say the legal expenses will run to 2,000, and where that's coming from I don't know. Helen and Misha are going to sue L.V. to get the room off her. The number of times we told Grandmother she should make a will, but she never would. Helen and Misha aren't very well either.

I wrote to you in the autumn once or twice I think. Aren't you getting my letters? If not, what can have happened to them?

I'm enclosing a forty kopeck stamp with this. Well, have you heard anything new? Are they going to let you out or not?

They're selling some very nice saucepans in the shops, they're made of aluminium.

Much love. Look after yourself.

There was now a damp spot on the paper, spreading and dissolving the ink. As before it was difficult to tell whether Dyrsin was still reading or whether he had finished.

'Well now,' Mishin said, 'do you see what I mean?'

But Dyrsin didn't stir.

'Write her an answer. A cheerful answer. You can write four pages if you like—you have my permission. You once wrote and told her to have faith in God. Well, that's all right, let her believe in God, it's better than nothing. But this really won't do, will it? You might calm her down by telling her you'll soon be back in a good job earning plenty of money.'

'But will they let me go back home? Won't they send me away somewhere after prison?'

579

'That will depend on the authorities. But in the meantime it's your duty to keep your wife's spirits up. After all she is your wife.' The major paused for a moment, then added, with a sympathetic wink: 'Or perhaps you were thinking of finding someone a little younger for yourself?'

Had he known that his favourite informer, Siromakha, was outside in the corridor, dying with impatience to see him, he would not have been sitting there so calmly.

CHAPTER SEVENTY-SIX

At those rare moments when Arthur Siromakha was not wholly absorbed by his constant efforts to give satisfaction to his employers—his very existence depended on this—and he was not on the alert like a prowling leopard, he gave the impression of being a lethargic young man of rather good build with the face of a tired actor, and eyes of an indefinable dull greyish-blue which always seemed moist and sorrowful.

Twice now Siromakha had been called an informer to his face but both his accusers had paid for it by being sent back to the camps shortly afterwards. Now people were too frightened of him to say anything. You were never confronted with the evidence supplied by an informer and he was free to accuse you of anything he liked: planning to escape, plotting terrorism or mutiny. You just never knew, and you were merely told to get your things together, not knowing whether you were simply being taken back to a camp, or whether you were on your way to face a new trial.

It has always been possible to exploit a man's will to survive, for few people court martyrdom by exposing the traitors in their midst until death is a certainty. A man will always wait silently and submissively for better times, clinging to whatever small blessings he may still enjoy. But when he has nothing more to lose and is ready to turn and fight it is more often than not too late, since he is already at bay or a captive who can do nothing but beat on the stone walls of his cell. Or, knowing he is condemned to death, he is totally indifferent to the affairs of this world.

So never accusing him to his face, never catching him in

the act, but not doubting that he was an informer, some of the prisoners simply avoided Siromakha, but others thought it safer to keep in with him, to play volley-ball and talk smut with him. This was how they behaved with the other informers too and on the surface life among the prisoners looked peaceful enough, despite the deadly struggle going on underneath.

Arthur's conversation wasn't limited to dirty stories. One of his favourite books was *The Forsyte Saga* and he could talk quite intelligently about it, though it must be said that apart from Galsworthy he was always reading a tattered copy of the thriller *The House without a Key*. He had a good ear and was particularly fond of Spanish and Italian music. He could hum snatches from Verdi and Rossini in tune and before he went to prison he felt his life was incomplete if he didn't go once a year to the Conservatoire.

He came from an old-established but poor family. At the beginning of the century one Siromakha was a composer and another was sent to Siberia for a criminal offence. Yet another member of his family had supported the Revolution and went to work for the Cheka.

When Arthur reached manhood his tastes and needs were such that he felt he must have his own source of income. Not for him the humdrum daily round of an office job with set hours, drawing his salary twice a month after it had been greatly depleted by tax deductions and obligatory contributions to the State loan. At the cinema he seriously wondered which of the famous actresses would suit him best and he could just see himself taking off for the Argentine with Deanna Durbin.

However, ambitions like this would never be realized by studying in an institute, so Arthur looked round for something which involved a little action and excitement. It was not long before he found exactly what he was looking for, and although the money wasn't as good as he would have liked, it at least spared him from service in the army during the war and thus probably saved his life. And while other fools rotted in the trenches Arthur spent his time very nicely in the restaurant of the Savoy Hotel.[1] He would walk in casually, his pale cheeks smoothly shaven and a solemn look

[1] A hotel in Moscow, now called the Hotel Berlin.

on his face. He loved the actual moment of entering the restaurant, with its warm air, the smell of good cooking and the orchestra playing, when he could take in the whole room with its dazzling chandeliers and mirrors, and the other diners watched him as he chose a table.

Arthur was sure that this was the life for him, and he was indignant that people thought his job despicable. This was because of ignorance or envy. The work was only for people with certain gifts: it demanded excellent powers of observation, a good memory, resourcefulness and the ability to pretend and play different roles. It was akin to that of an actor, though of course it was done in secret. But secrecy was only a basic tool of the trade. Anybody in this profession had to be shielded by secrecy just as a welder can only do his job if he wears a protective mask. Otherwise, Arthur would have been quite open about it—there was nothing to be ashamed of!

Once, having overspent his official allowance, Arthur got involved with some racketeers who were trying to make a profit at the expense of the State, and he landed in jail. Arthur didn't take offence and blamed only himself for getting caught. In the prison camp he immediately felt that he would be doing his old job again—only in rather different surroundings.

The Security Officers did not disappoint his hopes. He was not sent out to fell timber or hew coal, but was assigned to the recreation room. This was the only place in the camp where prisoners could feel human for a little while—they could come here for half an hour before lights out to look at a newspaper, play something on the guitar or talk with one another about their life before prison, which now seemed so remote and unreal. The recreation room was haunted by the intellectuals and Arthur seemed to fit in very well here with his artistic temperament, the understanding look in his eyes, his gossip about life in Moscow and his ability to make light conversation about anything under the sun.

Before long Arthur had informed on several individual prisoners for 'incitement' and a whole group which allegedly carried on 'anti-Soviet propaganda' in concerted fashion. He betrayed two prisoners who were supposed to have talked about escaping, though they had not even got to the stage of making plans. His greatest coup was to fabricate a case against the camp doctors by saying that they had kept prisoners in hospital much longer than necessary to prevent them working (though in fact their intention had been to give them a rest). All these people were given a second sentence, while Arthur's was reduced by two years as a reward for services rendered.

On being transferred to Mavrino, Arthur continued with the work in which he was now so experienced. He was the favourite of both Major Shikin and Major Mishin, and he was the most feared informer in the prison.

But though he was so well in with the two majors, he was not party to their secrets and he didn't know for which of them Doronin was working, and which of them it was most important to tell what had happened.

A lot has been written about how ungrateful and disloyal people are in the mass. But the opposite is sometimes true. With extraordinary recklessness, Doronin had told more than twenty other prisoners of his intention to play the double agent. Each of them had told one or two others, and Doronin's secret had become known to almost half the inmates of Mavrino—it had even been talked about aloud. And although every fifth or sixth prisoner was an informer, not one of them had got to know—or if so, had not reported it. And the keenest and most observant of them all, the king of the informers, Arthur Siromakha, had known nothing until today.

Now he felt that his honour was involved. It was understandable that the Security Officers, cooped up in their rooms, had not got wind of it—but what a disgrace that *he* had missed it! Not to mention that he had been in just as much danger as the others—he too could have been caught with a money order. He felt that Doronin's treachery was like a shot that had just missed his head. Doronin, it turned out, was someone to be taken very seriously and he would have to be dealt with drastically. (Thinking that Doronin had only shown his hand today or the day before, Arthur still didn't realize the full scale of the disaster.)

The awful thing was that Siromakha could not immediately get to see either Shikin or Mishin. He mustn't lose his head and try to barge into Shikin's room or even go up to his door too often, and there was this queue outside Mishin's office. Everybody had been sent away when the bell rang at three o'clock, but then some of the most persistent prisoners had stayed on to argue with the sergeant in the corridor of the staff building, and Siromakha had had to stand near the sick bay, holding his belly as though in pain, waiting for them to leave, only to see Dyrsin being called in to Mishin's office. Siromakha had thought Dyrsin wouldn't be in there long, but it seemed he would never come out. Risking Mamurin's wrath on account of his hour's absence from Number Seven, Siromakha waited in vain for Dyrsin to come out of Mishin's room.

But he was not supposed to give himself away even to the warders who stared at him as they passed by in the corridor. Losing patience he went over to Shikin's office on the third floor of the main building, came back again to Mishin's room and then returned once more to try and see Shikin. This time, standing by Shikin's door in the dark lobby, he was in luck: through the door he could hear the unmistakable sound of Spiridon's hoarse voice—there was no other voice like that in Mavrino.

He immediately knocked on the door in the special way he used to identify himself. The key turned and Shikin appeared in the narrow opening.

'Something very urgent!' Siromakha whispered.

'Just a moment,' Shikin said.

And walking rapidly so as not to be seen by Spiridon, Siromakha went a long way down the corridor, and then doubled back briskly and went straight into Shikin's room without knocking.

CHAPTER SEVENTY-SEVEN

At the end of a week's investigation, the Case of the Broken Lathe was still a mystery to Major Shikin. All he knew was that on Colonel Yakonov's orders, the lathe, with its open step pulley, hand-feed to the back mandrel and either hand or power support-feed—a good Russian lathe made at the height of the First World War in 1916—had been disconnected from its electric motor and, in this condition, transferred from Laboratory Number Three to the machine shop. As the two sides could not agree about transport, the laboratory was ordered to haul the lathe down the stairs from the first floor to the basement, and the machine shop to collect it from the basement corridor and heave it up some steps and across the back yard to their own building. (There was a shorter way, without stairs or steps—straight from the ground floor across the front yard, but as this was overlooked from the main road and the park, it was out of the question from the security point of view.)

Of course, now that the irreparable had happened, Major Shikin had to admit to himself that he was partly to blame: he had underestimated the importance of the operation and failed to give it his personal attention. Naturally, a leader's mistakes are always easier to spot after the event, in the perspective of history—but try to avoid making them at the time!

It so happened that the staff of Laboratory Number Three, consisting of its head, one other man, one girl and one invalid, found the job too much for them. Thereupon—believe it or not, totally irresponsibly—ten men were rounded up at random from various laboratories (no one bothered even to take their names!—and with a fortnight gone, it was only at the cost of considerable effort that the major had succeeded, by sifting the evidence, in reconstituting the complete list of the suspects). This team did manage to get the lathe down to the cellar. But the machine shop (where for some technical reason the man in charge was less than keen on this piece of equipment placed at his disposal) not only failed to provide its own labour force on time, but even to send anyone to check and take delivery at the meeting-point. So the ten prisoners mobilized for the task simply dumped the lathe down and, unsupervised, just dispersed. And there it stayed for several days, blocking the gangway (the major had tripped over it himself); and when the men from the machine shop at last turned up, they spotted a crack in the base, raised objections and left it for another three days, until they were finally ordered to take over.

It was that fatal crack in the bed-plate that led to the Case. It may not actually have been the crack that made the lathe unusable to this day (the major had heard such an opinion expressed) but the significance was much greater than the crack itself. The crack meant that enemy forces were secretly active in Mavrino. It also meant that the leadership of Mavrino had been blindly trusting and criminally lax. The success of the investigation in revealing the culprit and the true motives of the crime would not only mean that someone could be punished and others warned, but that, starting from the crack, a wide-scale educational campaign could be carried out among the staff. And, apart from anything else, for Major Shikin it was a matter of professional honour to unravel this sinister plot.

But it wasn't easy. Precious time had been wasted. The prisoners involved were by now in criminal collusion to protect each other. By a piece of shocking negligence, not a single free worker had been present at the time. Among the team of ten there happened to be only one informer, and a rotten one at that—the best he had ever done was a report on the sheet cut up into shirt-fronts. The only assistance he had been able to give was in re-establishing the complete list of the prisoners involved. For the rest, all ten, insolently counting on impunity, claimed that they had brought the lathe down safely, neither dragging it nor banging it by accident against the steps. Moreover, according to their evidence no one had held on to the part of the base under the back mandrel where the crack was later discovered—all had held it under the pulley or the spindle. In his eager pursuit of the truth, the major had even drawn several diagrams of the lathe, showing the position of the men around it. But if he had learned much about lathes, he had still found no one on whom to pin the blame for the crack. The only one who could be charged—if not with sabotage, at least with the intention of committing it—was Potapov. Exasperated by three hours' questioning, he let slip these revealing words:

'But if I wanted to damage the wretched thing, why on earth should I crack the base? All I needed to do was to put a handful of sand into the bearings.'

Shikin at once wrote this into the minutes of the interrogation, .but Potapov refused to sign.

That was the whole trouble with the investigation: Shikin was deprived of all the normal means of getting at the truth—solitary confinement, punishment-cell, reduced rations, beating-up, questioning at night, even the elementary precaution of separating the suspects—all were denied him. The prisoners were expected to do a full day's work, and for that they had to sleep and eat.

All the same, he did manage by Saturday to extract one prisoner's confession to the effect that, when they were at the bottom of the stairs and blocked by a narrow door, Spiridon ran into them and, with a shout of 'Wait, let me help', had grabbed hold of the lathe and helped them carry it. It was clear from the diagram that he could only have held it under the back mandrel.

This promising clue Shikin decided to follow up on Monday, putting on one side the two reports on the trial of Prince Igor, received that morning. Just before dinner, he summoned Spiridon who came in from the yard just as he was in his padded jacket with its canvas belt and, taking off his long-eared hat, stood twisting it guiltily, for all the world like the traditional peasant come to beg the landowner for a little piece of land. To avoid dirtying the floor, he never moved from the small rubber mat at the entrance. With a disapproving glance at his wet boots and a stern one at Spiridon himself, Shikin let him stand, while he himself sat in his armchair, reading various papers in silence. From time to time, as though impressed by what he read about Spiridon's wickedness, he looked up at him in amazement, as at a ravening beast who had at last been trapped (this technique was prescribed in the manuals as a psychological method of breaking the suspect down). A full half-hour went by in the undisturbed quiet of the locked room; the bell rang for lunch—this was when Spiridon had hoped to get his letter from home. It was clearly heard by him but evidently not by Shikin, for he continued to shift folders, take things out of one drawer and put them into another, frowning over his papers and again glancing in astonishment at Spiridon, who stood with bowed head, crushed and apologetic.

The last of the water had dripped off Spiridon's boots when Shikin said:

'Right. Come closer.' (Spiridon came closer.) 'Stop. Do you know this man?' Holding it at arm's length, he showed him the photograph of a young man in German uniform but without a cap.

Spiridon strained forward, screwed up his eyes and peered.

'Sorry, Major, I'm blind as a bat. Would you let me hold it?'

The major handed it over. Still clutching his floppy hat in one hand, Spiridon wrapped all five fingers of the other round the photograph; holding it by the edge, he turned it this way and that to catch the light from the window, then moved it slowly past his left eye, as though examining it inch by inch.

'No,' he said with a sigh of relief. 'Never seen him before.'

Shikin took the photograph back.

'That's bad, Yegorov,' he said sadly. 'Lies will do you no good, you know. Oh well, sit down.' He pointed to a chair some distance away. 'We'll have to have a long talk—too long for you to stay on your feet.'

He broke off and once again became absorbed in his papers.

Spiridon backed towards the chair and sat down. He put his hat on the chair next to him, but after looking at its clean, soft leather upholstery, took it back and kept it on his knees. His round head shrunk between his shoulders, he bent forward, his whole attitude expressing repentance and submissiveness.

But to himself he was thinking:

'You snake! You bastard! When will I get my letter from home now? Wonder if you've got it there all the time?' To Spiridon, who had been through interrogations and had met thousands of prisoners who had been interrogated, Shikin's game was crystal clear. But he knew he must pretend to be taken in.

'The trouble is, new evidence has come in against you, Yegorov.' Shikin sighed heavily. 'We know all about those tricks you were up to in Germany.'

'It might have been someone else, Major,' Spiridon reassured him. 'You'll hardly believe it—out there in Germany, we Yegorovs were as thick as flies. There was even a General Yegorov, so I've heard.'

'Not you, indeed! Of course it's you! Look at that!' he prodded his finger at a thick file. 'There's your name and patronymic—Spiridon Danilovich—and the date of your birth and everything.'

'Date of birth? Well, that proves it wasn't me. It can't be,' Spiridon said with conviction. 'You see, I added three years to my age when I was in Germany—just so they would be kinder to an old man.'

'Oh, by the way! Before I forget!' Shikin brightened up, pushed his papers aside and went on in casual voice. 'You know that lathe you helped to carry downstairs to the basement? About ten days ago?'

'What about it?'

'Where did it get that knock? On the stairs, was it, or in the passage?'

'Who got a knock?' Spiridon looked up in surprise. 'We didn't have a fight.'

'Who!—the lathe I mean!'

'Good Lord, Major! Why should anyone want to hit a lathe? A lathe wouldn't harm anyone, would it?'

'That's what I've been wondering myself—why should they break it? Did they drop it, perhaps?'

'Drop it? Never! Why, we carried it by its little paws as carefully as a baby!'

'Just how did you carry it yourself? How did you hold on to it?'

'How? Like this.'

'But where were you standing?'

'On one side of it.'

'Look, when you picked it up, where did you put your hands—under the back mandrel or under the spindle?'

589

'I don't know about all those mandrels and things, Major but look, I'll show you.' Throwing his hat down on the next chair he stood up and turned to the door, as though he were pulling the lathe through into the room.

'I was here, see? Backing. And the two of them got stuck in the door.'

'Which two?'

'How should I know? Can't remember. I got so winded I yelled "Stop, I'll change my grip," and held the thing like this . . .'

'What thing?'

'Can't you hear what I'm saying?' Spiridon snapped over his shoulder. 'The thing we were lugging along.'

'The lathe, you mean?'

'That's right, the lathe. I switched over quick, like that— see?' He demonstrated, knees bent, muscles tensed. 'Then one of them managed to squeeze through sideways, then the other, and with three of us on the job it was easy. Good lord!' He straightened up. 'We carried heavier weights than that on our collective farm! Your lathe is nothing! Put six women on to it and they'll cart it a mile! Where is it now? Come on, let's lift it, just for fun.'

'So you say you didn't drop it?' the major asked threateningly.

'That's what I'm telling you! No!'

'Then who broke it?'

'It's bust, is it?' Spiridon was amazed. 'Well . . .' He stopped demonstrating how to lift a lathe and sat down, all attention.

'It was all right before they moved it, wasn't it?'

'Well, I wouldn't know, I didn't see. It might have been broken at that.'

'And when they put it down?'

'Now that I did see—it was quite all right then.'

'Wasn't there a crack in the bed-plate?'

'No crack anywhere,' Spiridon asserted with conviction.

'But how could you see if it was there or not? You *are* blind, aren't you?'

'I'm blind for paper work, Major, that's true. But when it comes to my job, I see everything. Take you and the other officers, for instance, when you throw your cigarette ends away as you cross the yard—I sweep it all clean, I don't miss a single one, even if it's on the white snow. You can ask the governor.'

'Are you telling me you put the lathe down and inspected it?'

'Well, what d'you think? After we finished the job we had a smoke, naturally, and that's when we slapped it, like.'

'You slapped it? What with?'

'With our hands, of course, on the side, like that, like a sweating horse. One of the engineers said: "That's a good lathe. My grandfather worked on a lathe just like that".'

Shikin sighed and took a clean sheet of paper. 'It's a great pity, Yegorov, that you aren't being truthful with me about this either. I'll have to make a report. Obviously, you are the one who broke the lathe. If it hadn't been you, you'd have told me who did it.'

He spoke with assurance, but it was an assurance he had inwardly lost. True, he was on top, it was he who asked the questions, and the prisoner answered with every sign of readiness and in great detail; yet the first phase of the interrogation—the long silence, the photograph, the change of tone, the brisk chat about the lathe—had all been a waste of time. And if this red-headed handy-man with his obliging smile who still sat with his head sunk between his shoulders—if he had not broken then, there was even less chance of it now.

As for Spiridon—right from the start, even when he was talking about General Yegorov, he had already realized perfectly well that the reason he had been summoned had nothing to do with Germany. The photo was a bluff, Shikin was putting on an act: he had been summoned to talk about the lathe—and wouldn't it have been a miracle if he hadn't, after those other ten had been put through the mill for over a week? And, as all his life he had been accustomed to deceiving the authorities, he had no difficulty in entering into the bitter spirit of the game now. But all this empty talk grated on him. What annoyed him most was that he was still not getting his letter. And another thing: Shikin's office was warm and dry, but nobody was doing Spiridon's work in the yard, it was all piling up for tomorrow.

Time was passing, the bell for the end of the dinner break had gone long ago, but Shikin wanted him to sign a confession that, in violation of Section 95, he had given false evidence, and Shikin was writing the question and distorting Spiridon's answers as he put them down.

Just then there came a sharp knock at the door.

Tired of Spiridon's obtuseness, Shikin got rid of him and let in the serpent-tongued Siromakha who always knew how to get to the point and give his report in a dozen words.

Siromakha noiselessly slipped into the room. The shattering news he brought, as well as his special status among the Mavrino informers put him on an equal footing with the major. Shutting the door behind him, he leaned back against it in a dramatic pose. Very clearly, but so low that no one could possibly have heard him from the corridor, he announced:

'Doronin is going about showing his money order for a hundred and forty-seven roubles. Lyubimichev, Kagan and five others are blown. A crowd in the yard was waiting for them as they came out. Is Doronin one of your men?'

Shikin clutched at his collar and tugged it loose. His eyes bulged, his fat neck turned purple. He rushed to the telephone, his usually smug face so contorted with rage that he looked insane.

Silently crossing the room with a bound, Siromakha headed him off before he could lift the receiver. 'Comrade Major!'—as a prisoner he had no right to call him comrade but as a friend he had to—'Don't ring up yourself. Don't give him time to prepare himself.'

This was the very ABC of prison lore, yet Shikin had had to be reminded of it! Backing away, his eyes fixed on the major yet avoiding the furniture as though he had another pair at the back of his head, Siromakha reached the door.

Shikin drank a glass of water.

'May I go now, Comrade Major?' The question was perfunctory. 'I'll let you know whatever else I hear tonight or tomorrow morning.'

Shikin's staring eyes gradually assumed a saner expression.

'Nine grams of lead for him!' were the first words that burst from him. 'I'll see to it myself.'

Siromakha left without a sound, as though from a sick-room. He had done his duty according to his lights and was in no hurry to claim his reward.

He was beginning to doubt whether Shikin would remain a major of the MGB for long. Not only at Mavrino, but in the whole history of the Ministry, the situation was unprecedented.

The call to the head of the Vacuum Laboratory, for Doronin to be paraded before Colonel Yakonov at once, was not made by Shikin himself but by the Duty Officer whose desk stood on the landing.

It was only four in the afternoon, but the laboratory was always dark and the ceiling lights had already been switched on. The head was away, so Clara picked up the receiver. Later than usual, she had only just arrived on duty and, still in her fur coat and hat, stood talking to Tamara; she had not even looked once at Ruska although he was gazing at her passionately. Her hand in its scarlet glove holding the receiver, she answered, her eyes downcast, while he stood at his pump three paces away, devouring her with his eyes. He was thinking that tonight, when all the others had gone to supper, he would embrace her sweet head in his arms. Her nearness made him lose all sense of his surroundings.

Looking straight up at him (she had known all along that he was there) she said:

'Rostislav Vadimovich, Colonel Yakonov wants you urgently in his office.'

People could see and hear them so she could not have spoken differently, but the frightening thing was that her eyes had changed. They were no longer the same, but were dull and lifeless . . .

Thinking only of the look in her eyes and ignoring what Yakonov's unexpected summons might mean, he obeyed automatically. At the door, he looked round and saw that she was watching him, but she turned away at once. Shiftily, she averted her eyes in panic. What could have happened to her?

Thinking only of Clara and forgetting his normal cautious-ness and cunning which would have warned him to be ready for the unexpected question, the sudden attack, he climbed the stairs to the landing—and there the Duty Officer barred his way to Yakonov's room and pointed down the dark little passage which led to Shikin's door.

Had it not been for Siromakha, Shikin would have rung up the laboratory himself and Ruska would at once have expected the worst. He would have run to warn a dozen friends, he would have got Clara to talk to him, found out what was wrong and either gone away with a passionate faith in her or been released from his own allegiance. But now he guessed at the truth too late. On the offchance that he was wrong, that he was not suspected yet, he must not turn back or hesitate in front of the Duty Officer. Nevertheless, he turned and was just about to run down the stairs—but climbing them and already near the top was the prison Duty Officer, the former executioner, Lieutenant Zhvakun, who had been summoned by telephone.

Ruska went into Shikin's room.

In the time it took him to reach the door and cross the threshold, his expression changed. His two years of hiding from the police stood him in good stead and, thanks to his brilliant natural gift as a gambler, he mastered his feelings, brought his mind to bear on the situation and assumed a frank and boyish look of expectancy.

'You sent for me, Major?'

Shikin sat in an odd position, his chest slumped on his desk and one arm dangling like a lash at his side. Rising to meet Doronin, he swung it up and hit him in the face.

He swung the other, but Ruska dodged the blow and stood leaning back in a defensive position. Blood trickled from his mouth and his fair hair flopped over his ears.

The major, no longer able to reach Ruska's face, stood in front of him, glaring, spitting, his teeth bared.

'Judas!' he hissed. 'Sold out, have you? Well, that's the end of you. We'll shoot you in the cellar, like a dog.'

It was two and a half years since capital punishment had been abolished for ever by the benevolent Great Leader, but neither the major nor his renegade informer had any illusions: when a man's a nuisance, what can you do but shoot him?

Looking wild and dishevelled, the blood streaming down

his chin from his cut lip, Ruska nevertheless drew himself up and said insolently:

'As to shooting me, Major, you'd better think again. I'll see you in jail first. For four months now you've been a laughing stock—is that what they pay you for? You'll be stripped of your rank. Better think again!'

CHAPTER SEVENTY-EIGHT

The capacity to act with extraordinary courage—beyond the individual's normal strength—is partly due to our will, but partly, it seems, inborn. Hardest to achieve is an unpremeditated act of courage without preparation, by a sudden effort of will; easier to achieve of course if the effort has been steadily directed towards a goal for years; and blessedly easy if courage is part of us and to act by it comes to us as naturally and simply as breathing.

That was how Ruska Doronin had lived when he was on the all-Union wanted list—simply and cheerfully as a child. He had, it seemed, been born with a contempt for danger and the lust for adventure.

But it would have been unthinkable for the pampered Innokenty to roam about the country hiding under a false name. It would never even have occurred to him to evade his arrest, if the order to arrest him were put out.

He had acted on a swift upsurge of emotion which had now left him exhausted and spent. He could not have imagined, when he was making his call, how his fear would grow, burn him, consume his strength (if he had known, he would never have made the call!).

Only on that one night, at the Makarygins' party, had the tension left him. He had felt a kind of doomed gaiety, almost the thrill of playing with danger.

He had spent the rest of that night with his wife, forgetting everything.

When fear returned, the blow was all the harder. On Monday he had to force himself to start again, to live normally, to go to work, to be anxiously alert for any change, any hint of danger in the faces, the voices around him.

He still managed to behave with dignity, but inwardly he was destroyed; his will to resist, to look for a way out, to save himself, was already numbed.

A little before eleven he went to see his chief, but the secretary stopped him from going in and told him that his posting had been held up by the Deputy Minister.

The news, even though still unconfirmed, shook him so much that he could not bring himself to insist on an interview to find out what the truth was. His posting had long since been decided—there could be only one reason for the delay. He had been found out. . . .

Seeing everything in a blur and feeling his shoulders sagging, he returned to his office and only just had the strength to lock the door and remove the key so that they would think he had gone out. He could do this because the man with whom he shared the room was away on a mission.

Everything in him had gone horribly limp. He was afraid, he was torn with fear that now, at any moment, they would come and arrest him.

It flashed through his mind not to open the door—let them break in.

Or to hang himself before they came.

Or to jump out of the window. Straight down from the second floor to the pavement. . . . Two seconds' flight and a hideous crash—he would be snuffed out like a light.

His expense account, prepared by the book-keeper, lay on his desk. Before he went abroad, he had to have it audited. It made him sick just to look at it.

He shivered with cold in the heated room.

This nauseating impotence! To sit waiting for death and to do nothing! . . .

Innokenty stretched himself, face down, on the leather sofa. Only like this, his body lying upon it at full length, could he get some sort of support and comfort from it.

His thoughts were in a turmoil.

Could it really be he, Innokenty, who two days ago had rung up Dobroumov? How had he dared to do it? Where had he found such desperate courage?

Why had he done it? That stupid woman! 'And who are you? How can you prove it's true? . . .'

He ought never to have rung up. What a waste it all was. To die at thirty.

No, it was not that he was sorry he had rung up—more that he even lacked the will-power to regret his own action. Paralysed at the approach of danger, he lay prostrate, scarcely breathing, as though pinned down, only wishing it could all be over and done with—the sooner they came for him the better.

But happily no one came, no one tried the door. The telephone was silent.

He dozed off. One absurd, obsessive dream followed another, and he awoke unrefreshed, even more exhausted and bereft of will-power than before he went to sleep. But he had not the strength to get up, to shake off the nightmares or even to move. At last, he fell into a deep sleep and was only woken by the lunch-time noises in the corridor; the sofa was wet with saliva where he had dribbled in his sleep.

He got up, unlocked the door, went to wash. They were bringing round tea and sandwiches.

No one was coming to arrest him. The colleagues he met in the passage greeted him as usual.

Not that it proved anything. None of them would know.

All the same, the familiar, unchanged faces and voices restored his confidence a little. He asked the girl for stronger, hotter tea and drank two glasses; it made him feel better.

But he still could not muster up the strength to go in to see his chief and find out.

To kill himself would be only plain common sense—the instinct of self-preservation, the desire to spare oneself. But only if his arrest were certain.

But if it wasn't?

The telephone rang. Innokenty shuddered and, a moment later—not at once—his heart began to pound.

It was only Dottie. Her voice was affectionate—she was his wife again. She asked how he was getting on and suggested they should go out that evening. Once again, he felt warmth and gratitude towards her. Good or bad, she was his wife, the being closest to him on earth. He said nothing about the cancellation of his posting. Instead, he imagined himself at the theatre that evening, completely safe—they wouldn't arrest him in a theatre full of people!

'Yes, get the tickets. Something nice and cheerful,' he said.

'A musical comedy? There's a thing called *Akulina*. Apart from that, there's nothing. *The Law of Lycurgus* at the Red Army Theatre, the small one—it's a première—and *The Voice of America* at the big one. The Arts Theatre is doing *Unforgettable* 1919.'

'The *Law of Lycurgus* sounds too good. The worst plays have the best titles. Let's try *Akulina*. Then we'll go on to a restaurant.'

He'd keep away from the flat all night. They always came by night.

Gradually his will-power was returning. What if they did suspect him? Shchevronok and Zavarzin were even more complicated—they'd be suspected first. Suspicion wasn't proof.

But even suppose he was in real danger of arrest, what could he do about it? Get rid of the evidence? There was none. So why worry?

Now he had the strength to walk up and down, to think things out.

And suppose they did arrest him—it mightn't be today, it mightn't even be this week—why should he stop living? Shouldn't he, on the contrary, enjoy every moment of these few remaining days to the uttermost?

Why on earth had he been so frightened? He had put up a good case for Epicurus last night—why shouldn't he put some of his theories into practice? He had talked a lot of sense, or so he seemed to remember.

Thinking at the same time that he must look through his notebooks to see if there were anything to destroy, and remembering that he had once copied some passages from Epicurus into the last one, he leafed through it. There it was: 'The highest criteria of good and evil are our own feelings of pleasure or displeasure.'

His mind was too distracted to take this in. He went on to the next:

'Fear of death is fear of suffering after death.'

What nonsense. People are afraid of death because they are afraid of parting from life. You're wrong there, maestro.

He imagined the Athenian garden; seventy-year-old Epicurus, sunburnt, in a tunic, teaching from the marble steps—

and himself there, in modern dress, leaning casually against a pedestal.

'But we must remember,' he read on, 'that there is no immortality. Because there is no immortality, death is not a misfortune—it simply does not concern us. While we are here, death is absent, and when death comes we are gone.'

Good stuff!— Innokenty leaned back in his chair—and who was it, who was it who only the other day was saying the same thing? Oh, yes—that man at the party last night, who had fought in the war. . . .

'A belief in immortality arises from the insatiability of men's appetites. To the wise man the term of our life is quite sufficient to encompass the whole gamut of pleasures to which he may aspire and, when death comes, he rises, sated, from the banquet of life and makes room for others. One lifetime is long enough for the philosopher; a fool would not know what to do with eternity.'

Brilliant! There's only one trouble—what if, instead of dying a natural death at seventy, men with pistols drag you away from the banquet at thirty?

'Physical suffering is not to be feared. Those who know the limits of pain are immune to fear. Prolonged pain is never intense, intense pain is never prolonged. The philosopher will keep his peace of mind even under torture. Sensual and spiritual pleasure will come back to him from the past and restore the balance of his soul.'

Innokenty paced gloomily up and down.

Yes, that was what he feared—not death. What if they arrested him and tortured his body?

Well, Epicurus had said you could withstand torture. Oh, to have such strength!

But he could not find it in himself.

And death? Perhaps he wouldn't even mind dying if other people knew what he had died for, if it encouraged them to be strong themselves.

But no one would know, no one would witness his death. They would shoot him like a dog, in a cellar, and his 'file' would be locked away behind a thousand seals.

Yet with these thoughts he also began to feel a certain sense of peace. The cruellest of his despair seemed to be over.

As he closed his notebook he read a last sentence:
'Epicurus discouraged his followers from taking part in public life.'

How easy! . . . To philosophize. In a garden. . . .

He tipped back his head, like a bird, as though to let a trickle of water through his constricted throat.

But it was no good.

The fretted hands of the bronze clock stood at five to four.

It was dusk.

CHAPTER SEVENTY-NINE

At dusk the guardhouse gate opened, the long black Zim drove through, accelerated on the asphalt curves of the Mavrino drive—cleared by Spiridon's broad shovel and showing black against the surrounding snow—swept past Yakonov's car parked outside the staff building, and drew up sharply in front of the stone steps.

Major-General Oskolupov's aide jumped out of the front of the car and hurried to open the door at the back for the general. Oskolupov, stout in his tight grey overcoat and tall sheepskin hat, came out, squared his shoulders and—as the aide threw open the front door and then the inner one into the hall—went in and climbed up the stairs. He had a preoccupied look. On the first landing a cloakroom had been partitioned off behind the two antique wall-lamps. The attendants ran out, ready to take the general's coat (but knowing that he wouldn't leave it). He left neither coat nor hat, and continued up the right-hand flight of the great, curved double flight of steps. Higher up several prisoners and low-grade free workers hastily vanished. The general in his tall astrakhan hat moved with dignity, though—in view of the circumstances—also with haste. The aide left his things in the cloakroom and caught up with him.

'Go and find Roitman,' Oskolupov said over his shoulder. 'Tell him I'm coming to the new unit in half an hour, to see the results.'

On the second floor, instead of turning right to Yakonov's

office, he turned left into the corridor leading to Number Seven. Catching sight of his back, the Duty Officer grabbed the telephone to find Yakonov and warn him.

Number Seven was a shambles. Even a layman like Oskolupov could see that work was at a standstill, that the circuits, which had taken months to set up, were disconnected and broken up. The marriage of clipper to scrambler had started with each of the newly-weds being taken apart block by block, panel by panel, almost condenser by condenser. From various parts of the room came the smell of soldering flux and cigarettes, the whirring of a hand-drill, swearing, and Mamurin's despairing shouts on the telephone.

In spite of the noise and smoke, Siromakha saw the general coming in (he always kept the entrance door under observation); he rushed to warn Mamurin, who was standing by the telephone, seized his upholstered armchair and tiptoed with it to meet Oskolupov. In anyone else it would have looked like toadying, but in Siromakha it looked like a young man's zeal to help his senior officer.

Siromakha was not a trained engineer or technician and had become an electrician only at Mavrino, but because he was quick-witted, dedicated, ready to work twenty-four hours a day and to listen patiently whenever his superiors wished to think aloud, he was highly appreciated by them and the prison staff confided in him. He reckoned that this behaviour was less risky than his work as an informer and was more likely to lead to his release.

Without taking off his hat and undoing only the top buttons of his greatcoat, Oskolupov sat down.

The electric drill stopped, cigarettes were put out, voices grew silent—only Bobynin stayed in his corner of the room and went on ordering the electricians about and Pryanchikov with his soldering iron wandered like a lost soul around the stand of his ruined scrambler: all the rest waited for Oskolupov to speak.

Wiping the sweat off his brow after his arduous conversation over the telephone (he had been arguing with the head of the repair shop which had ruined three control panels), Mamurin came up and wearily greeted his former comrade, now immeasurably his superior. (Oskolupov held out three fingers.) His face was so deathly pale that it seemed a crime for him to be out of bed. He had felt the blows of the past twenty-four hours—the Minister's wrath and the break-up of the clipper—much more painfully than his colleagues. For over a year he had lived for nothing but the clipper, believing it to be the magic carpet on which he would fly to freedom. No gilding of the pill, such as the arrival of Pryanchikov with his scrambler, could blind him to the extent of the disaster.

Oskolupov had discovered the secret of how to run a project without knowing anything about its work. He had learned long ago that all you had to do was to stage a clash of opinions between the experts and base your directives on the outcome.

'Well, how are things? How's it going?' he now asked, thereby forcing his subordinates to speak first.

A long, useless, time-wasting discussion followed. People spoke reluctantly, sighed, and whenever two began to speak at once, both stopped.

There were two *leitmotifs*: 'we must' and 'how can we?' Markushev hotly insisted on 'we must' and was supported by Siromakha. An active little man with a spotty face, Markushev worked feverishly, day and night, planning means of making himself famous and obtaining an early release. The reason he had suggested amalgamating the clipper with the scrambler was not that, as an engineer, he believed in the success of the operation, but the fact that, once the two were amalgamated, the importance of Bobynin's and Pryanchikov's role would diminish and his own increase. So now—although he was anything but fond of working for someone else without credit unless he could turn the result to his advantage— he was indignant at the demoralization in Number Seven and, in oblique terms, complained of it to Oskolupov.

Siromakha managed to look agonized yet confident in the ultimate wisdom of his superiors.

For the first time in his career as head of Number Seven, Mamurin sat silent, his face sunk in his frail, yellowish hands.

Khorobrov scarcely bothered to conceal the malicious glint in his eyes. He, more than anyone else, opposed Markushev and stressed the difficulties.

Oskolupov picked on Dyrsin as the one who seemed most lacking in enthusiasm. Whenever Dyrsin became excited or suffered from a sense of injustice, he lost his voice. He was therefore always regarded as the culprit.

Yakonov arrived in the middle of the discussion and joined in it out of politeness, meaningless though this was in Oskolupov's presence. After a while he took Markushev aside, and the two of them started scribbling on scraps of paper on their knees, working out a variant of the scheme.

Oskolupov wished he could give vent to his feelings and yell at people, a technique which in his many years of service he had brought to a fine art—it was what he was best at. But he could see that at the moment shouting would do no good.

Whether he realized that the discussion was getting them nowhere, or because he wanted to enjoy a change of air while he still had his month of respite, Oskolupov rose, cutting Bulatov off in the middle of a sentence, and marched glumly to the door, leaving the entire staff of Number Seven to torment itself with the thought of having brought the Head of the Department to such a pass.

The rules of etiquette obliged Yakonov to get up too and drag his heavy body after the general, whose hat came up to his shoulder. They walked down the corridor in silence, but now side by side—which the Head of the Department disliked doing because his Chief Engineer was the taller by a head.

It was now Yakonov's duty, as well as to his advantage, to tell the major-general about Sologdin's wonderful, unexpected success with the scrambler: the news would at once dispel the bovine hostility Oskolupov had shown him since their interview with the Minister.

But the blue-print was not yet in his possession; and Sologdin's remarkable self-control, his readiness to be sent away to die rather than hand over the diagram, made Yakonov decide to keep his word to him by reporting directly to Sevastyanov tonight. Oskolupov would of course be furious, but he would have to climb down—nothing succeeds like success. (And Yakonov could always pretend to him afterwards that he had not been sure of Sologdin's success, regarding it only as an experiment.)

Apart from this simple reasoning, he had other motives

as well. Realizing how glum Oskolupov was, how terrified about his future, he enjoyed leaving him to stew in his own juice for a few more days. But he also felt an almost professional concern for the project, a sense of injustice as though it were his own. As Sologdin had foreseen, Oskolupov would certainly insist on sharing the credit. He would start by dismissing the work of the main group without so much as looking at it, then he would order Sologdin to be put in a room of his own and make access to him as difficult as possible for those who had to help him. He would summon Sologdin and threaten him and lay down impossible deadlines; and he would harry Yakonov, ring him up every two hours from the Ministry; and in the end boast that, if it hadn't been for him the work would never have got under way properly.

It was all so clear to him in advance, and all so sickening, that in the meantime Yakonov was happy to keep quiet for as long as he could.

When they came into his room, however, he did what he would never have done in front of witnesses—he helped Oskolupov off with his coat.

'What's Gerasimovich doing in your show?' Oskolupov asked, sitting down in Yakonov's armchair but still not taking off his hat.

Yakonov sat down.

'Gerasimovich? Let's see, when did he come from Streshnyovka? It must be last October. That's right. Well, ever since then he has been working on a television set for Comrade Stalin.'

'Call him in.'

Yakonov rang through.

Streshnyovka was another of Moscow's special prisons. There, under the leadership of Engineer Bobr, a very ingenious gadget, a listening device to be fitted to an ordinary telephone, had recently been developed. The cleverest thing about it was that it functioned when the receiver was on its rest and the telephone not in use. The design had been approved and released for production.

Already thinking ahead (as they always must) the authorities were now giving their minds to other appliances.

The Duty Officer looked in at the door.

'Prisoner Gerasimovich.'

'Send him in,' Yakonov nodded. He was sitting away from his desk, on a small chair, and almost falling off it.

Straightening his pince-nez as he came in, Gerasimovich stumbled over the edge of the carpet. Compared to the two stout men, he looked very narrow-shouldered and small.

'You sent for me,' he said drily, coming up to the desk and staring at the wall between Oskolupov and Yakonov.

'Yes. Sit down,' said Oskolupov.

He did so; his buttocks took up less than half the seat.

'Let's see . . . you are . . . ah, yes, an optician,' Oskolupov remembered. 'Actually, eyes are more in your line than ears, isn't that right?'

'Yes.'

'And you . . . er . . .' He rolled his tongue in his mouth as though rubbing his teeth with it. 'They say you're good at your job.'

He paused, shut one eye and fixed Gerasimovich with the other.

'Do you know the work of Engineer Bobr?'

'I've heard of it.'

'Good. And did you know that we have recommended his release?'

'No, I didn't.'

'Well, now you know. How long have you still got in prison?'

'Three years.'

'As long as that!' He sounded surprised, as though none of the prisoners in his care ever served longer than a few months, 'That's a very long time.' (To cheer a newcomer, he had recently said: 'Ten years! That's nothing. Other people are in for twenty-five.') 'You wouldn't mind earning a remission, I suppose?'

Gerasimovich (who never condescended to smile at his superiors) forced his lips into a grin.

'How could I? Remissions don't grow on trees.'

Oskolupov grunted and said:

'Certainly not by working on television sets! But suppose I transfer you to Streshnyovka and put you in charge of a project there? Six months' work and you'd be home by autumn.'

'May I know what the work would be?'

'Oh, there are plenty of jobs lined up. I can tell you this: they're on order for Comrade Beria himself. There's one idea, for instance: to fit microphones into the backs of park benches—that's where people let their hair down, you could pick up quite a lot that way. But that's not really your speciality, is it?'

'No.'

'But I've got something for you. Two things in fact, both equally important and both exactly in your line—isn't that so?' He turned for confirmation to Yakonov, who nodded. 'One is a camera for use at night. Works on . . . what d'you call'em? . . . infra-red rays. So that you can take a photo of someone, and whoever he's with, in the street at night and he'll never know anything about it. They've already done some of the work abroad—all it needs is a bit of improvement. And, of course, it'll have to be fairly simple to use. Our agents aren't as clever as you people! The other thing is this —I expect you'll say it's too simple, but we need it very badly: just an ordinary camera but so tiny it'll fit into a door jamb. An automatic one, so that every time the door opens it takes a photo of whoever goes through. So long as it works by day and by electric light—it doesn't necessarily have to work in the dark. That's another thing we'd like to mass-produce. Well, how about it? Will you take it on?'

His long, narrow face turned to the window, Gerasimovich stared away from the general.

The word 'anguished' was not in Oskolupov's vocabulary. He could therefore not have given a name to the expression on Gerasimovich's face.

Nor did he want to. He was waiting for the answer.

Here was the answer to Natasha's prayer! . . .

He saw her worn-out, tear-stained face.

For the first time in many years the idea of home—suddenly so near, so accessible—warmed his heart.

He had only to do like Bobr: invent a device that would put a couple of hundred unsuspecting fools behind bars in his place.

With great difficulty, falteringly, he asked:

'I couldn't . . . stay on television work?'

'You refuse?' Oskolupov frowned in amazement. His face

was particularly good at expressing anger. 'What's your reason?'

By all the laws of his ruthless tribe, every prisoner knew that to protect the stupid, gullible wretches who lived in the outside world was as absurd as not to slaughter pigs for lard. They lacked the immortal souls which prisoners earned through their endless years in prison; they were greedy and clumsy in using the freedom allotted to them; they were sunk in pettiness and vanity.

And Natasha was his lifelong companion. She had waited for him after his second sentence. Her life was on the point of flickering out, and his would go out with hers.

'I couldn't manage it,' said Gerasimovich in a very low, weak voice.

Yakonov, who until then had listened with only half an ear, looked up curiously. Was this another instance of irrational behaviour? But the universal law of 'charity begins at home' would surely prevail.

'It's a long time since you've been given a serious assignment, you've got unused to responsibility, that's why you feel reluctant,' Oskolupov was urging Gerasimovich. 'You're just the man for the job. All right, I'll give you time to think it over.'

Holding his forehead in his small hand, Gerasimovich was silent.

'But what have you got to think about? It's exactly in your line.'

He could keep quiet. He could cover himself. He could accept the job like any other prisoner, and then drag his feet, not do it. But Gerasimovich rose and looked with scorn at the bloated belly, fat cheeks, blunt snout and general's hat.

'No, it's not in my line!' His voice rose to a shrill squeak. 'Putting people in prison is not my line! I'm not a fisher of men. There are more than enough of us in prison as it is . . .'

CHAPTER EIGHTY

In the morning Rubin was still painfully obsessed by his discussion with Sologdin. He kept thinking of more and more arguments he could have used. Fortunately, as the day wore on, he became absorbed in his important task, and the memory faded.

He worked on the second floor, in the quiet, small top-secret room with a threadbare carpet, an old sofa and heavy curtains at the sides of the window and the door. The soft surfaces deadened sound, but there was hardly any sound anyway, as Rubin listened to the tapes through earphones, while Smolosidov said nothing all day long and scowled at him as though he were an enemy and not a colleague. Rubin took no notice of him except as a robot who was there to change the spools.

Putting on his earphones, he listened endlessly to the fateful conversations of the suspects. Sometimes he accepted the evidence of his ears, sometimes he despaired of it and turned to the violent squiggles of the voice-prints, recorded for each of the conversations; the many yards of paper tape overflowed the large desk and spiralled to the floor on either side. Anxious, he consulted his album of specimen voice-prints, classified by phonetic pattern and basic tone for a variety of male voices. Snatching up his red and blue pencil, worn to a blunt stub at either end (sharpening a pencil was always an undertaking for him), he marked the key passages on the tapes.

The work held him spellbound. His red-brown eyes seemed to burn, his long, unkempt, black beard was rough and straggling, grey ash rained steadily from the pipe or cigarette (one or the other was always in his mouth), on to his beard, the sleeves of his greasy denims with the missing button on one cuff, the desk, the album and the tapes.

He was in that mysterious state of mental exaltation for which physiologists have so far failed to account: forgetting his upset liver and the pains due to his high blood pressure, straight from his exhausting night, he did not even feel hungry although his last meal had been the pastry he had eaten at the birthday party the night before. His spirit soared, his eyes were preternaturally alert, his memory was ready to yield all it had stored up over the years.

He never once asked the time. When he first came in, he had tried to open the window, to let some air into the stuffy little room, but Smolosidov had growled, 'Don't do that, I've got a cold,' and Rubin had obeyed. Since then, he had not got up from his chair, not once looked out of the window at the snow turning grey and porous in the moist west wind. He had not so much as heard Shikin knock on the door, or Smolosidov telling him to stay out. As through a fog, he had seen Roitman come and go, and had muttered something over his shoulder without turning round. The bell had rung for dinner, and again for the end of the midday break, without his being aware of it. The instinct of the prisoner, for whom food is a sacred ritual, stirred in him only when Roitman shook him by the shoulder, pointing at a side table, where an omelette, cheese-cakes with sour cream and stewed fruit were laid out. His eyes widened in surprise, but he was still in a trance. Staring puzzled at this food fit for the gods, as though wondering why it was there, he changed tables and bolted it down, tasting nothing, only wanting to go back to his work.

Yet this meal, so little appreciated by Rubin, had cost Roitman more than if he had paid for it out of his own pocket. For two whole hours he had been on the phone, co-ordinating the arrangements with the Special Equipment Section of the Ministry, with General Bulbanyuk, with the Prison Administration, with Supplies and finally with Colonel Klimentyev. Those he spoke to, in their turn, rang up Accounts and various other departments. The difficulty was that Rubin was on 'third class' rations but, in view of the urgency of his task and its importance to the State, Roitman wanted him up-graded to 'first class', and to an 'invalid diet' as well. After everything had been settled, the prison authorities raised further difficulties: there was no such food in the prison store, the cook had to be paid extra for preparing special meals and there was no allowance for this in the budget.

Now, having achieved his end, Roitman sat looking across

the table at Rubin, not as a slave driver who wants to get the most out of his slave, but smiling fondly as at a grown-up child, admiring him, envying his enthusiasm, waiting for the right moment to ask him about his day's work, and longing to share in it himself.

Rubin ate everything to the last crumb and sat back, his relaxed face showed signs of returning consciousness. For the first time since that morning, he smiled:

'You shouldn't have fed me! *Sater venter non studet libenter.* The traveller should cover the greater part of his way before stopping for food.'

'Have you looked at the clock? It's a quarter past three.'

'What? I thought it wasn't twelve yet.'

'You know, I'm bursting with curiosity. What are your findings so far?'

So far from this being an order from a superior, Roitman spoke diffidently, as though afraid that Rubin would refuse to tell him. At moments when he was human, Roitman had great charm, in spite of his ungainly appearance and his full mouth that was always hanging open because of his adenoids.

'I'm just beginning. They're still only preliminary conclusions.'

'But what are they?'

'Some are open to argument, but there's one that's not. The technique of voice-printing, born on December 26th, 1949, *does* have a valid scientific basis.'

'You're not being carried away?' Roitman asked cautiously. He was as anxious to be convinced as Rubin himself. But his training in the exact sciences warned him that Rubin, the humanist, was capable of letting his enthusiasm get the better of his meticulousness as a scholar.

'When have you seen me carried away?' Rubin was almost offended. He stroked his tousled beard. 'The two years we spent collecting material, all those tonal and syllabic analyses of Russian speech, the study of sound shapes, the classification of voices, the research into national, group and individual speech mannerisms, all that work Yakonov thought was a waste of time—and, let's face it, even you had an occasional twinge of doubt—all that's paying off now. We ought to co-opt Nerzhin, don't you think?'

'If all goes well, why not? But at the moment we have to prove ourselves by succeeding in our first assignment.'

'Our first assignment! We don't know half enough for that yet! It can't be done as quickly as that!'

'But . . . I mean . . . Don't you realize how urgently it's wanted?'

Did he realize! 'Wanted' and 'urgently' were the words he had grown up with in the Komsomol. They were the ubiquitous slogans of the 'thirties. There was no steel, no electricity, no bread, no clothes, but all were 'urgently wanted' and so the blast furnaces had gone up and the mills had started to roll. Later, in the years before the war, the sedate pace of academic research, the leisureliness of the eighteenth century, which was his period, had spoiled him. But the call 'urgently wanted!' could always rouse him, it was always at the back of his mind and spurred him on to see a job through to the end.

The daylight coming through the window was growing dim. They switched on the ceiling light, sat at the desk and examined the patterns, characteristic sounds, groups of consonants and intonation lines marked off in blue and red pencil on the tapes. They worked together, paying no attention to Smolosidov, who sat all day without once leaving the room, guarding the magnetic tape like a surly black watchdog; he now sat looking at the backs of their heads—his heavy unblinking stare drilling through their skulls and pressing like a tumour on their brains. Smolosidov deprived them of the smallest yet the most important element in their work—spontaneity: he was the witness of their present hesitations as he would be the witness of their confident report to the authorities.

They swung from confidence to doubt and back—when one was up the other was down. Roitman was held back by his mathematical precision but driven on by fear of losing his job. Rubin was restrained by his unselfish desire to found a genuine new science but spurred on by his training as a Komsomol in the 'thirties.

Thus both decided not to add to the list of the five suspects. They dismissed from their minds the niggling suggestion that tapes should be made of the voices of the four who had been detained at the Arbat Metro Station (in any case they had been detained too late) or of the few others Bulbanyuk had promised to record if necessary. They also dismissed the possibility that the call might not have been made by the man who was in the secret, but at his request.

It was difficult enough to cope with the five they had already. They compared the voices with that of the criminal. They also compared the voice-prints.

'Look how much the analysis of the voice-prints gives us!' Rubin urged hotly. 'At first the criminal tried to change his voice, to disguise it—you can hear that. But look at the voice-prints—only the intensity of the frequencies is affected, there's no change in the individual speech type at all! That's our main discovery—the speech type! Even if he had disguised his voice to the end, he could not have concealed its individual character!'

'But we don't yet know enough about the extent to which a voice can be changed,' Roitman demurred. 'Perhaps in the micro-intonations. There the range is very wide.'

Although it was possible to doubt the evidence of the ear as to how the voices differed or were similar, the changing pattern of sound waves on the diagram seemed to bring the differences out more clearly. (The only trouble was the roughness of the visible record: the instrument picked out few of the frequency channels and showed the amplitude of the frequency only by indistinguishable smudges. It had not, after all, been designed for such precision work.)

Two of the five suspects—Zavarzin and Syagovity—could be eliminated at once (assuming that the method allowed any deduction to be made from a single conversation). With less certainty, Petrov could be eliminated as well (Rubin had no hesitation in doing so). On the other hand, the voices of both Volodin and Shchevronok had much in common with that of the criminal—they were alike in both individual type and the frequency of their basic tone, while the sounds o, r, l and sh were identical in all three.

The job in hand was ideal for testing the efficiency of the apparatus. Filled with triumph as its creators, Roitman and Rubin leaned back and surveyed the future. Already they could see the day when an elaborate organization, similar to that for fingerprinting, would exist: a central register, with the recorded voices of all who had ever been suspected. Every criminal's talk would be filed and the villain caught as surely as the burglar whose prints are on the safe.

But the door opened, and Oskolupov's aide announced the imminent arrival of his master.

The two men sobered up. Science was all very well but now they must agree their report and be ready to defend it in front of the head of the department.

Roitman thought they had achieved a great deal. Knowing that authorities dislike hypotheses and want everything clear-cut, he agreed to eliminate Petrov and to tell the major-general that the only suspects left were Shchevronok and Volodin; both were to be further investigated within the next couple of days.

'Of course,' said Roitman with a visionary look, 'we mustn't dismiss psychology altogether. We ought, after all, to try and imagine: what kind of man could bring himself to do such a thing? What could make him do it? And then compare our picture of him with what we know of the suspects. We ought to raise the question, you know—in future we shouldn't only be given a record of the suspect's voice and his name—we should know something about his position, what he does, his background, perhaps even an outline of his past. I feel even now I could make a psychological sketch of our criminal . . .'

But Rubin who only yesterday had maintained to the artist that objective knowledge is not coloured by emotion, had by now picked his man.

'Of course I've considered the psychological factors—on the whole they point to Volodin: in talking to his wife he uses that glum, depressed, even apathetic tone, like a criminal afraid of exposure, and I agree there's nothing of the sort about Shchevronok's cheerful patter—but how can we start by basing ourselves, not on the objective data of our science, but on something quite foreign to it? I've got a fair amount of experience in working with voice-prints now, and you must believe me—there are all sorts of elusive signs that make me absolutely certain it's Shchevronok. I've simply not had time to measure everything with a divider on the tapes and translate it into figures.' (This was just what Rubin, the humanist, never had time for.) 'But if you told me that at this moment I must pick one of the two names and vouch for it, I'd say Shchevronok almost without hesitation.'

'Yes, but we won't do that,' Roitman said mildly. 'We'll go to work with a divider and put down the result in figures—then we can talk.'

'But think of the time! The urgency!'

'But if it's the way to get at the truth?'

'Just look, look for yourself'—and seizing the paper tapes and scattering more ashes over them, Rubin furiously argued his case against Shchevronok.

That was how the major-general found them when he walked in, slowly and masterfully, on his short legs. They knew him well; the set of his sheepskin hat and the curl of his upper lip were enough to tell them the general was highly displeased.

They jumped up, while he sat down in a corner of the sofa, thrust his hands into his pockets and grunted:

'Well?'

Rubin was silent, as protocol required, leaving it to Roitman to report.

As he listened, Oskolupov's heavy face assumed an expression of deep thought, his eyelids drooped sleepily and he made no movement towards the pieces of tape offered as evidence.

Rubin listened to Roitman's report in anguish—clear and intelligent as it was, it omitted everything of the inspiration, the almost supernatural certainty which had guided him in his work. Roitman said in conclusion that both Shchevronok and Volodin were suspect, but further records of their conversations were needed for a final verdict. Looking up at Rubin, he said:

'But I think Lev Gregoryevich wants to add or to correct something.'

So far as Rubin was concerned, the general was wood from the neck up—he had not the slightest doubt about that. But at the moment he was also the eye of the State and, willy-nilly, the representative of those progressive forces to which Rubin was dedicated. So he spoke excitedly, brandishing the tapes and the album. He begged the general to understand that although it was true that their conclusion was

614

still ambiguous, there was no such ambiguity about the science of voice-printing itself—they had just not had the time to arrive at a definite verdict, but as for his own, Rubin's personal opinion . . .

No longer sleepy, Oskolupov looked at him with distaste. 'Think I care a damn about your "science"? It's the criminal I want. Now mind what you say—have you got him among that mess on your table or haven't you? He's not still at large? There's nobody apart from the five?'

He glowered at them while they stood in front of him with nothing to hold on to. Rubin dropped his arms, letting the tapes he was clutching trail on the floor. Like a black dragon at their back, Smolosidov crouched over the tape-recorder.

Rubin was confused. He had not expected to speak about this aspect of the matter.

More used to the ways of authority, Roitman mustered all his confidence:

'Yes . . . Actually I . . . We . . . we are sure he's one of the five.'

(What else could he say?)

Oskolupov narrowed his eyes.

'Are you prepared to stand by that?'

'Yes . . . yes . . . we vouch for it.'

'Well, I didn't put the words into your mouth. I'll go straight off and report to the Minister. We'll arrest both of the swine.'

(From the way he looked at them, he might have meant Roitman and Rubin.)

'Wait. Wait twenty-four hours,' protested Rubin. 'Give us a chance to produce the complete evidence.'

'You'll have your chance when the investigation begins. We'll put a microphone on the interrogator's table and you can listen for three hours on end if you like.'

'But one of them is innocent!' cried Rubin.

'Innocent? What d'you mean?' Oskolupov's green eyes opened wide in astonishment. 'Not guilty of anything at all? The security service will sort that one out.'

Having said this, he left without a word of praise for the two exponents of the new science.

Such was Oskolupov's style of leadership: never praise a subordinate—then he'll try all the harder. Nor was it only the personal style of the general, it came from above: the tone was set by 'Himself'.

Although they were used to it, they felt dejected.

They sat down on the same chairs on which they had sat such a short while ago, dreaming of the great future of their new-born science. They said nothing.

It was as if their whole beautiful fragile structure had been stamped on.

Since two could be arrested to make sure of one, why not arrest all five to make it easier still?

Roitman felt how precarious was the existence of the new unit; he remembered that half of the Acoustics Lab had been dispersed—and the same sense of loneliness and of the harshness of the world which he had felt last night came back to him again.

Relaxing after his intensive spell of work, Rubin, on the other hand, felt a certain relief: the simplicity of Oskolupov's decision showed that people would have been arrested anyway, without Rubin and his voice-prints—at least he had perhaps saved three of them.

The burning inspiration which had consumed him for so many hours was extinguished. He remembered his liver, his head ached, he remembered that his hair was falling out, that his wife was growing old, also that he still had more than five years of prison ahead of him; in the past few years everything seemed to be going wrong—and now Yugoslavia had been denounced.

Neither of the two men said anything of all this, they just sat in silence.

And Smolosidov was there, silent at their backs.

Rubin had already pinned a map of China to the wall, with the Communist-held territories pencilled over in red.

It was the only thing that heartened him now. In spite of everything we were winning . . .

There was a knock at the door and Roitman was called out. He had to make sure that the free workers from Acoustics would attend a lecture by a visiting speaker—today was Monday, the only evening in the week devoted to political studies.

CHAPTER EIGHTY- ONE

At the lecture, the only thought in the listeners' minds was how soon they could get away. By tram or bus or suburban train, all had set out from home at eight, some even seven that morning and by now they had no hope of being back before half past nine.

Most impatient of all was Simochka, even though she was on duty tonight. Waves of fear and hope assailed her and her legs were weak and numb as though she had drunk too much champagne. This was the evening she had arranged to meet Gleb. She couldn't bear that this solemn moment in her life should pass casually and take her off her guard. This was why, ever since Saturday, she had been preparing herself. All yesterday and half today had been like the eve of some great holiday. She had sat at the dressmaker's, hurrying her to finish the new frock that suited her so well. At home she had scrubbed herself hard in the tin bath which she had dragged into the middle of her cramped little Moscow room. She had spent a long time putting her hair into curlers before going to bed, and a long time too combing it out when she got up, all the time glancing at the mirror to convince herself that, from certain angles, she could look attractive.

She should have seen Nerzhin at three, after the lunch break, but in open disregard of the regulations (she really must speak to him tonight—he should be more careful) he had been late returning from the canteen. Meanwhile, she was sent to another room, to draw up lists and get answers to a questionnaire, and when she came back to Acoustics, shortly before six, he was again not there, although his desk was piled with folders and periodicals, and his light was on. So she had gone to the lecture without seeing him, and with no suspicion of the terrible news that yesterday, after a year of separation, he had unexpectedly had a meeting with his wife.

Small and fitting easily into the crowded row, she was invisible among her neighbours. Her cheeks getting hotter and hotter, she watched the hands of the big electric clock. Just after eight she would be alone with Gleb. . . .

When the lecture was over and everybody flocked to the cloak-room on the first floor, she went with the rest to see her girl-friends off. It was noisy and crowded—the men getting hastily into coats and lighting cigarettes to smoke on the way, the girls balancing on one foot as they pulled on their galoshes. But in spite of their hurry, her friends found time to admire her dress and discuss it in detail.

Made of brown silk, it flattered her figure. It clung to her wasp waist and fell in loose folds over her bust; two flounces, swinging lightly as she walked—one shiny, the other dull—gave a suggestion of fullness to her figure. Soft wide sleeves, gathered at the wrists, covered her thin, ethereal arms, while the collar had a charmingly naïve device: two long ends which tied in a bow in front and looked like the two wings of a butterfly.

To her suspicious colleagues it might seem strange that she should go to work wearing a new dress. But she explained that she was going on to a birthday party at her uncle's, where there would be young men.

Her friends admired the frock, said she looked 'really pretty' in it and asked where she had bought the satin crêpe.

Suddenly hesitant, she dawdled instead of going straight to the laboratory.

It was two minutes to eight when, encouraged by her friends' praise, yet with her heart thumping, she went into the Acoustics Laboratory. The prisoners were already handing over their secret papers to be locked up in the safe. From half-way across the room, left sadly bare by the removal of the scrambler to Number Seven, she saw Nerzhin's desk.

He had gone. (Couldn't he have waited? . . .) The desk light was out, the slats were shut, his papers handed in. Only one thing was unusual: in the space in the middle, which he always cleared before going away, were a large American magazine and a dictionary, both open. This might be a secret message to her: 'Coming back soon.'

Roitman's deputy handed her the seal (the room was always sealed for the night) and the keys of the safe and of the door. She was afraid of Roitman going to see Rubin again and coming back unexpectedly, but it must be all right, because Roitman was already wearing his coat and hat and, while pulling on his leather gloves, was telling his deputy to hurry up and get his things on; he looked depressed.

'Well, you're in charge now, good luck,' he said to her as he went out.

The bell rang in the corridor—it rang for a long time, and could be heard in all the rooms. The prisoners were trooping off to supper. Unsmiling, she walked up and down, watching the last of them leave. When she wasn't smiling, her face looked very stern, mostly because of the long thin nose with its sharp curve which spoiled her looks.

She was alone.

Now he might come.

She walked to and fro, twisting her fingers.

How unlucky that the thin curtains over the windows had, just today, been taken down and sent to the laundry. Three bare windows were left helplessly exposed to anyone who might be hiding in the pitch-dark yard and looking in. True, from the yard one couldn't see the whole room—the laboratory was on the first floor. But across the yard was the perimeter and directly opposite the window which she and Gleb shared, was a manned watch-tower: from there everything could be seen.

Could they put out all the lights? Then, with the door locked, people would think she had gone out.

But what if they broke in, or found a duplicate key? . . .

She went across to the acoustics booth. She did this without thinking, not connecting her action with the fact that the guard on the watch-tower couldn't see inside the booth. Stopping on the threshold, she leaned back against the thick, hollow door and closed her eyes. She didn't feel like going in alone, she wanted Gleb to take her in, carry her in.

She knew from other girls how it all happened, but she could only vaguely imagine it; her heart thumped and her cheeks burned more and more.

What in her youth she had regarded as her greatest treasure, was now a burden. . . .

Yes, she wanted to have his child and to look after it while Gleb was serving the rest of his sentence. It was only five years, after all!

She looked at the window. In the darkness, she could just make out the watch-tower and on it that dark blotch, symbol of the antithesis of love—a guard with a rifle.

Nerzhin's firm, swift step sounded in the corridor. Simochka flew over to her desk, sat down, pulled towards her the large amplifier, which lay on its side with its valve exposed, and examined it, a small screwdriver in her hand. Her heartbeats echoed in her head.

Softly, he opened the door half-way—every sound carried in the empty corridor—and in the distance, across the bare space left by Pryanchikov's scrambler, he saw Simochka, shamming dead behind her desk, like a quail behind a tussock.

That was how he thought of her, as he moved in swiftly to the kill.

She looked up at him with shining eyes and froze—his face had a gloomy expression which promised nothing good.

She had known exactly how it would be—he would come up to kiss her and she would stop him because of the windows, because of the guard. But instead of hurrying round the two desks, he said grimly and sadly:

'We can be seen, Simochka, I'll keep away.' Standing with his hands on his desk, he looked down at her as if he were a public prosecutor. 'If no one disturbs us, we must have an important talk.'

'A talk?'

'Yes.'

He unlocked the desk. One after the other, the slats in front of the desk-drawers fell open with a loud click. Without looking at her, he got out his books, files, periodicals, all the usual camouflage.

She sat motionless, her eyes fixed on his stony face. She still thought it was all because of Yakonov's summons on Saturday—they were bullying him, they would be sending him away soon—but if it was that, why didn't he come and kiss her?

'Has anything . . . what has happened?' she faltered, swallowing hard.

He sat down. Pushing the periodicals aside with his elbows, he propped his head on his hands and gave her a straight, hard look.

There was dead silence—not a sound anywhere. They were separated by the two desks—two desks lit by four ceiling lamps, two desk lights, and swept by the eye of the guard on the watch-tower.

His gaze was like a curtain of barbed wire, slowly coming down between them.

Gleb said:

'Simochka, it would be very wicked of me if I didn't confess something to you.'

'Confess?'

'I've treated you . . . thoughtlessly.'

She waited.

'Yesterday . . . I saw my wife.'

Simochka shrank into herself, became still smaller. The wings of her bow drooped, brushing the panel of the amplifier.

'Why . . . didn't you tell me . . . on Saturday?' she faltered.

'Simochka!' Gleb was horrified. 'Can you really think I'd have kept it from you if I'd known?'

('And why not?' she thought.)

'I only heard yesterday morning. It was quite unexpected. As you know, we hadn't seen each other for a whole year. But now that we have, after this meeting . . .' His voice sounded tortured, he knew what it meant for her to hear all this. 'I . . . She's the only person I can love. Besides, you know, she saved my life when I was in camp. And she gave up all her youth for me. You said you'd wait for me, but that's not possible. She's the one I'll go back to. I couldn't bear to hurt her. . . .'

He could have stopped there. The bullet—delivered with no sound except that low, hoarse voice—had found its target. She wasn't looking at him. She had crumpled up, her head lay on the crowded row of valves and condensers of the triple amplifier.

He stopped. He could hear her sobbing quietly.

'Simochka! Don't cry. Don't, my dear, you mustn't!' he said gently across the table, without moving from his chair.

But she went on crying silently; all he could see of her was the top of her head with its straight parting.

Had he met with resistance, anger, accusations, he would have answered with assurance and gone away relieved. But her defencelessness pierced him with remorse.

'Simochka, don't, please don't,' he muttered, leaning across the table. 'I beg you! I'm sorry! I've hurt you! I've caused you pain. But what else can I do? What other way is there?'

He was sorry to the point of tears for this weeping girl he had hurt so badly. But not for a moment could he think of making Nadya weep like this!

After his yesterday's meeting with her, his hands and lips were clean, and it seemed impossible to him now to go up to Simochka, draw her close to him and kiss her.

What a mercy the curtains had been taken down!

All he could do was to go on wretchedly begging her not to cry.

But she still wept.

He pleaded with her for some time longer, then stopped.

He lit a cigarette, as a man will when he finds himself in an embarrassing situation.

A comforting conviction whispered to him, very softly, that all this was superficial, that it would pass.

He turned towards the window. Pressing his nose and forehead to the glass, he stared in the direction of the guard. Dazzled by the light in the room, he couldn't see the turret, only the far away scattered lights, like blurred stars and, beyond them, the pale sky where it reflected the glow of nearby Moscow.

Looking down, he could also see that the snow in the yard was thawing.

Simochka raised her face.

He quickly turned to her.

Her tears shone as they trickled down her cheeks, but she didn't dry them. Wide open, radiating suffering, her eyes were beautiful.

Those clear eyes were fixed on Gleb with an unspoken question.

A question to which he would not give an answer.

Finally, he could hold out no longer and said:

'But she's given me all her life! I couldn't do such a thing! Are you sure you could?'

'She doesn't . . . want to divorce you?' Simochka asked softly, dragging the words.

She had sensed the most important thing. But he couldn't bring himself to admit it.

'No.'

'Is she . . . pretty?' she asked after a silence. The tears were still wet on her cheeks.

'Yes. For me, she is. . . .'

She sighed noisily; looking at the reflected points of light on the radio valves, she nodded to herself and said with sad conviction:

'If she is pretty, she won't wait for you.'

This woman, who was not after all a ghost, not an empty name—why had she insisted on seeing him in prison? What insatiable greed had made her stretch out her hand to a man who would never belong to her?

Simochka could not admit that this unseen woman had any of the rights of a wife. True, she had lived with Gleb for a short while, but that was eight years ago. Since then, Gleb had fought, had been in prison, and she, of course, had lived with other men—how could a pretty, childless young woman have waited for eight years! What difference could that meeting make? He could not belong to her now, or next year, or the year after that, but he could belong to Simochka. Simochka could become his wife this very day! . . .

'She won't wait for you!' she repeated.

Nerzhin was stunned.

'She has already waited eight years!' But his realistic mind corrected: of course it will be harder towards the end.

'She won't wait for you,' Simochka whispered with certainty.

She wiped her cheeks on which the tears were drying.

Nerzhin shrugged his shoulders and, looking at the scattered yellow lights beyond the window, replied:

'Well, if she won't, she won't! Perhaps she won't, but at least she'll have nothing to blame me for.'

He put out his cigarette.

Simochka exhaled a deep breath; it was as though she were emptying her lungs.

She was no longer crying.

But she no longer had any wish to live.

Carried away by what he had just said, Nerzhin explained:

'Simochka, it's not that I consider myself a good man. In fact I'm very bad—when I remember what I did during the war in Germany, what we all did. And the way I've behaved to you now. . . . But I picked up a lot of it in a corrupt world. What was wrong didn't seem wrong to me, but something normal, even praiseworthy. But the lower I sank in that inhumanly ruthless world, in some strange way the more I listened to those few who, even there, spoke to my conscience. You say she won't wait for me. Perhaps she won't. Perhaps I shall die forgotten in Siberia. But if you die knowing that you are not a swine, that's something, isn't it?'

He was on to his hobby horse. He could have gone on talking about it for a long time—especially as there was nothing else to talk about.

She hardly heard his sermon. He seemed to be talking on and on about himself. But what was to become of her? She thought with horror of how she would come home, say something offhand to her nagging mother and hurry off to bed. For months, she had gone to bed thinking of him. How humiliating to remember the way she had made ready for this evening! How she had scrubbed and scented herself!

But what could she do if one hour yesterday with his wife, even in the horrible circumstances of a prison visit, could outweigh their many months of friendship?

Of course, the conversation was over. Everything had been said—without any warning, or softening of the blow. There was nothing to hope for. She ought to go into the booth, cry a little longer and then tidy up her face.

But she neither had the strength to send him away nor to go herself. After all, there would never again be even this tenuous link between them.

Realizing that she wasn't listening, that his high-minded arguments were no use to her, he stopped.

They sat in silence.

It was then he realized that for him to sit in silence with her was embarrassing. He had spent too many years in the company of men, who got their explanations over briefly. Once everything has been said, why sit on and say nothing? It was this absurd way women had of clinging to one. Without turning his head, so that she shouldn't notice, he glanced at the clock. It was twenty-five to nine.

Still, he couldn't just get up and go for a stroll till the end of the break, it would be too insulting. He'd have to sit it out until the bell for roll-call.

Who was on duty tonight? Must be Shusterman. And tomorrow morning, Nadelashin.

Simochka sat hunched up over the amplifier, vacantly taking out the valves and putting them back again.

She had never understood how the amplifier worked and she understood less than ever now.

But Nerzhin's active mind needed something to do. Sticking out from under the inkstand was a strip of paper on which he had made a note of the day's broadcasts; he read:

20.30—Rs. S. (Obkh).

This meant: 'Russian songs sung by Obukhova.'

This was a rarity. And it was being transmitted during the break, at a time when no one would cut in with songs about the Leader.

On Gleb's left, within reach of his hand, stood the small wireless set Pryanchikov had given him, tuned in to Moscow —but was it tactful to put it on? The concert had started. By the end of the century people would remember Obukhova as they now remembered Chaliapin. And she was alive now. Out of the corner of his eye Nerzhin glanced at Simochka, who hadn't stirred, then with a stealthy movement, he put the wireless on very low.

The set warmed up; first the strings, then Obukhova's unmistakable deep, husky voice rang out in the quiet room:

> 'No, it isn't you I love,
> Your loveliness is not for me . . .'

It had to be that one! As though he had done it on

625

purpose! He fumbled, trying to switch off. Simochka started up and looked at the receiver in astonishment.

> *'My youth*
> *My youth*
> *My wasted youth . . .'*

Obukhova sang in her inimitable voice.

'Don't switch it off,' said Simochka. 'Put it on louder.'

After the long drawn out 'you-ou-th', the voice broke off to allow a brief outburst of despair from the violins, then continued to a melancholy waltz tune.

> *'When at times I gaze into your eyes . . .'*

Not for anything would he make it louder, but it was too late to switch off. How maddening that she should sing just that . . .

Simochka folded her hands on the amplifier and, looking at the radio set—neither sobbing nor shaking—wept openly and shamelessly.

Only when the song was over did Gleb put the wireless on louder. But the next song was no better:

> *'You will soon forget me . . .'*

Simochka wept and wept.

All her unspoken reproaches were set to music for Gleb to hear.

The song finished and was followed by a third, but the mysterious voice went on and on probing the same wound:

> *As you say good-bye*
> *You will tie a scarf—*
> *Your farewell gift—*
> *Around my neck.'*

'Forgive me!' said Gleb, shaken.

'I'll be all right.' She smiled helplessly, crying more than ever.

But the strange thing was that, as Obukhova sang, instead

of feeling more and more wretched, they somehow felt a little better. Ten minutes ago they had been so estranged that they had no words even to say good-bye, but now it was as though some gentle and calming presence had joined them.

And it so happened that in her present mood, in a special light that fell on her, now at this very moment, Simochka looked particularly attractive.

Nine out of ten men would have laughed at Gleb for giving her up voluntarily after so many years of celibacy. Who could force him to marry her later on? What prevented him from lying to her now?

But Gleb was profoundly glad that he had acted as he had. It even seemed as though the decision had not been his own.

Obukhova went on singing her heart-rending song:

> 'No joy, no comfort do I find,
>   I live for him alone! . . .'

No, of course it wasn't coincidence. All songs had been the same for a thousand years, as they would be for centuries to come. Songs are about parting—there are other things to do when people meet.

Nerzhin got up, walked round the two adjoining desks and without a thought for the guard, bent down and kissed Simochka's forehead.

The hand on the wall clock jumped again.

'Simochka, darling, go and wash your face. It's nearly time for roll-call. They'll be coming back.'

She shuddered, glanced at the clock, collected her thoughts. Then she raised her thin, fair eyebrows, as though only now she had realized with amazement what had happened this evening. Meekly and despondently, she went to the washbasin in the corner of the room.

Nerzhin pressed his forehead to the window again, and looked out into the darkness. And as sometimes happens when one looks at scattered lights at night, thinking of something else, they ceased to be those of the Moscow suburbs, he forgot where and what they were, they assumed a new significance, fell into a new, disturbing pattern.

CHAPTER EIGHTY-TWO

The day was safely over. Although Innokenty's anxiety had not left him for a moment, and he knew it might flare up tonight, the equilibrium he had reached by the afternoon had also remained with him. What he had to do now was to take cover in a theatre to prevent himself from jumping whenever the telephone rang.

The telephone did ring just as they were about to go. Flushed and pretty, Dottie came out of the bathroom in her dressing-gown and slippers.

Innokenty stood staring at the telephone like a dog at a hedgehog.

'You answer it, Dottie. Say I'm out, and you don't know when I'll be back. To hell with them, they'll only spoil our evening.'

Holding her bathrobe round her, Dottie lifted the receiver.

'Hallo. . . . He's out. . . . Who did you say?' Her expression changed. 'Yes, of course, Comrade General, now I recognize your voice.' Her hand over the receiver, she whispered. 'The boss, sounds very amiable.'

Innokenty hesitated. The boss in a good mood, ringing up himself, at this time. . . . She noticed his hesitation:

'Just a moment, I think I hear the door, it might be him. . . . Yes, here he is. Innokenty! Take off your coat and come along quick—the general is on the phone for you.'

Although, unlike Danera, she had never trained for the stage, Dottie was an excellent actress. Even if the man at the other end of the line were bristling with suspicion, her voice would almost make him see Innokenty at the door, wondering if he should first take his galoshes off, then making up his mind and crossing the carpet.

The general sounded in a good mood. He said Innokenty's posting had definitely been confirmed, he would be flying to Paris on Wednesday; he could hand over tomorrow, but must come round straight away to settle a few details, it would take only half an hour. The car had already been sent for him.

Innokenty rang off and took a deep breath—so deep and slow and happy that the air had time to spread right through his body and leave it emptied of all fear and doubt.

'Just imagine, Dottie, I'm flying Wednesday! And now . . .'

But Dottie, her ear close to the receiver, knew already.

Putting her head comically on one side, she asked: 'Do you think one of the "few details" might be me?'

'M-may be . . .'

'What did you tell them about me, anyway?' She pouted. 'Aren't you going to take your little kitten to Paris now? She does so want to go!'

'Of course I will, but not yet. First I'll have to present my credentials, and look round, and settle down . . .'

'Little kitten wants to go now! . . .'

Innokenty smiled indulgently and patted her shoulder:

'All right, I'll try. I didn't raise it before, so now I'll have to see what they say. Take your time over dressing. We'll miss the first act, but I don't suppose it matters with *Akulina*. . . . The second perhaps. . . . Anyway, I'll give you a ring from the Ministry.'

He just had time to put on his coat before the chauffeur rang at the door. It was not Viktor, who usually drove him, nor Kostya. This one was lanky, with quick movements and a pleasant intelligent face. Gaily twirling the keys of the car, he walked down the stairs almost shoulder to shoulder with Innokenty.

'I don't seem to remember you,' said Innokenty, buttoning up his coat as they went down.

'Don't you? I even remembered your staircase—I've been to your house twice.'

He had a cheerful yet slightly crafty smile. Innokenty thought it would be good to have a smart young fellow like this to drive his own car.

They set off. Innokenty sat in the back of the car. The driver tried a couple of times to joke with him, but Innokenty wasn't listening. Then they took a sharp turn and drew up close to the pavement. A young man in a soft hat and tight-waisted coat stood on the edge of the curb, one finger in the air.

'It's the mechanic from our garage,' the friendly driver

explained, fumbling with the door on his right. The door had jammed, something had gone wrong with the handle.

The driver swore within the bounds of politeness and asked:

'You wouldn't let him sit at the back with you, Comrade Counsellor? He's my boss, it's a bit awkward.'

'Of course!' Innokenty readily moved aside. Intoxicated, reckless, his mind was on his posting and his visa—not on danger.

A long cigarette between his teeth, the mechanic bent down, stepped into the car and, with a casual 'You don't mind?' dumped himself next to Volodin.

The car drove on.

Innokenty gave him a fastidious glance (what a lout!) but immediately forgot him; lost in his thoughts, he didn't notice the route they were taking.

Smoke from the mechanic's cigarette filled the back of the car.

'You might open the window!'—raising one eyebrow, Innokenty tried to put him in his place.

Impervious to irony and not opening the window, the mechanic sprawled back on the seat, took a piece of paper from an inside pocket and held it out to Innokenty.

'Would you mind reading this to me, comrade? I'll give you a light.'

The car turned into a dimly lit street—it looked like Pushechnaya. The mechanic shone a pocket torch on to the green sheet. Innokenty took it with a shrug and read without taking in the sense:

'. . . Deputy Prosecutor of the Supreme Court of the USSR . . .'

His head still in the clouds, he could not come out of them to wonder why he was being asked to read out something—was the mechanic illiterate, or couldn't understand what the paper was about, or was he drunk and trying to be familiar?
. . .

'Warrant for the arrest of,' he read, still absentmindedly, 'Volodin, Innokenty Artemyevich, b. 1919'—only now did the meaning pierce him from head to foot and his whole body seemed to fill with a searing heat—he opened his mouth but, before he could utter a sound, before the hand with the paper dropped to his knee, the 'mechanic' dug his fingers into his shoulder at the base of the neck and threatened:

'Quiet, keep still, or I'll choke you.'

Dazzling Innokenty with his torch, he continued to puff cigarette smoke in his face.

And, although he had read the warrant for his arrest—which meant his ruin, the end of his life—the one insufferable insult seemed to Innokenty to be this boorishness, the fingers digging into his arm, the smoke, the light in his face.

'Let go!' he shouted, trying with his own weak fingers to break free. It had reached his consciousness by now that this really was an order for his, Innokenty's, arrest, yet it seemed to him that he found himself in this car and had given a lift to the 'mechanic' by an unlucky chance. If only he could break away and reach his chief, the order would be cancelled.

He jerked the handle of the door on his left, but it too was jammed and there was something wrong with this lock as well.

'Driver! You'll answer for this! Is this some sort of a frame-up?' he shouted angrily.

'I serve the Soviet Union, Counsellor,' the chauffeur cheekily snapped back, using the official phrase.

Obeying the traffic regulations, the car circled Lubyanka Square—it drove round it, as though in farewell—to give Innokenty his last chance of seeing this world with its brilliant lights and the five-floor mass of the joint buildings of the Greater and Lesser Lubyanka, in which he was to end his life.

Cars queued up and moved on at the traffic lights, trolley-buses crawled, buses honked, crowds milled—and no one knew or saw the victim being dragged away under their eyes.

A small red flag, flood-lit from below, fluttered on the pillared turret of the Greater Lubyanka. Two reclining stone mermaids looked down unfeelingly on the tiny citizens scurrying in the square.

The car followed the façade of the world-famous building and turned into Greater Lubyanka Street.

'Let go, will you,' Innokenty was still trying to shake off the mechanic's grip on the base of his neck.

631

The black iron gates swung open as soon as the car pointed its radiator towards them, and swung shut the moment it had passed.

Gliding through a dark stone passage, the car stopped in the yard.

The 'mechanic' loosened his grip as they went through, and released it when they stopped. Getting out of his side of the car, he said in a businesslike voice:

'Out with you.'

It was now clear that he was perfectly sober.

The driver got out through the door—it wasn't jammed —and ordered:

'Get out! Hands behind your back!' No one could have recognized the icy voice as that of the cheeky chauffeur of ten minutes ago.

Innokenty slipped out through the open door of the decoy-car, straightened up and, although there seemed to be no reason for him to obey, clasped his hands behind his back.

Their manners were a bit rough, but being arrested wasn't nearly so frightening as he had imagined. He even felt a certain sense of relief—no more need to fear, to resist, to think of a way out—it was like a pleasant numbness spreading through a wounded body.

He looked round him at the small courtyard unevenly lit by a couple of lamps and by scattered windows on the upper floors. It was like the bottom of a well, with the walls of the buildings rising on all four sides.

'Don't look behind you!' snapped the 'chauffeur'. 'Quick march.'

In single file, with Innokenty in the middle, passing the impassive MGB men in uniform, they walked through a low archway, down a flight of steps into a lower, darker, covered courtyard and, turning left, came to a smart door, rather like the front door of a fashionable doctor's consulting room.

Beyond it was a short passage, neatly painted and brightly lit. The floor was freshly washed and had a carpet running down the middle.

The 'chauffeur' clicked his tongue as though to call a dog.

But there was no dog to be seen.

Further down, the passage was blocked by a glazed door

hung with faded curtains on the inside. It was reinforced with slats of wood, like the fence around a small railway station.

Instead of giving the doctor's surgery hours, the notice on the door said 'Prisoners' Reception'.

The 'mechanic' rang the bell—an old-fashioned one with a handle you had to turn. A few moments later, a warder with a long, impassive face and sky-blue epaulettes and a sergeant's white stripe, peered from behind the curtains and opened the door. The 'chauffeur' took the green warrant from the 'mechanic' and handed it to the warder, who read it with a bored expression, as a country chemist who had just been woken up might read a prescription—and the two of them went inside.

Innokenty and the 'mechanic' stood in the deep silence of the corridor in front of the closed door.

Innokenty had not even the curiosity to look at the joker in the tight-fitting coat, who had fooled him by his play-acting. Perhaps he ought to have protested, shouted, de-manded justice—but he forgot even that his hands were still clasped behind his back. His mind paralysed, he stood staring, spell-bound, at the notice: 'Prisoners' Reception'.

The soft sound of a Yale key came through the door. The long-faced warder called them in, and walked ahead, clicking his tongue as though he too were calling a dog.

But there was no dog here either.

The corridor was still as brightly lit and as clean as in a hospital. On one side were two doors, painted olive green. The sergeant opened one of them and said:

'Go inside.'

Innokenty went in. He hardly had time to see that the room had no window and was unfurnished except for a large rough table and two stools, when, from somewhere beside and behind him, the 'chauffeur' and the 'mechanic' seized him, held him in a four-armed grip and swiftly went through his pockets.

'Let me go!' Innokenty shouted weakly. 'How dare you!'

He struggled a little, but the knowledge that these men were no criminals but merely officials doing their job de-prived his movements of energy and his voice of confidence.

They removed his gold watch, two notebooks, a gold foun-

633

tain pen and handkerchief. He also saw one of them holding a pair of narrow silver epaulettes, and was amazed at the coincidence of their being exactly like his own.

They released him and the 'mechanic' held out his hand-kerchief:

'Take it.'

'What—after you've had it in your filthy paws?' Inno-kenty cried shrilly and jerked away.

The handkerchief fell to the ground and lay on the floor. 'You'll get a receipt for the valuables,' said the 'chauffeur', and the two of them hastily left the room.

The sergeant, however, was in no hurry. Glancing at the floor, he said:

'Better pick up your handkerchief.'

Innokenty did not bend down.

'They're crazy! They've ripped off my epaulettes!' he suddenly realized as he fumbled under his coat and found them missing from his tunic.

'Hands behind your back,' said the sergeant. 'Quick march.'

Walking down the passage, he clicked his tongue again, but there was still no dog.

Round a corner, they came into yet another passage. Close together on either side were narrow olive-green doors with shiny oval number plates. A drab, elderly woman in an army skirt and tunic with the same white stripe as the sergeant, came towards them. She had been peering through a peep-hole in one of the doors, but on seeing them she dimly covered it with its small shield and looked up at Innokenty as though she had seen him here a hundred times, and there was nothing surprising about his walking down this corridor again. She had a glum face. Fitting a long key into the lock of the door marked '8', she unlocked it noisily and nodded:

'In you go.'

He stepped through the door and, before he could turn round and ask for an explanation, it closed behind him and the key turned in the lock.

So this was where he was to live now! For how long? A day? or a month? or years? You couldn't call this a room, nor even a cell—for as he knew from books a cell must have a window and space, however small, in which to walk about; here you couldn't even sit down in comfort. A small table and a stool took up all the floor space. If you sat on the stool, you couldn't stretch your legs.

There was nothing else in this cupboard. Shoulder high, the walls were painted olive green; higher up, walls and ceiling were dazzling with whitewash and the light of a naked two-hundred-watt bulb hanging from the ceiling and protected by a wire guard.

Innokenty sat down. Twenty minutes ago he had still been thinking about his important new job in Paris. Twenty minutes ago, his past life had appeared to him as a harmonious whole, every step carefully considered, each event illuminated by the steady light of logic and all welded together, by flashes of success. And only twenty minutes later, he was here, in this mousetrap, and his whole past appeared to him, just as convincingly, as an accumulation of mistakes, a mountain of black debris.

No sound came from the corridor except, once or twice, the unlocking and the locking of a nearby door. Every minute the shield of the glazed peep-hole rose and a solitary, searching eye looked in. The door was four inches thick and the space for the peep-hole was cone-shaped, widening towards the room. He guessed why it was this shape: so that nowhere in this torture chamber could the prisoner find cover from the eye of the warden.

He felt cramped and hot. He took off his winter overcoat and looked sadly at the lining of the tunic, sticking out where the epaulettes had been ripped off. There was no nail or projection on the walls, where he could hang his hat and coat, so he put them on the table.

Now that lightning had struck—he had been arrested—he was no longer afraid. His mind started to work, pinpointing his mistakes.

Why hadn't he read the warrant right through? Was it even properly worded? Was it stamped? Was it authorized by the Public Prosecutor? Yes, it was, it said so in the first few words. What was the date of the signature? What was the charge? Had his chief known about it when he called him up? Of course he had! So the call had been a trick? But why the extraordinary mumbo-jumbo, the play-acting, the 'chauffeur' and the 'mechanic'?

He felt a small hard object in one of his pockets, and took it out. It was the elegant little pencil which had fallen from his notebook. He was overjoyed, he broke it in half and slipped the pieces inside his shoes: a pencil could come in very useful. What inefficient fools! They hadn't even searched him properly—here, at the Lubyanka!

But what a dreadful oversight not to have read the charge! It might, after all have nothing to do with his wretched telephone call. It might all be a mistake, a coincidence. What was he to do now?

He had not been here long, yet he had several times heard the hum of a machine behind the walls opposite the door of the passage. It stopped and started up again. Suddenly he was disturbed by the question: what sort of a machine could they have here? This was a prison, not a factory, then why a machine? Like everyone living in the 'forties, he had heard about mechanical methods of killing and the sound made him uneasy. The possibility occurred to him—absurd, yet oddly credible—that this was a machine for grinding to powder the bones of those who had been killed. He felt afraid.

Meanwhile he was again stung by the thought of the terrible mistake he had made by not reading the charge. He should have read it and—at once—protested, proclaimed his innocence. The very fact that he had given in so easily must have convinced them of his guilt! Why, why had he not protested? How was it possible that he hadn't? Obviously, the only conclusion they could come to was that he had been expecting, preparing for his arrest!

The realization of that fatal blunder cut him like a knife. His first instinct was to jump up, bang and kick at the door, shout at the top of his voice that he was innocent, that they must let him go—but this idea led to another, which sobered him; he would impress no one, they were used to people kicking and shouting, and it was too late anyway to undo the damage of those first few minutes of silence.

How could he have allowed himself to be caught so easily? A diplomat of high standing, picked up in his flat, in a Moscow street, letting himself be dragged off and locked up without a struggle, without a sound!

And now it was too late. He would never get out . . .

But suppose his chief was still waiting for him? Even if under escort, he must go to him, he must clear things up.

But instead of getting clearer, his mind was growing more and more confused.

The machine continued to hum intermittently.

Dazzled by the light, intolerable in this high but narrow space of one hundred cubic feet, his eyes had for some time rested with relief on the one small square of darkness on the white ceiling. The square, with its metal grating, was evidently an air-vent, though it was impossible to tell where it led.

All at once he imagined with the utmost clarity that the vent, instead of letting in air, was pumping poison gas into the room (perhaps a gas produced by the machine that hummed behind the wall)—that it had been pumping it from the moment he was locked up, that indeed this tiny cupboard with its close-fitting door could not be meant for anything else.

That was why they were watching him through the peep hole—to see if he was still conscious or had already passed out.

That was why his mind was confused, that was why he was fainting, that was why his head throbbed and he felt he was suffocating.

A colourless, odourless gas was filling the room!

Sheer terror—the primeval terror that unites beasts of prey and the animals they prey on, fleeing side by side from a forest fire—overcame Innokenty and, forgetting all his other thoughts and considerations, he hammered and kicked against the door, shouting for a living human presence.

'Open! Open up! I'm suffocating! I want air!'

A fanatical, unwinking eye gazed through the peep-hole, maliciously watching Innokenty's death pangs.

Oh, the sight of that disembodied eye, an eye without a face—an eye which alone expresses all that is behind it— that eye watching a man's death! . . .

There was no way out! . . .

Innokenty sank down on the stool.

The gas was choking him.

CHAPTER EIGHTY-THREE

The door (which had creaked when it was being locked) opened without a sound.

The long-faced warder stepped through the narrow opening and, only when he was inside, asked in a low, menacing voice:

'Why did you knock?'

Innokenty felt a weight lifted off his chest—if the warder ventured into the room, the air could not be poisoned.

'I feel faint,' he said haltingly. 'Please give me some water.'

'Remember, now,' the warder admonished him gravely: 'On no account must you knock, if you do, you will be punished.'

'But what if I'm ill? If I have to call somebody?'

'And you are not to raise your voice. If you need to call,' he continued in the same gloomy, flat, impassive tone: 'Wait until the peep-hole opens and raise your finger in silence.'

He stepped back and locked the door.

The machine started and stopped.

The door opened—this time it creaked. Innokenty began to understand: they were trained to open the door with or without noise, as it suited them.

The warder handed him a mug of water.

'Listen,' said Innokenty, taking it: 'I don't feel well, I need to lie down.'

'You're not supposed to in a box.'

'Where did you say? Where is one not supposed to?' (He wanted to talk, if only to this stone statue.)

But the warder had already stepped back and was closing the door.

'Listen to me, call your chief, why have I been arrested?' Innokenty remembered to say.

The door closed and the key turned in the lock.

He had said 'box', using the English word.

So they cynically called these cupboards 'boxes'! Well, they weren't far wrong!

He drank a mouthful of water. He no longer felt thirsty. The mug, about the size of a tea cup, had an odd picture on its green enamel: a cat in spectacles was pretending to read a book but, in fact, was watching a small bird which had hopped impudently near.

It was unlikely that they had chosen the picture specially for the Lubyanka—but how appropriate it was! The book was the law, and the cheeky sparrow was Innokenty yesterday.

He actually smiled, and the wry smile brought home to him the full measure of what had happened. Yet it also gave him a certain joy—the joy of this crumb of ordinary, everyday reality which had come to him.

If anyone had told him in advance that he would smile within half an hour of being locked up in a Lubyanka cell, he would not have believed it.

(Shchevronok, in the next cell, was having a worse time: not even the cat would have amused him at that moment.)

He pushed his overcoat aside and managed to put the mug on the table as well. The lock grated. The door opened. A lieutenant with a paper in his hand came in. The warder's haggard face could be seen over his shoulder.

Innokenty, the diplomat in his large grey tunic with gold embroidery, rose casually.

'I say, lieutenant, what's happened? What's this misunderstanding? Will you show me the warrant? I haven't read it.'

'Surname?' The lieutenant looked at him stonily.

'Volodin.' Innokenty gave in with good grace as though anxious to get the formalities over and clear the thing up.

'Name and patronymic?'

'Innokenty Artemyevich.'

'Year of birth?' The lieutenant checked the answers with his paper.

'Nineteen-nineteen.'

'Place of birth?'

'Leningrad.'

Just then when, presumably, the formalities were over and Innokenty was waiting for an explanation, the lieutenant stepped back and the door shut, nearly catching his toes.

Innokenty sat down and closed his eyes. He was beginning to feel the power of the vice now gripping him.

The machine started humming.

Then it stopped.

All sorts of major and minor matters came into his head, all had seemed so urgent an hour ago that even now he almost tried to get up to run and attend to them.

But there was no room in the box even to take a full pace, let alone run.

The peep-hole was uncovered. Innokenty raised his finger. The woman with the sky-blue epaulettes and the dull, heavy face, opened the door.

'I need to . . .' Innokenty made an expressive gesture.

'Hands behind your back! Come along,' she said in a commanding voice and, obedient to her nod, Innokenty went out into the corridor which, after the stuffy cell, struck him as pleasantly cool.

A short way down the passage, she nodded at a door: 'There.'

He went in. The door locked behind him.

Apart from the hole in the floor with two iron ledges for the feet, the floor and the walls were tiled red. Water gurgled refreshingly in the hole.

Glad, here at last, to escape from the watching eye, Innokenty squatted.

There came a click from the other side of the door. He raised his head and saw the same peep-hole with its cone-shaped opening, and the eye watching him, no longer intermittently but continuously.

Embarrassed, he stood up. The door opened before he had had time to raise his finger.

'Hands behind your back. Come along,' said the woman, unruffled.

Back in the box, Innokenty, without thinking, pushed up his sleeve to see the time—but time had ceased to exist.

He sighed and sat looking at the cat on the mug. But before he could become absorbed in his thoughts, the door was unlocked. A big-faced, broad-shouldered man in a grey linen coat asked:

'Surname?'

'I've already answered that question!' Innokenty said angrily.

With no change of tone—like a radio-operator calling a station—the man repeated:

'Surname?'

'Volodin, of course!'

'Pick up your things. Come along,' said greycoat dispassionately.

Innokenty picked up his coat and hat and went through the door. He was shown back to the room where he had first been—the one where they had ripped off his epaulettes and taken away his watch and his notebooks.

'You know, they've taken my things away,' he complained.

'Strip,' replied the warder in the grey coat.

'Why?' Innokenty was taken aback.

The warder met his eyes with a straight, hard look.

'Are you Russian?'

'Yes.' Usually so quick at repartee, he couldn't think of one at the moment.

'Strip.'

'You mean foreigners don't have to?' Innokenty joked feebly.

The warder waited in stony silence.

With a shrug and an attempt at a disdainful smile, Innokenty sat down on a stool, took his shoes off, removed his tunic and held it out to the warder. Although he attached no ritual importance to his uniform, he treated his gold-braided clothes with respect.

'Throw it down.' Greycoat pointed to the floor.

Innokenty hesitated. The warder tore the beige-grey tunic from his hands, flung it on the floor and snapped:

'Naked.'

'What do you mean?'

'Naked.'

'But that's quite impossible, comrade! It's much too cold here!'

'If you don't, you'll be undressed forcibly,' the man warned him.

Innokenty thought it over. They had set upon him once before and looked ready to do so again. Shivering with cold and disgust, he took off his trousers and his silk underclothes, and dropped them on to the heap on the floor.

'Take your socks off.'

He took them off and stood barefoot on the floorboards, his feet and hairless legs delicately white and soft like the rest of his body.

'Open your mouth. Wider. Say ah. Again. Say a-a-ah. Now raise your tongue.'

Like a horse dealer, his unwashed fingers prodding inside Innokenty's mouth, stretching one cheek, then the other, pulling down the lower eyelids, the warder convinced himself that there was nothing hidden in the eyes or mouth and tipped back the head so that the nostrils were lit up; then he checked both ears, pulling them back, told Innokenty to spread out his hands to show there was nothing between the fingers, and to swing his arms to show there was nothing under his armpits. In the same flat, irrefutable tone, he ordered:

'Take your penis in your hands. Turn back the foreskin. More. Right, that's enough. Move your penis up and right, up and left. Right, you can drop it. Turn your back to me. Straddle your legs. Wider. Bend down and touch the floor. Legs wider. Stretch your buttocks with your hands. Right. Now squat. Quickly! Once more!'

Thinking about his arrest before it happened, Innokenty had pictured to himself a duel of wits to the death. For this he was ready, prepared for a high-principled defence of his life and his convictions. Never had he imagined anything so simple, so dull and so irresistible as the reality. The people who had received him were petty-minded, low-grade officials, as uninterested in his personality as in what he had done, but alert and watchful in matters for which he was unprepared and which offered him no chance to resist. What, indeed, would resistance mean and what good would it do him? Every time on a different pretext, concessions were required of him, so trifling compared to the battle ahead that there was no point in making a fuss—yet taken as a whole, the minute thoroughness of the procedure effectively broke the prisoner's will.

Putting up with every humiliation, Innokenty stood in dejected silence.

The examiner nodded to him to go and sit on the stool

nearer the door. The idea of his bare body touching this new cold surface was unbearable, yet Innokenty sat down—and soon found with pleasure that the wooden stool actually made him feel warmer.

He had experienced many intense pleasures in his life, but this one was new to him. Pressing his arms to his sides and his knees to his stomach, he felt warmer still.

Meanwhile the examiner turned over the pile of clothes, shook and prodded them and held them up to the light. Showing a glimmer of humanity, he dealt with the underclothes first. After feeling inch by inch every seam and pleat of the pants and vest, he threw them over to Innokenty. He detached the socks from their suspenders, turned them inside out and threw them across to the door as well, so that now Innokenty was able to clothe his body and feel it revive in the blessed warmth.

Next the warder took a large jack-knife with a rough wooden handle, opened it and set about the shoes. Scornfully chucking out the pieces of pencil, he peeled off the galoshes and, with a concentrated air, bent the soles sharply again and again to see if there was any hard object concealed inside them. Inserting his knife, he did in fact dig out a small strip of metal and put it on the table. Then he took an awl and pierced one heel with it.

Watching him at work, Innokenty spared a thought for the poor man—how sick he must have been of going through people's underclothes, cutting up their shoes and looking up their anuses year after year.

But even this flicker of irony died down in him as he waited and watched in misery. After unpicking all the gold braid and cutting the buttons and button-loops off the tunic, the warder tore the lining and searched carefully inside. He took quite as long over the seams and pleats of the trousers, while the winter overcoat gave him even more trouble: deep in the interlining, he must have thought he touched something other than cottonwool (a hidden letter? An address? a capsule of poison?) for he prodded for a long time with as grave an air of concern as though he were operating on a heart.

The search must have taken at least an hour. Satisfied at last that the galoshes were made of nothing but solid rubber (they bent obediently this way and that) he threw them at Innokenty's feet and collected his trophies: braces, suspenders (he had warned Innokenty that neither were allowed in prison), tie, tie pin, cuff-links, the strip of metal from the shoe, the two halves of the pencil, the gold thread and insignia off the uniform and a large number of buttons. Only now did Innokenty appreciate the full extent of the damage. Not the ruined shoes, not the torn lining or the wadding sticking out of the armholes of the overcoat, but the removal of nearly all his buttons when he was also being deprived of his braces and suspenders, struck him for some reason as the ultimate humiliation.

'Why have you cut off the buttons?' he cried.

'Regulations,' grunted the warder.

'How am I going to keep my clothes on?'

'With bits of string,' came the surly answer as the man left the room.

'What's this nonsense? What string? Where am I to get it?' But the door had closed and the key turned in the lock.

Innokenty neither knocked on it nor shouted: he remembered that a few buttons had been left on the overcoat, and that he must be thankful for small mercies.

He was learning fast.

Holding up his trousers, he took a turn or two round the room, but had scarcely had time to enjoy its spaciousness and the exercise, when the key rattled once again and a different warder, also in a linen coat, but white and rather grubby, came in. Looking at Innokenty as at a familiar object always to be found in this room, he said:

'Take all your clothes off.'

Innokenty meant to answer in a stern, indignant voice, but all that came from his constricted throat was a hurt squeak:

'But I've only just put them on! Couldn't I have been told?'

Evidently he could not, for the warder merely looked at him with a blank, bored face, waiting for the order to be carried out.

What struck Innokenty most about the people he met here was their capacity for silence at moments when it would have been normal to reply.

Already getting into the way of implicit, spineless obedience, he took off his clothes and shoes.

'Sit down!' The warder pointed to the stool on which he had already sat for so long.

The naked prisoner sat down, without asking himself why. (Now that other people were doing his thinking for him, he was quickly losing the free man's habit of thinking before he acts.) The warder gripped the back of his neck and pressed a pair of clippers roughly to his temple.

'What are you doing?' Innokenty shuddered and made a weak attempt to free himself. 'You have no right! I'm not yet under arrest!' (He meant that he had not yet been convicted.)

Clutching his head as hard as ever, the barber continued to shave him in silence; Innokenty's flicker of resistance died down. The proud young diplomat who had walked with such an independent air down the gangways of international airports and glanced with such vague, *blasé* eyes at the busy daytime glitter of Europe's capitals around him, was now a drooping, raw-boned, naked man with a half-shaved head.

His fine, light-chestnut hair fell in soft curls, like sad, silent flakes of snow. Catching a strand, he rubbed it between his fingers. He sensed that he loved himself and his departing life.

He still remembered his deduction that meekness would be interpreted as guilt. He remembered his resolve to resist, object, argue, demand to see the Prosecutor, but while his reason still held on to it, his will was being sapped by the pleasant numbness of a man freezing to death in the snow.

Having shaved his head and ordered him to stand and raise each arm in turn, the barber shaved his armpits. Then he squatted on his heels and, with the same clipper, shaved the pubic hair. This tickled; Innokenty shivered; the barber snapped at him to keep still.

'May I dress?' asked Innokenty when this procedure was over. But the barber left without a word and locked the door.

This time he had the cunning not to hurry into his clothes. His shaved skin was unpleasantly prickly.

Passing his hand over his head and finding it unfamiliar

(it had never been clipped all over since early childhood), he felt an odd, short stubble, and bumps which he didn't know were there.

After a while he got into his underclothes, but just as he was pulling on his trousers the key rattled in the lock, and still another warder, with a fleshy purple nose, came in holding a large card.

'Surname?'

'Volodin,' the prisoner replied without arguing, although these senseless repetitions were making him feel sick.

'Name and patronymic?'

'Innokenty Artemyevich.'

'Year of birth?'

'Nineteen-nineteen.'

'Place of birth?'

'Leningrad.'

'Take all your clothes off.'

Half dazed, he took off those he had on. His vest slipped off the table where he had put it and fell to the floor, but this no longer upset him and he didn't bother to pick it up.

The warder inspected him carefully from all sides and wrote his observations on the card. From the attention paid to birthmarks and the detailed inspection of his face, Innokenty concluded that he was looking for identification marks.

The purple-nosed warder left in his turn.

Innokenty sat naked and apathetic.

The door rattled once again. A stout, dark-haired lady in a snow white linen coat came in. She had a coarse, arrogant face, but an educated manner.

Coming to, Innokenty dived for his underpants, to cover his nakedness. But the woman gave him a scornful, altogether unfeminine glance and, thrusting out her already prominent lower lip, asked:

'Have you got lice?'

Still holding his pants draped in front of him, Innokenty looked firmly into her dark Armenian eyes and said in a shocked voice: 'I'm a diplomat!'

'So what? Have you any complaints?'

'Why am I under arrest? Can I see the warrant? Can I see the Prosecutor?' he reeled off excitedly.

'That's not what I asked you,' said the woman with a weary frown. 'No venereal disease?'

'What?'

'Have you never had gonorrhoea, syphilis, soft chancre? Leprosy? Tuberculosis?'

She left the room without waiting for his answer.

The very first of the warders he had seen, the one with the long face, now came in. As he had neither harmed nor insulted him, Innokenty felt he was almost a friend.

'Why are you still undressed?' he asked severely. 'Get dressed at once.'

This was easier said than done. Locked up by himself, Innokenty struggled with his trousers, trying to make them keep up without braces and with hardly any buttons. Lacking the experience of generations of prisoners, he nevertheless solved the problem for himself, as had millions of his predecessors. He guessed where the 'bits of string' came from: all he had to do was tie his trousers at the waist and the flap with his shoe-laces. (Noticing for the first time that the metal tips had been torn off, he wondered why this had been done. Presumably the Lubyanka regulations assumed that prisoners could use them for making saws to cut through their bars.)

He made no attempt to tie up his diplomatic tunic.

Having checked through the peep-hole that the prisoner was now dressed, the sergeant unlocked the door, ordered him to keep his hands behind his back and led him to still another room, where the warder with the purple nose awaited him.

'Take your shoes off,' he greeted Innokenty.

There was a doctor's measuring scale against one of the walls. Purple-nose stood Innokenty with his back to it, measuring his height, noted it on his card and said: 'You can put your shoes on.'

'Hands behind your back,' added Long-face from the door —although from here to Box No. 8 was only two steps across the passage.

Once again, Innokenty was locked into his box.

The mysterious machine still hummed intermittently.

Holding his overcoat he sank listlessly on to the stool. All he had seen from the first moment he had found himself in the Lubyanka were dazzling lights, walls oppressively close to him and silent, blank-faced warders. Each procedure, more senseless than the last, struck him as a deliberate insult. He failed to see them as links in a considered, logical chain of events: preliminary search by the agents who had made the arrest; establishment of the prisoner's identity; his admission (in absentia, at the office) against a receipt from the prison administration; thorough search on admission; first hygienic precautions; listing of identification marks; medical examination. The procedure had lulled him, deprived him of his common sense and will to resist. His one longing was to sleep. He assumed now that he would be left alone for a while. His viewpoint altered by his three-hour stay in the Lubyanka, and seeing no other practical way to achieve his end, he stood the stool on the table, spread his fine cloth overcoat with its grey lambskin collar on the floor and lay down. His back was flat, he propped his head up against one corner of the box and bent his legs at the knees, resting his feet against the opposite corner. Yet for the few moments before his limbs grew numb he experienced bliss.

He was dozing off when the door flew open with a loud, deliberate noise:

'Stand up!' hissed the woman warder.

His eyelids barely moved.

'Stand up! Stand up!' the order rang out above him.

'But I want to sleep!'

'Stand up!' the woman shouted, bending over him like a vision of Medusa.

Getting up with difficulty from his cramped position, he muttered:

'Can't you take me somewhere where I can sleep?'

'It's forbidden,' the Medusa in sky-blue epaulettes snapped, and locked the door.

He leaned against the wall and waited, while she watched him through the door for a long time, raising the shield over the peep-hole again and again.

Finally she went and he took advantage of her absence to sink back on to the floor. He was almost asleep when the door creaked.

A tall, muscular man who would have done well as a road-mender or stonemason, came in, wearing a white coat.

'Take your things,' he said.

Innokenty took his hat and coat and followed him, tottering, his eyes dull and his feet by now unable to tell whether the floor was smooth or rough. He was in a state of extreme exhaustion, with no strength left to move, ready to lie down there and then in the middle of the corridor.

They went through a narrow opening in a thick wall to another corridor, not as clean as the first; there the man unlocked a door into a cabin—it was very like the dressing-room of a Russian bath—gave him a piece of kitchen soap no bigger than a match box and ordered him to wash.

For a long time Innokenty couldn't bring himself to do it. He was used to the shining cleanliness of tiled bathrooms, and although the cabin, with its plank walls and wooden benches, would have struck the average person as perfectly clean, to him it seemed filthy. At last he found a sufficiently dry patch on one of the benches to undress and, leaving his clothes, picked his way gingerly over the damp slats marked with the prints of both bare feet and shoes. He would much have preferred not to wash or undress at all, but the stonemason had unlocked the dressing-room door and ordered him to take a shower.

The shower-room door was like an ordinary—not a prison—door, with two glass panels, except that the glass panes were missing. Beyond it were more wooden slats, which seemed dirty to Innokenty, and four showers running with beautifully hot and cold water—but this he failed to appreciate. Four showers at the disposal of one man!—but this too gave him no pleasure. Had he known that in the world of prisoners it was more usual for four men to wash under one shower, he might have attached more value to his sixteenfold privilege. While still in the dressing-room, he had flung away the nasty evil-smelling soap in disgust (never in all his thirty years of life had he held such a thing in his hands or so much as known of its existence). Now he splashed himself for a couple of minutes, chiefly to wash off the bits of hair which had been pricking him in the tender parts of his body after the haircut. Then, feeling dirtier than before, he went back to the dressing-room for his clothes.

But there was nothing on any of the benches; all his splendid if ruined clothes had been taken away; only the galoshes and the shoes inside them stood with their toes pointing under the bench. The outer door was locked and the peep-hole covered. All Innokenty could do was to sit sculpturally naked like Rodin's 'Thinker', and think, while drying off.

After a time, he was issued with coarse, washed out, prison underclothes, stamped with the words 'Detention Centre' on the back and front, and a similarly stamped small square of turkish towelling folded in four, which he did not immediately recognize as a towel. The underclothes had buttons of some material which felt like cardboard, but there were too few of them, and there were tapes, but some were missing. The pants were too short and chafed between the legs, and the vest was so big that his hands were lost in the sleeves. His request to change them for another pair was refused, as he had soiled this one by putting it on.

Wearing this clumsy set of reach-me-downs, he still had to sit waiting in the dressing-room for a long time. He was told that his outer clothes were in the 'fryer'. The word was new to him. Even when the country was full of 'fryers' during the war, he had never come across one. But the 'frying' of his clothes was in keeping with his other senseless humiliations that night (he imagined a gigantic, devil's frying pan).

He tried to consider his position soberly, to think out what he should do about it, but his thoughts were confused and jumped from one thing to another—the tight underpants, the frying pan with his tunic in it, the constant, watchful eye outside the door, now hidden, now uncovered by the shield of the peep-hole.

The shower had woken him up, but he felt utterly weak and exhausted. He wished he could lie on something dry and not cold—lie motionless until the strength which was draining away from him returned. But he couldn't bring himself to lie half naked on the damp, sharp-edged planks which didn't even meet in the middle of the bench.

The door opened, but not for the arrival of his clothes from the fryer. Standing beside the bath attendant was a pink-cheeked, broad-faced girl in civilian dress. Modestly covering up what the inadequacies of his underclothes left exposed,

Innokenty went to the door. After ordering him to sign a carbon copy, the girl handed him a receipt, from the Detention Centre of the MGB of the USSR which, on December the 26th 1949, had taken for safe-keeping from Volodin I.A.: one fountain pen with yellow metal holder and nib; one tie-pin with inset red stone; one pair cuff-links of blue stone.

Again he sat and waited, dispirited. At last his clothes were brought—the overcoat cold and undamaged, the tunic, trousers and shirt crumpled, faded and still hot.

'Couldn't they have taken care of the tunic as well as the coat?' Innokenty protested.

'The coat has a fur trimming. Use your head,' the bath attendant admonished him.

After the fryer even his own clothes felt as though they were someone else's and disgusted him. Wearing all these alien, uncomfortable things, he was taken back to his Box No. 8.

He asked for water and drank two mugs full—it was the same mug with the picture of a cat.

Another girl came and gave him, against his signature, a blue receipt from the Detention Centre of the MGB of the USSR which, on December the 27th (already the 27th!) had taken from Volodin, I.A.: one silk vest, one pair silk pants, one pair braces and a tie.

The machine hummed intermittently and mysteriously as before.

Locked up once more, Innokenty rested his arms on the table, his head on his arms and tried to sleep.

'That's forbidden,' said a new warder, opening the door (the woman was off duty).

'What's forbidden?'

'To rest your head.'

His thoughts in total confusion, Innokenty continued to wait.

They brought him another receipt, this one on white paper, from the Detention Centre of the MGB of the USSR which had taken from Volodin I.A. 123 (one hundred and twenty-three roubles).

Then came a man wearing a blue linen coat over an expensive brown suit.

Every time they brought him a receipt, they asked his surname. Now, he was again asked: surname? name and patronymic? date of birth? place of birth?—after which the man said:

'Without.'

'What?' Innokenty was taken aback.

'Without your things, of course. Hands behind your back.'

In the corridor, all orders were given softly so that they could not be heard inside the boxes.

Clicking his tongue at the same invisible dog, the man in the brown suit took Innokenty through the main exit and another corridor, to a large room which was not of the prison type—it had curtains on the window, soft furniture and a desk. Innokenty was made to sit on a chair in the middle. He concluded that he was about to be questioned.

Instead, however, a camera was wheeled in from behind a curtain, two strong lights were switched on and he was photographed full face and in profile.

The officer who had brought Innokenty took each finger of his right hand and rolled it on a sticky roller covered with printer's ink, so that all five fingertips turned black. Spreading them evenly, he pressed them all together against a sheet of paper and tore it off.

The left hand was fingerprinted in the same way.

Above the fingerprints on the paper, there was a line of writing:

'Volodin, Innokenty Artemyevich, b. 1919, Leningrad.'

Above that was printed in bold characters:

TO BE KEPT IN PERPETUITY

Innokenty read the official formula and shivered. There was something mystical about it, something transcending man and his world.

He was allowed to scrub his hands with soap and a nail brush in cold water over a washbasin. The greasy ink was hard to remove by these inadequate means: the cold water ran off it. Innokenty scrubbed his fingertips with the soapy brush and did not question the inverted logic of making him have a bath before the fingerprinting.

His confused and exhausted mind was wholly in the power of that terrifying formula from another dimension:

TO BE KEPT IN PERPETUITY

CHAPTER EIGHTY-FOUR

Never had Innokenty lived through such an interminable night. He did not sleep for a moment, and more thoughts crowded through his mind in that one night than normally occurred to him in a month. There had been plenty of time to think during the slow process of unpicking the gold braid from his diplomatic uniform, during the long wait sitting half-naked in the bath-house and in the various boxes to which he had been confined throughout the night.

He had been struck by the aptness of the epitaph pronounced on him: 'To be kept in perpetuity.' For whether they proved he had made that telephone call or not (it had, in any case, obviously been monitored), having once arrested him they would never let him go again. He knew what it meant to be in Stalin's clutches—it was for life. The prospect of being sent to a labour camp was tolerable, but thanks to his position he might well be banished to a special place of monastic seclusion where he would not be allowed to sit down all day and forbidden to speak for years on end, where no one would ever discover what had become of him and he himself would be kept in total ignorance of events in the outside world, though whole continents might change their political allegiance and men might land on the moon. Prisoners held incommunicado could be quietly shot. It had happened before . . .

Was he afraid of death, he wondered?

All that evening Innokenty had welcomed every minor event, glad every time the door had opened to disturb his isolation, his unfamiliar state of confinement. Now, in contrast he wanted to be left alone to think something out, some great idea which was hovering just beyond the fringes of his consciousness, and he was glad that he had been put back in his previous box and left for a long time undisturbed except for constant surveillance through the peep-hole.

Suddenly he felt as if a thin veil were lifted from his brain and he remembered, clearly and quite involuntarily, the thought that had been in his mind earlier that day and the passage he had been reading:

'A belief in immortality arises from the insatiability of men's appetites. To the wise man the term of our life is quite sufficient to encompass the whole gamut of pleasures to which we may aspire. . . .'

If only pleasures were all that mattered! He had had money, good clothes, success, women, wine, travel; but now he was prepared to consign all these joys to perdition in exchange for one thing—justice. And there were all those others, unknown to him by sight or by name, walled up in this same building—how absurd to die without a chance to talk to them about the things which so disturbed his mind and spirit. How easy it had been for Epicurus to construct his philosophy under the spreading shade of a tree in that far-off era of immutable serenity and well-being! Now that Innokenty had neither pencil nor notebook he treasured all the more the fragments which came floating up from the recesses of his memory. He clearly recalled another passage:

'Physical suffering is not to be feared. Prolonged pain is never intense, intense pain is never prolonged.'

Take his present situation, for instance—cooped up sleepless and airless for days on end in a box like this, unable to stand up or stretch his legs—was this form of suffering prolonged or short-lived? Insignificant or intense? Or what about ten years in solitary, deprived of speech . . .?

In the room where he had been photographed and fingerprinted, Innokenty had noticed that it was nearly 2 a.m. By now it must be about three o'clock. A frivolous thought occurred to him, crowding out his serious reflections—his watch, which had been put in the prison safe-deposit, would go 'on working until the spring was unwound; then it would stop and no one else would wind it up again. The hands would remain fixed until either its owner died or all his possessions were confiscated. He wondered what time it would be showing. . . .

And was Dottie waiting for him at the theatre? Waiting

654

. . . and telephoning the Ministry? Probably not. Most likely the MVD had come immediately after his arrest to search the flat. It was such a big flat that it would take half a dozen men more than the whole night to search the place thoroughly. And what did they imagine they would find, the idiots?

Dottie would get a divorce and marry again. His father-in-law's career would suffer from this blot on the family escutcheon—they would undoubtedly treat him as partly guilty by association. Everybody who had known Counsellor Volodin would obediently erase him from their memory. He was being crushed by an implacable juggernaut and not a soul on earth would ever know what became of him. Yet he wanted to live on, to see what the future held. The world would be united. Armies, frontiers, would be abolished. A world parliament would be summoned, a universal president would be elected. He would stand bareheaded before the peoples of the world and say:

'Pick up your things!'

'What?'

'Pick up your things!'

'What things?'

'That junk.'

Innokenty stood up, holding his overcoat and fur hat. They were especially dear to him now that they were his only garments which had not been ruined by the fumigator. The duty warder stepped back from the open door to make way for the dark, cheerful-looking features of an MVD sergeant-major. As Innokenty wondered to himself how such men were recruited for a job like this, the man repeated the rigmarole of checking the prisoner's identity from a piece of paper:

'Surname?'

'Volodin.'

'Name and patronymic?'

'How many more times do I have to tell you?'

'Name and patronymic!'

'Innokenty Artemyevich.'

'Year of birth?'

'Nineteen-nineteen.'

'Place of birth?'

'Leningrad.'

'Pick up your things. Quick march!'

He led the way, clicking his tongue in the approved manner.

This time they went out into a dark covered yard and down a few steps. The thought occurred to him that they might be taking him off to be shot. They were always supposed to shoot people in cellars and always at night. However, a saving thought comforted him in this moment of anxiety: why, if they meant to shoot him, had they issued those three receipts? No, he was not going to be shot. (Innokenty still believed that all his jailors' actions were rational and coordinated.)

Still clicking his tongue, the cheerful sergeant-major led him into another building and through a dark lobby to a lift. A woman with a pile of ironed, greyish-yellow laundry stood and watched over her shoulder as Innokenty was escorted into the lift. Although the young laundress was ugly, although she was his social inferior and although she gave Innokenty exactly the same look of inscrutable, stony indifference as all the other automata-people employed in the Lubyanka, at the sight of her, as with the girls from the safe-deposit who had handed out the pink, blue and white receipts, Innokenty felt humiliated that she should see him in this miserable, ragged state and that she might feel a contemptuous sort of pity for him. But this thought passed as quickly as it had come—what did anything matter now?

The sergeant-major shut the lift doors and pressed a button for their destination, although none of the buttons were marked with floor-numbers. As soon as the lift-motor hummed into action, Innokenty immediately recognized it as the noise of that mysterious mechanical bone-crusher which he had heard through the walls of his box. Cheered by this happy discovery, he gave a mirthless smile.

The lift stopped. The sergeant-major ordered Innokenty out on to a landing, then along a wide corridor that swarmed with warders in blue epaulettes with white stripes of rank. One of them locked Innokenty into an unnumbered box. It was, however, a larger one than before, a dozen-odd square metres in area, dimly lit, with walls painted from floor to ceiling with olive-green oil paint. The box or cell was empty and gave an impression of being dirty. It had a worn concrete floor and a narrow wooden bench let into the wall that was just long enough to seat three people in a row. It was also chilly, which added to the general bleakness. The door contained the usual peep-hole, though its cover was seldom raised. From outside came the muffled tread of boots, a sign of the constant arrivals and departures which made up the busy night-time life of a detention centre.

Earlier Innokenty had imagined that he was due to be permanently shut up in the cramped, hot, blindingly lit conditions of Box No. 8, where he could never stretch out his legs, where the light hurt his eyes and it was difficult to breathe. He now saw that he had been wrong and that instead he would have to spend his days in this large, depressing, anonymous cell. His feet would suffer cold from the concrete floor, he would be tortured by the constant scurrying to and fro, by the shuffling of feet outside and the lack of proper light. If only there were a window—even a tiny one, even the kind of cell window that stage designers build for a prison scene at the opera; but there was none.

However many stories one may hear, however many memoirs one may read, it is impossible to imagine the reality of prison—the corridors, the staircases, the innumerable doors, the officers, sergeants and domestic staff moving ceaselessly to and fro in the busy nocturnal life of the Greater Lubyanka, yet with no more than one prisoner allowed out at a time, there is never a chance of meeting a fellow-prisoner, of hearing anything other than words of command. Each prisoner is made to feel that the whole Ministry is awake on his account alone, concerned with nothing but him and his crime. The first hours of imprisonment are designed to break the prisoner down by isolating him from contact with the other inmates, so that there is no one to keep his spirits up, so that the full force of the whole vast, ramified apparatus is felt to be bearing down on him and on him alone.

Innokenty's thoughts took a painful turn. He saw clearly that the telephone call, which only two days ago had seemed a noble act, had been merely stupid, pointless and suicidal. He now had enough space to walk up and down, but exhausted and confused by his treatment Innokenty lacked the strength to do so. He paced the cell a couple of times, then sat down on the bench and let his arms dangle slackly beside his legs. He thought of all the good and great intentions that lay buried behind these walls, locked up in these boxes, and he cursed his own soft-heartedness. It was today or tomorrow that Innokenty should have flown to Paris, and he could then have forgotten all about the miserable creature he had tried—and failed—to save. As he imagined himself making the trip abroad that should have started this coming day, the thought of the utter finality of his loss of freedom took his breath away. At that moment he could have clawed at the walls of his cell in an agony of frustration.

He was, however, prevented from committing such a breach of prison regulations by the door opening. Once again his 'personal data' were checked, to which Innokenty replied as in a dream, and he was ordered out with his 'things'. As he had felt rather cold in this cell he had put his fur hat on his head and thrown his overcoat over his shoulders. He made to leave the cell, unaware that by wearing his clothes in this way he might be concealing two loaded pistols or a couple of daggers. He was ordered to put on his overcoat with his arms in the sleeves and to hold his bared wrists behind his back.

With the guard clicking his tongue as before, Innokenty was led to the staircase by the lift-shaft and taken downstairs. In his situation the most interesting thing that Innokenty could have done would have been to have counted the number of turns they made and how many steps they took, so as to reconstruct the layout of the prison at his leisure. But his perception had become so blunted that he walked on unaware of his surroundings and of the number of steps they were taking. Suddenly, along another corridor, a tall warder came towards them, also vigorously clicking his tongue. The man escorting Innokenty hurriedly flung open the door of a green plywood cupboard, which was blocking the already narrow landing, pushed Innokenty into it and shut the door on him. Inside there was only just room enough to stand and a feeble light came in from the ceiling. The cupboard appeared to have no top, letting in the light from the staircase-well.

The natural human reaction would have been to protest

loudly, but Innokenty, who had by now grown used to the incomprehensible maltreatment and the silence which reigned in the Lubyanka, obeyed without a sound—behaving, in fact, exactly as the prison system intended he should. Now at last he realized why the Lubyanka warders clicked their tongues: it was a warning signal that they were escorting a prisoner. One prisoner must never be allowed to encounter another, never be allowed to draw comfort or support from the look in his eyes. . . .

The other prisoner was led away, then Innokenty was let out of his cupboard and escorted on.

It was there, on the steps of the last flight of stairs, that Innokenty noticed how deeply the steps were worn. He had never seen anything like it in his life before. From the edges to the centre they were worn down in oval con-cavities to half their thickness. He shuddered. How many feet must have scraped over them to wear out the stone to such a depth! Of every two who had passed that way, one had been a warder, the other—a prisoner.

On the landing of the next floor was a locked door with a small closed window behind a grille. Here Innokenty was introduced to a new experience—being made to stand with his face to the wall. Even so, out of the corner of his eye he could see the warder press an electric bell, at which the pane was suspiciously opened and then closed. Then, with much clanking of keys, the door was opened and the man who emerged from it, whom Innokenty could not see, began questioning him:

'Surname?'

Accustomed as all of us are to facing the person we are talking to, Innokenty naturally turned round, and just had time to catch sight of a puffy, effeminate face with a large red scald-mark and beneath the face a lieutenant's gold epaulettes, before the man bellowed at him:

'Face the wall!'

He then went on with the same wearisome set of questions, the answer to which Innokenty spoke to a patch of white plaster in front of his face.

Having satisfied himself that the prisoner still admitted to being the person described on the card and still remem-bered the year and place of his birth, the fleshy lieutenant rang the bell in the door, which had been locked behind him as a precaution. Once more the little window was drawn suspiciously back, someone looked through the opening, closed the window and opened the door with several loud turns of a key.

'Quick march!' said the fat lieutenant with the red scald-mark on his face.

They entered and the door was locked noisily behind them. Innokenty just had time to make out three branching corridors—one straight ahead, one to the right, another to the left—dimly lit, with rows of doors, and close at hand on his left a table, a filing cabinet and several more warders, before the lieutenant gave him an order in a quiet but steely voice:

'Face the wall. Stand still.'

It was an absurd situation—to have to stare at the dividing line between the olive-green paint below and the white-washed plaster above, feeling several hostile pairs of eyes on the back of one's neck . . .

After presumably checking his record-card, the lieutenant announced in a near-whisper that rang out clearly in the utter silence:

'Box No. 3!'

A warder moved away from the table and this time without the usual sound of clinking keys, set off along the burlap-covered floor of the right-hand corridor.

'Hands behind your back. Quick march!' he rapped out in a low voice.

On their right they followed the same olive-green wall round three corridors, while to their left they passed several doors marked with glazed number-plates—47, 48, 49. Beneath these were the covered peep-holes. Excited by the thought that his companions in misfortune were so near to him, Innokenty felt an urge to push one of the covers back, glance through for a moment and look in at the life inside the cell; but the warder was hurrying on and although he had nothing more to lose, Innokenty was already too thoroughly under the influence of the greatest deterrent of all—the prisoner's instinctive sense of obedience—to do anything so rash.

Unfortunately for us mortals and fortunately for the powers that be, it is in the nature of man that as long as he is alive there is always something which can be taken away from him. Even a man serving a life sentence, who cannot move, who is cut off from the sight of the sky, separated from his family and his property, can still be transferred to a damp cell in solitary confinement, deprived of hot food, beaten—and a man is just as sensitive to these refinements of punishment as he was to his first violent overthrow from his pinnacle of freedom and well-being. So to avoid the pain of these ultimate penalties a prisoner docilely carries out the hateful demands of a degrading prison régime, which slowly destroys him as a human being.

After the first bend in the corridor the doors were closer together and the glazed number-plates read: 1, 2, 3. The warder unlocked the door of Box No. 3, and with a wide sweeping gesture which seemed out of place and slightly comic, flung it open. Innokenty noticed the oddness of the warder's behaviour and looked closely at him. He was a short, broad-shouldered lad, with straight black hair and eye-sockets slashed crookedly into his face as though with a slanting blow from a sword. He had an ugly look about him, with unsmiling eyes and lips, but of the dozen or so expressionless Lubyanka faces that Innokenty had seen that night, there was something about this warder's evil face that he liked.

Locked inside the box, Innokenty looked round. By now he was something of a connoisseur of prison cells, having been in enough of them to draw comparisons. This box was a paradise—three and a half paces wide, seven and a half in length, with a parquet floor, one side almost completely taken up with a long and reasonably broad wooden bench fastened to the wall, and with a small free-standing hexagonal table near the doorway. The box had, of course, no windows, only a small ventilation grating far up on one wall. It was also very high—three and a half metres from floor to ceiling—and the whole of the wall was whitewashed, gleaming from a two-hundred-watt bulb in a wire casing over the door. The lamp warmed the box but it was painfully bright.

Prisoners learn fast and their knowledge sticks. This time Innokenty had no illusions; he did not expect to stay long in this comfortable box, but as he looked at the long bare bench, with his fast-growing prison experience he realized that his first and main need was sleep. Just as a young animal deprived of its mother will instinctively fend for itself, so Innokenty quickly discovered how to make a bed out of his overcoat, folding the astrakhan collar and the sleeves into a makeshift pillow. He lay down, and finding it very comfortable he closed his eyes and settled down to sleep.

But he could not sleep. He had so longed to be able to fall asleep earlier when it had been impossible, but he had passed through every stage of tiredness, had twice dropped into momentary sleep, and now that he could sleep, the sleep refused to come. The constant spasms of arousal had so unsettled him that he found it impossible to relax. Fighting off the wave of thoughts, regrets and reflections, Innokenty tried to breath evenly and count to himself. His inability to sleep was infuriating, now that he was warm, the bench felt quite comfortable, his legs were fully stretched and the warder, for some reason, was leaving him alone.

After lying like this for about half an hour, his thoughts began at last to lose coherence and a comforting warmth started creeping over his body from his legs upwards. It was then that Innokenty realized that he could not possibly sleep in that insanely bright light. Not only did the light penetrate his closed lids with an orange glow, but he could actually feel it pressing with unbearable force against his eyeballs. This physical pressure of the light, which Innokenty had never noticed before, drove him to fury. Turning in vain from side to side to find a position in which the light did not press on his eyes, Innokenty gave up in despair, sat up and put his feet on the ground.

The cover of his peep-hole was raised frequently—he could hear the noise it made—and the next time it was opened he quickly raised his finger.

The door opened noiselessly. The squinting warder looked at Innokenty in silence.

'Please—turn the light off!' Innokenty said imploringly.

'Not allowed to,' replied the warder imperturbably.

'Well, change the bulb, then. Put in one that's not so bright. What's the use of such a powerful bulb in such a small . . . box?'

'Don't talk so loud,' said the warder very quietly. The huge corridor behind him and the whole prison were as silent as the grave. 'The lamp has to be that bright—prison regulations.'

Innokenty had been right—there *was* a spark of life behind that death-like face. Having exhausted this topic of conversation and guessing that the door would immediately be closed again, Innokenty asked:

'Fetch me a drink of water, please.'

The man with the squint nodded and locked the door without a sound. He walked noiselessly away from the box along the burlap-covered floor, and returning with only the faintest grating of the key in the lock, stood in the doorway with a mug of water. As on the ground floor of the prison, the mug was decorated with a picture of a cat, but this cat had no spectacles, no book and no bird.

Innokenty drank gratefully and as he paused to draw breath he looked up at the warder. The man had taken one step into the room, shut the door as far as the width of his shoulders permitted and with a thoroughly non-regulation wink he asked in a low voice:

'What were you—outside?'

How odd it sounded—the first human remark of that night. Moved by the lively curiosity in the man's voice, by the low tone he used as a precaution against being overheard by someone in authority, and aroused by the unintentional callousness of that little word *were*, Innokenty whispered conspiratorially:

'Diplomat. Rank of counsellor.'

The man with the squint nodded sympathetically and said:

'I used to be a sailor in the Baltic Fleet.' He paused. 'What are you in for?'

'I've no idea,' said Innokenty cautiously. 'For nothing at all, as far as I know.'

The warder nodded sympathetically again.

'They all say that at first,' he said, then added coarsely, 'D'you want to go to the . . .?'

'No, thanks,' said Innokenty, not realizing in his innocence that the offer that had been made to him was the greatest privilege that a warder could grant and that for a prisoner one of the greatest joys on earth is to be allowed to relieve himself outside the regulation times.

After this interesting conversation the door was shut and Innokenty stretched out on the bench again, struggling in vain against the light pressing in through his defenceless eyelids. He tried covering them with his hand, but the hand slipped away. He realized how convenient it would be to fold his handkerchief into a strip and cover his eyes with it, but where was his handkerchief now? Oh God, why hadn't he picked it up from the floor? What a stupid fool he had been only a few hours ago. It is the little things—a handkerchief, an empty matchbox, a piece of strong thread or a plastic button—that are the prisoners' best friends. There will always come a time when one of them is suddenly indispensable for getting him out of a tight spot.

Suddenly the door opened and the squint-eyed warder handed Innokenty a great bulging red chequered mattress. It seemed like a miracle. Far from preventing him from sleeping, the Lubyanka was actually taking trouble over a prisoner's sleep! Rolled up in the mattress was a small down pillow, a pillow-slip and a sheet, both stamped 'Detention Centre', and even a grey blanket.

It was bliss—now he could sleep. His first impressions had made him judge the prison too harshly. With pleasurable anticipation (and doing it for the first time in his life) he pulled the slip over the pillow, made up his bed (because the bench was just too narrow the mattress hung slightly over the edge), undressed, lay down, covered his eyes with a sleeve of his tunic—he now lacked nothing. He was just beginning to drift off into that deep sleep once known as the arms of Morpheus, when the door opened with a crash and squint-eyes said:

'Take your arms out from under the blanket!'

'Take them out?' cried Innokenty, almost in tears. 'Why did you have to wake me up? It's hard enough for me to get to sleep.'

'Take your arms out,' repeated the warder, unmoved. 'Your arms must be outside the bedclothes.'

Innokenty did as he was told; but it proved to be no easy matter to fall asleep while keeping his arms above the blanket. It was a diabolical rule: a person's natural, ingrained habit is to keep his arms covered when he sleeps, to hold them close to his body. For a long time Innokenty tossed restlessly as he adapted himself to yet another form of humiliation, but at last sleep won the upper hand. A delicious numbness began to steal over his mind.

Suddenly he heard a noise along the corridor. Starting in the distance and drawing nearer came the sound of cell-doors being slammed, accompanied each time by a shouted word. There it was, next door. Then Innokenty's door was opened too and the ex-sailor from the Baltic announced mercilessly:

'Reveille!'

'What? Why?' groaned Innokenty. 'I haven't slept all night!'

'Six o'clock. Time to get up!' the sailor said and moved on to the next cell.

The desire to sleep now overcame Innokenty with peculiar force. He collapsed on to his bed and fell asleep instantly, but was only able to stay asleep for a minute or two before Squint-eyes noisily flung open his door and shouted:

'Reveille! Roll up your bedding.'

Innokenty raised himself on one elbow to stare at his tormentor, who only an hour before had seemed so likeable.

'But I haven't slept at all—don't you realize?'

'None of my business.'

'All right, so I get up, roll up my bedding—what do I do then?'

'Nothing. Sit there.'

'But—why?'

'Because the rule is—reveille at six.'

'Then I'll go to sleep sitting up!'

'I won't let you. I'll wake you.'

Innokenty clutched his head and rocked from side to side. Something that might have been sympathy showed in the warder's face.

'Want a wash?'

'All right,' said Innokenty after a moment's reflection and stretched out for his clothes.

'Hands behind your back! Quick march!'

The latrines were round the corner. Despairing of getting any more sleep that morning, Innokenty took the risk of stripping to the waist and thoroughly washing himself in cold water. He could splash around as much as he liked on the concrete floor of the large, chilly latrine with the door locked and without interruption from the warder. The man might be human, but why had he been so underhand as not to warn him in advance that reveille was at six o'clock?

The cold water banished the stupefying lassitude caused by Innokenty's interrupted sleep. In the corridor he tried asking about breakfast, but the warder cut him off. Back in the cell he replied:

'There's no breakfast.'

'What? Don't we get anything to eat?'

'At eight o'clock there's rations, tea and sugar.'

'What's "rations"?'

'It means bread.'

'And when's lunch?'

'Not allowed. Supper's the next meal.'

'And am I supposed to just sit here all that time?'

'That's enough talking.'

Innokenty just had time to raise his hand before the warder had fully closed the door.

'Well, what is it this time?' asked the sailor.

'My buttons have been cut off, and the lining's been ripped out of my coat—how can I get them mended?'

'How many buttons?'

They counted them, then the door was shut. After a short while it was opened again. Squint-eyes handed over a needle, a dozen separate pieces of thread and a few buttons of various sorts and sizes—some bone, some plastic and some wooden.

'These are no good! Where are my own buttons?'

'Take them and shut up, or you won't even get these,' shouted the warder.

Again for the first time in his life, Innokenty began to sew. It took him some time to discover how to stiffen the end of the thread, how to stitch, how to finish off sewing a button. Without the benefit of thousands of years of accumulated human experience, Innokenty discovered the art of sewing all over again. He pricked himself so often that his tender finger-tips began to hurt. He spent a long time sewing the lining of his tunic back into place and restoring

666

the torn-out padding to his overcoat. He sewed some of the buttons on in the wrong places, so that the hem of his tunic hung in wrinkles. But this absorbing, unhurried task not only made the time pass, it completely restored Innokenty's peace of mind. His anxiety subsided, his sense of fear and persecution ebbed away. It became obvious that even this legendary chamber of horrors, the Greater Lubyanka Prison, was not so terrible after all. There were people living in it, whom he longed to meet; and he had made a great discovery—that a person who has not slept all night, who is hungry and whose life has been turned drastically upside down in the space of a few hours, is granted his 'second wind', just as an athlete's aching body revives to a new access of freshness and strength.

The warder, a new one this time, took away the needle. Soon afterwards he was brought a pound of moist black bread with a triangular extra slice to make it up to the regulation weight and two lumps of sugar. Then they poured him out a mugful of hot, strong tea and told him he could have more if he wanted it.

The time was eight o'clock in the morning, the date December the 27th.

Innokenty tipped his whole day's ration of sugar into his mug and stupidly tried to stir it with his finger but found that it was too hot to bear. Then after stirring it by swilling it round in the mug he drank his tea with relish (he had no desire to eat anything) and asked for more by raising his hand. As the second mugful lacked sugar he tasted the flavour of the tea even more strongly and Innokenty gulped it down with a shiver of pleasure.

His mind now took on a rare degree of clarity. In expectation of the forthcoming battle of wits he began walking up and down in the narrow space between the bench and the opposite wall, squeezing past his rolled-up mattress—three short paces forward, three short paces back. He recalled another aphorism of Epicurus, which no one had so far refuted and which only yesterday, still a free man, he had found so hard to grasp:

'The highest criteria of good and evil are our own feelings of pleasure or displeasure.'

In other words, according to Epicurus, only what I like

667

is good, and what I do not like is evil. This was the philosophy of a savage. Because Stalin liked killing people, did this mean that he regarded killing as good? And if someone found displeasure in being imprisoned for having tried to save another man, was his action therefore evil? No—for Innokenty good and evil were now absolute and distinct, and visibly separated by the pale-grey door in front of him, by those whitewashed walls, by the experience of his first night in prison. Seen from the pinnacle of struggle and pain to which he was now ascending, the wisdom of Epicurus seemed no more than the babbling of a child.

The door opened with a crash.

'Surname?' barked another new warder, this time a man of Asiatic appearance.

'Volodin'.

'Interrogation. Hands behind your back!' Innokenty clasped his hands behind his back, and holding his head up like a bird drinking, marched out of his box.

CHAPTER EIGHTY-FIVE

At Mavrino, too, it was breakfast time.

The day had begun like any ordinary day, only marred by Senior Lieutenant Shusterman's efforts to prevent the prisoners from sleeping after reveille before he handed over to the next officer. All was not well, either, during exercise. After the previous day's thaw it had frozen again during the night and the path round the exercise yard was covered in a thin layer of ice. Several prisoners came out, took one turn round the yard, found it too slippery, and went back indoors. In the cells the prisoners sat on their bunks, either swinging their legs or tucking them up under them. They were in no hurry to get up, but instead scratched their chests, yawned, or cracked ill-tempered jokes about each other or about their miserable life, and described their dreams—a favourite pastime among prisoners. But although one man had dreamed of a stream of muddy water flowing towards a bridge and another had dreamed of pulling on a pair of long boots, none of the dreams had clearly predicted that a batch of prisoners would be transferred to a labour camp that day.

Sologdin, as usual, set off early to chop firewood. He had kept his window ajar all night and opened it wider before going out for firewood.

Rubin, lying with his head towards the same window, said nothing to Sologdin. He had suffered from insomnia all night, had gone to bed late and now he could feel a cold draught coming from the window, but he was determined to have nothing whatever to do with the man who had insulted him, so he put on his fur hat with the earflaps down and his quilted jerkin. Thus dressed he covered himself with his blanket and lay curled up in a ball; he did not get up for breakfast, but ignored both Shusterman and the general noise in the room in an attempt to make up his proper amount of sleep.

Potapov was one of the first to get up to take his exercise and to have breakfast. He had already drunk his tea, already made up his bunk into a severely tidy rectangle and had sat down to read a newspaper, although inwardly he was longing to get to work. Today he was due to calibrate an interesting new mechanism, designed by himself.

There was only buckwheat porridge for breakfast that morning, so several prisoners went without the meal, but Gerasimovich sat for a long time in the dining-hall, carefully and slowly spooning small quantities of porridge into his mouth. Nerzhin nodded to him from another corner of the half-empty dining-hall, also sat down at an empty table and ate listlessly.

When he had finished Nerzhin went back to his top bunk for the last quarter of an hour of free time, lay down and stared at the domed ceiling. People in the room were still discussing what had happened to Ruska. He had not come back to sleep in his bunk and it was now certain that he had been arrested. There was a little dark cell in the staff building and he had been locked up in there. They did not actually call him a double-crosser in so many words, but they implied it. The general opinion was that since he already had the maximum sentence, they might convert his sentence from twenty-five years in a labour camp to twenty-five years solitary (it was in that year that a number of special prisons were built consisting entirely of one-man cells and solitary confinement was becoming increasingly fashionable). Shikin, of course, would not charge him with being a double informer, but a man did not necessarily have to be charged with the actual offence of which he was guilty: if he had fair hair he could be charged with having black hair, yet still be sentenced to the punishment due for being fair-haired.

Nerzhin was not sure quite how far the affair between Ruska and Clara had gone, and whether, or how, he ought to commiserate with her.

Rubin threw off his blanket and got up, amid general mirth, wearing his fur hat and quilted jerkin. He never minded it, in fact, when people made fun of him personally. Removing his hat but keeping on his jerkin and without bothering to put on his boots as there was no longer much point in doing so (exercise, ablutions and breakfast were over anyway), Rubin asked someone to pour him out a glass of tea. Sitting on his bunk without raising his eyes, his beard matted and ragged, mechanically feeding himself with white bread and butter and washing it down with the hot liquid, he buried himself in a novel by Upton Sinclair which he held in the same hand as his glass of tea. He was in the blackest of moods.

Morning roll-call had begun. A junior lieutenant came in and counted heads, and Shusterman read out the day's orders. As he came into the semicircular room Shusterman announced, as he had done in the previous rooms:

'Pay attention! Prisoners are informed that no one will be allowed to go into the kitchen after dinnertime to fetch hot water, and no one is to knock on the door for it or call the duty cook!'

'Who gave that order?' shrieked Pryanchikov in fury, leaping up out of one of the caves between two of the sets of double bunks.

'The prison governor,' said Shusterman weightily.

'When?'

'Yesterday.'

With his thin, puny arms Pryanchikov shook his fists over his head as though calling on heaven and earth as his witness.

'It's impossible!' he protested indignantly. 'On Saturday evening the Minister himself, Abakumov, promised me that we could have hot water at night! It's only right—after all, we work until midnight!'

The prisoners greeted his retort with a roar of laughter.

'Your fault for working so late, you stupid c——' boomed Dvoyetyosov.

'We can't keep a cook working all night,' said Shusterman in a reasoned tone.

Then, taking a list from the junior lieutenant, in a chilling voice which produced instant silence, Shusterman announced:

'Pay attention! The following prisoners from this room will not report for work and will prepare for transfer: Khorobrov, Mikhailov, Nerzhin, Syomushkin. All articles of government property to be collected and handed in to the prison stores.'

And the two officers marched out.

Like a whirlwind, every man in the room crowded round the four whose names had been called out. People abandoned their tea, left half-eaten slices of bread and butter and gathered in groups. Four men out of twenty-five—it was a cruel, unusually heavy crop to take. Everybody started talking at once, excited voices mixed with others that were despondent or scornfully indignant. Some men stood up at full height on the upper bunks and waved their arms, others clasped their heads, others seemed to be trying to prove something, beating their breasts, while others were already shaking pillows out of their pillow-slips. The whole room was one explosive babel of grief, resignation, chagrin, determination, complaint and calculation. The upheaval was of such an intensity that Rubin got up from his bed as he was, in his jerkin and underpants, and screamed in a piercing voice:

'A historic day at Mavrino! The day of the great purge!'

He spread out his arms to embrace the whole scene.

His excitement did not mean that he was glad the men were being transferred. He would have laughed just as loudly if he himself were being shipped off. Nothing was sacred if it gave him a chance to coin a ringing phrase.

To be transferred is as fateful a juncture in a prisoner's life as it is for a soldier to be wounded. Just as a wound can be light or severe, curable or mortal, so a transfer can mean being sent near or far; it can be a pleasant change—or it can be death. Reading about the horrors of convict life in Dostoyevsky one is amazed at how peacefully the tsarist régime let its prisoners serve their sentences in one place, without a single transfer in ten years.

When a prisoner is kept permanently in one place he gets used to his comrades, to his work, to the prison officers. However much he may dislike the life, he inevitably adapts to it. He acquires a suitcase—either a fibre one sent from home or a prison-made plywood case; he acquires a little frame into which he puts a photograph of his wife or his daughter, he acquires a pair of felt slippers which he wears in the hut after work and which he hides in the daytime in case they are found during a search, he may even wangle himself a spare pair of cotton trousers or he may succeed in keeping a decent pair of shoes, all of which he keeps hidden when the camp officers make a check on the prisoners' belongings. He even has his own needle, his own buttons which he has securely sewn on—and a couple of spare ones as well. There is a modest store of tobacco in his pouch. And if he is a greenhorn he keeps some tooth-powder and occasionally cleans his teeth. He accumulates a pile of letters from his relatives, acquires a book and is able, by exchanging it, to read every other book in the camp.

But a transfer shatters his little world like a thunderbolt. It always comes without warning, and the prisoner is always told at the last possible moment in order to catch him unawares. Down the lavatory go all his letters from home. If the transfer is to be made in cattle trucks, the escort will cut off all the prisoner's buttons, scatter all his tooth-powder and tobacco to the four winds in case it might be used on the journey to blind one of the guards in the escort. If the party is to be transferred in special railway carriages with barred windows, the escort will ruthlessly trample on any suitcases which do not fit into the cramped cell-like compartments, smashing the little photograph frame as they do so. In either case they remove all books, which are forbidden on the journey, and they confiscate all needles, lest they be used to file through the bars or stab a member of the escort;

they throw out the prisoner's felt slippers as rubbish, grab any spare trousers and put them into the camp stores. Thus purged of sinful attachment to personal property, of any inclination to settle down to a sedentary existence, of any tendency to relapse into a life of bourgeois comfort (rightly condemned even by Chekhov), purged of his friends and his past, the prisoner clasps his hands behind his back and, lined up in columns of four (one step out of line and the escort will open fire without warning!), surrounded by dogs and armed men, he sets off for his railway wagon.

You will all have seen them at our railway stations, but in cowardly fashion you will have ignored them or obediently turned away like a good Soviet citizen so that the lieutenant in charge of the escort will not suspect you of criminal intent and arrest you.

The prisoner climbs aboard his wagon—and it is coupled on behind the mail car. Heavily barred on both sides, invisible from the platform, the prisoner travels in a normal scheduled train, taking with him in his stuffy, cramped, locked compartment a thousand memories, hopes and fears.

Where is he going? He is never told. What can he expect in the new place? The copper mines? A lumber camp? Or will he be detailed to farmwork, where you can occasionally roast yourself a potato or eat your fill of turnips. Perhaps he will be lucky enough to bribe someone or meet a friend who will help him to wangle a job as an orderly, a hospital attendant or even as assistant to the storekeeper. Will he be laid low by scurvy or muscular dystrophy in his first month? Will they allow him to send and receive letters at the new place? Or will they stop his correspondence for years on end, so that his family thinks he is dead? Maybe he will not even arrive at his destination. Will he die of dysentery in his cattle truck? Or die of hunger because the train does not stop for six days and no rations are issued? Or will the escort club him to death with rifle-butts for attempted escape? Or at the end of the journey will they throw the prisoners' frozen corpses out of an unheated wagon like so many logs of wood? A train of cattle trucks can take a month to reach the Pacific coast of eastern Siberia . . . Lord, have mercy on those who never arrive.

And although prisoners transferred from Mavrino were

treated lightly, even being allowed to keep their razors until the next stage in their transfer, every one of the twenty prisoners whose names were called out for transfer on Tuesday realized with dread what it might mean. The carefree life, half-way to freedom, which they had led at Mavrino, was over.

CHAPTER EIGHTY-SIX

Besides the shock and anxiety caused by the news of his transfer, Nerzhin felt a sudden and growing urge to get even with Major Shikin before he left. So when the bell rang for the start of work, despite the order to stay in the dormitory and wait for the warder, Nerzhin rushed through the swing doors along with the nineteen other men who were not due for transfer. He ran up to the third floor, knocked at Shikin's door and was told to enter.

Shikin was sitting at his desk, gloomy and depressed. Since yesterday he had been feeling a sharp twinge of anxiety. One foot had dangled over the abyss and he now had a feeling of the ground shifting under him. Unfortunately there was no quick and easy way to vent his hatred on that young puppy Doronin. The worst that Shikin could do (and the least dangerous for himself) was to make Doronin kick his heels in solitary for a while, write a really filthy report on him in his personal dossier and send him back to a labour camp at Vorkuta in the Arctic, where with such an adverse report he was bound to land up in a punitive brigade and that, before long, would be the end of him. The result would be the same as having him put on trial and shot. So far this morning he had not called in Doronin for interrogation because he expected several of the men listed for transfer to lodge protests.

He was not mistaken. The door opened and in came Nerzhin.

Major Shikin had always loathed this tough, scrawny prisoner with his mulish obstinacy and his sickeningly exact knowledge of the letter of the law. Shikin had long been trying to persuade Yakonov to have Nerzhin transferred and he felt a malicious pleasure at the sight of the man's face as he came in, presumably to demand an explanation of his transfer.

Nerzhin had an innate gift of being able spontaneously to phrase a complaint in a few sharp words, and to utter them in a single breath during that brief moment when the food-hatch of the cell door was opened, or to fit them in on the scrap of soggy lavatory paper supplied to prisoners for submitting written requests. During the five years of his sentence he had also developed his own special, very firm manner of talking to prison officers—the style known in prisoners' slang as the 'college leg-pull'.

'Major Shikin,' he began, as soon as he was in the doorway, 'I've come to get back my illegally confiscated book. I am sure that the means of public transport in Moscow being what they are, six weeks is long enough for you to have convinced yourself that my book has been passed by the censorship.'

'Book?' said Shikin in surprise (taken aback, he could think of nothing more intelligent to say). 'What book?'

'I am equally sure you know which book I am talking about. The selected poems of Sergei Yesenin.'

'Yesenin!' Major Shikin sat back in his chair as though just recalling this subversive name and being appalled by it. His bristly, greying crew-cut expressed horror and revulsion. 'How can you bring yourself to ask for . . . *Yesenin?*'

'Why not? He's published here, in the Soviet Union.'

'That means nothing.'

'Not only was this book published in the Soviet Union, but it happens to be dated 1940, in other words it does not fall within the forbidden period of 1917 to 1938.'

Shikin frowned.

'Why do you choose that period especially?'

Nerzhin's reply came as pat as if he had already learned it all by heart:

'It was kindly explained to me by the censor at one of the labour camps. Once during a pre-New Year search of the camp he took away my copy of Dahl's *Lexicon of the Russian Language*, on the grounds that it was published in 1935, and therefore had to be most carefully checked for errors of a political nature. However, when I pointed out to him that this dictionary was a photo-mechanical reprint of the 1881 edition, the censor gladly returned it to me, explaining that there was no objection to pre-revolutionary books because the enemies of the people had not yet emerged by then. And this edition of Yesenin, you see, was published in 1940.'

Shikin sat for a while in dignified silence.

'All right,' he said, 'suppose it was. But,' he went on earnestly, 'have you *read* this book? Have you read it at all? Would you confirm that in writing?'

'In the present circumstances you have no legal grounds for taking a signed statement from me under Article 95 of the Criminal Code of the RSFSR. However, I will make the following verbal statement: I have the unfortunate habit of reading the books which happen to be my property and vice-versa, I only keep books that I read.'

Shikin spread his hands.

'Bad luck!'

He intended this to be followed by a significant pause, but Nerzhin ruined it by saying:

'To repeat my request briefly—in accordance with Section 7, Sub-section B of the Prison Regulations, kindly return the book which was illegally confiscated from me.'

Wincing under this volley of words, Shikin stood up. Sitting at his desk his large head seemed to belong to a man of imposing proportions, but as soon as he stood up his arms and legs were so short that he appeared to shrink. Scowling, he walked over to a cupboard, unlocked it and took out the beautifully produced little volume of Yesenin, its dust-jacket patterned with maple leaves. Several passages were marked. Still without inviting Nerzhin to sit down, he settled comfortably in his armchair and began a leisurely inspection of the marked passages. Nerzhin calmly sat down, rested his hands on his knees and watched Shikin with a grim, unwavering stare.

'Well, take this for example,' said Shikin, and read out a verse in an insensitive monotone. 'That sounds pretty dubious to me.'

The prisoner looked at the Security Officer's flabby hands.

'Yesenin was limited by his class origins and there was a great deal about politics that he failed to understand.'

Nerzhin pursed his lips to express lofty commiseration. 'Like Pushkin, like Gogol . . .'

A new note was detectable in Nerzhin's voice which made Shikin glance up nervously at him. Whenever he was faced by prisoners who were not afraid of him, Shikin himself felt a secret fear—the usual fear of the ragged and unfortunate felt by people who are well dressed and well off. Now his authority was of little use as a defence. To be on the safe side he got up and opened the door a little.

Back in his armchair Shikin read out another passage:

' *"In earthly wedlock I tried to join*
The pure white rose and the black, black toad . . ."

. . . and so on. Now what is that supposed to mean?'

The prisoner's tight-stretched throat quivered.

'It's very simple,' he replied. 'It means that no one should ever try and reconcile the white rose of truth with the black toad of evil!'

The black toad was seated in front of him in the person of this grim-faced little policeman, with his short arms and his big head.

'I'm afraid, though, Major,' said Nerzhin in a rapid burst of words, 'that I haven't the time to discuss literature with you. The escort is waiting for me. Six weeks ago you said you would submit the question to the censorship. Have you done so?'

Shikin shrugged his shoulders and closed the little yellow book with a snap.

'I do not have to answer to you for my actions! I shall not return your book. In any case they wouldn't let you take it away with you.'

Nerzhin rose angrily, staring at the book. He reminded himself that the loving hands of his wife had once held it and had written a special inscription in it for him.

Smoothly and rapidly, each word a poisoned barb, he said:

'I hope you have not forgotten, Major, that for two years I petitioned the Ministry of State Security for the return of a sum of money in Polish zlotys, which had been removed from me in dubious circumstances, and although they had been converted to Russian money at a twentieth of their real value, they were nevertheless restored to me by order of the Supreme Soviet. I hope you haven't forgotten, either, how I once demanded five grams of top-grade flour. Everybody laughed at me, but I got them. And there are many more similar examples. I warn you that I am not going to let you keep that book. If I'm sent to my death at Kolyma, I shall get it back from you, even from there. I shall swamp the Party Central Committee and the Council of Ministers with complaints about you. Come on, hand it over!'

For all his rank and power, Shikin could not stand up to this prisoner—a man with no rights, condemned to be sent away to lingering death. Shikin actually had asked the censorship for a ruling on Yesenin and had been told, to his amazement, there was 'no formal objection' to the book. 'No formal objection' indeed! Shikin's infallible instinct told him that this was a mere phrase, that the book really ought to have been banned. It was more important, however, to make sure that this relentless troublemaker did not get him into any sort of danger.

'All right,' the major conceded, 'I'll give it back to you. But you won't be allowed to take it out of Mavrino.'

Nerzhin marched triumphantly towards the staircase clasping to himself the beloved, shiny dust-cover. It was a symbol of success at a moment when everything else had crumbled. On the landing he passed a group of prisoners discussing the latest news. Siromakha was among them, holding forth in a voice carefully modulated to prevent anyone in authority from hearing it:

'What the hell are they up to, sending men like that on transfer? What for? And what about Ruska Doronin? Who gave him away, I wonder?'

Clutching his little volume of Yesenin, Nerzhin hurried on to the Acoustics Laboratory, wondering how he could quickly destroy all his notes before a warder was sent to fetch him. Men due for transfer were not supposed to be allowed to walk freely round the prison. It was only due to the size of the transfer party or possibly to the leniency of the junior lieutenant, who was renowned for his inefficiency, that Nerzhin was able to enjoy this last, brief spell of comparative freedom. As he flung open the door of the Acoustics Laboratory he saw that the doors of the steel cupboard were open and Serafima standing between them, now back in her ugly striped dress and a grey mohair scarf round her shoulders. Not a word or a glance had passed between them since their bitter scene of the day before. She felt rather than saw Nerzhin come in, and numbly shuffled her feet as though deciding what to take out of the cupboard. Without thought or calculation Nerzhin slipped into the space between the steel cupboard doors, and said in a whisper:

'Serafima, after what happened yesterday I know it's cruel to talk to you. But if something isn't done, years of my work will be ruined. You wouldn't want me to burn it, would you? Will you look after it for me?'

She already knew that he was to be transferred. She had not moved a muscle when she heard the news, but now she raised her eyes, miserable and puffy from lack of sleep, and said:

'All right. Give it to me.'

Someone came in and Nerzhin moved swiftly on to his desk, where he found Major Roitman.

Roitman looked confused. Smiling awkwardly, he said:

'I am sorry about this, Nerzhin. I wasn't told, you see. . . . I had no idea. . . . And now it's too late to do anything about it.'

Nerzhin gave a look of chilling commiseration to this man, who until today he had thought was honest.

'Don't try and tell me that, I wasn't born yesterday, you know. A prisoner doesn't get transferred without the head of his laboratory being consulted.'

He began emptying the drawers of his desk.

Pain showed on Roitman's face: 'I was never asked, Nerzhin, believe me. Nobody warned me. . . .'

He said it aloud in front of everybody in the laboratory, preferring to lose authority in the eyes of those who were staying rather than seem to have done Nerzhin an injustice. Drops of sweat burst out on his forehead. He watched Nerzhin dully as he collected his belongings. It was true, he had not been consulted. It was just another blow by Yakonov in the running fight between the two men.

'Shall I give my notes on speech tests to Serafima?' Nerzhin enquired casually.

Roitman was too upset to reply and went slowly out of the room.

'Here, Serafima,' said Nerzhin as he carried envelopes, folders and calculation tables over to her desk. He almost put three of his private notebooks into one large envelope, but some inner guiding spirit prompted him not to. He glanced swiftly over Serafima's tense, blank features. Supposing this was a trap, a wronged woman taking her revenge, a lieutenant in the MGB doing her duty? Although her outstretched hands were warm, how long would she stay a virgin and faithful to him? Weather-vanes change with the first breeze that comes along, girls with the first man. She would show them to her husband—'Look darling, here are some old papers I was keeping . . .'

He transferred the notebooks to his pocket and gave the envelopes to Serafima without them. The Library of Alexandria had been burned; the monasteries had been burned, and the chronicles with them rather than be seized. And soot from the Lubyanka chimneys—the soot from countless reams of burned paper—fell on the prisoners as they were exercised in the compound on the prison roof.

More great ideas have been burned, perhaps, than have ever been made public. . . .

Nerzhin felt sure that as long as he was alive and sane he could reproduce the work he was destroying. He shook a box of matches, ran out, locked himself into the lavatory . . . and returned ten minutes later, looking pale and unconcerned.

Meanwhile Pryanchikov had come into the laboratory.

'It's incredible!' he said in a fury. 'And what do we do about it? Nothing—except sit there like logs of wood! We don't even kick up a row. Shipping them off in trucks! That's how you treat luggage, not people!'

Pryanchikov's impassioned speech struck an answering chord among the prisoners. Disturbed by the news of the transfer, none of the prisoners in the laboratory was working. A transfer was always a shock, a reminder that 'There but for the grace of God . . .' A transfer made every prisoner, even those unaffected by it, ponder on the insecurity of his fate, of how the whole apparatus of the MGB hung over his head like a sword of Damocles. They even had the habit of transferring perfectly harmless prisoners away from Mavrino, prisoners who had done nothing wrong but whose sentence was due to expire in a year or two; this was so that they would forget everything connected with their work and their knowledge would be out of date by the time they returned to normal life. Since men serving twenty-five years were effectively in for life, the security authorities were always glad to put them into special prisons like Mavrino.

The prisoners gathered round Nerzhin in a casual group. Some sat on desks instead of chairs, as if to emphasize the solemn nature of the occasion. Their mood was one of philosophic melancholy.

Just as mourners proclaim the virtues of the deceased, they now praised Nerzhin by recalling how he had always stood up for prisoners' rights. There had been the famous story of the flour, when he had deluged the Prison Commandant and the Ministry of Internal Affairs with complaints on the ground that *he personally* had been given five grams too little of flour in his daily rations. (According to prison regulations, no collective complaints were permitted, or complaints affecting all the prisoners as a whole. Although in theory the prisoners were being re-educated to be good socialists, they were forbidden to suffer for a common cause.) In those days the Mavrino prisoners had not yet been granted adequate rations, and the battle over the five grams of flour had been followed with much greater intensity than the news of international events. This gripping epic had ended by Nerzhin winning: the prison's Quartermaster had been dismissed from his job and out of the extra five grams of flour the prisoners had extra pancakes twice a week. The prisoners recalled, too, how Nerzhin had fought to have a longer exercise period on Sundays, although this particular attempt had been defeated —if the prisoners were allowed to wander around freely on Sundays, the authorities reasoned, how could they be made to work?

Nerzhin himself, however, hardly listened to these valedictions. It was a moment for action and he was in consequence bursting with energy. The worst had happened; its effects could be mitigated only by his own efforts. After handing his notes on speech tests to Serafima, and all the secret material to Roitman's assistant, having destroyed all his personal papers by burning them or tearing them up, having put all his library books in several piles, he then proceeded to clear the last remnants out of his drawers and distribute them among the other prisoners. It had already been decided who was to have his yellow revolving chair, who was to have his German-made desk with the roll-down wooden shutters in front of the drawers, who should have his inkwell, who should have his roll of coloured and marbled sheets of paper that was another piece of booty from Germany. With a gay smile the dying man disposed of his own legacies, while his heirs each presented him with two or three packets of cigarettes (this was the rule at Mavrino; cigarettes were plentiful in special prisons, while in the world of labour camps cigarettes were more precious than food).

Rubin came in from his top-secret work. He looked miserable, with bags under his eyes.

As they discussed books, Nerzhin said to him:

'If you were fond of Yesenin I'd give you this book here and now.'

'Would you really?' said Rubin in amazement.

'But you prefer Bagritsky, so there's nothing I can offer you.'

'You haven't got a shaving brush,' said Rubin, producing from his pocket a shaving brush with a bright plastic handle, an extremely fine one by prison standards. 'And since I've sworn not to shave until I'm pardoned, you'd better have it.'

Rubin never said 'until I'm released', because that would imply that he might serve out his sentence in full, but he always said 'until I'm pardoned', because of his persistent efforts to have his case reviewed.

'Thanks, old man, but you've got so used to Mavrino that you've forgotten what life's like in the camps. You don't think they let you shave yourself in a labour camp, do you? . . . Could you give me a hand with taking these books back to the library?'

They began gathering up his books and magazines. The other prisoners drifted away.

Each carrying an enormous pile of books they went out of the laboratory and up the main staircase, stopping by a window ledge in the upper corridor to re-arrange their untidy piles and to draw breath. Nerzhin's eyes, which had glittered with unnatural excitement while he had been disposing of his possessions, now looked fixed and grim.

'Look,' he said slowly, 'you and I have been living together for three years, and we've spent most of the time quarrelling or swearing at each other . . . now that I'm losing you, for ever probably, I realize that you're one of . . . my best . . .'

His voice broke.

Rubin's large brown eyes, which had so often flashed with anger, now shone with kindness and embarrassment.

'You're right,' he nodded. 'Let's kiss on it, you old brute.'

He clasped Nerzhin to his piratical black beard.

A short while later, just as they reached the library, Sologdin caught them up. He looked extremely worried. He carelessly slammed the glass door of the library so hard that the glass rattled and the librarian looked round in irritation.

'Well, Gleb,' said Sologdin. 'They've collared you at last.'

Completely ignoring Rubin, Sologdin only looked at Nerzhin; Rubin felt equally unwilling to bury the hatchet, and looked away.

'It's a great pity you're going. I'm really very sorry.'

How often they had talked and argued while chopping wood and at exercise; now all Sologdin's theories and rules of behaviour, which he had tried so hard and so unsuccessfully to preach, were useless and out of place.

'Listen,' he said. 'Time is money. It's not too late if you act now. Tell them you agree to working as a calculator, then I may be able to have you kept here. There's a new group being formed.' (Rubin gave Sologdin an astonished look.) 'But you'll have to work like a slave, I warn you.'

Nerzhin sighed.

'Thanks, Dmitry. I was given the chance, but somehow I've got used to the idea of leaving now. As the proverb says, "You won't drown at sea—but you may drown in a puddle!" I want to try swimming in the sea for a bit.'

'Do you? Well, take care.' Sologdin spoke briskly. 'It's really a pity, Gleb.'

He looked worried and, although trying not to, he found himself talking faster and faster. So the three of them stood and waited while the librarian, a woman who had dyed her hair, wore no lipstick and powdered her face heavily (she also had the rank of lieutenant) lazily completed Nerzhin's library card.

Then in the silence Gleb said to his two estranged friends:
'Listen, you two—you must make it up.'

Neither Sologdin nor Rubin turned their heads.

'Dmitry!' Gleb insisted.

Sologdin raised his cold blue eyes.

'Why ask me?' he said with surprise. 'I'm not the one . . .'

'Lev!' said Gleb.

Rubin gave him a pained look.

'Do you know why horses live so long?' And after a long pause he explained: 'Because they never try and analyse their relationships.'

Having disposed of his items of government property and of his working notes, Nerzhin was told by a warder to get back to his dormitory and prepare to leave. On the way there, laden with packets of cigarettes, he met Potapov hurrying down a passage with a box under his arm. Potapov's walk was quite different from the way he walked at exercise. In spite of his limp he walked fast, his neck jerking backwards and forwards, screwing up his eyes and looking into the distance, as though by gazing urgently ahead he could make up for his weak, old legs. Potapov very much wanted to say good-bye to Nerzhin and the other transferees, but as soon as he entered his laboratory he was gripped by the inner logic of his work and it drove all other thoughts and feelings out of his head. This ability to immerse himself completely in his work had been at the root of his success as an engineer while he had been a free man, and now in prison it helped him to bear many trials and discomforts.

'Well, I'm off,' Nerzhin said, stopping him. 'The corpse died happily and with a smile on his face.'

With an effort Potapov forced himself to grasp the meaning of this interruption. With the hand that was not holding the box, he touched the back of his neck as though to scratch it.

'It's a bad business . . .' he said slowly.

'I'd give you my copy of Yesenin, only apart from Pushkin you don't appreciate . . .'

Nerzhin sighed.

'Where shall we meet again? At the Kotlas transit camp? In the mines of Indigira? I somehow can't believe that we're ever likely to meet on some pavement in the street, can you?'

Wrinkling the corners of his eyes, Potapov quoted from his favourite Pushkin:

> *'My heart is dead to all*
> *But distant, fleeting hopes . . .'*

Markushev stuck his head angrily out of Number Seven and shouted:

'Come on, Potapov! Where are those filters? You're holding up the work.'

The joint authors of *The Smile of the Buddha* embraced awkwardly. Several packets of cigarettes fell to the floor.

'You know how it is,' said Potapov. 'The only way these people know how to do anything is "head down and charge".'

'Head down and charge' was Potapov's name for the rushed, sloppy, careless style of work which was the rule of Mavrino—and not only at Mavrino. It was what the newspapers called 'shock-work' or 'a crash programme'.

'Write to me,' said Potapov, and both men laughed. It was the most natural of remarks to make at a farewell, but in prison it sounded like a criminal conspiracy. The MVD made sure that each of its prisons was an island, with no communication from one to another. So, with his box of filters under his arm, jerking his head backwards and forwards, Potapov hurried off down the passage, his limp once more hardly noticeable.

Nerzhin hurried away, too, to his dormitory, where he began collecting his things, remembering from long practice all the unpleasant surprises that might be sprung on him at the body-searches to which he would be subjected, first at Mavrino, then at Butyrki. For the second time a warder looked in to hurry him up. The others had already left their rooms or been taken to prison headquarters. Just as Nerzhin was finishing his farewell rounds, fresh from walking out of doors, Spiridon came into the room wearing his black, belted sheepskin jerkin. Removing his large red-brown fur hat with its massive ear-flaps, and carefully lifting aside the bed-clothes on a bed near Nerzhin's, he sat down with his dirty quilted trousers on the steel frame.

'Look, Spiridon,' Nerzhin said, holding out the book to him. 'I got it back—my Yesenin.'

'So he coughed it up, did he, the swine?' Spiridon's glum, deeply wrinkled face lit up for a moment.

'I can't keep the book,' Nerzhin went on, 'but they have to be taught a lesson now and again.'

'You're right,' Spiridon nodded.

'Take it, will you? I want you to have the book as a present.'

'Don't you want to take it with you?' Spiridon asked awkwardly.

'Wait,' Nerzhin took back the book, opened it and began looking for a certain page. 'I'll find it in a moment, then you can read it . . .'

'It's time you were going, Gleb,' said Spiridon gloomily. 'You know all about labour camps—you get so fed up with the work that the only thing you can think about is wangling a spell in hospital.'

'Don't worry, Spiridon, I'm an old hand by now. I don't mind doing a bit of real work for a change.'

It was only then, as he looked at Spiridon, that Nerzhin realized that he was very upset, more so than would be caused by parting from a friend. And then he realized that after all the excitements of the day before—the discovery of the informers, Ruska's arrest, his talk with Simochka —he had completely forgotten that Spiridon had been due to get a letter from home. He put his book aside.

'What about the letter? Did you get one, Spiridon?'

Spiridon was holding the letter in his pocket. He pulled it out. The envelope was already tattered in the middle where it had been folded in two.

'There . . . You'd better . . .' Spiridon's lips trembled. Since yesterday he had folded and unfolded the letter countless times. The address was written in the large, round, childish hand of Spiridon's daughter, which she had retained ever since leaving school at the fifth class.

As had become their custom, Nerzhin read the letter aloud:

'Dear father, Its difficult enough writing to you, but I don't know how I can carry on living. People are so bad, father, they say one thing and then they cheat you . . .'

Nerzhin's voice dropped. He glanced at Spiridon, met his wide-open, steady, almost blind eyes under their bushy eyebrows. For several moments he felt incapable of thinking of anything to say to comfort him that would not sound false. Then the door was suddenly flung open and in flew Nadelashin, furious.

'Nerzhin!' he shouted. 'Taking advantage, are you? Get moving! Everybody else is ready—you're the last!'

The warders were in a hurry to get the transfer party over to the staff building before the lunch break, so that they would not have a chance to talk to any of the other prisoners again.

With one arm Nerzhin embraced Spiridon round his bristly, unshaven neck.

'Come on! I'm not waiting a minute longer!' screamed the junior lieutenant.

'Spiridon, Spiridon,' said Nerzhin, as he hugged his friend. Spiridon sighed hoarsely and waved his hand.

'Good-bye, Gleb.'

'Good-bye for ever, Spiridon.'

They kissed. Nerzhin grabbed his belongings and rushed out, followed by the Duty Officer.

With hands grimy with years of ingrained dirt, Spiridon picked up the little book from the bed, put his daughter's letter into his pocket and went off to his own room.

He did not notice that he had knocked his fur hat on to the floor with his knee, and it stayed where it had fallen.

CHAPTER EIGHTY-SEVEN

One by one, as the prisoners for transfer were rounded up and escorted to prison headquarters, they were searched. When each man had been searched he was pushed into an empty spare room furnished with two bare tables and a rough bench. Major Mishin was present throughout the entire search and Lieutenant-Colonel Klimentyev looked in from time to time. The stout major found it uncomfortable to bend down to inspect the prisoners' haversacks and suit-cases (it was in any case not in keeping with his rank), but the very fact that he was there inevitably made the warders more conscientious. Furiously they untied all the prisoners' rags and bundles, and they pounced with special vigour on any written matter. An order was in force that men leaving a special prison were not allowed to take out a scrap of paper that contained anything written, drawn or printed. For this reason most of the prisoners had already burned all their letters, destroyed notebooks of material on their work and had handed out their books to other prisoners.

One prisoner, an engineer called Romashev, who only had six months of his sentence to serve (he had already done nineteen and a half years) had openly brought along a large envelope containing several years' worth of notes and calculations concerned with the installation of hydro-electric power stations. He was expecting to be sent to the Krasnoyarsk region and greatly hoping to be allowed to work there on the job at which he was an expert. Although this envelope had already been inspected by Yakonov personally, who had stamped and signed it as suitable to be taken out, even though Major Shikin had also had it approved and stamped by the Security Office, all Romashev's months of persistence, care and forethought proved in vain: Major Mishin announced that *he* knew nothing about this envelope and ordered it to be confiscated. As it was removed Romashev's glazed, listless eyes watched it go. In his time he had survived both a death sentence and a transfer by cattle truck from Moscow to Vladivostok. At Kolyma he had stood in the way of a bucket so that it would break his leg, and in the resulting spell in hospital he had recuperated from the effects of forced labour in the Arctic Circle. After all that he saw no reason to weep at the mere destruction of ten years' work.

Another prisoner, on the other hand, the little bald designer called Syomushkin who had expended so much effort on Sunday darning his socks, was a novice; he had only been behind bars for two years, always in prisons and special prisons, and was terrified at the thought of being shipped off to a labour camp. Yet although he was desperately frightened, he still tried to keep a small volume of Lermontov which he and his wife had especially loved. He begged Major Mishin to let him keep the book, and he wrung his hands in childish supplication; embarrassing the other prisoners, who wanted no fuss or scenes, he tried to get into Klimentyev's office, but was not admitted. Suddenly with surprising violence he snatched the copy of Lermontov from Major Mishin (who leaped for the door in terror, thinking that this was the signal for a mutiny) and in one sweep he tore the green cardboard cover off the book, threw it aside and began tearing out the pages in clumps, convulsively sobbing and shouting as he hurled them round the room: 'All right, then! Keep it! Eat it if you like! I hope it chokes you!'

The search continued.

Emerging from the search, the prisoners could hardly recognize one another. They had been ordered to throw their blue denim overalls into one pile, their government-issue winter underwear into another and their overcoats (if there was anything left of them) into a third pile. Now the prisoners were dressed in nothing but their own clothes or in prison cast-offs. In all their years of work at Mavrino they had not earned the right to a change of clothing. This was not malice or parsimony on the part of the prison officers; they were completely dependent on the regulation enforced by the Accountancy Branch of the Ministry. This was the reason while, although it was in the depths of winter, several prisoners now found themselves without any underclothes and forced to wear nothing but the shorts and singlets they had been wearing on the day they were brought to the prison, and which had been lying untouched in their kitbags in the stores as unwashed as they had been when they had arrived. Some put on clumsy camp boots (anyone found with a pair of these boots had his 'civilian' shoes removed), others had leather boots with metal-tipped soles, while the lucky ones wore felt boots.

A pair of felt boots are the two best friends a prisoner will ever have. The most helpless of all living creatures, and with less influence over his own future than a frog, a toad or a fieldmouse, a prisoner is completely at the mercy of the whims of fate. Even snug in a warm bed a prisoner can never be certain that he will be safe from the horrors of winter, that he won't be grabbed that very night by some uniformed arm and dragged off to the North Pole. Woe then to anyone whose feet are not shod in felt boots! He will leave his feet in the Arctic, like two blocks of ice thrown off a lorry. Without his own pair of felt boots a prisoner spends all winter hiding, living a life of lies and pretence, putting up with insults from the dregs of prison society, or else he turns informer . . . anything to avoid being transferred in winter. But the prisoner wearing his own felt boots has not a care in the world. He can look the warders straight in the eye and take his orders smiling as serenely as Marcus Aurelius.

Although it was thawing outside, everybody who had their own felt boots, including Khorobrov and Nerzhin, put them on and stumped proudly around the empty room, partly in order to have less to carry but chiefly to feel their heartening warmth all the way up their legs, although today they would be going no further than Butyrki Prison, where it was just as warm as at Mavrino. Only the fearless Gerasimovich, who had refused to be a fisher of men, had nothing to wear of his own and the Quartermaster issued him instead with a second-hand long-sleeved sheepskin jacket that was too big for him and had no fastenings, and a pair of worn, blunt-toed leather boots. Dressed like this, Gerasimovich with his pince-nez looked especially ridiculous.

The search over, all twenty prisoners were shoved into an empty waiting-room together with those of their belongings which they had been allowed to take with them. The door was locked on them and a sentry mounted on it until the Black

Maria came. Another warder was detailed to patrol under the windows. His job, as he marched up and down slithering on the ice, was to chase away any prisoners who might try to wave good-bye to their comrades during the lunch break. Thus all contact between the twenty men who were leaving the two hundred and sixty-one who stayed behind was cut off.

The transferees were still physically at Mavrino, but effectively they were already gone. At first, as they sat down at random on their luggage or on the benches, no one spoke. They were all thinking about the search—about the things they had lost and the things they had managed to keep. They were thinking, too, about Mavrino—how easy life had been there, how much of their sentences they had spent there and how much still remained to serve. It is a habit of prisoners to count time—past time already lost and future time doomed to be lost. And they were thinking about their families and the difficulty of getting in touch with them, thinking how they would have to beg them for parcels again, because in the labour camps a grown man working twelve hours a day cannot get enough to eat.

They were thinking about the mistakes or the conscious decisions which they had made and which had led to their being transferred; they were wondering where they might be sent, what would happen when they got there and whether they would manage to fit in to the new surroundings. Each man was occupied by his own thoughts and none of them was cheerful.

Each man longed for some comfort and hope, so that when the talk started up again and somebody said that they might not be sent to a labour camp at all but to another special prison like Mavrino, even those who refused to believe this sat up and listened.

Thus Christ in the Garden of Gethsemane, though he knew that he must drink the bitter cup to its dregs, continued to hope and pray.

Trying to mend the handle of his suitcase, which was always breaking, Khorobrov swore loudly:

'Damn fools! Can't even make a simple suitcase properly! Some idiot dreams up a new method and all they do is bend a piece of wire at both ends and stick it through the handle. It holds as long as the suitcase is empty but just you try and put anything in it!'

Having pulled some pieces of brick from the stove, which had been built equally sloppily, Khorobrov was angrily knocking the wire loops back into the ends of the handle.

Nerzhin understood Khorobrov's feelings. Whenever he came up against humiliation, contempt, negligence and injustice, Khorobrov always lost his temper—but how could anyone discuss such things calmly? The howl of impotent frustration is something that cannot be expressed in carefully picked words. In fact Nerzhin himself, as he slipped back into the labour-camp mentality, actually felt a certain relief at regaining an important male freedom—the freedom to sprinkle one's talk with four-letter words.

Romashev was quietly describing to the novices the routes generally used for transporting prisoners to Siberia and compared the Kuibyshev transit prison very favourably with the ones at Gorky and Kirov. Khorobrov stopped banging his suitcase handle and threw down the piece of brick, smashing it into fragments like red crumbs.

Meanwhile Nerzhin, feeling the onset of a mutinous spirit induced in him by having to wear labour-camp clothes again, got up, persuaded the sentry to call for Junior Lieutenant Nadelashin and roared at the top of his voice:

'Lieutenant, we can see from this window that lunch has been in progress for half an hour. Why haven't we been brought any food?'

Nadelashin shuffled his feet awkwardly and replied sympathetically:

'I'm sorry, but you've been taken off the ration strength . . . as from this morning. . . .'

'Taken off?' Hearing a murmur of support and discontent rising behind his back, Nerzhin waded into the young officer: 'Tell the prison governor that we're not leaving this place until we're fed. And that we'll resist any attempt to ship us out by force.'

'All right, I'll tell him,' the junior lieutenant gave in at once and hurried off guiltily to report to his commanding officer.

None of the prisoners in the waiting-room had the slightest

doubt that it was worth making a fuss. Restraint and 'good manners' are luxuries that prisoners cannot afford.

'He's right!'

'Don't let 'em get away with it!'

'Trying to do us out of a meal, the bastards!'

'Cheeseparers! Can't spare us a lunch after slogging away here for three years.'

'We won't go—it's as simple as that. After all, what can they do to us?'

Even the men who were normally quiet and submissive now grew bold, already anticipating the freer atmosphere of the transit prisons. This was not just their last decent meat-meal before relapsing into years of subsistence on camp gruel—it was a symbol of their human dignity. And although there were some of them whose throats had gone completely dry with the anxiety and excitement and who would have been incapable of eating anything at that moment, even they completely disregarded their lack of appetite and expectantly demanded the meal.

From the window they could see the path which led from the staff building to the kitchen. They watched as a lorry, carrying a large fir tree, whose branches and tip projected over the sides and end, backed up to the prison log-pile. The prison Quartermaster climbed out of the cab, and a warder jumped down from the back. Yakonov had kept his word. Tomorrow or the day after the New Year's tree would be raised in the semicircular room and the prisoners, most of whom were fathers but who in the absence of their own children became like children themselves, would decorate it with baubles (which they had spent many hours of government time in making) including Clara's little basket and the shining little moon in its glass cage. These grown men, bearded and moustached, would form a circle round the tree and, laughing bitterly, they would sing traditional songs to the tree in voices loud enough to drown the wolf-like howl which was the voice of their fate.

They watched as the warder patrolling under the window chased away Pryanchikov, who had tried to reach the be-sieged prisoners and who was shouting and shaking his fists in the air.

They watched Junior Lieutenant Nadelashin trotting

anxiously from kitchen to headquarters, back to the kitchen and back again to headquarters. They saw, too, how Spiridon, without being given time to finish his lunch, was made to unload the fir tree from the lorry. As he went he wiped his moustache and tightened his belt.

At last the junior lieutenant came out again, this time not walking but running into the kitchen and soon reappeared with two cooks, lugging a container of hot food between them. A third woman followed them carrying a pile of soup-plates. Frightened of slipping and breaking the plates, she stopped. The lieutenant turned back and took some of them from her.

The thrill of victory filled the prisoners' room.

Lunch appeared. The soup was ladled out at one end of the table, the prisoners collected their plates and carried them away to their corners, to the window-sills or to their suitcases. A few managed to eat standing up, or kneeling down at the table, which was not provided with benches.

The junior lieutenant and the cooks went away. Silence, proper to all mealtimes, descended. Each man was enjoying the hot soup, a bit thin, but with a definitely meaty taste. As each spoonful went down, with its little blobs of fat and its boiled noodles, he revelled in the delicious warmth as it passed down his gullet and into his stomach. Blood and muscles rejoined in anticipation of new strength and reinforcement for their cells.

Nerzhin remembered the old proverb—'A woman marries for meat, a man marries for soup.' In his interpretation this proverb meant that it was the man's job to provide the meat, the woman's to make soup out of it. Russian proverbs were always down-to-earth, and direct; they meant what they said, with no high moral overtones. In its vast treasury of proverbs the Russian people has always been much franker about itself than even Tolstoy or Dostoyevsky had ever been.

As the soup was coming to an end and the aluminium spoons were beginning to scrape the plates, one of the men slowly sighed:

'Ye-e-e-s . . .'

From another corner came the response: 'Decent drop of soup, that.'

694

Someone else, not so easily satisfied, put in:

'Scooped it up out of the bottom of the pot, and the real meat floats on top. Bet they swiped all the meat for themselves.'

Another said gloomily:

'Let's hope we survive the camps, so that we can come back to eating this stuff again one day.'

Then Khorobrov banged his spoon on his empty plate and said in a dull voice, with a hint of mounting protest:

'No, you're wrong—any food is good as long as a man's free!'

No one answered.

Nerzhin began knocking on the door and demanding the next course. The lieutenant appeared immediately.

'Finished?' He smiled round at the prisoners. Noticing that they already had the satisfied look of men with full stomachs, he now announced the news which, as an experienced prison officer, he had withheld earlier: 'There's no second course, I'm afraid. None left. They're already washing out the pans. Sorry.'

Nerzhin glanced round at the prisoners, judging whether to kick up another row, but being easily satisfied, as Russians are, their pugnacity had already completely subsided.

'What was there for the second course?' growled a bass voice.

'Stew,' said the lieutenant, smiling awkwardly.

The men sighed, forgetting even to enquire about the third course.

The hum of a car engine could be heard outside. The lieutenant was called away to other duties, and the stern voice of Lieutenant-Colonel Klimentyev rang out in the corridor.

The men were led out one by one.

There was no roll-call from a list of names because a Mavrino escort was to take them to Butyrki, where the official handover would take place. Instead they counted them. Each man was ticked off as he took the familiar and always fateful step up from the ground on to the high step of the Black Maria, lowering his head to avoid bumping it on the steel lintel, bent under the weight of his luggage which bumped clumsily against the sides of the steps.

There was no one to see them off—the lunch-hour was over and the prisoners had been ordered indoors out of the exercise yard.

The Black Maria was backed right up to the steps of the staff building. Although there were no guard-dogs with their furious barking, the move into the vehicle was accompanied by the usual pushing, hustle and nervous haste on the part of the escort, which was designed to make their jobs quicker and easier, but which invariably communicated itself to the prisoners and prevented them from looking round and taking stock of their situation. Eighteen of the men boarded the truck in this way, without one of them so much as looking up for a farewell glance at the tall, motionless lime trees which had for so long spread their branches in impartial blessing over times of joy and sorrow.

The two prisoners, however, who did manage to glance around—Khorobrov and Nerzhin—did not look up at the lime trees, but at the sides of the lorry, with the special aim of noting what colour they were painted.

Their expectations were proved right.

In the past the prison vans had been painted leaden-grey and people had been terrified by the sight of them as they roared through the streets. After the war some genius had conceived the brilliant notion of making the prison vans identical with the lorries which carried bulk food, to paint their outsides in the same colours of orange and blue, and to write on them in four languages either:

ХЛЕБ. PAIN. BROT. BREAD

or

МЯСО. VIANDE. FLEISCH. MEAT.

Now, as he boarded the Black Maria, Nerzhin managed to glance at its side and read the English word: Meat. Taking his turn he squeezed through the first narrow little door, then through the even narrower second door, where he stepped over a pair of legs, dragged his suitcase and kit-bag over someone else's knees and sat down.

The interior of this three-ton Black Maria was not 'boxed',

that is to say it was not divided into ten narrow little steel-walled cells, each one just big enough to take a single prisoner. This was a 'general purpose' type of prison van, i.e. one designed not for transporting men awaiting trial but for moving convicted prisoners, which enabled it to carry a much larger live cargo. At the back, between outer and inner steel doors with small barred ventilators, the vehicle had a small compartment for the escort where, after locking the inner door from the outside and the outer door from the inside and communicating with the driver and escort commander by means of a special speaking-tube built into the coachwork of the truck, two men of the escort could just squeeze in. The rest of the space at the back was taken up with a small reserve cell, for use in case any prisoner grew obstreperous. All of the rest of the lorry was taken up by a low, enclosed, steel cabin like a rat-trap with room for exactly twenty men. (By applying pressure from a few pairs of boots you could even squeeze in a few more.)

A bench ran round three sides of this communal rat-trap, leaving very little space in the middle. Anybody who could find a place sat down, but they were not necessarily the luckiest ones, because as the truck filled up with other people their luggage bumped over knees and crashed into outstretched legs. There was no sense in getting annoyed or apologizing in all this jumble, and there was no chance of moving or changing one's position until the hour-long journey was over.

The warders shoved the last prisoner in, slammed the door and locked it, but the outside door of the rear chamber was left open. Another person could be heard climbing up the back steps, another shadow darkened the grating on the inner door.

'Hey,' came Ruska's voice, 'I'm going to Butyrki for interrogation. Who's in there? Who's being transferred?'

There was an immediate explosion of voices—twenty voices all shouted at once in reply, while both warders yelled at Ruska to shut up and Klimentyev roared at the warders to look sharp and stop the prisoners from talking.

'Quiet, you b—s,' roared a voice inside the van.

There was silence, except for the noises made by the warders, shoving Ruska into his box.

'Who gave you away, Ruska?' shouted Nerzhin.

'Siromakha.'

'The *ba-a*stard!' shouted several voices.

'How many of you are there?' shouted Ruska.

'Twenty.'

'Who's there?'

But the warders had pushed him into the box and locked the door.

'Keep your chin up, Ruska!' they shouted to him. 'See you in Siberia!'

A little light penetrated the interior as long as the outer door was open, but now it was shut, the heads of the two men of the escort blocked the last flicker of light that came in through the gratings of the two doors. The engine roared, the lorry shuddered and moved off, and as they swayed from side to side only a few fleeting shimmers occasionally lit up the prisoners' faces.

The brief exchange of shouts from cell to cell, like a spark leaping between flint and metal, was the kind of incident that always made prisoners very restless and uneasy.

They drove a short distance, then stopped. This was obviously the guardhouse.

'Ruska!' shouted one of the prisoners, 'did they beat you up?'

There was a pause, then the muffled reply:

'Yes, they did. . . .'

'Filthy swine!' shouted Nerzhin. 'Don't give in, Ruska!'

Several more voices shouted at once, making an inaudible babble.

The truck moved off from the guardhouse, then they were all swung sharply over to the right. This meant that they were turning left on to the main road. As they turned, Nerzhin's shoulder was pressed tightly up again Gerasimovich. They looked at each other, trying to make out each other's faces in the semi-darkness. They were now thrown together by something much more than the over-crowding in a prison van.

In the dark and discomfort Khorobrov boomed away:

'I shouldn't worry about leaving Mavrino if I were you. It's a lousy place. You bump into Siromakha wherever you go, one man in every half-dozen is a nark and you can't even fart without that swine Shikin finding out. No free Sundays for two years, bust your guts working a twelve-hour day for twenty grams of fat and they won't even allow you to write home, the bastards. And they expect you to work. It's hell, I tell you!'

Khorobrov stopped, overcome with indignation.

In the silence that followed him, broken only by the even hum of the engine as it drove the van steadily over the asphalt, Nerzhin's crisp reply rang out:

'No, Ilya, it's not hell. *That's* not hell! Where we're going —*that's* hell. Mavrino is the best, the highest, the first circle of hell. It's almost Paradise. . . .'

He said no more, feeling it unnecessary. They all knew well enough that what awaited them was incomparably worse than Mavrino. They all knew that when they were in their labour camps they would dream nostalgically of Mavrino as of a golden age. For the moment, however, to bolster their morale they felt a need to curse the special prison so that none of them might actually feel any regrets about it or blame himself for whatever action had led to his transfer.

But Khorobrov insisted:

'There's no such place as a *good* prison.'

Half-listening to the noise of the engine, the prisoners said nothing.

The prospects that awaited them were the taiga and the tundra, the Cold Pole at Oi-Myakoi and the copper mines of Dzhezkazgan, kicking and shoving, starvation rations, soggy bread, hospital, death. No fate on earth could possibly be worse. Yet they were at peace within themselves. They were as fearless as men are who have lost everything they ever had—fearlessness hard to attain but enduring once it is reached.

Buffeting its load of tightly packed bodies, the gaily painted orange and blue truck drove on through the streets, passed a railway station and stopped at a crossroads. There, halted by a traffic-light, stood the dark-red car belonging to the Moscow correspondent of the Paris newspaper *Libération*, on his way to a hockey match at the Dynamo Stadium. On the side of the van the correspondent read the words:

МЯСО. VIANDE. FLEISCH. MEAT.

He remembered having seen several trucks like this today in various parts of Moscow. Taking out his notebook he wrote with his dark-red fountain pen:

'Now and again on the streets of Moscow you meet food delivery vans, clean, well-designed and hygienic. One must admit that the city's food supplies are admirably well organized.'

1955-1964

Fontana Modern Novels

The First Circle Alexander Solzhenitsyn *75p*
The unforgettable novel of Stalin's post-war Terror. 'The greatest novel of the 20th Century.' *Spectator.* 'An unqualified masterpiece—this immense epic of the dark side of Soviet life.' *Observer.* 'At once classic and contemporary . . . future generations will read it with wonder and awe.' *New York Times*

Doctor Zhivago Boris Pasternak *60p*
The world-famous novel of life in Russia during and after the Revolution. '*Dr. Zhivago* will, I believe, come to stand as one of the great events in man's literary and moral history.' *New Yorker.* 'One of the most profound descriptions of love in the whole range of modern literature.' *Encounter*

The Master and Margarita Mikhail Bulgakov *50p*
'The fantastic scenes are done with terrific verve and the nonsense is sometimes reminscent of Lewis Carroll . . . on another level, Bulgakov's intentions are mystically serious. You need not catch them all to appreciate his great imaginative power and ingenuity.' *Sunday Times.* 'A grim and beautiful tale . . . just as you think the whole thing is a very funny satire, a chilling wind out of the Ingmar Bergman country blows, and, yet again, as you search for some moral significance, there are pages of sheer and beautiful fantasy *Times Educational Supplement*

The White Guard Mikhail Bulgakov *40p*
'A powerful reverie . . . the city is so vivid to the eye that it is the real hero of the book.' *V. S. Pritchett, New Statesman.* 'Set in Kiev in 1918 . . . the tumultuous atmosphere of the Ukranian capital in revolution and civil war is brilliantly evoked.' *Daily Telegraph.* 'A beautiful novel.' *The Listener*

Fontana Modern Novels

Simone de Beauvoir

The Woman Destroyed   *35p*

'Immensely intelligent, basically passionless stories about the decay of passion. Simone de Beauvoir shares, with other women novelists, the ability to write about emotion in terms of direct experience . . . The middle-aged women at the centre of the three stories in *The Woman Destroyed* all suffer agonisingly the pains of growing older and of being betrayed by husbands and children.'   *Sunday Times*

Les Belles Images   *35p*

Her totally absorbing story of upper-class Parisian life. 'A brilliant sortie into Jet Set France.' *Daily Mirror.* 'As compulsively readable as it is profound, serious and disturbing.'
Queen

The Mandarins   *75p*

'A magnificent satire by the author of *The Second Sex. The Mandarins* gives us a brilliant survey of the post-war French intellectual . . . a dazzling panorama.' *New Statesman.* 'A superb document . . . a remarkable novel.' *Sunday Times*

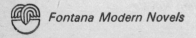 *Fontana Modern Novels*

Fontana Modern Novels

The Tin Men   Michael Frayn   *35p*
'One knew, sourly, that this book was going to be funny; one did not see how it could be so continuously funny . . . The fun of *The Tin Men* is outrageous because it is so serious.'
Guardian

Ordinary Families   E. Arnot Robertson   *35p*
'The loves and jealousies, miseries and raptures of adolescence, woven with a very dexterous hand.' *Observer*. 'A splendid book . . . It is one of the few books to yield treasures on a second reading.' *Evening Standard*. 'A wise, witty and brilliant book.' *Sunday Times*

The Once and Future King   T. H. White   *75p*
'T. H. White is much more than a spinner of good plots; his prose gives as much pleasure as his matter. There are witty and learned asides on every subject under the sun. He can draw living people; he can describe a landscape; and he can enter into the inmost minds of birds and beasts. This ambitious work will long remain a memorial to an author who is at once civilised, learned, witty and humane.'
Times Literary Supplement

Fontana Books

Fontana is best known as one of the leading paperback publishers of popular fiction and non-fiction. It also includes an outstanding, and expanding, section of books on history, natural history, religion and social sciences.

Most of the fiction authors need no introduction. They include Agatha Christie, Hammond Innes, Alistair MacLean, Catherine Gaskin, Victoria Holt and Lucy Walker. Desmond Bagley and Maureen Peters are among the relative newcomers.

The non-fiction list features a superb collection of animal books by such favourites as Gerald Durrell and Joy Adamson.

All Fontana books are available at your bookshop or newsagent; or can be ordered direct. Just fill in the form below and list the titles you want.

_____

FONTANA BOOKS, Cash Sales Department, P.O. Box 4, Godalming, Surrey, GU7 1JY. Please send purchase price plus 7p postage per book by cheque, postal or money order. No currency.

NAME (Block letters) _____

ADDRESS _____

_____

_____